Praise for Robert Jordan and The Wheel of Time®

"His huge, ambitious Wheel of Time series helped redefine the genre." —George R. R. Martin, internationally bestselling author of *A Game of Thrones*

"Anyone who's writing epic secondary world fantasy knows Robert Jordan isn't just a part of the landscape, he's a monolith within the landscape." —Patrick Rothfuss, internationally bestselling author of The Kingkiller Chronicle

"*The Eye of the World* was a turning point in my life. I read, I enjoyed. (Then continued on to write my larger fantasy novels.)" —Robin Hobb, *New York Times* bestselling author of The Farseer Trilogy

"Robert Jordan's work has been a formative influence and an inspiration for a generation of fantasy writers." —Brent Weeks, *New York Times* bestselling author of *The Way of Shadows*

"Jordan has come to dominate the world Tolkien began to reveal." —*The New York Times*

"One of fantasy's most acclaimed series." —*USA Today*

"Robert Jordan was a giant of fiction whose words helped a whole generation of fantasy writers, including myself, find our true voices. I thanked him then, but I didn't thank him enough." —Peter V. Brett, internationally bestselling author of The Demon Cycle

"[Robert Jordan's] impact on the place of fantasy in the culture is colossal. . . . He brought innumerable readers to fantasy. He became the *New York Times* Best Seller List's face of fantasy." —Guy Gavriel Kay, internationally bestselling author of *Tigana*

"Jordan's writing is so amazing! The characterization, the attention to detail!" —Clint McElroy, cocreator of the #1 podcast *The Adventure Zone*

"The Wheel of Time [is] rapidly becoming the definitive American fantasy saga. It is a fantasy tale seldom equaled and still less often surpassed in English." —*Chicago Sun-Times*

"Hard to put down for even a moment. A fittingly epic conclusion to a fantasy series that many consider one of the best of all time." —*San Francisco Book Review* on *A Memory of Light*

The Wheel of Time®

By Robert Jordan

By Robert Jordan and Brandon Sanderson

By Robert Jordan and Teresa Patterson

By Robert Jordan, Harriet McDougal, Alan Romanczuk, and Maria Simons

THE
DRAGON
REBORN

ROBERT JORDAN

A TOM DOHERTY ASSOCIATES BOOK
NEW YORK

Dedicated to
James Oliver Rigney, Sr.
(1920–1988)

He taught me always to follow the dream,
and when I caught it, to live it.

THE DRAGON REBORN

Copyright © 1991 by Bandersnatch Group, Inc.

Excerpt from *The Shadow Rising* copyright © 1992 by Bandersnatch Group, Inc.

The phrase "The Wheel of Time" and the snake-wheel symbol are trademarks of Bandersnatch Group, Inc.

Maps by Ellisa Mitchell
Interior illustrations by Matthew C. Nielsen and Ellisa Mitchell

A Tor Book
Published by Tom Doherty Associates
120 Broadway
New York, NY 10271

www.tor-forge.com

Tor® is a registered trademark of Macmillan Publishing Group, LLC.

ISBN 978-1-250-25149-7

Our books may be purchased in bulk for promotional, educational, or business use. Please contact your local bookseller or the Macmillan Corporate and Premium Sales Department at 1-800-221-7945, extension 5442, or by email at MacmillanSpecialMarkets@macmillan.com.

First Edition: November 1991
First Premium Mass Market Edition: November 2019

Printed in the United States of America

0   9   8   7   6

Contents

And his paths shall be many, and who shall know his name, for he shall be born among us many times, in many guises, as he has been and ever will be, time without end. His coming shall be like the sharp edge of the plow, turning our lives in furrows from out of the places where we lie in our silence. The breaker of bonds; the forger of chains. The maker of futures; the unshaper of destiny.

—from *Commentaries
on the Prophecies of the Dragon,*
by Jurith Dorine, Right Hand to the
Queen of Almoren, 742 AB, the Third Age

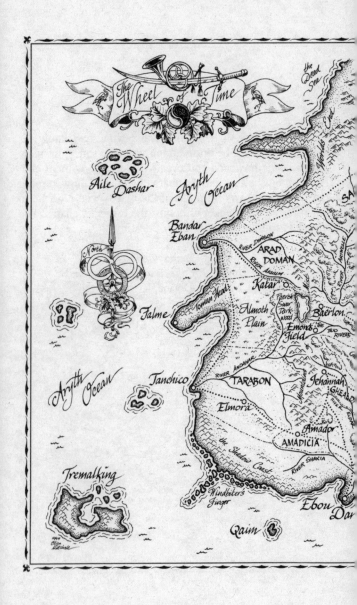

The Wheel of Time

Aile Dashar

Aryth Ocean

Bandar Eban

North

Falme

Aryth Ocean

Tanchico

Tremalking

the Dead Sea

World's End

RIVER DHAGON

ARAD DOMAN

RIVER ARMAHN

Katar

SA

Toman Head

Almoth Plain

Faerish Snur Fork road

Baerlon

Emond's Field

THE TWO RIVERS

RIVER ANDAHAR

TARABON

Elmora

Jehannah

GHEALDAN

Amador

AMADICIA

RIVER SHADRA

the Shadow Coast

Windbiter's Finger

Ebou Dar

Qaim

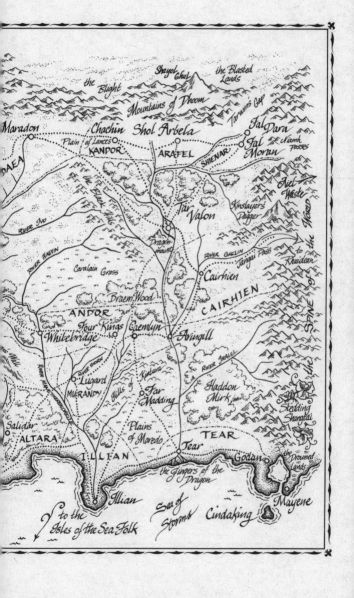

PROLOGUE

Fortress of the Light

Pedron Niall's aged gaze wandered about his private audience chamber, but dark eyes hazed with thought saw nothing. Tattered wall hangings, once battle banners of the enemies of his youth, faded into dark wood paneling laid over stone walls, thick even here in the heart of the Fortress of the Light. The single chair in the room—heavy, high-backed, and almost a throne—was as invisible to him as the few scattered tables that completed the furnishings. Even the white-cloaked man kneeling with barely restrained eagerness on the great sunburst set in the wide planks of the floor had vanished from Niall's mind for the moment, though few would have dismissed him so lightly.

Jaret Byar had been given time to wash before being brought to Niall, but both his helmet and his breastplate were dulled from travel and battered from use. Dark, deep-set eyes shone with a feverish, urgent light in a face that seemed to have had every spare scrap of flesh boiled away. He wore no sword—none was allowed in Niall's presence—but he seemed poised on the edge of violence, like a hound awaiting the loosing of the leash.

Twin fires on long hearths at either end of the room held off the late winter cold. It was a plain, soldier's room, really, everything well made but nothing extravagant—except for the sunburst. Furnishings came to the audience chamber of the Lord Captain Commander of the Children of the Light with the man who rose to the office; the flaring sun of coin gold had been worn smooth by generations of petitioners, replaced and worn smooth again. Gold enough to buy any estate in Amadicia, and the patent of nobility to go with it.

For ten years Niall had walked across that gold and never thought of it twice, any more than he thought of the sunburst embroidered across the chest of his white tunic. Gold held little interest for Pedron Niall.

Eventually his eyes went back to the table next to him, covered with maps and scattered letters and reports. Three loosely rolled drawings lay among the jumble. He took one up reluctantly. It did not matter which; all depicted the same scene, though by different hands.

Niall's skin was as thin as scraped parchment, drawn tight by age over a body that seemed all bone and sinew, but there was nothing of frailty about him. No man held Niall's office before his hair was white, nor did any man softer than the stones of the Dome of Truth. Still, he was suddenly aware of the tendon-ridged back of the hand holding the drawing, aware of the need for haste. Time was growing short. *His* time was growing short. It had to be enough. He had to make it enough.

He made himself unroll the thick parchment halfway, just enough to see the face that interested him. The chalks were a little smudged from travel in saddlebags, but the face was clear. A gray-eyed youth with reddish hair. He looked tall, but it was hard to say for certain. Aside from the hair and the eyes, he could have been set down in any town without exciting comment.

"This . . . this *boy* has proclaimed himself the Dragon Reborn?" Niall muttered.

The Dragon. The name made him feel the chills of winter and age. The name borne by Lews Therin Telamon when he doomed every man who could channel the One Power, then or ever after, to insanity and death, himself among them. It was more than three thousand years since Aes Sedai pride and the War of the Shadow had brought an end to the Age of Legends. Three thousand years, but prophecy and legend helped men remember—the heart of it, at least, if the details were gone. Lews Therin Kinslayer. The man who had begun the Breaking of the World, when madmen who could tap the power that drove the universe leveled mountains and sank ancient lands beneath the seas, when the whole face of the earth had been changed and all who survived fled like beasts before a wildfire. It had not ended until the last male Aes Sedai lay dead, and a scattered human race could begin trying to rebuild from the rubble—where even rubble remained. It was burned into memory by the stories mothers told children. And prophecy said the Dragon would be born again.

Niall had not really meant it for a question, but Byar took it for one. "Yes, my Lord Captain Commander, he has. It is a worse madness than any false Dragon I've ever heard of. Thousands have declared for him already. Tarabon and Arad Doman are in civil war, as well as at war with each other. There is fighting all across Almoth Plain and Toman Head, Taraboner against Domani against Darkfriends crying for the Dragon—or there was fighting until winter chilled most of it. I've never seen it spread so quickly, my Lord Captain Commander. Like throwing a lantern into a hay barn. The snow may have damped it down, but come spring, the flames will burst out hotter than before."

Niall cut him off with a raised finger. Twice already Niall had let him tell his story through, his voice burning with anger and hate. Parts of it Niall knew from other sources, and in some areas he knew more than Byar, but each time he heard it, it goaded him anew. "Geofram Bornhald and a thousand of the Children dead. And Aes Sedai did it. You have no doubts, Child Byar?"

"None, my Lord Captain Commander. After a skirmish on the way to Falme, I saw two of the Tar Valon witches. They cost us more than fifty dead before we stuck them full of arrows."

"You are *sure*—sure they were Aes Sedai?"

"The ground erupted under our feet." Byar's voice was firm and full of belief. He had little imagination, did Jaret Byar; death was part of a soldier's life, however it came. "Lightnings struck our ranks out of a clear sky. My Lord Captain Commander, what else could they have been?"

Niall nodded grimly. There had been no male Aes Sedai since the Breaking of the World, but the women who still claimed that title were bad enough. They prated of their Three Oaths: to speak no word that was not true, to make no weapon for one man to kill another, to use the One Power as a weapon only against Darkfriends or Shadowspawn. But now they had showed those oaths for the lies they were. He had always known no one could want the power they wielded except to challenge the Creator, and that meant to serve the Dark One.

"And you know nothing of those who took Falme and killed half of one of my legions?"

"Lord Captain Bornhald said they called themselves Seanchan, my Lord Captain Commander," Byar said stolidly. "He said they were Darkfriends. And his charge broke them, even if they killed him." His voice gained intensity. "There were many refugees from the city. Everyone I spoke to agreed the strangers had broken and fled. Lord Captain Bornhald did that."

Niall sighed softly. They were almost the same words Byar had used the first two times about the army that had seemingly come out of nowhere to take Falme. *A good soldier*, Niall thought, *so Geofram Bornhald always said, but not a man to think for himself.*

"My Lord Captain Commander," Byar said suddenly, "Lord Captain Bornhald *did* command me to stand aside from the battle. I was to watch, and report to you. And tell his son, Lord Dain, how he died."

"Yes, yes," Niall said impatiently. For a moment he studied Byar's hollow-cheeked face, then added, "No one doubts your honesty or courage. It is exactly the sort of thing Geofram Bornhald would do, facing a battle in which he feared his entire command might die." *And not the sort of thing you have imagination enough to think up.*

There was nothing more to learn from the man. "You have done well, Child Byar. You have my leave to carry word of Geofram Bornhald's death to his son. Dain Bornhald is with Eamon Valda—near Tar Valon at last report. You may join them."

"Thank you, my Lord Captain Commander. Thank you." Byar rose to his feet and bowed deeply. Yet as he straightened, he hesitated. "My Lord Captain Commander, we *were* betrayed." Hatred gave his voice a saw-toothed edge.

"By this one Darkfriend you spoke of, Child Byar?" He could not keep an edge out of his own voice. A year's planning lay in ruins amid the corpses of a thousand of the Children, and Byar wanted to talk only of this one man. "This young blacksmith you've only seen twice, this Perrin from the Two Rivers?"

"Yes, my Lord Captain Commander. I do not know how, but I know he is to blame. I know it."

"I will see what can be done about him, Child Byar." Byar opened his mouth again, but Niall raised a thin hand to forestall him. "You may leave me now." The gaunt-faced man had no choice but to bow again and leave.

As the door closed behind him, Niall lowered himself into his high-backed chair. What had brought on Byar's hatred of this Perrin? There were far too many Darkfriends to waste energy on hating any particular one. Too many Darkfriends, high and low, hiding behind glib tongues and open smiles, serving the Dark One. Still, one more name added to the lists would do no harm.

He shifted on the hard chair, trying to find comfort for his old bones. Not for the first time he thought vaguely that perhaps a cushion would not be too much luxury. And not for the first time, he pushed the thought away. The world tumbled toward chaos, and he had no time to give in to age.

He let all the signs that foretold disaster swirl through his mind. War gripped Tarabon and Arad Doman, civil war ripped at Cairhien, and war fever was rising in Tear and Illian, old enemies as they were. Perhaps these wars meant nothing in themselves—men fought wars—but they usually came one at a time. And aside from the false Dragon somewhere on Almoth Plain, another tore at Saldaea, and a third plagued Tear. Three at once. *They must all be false Dragons. They* must *be!*

A dozen small things besides, some perhaps only baseless rumors, but taken together with the rest. . . . Sightings of Aiel reported as far west as Murandy, and Kandor. Only two or three in one place, but one or a thousand, Aiel had come out of the Waste just once in all the years since the Breaking. Only in the Aiel War had they ever left that desolate wilderness. The Atha'an Miere, the Sea Folk, were said to be ignoring trade to seek signs and portents—of what, exactly, they did not say—sailing with ships half full or even empty. Illian had called the Great Hunt of the Horn for the first time in almost four hundred years, had sent out the Hunters to seek the fabled Horn of Valere, which prophecy said would summon dead heroes from the grave to fight in Tarmon Gai'don, the Last Battle against the Shadow. Rumor said the Ogier, always so reclusive that most common people thought them only legend, had called meetings between their far-flung *stedding*.

Most telling of all, to Niall, the Aes Sedai had apparently come into the open. It was said they had sent some of their sisters to Saldaea to confront the false Dragon Mazrim Taim. Rare as it was in men, Taim could channel the One Power. That was a thing to fear and despise in itself, and few thought a man like that could be defeated except with the aid of Aes Sedai. Better to allow Aes Sedai help than to face the inevitable horrors when he went mad, as such men inevitably did. But Tar Valon had apparently sent other Aes Sedai to support the other false Dragon at Falme. Nothing else fit the facts.

The pattern chilled the marrow in his bones. Chaos multiplied; what was unheard of, happening again and again. The whole world seemed to be milling, stirring near the boil. It was clear to him. The Last Battle really was coming.

All his plans were destroyed, the plans that would have secured his name among the Children of the Light for a hundred generations. But turmoil meant opportunity, and he had new plans, with new objectives. If he could keep the strength and will to carry them out. *Light, let me hold on to life long enough.*

A deferential tap on the door brought him out of his dark thoughts. "Come!" he snapped.

A servant in coat and breeches of white-and-gold bowed his way in. Eyes to the floor, he announced that Jaichim Carridin, Anointed of the Light, Inquisitor of the Hand of the Light, came at the command of the Lord Captain Commander. Carridin appeared on the man's heels, not waiting for Niall to speak. Niall gestured the servant to leave.

Before the door was fully closed again, Carridin dropped to one knee with a flourish of his snowy cloak. Behind the sunburst on the cloak's breast lay the scarlet shepherd's crook of the Hand of the Light, called the Questioners by many, though seldom to their faces. "As you have commanded my presence, my Lord Captain Commander," he said in a strong voice, "so have I returned from Tarabon."

Niall examined him for a moment. Carridin was tall, well into his middle years, with a touch of gray in his hair, yet fit and hard. His dark, deep-set eyes had a knowing look about them, as always. And he did not blink under the silent study of the Lord Captain Commander. Few men had consciences so clear or nerves so steady. Carridin knelt there, waiting as calmly as if it were an everyday matter to be ordered curtly to leave his command and return to Amador without delay, no reasons given. But then, it was said Jaichim Carridin could outwait a stone.

"Rise, Child Carridin." As the other man straightened, Niall added, "I have had disturbing news from Falme."

Carridin straightened the folds of his cloak as he answered. His voice rode the edge of suitable respect, almost as if he spoke to an equal rather than to the man he had sworn to obey to the death. "My Lord Captain Commander refers to the news brought by Child Jaret Byar, late second to Lord Captain Bornhald."

The corner of Niall's left eye fluttered, an old presage of anger. Supposedly only three men knew Byar was in Amador, and none besides Niall knew from where he came. "Do not be too clever, Carridin. Your desire to know everything may one day lead you into the hands of your own Questioners."

Carridin showed no reaction beyond a slight tightening of his mouth at the name. "My Lord Captain Commander, the Hand seeks out truth everywhere, to serve the Light."

To serve the Light. Not to serve the Children of the Light. All the Children served the Light, but Pedron Niall often wondered if the Questioners really considered themselves part of the Children at all. "And what truth do you have for me about what occurred in Falme?"

"Darkfriends, my Lord Captain Commander."

"Darkfriends?" Niall's chuckle held no amusement. "A few weeks gone I was receiving reports from you that Geofram Bornhald was a servant of the Dark One because he moved soldiers onto Toman Head against your orders." His voice became dangerously soft. "Do you now mean me to believe that Bornhald, as a Darkfriend, led a thousand of the Children to their deaths fighting other Darkfriends?"

"Whether or not he was a Darkfriend will never be known," Carridin said blandly, "since he died before he could be put to the question. The Shadow's plots are murky, and often seem mad to those who walk in the Light. But that those who seized Falme were Darkfriends, I have no doubt. Darkfriends and Aes Sedai, in support of a false Dragon. It was the One Power that destroyed Bornhald and his men, of that I am sure, my Lord Captain Commander, just as it destroyed the armies that Tarabon and Arad Doman sent against the Darkfriends in Falme."

"And what of the stories that those who took Falme came from across the Aryth Ocean?"

Carridin shook his head. "My Lord Captain Commander, the people are full of rumors. Some claim they were the armies Artur Hawkwing sent across the ocean a thousand years ago, come back to claim the land. Why, some even claim to have seen Hawkwing himself in Falme. And half the heroes of legend besides. The west is boiling from Tarabon to Saldaea, and a hundred new rumors bubble to the surface every day, each more outrageous than the last. These so-called Seanchan were no more than another rabble of Darkfriends gathered to support a false Dragon, only this time with open Aes Sedai support."

"What proof have you?" Niall made his voice sound as if he doubted the point. "You have prisoners?"

"No, my Lord Captain Commander. As Child Byar no doubt told you, Bornhald managed to hurt them badly enough that they dispersed. And certainly no one we've questioned would admit to supporting a false Dragon. As for proof . . . it lies in two parts. If my Lord Captain Commander will permit me?"

Niall gestured impatiently.

"The first part is negative. Few ships have tried to cross the Aryth Ocean, and most never returned. Those that did, turned back before they ran out of food and water. Even the Sea Folk will not cross the Aryth, and they sail wherever there is trade, even to the lands beyond the Aiel Waste. My Lord Captain Commander, if there *are* any lands across the ocean, they are too far to reach, the ocean too wide. To carry an army across it would be as impossible as flying."

"Perhaps," Niall said slowly. "It is certainly indicative. What is your second part?"

"My Lord Captain Commander, many of those we questioned spoke of monsters fighting for the Darkfriends, and held to their claims even under the last degree of the question. What could they be but Trollocs and other Shadowspawn, in some way brought down from the Blight?" Carridin spread his hands as if that were conclusive. "Most people think Trollocs are only travelers' tales and lies, and most of the rest think they were all killed in the Trolloc Wars. What other name would they put to a Trolloc but monster?"

"Yes. Yes, you may be right, Child Carridin. May be, I say." He would not give Carridin the satisfaction of knowing he agreed. *Let him work awhile.* "But what of him?" He indicated the rolled drawings. If he knew Carridin, the Inquisitor had copies in his own chambers. "How dangerous is he? Can he channel the One Power?"

The Inquisitor merely shrugged. "Perhaps he can channel, perhaps not. Aes Sedai could no doubt make people believe a cat could channel, if they wanted to. As to how dangerous he is. . . . Any false Dragon is dangerous until he is put down, and one with Tar Valon openly behind him is ten times dangerous. But he is less dangerous now than he will be in half a year, unchecked. The captives I questioned had never seen him, had no idea where he is now. His forces are fragmented. I doubt there are more than two hundred gathered in any one place. The Taraboners or the Domani, either one, could sweep them away if they weren't so busy fighting each other."

"Even a false Dragon," Niall said dryly, "is not enough to make them forget four hundred years of squabbling over possession of Almoth Plain. As if either of them ever had the strength to hold it." Carridin's face did not change, and Niall wondered how he could keep so calm. *You will not be calm much longer, Questioner.*

"It is of no import, my Lord Captain Commander. Winter keeps them all in their camps, except for scattered skirmishes and raids. When the weather warms enough for troops to move. . . . Bornhald took only half his legion to their deaths on Toman Head. With the other half, I will hunt this false Dragon to his death. A corpse is not dangerous to anyone."

"And if you face what it seems Bornhald faced? Aes Sedai channeling the Power to kill?"

"Their witchery doesn't protect them from arrows, or a knife in the dark. They die as quickly as anyone else." Carridin smiled. "I promise you, I will be successful before summer."

Niall nodded. The man was confident, now. Sure the dangerous questions would already have come, if they were coming. *You should have remembered, Carridin, I was accounted a fine tactician.* "Why," he said quietly, "did you not take your own forces to Falme? With Darkfriends on Toman Head, an army of them holding Falme, why did you try to stop Bornhald?"

Carridin blinked, but his voice remained steady. "At first they were only rumors, my Lord Captain Commander. Rumors so wild, no one could believe. By the time I learned the truth, Bornhald had joined battle. He was dead, and the Darkfriends scattered. Besides, my task was to bring the Light to Almoth Plain. I could not disobey my orders to chase after rumors."

"Your task?" Niall said, his voice rising as he stood. Carridin topped him by a head, but the Inquisitor stepped back. "Your task? Your task was to seize Almoth Plain! An empty bucket that no one holds except by words and claims, and all you had to do was fill it. The nation of Almoth would have lived again, ruled by the Children of the Light, with no need to pay lip service to a fool of a king. Amadicia and Almoth, a vise gripping Tarabon. In five years we would have held sway there as much as here in Amadicia. And you made a dog's dinner of it!"

The smile went at last. "My Lord Captain Commander," Carridin protested. "How could I foresee what happened? Yet another false Dragon. Tarabon and Arad Doman finally going to war after so long merely growling at each other. And Aes Sedai revealing their true selves after three thousand years of dissembling! Even with that, though, all is not lost. I can find and destroy this false Dragon before his followers unite. And once the Taraboners and Domani have weakened themselves, they can be cleared from the plain without—"

"No!" Niall snapped. "Your plans are done with, Carridin. Perhaps I should hand you over to your own Questioners right now. The High Inquisitor would not object. He is gnashing his teeth to find someone to blame for what happened. He would never put forward one of his own, but I doubt he'd quibble if I named you. A few days under the question, and you would confess to anything. Name yourself Darkfriend, even. You would go under the headsman's axe inside a week."

There was sweat beading on Carridin's forehead. "My

Lord Captain Commander. . . ." He stopped to swallow. "My Lord Captain Commander seems to be saying there is another way. If he will but speak it, I am sworn to obey."

Now, Niall thought. *Now to toss the dice.* Prickles ran across his skin, as if he were in battle and had suddenly realized that every man for a hundred paces around him was an enemy. Lord Captain Commanders did not go to the headsman, but more than one had been known to die suddenly and unexpectedly, swiftly mourned and swiftly replaced by men with less dangerous ideas.

"Child Carridin," he said firmly, "you will make certain that this false Dragon does not die. And if any Aes Sedai come to oppose rather than support him, you will make use of your 'knives in the dark.'"

The Inquisitor's jaw dropped. Yet he recovered quickly, eyeing Niall in a speculative fashion. "To kill Aes Sedai is a duty, but. . . . To allow a false Dragon to roam free? That . . . that would be . . . treason. And blasphemy."

Niall drew a deep breath. He could sense the unseen knives waiting in the shadows. But he was committed, now. "It is no treason to do what must be done. And even blasphemy can be tolerated for a cause." Those two sentences alone were enough to kill him. "Do you know how to unite people behind you, Child Carridin? The quickest way? No? Loose a lion—a rabid lion—in the streets. And when panic grips the people, once it has turned their bowels to water, calmly tell them you will deal with it. Then you kill it, and order them to hang the carcass up where everyone can see. Before they have time to think, you give another order, and it will be obeyed. And if you continue to give orders, they will continue to obey, for you will be the one who saved them, and who better to lead?"

Carridin moved his head uncertainly. "Do you mean to . . . take it all, my Lord Captain Commander? Not just Almoth Plain, but Tarabon and Arad Doman as well?"

"What I mean is for me to know. It is for you to obey as you are sworn to do. I expect to hear of messengers on fast horses leaving for the plain by tonight. I am certain you know how to word the orders so no one suspects what they should not. If you must harry someone, let it be the Taraboners and Domani. It would not do to have them kill my lion. No, under the Light, we shall force peace between them."

"As my Lord Captain Commander commands," Carridin said smoothly. "I hear and obey." Too smoothly.

Niall smiled a cold smile. "In case your oath is not strong enough, know this. If this false Dragon dies before I command his death, or if he is taken by the Tar Valon witches, you will be found one morning with a dagger in your heart. And should any . . . accident . . . befall me—even if I should die of old age—you will not survive me the month."

"My Lord Captain Commander, I have sworn to obey—"

"So you have." Niall cut him off. "See that you remember it. Now, go!"

"As my Lord Captain Commander commands." This time Carridin's voice was not so steady.

The door closed behind the Inquisitor. Niall rubbed his hands together. He felt cold. The dice were spinning, with no way of telling what pips would show when they stopped. The Last Battle truly was coming. Not the Tarmon Gai'don of legend, with the Dark One breaking free to be faced by the Dragon Reborn. Not that, he was sure. The Aes Sedai of the Age of Legends might have made a hole in the Dark One's prison at Shayol Ghul, but Lews Therin Kinslayer and his Hundred Companions had sealed it up again. The counterstroke had tainted the male half of the True Source forever and driven them mad, and so begun the Breaking, but one of those ancient Aes Sedai could do what ten of the Tar Valon witches of today could not. The seals they had made would hold.

Pedron Niall was a man of cold logic, and he had reasoned out how Tarmon Gai'don would be. Bestial Trolloc hordes rolling south out of the Great Blight as they had in the Trolloc Wars, two thousand years before, with the Myrddraal—the Halfmen—leading, and perhaps even new human Dreadlords from among the Darkfriends. Humankind, split into nations squabbling among themselves, could not stand against that. But he, Pedron Niall, would unite humankind behind the banners of the Children of the Light. There would be new legends, to tell how Pedron Niall had fought Tarmon Gai'don, and won.

"First," he murmured, "loose a rabid lion in the streets."

"A rabid lion?"

Niall spun on his heel as a bony little man with a huge beak of a nose slipped from behind one of the hanging banners. There was just a glimpse of a panel swinging shut as the banner fell back against the wall.

"I showed you that passage, Ordeith," Niall snapped, "so you could come when I summoned you without half the fortress knowing, not so you could listen to my private conversation."

Ordeith made a smooth bow as he crossed the room. "Listen, Great Lord? I would never do such a thing. I only just arrived and could not avoid hearing your final words. No more than that." He wore a half-mocking smile, but it never left his face that Niall had ever seen, even when the fellow had no reason to know anyone was watching.

A month before, in the dead of winter, the gangly little man had arrived in Amadicia, ragged and half-frozen, and somehow managed to talk his way through all the layers of guards to Pedron Niall himself. He seemed to know things about events on Toman Head that were not in Carridin's voluminous if obscure reports, or in Byar's tale, or in any other report or rumor that had come to Niall. His name was a lie, of course. In the Old Tongue, Ordeith meant "wormwood." When Niall challenged him on it, though, all he said was, "Who we were is lost to all men, and life is bitter." But he was clever. It had been he who helped Niall see the pattern emerging in events.

Ordeith moved to the table and took up one of the drawings. As he unrolled it enough to reveal the young man's face, his smile deepened to nearly a grimace.

Niall was still irritated that the man had come unsummoned. "You find a false Dragon funny, Ordeith. Or does he frighten you?"

"A false Dragon?" Ordeith said softly. "Yes. Yes, of course, it must be. Who else could it be." And he barked a shrill laugh that grated on Niall's nerves. Sometimes Niall thought Ordeith was at least half-mad.

But he is clever, mad or not. "What do you mean, Ordeith? You sound as if you know him."

Ordeith gave a start, as though he had forgotten the Lord Captain Commander was there. "Know him? Oh, yes, I know him. His name is Rand al'Thor. He comes from the Two Rivers, in the backcountry of Andor, and he is a Darkfriend so deep in the Shadow it would make your soul cringe to know the half."

"The Two Rivers," Niall mused. "Someone else mentioned another Darkfriend from there, another youth. Strange to think of Darkfriends coming from a place like that. But truly they are everywhere."

"Another, Great Lord?" Ordeith said. "From the Two Rivers? Would that be Matrim Cauthon or Perrin Aybara? They are of an age with him, and close behind in evil."

"His name was given as Perrin," Niall said, frowning. "Three of them, you say? Nothing comes out of the Two Rivers but wool and tabac. I doubt if there is another place men live that is more isolated from the rest of the world."

"In a city, Darkfriends must hide their nature to one extent or another. They must associate with others, with strangers come from other places and leaving to take word of what they have seen. But in quiet villages, cut off from the world, where few outsiders ever go. . . . What better places for all to be Darkfriends?"

"How is it you know the names of three Darkfriends, Ordeith? Three Darkfriends from the far end of forever. You keep too many secrets, Wormwood, and pull more surprises from your sleeve than a gleeman."

"How can any man tell *all* that he knows, Great Lord," the little man said smoothly. "It would be only prattle, until it becomes useful. I will tell you this, Great Lord. This Rand al'Thor, this Dragon, has deep roots in the Two Rivers."

"False Dragon!" Niall said sharply, and the other man bowed.

"Of course, Great Lord. I misspoke myself."

Suddenly Niall became aware of the drawing crumpled and torn in Ordeith's hands. Even while the man's face remained smooth except for that sardonic smile, his hands twitched convulsively around the parchment.

"Stop that!" Niall commanded. He snatched the drawing away from Ordeith and smoothed it as best he could. "I do not have so many likenesses of this man that I can allow them to be destroyed." Much of the drawing was only a smudge, and a rip ran across the young man's breast, but miraculously the face was untouched.

"Forgive me, Great Lord." Ordeith made a deep bow, his smile never slipping. "I hate Darkfriends."

Niall studied the face in chalks. *Rand al'Thor, of the*

Two Rivers. "Perhaps I must make plans for the Two Rivers. When the snows clear. Perhaps."

"As the Great Lord wishes," Ordeith said blandly.

The grimace on Carridin's face as he strode through the halls of the Fortress made other men avoid him, though in truth few sought the company of Questioners. Servants, hurrying about their tasks, tried to fade into the stone walls, and even men with golden knots of rank on their white cloaks took side corridors when they saw his face.

He flung open the door to his rooms and slammed it behind him, feeling none of the usual satisfaction at the fine carpets from Tarabon and Tear in lush reds and golds and blues, the beveled mirrors from Illian, the gold-leaf work on the long, intricately carved table in the middle of the floor. A master craftsman from Lugard had worked nearly a year on that. This time he barely saw it.

"Sharbon!" For once his body servant did not appear. The man was supposed to be readying the rooms. "The Light burn you, Sharbon! Where are you?"

A movement caught the corner of his eye, and he turned ready to shrivel Sharbon with his curses. The curses themselves shriveled as a Myrddraal took another step toward him with the sinuous grace of a serpent.

It was a man in form, no larger than most, but there the resemblance ended. Dead black clothes and cloak, hardly seeming to stir as it moved, made its maggot-white skin appear ever paler. And it had no eyes. That eyeless gaze filled Carridin with fear, as it had filled thousands before.

"Wha. . . ." Carridin stopped to work moisture back into his mouth, to try bringing his voice back down to its normal register. "What are you doing here?" It still sounded shrill.

The Halfman's bloodless lips quirked in a smile. "Where there is shadow, there may I go." Its voice sounded like a snake rustling through dead leaves. "I like to keep a watch on all those who serve me."

"I ser. . . ."

It was no use. With an effort Carridin jerked his eyes away from that smooth expanse of pale, pasty face and turned his back. A shiver ran down his spine, having his back to a Myrddraal. Everything was sharp in the mirror

on the wall in front of him. Everything but the Halfman.
The Myrddraal was an indistinct blur. Hardly soothing to
look at, but better than meeting that stare. A little strength
returned to Carridin's voice.

"I serve the. . . ." He cut off, suddenly aware of where he
was. In the heart of the Fortress of the Light. The rumor
of a whisper of the words he was about to say would have
him given to the Hand of the Light. The lowest of the Children would strike him down on the spot if he heard. He was
alone except for the Myrddraal, and perhaps Sharbon—
Where is that cursed man? It would be good to have someone to share the Halfman's stare, even if the other would
have to be disposed of afterwards—but still he lowered his
voice. "I serve the Great Lord of the Dark, as you do. We
both serve."

"If you wish to see it so." The Myrddraal laughed, a
sound that made Carridin's bones shiver. "Still, I will know
why you are here instead of on Almoth Plain."

"I . . . I was commanded here by word of the Lord Captain Commander."

The Myrddraal grated, "Your Lord Captain Commander's words are dung! You were commanded to find the human called Rand al'Thor and kill him. That before all else.
Above all else! Why are you not obeying?"

Carridin took a deep breath. That gaze on his back felt
like a knife blade grating along his spine. "Things . . . have
changed. Some matters are not as much in my control as
they were." A harsh, scraping noise jerked his head around.

The Myrddraal was drawing a hand across the tabletop,
and thin tendrils of wood curled away from its fingernails.
"Nothing has changed, human. You forswore your oaths to
the Light and swore new oaths, and *those* oaths you will
obey."

Carridin started at the gouges marring the polished
wood and swallowed hard. "I don't understand. Why is it
suddenly so important to kill him? I thought the Great Lord
of the Dark meant to use him."

"You question me? I should take your tongue. It is not
your part to question. Or to understand. It is your part to
obey! You will give dogs lessons in obedience. Do you understand *that*? Heel, dog, and obey your master."

Anger wormed its way through the fear, and Carridin's

hand groped at his side, but his sword was not there. It lay in the next room now, where he had left it on going to attend Pedron Niall.

The Myrddraal moved faster than a striking viper. Carridin opened his mouth to scream as its hand closed on his wrist in a crushing grip; bones grated together, sending jolts of agony up his arm. The scream never left his mouth, though, for the Halfman's other hand gripped his chin and forced his jaws shut. His heels rose up, and then his toes left the floor. Grunting and gurgling, he dangled in the Myrddraal's grasp.

"Hear me, human. You will find this youth and kill him as quickly as possible. Do not think you can dissemble. There are others of your *children* who will tell me if you turn aside in your purpose. But I will give you this to encourage you. If this Rand al'Thor is not dead in a month, I will take one of your blood. A son, a daughter, a sister, an uncle. You will not know who until the chosen has died screaming. If he lives another month, I will take another. And then another, and another. And when there is no one of your blood living except yourself, if he still lives, I will take you to Shayol Ghul itself." It smiled. "You will be years in the dying, human. Do you understand me, now?"

Carridin made a sound, half groan, half whimper. He thought his neck was going to break.

With a snarl, the Myrddraal hurled him across the room. Carridin slammed against the far wall and slid to the rug, stunned. Facedown, he lay fighting for breath.

"Do you understand me, human?"

"I . . . I hear and obey," Carridin managed into the carpet. There was no answer.

He turned his head, wincing at the pain in his neck. The room was empty except for him. Halfmen rode shadows like horses, so the legends said, and when they turned sideways, they disappeared. No wall could keep them out. Carridin wanted to weep. He levered himself up, cursing the jolt of pain from his wrist.

The door opened, and Sharbon hurried in, a plump man with a basket in his arms. He stopped to stare at Carridin. "Master, are you all right? Forgive me for not being here, master, but I went to buy fruits for your—"

With his good hand Carridin struck the basket from

Sharbon's hands, sending withered winter apples rolling across the carpets, and backhanded the man across the face.

"Forgive me, master," Sharbon whispered.

"Fetch me paper and pen and ink," Carridin snarled. "Hurry, fool! I must send orders." *But which? Which?* As Sharbon scurried to obey, Carridin stared at the gouges in the tabletop and shivered.

CHAPTER
I

Waiting

The Wheel of Time turns, and Ages come and pass, leaving memories that become legend. Legend fades to myth, and even myth is long forgotten when the Age that gave it birth comes again. In one Age, called the Third Age by some, an Age yet to come, an Age long past, a wind rose in the Mountains of Mist. The wind was not the beginning. There are neither beginnings nor endings to the turning of the Wheel of Time. But it was *a* beginning.

Down long valleys the wind swept, valleys blue with morning mist hanging in the air, some forested with evergreens, some bare where grasses and wildflowers would soon spring up. It howled across half-buried ruins and broken monuments, all as forgotten as those who had built them. It moaned in the passes, weatherworn cuts between peaks capped with snow that never melted. Thick clouds clung to the mountaintops so that snow and white billows seemed one.

In the lowlands winter was going or gone, yet here in the heights it held awhile, quilting the mountainsides with broad, white patches. Only evergreens clung to leaf or needle; all other branches stood bare, brown or gray against the rock and not yet quickened ground. There was no sound but the crisp rush of wind over snow and stone. The land seemed to be waiting. Waiting for something to burst.

Sitting his horse just inside a thicket of leatherleaf and pine, Perrin Aybara shivered and tugged his fur-lined cloak closer, as close as he could with a longbow in one hand and a great, half-moon axe at his belt. It was a good axe of cold steel; Perrin had pumped the bellows the day master Luhhan had made it. The wind jerked at his cloak, pulling the hood back from his shaggy curls, and cut through his coat; he wiggled his toes in his boots for warmth and shifted on his high-cantled saddle, but his mind was not really on the cold. Eyeing his five companions, he wondered if they, too, felt it. Not the waiting they had been sent there for, but something more.

Stepper, his horse, shifted and tossed his head. He had named the dun stallion for his quick feet, but now Stepper seemed to feel his rider's irritation and impatience. *I am tired of all this waiting, all this sitting while Moiraine holds us as tight as tongs. Burn the Aes Sedai! When will it end?*

He sniffed the wind without thinking. The smell of horse predominated, and of men and men's sweat. A rabbit had gone through those trees not long since, fear powering its run, but the fox on its trail had not killed there. He realized what he was doing, and stopped it. *You'd think I would get a stuffed nose with all this wind.* He almost wished he did have one. *And I wouldn't let Moiraine do anything about it, either.*

Something tickled the back of his mind. He refused to acknowledge it. He did not mention his feeling to his companions.

The other five men sat their saddles, short horsebows at the ready, eyes searching the sky above as well as the thinly treed slopes below. They seemed unperturbed by the wind flaring their cloaks out like banners. A two-handed sword hilt stuck up above each man's shoulder through a slit in his cloak. The sight of their bare heads, shaven except for topknots, made Perrin feel colder. For them, this weather was already well into spring. All softness had been hammered out of them at a harder forge than he had ever known. They were Shienarans, from the Borderlands up along the Great Blight, where Trolloc raids could come in any night, and even a merchant or a farmer might well have to take up sword or bow. And these men were no farmers, but soldiers almost from birth.

He sometimes wondered at the way they deferred to him and followed his lead. It was as if they thought he had some special right, some knowledge hidden from them. *Or maybe it's just my friends*, he thought wryly. They were not as tall as he, nor as big—years as a blacksmith's apprentice had given him arms and shoulders to make two of most men's—but he had begun shaving every day to stop their jokes about his youth. Friendly jokes, but still jokes. He would not have them start again because he spoke of a feeling.

With a start, Perrin reminded himself that he was supposed to be keeping watch, too. Checking the arrow nocked to his longbow, he peered down the valley running off to the west, widening as it fell away, the ground streaked with broad, twisted ribbons of snow, remnants of winter. Most of the scattered trees down there still clawed the sky with stark winter branches, but enough evergreens—pine and leatherleaf, fir and mountain holly, even a few towering greenwoods—stood on the slopes and the valley floor to give cover for anyone who knew how to use it. But no one would be there without a special purpose. The mines were all far to the south or even further north; most people thought there was ill luck in the Mountains of Mist, and few entered them who could avoid it. Perrin's eyes glittered like burnished gold.

The tickling became an itch. *No!*

He could push the itch aside, but the expectation would not go. As if he teetered on a brink. As if everything teetered. He wondered whether something unpleasant lay in the mountains around them. There was a way to know, perhaps. In places like this, where men seldom came, there were almost always wolves. He crushed the thought before it had a chance to firm. *Better to wonder. Better than that.* Their numbers were not many, but they had scouts. If there was anything out there, the outriders would find it. *This is my forge; I'll tend it, and let them tend theirs.*

He could see further than the others, so he was first to spot the rider coming from the direction of Tarabon. Even to him the rider was only a spot of bright colors on horseback winding its way through the trees in the distance, now seen, now hidden. A piebald horse, he thought. *And not before time!* He opened his mouth to announce her—it would be a woman; each rider before had been—when Masema suddenly muttered, "Raven!" like a curse.

Perrin jerked his head up. A big black bird was quartering over the treetops no more than a hundred paces away.

Its quarry might have been carrion dead in the snow or some small animal, yet Perrin could not take the chance. It did not seem to have seen them, but the oncoming rider would soon be in its sight. Even as he spotted the raven, his bow came up, and he drew—fletchings to cheek, to ear— and loosed, all in one smooth motion. He was dimly aware of the slap of bowstrings beside him, but his attention was all on the black bird.

Of a sudden it cartwheeled in a shower of midnight feathers as his arrow found it, and tumbled from the sky as two more arrows streaked through the place where it had been. Bows half-drawn, the other Shienarans searched the sky to see if it had a companion.

"Does it have to report," Perrin asked softly, "or does . . . *he* . . . see what it sees?" He had not meant anyone to hear, but Ragan, the youngest of the Shienarans, less than ten years his elder, answered as he fitted another arrow to his short bow.

"It has to report. To a Halfman, usually." In the Borderlands there was a bounty on ravens; no one there ever dared assume any raven was just a bird. "Light, if Heartsbane saw what the ravens saw, we would all have been dead before we reached the mountains." Ragan's voice was easy; it was a matter of every day to a Shienaran soldier.

Perrin shivered, not from the cold, and in the back of his head something snarled a challenge to the death. Heartsbane. Different names in different lands—Soulsbane and Heartfang, Lord of the Grave and Lord of the Twilight— and everywhere Father of Lies and the Dark One, all to avoid giving him his true name and drawing his attention. The Dark One often used ravens and crows, rats in the cities. Perrin drew another broadhead arrow from the quiver on his hip that balanced the axe on the other side.

"That may be as big as a club," Ragan said admiringly, with a glance at Perrin's bow, "but it can shoot. I would hate to see what it could do to a man in armor." The Shienarans wore only light mail, now, under their plain coats, but usually they fought in armor, man and horse alike.

"Too long for horseback," Masema sneered. The triangular scar on his dark cheek twisted his contemptuous grin even more. "A good breastplate will stop even a pile arrow except at close range, and if your first shot fails, the man you're shooting at will carve your guts out."

"That is just it, Masema." Ragan relaxed a bit as the sky remained empty. The raven must have been alone. "With this Two Rivers bow, I'll wager you don't have to be so close." Masema opened his mouth.

"You two stop flapping your bloody tongues!" Uno snapped. With a long scar down the left side of his face and that eye gone, his features were hard, even for a Shienaran. He had acquired a painted eyepatch on their way into the mountains during the autumn; a permanently frowning eye in a fiery red did nothing to make his stare easier to face. "If you can't keep your bloody minds on the bloody task at hand, I'll see if extra flaming guard duty tonight will bloody settle you." Ragan and Masema subsided under his stare. He gave them a last scowl that faded as he turned to Perrin. "Do you see anything yet?" His tone was a little gruffer than he might have used with a commander put over him by the King of Shienar, or the Lord of Fal Dara, yet there was something in it of readiness to do whatever Perrin suggested.

The Shienarans knew how far he could see, but they seemed to take it as a matter of course, that and the color of his eyes, as well. They did not know everything, not by half, but they accepted him as he was. As they thought he was. They seemed to accept everything and anything. The world was changing, they said. Everything spun on the wheels of chance and change. If a man had eyes a color no man's eyes had ever been, what did it matter, now?

"She's coming," Perrin said. "You should just see her now. There." He pointed, and Uno strained forward, his one real eye squinting, then finally nodded doubtfully.

"There's bloody something moving down there." Some of the others nodded and murmured, too. Uno glared at them, and they went back to studying the sky and the mountains.

Suddenly Perrin realized what the bright colors on the distant rider meant. A vivid green skirt peeking out beneath a bright red cloak. "She's one of the Traveling People," he said, startled. No one else he had ever heard of dressed in such brilliant colors and odd combinations, not by choice.

The women they had sometimes met and guided even deeper into the mountains included every sort: a beggar woman in rags struggling afoot through a snowstorm; a merchant by herself leading a string of laden packhorses; a lady in silks and fine furs, with red-tasseled reins on her palfrey and gold worked on her saddle. The beggar departed with a purse of silver—more than Perrin thought they could afford to give, until the lady left an even fatter purse of gold. Women from every station in life, all alone, from Tarabon, and Ghealdan, and even Amadicia. But he had never expected to see one of the Tuatha'an.

"A bloody Tinker?" Uno exclaimed. The others echoed his surprise.

Ragan's topknot waved as he shook his head. "A Tinker wouldn't be mixed in this. Either she's not a Tinker, or she is not the one we are supposed to meet."

"Tinkers," Masema growled. "Useless cowards."

Uno's eye narrowed until it looked like the pritchel hole of an anvil; with the red painted eye on his patch, it gave him a villainous look. "Cowards, Masema?" he said softly. "If you were a woman, would you have the flaming nerve to ride up here, alone and bloody unarmed?" There was no doubt she would be unarmed if she was of the Tuatha'an. Masema kept his mouth shut, but the scar on his cheek stood out tight and pale.

"Burn me, if I would," Ragan said. "And burn me if you would either, Masema." Masema hitched at his cloak and ostentatiously searched the sky.

Uno snorted. "The Light send that flaming carrion eater was flaming alone," he muttered.

Slowly the shaggy brown-and-white mare meandered closer, picking a way along the clear ground between broad snowbanks. Once the brightly clad woman stopped to peer at something on the ground, then tugged the cowl of her cloak further over her head and heeled her mount forward in a slow walk. *The raven*, Perrin thought. *Stop looking at that bird and come on, woman. Maybe you've brought the word that finally takes us out of here. If Moiraine means to let us leave before spring. Burn her!* For a moment he was not sure whether he meant the Aes Sedai, or the Tinker woman who seemed to be taking her own time.

If she kept on as she was, the woman would pass a good

thirty paces to one side of the thicket. With her eyes fixed on where her piebald stepped, she gave no sign that she had seen them among the trees.

Perrin nudged the stallion's flanks with his heels, and the dun leaped ahead, sending up sprays of snow with his hooves. Behind him, Uno quietly gave the command, "Forward!"

Stepper was halfway to her before she seemed to become aware of them, and then she jerked her mare to a halt with a start. She watched as they formed an arc centered on her. Embroidery of eye-wrenching blue, in the pattern called a Tairen maze, made her red cloak even more garish. She was not young—gray showed thick in her hair where it was not hidden by her cowl—but her face had few lines, other than the disapproving frown she ran over their weapons. If she was alarmed at meeting armed men in the heart of mountain wilderness, though, she gave no sign. Her hands rested easily on the high pommel of her worn but well-kept saddle. And she did not smell afraid.

Stop that! Perrin told himself. He made his voice soft so as not to frighten her. "My name is Perrin, good mistress. If you need help, I will do what I can. If not, go with the Light. But unless the Tuatha'an have changed their ways, you are far from your wagons."

She studied them a moment more before speaking. There was a gentleness in her dark eyes, not surprising in one of the Traveling People. "I seek an . . . a woman."

The skip was small, but it was there. She sought not any woman, but an Aes Sedai. "Does she have a name, good mistress?" Perrin asked. He had done this too many times in the last few months to need her reply, but iron was spoiled for want of care.

"She is called. . . . Sometimes, she is called Moiraine. My name is Leya."

Perrin nodded. "We will take you to her, Mistress Leya. We have warm fires, and with luck something hot to eat." But he did not lift his reins immediately. "How did you find us?" He had asked before, each time Moiraine sent him out to wait at a spot she named, for a woman she knew would come. The answer would be the same as it always was, but he had to ask.

Leya shrugged and answered hesitantly. "I . . . knew that

if I came this way, someone would find me and take me to her. I . . . just . . . knew. I have news for her."

Perrin did not ask what news. The women gave the information they brought only to Moiraine.

And the Aes Sedai tells us what she chooses. He thought. Aes Sedai never lied, but it was said that the truth an Aes Sedai told you was not always the truth you thought it was. *Too late for qualms, now. Isn't it?*

"This way, Mistress Leya," he said, gesturing up the mountain. The Shienarans, with Uno at their head, fell in behind Perrin and Leya as they began to climb. The Borderlanders still studied the sky as much as the land, and the last two kept a special watch on their backtrail.

For a time they rode in silence except for the sounds the horses' hooves made, sometimes crunching through old snowcrust, sometimes sending rocks clattering as they crossed bare stretches. Now and again Leya cast glances at Perrin, at his bow, his axe, his face, but she did not speak. He shifted uncomfortably under the scrutiny, and avoided looking at her. He always tried to give strangers as little chance to notice his eyes as he could manage.

Finally he said, "I was surprised to see one of the Traveling People, believing as you do."

"It is possible to oppose evil without doing violence." Her voice held the simplicity of someone stating an obvious truth.

Perrin grunted sourly, then immediately muttered an apology. "Would it were as you say, Mistress Leya."

"Violence harms the doer as much as the victim," Leya said placidly. "That is why we flee those who harm us, to save them from harm to themselves as much for our own safety. If we do violence to oppose evil, soon we would be no different from what we struggle against. It is with the strength of our belief that we fight the Shadow."

Perrin could not help snorting. "Mistress, I hope you never have to face Trollocs with the strength of your belief. The strength of their swords will cut you down where you stand."

"It is better to die than to—" she began, but anger made him speak right over her. Anger that she just would not see. Anger that she really would die rather than harm anyone, no matter how evil.

"If you run, they will hunt you, and kill you, and eat your corpse. Or they might not wait till it *is* a corpse. Either way, you are dead, and it's evil that has won. And there are men just as cruel. Darkfriends and others. More others than I would have believed even a year ago. Let the Whitecloaks decide you Tinkers don't walk in the Light and see how many of you the strength of your belief can keep alive."

She gave him a penetrating look. "And yet you are not happy with your weapons."

How did she know that? He shook his head irritably, shaggy hair swaying. "The Creator made the world," he muttered, "not I. I must live the best I can in the world the way it is."

"So sad for one so young," she said softly. "Why so sad?"

"I should be watching, not talking," he said curtly. "You won't thank me if I get you lost." He heeled Stepper forward enough to cut off any further conversation, but he could feel her looking at him. *Sad? I'm not sad, just. . . . Light, I don't know. There ought to be a better way, that's all.* The itching tickle came again at the back of his head, but absorbed in ignoring Leya's eyes on his back, he ignored that, too.

Over the slope of the mountain and down they rode, across a forested valley with a broad stream running cold along its bottom, knee-deep on the horses. In the distance, the side of a mountain had been carved into the semblance of two towering forms. A man and a woman, Perrin thought they might be, though wind and rain had long since made that uncertain. Even Moiraine claimed to be unsure who they were supposed to be, or when the granite had been cut.

Pricklebacks and small trout darted away from the horses' hooves, silver flashes in the clear water. A deer raised its head from browsing, hesitated as the party rode up out of the stream, then bounded off into the trees, and a large mountain cat, gray striped and spotted with black, seemed to rise out of the ground, frustrated in its stalk. It eyed the horses a moment, and with a lash of its tail vanished after the deer. But there was little life visible in the mountains yet. Only a handful of birds perched on limbs or pecked at the ground where the snow had melted. More would return to the heights in a few weeks, but not yet. They saw no other ravens.

It was late afternoon by the time Perrin led them between

two steep-sloped mountains, snowy peaks as ever wrapped
in cloud, and turned up a smaller stream that splashed
downward over gray stones in a series of tiny waterfalls.
A bird called in the trees, and another answered it from
ahead.

Perrin smiled. Bluefinch calls. A Borderland bird. No
one rode this way without being seen. He rubbed his nose,
and did not look at the tree the first "bird" had called from.

Their path narrowed as they rode up through scrubby
leatherleaf and a few gnarled mountain oaks. The ground
level enough to ride beside the stream became barely wider
than a man on horseback, and the stream itself no more
than a tall man could step across.

Perrin heard Leya behind him, murmuring to herself.
When he looked over his shoulder, she was casting worried
glances up the steep slopes to either side. Scattered trees
perched precariously above them. It appeared impossible
they would not fall. The Shienarans rode easily, at last beginning to relax.

Abruptly a deep, oval bowl between the mountains
opened out before them, its sides steep but not nearly so
precipitous as the narrow passage. The stream rose from
a small spring at its far end. Perrin's sharp eyes picked out
a man with the topknot of a Shienaran, up in the limbs of
an oak to his left. Had a redwinged jay called instead of a
bluefinch, he would not have been alone, and the way in
would not have been so easy. A handful of men could hold
that passage against an army. If an army came, a handful
would have to.

Among the trees around the bowl stood log huts, not
readily visible, so that those gathered around the cook fires
at the bottom of the bowl seemed at first to be without shelter. There were fewer than a dozen in sight. And not many
more out of sight, Perrin knew. Most of them looked around
at the sound of horses, and some waved. The bowl seemed
filled with the smells of men and horses, of cooking and
burning wood. A long white banner hung limply from a tall
pole near them. One form, at least half again as tall as anyone else, sat on a log engrossed in a book that was small in
his huge hands. That one's attention never wavered, even
when the only other person without a topknot shouted, "So
you found her, did you? I thought you'd be gone the night,

this time." It was a young woman's voice, but she wore a boy's coat and breeches and had her hair cut short.

A burst of wind swirled into the bowl, making cloaks flap and rippling the banner out to its full length. For a moment the creature on it seemed to ride the wind. A four-legged serpent scaled in gold and scarlet, golden maned like a lion, and its feet each tipped with five golden claws. A banner of legend. A banner most men would not know if they saw it, but would fear when they learned its name.

Perrin waved a hand that took it all in as he led the way down into the bowl. "Welcome to the camp of the Dragon Reborn, Leya."

CHAPTER
2

Saidin

Face expressionless, the Tuatha'an woman stared at the banner as it drooped again, then turned her attention to those around the fire. Especially the one reading, the one half again as tall as Perrin and twice as big. "You have an Ogier with you. I would not have thought. . . ." She shook her head. "Where is Moiraine Sedai?" It seemed the Dragon banner might as well not exist as far as she was concerned.

Perrin gestured toward the rough hut that stood furthest up the slope, at the far end of the bowl. With walls and sloping roof of unpeeled logs, it was the largest, though not very big at that. Perhaps just barely large enough to be called a cabin rather than a hut. "That one is hers. Hers and Lan's. He is her Warder. When you have had something hot to drink—"

"No. I must speak to Moiraine."

He was not surprised. All the women who came insisted on speaking to Moiraine immediately, and alone. The news that Moiraine chose to share with the rest of them did not always seem very important, but the women held the intensity of a hunter stalking the last rabbit in the world for his starving family. The half-frozen old beggar woman had refused blankets and a plate of hot stew and tramped up to Moiraine's hut, barefoot in still-falling snow.

Leya slid from her saddle and handed the reins up to Perrin. "Will you see that she is fed?" She patted the piebald mare's nose. "Piesa is not used to carrying me over such rugged country."

"Fodder is scarce, still," Perrin told her, "but she'll have what we can give her."

Leya nodded, and went hurrying away up the slope without another word, holding her bright green skirts up, the blue-embroidered red cloak swaying behind her.

Perrin swung down from his saddle, exchanging a few words with the men who came from the fires to take the horses. He gave his bow to the one who took Stepper. No, except for one raven, they had seen nothing but the mountains and the Tuatha'an woman. Yes, the raven was dead. No, she had told them nothing of what was happening outside the mountains. No, he had no idea whether they would be leaving soon.

Or ever, he added to himself. Moiraine had kept them there all winter. The Shienarans did not think she gave the orders, not here, but Perrin knew that Aes Sedai somehow always seemed to get their way. Especially Moiraine.

Once the horses were led away to the rude log stable, the riders went to warm themselves. Perrin tossed his cloak back over his shoulders and held his hands out to the flames gratefully. The big kettle, Baerlon work by the look of it, gave off smells that had been making his mouth water for some time already. Someone had been lucky hunting today, it seemed, and lumpy roots circled another fire close by, giving off an aroma faintly like turnips as they roasted. He wrinkled his nose and concentrated on the stew. More and more he wanted meat above anything else.

The woman in men's clothes was peering toward Leya, who was just disappearing into Moiraine's hut.

"What do you see, Min?" he asked.

She came to stand beside him, her dark eyes troubled. He did not understand why she insisted on breeches instead of skirts. Perhaps it was because he knew her, but he could not see how anyone could look at her and see a too-handsome youth instead of a pretty young woman.

"The Tinker woman is going to die," she said softly, eyeing the others near the fires. None was close enough to hear.

He was still, thinking of Leya's gentle face. *Ah, Light! Tinkers never harm anyone!* He felt cold despite the warmth of the fire. *Burn me, I wish I'd never asked.* Even the few

Aes Sedai who knew of it did not understand what Min did. Sometimes she saw images and auras surrounding people, and sometimes she even knew what they meant.

Masuto came to stir the stew with a long wood spoon. The Shienaran eyed them, then laid a finger alongside his long nose and grinned widely before he left.

"Blood and ashes!" Min muttered. "He's probably decided we are sweethearts murmuring to each other by the fire."

"Are you sure?" Perrin asked. She raised her eyebrows at him, and he hastily added, "About Leya."

"Is that her name? I wish I didn't know. It always makes it worse, knowing and not being able to. . . . Perrin, I saw her own face floating over her shoulder, covered in blood, eyes staring. It's never any clearer than that." She shivered and rubbed her hands together briskly. "Light, but I wish I saw more happy things. All the happy things seem to have gone away."

He opened his mouth to suggest warning Leya, then closed it again. There was never any doubt about what Min saw and knew, for good or bad. If she was certain, it happened.

"Blood on her face," he muttered. "Does that mean she'll die by violence?" He winced that he said it so easily. *But what can I do? If I tell Leya, if I make her believe somehow, she'll live her last days in fear, and it will change nothing.*

Min gave a short nod.

If she's going to die by violence, it could mean an attack on the camp. But there were scouts out every day, and guards set day and night. And Moiraine had the camp warded, so she said; no creature of the Dark One would see it unless he walked right into it. He thought of the wolves. *No!* The scouts would find anyone or anything trying to approach the camp. "It's a long way back to her people," he said half to himself. "Tinkers wouldn't have brought their wagons any further than the foothills. Anything could happen between here and there."

Min nodded sadly. "And there aren't enough of us to spare even one guard for her. Even if it would do any good."

She had told him; she had tried warning people about bad things when, at six or seven, she had first realized not everyone could see what she saw. She would not say more, but he had the impression that her warnings had only made matters worse, when they were believed at all. It took some doing to believe in Min's viewings until you had proof.

"When?" he said. The word was cold in his ears, and hard as tool steel. *I can't do anything about Leya, but maybe I can figure out whether we're going to be attacked.*

As soon as the word was out of his mouth, she threw up her hands. She kept her voice down, though. "It isn't like that. I can never tell *when* something is going to happen. I only know it will, if I even know what I see means. You don't understand. The seeing doesn't come when I want it to, and neither does knowing. It just happens, and sometimes I know. Something. A little bit. It just happens." He tried to get a soothing word in, but she was letting it all out in a flood he could not stem. "I can see things around a man one day and not the next, or the other way 'round. Most of the time, I don't see anything around anyone. Aes Sedai always have images around them, of course, and Warders, though it's always harder to say what it means with them than with anyone else." She gave Perrin a searching look, half squinting. "A few others always do, too."

"Don't tell me what you see when you look at me," he said harshly, then shrugged his heavy shoulders. Even as a child he had been bigger than most of the others, and he had quickly learned how easy it was to hurt people by accident when you were bigger than they. It had made him cautious and careful, and regretful of his anger when he let it show. "I am sorry, Min. I shouldn't have snapped at you. I did not mean to hurt you."

She gave him a surprised look. "You didn't hurt me. Blessed few people *want* to know what I see. The Light knows, I would not, if it were someone else who could do it." Even the Aes Sedai had never heard of anyone else who had her gift. "Gift" was how they saw it, even if she did not.

"It's just that I wish there were something I could do about Leya. I couldn't stand it the way you do, knowing and not able to do anything."

"Strange," she said softly, "how you seem to care so much about the Tuatha'an. They are utterly peaceful, and I always see violence around—"

He turned his head away, and she cut off abruptly.

"Tuatha'an?" came a rumbling voice, like a huge bumble-bee. "What about the Tuatha'an?" The Ogier came to join them at the fire, marking his place in his book with a finger the size of a large sausage. A thin streamer of tabac smoke rose from the pipe in his other hand. His high-necked coat of dark brown wool buttoned up to the neck, and flared at the knee over turned-down boot tops. Perrin stood hardly as high as his chest.

Loial's face had frightened more than one person, with his nose broad enough almost to be called a snout and his too-wide mouth. His eyes were the size of saucers, with thick eyebrows that dangled like mustaches almost to his cheeks, and his ears poked up through long hair in tufted points. Some who had never seen an Ogier took him for a Trolloc, though Trollocs were as much legend to most of them as Ogier.

Loial's wide smile wavered and his eyes blinked as he became aware of having interrupted them. Perrin wondered how anyone could be frightened of the Ogier for long. *Yet some of the old stories call them fierce, and implacable as enemies.* He could not believe it. Ogier were enemies to no one.

Min told Loial of Leya's arrival, but not of what she had seen. She was usually closemouthed about those seeings, especially when they were bad. Instead, she added, "You should know how I feel, Loial, suddenly caught up by Aes Sedai and these Two Rivers folk."

Loial made a noncommittal sound, but Min seemed to take it for agreement.

"Yes," she said emphatically. "There I was, living my life in Baerlon as I liked it, when suddenly I was grabbed up by the scruff of the neck and jerked off to the Light knows where. Well, I might as well have been. My life has not been my own since I met Moiraine. And these Two Rivers farmboys." She rolled her eyes at Perrin, a wry twist to her mouth. "All I wanted was to live as I pleased, fall in love with a man I chose. . . ." Her cheeks reddened suddenly, and she cleared her throat. "I mean to say, what is wrong with wanting to live your life without all this up-heaval?"

"Ta'veren," Loial began. Perrin waved at him to stop,

but the Ogier could seldom be slowed, much less stopped, when one of his enthusiasms had him in its grip. He was accounted extremely hasty, by the Ogier way of looking at things. Loial pushed his book into a coat pocket and went on, gesturing with his pipe. "All of us, all of our lives, affect the lives of others, Min. As the Wheel of Time weaves us into the Pattern, the life-thread of each of us pulls and tugs at the life-threads around us. *Ta'veren* are the same, only much, much more so. They tug at the entire Pattern—for a time, at least—forcing it to shape around them. The closer you are to them, the more you are affected personally. It's said that if you were in the same room with Artur Hawkwing, you could feel the Pattern rearranging itself. I don't know how true that is, but I've read that it was. But it doesn't only work one way. *Ta'veren* themselves are woven to a tighter line than the rest of us, with fewer choices."

Perrin grimaced. *Bloody few of the ones that matter.*

Min tossed her head. "I just wish they didn't have to be so . . . so bloody *ta'veren* all the time. *Ta'veren* tugging on one side, and Aes Sedai meddling on the other. What chance does a woman have?"

Loial shrugged. "Very little, I suppose, as long as she stays close to *ta'veren.*"

"As if I had a choice," Min growled.

"It was your good fortune—or misfortune, if you see it that way—to fall in with not one, but three *ta'veren.* Rand, Mat, and Perrin. I myself count it very good fortune, and would even if they weren't my friends. I think I might even. . . ." The Ogier looked at them, suddenly shy, his ears twitching. "Promise you will not laugh? I think I might write a book about it. I have been taking notes."

Min smiled, a friendly smile, and Loial's ears pricked back up again. "That's wonderful," she told him. "But some of us feel as if we're being danced about like puppets by these *ta'veren.*"

"I didn't ask for it," Perrin burst out. "I did not ask for it."

She ignored him. "Is that what happened to you, Loial? Is that why you travel with Moiraine? I know you Ogier almost never leave your *stedding.* Did one of these *ta'veren* tug you along with him?"

Loial became engrossed in a study of his pipe. "I just

wanted to see the groves the Ogier planted," he muttered.
"Just to see the groves." He glanced at Perrin as if asking
for help, but Perrin only grinned.

Let's see how the shoe nails onto your hoof. He did not
know all of it, but he did know Loial had run away. He
was ninety years old, but not yet old enough by Ogier standards to leave the *stedding*—going Outside, they called
it—without the permission of the Elders. Ogier lived a very
long time, as humans saw things. Loial said the Elders
would not be best pleased when they put their hands on him
again. He seemed intent on putting that moment off as long
as possible.

There was a stir among the Shienarans, men getting to
their feet. Rand was coming out of Moiraine's hut.

Even at that distance Perrin could make him out clearly,
a young man with reddish hair and gray eyes. He was of
an age with Perrin, and would stand half a head taller if
they were side by side, though Rand was more slender, if
still broad across the shoulders. Embroidered golden thorns
ran up the sleeves of his high-collared, red coat, and on
the breast of his dark cloak stood the same creature as on
the banner, the four-legged serpent with the golden mane.
Rand and he had grown up together as friends. *Are we still
friends? Can we be? Now?*

The Shienarans bowed as one, heads held up but hands to
knees. "Lord Dragon," Uno called, "we stand ready. Honor
to serve."

Uno, who could hardly say a sentence without a curse,
spoke now with the deepest respect. The others echoed
him. "Honor to serve." Masema, who saw ill in everything,
and whose eyes now shone with utter devotion; Ragan; all
of them, awaiting a command if it were Rand's pleasure to
give one.

From the slope Rand stared down at them a moment,
then turned and disappeared into the trees.

"He has been arguing with Moiraine again," Min said
quietly. "All day, this time."

Perrin was not surprised, yet he still felt a small shock.
Arguing with an Aes Sedai. All the childhood tales came
back to him. Aes Sedai, who made thrones and nations
dance to their hidden strings. Aes Sedai, whose gift always
had a hook in it, whose price was always smaller than you

could believe, yet always turned out to be greater than you could imagine. Aes Sedai, whose anger could break the ground and summon lightning. Some of the stories were untrue, he knew now. And at the same time, they did not tell the half.

"I had better go to him," he said. "After they argue, he always needs someone to talk to." And aside from Moiraine and Lan, there were only the three of them—Min, Loial, and him—who did not stare at Rand as if he stood above kings. And of the three only Perrin knew him from before.

He strode up the slope, pausing only to glance at the closed door of Moiraine's hut. Leya would be in there, and Lan. The Warder seldom let himself get far from the Aes Sedai's side.

Rand's much smaller hut was a little lower down, well hidden in the trees, away from all the rest. He had tried living down among the other men, but their constant awe drove him off. He kept to himself, now. Too much to himself, to Perrin's thinking. But he knew Rand was not headed to his hut now.

Perrin hurried on to where one side of the bowl-shaped valley suddenly became sheer cliff, fifty paces high and smooth except for tough brush clinging tenaciously here and there. He knew exactly where a crack in the gray rock wall lay, an opening hardly wider than his shoulders. With only a ribbon of late-afternoon light overhead, it was like walking down a tunnel.

Half a mile the crack ran, abruptly opening out into a narrow vale, less than a mile long, its floor covered with rocks and boulders, and even the steep slopes were thickly forested with tall leatherleaf and pine and fir. Long shadows stretched away from the sun sitting on the mountaintops. The walls of this place were unbroken save for the crack, and as steep as if a giant axe had buried itself in the mountains. It could be even more easily defended by a few than the bowl, but it had neither stream nor spring. No one went there. Except Rand, after he argued with Moiraine.

Rand stood not far from the entrance, leaning against the rough trunk of a leatherleaf, staring at the palms of his hands. Perrin knew that on each there was a heron, branded into the flesh. Rand did not move when Perrin's boot scraped on stone.

Suddenly Rand began to recite softly, never looking up from his hands.

> Twice and twice shall he be marked,
> twice to live, and twice to die.
> Once the heron, to set his path.
> Twice the heron, to name him true.
> Once the Dragon, for remembrance lost.
> Twice the Dragon, for the price he must pay.

With a shudder he tucked his hands under his arms. "But no Dragons, yet." He chuckled roughly. "Not yet."

For a moment Perrin simply looked at him. A man who could channel the One Power. A man doomed to go mad from the taint on *saidin*, the male half of the True Source, and certain to destroy everything around him in his madness. A man—a thing!—everyone was taught to loathe and fear from childhood. Only . . . it was hard to stop seeing the boy he had grown up with. *How do you just* stop *being somebody's friend?* Perrin chose a small boulder with a flat top, and sat, waiting.

After a while Rand turned his head to look at him. "Do you think Mat is all right? He looked so sick, the last I saw him."

"He must be all right by now." *He should be in Tar Valon, by now. They'll Heal him, there. And Nynaeve and Egwene will keep him out of trouble.* Egwene and Nynaeve, Rand and Mat and Perrin. All five from Emond's Field in the Two Rivers. Few people had come into the Two Rivers from outside, except for occasional peddlers, and merchants once a year to buy wool and tabac. Almost no one had ever left. Until the Wheel chose out its *ta'veren*, and five simple country folk could stay where they were no longer. Could be what they had been no longer.

Rand nodded and was silent.

"Lately," Perrin said, "I find myself wishing I was still a blacksmith. Do you. . . . Do you wish you were still just a shepherd?"

"Duty," Rand muttered. "Death is lighter than a feather, duty heavier than a mountain. That's what they say in Shienar. 'The Dark One is stirring. The Last Battle is coming. And the Dragon Reborn has to face the Dark One in the Last Battle, or the Shadow will cover everything. The Wheel of Time broken. Every Age remade in the Dark One's image.' There's only me." He began to laugh mirthlessly, his shoulders shaking. "I have the duty, because there isn't anybody else, now is there?"

Perrin shifted uneasily. The laughter had a raw edge that made his skin crawl. "I understand you were arguing with Moiraine again. The same thing?"

Rand drew a deep, ragged breath. "Don't we always argue about the same thing? They're down there, on Almoth Plain, and the Light alone knows where else. Hundreds of them. Thousands. They declared for the Dragon Reborn because I raised that banner. Because I let myself be called the Dragon. Because I could see no other choice. And they're dying. Fighting, searching, and praying for the man who is supposed to lead them. Dying. And I sit here safe in the mountains all winter. I . . . I owe them . . . something."

"You think I like it?" Perrin swung his head in irritation.

"You take whatever she says to you," Rand grated. "You never stand up to her."

"Much good it has done you, standing up to her. You have argued all winter, and we have sat here like lumps all winter."

"Because she is right." Rand laughed again, that chilling laugh. "The Light burn me, she is right. They are all split up into little groups all over the plain, all across Tarabon and Arad Doman. If I join any one of them, the Whitecloaks and the Domani army and the Taraboners will be on top of them like a duck on a beetle."

Perrin almost laughed himself, in confusion. "If you agree with her, why in the Light do you argue all the time?"

"Because I have to do something. Or I'll . . . I'll—burst like a rotted melon!"

"Do what? If you listen to what she says—"

Rand gave him no chance to say they would sit there forever. "Moiraine says! Moiraine says!" Rand jerked erect, squeezing his head between his hands. "Moiraine has something to say about everything! Moiraine says I mustn't go to the men who are dying in my name. Moiraine says I'll know what to do next because the Pattern will force me to it. Moiraine says! But she never says how I'll know. Oh, no! She doesn't know that." His hands fell to his sides, and he turned toward Perrin, head tilted and eyes narrowed. "Sometimes I feel as if Moiraine is putting me through my paces like a fancy Tairen stallion doing his steps. Do you ever feel that?"

Perrin scrubbed a hand through his shaggy hair. "I. . . . Whatever is pushing us, or pulling us, I know who the enemy is, Rand."

"Ba'alzamon," Rand said softly. An ancient name for the Dark One. In the Trolloc tongue, it meant Heart of the Dark. "And I must face him, Perrin." His eyes closed in a grimace, half smile, half pain. "Light help me, half the time I want it to happen now, to be over and done with, and the other half. . . . How many times can I manage to. . . . Light, it pulls at me so. What if I can't. . . . What if I. . . ." The ground trembled.

"Rand?" Perrin said worriedly.

Rand shivered; despite the chill, there was sweat on his face. His eyes were still shut tight. "Oh, Light," he groaned, "it pulls so."

Suddenly the ground heaved beneath Perrin, and the valley echoed with a vast rumble. It seemed as if the ground was jerked out from under his feet. He fell—or the earth leaped up to meet him. The valley shook as though a vast hand had reached down from the sky to wrench it out of the land. He clung to the ground while it tried to bounce him like a ball. Pebbles in front of his eyes leaped and tumbled, and dust rose in waves.

"Rand!" His bellow was lost in the grumbling roar.

Rand stood with his head thrown back, his eyes still shut tight. He did not seem to feel the thrashing of the ground that had him now at one angle, now at another. His balance never shifted, no matter how he was tossed. Perrin could not be certain, being shaken as he was, but he thought Rand wore a sad smile. The trees flailed about, and the leatherleaf suddenly cracked in two, the greater part of its trunk crashing down not three paces from Rand. He noticed it no more than he noticed any of the rest.

Perrin struggled to fill his lungs. "Rand! For the love of the Light, Rand! Stop it!"

As abruptly as it had begun, it was done. A weakened branch cracked off of a stunted oak with a loud snap. Perrin got to his feet slowly, coughing. Dust hung in the air, sparkling motes in the rays of the setting sun.

Rand was staring at nothing, now, chest heaving as if he had run ten miles. This had never happened before, nor anything remotely like it.

"Rand," Perrin said carefully, "what—?"

Rand still seemed to be looking into a far distance. "It is always there. Calling to me. Pulling at me. *Saidin.* The male half of the True Source. Sometimes I can't stop myself from reaching out for it." He made a motion of plucking something out of the air, and transferred his stare to his closed fist. "I can feel the taint even before I touch it. The Dark One's taint, like a thin coat of vileness trying to hide the Light. It turns my stomach, but I cannot help myself. I cannot! Only sometimes, I reach out, and it's like trying to catch air." His empty hand sprang open, and he gave a bitter laugh. "What if that happens when the Last Battle comes? What if I reach out and catch nothing?"

"Well, you caught something that time," Perrin said hoarsely. "What were you doing?"

Rand looked around as if seeing things for the first time. The fallen leatherleaf, and the broken branches. There was, Perrin realized, surprisingly little damage. He had expected gaping rents in the earth. The wall of trees looked almost whole.

"I did not mean to do this. It was as if I tried to open a tap, and instead pulled the whole tap out of the barrel. It . . . filled me. I had to send it somewhere before it burned me up, but I . . . I did not mean this."

Perrin shook his head. *What use to tell him to try not to do it again? He barely knows more about what he's doing than I do.* He contented himself with, "There are enough who want you dead—and the rest of us—without you doing the job for them." Rand did not seem to be listening. "We had best get on back to the camp. It will be dark soon, and I don't know about you, but I am hungry."

"What? Oh. You go on, Perrin. I will be along. I want to be alone again a while."

Perrin hesitated, then turned reluctantly toward the crack in the valley wall. He stopped when Rand spoke again.

"Do you have dreams when you sleep? Good dreams?"

"Sometimes," Perrin said warily. "I don't remember much of what I dream." He had learned to set guards on his dreaming.

"They're always there, dreams," Rand said, so softly Perrin barely heard. "Maybe they tell us things. True things." He fell silent, brooding.

"Supper's waiting," Perrin said, but Rand was deep in his own thoughts. Finally Perrin turned and left him standing there.

CHAPTER

3

News from the Plain

Darkness shrouded part of the crack, for in one place the tremors had collapsed a part of the wall against the other side, high up. He stared up at the blackness warily before hurrying underneath, but the slab of stone seemed to be solidly wedged in place. The itch had returned to the back of his head, stronger than before. *No, burn me! No!* It went away.

When he came out above the camp, the bowl was filled with odd shadows from the sinking sun. Moiraine was standing outside her hut, peering up at the crack. He stopped short. She was a slender, dark-haired woman no taller than his shoulder, and pretty, with the ageless quality of all Aes Sedai who had worked with the One Power for a time. He could not put any age at all to her, with her face too smooth for many years and her dark eyes too wise for youth. Her dress of deep blue silk was disarrayed and dusty, and wisps stuck out in her usually well-ordered hair. A smudge of dust lay across her face.

He dropped his eyes. She knew about him—she and Lan alone, of those in the camp—and he did not like the knowing in her face when she looked into his eyes. Yellow eyes. Someday, perhaps, he could bring himself to ask her what she knew. An Aes Sedai must know more of it than he did. But this was not the time. There never seemed to be a time. "He. . . . He didn't mean. . . . It was an accident."

"An accident," she said in a flat voice, then shook her head and vanished back inside the hut. The door banged shut a little loudly.

Perrin drew a deep breath and continued on down toward

the cook fires. There would be another argument between Rand and the Aes Sedai, in the morning if not tonight.

Half a dozen trees lay toppled on the slopes of the bowl, roots ripped out of the earth in arcs of soil. A trail of scrapes and churned ground led down to the streamside and a boulder that had not been there before. One of the huts up the opposite slope had collapsed in the tremors, and most of the Shienarans were gathered around it, rebuilding it. Loial was with them. The Ogier could pick up a log it would take four men to lift. Uno's curses occasionally drifted down.

Min stood by the fires, stirring a kettle with a disgruntled expression. There was a small bruise on her cheek, and a faint smell of burned stew hung in the air. "I hate cooking," she announced, and peered doubtfully into the kettle. "If something goes wrong with it, it isn't my fault. Rand spilled half of it on the fire with his. . . . What right does he have to bounce us around like sacks of grain?" She rubbed the seat of her breeches and winced. "When I get my hands on him, I'll thump him so he never forgets." She waved the wooden spoon at Perrin as if she intended to start the thumping with him.

"Was anyone hurt?"

"Only if you count bruises," Min said grimly. "They were upset, all right, at first. Then they saw Moiraine staring off toward Rand's hidey-hole, and decided it was his work. If the *Dragon* wants to shake the mountain down on our heads, then the *Dragon* must have a good reason for it. If he decided to make them take off their skins and dance in their bones, they would think it all right." She snorted and rapped the spoon on the edge of the kettle.

He looked back toward Moiraine's hut. If Leya had been hurt—if she were dead—the Aes Sedai would not simply have gone back inside. The sense of waiting was still there. *Whatever it is, it hasn't happened yet.* "Min, maybe you had better go. First thing in the morning. I have some silver I can let you have, and I'm sure Moiraine would give you enough to take passage with a merchant's train out of Ghealdan. You could be back in Baerlon before you know it."

She looked at him until he began to wonder if he had said something wrong. Finally, she said, "That is very sweet of you, Perrin. But, no."

"I thought you wanted to go. You're always carrying on about having to stay here."

"I knew an old Illianer woman; once," she said slowly. "When she was young, her mother arranged a marriage for her with a man she had never even met. They do that down in Illian, sometimes. She said she spent the first five years raging against him, and the next five scheming to make his life miserable without his knowing who was to blame. It was only years later, she said, when he died, that she realized he really had been the love of her life."

"I don't see what that has to do with this."

Her look said he obviously was not trying to understand, and her voice became overly patient. "Just because fate has chosen something for you instead of you choosing it for yourself doesn't mean it has to be bad. Even if it's something you are sure you would never have chosen in a hundred years. 'Better ten days of love than years of regretting,'" she quoted.

"I understand that even less," he told her. "You don't have to stay if you don't want to."

She hung the spoon on a tall forked stick stuck in the ground, then surprised him by rising on tiptoe to kiss his cheek. "You are a very nice man, Perrin Aybara. Even if you don't understand anything."

Perrin blinked at her uncertainly. He wished that he could be certain Rand was in his right mind, or that Mat were there. He was never sure of his ground with girls, but Rand always seemed to know his way. So did Mat; most of the girls back home in Emond's Field had sniffed that Mat would never grow up, but he had seemed to have a way with them.

"What about you, Perrin? Don't you ever want to go home?"

"All the time," he said fervently. "But I . . . I do not think I can. Not yet." He looked off toward Rand's vale. *We are tied together, it seems, aren't we, Rand?* "Maybe not ever." He thought he had said that too softly for her to hear, but the look she gave him was full of sympathy. And agreement.

His ears caught faint footsteps behind him, and he looked back up toward Moiraine's hut. Two shapes were making their way down through the deepening twilight, one a woman, slender and graceful even on the rough, slanting ground. The man, head and shoulders taller than his companion, turned off toward where the Shienarans were working. Even to Perrin's eyes he was indistinct, sometimes seeming to vanish altogether, then reappear in midstride, parts of him fading into the night and fading back as the wind gusted. Only a Warder's shifting cloak could do that, which made the larger figure Lan, just as the smaller was certainly Moiraine.

Well behind them, another shape, even dimmer, slipped between the trees. *Rand*, Perrin thought, *going back to his hut. Another night when he won't eat because he can't stand the way everybody looks at him.*

"You must have eyes in the back of your head," Min said, frowning toward the approaching woman. "Or else the sharpest ears I have ever heard of. Is that Moiraine?"

Careless. He had grown so used to the Shienarans knowing how well he could see—in daylight at least; they did not know about the night—that he was beginning to slip about other things. *Carelessness might kill me yet.*

"Is the Tuatha'an woman all right?" Min asked as Moiraine came to the fire.

"She is resting." The Aes Sedai's low voice had its usual musical quality, as if speaking were halfway to singing, and her hair and clothes were back in perfect order again. She rubbed her hands over the fire. There was a golden ring on her left hand, a serpent biting its own tail. The Great Serpent, an even older symbol for eternity than the Wheel of Time. Every woman trained in Tar Valon wore such a ring.

For a moment Moiraine's gaze rested on Perrin, and seemed to penetrate too deeply. "She fell and split her scalp when Rand. . . ." Her mouth tightened, but in the next instant her face was utter calm again. "I Healed her, and she is sleeping. There is always a good deal of blood with even a minor scalp wound, but it was not serious. Did you see anything about her, Min?"

Min looked uncertain. "I saw. . . . I thought I saw her death. Her own face, all over blood. I was sure I knew what it meant, but if she split her scalp. . . . Are you sure she is all right?" It was a measure of her discomfort that she asked. An Aes Sedai did not Heal and leave anything wrong that could be Healed. And Moiraine's Talents were particularly strong in that area.

Min sounded so troubled that Perrin was surprised for

a moment. Then he nodded to himself. She did not really like doing what she did, but it was a part of her; she thought she knew how it worked, or some of it, at least. If she was wrong, it would almost be like finding out she did not know how to use her own hands.

Moiraine considered her for a moment, serene and dispassionate. "You have never been wrong in any reading for me, not one about which I had any way of knowing. Perhaps this is the first time."

"When I know, I know," Min whispered obstinately. "Light help me, I do."

"Or perhaps it is yet to come. She has a long way yet to travel, to return to her wagons, and she must ride through unsettled lands."

The Aes Sedai's voice was a cool song, uncaring. Perrin made an involuntary sound in his throat. *Light, did I sound like that? I won't let a death matter that little to me.*

As if he had spoken aloud, Moiraine looked at him. "The Wheel weaves as the Wheel wills, Perrin. I told you long ago that we were in a war. We cannot stop just because some of us may die. Any of us may die before it is done. Leya's weapons may not be the same as yours, but she knew that when she became part of it."

Perrin dropped his eyes. *That's as may be, Aes Sedai, but I will never accept it the way you do.*

Lan joined them across the fire, with Uno and Loial. The flames cast flickering shadows across the Warder's face, making it seem more carved from stone even than it normally did, all hard planes and angles. His cloak was not much easier to look at in the firelight. Sometimes it seemed only a dark gray cloak, or black, but the gray and black appeared to crawl and change if you looked too closely, shades and shadows sliding across it, soaking into it. Other times, it looked as if Lan had somehow made a hole in the night and pulled darkness 'round his shoulders. Not at all an easy thing to watch, and not made any easier by the man who wore it.

Lan was tall and hard, broad-shouldered, with blue eyes like frozen mountain lakes, and he moved with a deadly grace that made the sword on his hip seem a part of him. It was not that he seemed merely capable of violence and death; this man had tamed violence and death and kept

them in his pocket, ready to be loosed in a heartbeat, or embraced, should Moiraine give the word. Beside Lan, even
Uno appeared less dangerous. There was a touch of gray in
the Warder's long hair, held back by a woven leather cord
around his forehead, but younger men stepped back from
confronting Lan—if they were wise.

"Mistress Leya has the usual news from Almoth Plain,"
Moiraine said. "Everyone fighting everyone else. Villages
burned. People fleeing in every direction. And Hunters have
appeared on the plain, searching for the Horn of Valere."
Perrin shifted—the Horn was where no Hunter on Almoth
Plain would find it; where he hoped no Hunter ever would
find it—and she gave him a cool look before continuing.
She did not like any of them to speak of the Horn. Except
when she chose to, of course.

"She brought different news, as well. The Whitecloaks
have perhaps five thousand men on Almoth Plain."

Uno grunted. "That's flamin'—uh, pardon, Aes Sedai.
That must be half their strength. They've never committed
so much to one place before."

"Then I suppose all those who declared for Rand are dead
or scattered," Perrin muttered. "Or they soon will be. You
were right, Moiraine." He did not like the thought of Whitecloaks. He did not like the Children of the Light at all.

"That is what is odd," Moiraine said. "Or the first part
of it. The Children have announced that their purpose is to
bring peace, which is not unusual for them. What *is* unusual
is that while they are trying to force the Taraboners and the
Domani back across their respective borders, they have not
moved in any force against those who have declared for the
Dragon."

Min gave an exclamation of surprise. "Is she certain?
That does not sound like any Whitecloaks I ever heard of."

"There can't be many blood—uh—many Tinkers left on
the plain," Uno said. His voice creaked from the strain of
watching his language in front of an Aes Sedai. His real eye
matched the frown of the painted one. "They don't like to
stay where there's any kind of trouble, especially fighting.
There can't be enough of them to see everywhere."

"There are enough for my purposes," Moiraine said
firmly. "Most have gone, but some few remained because I
asked them to. And Leya is quite certain. Oh, the Children

have snapped up some of the Dragonsworn, where there were only a handful gathered. But though they proclaim they will bring down this *false* Dragon, though they have a thousand men supposedly doing nothing but hunting him, they avoid contact with any party of as many as fifty Dragonsworn. Not openly, you understand, but there is always some delay, something that allows those they chase to slip away."

"Then Rand can go down to them as he wants." Loial blinked uncertainly at the Aes Sedai. The whole camp knew of her arguments with Rand. "The Wheel weaves a way for him."

Uno and Lan opened their mouths at the same time, but the Shienaran gave way with a small bow. "More likely," the Warder said, "it is some Whitecloak plot, though the Light burn me if I can see what it is. But when the Whitecloaks give me a gift, I search for the poisoned needle hidden in it." Uno nodded grimly. "Besides which," Lan added, "the Domani and the Taraboners are still trying as hard to kill the Dragonsworn as they are to kill each other."

"And there is another thing," Moiraine said. "Three young men have died in villages Mistress Leya's wagons passed near." Perrin noticed a flicker of Lan's eyelid; for the Warder, it was as much a sign of surprise as a shout from another man. Lan had not expected her to tell this. Moiraine went on. "One died by poison, two by the knife. Each in circumstances where no one should have been able to come close unseen, but that is how it happened." She peered into the flames. "All three young men were taller than most, and had light-colored eyes. Light eyes are uncommon on Almoth Plain, but I think it is very unlucky right now to be a tall young man with light eyes there."

"How?" Perrin asked. "How could they be killed if no one could get close to them?"

"The Dark One has killers you don't notice until it is too late," Lan said quietly.

Uno gave a shiver. "The Soulless. I never heard of one south of the Borderlands before."

"Enough of such talk," Moiraine said firmly.

Perrin had questions—*What in the Light are the Soulless? Are they like a Trolloc, or a Fade? What?*—but he left them unasked. When Moiraine decided enough had been said about something, she would not talk of it anymore.

And when she shut her mouth, you could not pry Lan's open with an iron bar. The Shienarans followed her lead, too. No one wanted to anger an Aes Sedai.

"Light!" Min muttered, uneasily eyeing the deepening darkness around them. "You don't *notice* them? Light!"

"So nothing has changed," Perrin said glumly. "Not really. We cannot go down to the plain, and the Dark One wants us dead."

"Everything changes," Moiraine said calmly, "and the Pattern takes it all in. We must ride on the Pattern, not on the changes of a moment." She looked at them each in turn, then said, "Uno, are you certain your scouts missed nothing suspicious? Even something small?"

"The Lord Dragon's Rebirth has loosed the bonds of certainty, Moiraine Sedai, and there is never certainty if you fight Myrddraal, but I will stake my life that the scouts did as good a job as any Warder." It was one of the longest speeches Perrin had ever heard out of Uno without any curses. There was sweat on the man's forehead from the effort.

"We all may," Moiraine said. "What Rand did might as well have been a fire on the mountaintop for any Myrddraal within ten miles."

"Maybe . . ." Min began hesitantly. "Maybe you ought to set wards that will keep them out." Lan gave her a hard stare. He sometimes questioned Moiraine's decisions himself, though he seldom did so where anyone could overhear, but he did not approve of others doing the same. Min frowned right back at him. "Well, Myrddraal and Trollocs are bad enough, but at least I can see them. I don't like the idea that one of these . . . these Soulless might sneak in here and slit my throat before I even noticed him."

"The wards I set will hide us from the Soulless as well as from any other Shadowspawn," Moiraine said. "When you are weak, as we are, the best choice is often to hide. If there *is* a Halfman close enough to have. . . . Well, to set wards that would kill them if they tried to enter camp is beyond my abilities, and even if I could, such a warding would only pen us here. Since it is not possible to set two kinds of warding at once, I leave the scouts and the guards—and Lan—to defend us, and use the one warding that may do some good."

"I could make a circuit around the camp," Lan said. "If

there is anything out there that the scouts missed, I will find it." It was not a boast, just a statement of fact. Uno even nodded agreement.

Moiraine shook her head. "If you are needed tonight, my Gaidin, it will be here." Her gaze rose toward the dark mountains around them. "There is a feeling in the air."

"Waiting." The word left Perrin's tongue before he could stop it. When Moiraine looked at him—into him—he wished he had it back.

"Yes," she said. "Waiting. Make sure your guards are especially alert tonight, Uno." There was no need to suggest that the men sleep with their weapons close at hand; Shienarans always did that. "Sleep well," she added to them all, as if there were any chance of that now, and started back for her hut. Lan stayed long enough to spoon up three dishes of stew, then hurried after her, quickly swallowed by the night.

Perrin's eyes shone golden as they followed the Warder through the darkness. "Sleep well," he muttered. The smell of cooked meat suddenly made him queasy. "I have the third watch, Uno?" The Shienaran nodded. "Then I will try to take her advice." Others were coming to the fires, and murmurs of conversation followed him up the slope.

He had a hut to himself, a small thing of logs barely tall enough to stand in, the chinks filled with dried mud. A rough bed, padded with pine boughs beneath a blanket, took up nearly half of it. Whoever had unsaddled his horse had also propped his bow just inside the door. He hung up his belt, with axe and quiver, on a peg, then stripped down to his smallclothes, shivering. The nights were cold still, but cold kept him from sleeping too deeply. In deep sleep, dreams came that he could not shake off.

For a time, with a single blanket over him, he lay staring at the log roof, shivering. Then sleep came, and with it, dreams.

CHAPTER
4

Shadows Sleeping

Cold filled the common room of the inn despite the fire blazing on the long, stone hearth. Perrin rubbed his hands before the flames, but he could get no warmth in them. There was an odd comfort in the cold, though, as if it were a shield. A shield against what, he could not think. Something murmured in the back of his mind, a dim sound only vaguely heard, scratching to get in.

"So you will give it up, then. It is the best thing for you. Come. Sit, and we will talk."

Perrin turned to look at the speaker. The round tables scattered about the room were empty except for the lone man seated in a corner, in the shadows. The rest of the room seemed in some way hazy, almost an impression rather than a place, especially anything he was not looking at directly. He glanced back at the fire; it burned on a brick hearth, now. Somehow, none of it bothered him. *It should.* But he could not have said why.

The man beckoned, and Perrin walked closer to his table. A square table. The tables were square. Frowning, he reached out to finger the tabletop, but pulled his hand back. There were no lamps in that corner of the room, and despite the light elsewhere, the man and his table were almost hidden, nearly blended with the dimness.

Perrin had a feeling that he knew the man, but it was as vague as what he saw out of the corner of his eye. The fellow was in his middle years, handsome and too well dressed for a country inn, in dark, nearly black, velvets with white lace falls at his collar and cuffs. He sat stiffly, sometimes pressing a hand to his chest, as if moving hurt him.

His dark eyes were fixed on Perrin's face; they appeared like glistening points in the shadows.

"Give up what?" Perrin asked.

"That, of course." The man nodded to the axe at Perrin's waist. He sounded surprised, as if it were a conversation they had had before, an old argument taken up again.

Perrin had not realized the axe was there, had not felt the weight of it pulling at his belt. He ran a hand over the half-moon blade and the thick spike that balanced it. The steel felt—solid. More solid than anything else there. Maybe even more solid than he was himself. He kept his hand there, to hold onto something real.

"I have thought of it," he said, "but I do not think I can. Not yet." *Not yet?* The inn seemed to flicker, and the murmur sounded again in his head. *No!* The murmur faded.

"No?" The man smiled, a cold smile. "You are a blacksmith, boy. And a good one, from what I hear. Your hands were made for a hammer, not an axe. Made to make things, not to kill. Go back to that before it is too late."

Perrin found himself nodding. "Yes. But I'm *ta'veren*." He had never said that out loud before. *But he knows it already.* He was sure of that, though he could not say why.

For an instant the man's smile became a grimace, but then it returned in more strength than before. A cold strength. "There are ways to change things, boy. Ways to avoid even fate. Sit, and we will talk of them." The shadows appeared to shift and thicken, to reach out.

Perrin took a step back, keeping well in the light. "I don't think so."

"At least have a drink with me. To years past and years to come. Here, you will see things more clearly after." The cup the man pushed across the table had not been there a moment before. It shone bright silver, and dark, blood-red wine filled it to the brim.

Perrin peered at the man's face. Even to his sharp eyes, the shadows seemed to shroud the other man's features like a Warder's cloak. Darkness molded the man like a caress. There was something about the man's eyes, something he thought he could remember if he tried hard enough. The murmur returned.

"No," he said. He spoke to the soft sound inside his head, but when the man's mouth tightened in anger, a flash of rage suppressed as soon as begun, he decided it would do for the wine as well. "I am not thirsty."

He turned and started for the door. The fireplace was rounded river stones; a few long tables lined by benches filled the room. He suddenly wanted to be outside, anywhere away from this man.

"You will not have many chances," the man said behind him in a hard voice. "Three threads woven together share one another's doom. When one is cut, all are. Fate can kill you, if it does not do worse."

Perrin felt a sudden heat against his back, rising then fading just as quickly, as if the doors of a huge smelting furnace had swung open and closed again. Startled, he turned back to the room. It was empty.

Only a dream, he thought, shivering from the cold, and with that everything shifted.

He stared into the mirror, a part of him not comprehending what he saw, another part accepting. A gilded helmet, worked like a lion's head, sat on his head as if it belonged there. Gold leaf covered his ornately hammered breastplate, and gold-work embellished the plate and mail on his arms and legs. Only the axe at his side was plain. A voice—his own—whispered in his mind that he would take it over any other weapon, had carried it a thousand times, in a hundred battles. *No!* He wanted to take it off, throw it away. *I can't!* There was a sound in his head, louder than a murmur, almost at the level of understanding.

"A man destined for glory."

He spun away from the mirror and found himself staring at the most beautiful woman he had ever seen. He noticed nothing else about the room, cared to see nothing but her. Her eyes were pools of midnight, her skin creamy pale and surely softer, more smooth than her dress of white silk. When she moved toward him, his mouth went dry. He realized that every other woman he had ever seen was clumsy and ill-shaped. He shivered, and wondered why he felt cold.

"A man should grasp his destiny with both hands," she said, smiling. It was almost enough to warm him, that smile. She was tall, less than a hand short of being able to look him in the eyes. Silver combs held hair darker than a raven's wing. A broad belt of silver links banded a waist he could have encircled with his hands.

"Yes," he whispered. Inside him, startlement fought with acceptance. He had no use for glory. But when she said it, he wanted nothing else. "I mean. . . ." The murmuring sound dug at his skull. "No!" It was gone, and for a moment, so was acceptance. Almost. He put a hand to his head, touched the golden helmet, took it off. "I . . . I don't think I want this. It is not mine."

"Don't want it?" She laughed. "What man with blood in his veins would not want glory? As much glory as if you had sounded the Horn of Valere."

"I don't," he said, though a piece of him shouted that he lied. The Horn of Valere. *The Horn rang out, and the wild charge began. Death rode at his shoulder, and yet she waited ahead, too. His lover. His destroyer.* "No! I am a blacksmith."

Her smile was pitying. "Such a little thing to want. You must not listen to those who would try to turn you from your destiny. They would demean you, debase you. Destroy you. Fighting fate can only bring pain. Why choose pain, when you can have glory? When your name can be remembered alongside all the heroes of legend?"

"I am no hero."

"You don't know the half of what you are. Of what you can be. Come, share a cup with me, to destiny and glory." There was a shining silver cup in her hand, filled with blood-red wine. "Drink."

He stared at the cup, frowning. There was something . . . familiar about it. A growling chewed at his brain. "No!" He fought away from it, refusing to listen. "No!"

She held out the golden cup to him. "Drink."

Golden? I thought the cup was. . . . It was. . . . The rest of the thought would not come. But in his confusion the sound came again, inside, gnawing, demanding to be heard. "No," he said. "No!" He looked at the golden helmet in his hands and threw it aside. "I am a blacksmith. I am. . . ." The sound within his head fought him, struggling toward being heard. He wrapped his arms around his head to shut it out, and only shut it in. "I—am—a—man!" he shouted.

Darkness enfolded him, but her voice followed, whispering. "The night is always there, and dreams come to all men. Especially you, my wildling. And I will always be in your dreams."

Stillness.

He lowered his arms. He was back in his own coat and breeches again, sturdy and well made, if plain. Suitable garb for a blacksmith, or any country man. Yet he barely noticed them.

He stood on a low-railed bridge of stone, arching from one wide, flat-topped stone spire to another, spires that rose from depths too far for even his eyes to penetrate. The light would have been dim to any other eyes, and he could not make out from where it came. It just was. Everywhere he looked, left and right, up or down, were more bridges, more spires, and railless ramps. There seemed no end to them, no pattern. Worse, some of those ramps climbed to spire tops that had to be directly above the ones they had left. Splashing water echoed, the sound seeming to come from everywhere at once. He shivered with cold.

Suddenly, from the corner of his eye, he caught a motion, and without thinking, he crouched behind the stone railing. There was danger in being seen. He did not know why, but he knew it was true. He just knew.

Cautiously peering over the top of the rail, he sought what he had seen moving. A flash of white flickered on a distant ramp. A woman, he was sure, though he could not quite make her out. A woman in a white dress, hurrying somewhere.

On a bridge slightly below him, and much closer than the ramp where the woman had been, a man suddenly appeared, tall and dark and slender, the silver in his black hair giving him a distinguished look, his dark green coat thickly embroidered with golden leaves. Gold-work covered his belt and pouch, and gems sparkled on his dagger sheath, and golden fringe encircled his boot tops. Where had he come from?

Another man started across the bridge from the other side, his appearance as sudden as the first man's. Black stripes ran down the puffy sleeves of his red coat, and pale lace hung thick at his collar and cuffs. His boots were so worked with silver that it was hard to see the leather. He was shorter than the man he went to meet, more stocky, with close-cropped hair as white as his lace. Age did not make him frail, though. He strode with the same arrogant strength the other man showed.

The two of them approached each other warily. *Like two horse traders who know the other fellow has a spavined mare to sell*, Perrin thought.

The men began to talk. Perrin strained his ears, but he could not hear so much as a murmur above the splashing echoes. Frowns, and glares, and sharp motions as if half on the point of striking. They did not trust one another. He thought they might even hate each other.

He glanced up, searching for the woman, but she was gone. When he looked back down, another man had joined the first two. And somehow, from somewhere, Perrin knew him with the vagueness of an old memory. A handsome man in his middle years, wearing nearly black velvet and white lace. *An inn*, Perrin thought. *And something before that. Something. . . .* Something a long time ago, it seemed. But the memory would not come.

The first two men stood side by side, now, made uncomfortable allies by the presence of the newcomer. He shouted at them and shook his fist, while they shifted uneasily, refusing to meet his glares. If the two hated each other, they feared him more.

His eyes, Perrin thought. *What is strange about his eyes?*

The tall, dark man began to argue back, slowly at first, then with increasing fervor. The white-haired man joined in, and suddenly their temporary alliance broke. All three shouted at once, each at both of the others in turn. Abruptly the man in dark velvets threw his arms wide, as if demanding an end to it. And an expanding ball of fire enveloped them, hid them, spreading out and out.

Perrin threw his arms around his head and dropped behind the stone railing, huddling there as wind buffeted him and tore at his clothes, a wind as hot as fire. A wind that was fire. Even with his eyes shut, he could see it, flame billowing across everything, flame blowing through everything. The fiery gale roared through him, too; he could feel it, burning, tugging, trying to consume him and scatter the ashes. He yelled, trying to hang onto himself, knowing it was not enough.

And between one heartbeat and the next, the wind was gone. There was no diminishing. One instant a storm of flame pummeled him; the next, utter stillness. The echoes of falling water were the only sound.

Slowly, Perrin sat up, examining himself. His clothes were unsinged and whole, his exposed skin unburned. Only the memory of heat made him believe it had happened. A memory in the mind alone; his body felt no memory of it.

Cautiously he peeked over the railing. Only a few paces of half-melted footing at either end remained of the bridge where the men had been standing. Of them, there was no sign.

A prickling in the hair on the back of his neck made him look up. On a ramp above him and to the right, a shaggy gray wolf stood looking at him.

"No!" He scrambled to his feet and ran. "This is a dream! A nightmare! I want to wake up!" He ran, and his vision blurred. The blurs shifted. A buzzing filled his ears, then faded, and as it went, the shimmering in his eyes steadied.

He shivered with the cold and knew this for a dream, certain and sure, from the first moment. He was dimly aware of some shadowy memory of dreams preceding this, but this one he knew. He had been in this place before, on previous nights, and if he understood nothing of it, he still knew it for a dream. For once, knowing changed nothing.

Huge columns of polished redstone surrounded the open space where he stood, beneath a domed ceiling fifty paces or more above his head. He and another man as big could not have encircled one of those columns with their arms. The floor was paved with great slabs of pale gray stone, hard yet worn by countless generations of feet.

And centered beneath the dome was the reason why all those feet had come to this chamber. A sword, hanging hilt down in the air, apparently without support, seemingly where anyone could reach out and take it. It revolved slowly, as if some breath of air caught it. Yet it was not really a sword. It seemed made of glass, or perhaps crystal, blade and hilt and crossguard, catching such light as there was and shattering it into a thousand glitters and flashes.

He walked toward it and put out his hand, as he had done each time before. He clearly remembered doing it. The hilt hung there in front of his face, within easy reach. A foot from the shining sword, his hand splayed out against empty air as if it had touched stone. As he had known it would. He pushed harder, but he might as well have been shoving against a wall. The sword turned and sparkled, a foot away and as far out of reach as if on the other side of an ocean.

Callandor. He was not certain whether the whisper came inside his head or out; it seemed to echo 'round the columns, as soft as the wind, everywhere at once, insistent. *Callandor. Who wields me wields destiny. Take me, and begin the final journey.*

He took a step back, suddenly frightened. That whisper had never come before. Four times before he had had this dream—he could remember that even now; four nights, one after the other—and this was the first time anything had changed in it.

The Twisted Ones come.

It was a different whisper, from a source he knew, and he jumped as if a Myrddraal had touched him. A wolf stood there among the columns, a mountain wolf, almost waist-high and shaggy white and gray. It stared at him intently with eyes as yellow as his own.

The Twisted Ones come.

"No," Perrin rasped. "No! I will not let you in! I—will—not!"

He clawed his way awake and sat up in his hut, shaking with fear and cold and anger. "I will not," he whispered hoarsely.

The Twisted Ones come.

The thought was clear in his head, but the thought was not his own.

The Twisted Ones come, brother.

CHAPTER

5

Nightmares Walking

Leaping from his bed, Perrin snatched his axe and ran outside, barefoot and wearing nothing but thin linen, heedless of the cold. The moon bathed the clouds with pale white. More than enough light for his eyes, more than enough to see the shapes slipping through the trees from all sides, shapes almost as big as Loial, but with faces distorted by muzzles and beaks, half-human heads wearing horns and feathered crests, stealthy forms stalking on hooves or paws as often as booted feet.

He opened his mouth to shout warning, and suddenly the door of Moiraine's hut burst open and Lan dashed out, sword in hand and shouting, "Trollocs! Wake, for your lives! Trollocs!" Shouts answered him as men began to tumble from their huts, garbed for sleep, which for most meant not at all, but with swords ready. With a bestial roar, the Trollocs rushed forward to be met with steel and cries of "Shienar!" and "The Dragon Reborn!"

Lan was fully clothed—Perrin would have bet the Warder had not slept—and he flung himself among the Trollocs as if his wool were armor. He seemed to dance from one to another, man and sword flowing like water or wind, and where the Warder danced, Trollocs screamed and died.

Moiraine was out in the night as well, dancing her own dance among the Trollocs. Her only apparent weapon was a switch, but where she slashed a Trolloc, a line of flame grew on its flesh. Her free hand threw fiery balls summoned from thin air, and Trollocs howled as flames consumed them, thrashing on the ground.

An entire tree burst into flame from root to crown, then

another, and another. Trollocs shrieked at the sudden light, but they did not stop swinging their spiked axes and swords curved like scythes.

Abruptly Perrin saw Leya step hesitantly out of Moiraine's cabin, halfway around the bowl from him, and all thought of anything else left him. The Tuatha'an woman pressed her back against the log wall, a hand to her throat. The light from the burning trees showed him the pain and horror, the loathing on her face as she watched the carnage.

"Hide!" Perrin shouted at her. "Get back inside and hide!" The swelling roar of fighting and dying swallowed his words. He ran toward her. "Hide, Leya! For the love of the Light, hide!"

A Trolloc loomed up over him, a cruelly hooked beak where its mouth and nose should have been. Black mail and spikes covered it from shoulders to knees, and it moved on a hawk's talons as it swung one of those strangely curved swords. It smelled of sweat and dirt and blood.

Perrin crouched under the slash, shouting wordlessly as he struck out with his axe. He knew he should have been afraid, but urgency suppressed fear. All that mattered was that he had to reach Leya, had to get her to safety, and the Trolloc was in the way.

The Trolloc fell, roaring and kicking; Perrin did not know where he had hit it, or if it were dying or merely hurt. He leaped over it, where it lay thrashing, and ran scrambling up the slope.

Burning trees cast lurid shadows across the small valley. A flickering shadow beside Moiraine's hut suddenly resolved into a Trolloc, goat-snouted and horned. Gripping a wildly spiked axe with both hands, it seemed on the point of rushing down into the fray when its eyes fell on Leya.

"No!" Perrin shouted. "Light, no!" Rocks skittered away under his bare feet; he did not feel the bruises. The Trolloc's axe rose. "Leyaaaaaaaa!"

At the last instant the Trolloc spun, axe flashing toward Perrin. He threw himself down, yelling as steel scored his back. Desperately he flung out a hand, caught a goat hoof, and pulled with all his strength. The Trolloc's feet came out from under it, and it fell with a crash, but as it slid down the slope, it seized Perrin in hands big enough to make two of his, pulling him along to roll over and over. The stink of it filled his nostrils, goat-stench and sour man-sweat. Massive arms snaked around his chest, squeezing the air out; his ribs creaked on the point of breaking. The Trolloc's axe was gone in the fall, but blunt goat-teeth sank into Perrin's shoulder, powerful jaws chewing. He groaned as pain jolted down his left arm. His lungs labored for breath, and blackness crept in on the edges of his vision, but dimly he was aware that his other arm was free, that somehow he had held on to his own axe. He held it short on the handle, like a hammer, with the spike foremost. With a roar that took the last of his air, he drove the spike into the Trolloc's temple. Soundlessly it convulsed, limbs flinging wide, hurling him away. By instinct alone his hand tightened on the axe, ripping it loose as the Trolloc slid further down the slope, still twitching.

For a moment Perrin lay there, fighting for breath. The gash across his back burned, and he felt the wetness of blood. His shoulder protested as he pushed himself up. "Leya?"

She was still there, huddled in front of the hut, not more than ten paces upslope. And watching him with such a look on her face that he could barely meet her eyes.

"Don't pity me!" he growled at her. "Don't you—!"

The Myrddraal's leap from the roof of the hut seemed to take too long, and its dead black cloak hung during the slow fall as if the Halfman were standing on the ground already. Its eyeless gaze was fixed on Perrin. It smelled like death.

Cold seeped through Perrin's arms and legs as the Myrddraal stared at him. His chest felt like a lump of ice. "Leya," he whispered. It was all he could do not to run. "Leya, please hide. Please."

The Halfman started toward him, slowly, confident that fear held him in a snare. It moved like a snake, unlimbering a sword so black only the burning trees made it visible. "Cut one leg of the tripod," it said softly, "and all fall down." Its voice sounded like dry-rotted leather crumbling.

Suddenly Leya moved, throwing herself forward, attempting to wrap her arms around the Myrddraal's legs. It gave an almost casual backwards swing of its dark sword, never even looking around, and she crumpled.

Tears started in the corners of Perrin's eyes. *I should have helped her . . . saved her. I should have done . . .*

something! But so long as the Myrddraal stared at him with its eyeless gaze, it was an effort even to think.

We come, brother. We come, Young Bull.

The words inside his mind made his head ring like a struck bell; the reverberations shivered through him. With the words came the wolves, scores of them, flooding into his mind as he was aware of them flooding into the bowl-shaped valley. Mountain wolves almost as tall as a man's waist, all white and gray, coming out of the night at the run, aware of the two-legs' surprise as they darted in to take on the Twisted Ones. Wolves filled him till he could barely remember being a man. His eyes gathered the light, shining golden yellow. And the Halfman stopped its advance as if suddenly uncertain.

"Fade," Perrin said roughly, but then a different name came to him, from the wolves. Trollocs, the Twisted Ones, made during the War of the Shadow from melding men and animals, were bad enough, but the Myrddraal—. "Neverborn!" Young Bull spat. Lip curling back in a snarl, he threw himself at the Myrddraal.

It moved like a viper, sinuous and deadly, black sword quick as lightning, but he was Young Bull. That was what the wolves called him. Young Bull, with horns of steel that he wielded with his hands. He was one with the wolves. He was a wolf, and any wolf would die a hundred times over to see one of the Neverborn go down. The Fade fell back before him, its darting blade now trying to deflect his slashes.

Hamstring and throat, that was how wolves killed. Young Bull suddenly threw himself to one side and dropped to a knee, axe slicing across the back of the Halfman's knee. It screamed—a bone-burrowing sound to raise his hair at any other time—and fell, catching itself with one hand. The Halfman—the Neverborn—still held its sword firmly, but before it could set itself, Young Bull's axe struck again. Half severed, the Myrddraal's head flopped over to hang down its back; yet still leaning there on one hand, the Neverborn slashed wildly with its sword. Neverborn were always long in dying.

From the wolves as much as his own eyes Young Bull received impressions of Trollocs thrashing on the ground, shrieking, untouched by wolf or man. Those would have been linked to this Myrddraal, and would die when it did—if no one killed them first.

The urge to rush down the slope and join his brothers, join in killing the Twisted Ones, in hunting the remaining Neverborn, was strong, but a buried fragment that was still man remembered. *Leya.*

He dropped his axe and turned her over gently. Blood covered her face, and her eyes stared up at him, glazed with death. An accusing stare, it seemed to him. "I tried," he told her. "I tried to save you." Her stare did not change. "What else could I have done? It would have killed you if I hadn't killed it!"

Come, Young Bull. Come kill the Twisted Ones.

Wolf rolled over him, enveloped him. Letting Leya back down, Perrin took up his axe, blade gleaming wetly. His eyes shone as he raced down the rocky slope. He was Young Bull.

Trees scattered around the bowl-shaped valley burned like torches; a tall pine flared into flame as Young Bull joined the battle. The night air flashed actinic blue, like sheet lightning, as Lan engaged another Myrddraal, ancient Aes Sedai–made steel meeting black steel wrought in Thakan'dar, in the shadow of Shayol Ghul. Loial wielded a quarterstaff the size of a fence rail, the whirling timber marking a space no Trolloc entered without falling. Men fought desperately in the dancing shadows, but Young Bull—Perrin—noted in a distant way that too many of the Shienaran two-legs were down.

The brothers and sisters fought in small packs of three or four, dodging scythe-like swords and spiked axes, darting in with slashing teeth to sever hamstrings, lunging to bite out throats as their prey fell. There was no honor in the way they fought, no glory, no mercy. They had not come for battle, but to kill. Young Bull joined one of the small packs, the blade of his axe serving for teeth.

He no longer thought of the greater battle. There was only the Trolloc he and the wolves—the brothers—cut off from the rest and brought down. Then there would be another, and another, and another, until none were left. None here, none anywhere. He felt the urge to hurl the axe aside and use his teeth, to run on all fours as his brothers did. Run through the high mountain passes. Run belly-deep in powdery snow pursuing deer. Run, with the cold wind ruffling his fur. He snarled with his brothers, and Trollocs howled with fear at his yellow-eyed gaze even more than they did at the other wolves.

Abruptly he realized there were no more Trollocs standing anywhere in the bowl, though he could feel his brothers pursuing others as they fled. A pack of seven had a different prey, somewhere out there in the darkness. One of the Neverborn ran for its hard-footed four-legs—its horse, a distant part of him said—and his brothers followed, noses filled with its scent, its essence of death. Inside his head, he was with them, seeing with their eyes. As they closed in, the Neverborn turned, cursing, black blade and black-clad Neverborn like part of the night. But night was where his brothers and sisters hunted.

Young Bull snarled as the first brother died, its death pain lancing him, yet the others closed in and more brothers and sisters died, but snapping jaws dragged the Neverborn down. It fought back with its own teeth now, ripping out throats, slashing with fingernails that sliced skin and flesh like the hard claws the two-legs carried, but brothers savaged it even as they died. Finally a lone sister heaved herself out of the still-twitching pile and staggered to one side. Morning Mist, she was called, but as with all their names, it was more than that: a frosty morning with the bite of snows yet to come already in the air, and the mist curling thick across the valley, swirling with the sharp breeze that carried the promise of good hunting. Raising her head, Morning Mist howled to the cloud-hidden moon, mourning her dead.

Young Bull threw back his head and howled with her, mourned with her.

When he lowered his head, Min was staring at him. "Are you all right, Perrin?" she asked hesitantly. There was a bruise on her cheek, and a sleeve half torn from her coat. She had a cudgel in one hand and a dagger in the other, and there was blood and hair on both.

They were all staring at him, he saw, all those who were still on their feet. Loial, leaning wearily on his tall staff. Shienarans, who had been carrying their fallen down to where Moiraine crouched over one of their number with Lan standing at her side. Even the Aes Sedai was looking his way. The burning trees, like huge torches, cast a wavering light.

Dead Trollocs lay everywhere. There were more Shienarans down than standing, and the bodies of his brothers
were scattered among them. So many. . . .

Perrin realized he wanted to howl again. Frantically he
walled himself off from contact with the wolves. Images
seeped through, emotions, as he tried to stop them. Finally,
though, he could no longer feel them, feel their pain, or
their anger, or the desire to hunt the Twisted Ones, or to
run. . . . He gave himself a shake. The wound on his back
burned like fire, and his torn shoulder felt as if it had been
hammered on an anvil. His bare feet, scraped and bruised,
throbbed with his pain. The smell of blood was everywhere.
The smell of Trollocs, and death.

"I. . . . I'm all right, Min."

"You fought well, blacksmith," Lan said. The Warder
raised his still-bloody sword above his head. *"Tai'shar
Manetheren! Tai'shar Andor!"* True Blood of Manetheren.
True Blood of Andor.

The Shienarans still standing—so few—lifted their blades
and joined him. *"Tai'shar Manetheren! Tai'shar Andor!"*

Loial nodded. *"Ta'veren,"* he added.

Perrin lowered his eyes in embarrassment. Lan had saved
him from the questions he did not want to answer, but had
given him an honor he did not deserve. The others did not
understand. He wondered what they would say if they knew
the truth. Min moved closer, and he muttered, "Leya's dead.
I couldn't. . . . I almost reached her in time."

"It wouldn't have made any difference," she said softly.
"You know that." She leaned to look at his back, and winced.
"Moiraine will take care of that for you. She's Healing those
she can."

Perrin nodded. His back felt sticky with drying blood all
the way to his waist, but despite the pain he hardly noticed
it. *Light, I almost didn't come back that time. I can't let that
happen again. I won't. Never again!*

But when he was with the wolves, it was all so different.
He did not have to worry about strangers being afraid of
him just because he was big, then. There was no one thinking he was slow-witted just because he tried to be careful.
Wolves knew each other even if they had never met before,
and with them he was just another wolf.

No! His hands tightened on the haft of his axe. *No!* He gave a start as Masema suddenly spoke up.

"It was a sign," the Shienaran said, turning in a circle to address everyone. There was blood on his arms and his chest—he had fought in nothing but his breeches—and he moved with a limp, but the light in his eyes was as fervent as it had ever been. More fervent. "A sign to confirm our faith. Even wolves came to fight for the Dragon Reborn. In the Last Battle, the Lord Dragon will summon even the beasts of the forest to fight at our sides. It is a sign for us to go forth. Only Darkfriends will fail to join us." Two of the Shienarans nodded.

"You shut your bloody mouth, Masema!" Uno snapped. He seemed untouched, but then Uno had been fighting Trollocs since before Perrin was born. Yet he sagged with weariness; only the painted eye on his eyepatch seemed fresh. "We'll flaming go forth when the Lord Dragon bloody well tells us, and not before! You sheep-headed farmers flaming remember that!" The one-eyed man looked at the growing row of men being tended by Moiraine—few were able to as much as sit up, even after she was done with them—and shook his head. "At least we'll have plenty of flaming wolf hides to keep the wounded warm."

"No!" The Shienarans seemed surprised at the vehemence in Perrin's voice. "They fought for us, and we'll bury them with our dead."

Uno frowned, and opened his mouth as if to argue, but Perrin fixed him with a steady, yellow-eyed stare. It was the Shienaran who dropped his gaze first, and nodded.

Perrin cleared his throat, embarrassed all over again as Uno gave orders for the Shienarans who were fit to gather the dead wolves. Min was squinting at him the way she did when she saw things. "Where's Rand?" he asked her.

"Out there in the dark," she said, nodding upslope without taking her eyes off him. "He will not talk to anyone. He just sits there, snapping at anyone who comes near him."

"He will talk to me," Perrin said. She followed him, protesting all the while that he ought to wait until Moiraine had seen to his injuries. *Light, what does she see when she looks at me? I don't want to know.*

Rand was seated on the ground just beyond the light

of the burning trees, with his back against the trunk of a
stunted oak. Staring at nothing, he had his arms wrapped
around himself, hands under his red coat, as if feeling the
cold. He did not appear to notice their approach. Min sat
down beside him, but he did not move even when she laid
a hand on his arm. Even here Perrin smelled blood, and not
only his own.

"Rand," Perrin began, but Rand cut him off.

"Do you know what I did during the fight?" Still staring into the distance, Rand addressed the night. "Nothing!
Nothing useful. At first, when I reached out for the True
Source, I couldn't touch it, couldn't grasp it. It kept sliding away. Then, when I finally had hold of it, I was going
to burn them all, burn all the Trollocs and Fades. And all
I could do was set fire to some trees." He shook with silent
laughter, then stopped with a pained grimace. "*Saidin* filled
me till I thought I'd explode like fireworks. I had to channel it somewhere, get rid of it before it burned me up, and
I found myself thinking about pulling the mountain down
and burying the Trollocs. I almost tried. That was my fight.
Not against the Trollocs. Against myself. To keep from
burying us all under the mountain."

Min gave Perrin a pained look, as if asking for help.

"We . . . dealt with them, Rand," Perrin said. He shivered, thinking of all the wounded men down below. And
the dead. *Better that than the mountain down on top of us.*
"We didn't need you."

Rand's head fell back against the tree and his eyes closed.
"I felt them coming," he said, nearly whispering. "I didn't
know what it was, though. They feel like the taint on *saidin*.
And *saidin* is always there, calling to me, singing to me. By
the time I knew the difference, Lan was already shouting
his warning. If I could only control it, I could have given
warning before they were even close. But half the time
when I actually manage to touch *saidin*, I don't know what
I am doing at all. The flow of it just sweeps me along. I
could have given warning, though."

Perrin shifted his bruised feet uncomfortably. "We had
warning enough." He knew he sounded as if he were trying
to convince himself. *I could have given warning, too, if I'd
talked with the wolves. They knew there were Trollocs and
Fades in the mountains. They were trying to tell me.* But

he wondered: If he did not keep the wolves out of his mind, might he not be running with them now? There had been a man, Elyas Machera, who also could talk to wolves. Elyas ran with the wolves all the time, yet seemed able to remember he was a man. But he had never told Perrin how he did it, and Perrin had not seen him in a long time.

The crunch of boots on rock announced two people coming, and a swirl of air carried their scents to Perrin. He was careful not to speak names, though, until Lan and Moiraine were close enough for even ordinary eyes to make them out.

The Warder had a hand under the Aes Sedai's arm, as if trying to support her without letting her know it. Moiraine's eyes were haggard, and she carried a small, age-dark ivory carving of a woman in one hand. Perrin knew it for an *angreal*, a remnant from the Age of Legends that allowed an Aes Sedai to safely channel more of the Power than she could alone. It was a measure of her tiredness that she was using it for Healing.

Min got to her feet to help Moiraine, but the Aes Sedai motioned her away. "Everyone else is seen to," she told Min. "When I am done here, I can rest." She shook off Lan as well, and a look of concentration appeared on her face as she traced a cool hand across Perrin's bleeding shoulder, then along the wound on his back. Her touch made his skin tingle. "This is not too bad," she said. "The bruising of your shoulder goes deep, but the gashes are shallow. Brace yourself. This will not hurt, but. . . ."

He had never found it easy being near someone he knew was channeling the One Power, and still less if it actually involved him. Yet there had been one or two of those times, and he thought he had some idea what the channeling entailed, but those Healings had been minor, simply washing away tiredness when Moiraine could not afford to have him weary. They had been nothing like this.

The Aes Sedai's eyes suddenly seemed to be seeing inside him, seeing through him. He gasped and almost dropped his axe. He could feel the skin on his back crawling, muscles writhing as they knit back together. His shoulder quivered uncontrollably, and everything blurred. Cold seared him to the bone, then deeper still. He had the impression of moving, falling, flying; he could not tell which, but he felt as if he were rushing—somewhere, somehow—at great

speed, forever. After an eternity the world came into focus
again. Moiraine was stepping back, half staggering until
Lan caught her arm.

Gaping, Perrin looked down at his shoulder. The gashes
and bruises were gone; not so much as a twinge remained.
He twisted carefully, but the pain in his back had vanished
as well. And his feet no longer hurt; he did not need to look
to know all the bruises and scrapes were gone. His stomach
rumbled loudly.

"You should eat as soon as you can," Moiraine told him.
"A good bit of the strength for that came from you. You
need to replace it."

Hunger—and images of food—were already filling Perrin's head. Blood rare beef, and venison, and mutton, and. . . .
With an effort he made himself stop thinking of meat. He
would find some of those roots that smelled like turnips
when they were roasted. His stomach growled in protest.

"There's barely even a scar, blacksmith," Lan said behind
him.

"Most of the wolves who were hurt made their own
way to the forest," Moiraine said, knuckling her back and
stretching, "but I Healed those I could find." Perrin gave
her a sharp look, yet she seemed to be just making conversation. "Perhaps they came for their own reasons, yet we
would likely all be dead without them." Perrin shifted uneasily and dropped his eyes.

The Aes Sedai reached toward the bruise on Min's cheek,
but Min stepped back, saying, "I'm not really hurt, and you're
tired. I've had worse falling over my own feet."

Moiraine smiled and let her hand fall. Lan took her arm;
she swayed in his grip. "Very well. And what of you, Rand?
Did you take any hurt? Even a nick from a Myrddraal's
blade can be deadly, and some Trolloc blades are almost
as bad."

Perrin noticed something for the first time. "Rand, your
coat is wet."

Rand pulled his right hand from under his coat, a hand
covered in blood. "Not a Myrddraal," he said absently,
peering at his hand. "Not even a Trolloc. The wound I took
at Falme broke open."

Moiraine hissed and jerked her arm free from Lan, half
fell to her knees beside Rand. Pulling back the side of his

coat, she studied his wound. Perrin could not see it, for her head was in the way, but the smell of blood was stronger, now. Moiraine's hands moved, and Rand grimaced in pain. "'The blood of the Dragon Reborn on the rocks of Shayol Ghul will free mankind from the Shadow.' Isn't that what the Prophecies of the Dragon say?"

"Who told you that?" Moiraine said sharply.

"If you could get me to Shayol Ghul now," Rand said drowsily, "by Waygate or Portal Stone, there could be an end to it. No more dying. No more dreams. No more."

"If it were as simple as that," Moiraine said grimly, "I would, one way or another, but not all in *The Karaethon Cycle* can be taken at its face. For every thing it says straight out, there are ten that could mean a hundred different things. Do not think you know anything at all of what *must* be, even if someone has told you the whole of the Prophecies." She paused, as if gathering strength. Her grip tightened on the *angreal*, and her free hand slid along Rand's side as if it were not covered in blood. "Brace yourself."

Suddenly Rand's eyes opened wide, and he sat straight up, gasping and staring and shivering. Perrin had thought, when she Healed him, that it went on forever, but in moments she was easing Rand back against the oak.

"I have . . . done as much as I can," she said faintly. "As much as I can. You must be careful. It could break open again if. . . ." As her voice trailed off, she fell.

Rand caught her, but Lan was there in an instant to scoop her up. As the Warder did so, a look passed across his face, a look as close to tenderness as Perrin ever expected to see from Lan.

"Exhausted," the Warder said. "She has cared for everyone else, but there's no one to take her fatigue. I will put her to bed."

"There's Rand," Min said slowly, but the Warder shook his head.

"It isn't that I do not think you would try, sheepherder," he said, "but you know so little you might as soon kill her as help her."

"That's right," Rand said bitterly. "I'm not to be trusted. Lews Therin Kinslayer killed everyone close to him. Maybe I'll do the same before I am done."

"Pull yourself together, sheepherder," Lan said harshly. "The whole world rides on your shoulders. Remember you're a man, and do what needs to be done."

Rand looked up at the Warder, and surprisingly, all of his bitterness seemed to be gone. "I will fight the best I can," he said. "Because there's no one else, and it has to be done, and the duty is mine. I'll fight, but I do not have to like what I've become." He closed his eyes as if going to sleep. "I will fight. Dreams. . . ."

Lan stared down at him a moment, then nodded. He raised his head to look across Moiraine at Perrin and Min. "Get him to his bed, then see to some sleep yourselves. We have plans to make, and the Light alone knows what happens next."

CHAPTER
6

The Hunt Begins

Perrin did not expect to sleep, but a stomach stuffed with cold stew—his resolve about the roots had lasted until the smells of supper's leftovers hit his nose—and bone weariness pulled him down on his bed. If he dreamed, he did not remember. He awoke to Lan shaking his shoulders, dawn through the open door turning the Warder to a shadow haloed with light.

"Rand is gone," was all Lan said before he left at a run, but it was more than enough.

Perrin dragged himself up yawning and dressed quickly in the early chill. Outside, only a handful of Shienarans were in sight, using their horses to drag Trolloc bodies into the woods, and most of those moved as if they should be in a sickbed. A body took time to build back the strength that being Healed took.

Perrin's stomach muttered at him, and his nose tested the breeze in the hope that someone had already started cooking. He was ready to eat those turnip-like roots, raw if need be. There were only the lingering stench of slain Myrddraal, the smells of dead Trollocs and men, alive and dead, of horses and the trees. And dead wolves.

Moiraine's hut, high on the other side of the bowl, seemed a center of activity. Min hurried inside, and moments later Masema came out, then Uno. At a trot the one-eyed man vanished into the trees, toward the sheer rock wall beyond the hut, while the other Shienaran limped down the slope.

Perrin started toward the hut. As he splashed across the shallow stream, he met Masema. The Shienaran's face was haggard, the scar on his cheek prominent, and his eyes even more sunken than usual. In the middle of the stream, he raised his head suddenly and caught Perrin's coat sleeve.

"You're from his village," Masema said hoarsely. "You must know. Why did the Lord Dragon abandon us? What sin did we commit?"

"Sin? What are you talking about? Whyever Rand went, it was nothing you did or didn't do." Masema did not appear satisfied; he kept his grip on Perrin's sleeve, peering into his face as if there were answers there. Icy water began to seep into Perrin's left boot. "Masema," he said carefully, "whatever the Lord Dragon did, it was according to his plan. The Lord Dragon would not abandon us." *Or would he? If I were in his place, would I?*

Masema nodded slowly. "Yes. Yes, I see that, now. He has gone out alone to spread the word of his coming. We must spread the word, too. Yes." He limped on across the stream, muttering to himself.

Squelching at every other step, Perrin climbed to Moiraine's hut and knocked. There was no answer. He hesitated a moment, then went in.

The outer room, where Lan slept, was as stark and simple as Perrin's own hut, with a rough bed built against one wall, a few pegs for hanging possessions, and a single shelf. Not much light entered through the open door, and the only other illumination came from crude lamps on the shelf, slivers of oily fat-wood wedged into cracks in pieces of rock. They gave off thin streamers of smoke that made a layer of haze under the roof. Perrin's nose wrinkled at the smell.

The low roof was only a little higher than his head. Loial's head actually brushed it, even seated as he was on one end of Lan's bed, with his knees drawn up to make himself small. The Ogier's tufted ears twitched uneasily. Min sat cross-legged on the dirt floor beside the door that led to Moiraine's room, while the Aes Sedai paced back and forth in thought. Dark thoughts, they must have been. Three paces each way was all she had, but she made vigorous use of the space, the calm on her face belied by the quickness of her step.

"I think Masema is going crazy," Perrin said.

Min sniffed. "With him, how can you tell?"

Moiraine rounded on him, a tightness to her mouth. Her

voice was soft. Too soft. "Is Masema the most important thing in your mind this morning, Perrin Aybara?"

"No. I'd like to know when Rand left, and why. Did anyone see him go? Does anyone know where he went?" He made himself meet her look with one just as level and firm. It was not easy. He loomed over her, but she was Aes Sedai. "Is this of your making, Moiraine? Did you rein him in until he was so impatient he'd go anywhere, do anything, just to stop sitting still?" Loial's ears went stiff, and he motioned a surreptitious warning with one thick-fingered hand.

Moiraine studied Perrin with her head tilted to one side, and it was all he could do not to drop his eyes. "This is none of my doing," she said. "He left sometime during the night. When and how and why, I yet hope to learn."

Loial's shoulders heaved in a quiet sigh of relief. Quiet for an Ogier, it sounded like steam rushing out from quenching red-hot iron. "Never anger an Aes Sedai," he said in a whisper obviously meant just for himself, but audible to everyone. "'Better to embrace the sun than to anger an Aes Sedai.'"

Min reached up enough to hand Perrin a folded piece of paper. "Loial went to see him after we got him to bed last night, and Rand asked to borrow pen and paper and ink."

The Ogier's ears jerked, and he frowned worriedly until his long eyebrows hung down on his cheeks. "I did not know what he was planning. I didn't."

"We know that," Min said. "No one is accusing you of anything, Loial."

Moiraine frowned at the paper, but she did not try to stop Perrin from reading. It was in Rand's hand.

What I do, I do because there is no other way. He is hunting me again, and this time one of us has to die, I think. There is no need for those around me to die, also. Too many have died for me already. I do not want to die either, and will not, if I can manage it. There are lies in dreams, and death, but dreams hold truth, too.

That was all, with no signature. There was no need for Perrin to wonder who Rand meant by "he." For Rand, for all of them, there could be only one. Ba'alzamon.

"He left that tucked under the door there," Min said in a tight voice. "He took some old clothes the Shienarans had hanging out to dry, and his flute, and a horse. Nothing else but a little food, as far as we can tell. None of the guards saw him go, and last night they would have seen a mouse creeping."

"And would it have done any good if they had?" Moiraine said calmly. "Would any of them have stopped the *Lord Dragon*, or even challenged him? Some of them— Masema for one—would slit their own throats if the *Lord Dragon* told them to."

It was Perrin's turn to study her. "Did you expect anything else? They swore to follow him. Light, Moiraine, he'd never have named himself Dragon if not for you. What did you expect of them?" She did not speak, and he went on more quietly. "Do you believe, Moiraine? That he's really the Dragon Reborn? Or do you just think he's someone you can use before the One Power kills him or drives him mad?"

"Go easy, Perrin," Loial said. "Not so angry."

"I'll go easy when she answers me. Well, Moiraine?"

"He is what he is," she said sharply.

"You said the Pattern would force him to the right path eventually. Is that what this is, or is he just trying to get away from you?" For a moment he thought he had gone too far—her dark eyes sparkled with anger—but he refused to back down. "Well?"

Moiraine took a deep breath. "This may well be what the Pattern has chosen, yet I did not mean for him to go off alone. For all his power, he is as defenseless as a babe in many ways, and as ignorant of the world. He channels, but he has no control over whether or not the One Power comes when he reaches for it and almost as little over what he does with it if it does come. The power itself will kill him before he has a chance to go mad if he does not learn that control. There is so much he must learn, yet. He wants to run before he has learned to walk."

"You split hairs and lay false trails, Moiraine." Perrin snorted. "If he is what you say he is, did it never occur to you that he might know what he has to do better than you?"

"He is what he is," she repeated firmly, "but I must keep him alive if he is to do anything. He will fulfill no prophecies dead, and even if he manages to avoid Darkfriends and Shadowspawn, there are a thousand other hands ready to slay him. All it will take is a hint of the hundredth part of what he is. Yet if that were all he might face, I would not worry half so much as I do. There are the Forsaken to be accounted for."

Perrin gave a start; from the corner, Loial moaned. "'The Dark One and all the Forsaken are bound in Shayol Ghul,'" Perrin began by rote, but she gave him no time to finish.

"The seals are weakening, Perrin. Some are broken, though the world does not know that. Must not know that. The Father of Lies is not free. Yet. But as the seals weaken, more and more, which of the Forsaken may be loosed already? Lanfear? Sammael? Asmodean, or Be'lal, or Ravhin? Ishamael himself, the Betrayer of Hope? They were thirteen altogether, Perrin, and bound in the sealing, not in the prison that holds the Dark One. Thirteen of the most powerful Aes Sedai of the Age of Legends, the weakest of them stronger than the ten strongest Aes Sedai living today, the most ignorant with all the knowledge of the Age of Legends. And every man and woman of them gave up the Light and dedicated their souls to the Shadow. What if they are free, and out there waiting for him? I will not let them have him."

Perrin shivered, partly from the icy iron in her last words, and partly from thought of the Forsaken. He did not want to think of even one of the Forsaken loose in the world. His mother had frightened him with those names when he was little. *Ishamael comes for boys who do not tell their mothers the truth. Lanfear waits in the night for boys who do not go to bed when they are supposed to.* Being older did not help, not when he knew now they were all real. Not when Moiraine said they might be free.

"Bound in Shayol Ghul," he whispered, and wished he still believed it. Troubled, he studied Rand's letter again. "Dreams. He was talking about dreams yesterday, too."

Moiraine stepped closer, and peered up into his face. "Dreams?" Lan and Uno came in, but she waved them to silence. The small room was more than crowded now, with five people in it besides the Ogier. "What dreams have *you* had the last few days, Perrin?" She ignored his protest that there was nothing wrong with his dreams. "Tell me," she insisted. "What dream have you had that was not ordinary? Tell me." Her gaze seized him like smithy tongs, willing him to speak.

He looked at the others—they were all watching him fixedly, even Min—then hesitantly told of the one dream that seemed unusual to him, the dream that came every night. The dream of the sword he could not touch. He did not mention the wolf that had appeared in the last.

"Callandor," Lan breathed when he was done. Rock-hard face or no, he looked stunned.

"Yes," Moiraine said, "but we must be absolutely certain. Speak to the others." As Lan hurried out, she turned to Uno. "And what of your dreams? Did you dream of a sword, too?"

The Shienaran shifted his feet. The red eye painted on his patch stared straight at Moiraine, but his real eye blinked and wavered. "I dream about flam—uh, about swords all the time, Moiraine Sedai," he said stiffly. "I suppose I've dreamed about a sword the last few nights. I don't remember my dreams the way Lord Perrin here does."

Moiraine said, "Loial?"

"My dreams are always the same, Moiraine Sedai. The groves, and the Great Trees, and the *stedding.* We Ogier always dream of the *stedding* when we are away from them."

The Aes Sedai turned back to Perrin.

"It was just a dream," he said. "Nothing but a dream."

"I doubt it," she said. "You describe the hall called the Heart of the Stone, in the fortress called the Stone of Tear, as if you had stood in it. And the shining sword is *Callandor,* the Sword That Is Not a Sword, the Sword That Cannot Be Touched."

Loial sat up straight, bumping his head on the roof. He did not seem to notice. "The Prophecies of the Dragon say the Stone of Tear will never fall till *Callandor* is wielded by the Dragon's hand. The fall of the Stone of Tear will be one of the greatest signs of the Dragon's Rebirth. If Rand holds *Callandor,* the whole world must acknowledge him as the Dragon."

"Perhaps." The word floated from the Aes Sedai's lips like a shard of ice on still water.

"Perhaps?" Perrin said. "Perhaps? I thought that was the final sign, the last thing to fulfill your Prophecies."

"Neither the first nor the last," Moiraine said. "*Callandor* will be but one fulfillment of *The Karaethon Cycle*, as his birth on the slopes of Dragonmount was the first. He has yet to break the nations, or shatter the world. Even scholars who have studied the Prophecies for their entire lives do not know how to interpret them all. What does it mean that he 'shall slay his people with the sword of peace, and destroy them with the leaf'? What does it meant that he 'shall bind the nine moons to serve him'? Yet these are given equal weight with *Callandor* in the *Cycle*. There are others. What 'wounds of madness and cutting of hope' has he healed? What chains has he broken, and who put into chains? And some are so obscure that he may already have fulfilled them, although I am not aware of it. But, no. *Callandor* is far from the end of it."

Perrin shrugged uneasily. He knew only bits and pieces of the Prophecies; he had liked hearing them even less since Rand had let Moiraine put that banner in his hands. No, it had been before that, even. Since a journey by Portal Stone had convinced him his life was bound to Rand's.

Moiraine was continuing. "If you think he has simply to put out his hand, Loial son of Arent son of Halan, you are a fool, as is he if he thinks it. Even if he lives to reach Tear, he may never attain the Stone.

"Tairens have no love for the One Power, and less for any man claiming to be the Dragon. Channeling is outlawed, and Aes Sedai are tolerated at best, so long as they do not channel. Telling the Prophecies of the Dragon, or even possessing a copy of them, is enough to put you in prison, in Tear. And no one enters the Stone of Tear without permission of the High Lords; none but the High Lords themselves enter the Heart of the Stone. He is not ready for this. Not ready."

Perrin grunted softly. The Stone would never fall till the Dragon Reborn held *Callandor. How in the Light is he supposed to reach it—inside a bloody fortress!—before the fortress falls? It is madness!*

"Why are we just sitting here?" Min burst out. "If Rand is going to Tear, why aren't we following him? He could be killed, or . . . or. . . . Why are we sitting here?"

Moiraine put a hand on Min's head. "Because I must be sure," she said gently. "It is not comfortable being chosen by the Wheel, to be great or to be near greatness. The chosen of the Wheel can only take what comes."

"I am tired of taking what comes." Min scrubbed a hand across her eyes. Perrin thought he saw tears. "Rand could be dying while we wait." Moiraine smoothed Min's hair; there was a look almost of pity on the Aes Sedai's face.

Perrin sat down on the end of Lan's bed opposite Loial. The smell of people was thick in the room—people and worry and fear; Loial smelled of books and trees as well as worry. It felt like a trap, with the walls around them, and all so close. The burning slivers stank. "How can my dream tell where Rand is going?" he asked. "It was my dream."

"Those who can channel the One Power," Moiraine said quietly, "those who are particularly strong in Spirit, can sometimes force their dreams on others." She did not stop her soothing of Min. "Especially on those who are— susceptible. I do not believe Rand did it on purpose, but the dreams of those touching the True Source can be powerful. For one as strong as he, they could possibly seize an entire village, or perhaps even a city. He knows little of what he does, and even less of how to control it."

"Then why didn't you have it, too?" he demanded. "Or Lan." Uno stared straight ahead, looking as if he would rather be anywhere else, and Loial's ears wilted. Perrin was too tired and too hungry to care whether he showed proper respect for an Aes Sedai. And too angry, as well, he realized. "Why?"

Moiraine answered calmly. "Aes Sedai learn to shield their dreams. I do it without thinking, when I sleep. Warders are given something much the same in the bonding. The Gaidin could not do what they must if the Shadow could steal into their dreams. We are all vulnerable when we sleep, and the Shadow is strong in the night."

"There's always something new from you," Perrin growled. "Can't you tell us what to expect once in a while, instead of explaining after it happens?" Uno looked as though he was trying to think of a reason to leave.

Moiraine gave Perrin a flat look. "You want me to share a lifetime of knowledge with you in a single afternoon? Or even a single year? I will tell you this. Be wary of dreams, Perrin Aybara. Be very wary of dreams."

He pulled his eyes away from hers. "I am," he murmured. "I am."

After that, silence, and no one seemed to want to break it. Min sat staring at her crossed ankles, but apparently taking some comfort from Moiraine's presence. Uno stood against the wall, not looking at anyone. Loial forgot himself enough to pull a book from his coat pocket and try to read in the dim light. The wait was long, and far from easy for Perrin. *It's not the Shadow in my dreams I'm afraid of. It's wolves. I will not let them in. I won't!*

Lan returned, and Moiraine straightened eagerly. The Warder answered the question in her eyes. "Half of them remember dreaming of swords the last four nights running. Some remember a place with great columns, and five say the sword was crystal, or glass. Masema says he saw Rand holding it last night."

"That one would," Moiraine said. She rubbed her hands together briskly; she seemed suddenly full of energy. "Now I *am* certain. Though I still wish I knew how he left here unseen. If he has rediscovered some Talent from the Age of Legends. . . ."

Lan looked at Uno, and the one-eyed man shrugged in dismay. "I bloody forgot, with all this flaming talk about bloo—" He cleared his throat, shooting a glance at Moiraine. She looked back expectantly, and he went on. "I mean . . . uh . . . that is, I followed the Lord Dragon's tracks. There's another way into that closed valley, now. The . . . the earthquake brought down the far wall. It's a hard climb, but you can get a horse up it. I found more tracks at the top, and there's an easy way from there around the mountain." He let out a long breath when he was done.

"Good," Moiraine said. "At least he has not rediscovered how to fly, or make himself invisible, or something else out of legend. We must follow him without delay. Uno, I will give you enough gold to take you and the others as far as Jehannah, and the name of someone there who will see that you get more. The Ghealdanin are wary of strangers, but if you keep to yourselves, they should not trouble you. Wait there until I send word."

"But we will go with you," he protested. "We have all sworn to follow the Dragon Reborn. I do not see how the

few of us can take a fortress that has never fallen, but with
the Lord Dragon's aid, we will do what must be done."

"So we are 'the People of the Dragon,' now." Perrin
laughed mirthlessly. "'The Stone of Tear will never fall till
the People of the Dragon come.' Have you given us a new
name, Moiraine?"

"Watch your tongue, blacksmith," Lan growled, all ice
and stone.

Moiraine gave them both sharp looks, and they fell silent.
"Forgive me, Uno," she said, "but we must travel quickly if
we are to have a hope of overtaking him. You are the only
Shienaran fit enough for a hard ride, and we cannot afford
the days the others will need to regain full strength. I will
send for you when I can."

Uno grimaced, but he bowed in acquiescence. At her dismissal, he squared his shoulders and left to tell the others.

"Well, I am going along, whatever you say," Min put in
firmly.

"You are going to Tar Valon," Moiraine told her.

"I am no such thing!"

The Aes Sedai went on smoothly as if the other woman
had not spoken. "The Amyrlin Seat must be told what has
happened, and I cannot count on finding one I can trust who
has messenger pigeons. Or that the Amyrlin will see any
message I send by pigeon. It is a long journey, and hard. I
would not send you alone if there were anyone to send with
you, but I will see you have money, and letters to those who
might help you on your way. You must ride quickly, though.
When your horse tires, buy another—or steal one, if you
must—but ride quickly."

"Let Uno take your message. He's fit; you said so. I am
going after Rand."

"Uno has his duties, Min. And do you think a man could
simply walk up to the gates of the White Tower and demand
an audience with the Amyrlin Seat? Even a king would be
made to wait days if he arrived unannounced, and I fear
any of the Shienarans would be left kicking their heels for
weeks, if not forever. Not to mention that something so
unusual would be known to everyone in Tar Valon before
the first sunset. Few women seek audiences with the Amyrlin herself, but it does happen, and it should occasion no
great comment. No one must learn even as much as that the

Amyrlin Seat has received a message from me. Her life—and ours—could depend on it. You are the one who must go."

Min sat there opening and closing her mouth, obviously searching for another argument, but Moiraine had already gone on. "Lan, I very much fear we will find more evidence of his passing than I would like, but I will rely on your tracking." The Warder nodded. "Perrin? Loial? Will you come with me after Rand?" From her place against the wall, Min gave an indignant squawk, but the Aes Sedai ignored it.

"I will come," Loial said quickly. "Rand is my friend. And I will admit it; I would not miss anything. For my book, you see."

Perrin was slower to answer. Rand was his friend, whatever he had become in the forging. And there was that near certainty of their futures being linked, though he would have avoided that part of it if he could. "It has to be done, doesn't it?" he said finally. "I will come."

"Good." Moiraine rubbed her hands together again, with the air of someone settling to work. "You must all ready yourselves at once. Rand has hours on us. I mean to be well along his trail before midday."

Slender as she was, the force of her presence herded all of them but Lan toward the door, Loial walking stooped over until he was through the doorway. Perrin thought of a goodwife herding geese.

Once outside, Min hung back for a moment to address Lan with a too-sweet smile. "And is there any message you want carried? To Nynaeve, perhaps?"

The Warder blinked as if caught off guard, like a horse on three legs. "Does everyone know—?" He regained his balance almost immediately. "If there is anything else she needs to hear from me, I will tell her myself." He closed the door nearly in her face.

"Men!" Min muttered at the door. "Too blind to see what a stone could see, and too stubborn to be trusted to think for themselves."

Perrin inhaled deeply. Faint smells of death still hung in the valley air, but it was better than the closeness inside. Some better.

"Clean air," Loial sighed. "The smoke was beginning to bother me a little."

They started down the slope together. Beside the stream below, the Shienarans who could stand were gathered around Uno. From his gestures the one-eyed man was making up for lost time with his cursing.

"How did you two become privileged?" Min demanded abruptly. "She *asked* you. She didn't do me the courtesy of asking."

Loial shook his head. "I think she asked because she knew what we would answer, Min. Moiraine seems able to read Perrin and me; she knows what we'll do. But you are a closed book to her."

Min appeared only a little mollified. She looked up at them, Perrin head and shoulders taller on one side and Loial towering even higher on the other. "Much good it does me. I am still going where she wants as easily as you two little lambs. You were doing well for a while, Perrin. Standing up to her like she'd sold you a coat and the seams were popping open."

"I did stand up to her, didn't I," Perrin said wonderingly. He had not really realized he had done that. "It was not so bad as I'd have thought it would be."

"You were lucky," Loial rumbled. "'To anger an Aes Sedai is to put your head in a hornet's nest.'"

"Loial," Min said, "I need to speak to Perrin. Alone. Would you mind?"

"Oh. Of course not." He lengthened his stride to its normal span and quickly moved ahead of them, pulling his pipe and tabac pouch from a coat pocket.

Perrin eyed her warily. She was biting her lip, as if considering what to say. "Do you ever see things about him?" he asked, nodding after the Ogier.

She shook her head. "I think it only works with humans. But I've seen things around you that you ought to know about."

"I've told you—"

"Don't be more thickheaded than you have to be, Perrin. Back there, right after you said you'd go. They were not there before. They must have to do with this journey. Or at least with you deciding to go."

After a moment he said reluctantly, "What did you see?"

"An Aielman in a cage," she said promptly. "A Tuatha'an with a sword. A falcon and a hawk, perching on your shoulders. Both female, I think. And all the rest, of course. What is always there. Darkness swirling 'round you, and—"

"None of that!" he said quickly. When he was sure she had stopped, he scratched his head, thinking. None of it made any sense to him. "Do you have any idea what it all means? The new things, I mean."

"No, but they're important. The things I see always are. Turning points in people's lives, or what's fated. It's always important." She hesitated for a moment, glancing at him. "One more thing," she said slowly. "If you meet a woman— the most beautiful woman you've ever seen—run!"

Perrin blinked. "You saw a beautiful woman? Why should I run from a beautiful woman?"

"Can't you just take advice?" she said irritably. She kicked at a stone and watched it roll down the slope.

Perrin did not like jumping to conclusions—it was one of the reasons some people thought him slow-witted—but he totaled up a number of things Min had said in the last few days and came to a startling conclusion. He stopped dead, hunting for words. "Uh . . . Min, you know I like you. I like you, but. . . . Uh . . . you sort of remind me of my sisters. I mean, you. . . ." The flow stumbled to a halt as she raised her head to look at him, eyebrows arched. She wore a small smile.

"Why, Perrin, you must know that I love you." She stood there, watching his mouth work, then spoke slowly and carefully. "Like a brother, you great wooden-headed lummox! The arrogance of men never ceases to amaze me. You all think everything has to do with you, and every woman has to desire you."

Perrin felt his face growing hot. "I never. . . . I didn't. . . ." He cleared his throat. "What did you see about a woman?"

"Just take my advice," she said, and started down toward the stream again, walking fast. "If you forget all the rest," she called over her shoulder, "heed that!"

He frowned after her—for once his thoughts seemed to arrange themselves quickly—then caught up in two strides. "It's Rand, isn't it?"

She made a sound in her throat and gave him a sidelong look. She did not slow down, though. "Maybe you aren't so boneheaded after all," she muttered. After a moment she added, as if to herself, "I'm bound to him as surely as a stave is bound to the barrel. But I can't see if he'll ever love me in return. And I am not the only one."

"Does Egwene know?" he asked. Rand and Egwene had been all but promised since childhood. Everything but kneeling in front of the Women's Circle of the village to speak the betrothal. He was not sure how far they had drifted from that, if at all.

"She knows," Min said curtly. "Much good it does either of us."

"What about Rand? Does he know?"

"Oh, of course," she said bitterly. "I told him, didn't I? 'Rand, I did a viewing of you, and it seems I have to fall in love with you. I have to share you, too, and I don't much like that, but there it is.' You're a wooden-headed wonder after all, Perrin Aybara." She dashed a hand across her eyes angrily. "If I could be with him, I know I could help. Somehow. Light, if he dies, I don't know if I can stand it."

Perrin shrugged uncomfortably. "Listen, Min. I'll do what I can to help him." *However much that is.* "I promise you that. It really is best for you to go to Tar Valon. You'll be safe there."

"Safe?" She tasted the word as if wondering what it meant. "You think Tar Valon is safe?"

"If there's no safety in Tar Valon, there's no safety anywhere."

She sniffed loudly, and in silence they went to join those preparing to leave.

CHAPTER
7

The Way Out of the Mountains

The way down out of the mountains was hard, but the lower they went, the less Perrin needed his fur-lined cloak. Hour by hour, they rode out of the tailings of winter and into the first days of spring. The last remnants of snow vanished, and grasses and wildflowers—white maiden's hope and pink jump up—began to cover the high meadows they crossed. Trees appeared more often, with more leaves, and grasslarks and robins sang in the branches. And there were wolves. Never in sight—not even Lan mentioned seeing one—but Perrin knew. He kept his mind firmly closed to them, yet now and again a feather-light tickle at the back of his mind reminded him they were there.

Lan spent most of his time scouting their path on his black warhorse, Mandarb, following Rand's tracks as the rest of them followed the signs the Warder left for them. An arrow of stones laid out on the ground, or one lightly scratched in the rock wall of a forking pass. Turn this way. Cross that saddlepass. Take this switchback, this deer trail, this way through the trees and down along a narrow stream, even though there is nothing to indicate anyone has ever gone that way before. Nothing but Lan's signs. A tuft of grass or weeds tied one way to say bear left, another for bear right. A bent branch. A pile of pebbles for a rough climb ahead, two leaves caught on a thorn for a steep descent. The Warder had a hundred signs, it seemed to Perrin, and Moiraine knew them all. Lan rarely came back except when they made camp, to confer with Moiraine quietly, away from the fire. When the sun rose, most often he was hours gone already.

Moiraine was always first into the saddle after him, while the eastern sky was just turning pink. The Aes Sedai would not have climbed down from Aldieb, her white mare, until full dark or later, except that Lan refused to track further once the light began to fail.

"We'll go even slower if a horse breaks a leg," the Warder would tell Moiraine when she complained.

Her reply was always very much the same. "If you cannot move any faster than this, perhaps I should send you off to Myrelle before you get any older. Well, perhaps that can wait, but you must move us faster."

She half sounded as if the threat were irritated truth, half as if she were making a joke. There was something of a threat in it, or maybe a warning, Perrin was sure, from the way Lan's mouth tightened even when she smiled afterwards and reached up to pat his shoulder soothingly.

"Who is Myrelle?" Perrin asked suspiciously, the first time it happened. Loial shook his head, murmuring something about unpleasant things happening to those who pried into Aes Sedai affairs. The Ogier's hairy-fetlocked horse was as tall and heavy as a Dhurran stallion, but with Loial's long legs dangling to either side, the animal looked undersized, like a large pony.

Moiraine gave an amused, secretive smile. "Just a Green sister. Someone to whom Lan must one day deliver a package for safekeeping."

"No day soon," Lan said, and surprisingly, there was open anger in his voice. "Never, if I can help it. You will outlive me long, Moiraine Aes Sedai!"

She has too many secrets, Perrin thought, but asked no more about a subject that could crack the Warder's iron self-control.

The Aes Sedai had a blanket-wrapped bundle tied behind her saddle: the Dragon banner. Perrin was uneasy about having it with them, but Moiraine had neither asked his opinion nor listened when he offered it. Not that anyone was likely to recognize it if he saw it, yet he hoped she was as good at keeping secrets from other people as she was at keeping them from him.

In the beginning, at least, it was a boring journey. One

cloud-capped mountain was very much like another, one pass little different from the next. Supper was usually rabbit, dropped by stones from Perrin's sling. He did not have so many arrows as to risk shooting at rabbits in that rocky country. Breakfast was cold rabbit, more often than not, and the midday meal the same, eaten in the saddle.

Sometimes when they camped near a stream and there was still light enough to see, he and Loial caught mountain trout, lying on their bellies, hands elbow-deep in the cold water, tickling the green-backed fish out from under the rock ledges where they hid. Loial's fingers, big as they were, were even more deft at it than Perrin's.

Once, three days after setting out, Moiraine joined them, stretching herself out on the streamside and undoing rows of pearl buttons to roll up her sleeves as she asked how the thing was done. Perrin exchanged surprised looks with Loial. The Ogier shrugged.

"It is not that hard, really," Perrin told her. "Just bring your hand up from behind the fish, and underneath, as if you're trying to tickle its belly. Then you pull it out. It takes practice, though. You might not catch anything the first few times you try."

"I tried for days before I ever caught anything," Loial added. He was already easing his huge hands into the water, careful to keep his shadow from scaring the fish.

"As difficult as that?" Moiraine murmured. Her hands slipped into the water—and a moment later came out with a splash, holding a fat trout that thrashed the surface. She laughed with delight as she tossed it up onto the bank.

Perrin blinked at the big fish flopping in the fading sunlight. It must have weighed at least five pounds. "You were very lucky," he said. "Trout that size don't often shelter under a ledge this small. We'll have to move upstream a bit. It will be dark before any of them settle under this ledge again."

"Is that so?" Moiraine said. "You two go ahead. I think I will just try here again."

Perrin hesitated a moment before moving up the bank to another overhang. She was up to something, but he could not imagine what. That troubled him. Belly down, and careful not to let his shadow fall on the water, he peered over the edge. Half a dozen slender shapes hung suspended in the water, barely moving a fin to hold their places. All of them together would not weigh as much as Moiraine's fish, he decided with a sigh. If they were lucky, he and Loial might take two apiece, but the shadows of trees on the far bank already stretched across the water. Whatever they caught now would be it, and Loial's appetite was big enough by itself to swallow those four and most of the bigger fish, too. Loial's hands were already easing up behind one of the trout.

Before Perrin could even slide his hands into the water, Moiraine gave a shout. "Three should be enough, I think. The last two are bigger than the first."

Perrin gave Loial a startled look. "She can't have!"

The Ogier straightened, sending the small trout scattering. "She is Aes Sedai," he said simply.

Sure enough, when they returned to Moiraine, three big trout lay on the bank. She was already buttoning her sleeves up again.

Perrin thought about reminding her that whoever took the fish was supposed to clean them, too, but just at that moment she caught his eye. There was no particular expression on her smooth face, but her dark eyes did not waver, and they appeared to know what he was going to say, and to have dismissed it out of hand already. When she turned away, it seemed somehow too late to say anything.

Muttering to himself, Perrin pulled out his beltknife and set to the gutting and heading. "All of a sudden she's forgotten about sharing the chores, it seems. I suppose she'll want us to do the cooking, as well, and the cleaning up after."

"No doubt she will," Loial said without pausing over the fish he was working on. "She is Aes Sedai."

"I seem to remember hearing that somewhere." Perrin's knife ripped into the fish. "The Shienarans might have been willing to run around fetching and carrying for her, but there are only four of us now. We should keep on turn and turn about. It's only fair."

Loial gave a great snort of laughter. "I doubt she sees it that way. First she had to put up with Rand arguing with her all the time, and now you're ready to take over for him. As a rule, Aes Sedai do not let anyone argue with them. I expect she means to have us back in the habit of doing what she says by the time we reach the first village."

"A good habit to be in," Lan said, throwing back his cloak. In the fading light he had appeared out of nowhere.

Perrin nearly fell over from surprise, and Loial's ears went stiff with shock. Neither of them had heard the Warder's step.

"A habit you should never have lost," Lan added, then strode off toward Moiraine and the horses. His boots barely made a sound, even on that rocky ground, and once he was a few paces away the cloak hanging down his back gave him the uneasy appearance of a disembodied head and arms drifting up from the stream.

"We need her to find Rand," Perrin said softly, "but I am not going to let her shape my life anymore." He went back to his cleaning vigorously.

He meant to keep that promise—he really did—but during the days that followed, in some way he did not quite understand, he found that he and Loial were doing the cooking, and the cleaning up, and any other little chore that Moiraine thought of. He even discovered that somehow or other he had taken over tending Aldieb every night, unsaddling the mare and rubbing her down while Moiraine settled herself, apparently deep in thought.

Loial gave in to it as inevitable, but not Perrin. He tried refusing, resisting, but it was hard to resist when she made a reasonable suggestion, and a small one at that. Only there was always another suggestion behind it, as reasonable and small as the first, and then another. The simple force of her presence, the strength of her gaze, made it difficult to protest. Her dark eyes would catch his at the moment he opened his mouth. A lift of her eyebrow to suggest he was being rude, a surprised widening of her eyes that he could object to so small a request, a level stare that held in it everything that was Aes Sedai, all these things could make him hesitate, and once he hesitated there was never any recovering lost ground. He accused her of using the One Power on him, though he did not really think that was it, and she told him not to be a fool. He began to feel like a piece of iron trying to stop a smith from hammering it into a scythe.

The Mountains of Mist gave way abruptly to the forested foothills of Ghealdan, to land that seemed all up and down, but never very high. Deer, which in the mountains had often watched them warily, as if uncertain what a man was, began to bound away, white tails flickering, at the first sight of the horses. Even Perrin now caught only the faintest glimpses of the gray-striped mountain cats that seemed to fade away like smoke. They were coming into the lands of men.

Lan stopped wearing his color-shifting cloak and began riding back to the rest of them more often, telling them what lay ahead. In many places the trees had all been cut down. Soon, fields encircled by rough stone walls and farmers plowing 'round the sides of hills were common sights, if not exactly frequent, along with lines of people moving across the plowed ground, sowing seed from sacks slung from their shoulders. Scattered farmhouses and barns of gray stone sat on hilltops and ridges.

The wolves should not have been there. Wolves avoided places where men were, but Perrin could still sense them, an unseen screen and escort ringing the mounted party. Impatience filled him; impatience to reach a village or a town, any place where there were enough men to make the wolves go away.

A day after sighting the first field, just as the sun touched the horizon behind them, they came to the village of Jarra, not far north of the border with Amadicia.

CHAPTER
8

Jarra

Gray stone houses with slate roofs lay clustered along the few narrow streets of Jarra, clinging to a hillside above a little stream spanned by a low wooden bridge. The muddy streets were empty, and so was the sloping village green, except for one man sweeping the steps of the village's only inn, standing beside its stone stable; but it looked as if there had been a good many people on the green not long before. Half a dozen arches, woven of green branches and dotted with such few flowers as could be found this early in the year, stood in a circle in the middle of the grass. The ground had a trampled look, and there were other signs of a gathering; a woman's red scarf lying tangled at the foot of one of the arches, a child's knitted cap, a pewter pitcher tumbled on its side, a few half-eaten scraps of food.

The aromas of sweet wine and spiced cakes clung about the green, mixed in with smoke from dozens of chimneys and evening meals cooking. For an instant Perrin's nose caught another odor, one he could not identify, a faint trail that raised the hair on the back of his neck with its vileness. Then it was gone. But he was sure something had passed that way, something—wrong. He scrubbed at his nose as if to rub away the memory of it. *That can't be Rand. Light, even if he has gone mad, that can't be him. Can it?*

A painted sign hung above the inn door, a man standing on one foot with his arms thrown in the air: Harilin's Leap. As they drew rein in front of the square stone building, the sweeper straightened, yawning fiercely. He gave a start at Perrin's eyes, but his own already protruding eyes went wide when they fell on Loial. With his wide mouth and no chin to speak of, he looked something like a frog. There was an old smell of sour wine about him—to Perrin, at least. The fellow had certainly been part of the celebration.

The man gave himself a shake, and turned it into a bow with one hand resting on the double row of wooden buttons running down his coat. His eyes flickered from one to another of them, popping even more every time they rested on Loial. "Welcome, good mistress, and the Light illumine your way. Welcome, good masters. You wish food, rooms, baths? All to be had, here at the Leap. Master Harod, the innkeeper, keeps a good house. I am called Simion. If you wish anything, ask for Simion, and he will get it for you." He yawned again, covering his mouth in embarrassment and bowing to hide it. "I beg your pardon, good mistress. You have come far? Have you word of the Great Hunt? The Hunt for the Horn of Valere? Or the false Dragon? It's said there's a false Dragon in Tarabon. Or maybe Arad Doman."

"We have not come that far," Lan said, swinging down from his saddle. "No doubt you know more than I." They all began dismounting.

"You have had a wedding here?" Moiraine said.

"A wedding, good mistress? Why, we've had a lifetime of weddings. A plague of them. All in the last two days. There isn't a woman old enough to speak the betrothal remains unmarried, not in the whole village, not for a mile in any direction. Why, even Widow Jorath dragged old Banas through the arches, and they'd both sworn they'd never marry again. It was like a whirlwind just snatched everybody up. Rilith, the weaver's daughter, she started it, asking Jon the blacksmith to marry her, and him old enough to be her father and more. The old fool just took off his apron and said yes, and she demanded the arches be put up right then and there. Wouldn't hear of a proper wait, and all the other women sided with her. Since then we've had marriages day and night. Why, nobody's had any sleep at all hardly."

"That's very interesting," Perrin said when Simion paused to yawn again, "but have you seen a young—"

"It is very interesting," Moiraine said, cutting him off, "and I would hear more of it later, perhaps. For now, we would like rooms, and a meal." Lan made a small gesture toward Perrin, down low, as if telling him to hold his tongue.

"Of course, good mistress. A meal. Rooms." Simion hesitated, eyeing Loial. "We'll have to push two beds together for—" He leaned closer to Moiraine and dropped his voice. "Pardon, good mistress, but—uh—what exactly—is he? Meaning no disrespect," he added hastily.

He had not spoken softly enough, for Loial's ears twitched irritably. "I am an Ogier! What did you think I was? A Trolloc?"

Simion took a step back at the booming voice. "Trolloc, good—uh—master? Why, I'm a grown man. I don't believe in children's tales. Uh, did you say Ogier? Why, Ogier are childr—I mean . . . that is. . . ." In desperation, he turned to bellow toward the stable next to the inn. "Nico! Patrim! Visitors! Come see to their horses!" After a moment two boys with hay in their hair tumbled out of the stable, yawning and rubbing their eyes. Simion gestured to the steps, bowing, as the boys gathered reins.

Perrin slung his saddlebags and blanketroll over his shoulder and carried his bow as he followed Moiraine and Lan inside, with Simion bowing and bobbing ahead of them. Loial had to duck low under the lintel, and the ceiling inside only cleared his head by a foot. He kept rumbling to himself about not understanding why so few humans remembered the Ogier. His voice was like distant thunder. Even Perrin, right in front of him, could only understand half of his words.

The inn smelled of ale and wine, cheese and weariness, and the aroma of roasting mutton drifted from somewhere in the back. The few men in the common room sagged over their mugs as if they would really like to lie down on the benches and go to sleep. One plump serving woman was drawing a mug of ale from one of the barrels at the end of the room. The innkeeper himself, in a long white apron, sat on a tall stool in the corner, leaning against the wall. As the newcomers entered, he lifted his head, bleary-eyed. His jaw dropped at the sight of Loial.

"Visitors, Master Harod," Simion announced. "They want rooms. Master Harod? He's an Ogier, Master Harod." The serving woman turned and saw Loial, and dropped the mug with a clatter. None of the weary men at the tables even looked up. One had put his head down on the table and was snoring.

Loial's ears twitched violently.

Master Harod got to his feet slowly, eyes fastened on Loial, smoothing his apron all the while. "At least he isn't a Whitecloak," he said at last, then gave a start as if surprised he had spoken aloud. "That is to say, welcome, good mistress. Good masters. Forgive my lack of manners. I can only plead tiredness, good mistress." He darted another glance at Loial, and mouthed "Ogier?" with a look of disbelief.

Loial opened his mouth, but Moiraine forestalled him. "As your man said, good innkeeper, I wish rooms for my party for the night, and a meal."

"Oh! Of course, good mistress. Of course. Simion, show these good people to my best rooms, so they can put down their belongings. I'll have a fine meal laid out for you when you return, good mistress. A fine meal."

"If it pleases you to follow me, good mistress," Simion said. "Good masters." He bowed the way to stairs at one side of the common room.

Behind them, one of the men at the tables suddenly exclaimed, "What in the name of the Light is that?" Master Harod began explaining about Ogier, making it sound as if he were quite familiar with them. Most of what Perrin heard before they left the voices behind was wrong. Loial's ears twitched without stop.

On the second floor, the Ogier's head came near to brushing along the ceiling. The narrow corridor was growing dark, with only the sharp light of sunset through a window next to the door at the far end.

"Candles in the rooms, good mistress," Simion said. "I should have brought a lamp, but my head is still spinning from all those weddings. I'll send someone up to light the fire, if you wish. And you'll want wash water, of course." He pushed open a door. "Our best room, good mistress. We don't have many—not many strangers, you see—but this is our best."

"I'll take the one next to it," Lan said. He had Moiraine's blanketroll and saddlebags on his shoulder as well as his own, and the bundle containing the Dragon banner, too.

"Oh, good master, that's not a very good room at all. Narrow bed. Cramped. Meant for a servant, I suspect, as if we'd ever have anybody here who had a servant. Begging your pardon, good mistress."

"I will take it anyway," Lan said firmly.

"Simion," Moiraine said, "does Master Harod dislike the Children of the Light?"

"Well, he does, good mistress. He didn't, but he does. It isn't good policy, disliking the Children, not so close to the border as we are. They come through Jarra all the time, like there wasn't any border at all. But there was trouble, yesterday. A fistful of trouble. And with the weddings going on, and all."

"What happened, Simion?"

The man looked at her sharply before answering. Perrin did not think anyone else saw how sharply, in the dimness. "There was about twenty of them, come day before yesterday. No trouble then. But yesterday. . . . Why, three of them up and announced they weren't Children of the Light anymore. They took off their cloaks and just rode away."

Lan grunted. "Whitecloaks swear for life. What did their commander do?"

"Why, he would have done something, you can be sure, good master, but another of them announced he was off to find the Horn of Valere. Anyway, still another said they should be hunting the Dragon. That one said he was going to Almoth Plain when he left. Then some of them started saying things to women in the streets, things they shouldn't have, and grabbing at them. The women were screaming, and Children yelling at the ones bothering the women. I never saw such commotion."

"Didn't any of you try to stop them?" Perrin said.

"Good master, you carry that axe like you know how to use it, but it isn't so easy to face up to men with swords and armor and all, when all you know how to use is a broom or a hoe. The rest of the Whitecloaks, those as hadn't gone off, put an end to it. Almost came to drawing swords. And that wasn't the worst. Two more just went mad—if the others weren't. Those two started raving that Jarra was full of Darkfriends. They tried to burn the village down—said they would!—beginning with the Leap. You can see the burn marks out back, where they got it started. Fought the other Whitecloaks when they tried to stop them. The Whitecloaks that were left, they helped us put it out, tied those two up tight, and rode out of here, back toward Amadicia. Good riddance, I say, and if they never come back, it'll be too soon."

"Rough behavior," Lan said, "even for Whitecloaks."

Simion bobbed his head in agreement. "As you say, good master. They never acted like that before. Swagger around, yes. Look at you like you were dirt, and poke their noses in where they hadn't any business. But they never caused trouble before. Not like that, anyway."

"They are gone now," Moiraine said, "and troubles with them. I am sure we will pass a quiet night."

Perrin kept his mouth shut, but he was not quiet inside. *All these weddings and Whitecloaks are all very well, but I'd sooner know if Rand stopped here, and which way he went when he left. That smell couldn't have been him.*

He let Simion guide him on down the hall to another room, with two beds and a washstand, a pair of stools and not much else. Loial stooped to put his head through the doorway. Only a little light came in by the narrow windows. The beds were big enough, with blankets and comforters folded at the foot, but the mattresses looked lumpy. Simion fumbled on the mantel above the fireplace until he found a candle, and a tinderbox to get it alight.

"I'll see about getting some beds put together for you, good—uh—Ogier. Yes, just a moment, now." He showed no sign of hurry to be about it, though, fussing with the candlestick as if he had to place it just right. Perrin thought he looked uneasy.

Well, I'd be more than uneasy if Whitecloaks had been acting like that in Emond's Field. "Simion, has another stranger passed through here in the last day or two? A young man, tall, with gray eyes and reddish hair? He might have played the flute for a meal or a bed."

"I remember him, good master," Simion said, still shifting the candlestick. "Came yesterday morning, early. Looked hungry, he did. He played the flute for all the weddings, yesterday. Good-looking young fellow. Some of the women eyed him, at first, but. . . ." He paused, looking at Perrin sideways. "Is he a friend of yours, good master?"

"I know him," Perrin said. "Why?"

Simion hesitated. "No reason, good master. He was an odd fellow, that's all. He talked to himself, sometimes, and sometimes he laughed when nobody had said anything. Slept in this very room, last night, or part of it. Woke us all in the middle of the night, yelling. It was just a nightmare, but he wouldn't stay any longer. Master Harod didn't make much effort to talk him into it, after all that noise." Simion paused again. "He said something strange when he left."

"What?" Perrin demanded.

"He said somebody was after him. He said. . . ." The chinless man swallowed and went on more slowly. "Said they'd kill him if he didn't go. 'One of us has to die, and I mean it to be him.' His very words."

"He did not mean us," Loial rumbled. "We are his friends."

"Of course, good—uh—good Ogier. Of course, he didn't mean you. I—uh—I don't mean to say anything about a friend of yours, but I—uh—I think he's sick. In the head, you know."

"We will take care of him," Perrin said. "That's why we're following him. Which way did he go?"

"I knew it," Simion said, bouncing on his toes. "I knew she could help as soon as I saw you. Which way? East, good master. East, like the Dark One himself was on his heels. Do you think she'll help me? Help my brother, that is? Noam's bad sick, and Mother Roon says she can't do anything."

Perrin kept his face expressionless, and bought a little time to think by propping his bow in the corner and setting his blanketroll and saddlebags on one of the beds. The problem was that thinking did not help much. He looked at Loial, but found no help there; consternation had the Ogier's ears drooping and his long eyebrows hanging down on his cheeks. "What makes you think she can help your brother?" *Stupid question! The right question is, what does he mean to do about it?*

"Why, I traveled to Jehannah, once, good master, and I saw two . . . two women like her. I couldn't mistake her after that." His voice dropped to a whisper. "It's said *they* can raise the dead, good master."

"Who else knows this?" Perrin asked sharply, and at the same time Loial said, "If your brother is dead, there is nothing anyone can do."

The frog-faced man looked from one to the other of them anxiously, and his words came in a babble. "No one knows but me, good master. Noam isn't dead, good Ogier, only sick. I swear nobody else could recognize her. Even Master Harod's never been more than twenty miles from here in his life. He's so bad sick. I'd ask her myself, only my knees'd be shaking so hard she couldn't hear me talk. What if she took offense and called down lightning on me? And what if I'd been wrong? It isn't the kind of thing you accuse a woman of without. . . . I mean . . . uh. . . ." He raised his hands, half in pleading, half as if to defend himself.

"I can make no promises," Perrin said, "but I'll speak to her. Loial, why don't you keep Simion company till I've spoken to Moiraine?"

"Of course," the Ogier boomed. Simion gave a start when Loial's hand swallowed his shoulder. "He will show me my room, and we will talk. Tell me, Simion, what do you know of trees?"

"T-t-trees, g-good Ogier?"

Perrin did not wait any longer. He hurried back down the dark hall and knocked on Moiraine's door, barely waiting for her peremptory "Come!" before pushing in.

Half a dozen candles showed that the Leap's best room was none too good, though the one bed had four tall posts supporting a canopy, and the mattress looked less full of lumps than Perrin's. There was a scrap of carpet on the floor, and two cushioned chairs instead of stools. Other than that, it looked no different from his room. Moiraine and Lan stood in front of the cold hearth as if they had been discussing something, and the Aes Sedai did not look pleased at being interrupted. The Warder's face was as imperturbable as a carving.

"Rand's been here, all right," Perrin started off. "That fellow Simion remembers him." Moiraine hissed through her teeth.

"You were told to keep your mouth shut," Lan growled.

Perrin squared his feet to face the Warder. That was easier than facing Moiraine's glare. "How could we find out whether he had been here without asking questions? Tell me that. He left last night, if you are interested, heading east. And he was carrying on about somebody following him, trying to kill him."

"East." Moiraine nodded. The utter calm of her voice

was at odds with her disapproving eyes. "That is good to know, though it had to be so if he is going to Tear. But I was fairly certain he had been here even before I heard about the Whitecloaks, and they made it a certainty. Rand is almost surely right about one thing, Perrin. I cannot believe we are the only ones trying to find him. And if they find out about us, they may well try to stop us. We have enough to contend with trying to catch up to Rand without that. You must learn to hold your tongue until I tell you to speak."

"The Whitecloaks?" Perrin said incredulously. *Hold my tongue? Burn me, if I will!* "How could they tell you—? Rand's madness. It is *catching*?"

"Not his madness," Moiraine said, "if he is far enough gone yet to be called mad. Perrin, he is more strongly *ta'veren* than anyone since the Age of Legends. Yesterday, in this village, the Pattern . . . moved, shaped itself around him like clay shaped on a mold. The weddings, the Whitecloaks, these were enough to say Rand had been here, for anyone who knew to listen."

Perrin drew a long breath. "And this is what we'll find everywhere he's been? Light, if there are Shadowspawn after him, they can track him as easily as we can."

"Perhaps," Moiraine said. "Perhaps not. No one knows anything about *ta'veren* as strong as Rand." For just a moment she sounded vexed at not knowing. "Artur Hawkwing was the most strongly *ta'veren* of whom any writings remain. And Hawkwing was in no way as strong as Rand."

"It is said," Lan put in, "that there were times when people in the same room with Hawkwing spoke truth when they meant to lie, made decisions they had not even known they were contemplating. Times when every toss of the dice, every turn of the cards, went his way. But only times."

"You mean you don't know," Perrin said. "He could leave a trail of weddings and Whitecloaks gone mad all the way to Tear."

"I mean I know as much as there is to know," Moiraine said sharply. Her dark-eyed gaze chastised Perrin like a whip. "The Pattern weaves finely around *ta'veren*, and others can follow the shape of those threads if they know where to look. Be careful your tongue does not unravel more than you can know."

In spite of himself Perrin hunched his shoulders as if she were delivering real blows. "Well, you had better be glad I opened my mouth this time. Simion knows you're Aes Sedai. He wants you to Heal his brother Noam of some sickness. If I hadn't talked to him, he would never have worked up nerve enough to ask, but he might have started talking among his friends."

Lan caught Moiraine's eye, and for a moment they stared at one another. The Warder had the air about him of a wolf about to leap. Finally, Moiraine shook her head. "No," she said.

"As you wish. It is your decision." Lan sounded as if he thought she had made the wrong one, but the tension left him.

Perrin stared at them. "You were thinking of. . . . Simion couldn't tell anyone if he were dead, could he?"

"He will not die by my actions," Moiraine said. "But I cannot, and will not, promise that it will always be so. We must find Rand, and I will not fail in that. Is that spoken plainly enough for you?" Caught in her gaze, Perrin could make no answer. She nodded as if his silence were answer enough. "Now take me to Simion."

The door to Loial's room stood open, spilling a pool of candlelight into the hall. The two beds inside had been pushed together, and Loial and Simion were seated on the edge of one. The chinless man was staring up at Loial with his mouth open and an expression of wonder on his face.

"Oh, yes, the *stedding* are wonderful," Loial was saying. "There is such peace there, under the Great Trees. You humans may have your wars and strife, but nothing ever troubles the *stedding*. We tend the trees and live in harmony. . . ." He trailed off when he saw Moiraine, with Lan and Perrin behind her.

Simion scrambled to his feet, bowing and backing away until he came up against the far wall. "Uh . . . good mistress. . . . Uh . . . uh. . . ." Even then, he continued bobbing like a toy on a string.

"Show me to your brother," Moiraine commanded, "and I will do what I can. Perrin, you will come, too, since this good man spoke to you first." Lan lifted an eyebrow, and she shook her head. "If we all go, we might attract attention. Perrin can give me what protection I need."

Lan nodded reluctantly, then gave Perrin a hard look. "See that you do, blacksmith. If any harm befalls her. . . ." His cold blue eyes finished the promise.

Simion snatched one of the candles and scurried into the hallway, still bowing so the candlelight made their shadows dance. "This way—uh—good mistress. This way."

Beyond the door at the end of the hall, outside stairs led down to a cramped alleyway, between inn and stable. Night shrank the candle to a flickering pinpoint. The half moon was up in a star-flecked sky, giving more than enough light for Perrin's eyes. He wondered when Moiraine would tell Simion he did not have to keep bowing, but she never did. The Aes Sedai glided along, clutching her skirts to keep them out of the mud, as though the dark passage were a palace hall and she a queen. The air was already cooling; nights still carried echoes of winter.

"This way." Simion led them back to a small shed behind the stable and hurriedly unbarred the door. "This way." Simion pointed. "There, good mistress. There. My brother. Noam."

The far end of the shed had been barred off with slats of wood; hastily, by the rough look of it. A stout iron lock in a hasp held shut a crude door of wooden slats. Behind those bars, a man lay sprawled on his stomach on the straw-covered floor. He was barefoot, his shirt and breeches ripped as if he had torn at them without knowing how to take them off. There was an odor of unwashed flesh that Perrin thought even Simion and Moiraine must smell.

Noam lifted his head and stared at them silently, without expression. There was nothing at all about him to suggest he was Simion's brother—he had a chin, for one thing, and he was a big man, with heavy shoulders—but that was not what staggered Perrin. Noam stared at them with burnished golden eyes.

"He'd been talking crazy almost a year, good mistress, saying he could . . . could talk with wolves. And his eyes. . . ." Simion darted a glance at Perrin. "Well, he'd talk about it when he'd drunk too much. Everybody laughed at him. Then a month or so ago, he didn't come to town. I went out to see what was the matter, and I found him— like this."

Cautiously, unwillingly, Perrin reached out toward Noam

as he would have toward a wolf. *Running through the woods with the cold wind in his nose. Quick dash from cover, teeth snapping at hamstrings. Taste of blood, rich on the tongue. Kill.* Perrin jerked back as he would have from a fire, sealed himself off. They were not thoughts at all, really, just a chaotic jumble of desires and images, part memory, part yearning. But there was more wolf there than anything else. He put a hand to the wall to steady himself; his knees felt weak. *Light help me!*

Moiraine put a hand on the lock.

"Master Harod has the key, good mistress. I don't know if he'll—"

She gave a tug, and the lock sprang open. Simion gaped at her. She lifted the lock free of the hasp, and the chinless man turned to Perrin.

"Is that safe, good master? He's my brother, but he bit Mother Roon when she tried to help, and he . . . he killed a cow. With his teeth," he finished faintly.

"Moiraine," Perrin said, "the man is dangerous."

"All men are dangerous," she replied in a cool voice. "Now be quiet." She opened the door and went in. Perrin held his breath.

At her first step, Noam's lips peeled back from his teeth, and he began to growl, a rumble that deepened till his whole body quivered. Moiraine ignored it. Still growling, Noam wriggled backwards in the straw as she came closer to him, until he had backed himself into a corner. Or she had backed him.

Slowly, calmly, the Aes Sedai knelt and took his head between her hands. Noam's growl heightened to a snarl, then tailed off in a whimper before Perrin could move. For a long moment Moiraine held Noam's head, then just as calmly released it and rose. Perrin's throat tightened as she turned her back on Noam and walked out of the cage, but the man only stared after her. She pushed the slatted door to, slipped the lock back through the hasp, not bothering to snap it shut— and Noam hurled himself snarling against the wooden bars. He bit at them, and battered them with his shoulders, tried to force his head between them, all the while snarling and snapping.

Moiraine brushed straw from her skirt with a steady hand and no expression.

"You do take chances," Perrin breathed. She looked at him—a steady, knowing gaze—and he dropped his eyes. His yellow eyes.

Simion was staring at his brother. "Can you help him, good mistress?" he asked hoarsely.

"I am sorry, Simion," she said.

"Can't you do anything, good mistress? Something? One of those"—his voice fell to a whisper—"Aes Sedai things?"

"Healing is not a simple matter, Simion, and it comes from within as much as from the Healer. There is nothing here that remembers being Noam, nothing that remembers being a man. There are no maps remaining to show him the path back, and nothing left to take that path. Noam is gone, Simion."

"He—he just used to talk funny, good mistress, when he'd had too much to drink. He just. . . ." Simion scrubbed a hand across his eyes and blinked. "Thank you, good mistress. I know you'd have done something if you could." She put a hand on his shoulder, murmured comforting words, and then she was gone from the shed.

Perrin knew he should follow her, but the man—what had once been a man—snapping at the wooden bars, held him. He took a quick step and surprised himself by removing the dangling lock from the hasp. The lock was a good one, the work of a master smith.

"Good master?"

Perrin stared at the lock in his hand, at the man behind in the cage. Noam had stopped biting at the slats; he stared back at Perrin warily, panting. Some of his teeth had broken off jaggedly.

"You can leave him in here forever," Perrin said, "but I—I don't think he'll ever get any better."

"If he gets out, good master, he'll die!"

"He will die in here or out there, Simion. Out there, at least he'll be free, and as happy as he can be. He is not your brother anymore, but you're the one who has to decide. You can leave him in here for people to stare at, leave him to stare at the bars of his cage until he pines away. You cannot cage a wolf, Simion, not and expect it to be happy. Or live long."

"Yes," Simion said slowly. "Yes, I see." He hesitated, then nodded, and jerked his head toward the shed door.

That was all the answer Perrin needed. He swung back the slatted door and stood aside.

For a moment Noam stared at the opening. Abruptly he darted out of the cage, running on all fours, but with surprising agility. Out of the cage, out of the shed, and into the night. *The Light help us both*, Perrin thought.

"I suppose it's better for him to be free." Simion gave himself a shake. "But I don't know what Master Harod will say when he finds that door standing open and Noam gone."

Perrin shut the cage door; the big lock made a sharp click as he refastened it. "Let him puzzle that out."

Simion barked a quick laugh, abruptly cut off. "He'll make something out of it. They all will. Some of them say Noam turned into a wolf—fur and all!—when he bit Mother Roon. It's not true, but they say it."

Shivering, Perrin leaned his head against the cage door. *He may not have fur, but he's a wolf. He's wolf, not man. Light, help me.*

"We didn't keep him here always," Simion said suddenly. "He was at Mother Roon's house, but she and I got Master Harod to move him here after the Whitecloaks came. They always have a list of names, Darkfriends they're looking for. It was Noam's eyes, you see. One of the names the Whitecloaks had was a fellow named Perrin Aybara, a blacksmith. They said he has yellow eyes, and runs with wolves. You can see why I didn't want them to know about Noam."

Perrin turned his head enough to look at Simion over his shoulder. "Do you think this Perrin Aybara is a Darkfriend?"

"A Darkfriend wouldn't care if my brother died in a cage. I suppose she found you soon after it happened. In time to help. I wish she'd come to Jarra a few months ago."

Perrin was ashamed that he had ever compared the man to a frog. "And I wish she could have done something for him." *Burn me, I wish she could.* Suddenly it burst on him that the whole village must know about Noam. About his eyes. "Simion, would you bring me something to eat in my room?" Master Harod and the rest might have been too taken with staring at Loial to notice his eyes before, but they surely would if he ate in the common room.

"Of course. And in the morning, too. You don't have to come down until you are ready to get on your horse."

"You are a good man, Simion. A good man." Simion looked so pleased that Perrin felt ashamed all over again.

CHAPTER
9

Wolf Dreams

Perrin returned to his room by the back way, and after a time Simion came up with a covered tray. The cloth did not hold in the smells of roasted mutton, sweetbeans, turnips, and freshly baked bread, but Perrin lay on his bed, staring at the whitewashed ceiling, until the aromas grew cold. Images of Noam ran through his head over and over again. Noam chewing at the wooden slats. Noam running off into the darkness. He tried to think of lock-making, of the careful quenching and shaping of the steel, but it did not work.

Ignoring the tray, he rose and made his way down the hall to Moiraine's room. She answered his rap on the door with, "Come in, Perrin."

For an instant all the old stories about Aes Sedai stirred again, but he pushed them aside and opened the door.

Moiraine was alone—for which he was grateful—sitting with an ink bottle balanced on her knee, writing in a small, leather-bound book. She corked the bottle and wiped the steel nib of her pen on a small scrap of parchment without looking at him. There was a fire in the fireplace.

"I have been expecting you for some time," she said. "I have not spoken about this before because it was obvious you did not want me to. After tonight, though. . . . What do you want to know?"

"Is that what I can expect?" he asked. "To end like that?"

"Perhaps."

He waited for more, but she only put pen and ink away in their small case of polished rosewood and blew on her writing to dry it. "Is that all? Moiraine, don't give me slippery Aes Sedai answers. If you know something, tell me. Please."

"I know very little, Perrin. While searching for other answers among the books and manuscripts two friends keep for their researches, I found a copied fragment of a book from the Age of Legends. It spoke of . . . situations like yours. That may be the only copy anywhere in the world, and it did not tell me much."

"What *did* it tell you? Anything at all is more than I know now. Burn me, I've been worrying about Rand going mad, but I never thought I had to worry about myself!"

"Perrin, even in the Age of Legends, they knew little of this. Whoever wrote it seemed uncertain whether it was truth or legend. And I only saw a fragment, remember. She said that some who talked to wolves lost themselves, that what was human was swallowed up by wolf. Some. Whether she meant one in ten, or five, or nine, I do not know."

"I can shut them out. I don't know how I do it, but I can refuse to listen to them. I can refuse to hear them. Will that help?"

"It may." She studied him, seeming to choose her words carefully. "Mostly, she wrote of dreams. Dreams can be dangerous for you, Perrin."

"You said that once before. What do you mean?"

"According to her, wolves live partly in this world, and partly in a world of dreams."

"A world of dreams?" he said disbelievingly.

Moiraine gave him a sharp look. "That is what I said, and that is what she wrote. The way wolves talk to one another, the way they talk to you, is in some way connected to this world of dreams. I do not claim to understand how." She paused, frowning slightly. "From what I have read of Aes Sedai who had the Talent called Dreaming, Dreamers sometimes spoke of encountering wolves in their dreams, even wolves that acted as guides. I fear you must learn to be as careful sleeping as waking, if you intend to avoid wolves. If that is what you decide to do."

"If that is what I decide? Moiraine, I will not end up like Noam. I won't!"

She eyed him quizzically, shaking her head slowly. "You speak as if you can make all your own choices, Perrin. You are *ta'veren*, remember." He turned his back on her, staring at the night-dark windows, but she continued: "Perhaps, knowing what Rand is, knowing how strongly *ta'veren* he is, I have paid too little attention to the other two *ta'veren* I found with him. Three *ta'veren* in the same village, all born within weeks of one another? That is unheard of. Perhaps you—and Mat—have larger purposes in the Pattern than you, or I, thought."

"I do not want any *purpose* in the Pattern," Perrin muttered. "I surely can't have one if I forget I am a man. Will you help me, Moiraine?" It was hard to say that. *What if it means her using the One Power? Would I rather forget I'm a man?* "Help me keep from—losing myself?"

"If I can keep you whole, I will. I promise you that, Perrin. But I will not endanger the struggle against the Shadow. You must know that, too."

When he turned to look at her, she was regarding him unblinkingly. *And if your struggle means putting me in my grave tomorrow, will you do that, too?* He was icily sure that she would. "What have you not told me?"

"Do not presume too far, Perrin," she said coldly. "Do not press me further than I think proper."

He hesitated before asking the next question. "Can you do for me what you did for Lan? Can you shield my dreams?"

"I already have a Warder, Perrin." Her lips quirked almost into a smile. "And one is all I will have. I am of the Blue Ajah, not the Green."

"You know what I mean. I don't want to be a Warder." *Light, bound to an Aes Sedai the rest of my life? That's as bad as the wolves.*

"It would not aid you, Perrin. The shielding is for dreams from the outside. The danger in your dreams is within you." She opened the small book again. "You should sleep," she said in dismissal. "Be wary of your dreams, but you must sleep sometime." She turned a page, and he left.

Back in his own room, he eased the hold he kept on himself, eased it just a trifle, let his senses spread. The wolves were out there still, beyond the edges of the village, ringing Jarra. Almost immediately he snapped back to rigid self-control. "What I need is a city," he muttered. That would keep them at bay. *After I find Rand. After I finish whatever has to be finished with him.* He was not sure how sorry he

was that Moiraine could not shield him. The One Power or
the wolves; that was a choice no man should have to make.

He left the fire laid on the hearthstone unlit, and threw
open both windows. Cold night air rushed in. Tossing blankets and comforter on the floor, he lay down fully clothed
on the lumpy bed, not bothering to try to find a comfortable position. His last thought before sleep came was that
if anything would keep him from deep sleep and dangerous
dreams, that mattress would.

He was in a long hallway, its high stone ceiling and walls
glistening with damp and streaked by odd shadows. They
lay in contorted strips, stopping as abruptly as they began,
too dark for the light between them. He had no idea where
the light came from.

"No," he said, then louder, "No! This is a dream. I need
to wake up. Wake up!"

The hallway did not change.

Danger. It was a wolf's thought, faint and distant.

"I will wake up. I will!" He pounded a fist against the
wall. It hurt, but he did not wake. He thought one of the
sinuous shadows shifted away from his blow.

Run, brother. Run.

"Hopper?" he said wonderingly. He was sure he knew
the wolf whose thoughts he heard. Hopper, who had envied
the eagles. "Hopper is dead!"

Run!

Perrin lurched into a run, one hand holding his axe to
keep the haft from banging against his leg. He had no idea
where he was running, or why, but the urgency of Hopper's
sending could not be ignored. *Hopper's dead*, he thought.
He's dead! But Perrin ran.

Other hallways crossed the one he ran along, at odd
angles, sometimes descending, sometimes climbing. None
looked any different from the passage he was in, though.
Damp stone walls unbroken by doors, and strips of darkness.

As he came on one of those crossing halls, he skidded
to a halt. A man stood there, blinking at him uncertainly,
in strangely cut coat and breeches, the coat flaring over his
hips as the bottoms of the breeches flared over his boots.

Both were bright yellow, and his boots were only a little paler.

"This is more than I can stand," the man said, to himself, not Perrin. He had an odd accent, quick and sharp. "Not only do I dream of peasants, now, but foreign peasants, from those clothes. Begone from my dreams, fellow!"

"Who are you?" Perrin asked. The man's eyebrows rose as if he were offended.

The strips of shadow around them writhed. One detached from the ceiling at one end and drifted down to touch the strange man's head. It appeared to tangle in his hair. The man's eyes widened, and everything seemed to happen at once. The shadow jerked back to the ceiling, ten feet overhead, trailing something pale. Wet drops splattered Perrin's face. A bone-rattling shriek shattered the air.

Frozen, Perrin stared at the bloody shape wearing the man's clothes, screaming and thrashing on the floor. Unbidden, his eyes rose to the pale thing like an empty sack that dangled from the ceiling. Part of it was already absorbed by the black strip, but he had no trouble recognizing a human skin, apparently whole and unbroken.

The shadows around him danced in agitation, and Perrin ran, pursued by dying screams. Ripples ran along the shadow strips, pacing him.

"Change, burn you!" he shouted. "I know it's a dream! Light burn you, change!"

Colorful tapestries hung along the walls between tall golden stands holding dozens of candles that illuminated white floor tiles and a ceiling painted with fluffy clouds and fanciful birds in flight. Nothing moved but the flickering candle flames along the length of that hall, stretching as far as he could see, or in the pointed arches of white stone that occasionally broke the walls.

Danger. The sending was even fainter than before. And more urgent, if that were possible.

Axe in hand, Perrin started warily down the hall, muttering to himself. "Wake up. Wake up, Perrin. If you know it's a dream, it changes or you wake up. Wake up, burn you!" The hallway stayed as solid as any he had ever walked.

He came abreast of the first of the pointed white archways. It let into a huge room, apparently windowless, but furnished as ornately as any palace, the furniture all carved and gilded and inlaid with ivory. A woman stood in the middle of the room, frowning at a tattered manuscript lying open on a table. A black-haired, black-eyed, beautiful woman clothed in white and silver.

Even as he recognized her, she lifted her head and looked straight at him. Her eyes widened, in shock, in anger. "You! What are you doing here? How did you—? You'll ruin things you could not begin to imagine!"

Abruptly the space seemed to flatten, as if he were suddenly staring at a picture of a room. The flat image appeared to turn sideways, become only a bright vertical line down the middle of blackness. The line flashed white, and was gone, leaving only the dark, blacker than black.

Just in front of Perrin's boots, the floor tiles came to an abrupt end. As he watched, the white edges dissolved into the black like sand washed away by water. He stepped back hastily.

Run.

Perrin turned, and Hopper was there, a big gray wolf, grizzled and scarred. "You are dead. I saw you die. I *felt* you die!" A sending flooded Perrin's mind.

Run now! You must not be here now. Danger. Great danger. Worse than all the Neverborn. You must go. Go now! Now!

"How?" Perrin shouted. "I want to go, but how?"

Go! Teeth bared, Hopper leaped for Perrin's throat.

With a strangled cry, Perrin sat up on the bed, hands going to his throat to hold in lifeblood. They met unbroken skin. He swallowed with relief, but the next moment his fingers touched a damp spot.

Almost falling in his haste, he scrambled off the bed, stumbled to the washstand and seized the pitcher, splashed water everywhere as he filled the basin. The water turned pink as he washed his face. Pink with the blood of that strangely dressed man.

More dark spots dotted his coat and breeches. He tore them off and tossed them into the furthest corner. He meant to leave them there. Simion could burn them.

A gust of wind whipped in the open window. Shivering in shirt and smallclothes, he sat on the floor and leaned back against the bed. *This should be uncomfortable enough.* Sourness tinged his thoughts, and worry, and fear. And determination. *I won't give in to this. I won't!*

He was still shivering when sleep finally came, a shallow half sleep filled with vague awareness of the room around him and thoughts of the cold. But the bad dreams that came were better than some others.

Rand huddled under the trees in the night, watching the heavy-shouldered black dog come nearer his hiding place. His side ached, the wound Moiraine could not quite Heal, but he ignored it. The moon gave barely enough light for him to make out the dog, waist-high, with its thick neck and massive head, and its teeth that seemed to shine like wet silver in the night. It sniffed the air and trotted toward him.

Closer, he thought. *Come closer. No warning for your master this time. Closer. That's it.* The dog was only ten paces away, now, a deep growl rumbling in its chest as it suddenly bounded forward. Straight at Rand.

The Power filled him. Something leaped from his outstretched hands; he was not sure what it was. A bar of white light, solid as steel. Liquid fire. For an instant, in the middle of that something, the dog seemed to become transparent, and then it was gone.

The white light faded except for the afterimage burned across Rand's vision. He sagged against the nearest tree trunk, the bark rough on his face. Relief and silent laughter shook him. *It worked. Light save me, it worked this time.* It had not always. There had been other dogs this night.

The One Power pulsed in him, and his stomach twisted with the Dark One's taint on *saidin*, wanted to empty itself. Sweat beaded on his face despite the cold night wind, and his mouth tasted full of sickness. He wanted to lie down and die. He wanted Nynaeve to give him some of her medicines, or Moiraine to Heal him, or. . . . Something, anything, to stop the sick feeling that was suffocating him.

But *saidin* flooded him with life, too, life and energy and awareness larded through the illness. Life without *saidin* was a pale copy. Anything else was a wan imitation.

But they can find me if I hold on. Track me, find me. I have to reach Tear. I'll find out there. If I am the Dragon, there'll be an end to it. And if I am not. . . . If it's all a lie, there will be an end to that, too. An end.

Reluctantly, with infinite slowness, he severed contact with *saidin*, gave up its embrace as if giving up life's breath. The night seemed drab. The shadows lost their infinite sharp shadings and washed together.

In the distance, to the west, a dog howled, a shivering cry in the silent night.

Rand's head came up. He peered in that direction as though he could see the dog if he tried hard enough.

A second dog answered the first, then another, and two more together, all spread out somewhere west of him.

"Hunt me," Rand snarled. "Hunt me if you will. I'm no easy meat. No more!"

Pushing himself away from the tree, he waded a shallow, icy stream, then settled into a steady trot eastward. Cold water filled his boots, and his side hurt, but he ignored both. The night was quiet again behind him, but he ignored that, too. *Hunt me. I can hunt, too. I am no easy meat.*

CHAPTER
10

Secrets

Ignoring her companions for a moment, Egwene al'Vere stood in her stirrups hoping for a glimpse of Tar Valon in the distance, but all she could see was something indistinct, gleaming white in the morning sunlight. It had to be the city on the island, though. The lone, broken-topped mountain called Dragonmount, rising out of the rolling plain, had first appeared on the horizon late the afternoon before, and that lay just this side of the River Erinin from Tar Valon. It was a landmark; that mountain—one jagged fang sticking up out of rolling flatlands—easily seen for many miles, easy to avoid, as all did, even those who went to Tar Valon.

Dragonmount was where Lews Therin Kinslayer had died, so it was said; and other words had been spoken of the mountain, prophecy and warning. Rich reasons to stay away from its black slopes.

She had reason not to stay away, and more than one. Only in Tar Valon could she find the training she needed, the training she had to have. *I will never be collared again!* She pushed the thought away, but it came back turned end about. *I will never lose my freedom again!* In Tar Valon, Anaiya would resume testing her dreams; the Aes Sedai would have to, though she had found no real evidence that Egwene was a Dreamer, as Anaiya suspected. Egwene's dreams had been troubling since leaving Almoth Plain. Aside from dreams of the Seanchan—and those still made her wake sweating—she dreamed more and more of Rand. Rand running. Running toward something, but running away from something, too.

She peered harder toward Tar Valon. Anaiya would be there. *And Galad, too, perhaps.* She blushed in spite of herself, and banished him from her mind entirely. *Think about the weather. Think about anything else. Light, but it feels warm.*

This early in the year, with winter only yesterday's memory, white still capped Dragonmount, but here below, the snows were melted. Early shoots poked through the matted brown of last year's grasses, and where trees topped a low hill here and there, the first red of new growth was showing. After a winter spent traveling, sometimes trapped in village or camp for days by storms, sometimes covering less ground between sunrise and sunset, with snowdrifts belly-deep on the horses, than she could have walked by noon in better weather, it was good to see signs of spring.

Sweeping her thick wool cloak back out of her way, Egwene let herself drop down in the high-cantled saddle, and smoothed her skirts in a gesture of impatience. Her dark eyes filled with distaste. She had worn the dress, divided for riding by her own skill with a needle, for far too long, but the only other she had was even more grubby. And the same color, the dark gray of the Leashed Ones. The choice all those weeks ago, on beginning their ride to Tar Valon, had been dark gray or nothing.

"I swear I will never wear gray again, Bela," she told her shaggy mount, patting the mare's neck. *Not that I'll have much choice once we're back in the White Tower,* she thought. In the Tower, all novices wore white.

"Are you talking to yourself again?" Nynaeve asked, pulling her bay gelding closer. The two women were of a height as well as dressed alike, but the difference in their horses put the former Wisdom of Emond's Field a head taller. Nynaeve frowned now, and tugged at the thick braid of dark hair hanging over her shoulder, the way she did when worried or troubled, or sometimes when she was preparing to be particularly stubborn even for her. A Great Serpent ring on her finger marked her as one of the Accepted, not yet Aes Sedai, but a long step closer than Egwene. "Better you should be keeping watch."

Egwene held her tongue on the retort that she had been watching for Tar Valon. *Did she think I was standing in my stirrups because I do not like my saddle?* Nynaeve seemed to forget too often that she was not the Wisdom of Emond's Field any longer, and Egwene was no longer a child. *But she wears the ring and I do not—yet!—and for her, that means nothing has changed!*

"Do you wonder how Moiraine is treating Lan?" she asked sweetly, and had a moment of pleasure at the sharp jerk Nynaeve gave her braid. The pleasure faded quickly, though. Wounding remarks did not come naturally to her, and she knew Nynaeve's emotions concerning the Warder were like skeins of yarn after a kitten had gotten into the knitting basket. But Lan was no kitten, and Nynaeve would have to do something about the man before his stubborn-stupid nobility made her mad enough to kill him.

They were six altogether, all plainly dressed enough not to stand out in the villages and small towns they had encountered, yet perhaps as odd a party as had crossed the Caralain Grass anytime recently, four of them women, and one of the men in a litter slung between two horses. The litter horses carried light packs, as well, with supplies for the long stretches between villages the way they had come.

Six people, Egwene thought, *and how many secrets?* They all shared more than one, secrets that would have to be kept, perhaps, even in the White Tower. *Life was simpler back home.*

"Nynaeve, do you think Rand is all right? And Perrin?" she added hastily. She could not afford to pretend any longer that one day she would marry Rand; pretending would be all it was, now. She did not like that—she was not entirely reconciled to it—but she knew it.

"Your dreams? Have they been troubling you again?" Nynaeve sounded concerned, but Egwene was in no mood to accept sympathy.

She made her voice sound as everyday as she could manage. "From the rumors we heard, I can't tell what might be going on. They have everything I know about so twisted, so wrong."

"Everything has been wrong since Moiraine came into our lives," Nynaeve said brusquely. "Perrin and Rand. . . ." She hesitated, grimacing. Egwene thought Nynaeve believed everything that Rand had become was Moiraine's doing. "They will have to take care of themselves for now.

I'm afraid we have something to worry about ourselves. Something is not right. I can . . . feel it."

"Do you know what?" Egwene asked.

"It feels almost like a storm." Nynaeve's dark eyes studied the morning sky, clear and blue, with only a few scattered white clouds, and she shook her head again. "Like a storm coming." Nynaeve had always been able to foretell the weather. Listening to the wind, it was called, and the Wisdom of every village was expected to do it, though many really could not. Yet since leaving Emond's Field, Nynaeve's ability had grown, or changed. The storms she felt sometimes had to do with men rather than wind, now.

Egwene bit her underlip, thinking. They could not afford to be stopped or slowed, not after coming so far, not so close to Tar Valon. For Mat's sake, and for reasons that her mind might tell her were more important than the life of one village youth, one childhood friend, but that her heart could not rate so high. She looked at the others, wondering if any of them had noticed something.

Verin Sedai, short and plump and all in shades of brown, rode apparently lost in thought, the hood of her cloak pulled forward till it all but hid her face, in the lead but letting her horse amble at its own pace. She was of the Brown Ajah, and the Brown sisters usually cared more for seeking out knowledge than for anything in the world around them. Egwene was not so sure of Verin's detachment, though. Verin had put herself hip-deep in the affairs of the world by being with them.

Elayne, of an age with Egwene and also a novice, but golden-haired and blue-eyed where Egwene was dark, rode back beside the litter where Mat lay unconscious. In the same gray as Egwene and Nynaeve, she was watching him with the worry they all felt. Mat had not roused in three days, now. The lean, long-haired man riding on the other side of the litter seemed to be trying to look everywhere without anyone noticing, and the lines of his face had deepened in concentration.

"Hurin," Egwene said, and Nynaeve nodded. They slowed to let the litter catch up to them. Verin ambled on ahead.

"Do you sense something, Hurin?" Nynaeve asked. Elayne lifted her eyes, suddenly intent, from Mat's litter.

With the three of them looking at him, the lean man

shifted in his saddle and rubbed the side of his long nose. "Trouble," he said, curt and reluctant at the same time. "I think maybe . . . trouble."

A thief-taker for the King of Shienar, he did not wear a Shienaran warrior's topknot, yet the short sword and notched sword-breaker at his belt were worn with use. Years of experience seemed to have given him some talent at sniffing out wrongdoers, especially those who had done violence.

Twice on the journey he had advised them to leave a village after being there less than an hour. The first time, they had all refused, saying they were too tired, but before the night was done the innkeeper and two other men of the village had tried to murder them in their beds. They were only simple thieves, not Darkfriends, just greedy for the horses and whatever they had in their saddlebags and bundles. But the rest of the village knew of it, and apparently considered strangers fair gleanings. They had been forced to flee a mob waving axe handles and pitchforks. The second time, Verin ordered them to ride on as soon as Hurin spoke.

But the thief-taker was always wary when talking to any of his companions. Except Mat, back when Mat could talk; the two of them had joked and played at dice, when the women were not too close at hand. Egwene thought he might be uneasy at being alone, for all practical purposes, with an Aes Sedai and three women in training for sisterhood. Some men found facing a fight easier than facing Aes Sedai.

"What kind of trouble?" Elayne said.

She spoke easily, but with such a clear note of expecting to be answered, immediately and in detail, that Hurin opened his mouth. "I smell—" He cut himself short and blinked as if surprised, eyes darting from one woman to another. "Just a feeling," he said finally. "A . . . a hunch. I've seen some tracks, yesterday, and today. A lot of horses. Twenty or thirty going this way, twenty or thirty that. It makes me wonder. That's all. A feeling. But I say it's trouble."

Tracks? Egwene had not noticed them. Nynaeve said sharply, "I did not see anything worrisome in them." Nynaeve prided herself on being as good a tracker as any man. "They were days old. What makes you think they are trouble?"

"I just think they are," Hurin said slowly, as if he wanted to say more. He dropped his eyes, rubbing at his nose and inhaling deeply. "It's been a long time since we saw a village," he muttered. "Who knows what news from Falme has come before us? We might not find so good a welcome as we expect. I'm thinking these men could be brigands, killers. We should be wary, I'm thinking. If Mat was on his feet, I'd scout ahead, but maybe it's best I don't leave you alone."

Nynaeve's eyebrows lifted. "Do you believe we cannot look after ourselves?"

"The One Power won't do you much good if somebody kills you before you can use it," Hurin said, addressing the tall pommel of his saddle. "Begging your pardon, but I think I. . . . I'll just ride up with Verin Sedai for a time." He dug in his heels and galloped forward before any of them could speak again.

"Now that is a surprise," Elayne said as Hurin slowed a little distance from the Brown sister. Verin did not seem to notice him any more than she noticed anything else, and he appeared content to leave it so. "He has been staying as far from Verin as he could ever since we left Toman Head. He always looks at her as if he's afraid of what she might say."

"Respecting Aes Sedai doesn't mean he is not afraid of them," Nynaeve said, then added, reluctantly, "Of us."

"If he thinks there might be trouble, we ought to send him out scouting." Egwene took a deep breath and gave the other two women as level a look as she could manage. "If there is trouble, we can defend ourselves better than he could with a hundred soldiers to help him."

"He doesn't know that," Nynaeve said flatly, "and I am not about to tell him. Or anyone else."

"I can imagine what Verin would have to say about it." Elayne sounded anxious. "I wish I had some idea how much she does know. Egwene, I don't know if my mother could help me if the Amyrlin found out, much less help the pair of you. Or even whether she would try." Elayne's mother was Queen of Andor. "She was only able to learn a little of the Power before she left the White Tower, for all she has lived as if she had been raised to full sister."

"We cannot hope to rely on Morgase," Nynaeve said. "She is in Caemlyn, and we will be in Tar Valon. No, we may be in enough trouble already for going off as we did, no matter what we've brought back. It will be best if we stay low, behave humbly, and do nothing to attract more attention than we already have."

Another time, Egwene would have laughed at the idea of Nynaeve pretending to be humble. Even Elayne managed a better job of it. But at present she did not feel like laughing. "And if Hurin is right? If we are attacked? He cannot defend us against twenty or thirty men, and we might be dead if we wait for Verin to do something. You said you sense a storm, Nynaeve."

"You do?" Elayne said. Red-gold curls swung as she shook her head. "Verin will not like it if we. . . ." She trailed off. "Whatever Verin likes or doesn't like, we may have to."

"I will do what must be done," Nynaeve said sharply, "if there is anything to be done, and you two will run, if need be. The White Tower may be all abuzz with your potential, but don't think they will not still you both if the Amyrlin Seat or the Hall of the Tower decides it is necessary."

Elayne swallowed hard. "If they would still us for it," she said in a faint voice, "they would still you, too. We should all run together; or act together. Hurin has been right before. If we want to live to be in trouble in the Tower, we may have to . . . to do what we must."

Egwene shivered. Stilled. Cut off from *saidar*, the female half of the True Source. Few Aes Sedai had ever incurred that penalty, yet there were deeds for which the Tower demanded stilling. Novices were required to learn the names of every Aes Sedai who had ever been stilled, and their crimes.

She could always feel the Source there, now, just out of sight, like the sun at noon over her shoulder. If she often caught nothing when she tried to touch *saidar*, she still wanted to touch it. The more she touched it, the more she wanted to, all the time, no matter what Sheriam Sedai, the Mistress of Novices, said about the dangers of growing too fond of the feel of the One Power. To be cut off from it; still able to sense *saidar*, but never to touch it again. . . .

Neither of the others seemed to want to talk, either.

To cover her shaking, she bent from her saddle to the gently swaying litter. Mat's blankets had become disarrayed, exposing a curved dagger in a golden sheath clutched in one hand, a ruby the size of a pigeon's egg capping the hilt. Careful not to touch the dagger, she eased the blankets back over his hand. He was only a few years older than she, but gaunt cheeks and sallow skin had aged him. His chest barely moved as he breathed hoarsely. A lumpy leather sack lay at his feet. She shifted the blanket to cover that, too. *We have to get Mat to the Tower*, she thought. *And the sack.*

Nynaeve leaned down as well, and felt Mat's forehead. "His fever is worse." She sounded worried. "If only I had some worrynot root or feverbane."

"Perhaps if Verin tried Healing again," Elayne said.

Nynaeve shook her head. She smoothed Mat's hair back and sighed, then straightened before speaking. "She says it is all she can do to keep him alive, now, and I believe her. I—I tried Healing last night myself, but nothing happened."

Elayne gasped. "Sheriam Sedai says we mustn't try to Heal until we've been guided step by step a hundred times."

"You could have killed him," Egwene said sharply.

Nynaeve sniffed loudly. "I was Healing before I ever thought of going to Tar Valon, even if I didn't know I was. But it seems I need my medicines to make it work for me. If I only had some feverbane. I do not think he has much time left. Hours, maybe."

Egwene thought she sounded almost as unhappy about knowing, about how she knew, as she did about Mat. She wondered again why Nynaeve had chosen to go to Tar Valon for training at all. She had learned to channel unknowingly, even if she could not always control the act, and had passed the crisis that killed three out of four women who learned without Aes Sedai guidance. Nynaeve said she wanted to learn more, but often she was as reluctant about it as a child being dosed with sheepstongue root.

"We will have him in the White Tower soon," Egwene said. "They can Heal him there. The Amyrlin will take care of him. She will take care of everything." She did not look at where Mat's blanket covered the sack at his feet. The other two women were studiously not looking at it, either. There were some secrets they would all be relieved to shed.

"Riders," Nynaeve said suddenly, but Egwene had already seen them. Two dozen men appearing over a low rise ahead, white cloaks flapping as they galloped, angling toward them.

"Children of the Light," Elayne said, like a curse. "I think we have found your storm, and Hurin's trouble."

Verin had pulled up, a hand on Hurin's arm to stop him drawing his sword. Egwene touched the lead litter horse to stop it just behind the plump Aes Sedai.

"Let me do all the talking, children," the Aes Sedai said placidly, pushing her cowl back to reveal gray in her hair. Egwene was not sure how old Verin was; she thought old enough to be a grandmother, but the gray streaks were the Aes Sedai's only signs of age. "And whatever you do, do not allow them to make you angry."

Verin's face was as calm as her voice, but Egwene thought she saw the Aes Sedai measuring the distance to Tar Valon. The tops of the towers were visible now, and a high bridge arching over the river to the island, tall enough for the trading ships that plied the river to sail beneath.

Close enough to see, Egwene thought, *but too far to do any good.*

For a moment she was sure the oncoming Whitecloaks meant to charge them, but their leader raised a hand and they abruptly drew rein a scant forty paces off, scattering dust and dirt ahead of them.

Nynaeve muttered angrily under her breath, and Elayne sat straight and full of pride, appearing likely to berate the Whitecloaks for ill manners. Hurin still had a grip on his sword hilt; he looked ready to put himself between the women and the Whitecloaks no matter what Verin said. Verin mildly waved a hand in front of her face to dispel the dust. The white-cloaked riders spread out in an arc, blocking the way firmly.

Their breastplates and conical helmets shone from polishing, and even the mail on their arms gleamed brightly. Each man had the flaring, golden sun on his breast. Some fitted arrows to bows, which they did not raise, but held ready. Their leader was a young man, yet he wore two golden knots of rank beneath the sunburst on his cloak.

"Two Tar Valon witches, unless I miss my guess, yes?" he said with a tight smile that pinched his narrow face. Arrogance brightened his eyes, as if he knew some truth others were too stupid to see. "And two nits, and a pair of lapdogs, one sick and one old." Hurin bristled, but Verin's hand restrained him. "Where do you come from?" the Whitecloak demanded.

"We come from the west," Verin said placidly. "Move out of our way, and let us continue. The Children of the Light have no authority here."

"The Children have authority wherever the Light is, witch, and where the Light is not, we bring it. Answer my questions! Or must I take you to our camp and let the Questioners ask?"

Mat could not afford any more delay in reaching help in the White Tower. And more importantly—Egwene winced to think of it that way—more importantly, they could not let the contents of that sack fall into Whitecloak hands.

"I have answered you," Verin said, still calm, "and more politely than you deserve. Do you really believe you can stop us?" Some of the Whitecloaks raised their bows as if she had uttered a threat, but she went on, her voice never rising. "In some lands you may hold sway by your threats, but not here, in sight of Tar Valon. Can you truly believe that in this place, you will be allowed to carry off Aes Sedai?"

The officer shifted uneasily in his saddle, as though suddenly doubting whether he could back up his words. Then he glanced back at his men—either to remind himself of their support or because he had remembered they were watching—and with that he took himself in hand. "I have no fear of your Darkfriend ways, witch. Answer me, or answer the Questioners." He did not sound as forceful as he had.

Verin opened her mouth as if for idle conversation, but before she could speak, Elayne jumped in, voice ringing with command. "I am Elayne, Daughter-Heir of Andor. If you do not move aside at once, you will have Queen Morgase to answer to, Whitecloak!" Verin hissed with vexation.

The Whitecloak looked taken aback for an instant, but then he laughed. "You think it so, yes? Perhaps you will discover Morgase no longer has so much love for witches, girl. If I take you from them and return you to her side, she will thank me for it. Lord Captain Eamon Valda would like very much to speak to you, Daughter-Heir of Andor." He raised a hand, whether to gesture or signal his men, Egwene could not say. Some of the Whitecloaks gathered their reins.

There's no more time to wait, Egwene thought. *I will not be chained again!* She opened herself to the One Power. It was a simple exercise, and after long practice, it went much more swiftly than the first time she had tried. In a heartbeat her mind emptied of everything, everything but a single rosebud, floating in emptiness. She was the rosebud, opening to the light, opening to *saidar,* the female half of the True Source. The Power flooded her, threatening to sweep her away. It was like being filled with light, with the Light, like being one with the Light, a glorious ecstasy. She fought to keep from being overwhelmed, and focused on the ground in front of the Whitecloak officer's horse. A small patch of ground; she did not want to kill anyone. *You will not take me!*

The man's hand was still going up. With a roar the ground in front of him erupted in a narrow fountain of dirt and rocks higher than his head. Screaming, his horse reared, and he rolled out of his saddle like a sack.

Before he hit the ground, Egwene shifted her focus closer to the other Whitecloaks, and the ground threw up another small explosion. Bela danced sideways, but she controlled the mare with reins and knees without even thinking of it. Wrapped inside emptiness, she was still surprised at a third eruption, not of her making, and a fourth. Distantly, she was aware of Nynaeve and Elayne, both enveloped in the glow that said they, too, had embraced *saidar,* had been embraced by it. That aura would not be visible to any but another woman who could channel, but the results were visible to all. Explosions harried the Whitecloaks on every side, showering them with dirt, shaking them with noise, sending their horses plunging wildly.

Hurin stared around him, mouth open and obviously as frightened as the Whitecloaks, as he tried to keep the litter horses and his own mount from bolting. Verin was wide-eyed with astonishment and anger. Her mouth worked furiously, but whatever she might be saying was lost in the thunder.

And then the Whitecloaks were running away, some dropping their bows in panic, galloping as if the Dark One himself were at their backs. All but the young officer, who was picking himself up off the ground. Shoulders hunched, he stared at Verin, the whites of his eyes showing all the way 'round. Dust stained his fine white cloak, and his face, but he did not seem to notice. "Kill me, then, witch," he said shakily. "Go ahead. Kill me, as you killed my father!"

The Aes Sedai ignored him. Her attention was all on her companions. As if they, too, had forgotten their officer, the fleeing Whitecloaks vanished over the same rise where they had first appeared, all in a body and none looking back. The officer's horse ran with them.

Under Verin's furious gaze, Egwene let go of *saidar*, slowly, unwillingly. It was always hard, letting go. Even more slowly, the glow around Nynaeve vanished. Nynaeve was frowning hard at the pinch-faced Whitecloak before them, as if he might still be capable of some sort of trickery. Elayne looked shocked by what she had done.

"What you have done," Verin began, then stopped to take a deep breath. Her stare took in all three of the younger women. "What you have done is an abomination. An abomination! An Aes Sedai does not use the Power as a weapon except against Shadowspawn, or in the last extreme to defend her life. The Three Oaths—"

"They were ready to kill us," Nynaeve broke in heatedly. "Kill us, or carry us off to be tortured. He was giving the order."

"It . . . it was not really using the Power as a weapon, Verin Sedai." Elayne held her chin high, but her voice shook. "We did not hurt anyone, or even try to hurt anyone. Surely—"

"Do not split hairs with me!" Verin snapped. "When you become full Aes Sedai—if you ever become full Aes Sedai!—you will be bound to obey the Three Oaths, but even novices are expected to do their best to live as if already bound."

"What about him?" Nynaeve gestured to the Whitecloak officer, still standing there and looking stunned. Her face was as tight as a drum; she seemed almost as angry as the Aes Sedai. "He was about to take us prisoner. Mat will die if he doesn't reach the Tower soon, and . . . and. . . ."

Egwene knew what Nynaeve was struggling not to say aloud. *And we can't let that sack fall into any hands but the Amyrlin's.*

Verin regarded the Whitecloak wearily. "He was only trying to bully us, child. He knew very well he could not make us go where we did not want, not without more trouble than he was willing to accept. Not here, not in sight of Tar Valon. I could have talked us past him, with a little time and a little patience. Oh, he might well have tried to kill us if he could have done it from hiding, but no Whitecloak with the brains of a goat will try harming an Aes Sedai who knows he is there. See what you have done! What stories will those men tell, and what harm will it do?"

The officer's face had reddened when she mentioned hiding. "It is no cowardice not to charge the powers that Broke the World," he burst out. "You witches want to Break the World again, in the service of the Dark One!" Verin shook her head in tired disbelief.

Egwene wished she could mend some of the damage she had done. "I am very sorry for what I did," she told the officer. She was glad she was not bound to speak no word that was not true, as full Aes Sedai were, because what she had said was only half true at best. "I should not have, and I apologize. I am sure Verin Sedai will Heal your bruises." He stepped back as if she had offered to have him skinned alive, and Verin sniffed loudly. "We have come a long way," Egwene went on, "all the way from Toman Head, and if I weren't so tired, I would never have—"

"Be quiet, girl!" Verin shouted at the same time the Whitecloak snarled, "Toman Head? Falme! You were at Falme!" He stumbled back another step and half drew his sword. From the look on his face, Egwene did not know whether he meant to attack, or to defend himself. Hurin moved his horse closer to the Whitecloak, a hand on his sword-breaker, but the narrow-faced man went on in a rant, spittle flying with his fury. "My father died at Falme! Byar told me! You witches killed him for your false Dragon! I'll see you dead for it! I will see you burn!"

"Impetuous children," Verin sighed. "Almost as bad as boys for letting your mouths run away with you. Go with the Light, my son," she told the Whitecloak.

Without another word, she guided them around the man, but his shouts followed after. "My name is Dain Bornhald! Remember it, Darkfriends! I will make you fear my name! Remember my name!"

As Bornhald's shouts faded behind them, they rode in

silence for a time. Finally, Egwene said to no one in particular, "I was only trying to make things better."

"Better!" Verin muttered. "You must learn there is a time to speak all of the truth, and a time to govern your tongue. The least of the lessons you must learn, but important, if you mean to live long enough to wear the shawl of a full sister. Did it never occur to you that word of Falme might have come ahead of us?"

"Why should it have occurred to her?" Nynaeve asked. "No one we've met before this had heard more than rumors, if that, and we have outrun even rumor in the last month."

"And all word has to come along the same roads we used?" Verin replied. "We have moved slowly. Rumor takes wing along a hundred paths. Always plan for the worst, child; that way, all your surprises will be pleasant ones."

"What did he mean about my mother?" Elayne said suddenly. "He must have been lying. She would never turn against Tar Valon."

"The Queens of Andor have always been friends to Tar Valon, but all things change." Verin's face was calm again, yet there was a tightness in her voice. She turned in her saddle to look over them, the three young women, Hurin, Mat in the litter. "The world is strange, and all things change." They capped the ridge; a village was in sight ahead of them now, yellow tile roofs clustered around the great bridge that led to Tar Valon. "Now you must truly be on your guard," Verin told them. "Now the real danger begins."

CHAPTER

11

Tar Valon

The small village of Darein had lain beside the River Erinin almost as long as Tar Valon had occupied its island. Darein's small, red and brown brick houses and shops, its stone-paved streets, gave a feel of permanence, but the village had been burned in the Trolloc Wars, sacked when Artur Hawkwing's armies besieged Tar Valon, looted more than once during the War of the Hundred Years, and put to the torch again in the Aiel War, not quite twenty years before. An unquiet history for a little village, but Darein's place, at the foot of one of the bridges leading out to Tar Valon, ensured it would always be rebuilt, however many times it was destroyed. So long as Tar Valon stood, at least.

At first it seemed to Egwene that Darein was expecting war again. A square of pikemen marched along the streets, ranks and files bristling like a carding comb, followed by bowmen in flat, rimmed helmets, with filled quivers riding at their hips and bows slanted across their chests. A squadron of armored horsemen, faces hidden behind the steel bars of their helmets, gave way to Verin and her party at a wave of their officer's gauntleted hand. All wore the White Flame of Tar Valon, like a snowy teardrop, on their breasts.

Yet townspeople went about their business with apparent unconcern, the market throng dividing around the soldiers as if marching men were obstructions they were long used to. A few men and women carrying trays of fruit kept pace with the soldiers, trying to interest them in wrinkled apples and pears pulled from winter cellars, but aside from

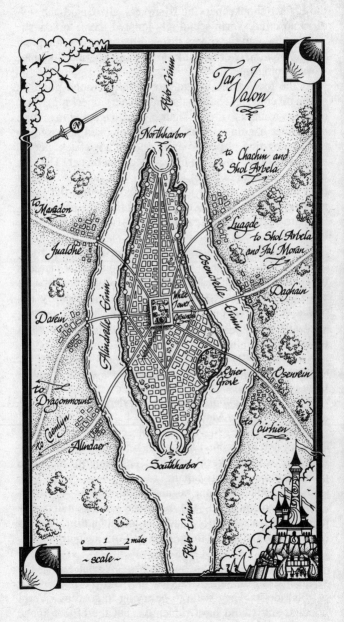

those few, shopkeepers and hawkers alike paid the soldiers no mind. Verin seemingly ignored them, too, as she led Egwene and the others through the village to the great bridge, arching over half a mile or more of water like lace woven from stone.

At the foot of the bridge more soldiers stood guard, a dozen pikemen and half that many archers, checking everyone who wanted to cross. Their officer, a balding man with his helmet hanging on his sword hilt, looked harassed by the waiting line of people afoot and on horseback, people with carts drawn by oxen or horses or the owner. The line was only a hundred paces long, but every time one was let onto the bridge, another joined the far end. Just the same, the balding man seemed to be taking his time about making sure each one had a right to enter Tar Valon before he let them go.

He opened his mouth angrily when Verin led her party to the head of the line, then caught a good look at her face and hurriedly stuffed his helmet onto his head. No one who really knew them needed a Great Serpent ring to identify Aes Sedai. "Good morrow to you, Aes Sedai," he said, bowing with a hand to his heart. "Good morrow. Go right across, if it please you."

Verin reined in beside him. A murmur rose from the waiting line, but no one voiced a complaint aloud. "Trouble from the Whitecloaks, guardsman?"

Why are we stopping? Egwene wondered urgently. "Has she forgotten about Mat?"

"Not really, Aes Sedai," the officer said. "No fighting. They tried to move into Eldone Market, the other side of the river, but we showed them better. The Amyrlin means to make sure they don't try again."

"Verin Sedai," Egwene began carefully, "Mat—"

"In a moment, child," the Aes Sedai said, sounding only halfway absentminded. "I have not forgotten him." Her attention went right back to the officer. "And the outlying villages?"

The man shrugged uncomfortably. "We can't keep the Whitecloaks out, Aes Sedai, but they move off when our patrols ride in. They seem to be trying to goad us." Verin nodded, and would have ridden on, but the officer spoke again. "Pardon, Aes Sedai, but you've obviously come from a distance. Have you any news? Fresh rumors come up-river with every trading vessel. They say there's a new false Dragon out west somewhere. Why, they even say he has Artur Hawkwing's armies, back from the dead, following him, and that he killed a lot of Whitecloaks and destroyed a city—Falme, they call it—in Tarabon, some say."

"They say Aes Sedai helped him!" a man's voice shouted from the waiting line. Hurin breathed deeply, and shifted himself as if he expected violence.

Egwene looked 'round, but there was no sign of who-ever had shouted. Everyone appeared to be concerned only with waiting, patiently or impatiently, for his turn to cross. Things had changed, and not for the better. When she had left Tar Valon, any man who spoke against Aes Sedai would have been lucky to escape with a punch in the nose from whoever overheard. Red in the face, the officer was glaring down the line.

"Rumors are seldom true," Verin told him. "I can tell you that Falme still stands. It isn't even in Tarabon, guardsman. Listen less to rumor, and more to the Amyrlin Seat. The Light shine on you." She lifted her reins, and he bowed as she led the others past him.

The bridge struck Egwene with wonder, as the bridges of Tar Valon always did. The openwork walls looked intricate enough to tax the best craftswoman at her lace-frame. It hardly seemed that such could have been done with stone, or that it could stand even its own weight. The river rolled, strong and steady, fifty paces or more below, and for all that half mile the bridge flowed unsupported from riverbank to island.

Even more wondrous, in its own way, was the feeling that the bridge was taking her home. More wondrous, and shocking. *Emond's Field is my home.* But it was in Tar Valon that she would learn what she must to keep her alive, to keep her free. It was in Tar Valon that she would learn—must learn—why her dreams disturbed her so, and why they sometimes seemed to have meanings she could not puzzle out. Tar Valon was where her life was tied, now. If she ever returned to Emond's Field—the "if" hurt, but she had to be honest—if she returned, it would be to visit, to see her parents. She had already gone beyond being an inn-keeper's daughter. Those bonds would not hold her again, either, not because she hated them, but because she had out-grown them.

The bridge was only the beginning. It arched straight to the walls that surrounded the island, high walls of gleaming white, silver-streaked stone, whose tops looked down on the bridge's height. At intervals, guard towers interrupted the walls, of the same white stone, their massive footings washed by the river. But above the walls and beyond rose the true towers of Tar Valon, the towers of story, pointed spires and flutes and spirals, some connected by airy bridges a good hundred paces or more above the ground. And still only the beginning.

There were no guards on the bronze-clad gates, and they stood wide enough for twenty abreast to ride through, opening onto one of the broad avenues that crisscrossed the island. Spring might barely have come, but the air already smelled of flowers and perfumes and spices.

The city took Egwene's breath as if she had never seen it before. Every square and street crossing had its fountain, or its monument or statue, some atop great columns as high as towers, but it was the city itself that dazzled the eye. What was plain in form might have so many ornaments and carvings that it seemed an ornament itself, or, lacking decoration, used its form alone for grandeur. Great buildings and small, in stone of every color, looking like shells, or waves, or wind-sculpted cliffs, flowing and fanciful, captured from nature or the flights of men's minds. The dwellings, the inns, the very stables—even the most insignificant buildings in Tar Valon had been made for beauty. Ogier stonemasons had built most of the city in the long years after the Breaking of the World, and they maintained it had been their finest work.

Men and women of every nation thronged the streets. They were dark of skin, and pale, and everything in between, their garments in bright colors and patterns, or drab, but decked with fringes and braids and shining buttons, or stark and severe; showing more skin than Egwene thought proper, or revealing nothing but eyes and fingertips. Sedan chairs and litters wove through the crowds, the trotting bearers crying "Give way!" Closed carriages inched along, liveried coachmen shouting "Hiya!" and "Ho!" as if they believed they might achieve more than a walk. Street musicians played flute or harp or pipes, sometimes accompanying a juggler or an acrobat, always with a cap set out for coins. Wandering hawkers cried their wares, and shopkeepers standing in front of their shops shouted the excellence of their goods. A hum filled the city like the song of a thing alive.

Verin had pulled her cowl back up, hiding her face. No one seemed to be paying them any mind in these crowds, Egwene thought. Not even Mat in his horse litter drew a second glance, though some folk did edge away from it as they hurried past. People sometimes brought their sick to the White Tower for Healing, and whatever he had might be catching.

Egwene rode up beside Verin and leaned close. "Do you really expect trouble now? We are in the city. We are almost there." The White Tower stood in plain sight now, the great building gleaming broad and tall above the rooftops.

"I always expect trouble," Verin replied placidly, "and so should you. In the Tower most of all. You must all of you be more careful than ever, now. Your . . . tricks"—her mouth tightened for an instant before serenity returned—"frightened away the Whitecloaks, but inside the Tower they may well bring you death or stilling."

"I would not do that in the Tower," Egwene protested. "None of us would." Nynaeve and Elayne had joined them, leaving Hurin to mind the litter horses. They nodded, Elayne fervently, and Nynaeve, it seemed to Egwene, as if she had reservations.

"You should not do it ever again, child. You must not! Ever!" Verin eyed them sideways 'round the edge of her cowl, and shook her head. "And I truly hope you have learned the folly of speaking when you should be silent." Elayne's face went crimson, and Egwene's cheeks grew hot. "Once we enter the Tower grounds, hold your tongues and accept whatever happens. *Whatever* happens! You know nothing of what awaits us in the Tower, and if you did, you would not know how to handle it. So be silent."

"I will do as you say, Verin Sedai," Egwene said, and Elayne echoed her. Nynaeve sniffed. The Aes Sedai stared at her, and she nodded reluctantly.

The street opened into a vast square, centered in the city, and in the middle of the square stood the White Tower, shining in the sun, rising until it seemed to touch the sky from a palace of domes and delicate spires and other shapes surrounded by the Tower grounds. There were surprisingly few people in the square. No one intruded on the Tower unless he had business there, Egwene reminded herself uneasily.

Hurin led the horse litter forward as they entered the square. "Verin Sedai, I must leave you now." He eyed the Tower once, then managed not to look at it again, though it was hard to look at anything else. Hurin came from a land where Aes Sedai were respected, but it was one thing to respect them and quite another to be surrounded by them.

"You have been a great help on our journey, Hurin," Verin told him, "and a long journey it has been. There will be a place in the Tower for you to rest before you travel on."

Hurin shook his head emphatically. "I cannot waste a day, Verin Sedai. Not another hour. I must return to Shienar, to tell King Easar, and Lord Agelmar, the truth of what happened at Falme. I must tell them about—" He cut off abruptly and looked around. There was no one close enough to overhear, but he still lowered his voice and said only, "About Rand. That the Dragon is Reborn. There must be trading ships heading upriver, and I mean to be on the next to sail."

"Go in the Light, then, Hurin of Shienar," Verin said.

"The Light illumine all of you," he replied, gathering his reins. Yet he hesitated a moment, then added, "If you need me—ever—send word to Fal Dara, and I'll find a way to come." Clearing his throat as if embarrassed, he turned his horse and trotted away, heading beyond the Tower. All too soon he was lost to sight.

Nynaeve gave an exasperated shake of her head. "Men! They always say to send for them if you need them, but when you do need one, you need him right then."

"No man can help where we are going now," Verin said dryly. "Remember. Be silent."

Egwene felt a sense of loss with Hurin's going. He would barely talk to any of them, except Mat, and Verin was right. He was only a man, and helpless as a babe when it came to facing whatever might await them in the Tower. Yet his leaving made their number one less, and she could never help thinking that a man with a sword was useful to have around. And he had been a link to Rand, and Perrin. *I have my own troubles to worry about.* Rand and Perrin would have to make do with Moiraine to look after them. *And Min will certainly look after Rand*, she thought with a flash of jealousy that she tried to suppress. She almost succeeded.

With a sigh, she took up the lead of the horse litter. Mat lay bundled to his chin; his breathing was a dry rasp. *Soon*, she thought. *You'll be Healed soon, now. And we'll find out what's waiting for us.* She wished Verin would stop trying to frighten them. She wished she did not think Verin had reason to frighten them.

Verin took them around the Tower grounds to a small side gate that stood open, with two guards. Pausing, the Aes Sedai pushed back her cowl and leaned from her saddle to speak softly to one of the men. He gave a start, and a surprised look at Egwene and the others. With a quick, "As you command, Aes Sedai," he took off into the grounds at a run. Verin was already riding through the gates as he spoke. She rode as if there were no hurry.

Egwene followed with the litter, exchanging glances with Nynaeve and Elayne, wondering what Verin had told the man.

A gray stone guardhouse stood just inside the gate, shaped like a six-pointed star lying on its side. A small knot of guards lounged in the doorway; they left off talking and bowed as Verin rode past.

This part of the Tower grounds could have been some lord's park, with trees and pruned shrubs and wide graveled paths. Other buildings were visible through the trees, and the Tower itself loomed over everything.

The path led them to a stableyard among the trees, where grooms in leather vests came running to take their horses. At the Aes Sedai's direction, some of the grooms unfastened the litter and set it gently off to one side. As the horses were led away into the stable, Verin took the leather sack from Mat's feet and tucked it carelessly under one arm.

Nynaeve paused in knuckling her back and frowned at the Aes Sedai. "You said he has hours, perhaps. Are you just going to—"

Verin held up a hand, but whether it was the gesture that stopped Nynaeve or the crunch of feet approaching on gravel, Egwene could not say.

In a moment Sheriam Sedai appeared, followed by three of the Accepted, their white dresses ringed at the hem with the colors of all seven Ajahs from Blue to Red, and two husky men in rough, laborer's coats. The Mistress of Novices was a slightly plump woman, with the high cheekbones that were common in Saldaea. Flame-red hair and clear, tilted green eyes made her smooth Aes Sedai features striking. She eyed Egwene and the others calmly, but her mouth was tight.

"So you have brought back our three runaways, Verin. With everything that happened, I could almost wish you had not."

"We did not—" Egwene began, but Verin cut her off with a sharp, "BE SILENT!" Verin stared at her—at each of the three of them—as if the intensity of her look could hold their mouths shut.

Egwene was sure that, for her part, it could. She had never seen Verin angry before. Nynaeve crossed her arms beneath her breasts and muttered under her breath, but she said nothing. The three Accepted behind Sheriam kept their silence, of course, but Egwene thought she could see their ears grow from listening.

When she was certain Egwene and the others would remain still, Verin turned back to Sheriam. "The boy must be taken somewhere away from everyone. He is ill, dangerously so. Dangerous to others as well as to himself."

"I was told you had a litter to be carried." Sheriam motioned the two men to the litter, spoke a quiet word to one, and as quickly as that Mat was whisked away.

Egwene opened her mouth to say he needed help now, but at Verin's stare, quick and furious, she closed it again. Nynaeve was tugging her braid nearly hard enough to pull it out of her head.

"I suppose," Verin said, "that the whole Tower knows we have returned by now?"

"Those who do not know," Sheriam told her, "will know before much longer. Comings and goings have become the first topic of conversation and gossip. Even before Falme, and far ahead of the war in Cairhien. Did you think to keep it secret?"

Verin gathered the leather sack in both arms. "I must see the Amyrlin. Immediately."

"And what of these three?"

Verin considered Egwene and her friends, frowning. "They must be closely held until the Amyrlin wishes to see them. If she does wish to. Closely held, mind. Their own rooms will do, I think. No need for cells. Not a word to anyone."

Verin was still speaking to Sheriam, but Egwene knew the last had been meant as a reminder to her and the others. Nynaeve's brows were drawn down, and she jerked at her braid as if she wanted to hit something. Elayne's blue eyes were open wide, and her face was even paler than usual. Egwene was not sure which feelings she shared, anger or fear or worry. Some of all three, she thought.

With a last, searching glance at her three traveling companions, Verin hurried off, clutching the sack to her chest, cloak flapping behind her. Sheriam put her fists on her hips and studied Egwene and the other two. For a moment Egwene felt a lessening of tension. The Mistress of Novices always kept a steady temper and a sympathetic sense of humor even when she was giving you extra chores for breaking the rules.

But Sheriam's voice was grim when she spoke. "Not a word, Verin Sedai said, and not a word shall it be. If one of you speaks—except to answer an Aes Sedai, of course— I'll make you wish you had nothing but a switching and a few hours scrubbing floors to worry about. Do you understand me?"

"Yes, Aes Sedai," Egwene said, and heard the other two say the same, although Nynaeve pronounced the words like a challenge.

Sheriam made a disgusted sound in her throat, almost a growl. "Fewer girls now come to the Tower to be trained than once did, but they still come. Most leave never having learned to sense the True Source, much less touch it. A few learn enough not to harm themselves before they go. A bare handful can aspire to be raised to the Accepted, and fewer still to wear the shawl. It is a hard life, a hard discipline, yet every novice fights to hold on, to attain the ring and the shawl. Even when they are so afraid they cry themselves to sleep every night, they struggle to hold on. And you three, who have more ability born in you than I ever hoped to see in my lifetime, left the Tower without permission, ran away not even half-trained, like irresponsible children, stayed away for months. And now you ride back in as if nothing has happened, as if you can take up your training again on the morrow." She let out a long breath as if she might explode otherwise. "Faolain!"

The three Accepted jumped as if they had been caught eavesdropping, and one, a dark, curly-haired woman, stepped forward. They were all young women, but still older than Nynaeve. Nynaeve's rapid Acceptance had been extraordinary. In the normal course of things, it took years as a novice to earn the Great Serpent rings they wore, and would take years more before they could hope to be raised to full Aes Sedai.

"Take them to their rooms," Sheriam commanded, "and keep them there. They may have bread, cold broth, and water until the Amyrlin Seat says otherwise. And if one of them speaks even a word, you may take her to the kitchens and set her to scrubbing pots." She whirled and stalked away, even her back expressing anger.

Faolain eyed Egwene and the others with almost a hopeful air, especially Nynaeve, who wore a glower like a mask. Faolain's round face held no love for those who broke the rules so extravagantly, and less for one like Nynaeve, a wilder who had earned her ring without ever being a novice, who had channeled power before she ever entered Tar Valon. When it became obvious that Nynaeve meant to keep her anger to herself, Faolain shrugged. "When the Amyrlin sends for you, you'll probably be stilled."

"Give over, Faolain," another of the Accepted said. The oldest of the three, she had a willowy neck and coppery skin, and a graceful way of moving. "I will take you," she told Nynaeve. "I am called Theodrin, and I, too, am a wilder. I will hold you to Sheriam Sedai's order, but I will not bait you. Come."

Nynaeve gave Egwene and Elayne a worried look, then sighed and let Theodrin lead her away.

"Wilders," Faolain muttered. On her tongue, it sounded like a curse. She turned her stare to Egwene.

The third Accepted, a pretty, apple-cheeked young woman, stationed herself beside Elayne. Her mouth was turned up at the corners as if she liked to smile, but the

stern look she gave Elayne said she would brook no nonsense now.

Egwene returned Faolain's stare with as much calm
as she could manage, and, she hoped, a measure of the
haughty, silent contempt that Elayne had adopted. *Red
Ajah*, she thought. *This one will definitely choose the Reds.*
But it was hard not to think of her own troubles. *Light, what
are they going to do to us?* She meant the Aes Sedai, the
Tower, not these women.

"Well, come along," Faolain snapped. "It's bad enough I
have to stand guard on your door without standing here all
day. Come along."

Taking a deep breath, Egwene gripped Elayne's hand and
followed. *Light, let them be Healing Mat.*

CHAPTER

12

The Amyrlin Seat

S iuan Sanche paced the length of her study, pausing now and again to glance, with a blue-eyed gaze that had made rulers stammer, at a carved nightwood box on a long table centered in the room. She hoped she would not have to use any of the carefully drawn documents within it. They had been prepared and sealed in secret, by her own hand, to cover a dozen possible eventualities. She had laid a warding on the box so that if any hand but hers opened it, the contents would flash to ash in an instant; very likely the box itself would burst into flame.

"And burn the thieving fisher-bird, whoever she might be, so she never forgets it, I hope," she muttered. For the hundredth time since being told that Verin had returned, she readjusted her stole on her shoulders without realizing what she was doing. It hung below her waist, broad and striped with the colors of the seven Ajahs. The Amyrlin Seat was of all Ajahs and of none, no matter from which she had been raised.

The room was ornate, for it had belonged to generations of women who had worn the stole. The tall fireplace and broad, cold hearth were all carved golden marble from Kandor, and the diamond-shaped floor tiles, polished redstone from the Mountains of Mist. The walls were panels of some pale striped wood, hard as iron and carved in fantastic beasts and birds of unbelievable plumage, panels brought from the lands beyond the Aiel Waste by the Sea Folk before Artur Hawkwing was born. Tall, arched windows, open now to let in the new, green smells, let onto a balcony overlooking her small private garden, where she seldom had time to walk.

All that grandeur was in stark contrast to the furnishings Siuan Sanche had brought to the room. The one table and the stout chair behind it were plain, if well polished with age and beeswax, as was the only other chair in the room. That stood off to one side, close enough to be drawn up if she wished a visitor to sit. A small Tairen rug lay in front of the table, woven in simple patterns of blue and brown and gold. A single drawing, tiny fishing boats among reeds, hung above the fireplace. Half a dozen stands held open books about the floor. That was all. Even the lamps would not have been out of place in a farmer's house.

Siuan Sanche had been born poor in Tear, and had worked on her father's fishing boat, one just like the boats in the drawing, in the delta called the Fingers of the Dragon, before ever she dreamed of coming to Tar Valon. Even the nearly ten years since she had been raised to the Seat had not made her comfortable with too much luxury. Her bedchamber was more simple still.

Ten years with the stole, she thought. *Nearly twenty since I decided to sail these dangerous waters. And if I slip now, I'll wish I were back hauling nets.*

She spun at a sound. Another Aes Sedai had slipped into the room, a copper-skinned woman with dark hair cut short. She caught herself in time to keep her voice steady and say only what was expected. "Yes, Leane?"

The Keeper of the Chronicles bowed, just as deeply as she would had others been present. The tall Aes Sedai, as tall as most men, was second only to the Amyrlin in the White Tower, and though Siuan had known her since they were novices together, sometimes Leane's insistence on upholding the dignity of the Amyrlin Seat was enough to make Siuan want to scream.

"Verin is here, Mother, asking leave to speak with you. I have told her you are busy, but she asks—"

"Not too busy to speak to her," Siuan said. Too quickly, she knew, but she did not care. "Send her in. There's no need for you to remain, Leane. I will speak to her alone."

A twitch of her eyebrows was the Keeper's only sign of surprise. The Amyrlin seldom saw anyone, even a queen, without the Keeper present. But the Amyrlin was the Amyrlin. Leane bowed her way out, and in moments Verin took her place, kneeling to kiss the Great Serpent ring on

Siuan's finger. The Brown sister had a good-sized leather sack under her arm.

"Thank you for seeing me, Mother," Verin said as she straightened. "I have urgent news from Falme. And more. I scarcely know where to begin."

"Begin where you will," Siuan said. "These rooms are warded, in case anyone thinks to use childhood tricks of eavesdropping." Verin's eyebrows lifted in surprise, and the Amyrlin added, "Much has changed since you left. Speak."

"Most importantly, then, Rand al'Thor has proclaimed himself the Dragon Reborn."

Siuan felt a tightness loosen in her chest. "I hoped it was he," she said softly. "I have had reports from women who could only tell what they had heard, and rumors by the score come with every trader's boat and merchant's wagon, but I could not be sure." She took a deep breath. "Yet I think I can name the day it happened. Did you know the two false Dragons no longer trouble the world?"

"I had not heard, Mother. That is good news."

"Yes. Mazrim Taim is in the hands of our sisters in Saldaea, and the poor fellow in Haddon Mirk, the Light have pity on his soul, was taken by the Tairens and executed on the spot. No one even seems to know what his name was. Both were taken on the same day and, according to rumor, under the same circumstances. They were in battle, and winning, when suddenly a great light flashed in the sky, and a vision appeared, just for an instant. There are a dozen different versions of what it was, but in both cases the result was exactly the same. The false Dragon's horse reared up and threw him. He was knocked unconscious, and his followers cried out that he was dead, and fled the field, and he was taken. Some of my reports speak of visions in the sky at Falme. I'll wager a gold mark to a week-old delta perch that was the instant Rand al'Thor proclaimed himself."

"The true Dragon has been Reborn," Verin said almost to herself, "and so the Pattern has no room for false Dragons anymore. We have loosed the Dragon Reborn on the world. The Light have mercy on us."

The Amyrlin shook her head irritably. "We have done what must be done." *And if even the newest novice learns of it, I will be stilled before the next sunrise, if I'm not torn to pieces first. Me, and Moiraine, and Verin, and likely any-*

one thought to be a friend of ours, as well. It was not easy to carry on so great a conspiracy when only three women knew of it, when even a close friend would betray them and consider it a duty well done. *Light, but I wish I could be sure they would not be right to do it.* "At least he is safely in Moiraine's hands. She will guide him, and do what must be done. What else have you to tell me, Daughter?"

For answer, Verin placed the leather sack on the table and took out a curled, gold horn, with silver script inlaid around its flaring bell mouth. She laid the horn on the table, then looked to the Amyrlin with quiet expectation.

Siuan did not have to be close enough to read the script to know what it said. *Tia mi aven Moridin isainde vadin.* "The grave is no bar to my call." "The Horn of Valere?" she gasped. "You brought that all the way here, across hundreds of leagues, with the Hunters looking everywhere for it? Light, woman, it was to be left with Rand al'Thor."

"I know, Mother," Verin said calmly, "but the Hunters all expect to find the Horn in some great adventure, not in a sack with four women escorting a sick youth. And it would do Rand no good."

"What do you mean? He is to fight Tarmon Gai'don. The Horn is to summon dead heroes from the grave to fight in the Last Battle. Has Moiraine once again made some new plan without consulting me?"

"This is none of Moiraine's doing, Mother. We plan, but the Wheel weaves the Pattern as it wills. Rand was not first to sound the Horn. Matrim Cauthon did that. And Mat now lies below, dying of his ties to the Shadar Logoth dagger. Unless he can be Healed here."

Siuan shivered. Shadar Logoth, that dead city so tainted that even Trollocs feared to enter, and with reason. By chance, a dagger from that place had come into young Mat's hands, twisting and tainting him with the evil that had killed the city long ago. Killing him. *By chance? Or by the Pattern? He is* ta'veren, *too, after all. But . . .* Mat *sounded the Horn.* Then—

"So long as Mat lives," Verin went on, "the Horn of Valere is no more than a horn to anyone else. If he dies, of course, another can sound it and forge a new link between man and Horn." Her gaze was steady and untroubled by what she seemed to be suggesting.

"Many will die before we are done, Daughter." *And who else could I use to sound it again? I'll not take the risk of trying to return it to Moiraine, now. One of the Gaidin, perhaps. Perhaps.* "The Pattern has yet to make his fate clear."

"Yes, Mother. And the Horn?"

"For the moment," the Amyrlin said finally, "we will find some place to hide this where no one but we two know. I will consider what to do after that."

Verin nodded. "As you say, Mother. Of course, a few hours will make one decision for you."

"Is that all you have for me?" Siuan snapped. "If it is, I have those three runaways to deal with."

"There is the matter of the Seanchan, Mother."

"What of them? All my reports say they have fled back across the ocean, or to wherever they came from."

"It seems so, Mother. But I fear we may have to deal with them again." Verin pulled a small leather notebook from behind her belt and began leafing through it. "They spoke of themselves as the Forerunners, or Those Who Come Before, and talked of the Return, and of reclaiming this land as theirs. I've taken notes on everything I heard of them. Only from those who actually saw them, of course, or had dealings with them."

"Verin, you are worrying about a lionfish out in the Sea of Storms, while here and now the silverpike are chewing our nets to shreds."

The Brown sister continued turning pages. "An apt metaphor, Mother, the lionfish. Once I saw a large shark that a lionfish had chased into the shallows, where it died." She tapped one page with a finger. "Yes. This is the worst. Mother, the Seanchan use the One Power in battle. They use it as a weapon."

Siuan clasped her hands tightly at her waist. The reports the pigeons had brought spoke of that, too. Most had only secondhand knowledge, but a few women wrote of seeing for themselves. The Power used as a weapon. Even dry ink on paper carried an edge of hysteria when they wrote of that. "That is already causing us trouble, Verin, and will cause more as the stories spread, and grow with the spreading. But I can do nothing about that. I am told these people are gone, Daughter. Do you have any evidence otherwise?"

"Well, no, Mother, but—"

"Until you do, let us deal with getting the silverpike out of our nets before they start chewing holes in the boat, too."

With reluctance, Verin closed the notebook and tucked it back behind her belt. "As you say, Mother. If I might ask, what do you intend to do to Nynaeve and the other two girls?"

The Amyrlin hesitated, considering. "Before I am done with them, they will wish they could go down to the river and sell themselves for fishbait." It was the simple truth, but it could be taken in more than one way. "Now. Seat yourself, and tell me everything those three have said and done in the time they were with you. Everything."

CHAPTER
13

Punishments

Lying on her narrow bed, Egwene frowned up at the flickering shadows cast on the ceiling by her single lamp. She wished she could form some plan of action, or reason out what to expect next. Nothing came. The shadows had more pattern than her thoughts. She could hardly even make herself worry about Mat, yet the shame she felt at that was small, crushed by the walls around her.

It was a stark, windowless room, like all those in the novices' quarters, small and square and painted white, with pegs on one wall for hanging her belongings, the bed built against a second, and a tiny shelf on a third, where in other days she had kept a few books borrowed from the Tower library. A washstand and a three-legged stool completed the furnishings. The floorboards were almost white from scrubbing. She had done that task, on hands and knees, every day she had lived there, in addition to her other chores and lessons. Novices lived simply, whether they were innkeepers' daughters or the Daughter-Heir of Andor.

She wore the plain white dress of a novice again—even her belt and pouch were white—but she felt no joy at having rid herself of the hated gray. Her room had become too much of a prison cell. *What if they mean to keep me here. In this room. Like a cell. Like a collar and. . . .*

She glanced at the door—the dark Accepted would still be standing guard on the other side, she knew—and rolled close to the white plastered wall. Just above the mattress was a small hole, almost invisible unless you knew where to look, drilled through into the next room by novices long ago. Egwene kept her voice to a whisper.

"Elayne?" There was no answer. "Elayne? Are you asleep?"

"How could I sleep?" came Elayne's reply, a reedy whisper through the hole. "I thought we might be in some trouble, but I did not expect this. Egwene, what are they going to do to us?"

Egwene had no answer, and her guesses were not of the sort she wanted to voice aloud. She did not even want to think of them. "I actually thought we might be heroes, Elayne. We brought back the Horn of Valere safely. We discovered Liandrin is Black Ajah." Her voice skipped on that. Aes Sedai had always denied the existence of a Black Ajah, an Ajah that served the Dark One, and were known to become angry with anyone who even suggested it was real. *But we know it's real.* "We should be heroes, Elayne."

"'Should and would build no bridges,'" Elayne said. "Light, I used to hate it when Mother said that to me, but it's true. Verin said we mustn't speak of the Horn, or Liandrin, to anyone but her or the Amyrlin Seat. I do not think any of this will work out the way we thought. It is not fair. We've been through so much; you've been through so much. It just is not fair."

"Verin says. Moiraine says. I know why people think Aes Sedai are puppetmasters. I can almost feel the strings on my arms and legs. Whatever they do, it will be what they decide is good for the White Tower, not what is good or fair for us."

"But you still want to be Aes Sedai. Don't you?"

Egwene hesitated, but there was never any real question as to her answer. "Yes," she said. "I still do. It is the only way we will ever be safe. But I will tell you this. I'll not let myself be stilled." That was a new thought, voiced as soon as it came to her, but she realized she did not want to take it back. *Give up touching the True Source?* She could sense it there, even now, the glow just over her shoulder, the shining just out of sight. She resisted the desire to reach out to it. *Give up being filled with the One Power, feeling more alive than I ever have before? I won't!* "Not without a fight."

There was a long silence from the other side of the wall. "How could you stop it? You may be as strong as any of them, now, but neither one of us knows enough yet to stop

even one Aes Sedai from shielding us from the Source, and
there are dozens of them here."

Egwene considered. Finally she said, "I could run away.
Really run away, this time."

"They would come after us, Egwene. I'm sure they
would. Once you show any ability at all, they don't let you
go until you've learned enough not to kill yourself. Or just
die from it."

"I am not a simple village girl anymore. I have seen
something of the world. I can keep out of Aes Sedai hands
if I want to." She was trying to convince herself as much
as Elayne. *And what if I don't know enough, yet? Enough
about the world, enough about the Power? What if just
channeling can still kill me?* She refused to think of that. *So
much I have to learn yet. I won't let them stop me.*

"My mother might protect us," Elayne said, "if what that
Whitecloak said is true. I never thought I would hope something like that was the truth. But if it isn't, Mother is just
as likely to send us both back in chains. Will you teach me
how to live in a village?"

Egwene blinked at the wall. "You will come with me? If
it comes to that, I mean?"

There was another long silence, then a faint whisper. "I
do not want to be stilled, Egwene. I will not be. I will not
be!"

The door swung open, crashing against the wall, and
Egwene sat up with a start. She heard the bang of a door
from the other side of the wall. Faolain stepped into
Egwene's room, smiling as her eyes went to the tiny hole.
Similar holes joined most of the novice rooms; any woman
who had been a novice knew of them.

"Whispering with your friend, eh?" the curly-haired Accepted said with surprising warmth. "Well, it grows lonely,
waiting by yourself. Did you have a nice chat?"

Egwene opened her mouth, then closed it again hastily.
She could answer Aes Sedai, Sheriam had said. No one
else. She regarded the Accepted with a level expression and
waited.

The false sympathy slid off Faolain's face like water running off a roof. "On your feet. The Amyrlin's not to be kept
waiting by the likes of you. You are lucky I did not come in
in time to hear you. Move!"

Novices were supposed to obey the Accepted almost as quickly as they obeyed Aes Sedai, but Egwene got to her feet slowly, and took as much time as she dared in smoothing her dress. She gave Faolain a small curtsy and a tiny smile. The scowl that rolled across the Accepted's face made Egwene's smile grow before she remembered to rein it in; there was no point in pushing Faolain too far. Holding herself straight, pretending her knees were not shaking, she preceded the Accepted out of the room.

Elayne was already waiting outside with the apple-cheeked Accepted, looking fiercely determined to be brave. Somehow, she managed to give the impression that the Accepted was a handmaid carrying her gloves. Egwene hoped that she herself was doing half so well.

The railed galleries of the novices' quarters rose tier on tier above, in a hollow column, and fell as many below, to the Novices' Court. There were no other women in sight. Even if every novice in the Tower had been there, though, less than a quarter of the rooms would have been filled. The four of them walked 'round the empty galleries and down the spiraling ramps in silence; none could bear to have the sounds of voices emphasize the emptiness.

Egwene had never before been into the part of the Tower where the Amyrlin had her rooms. The corridors there were wide enough for a wagon to pass down easily, and taller than they were wide. Colorful tapestries hung on the walls, tapestries in a dozen styles, of floral designs and forest scenes, of heroic deeds and intricate patterns, some so old they looked as if they might break if handled. Their shoes made loud clicks on diamond-shaped floor tiles that repeated the colors of the seven Ajahs.

There were few other women in evidence—an Aes Sedai now and then, sweeping majestically along with no time to notice Accepted or novices; five or six Accepted hurrying self-importantly about their tasks or studies; a sprinkling of serving women with trays, or mops, or armfuls of sheets or towels; a few novices moving on errands even more quickly than the servants.

Nynaeve and her slim-necked escort, Theodrin, joined them. Neither spoke. Nynaeve wore an Accepted's dress, now, white with the seven colored bands at the hem, but her belt and pouch were her own. She gave Egwene and Elayne each a reassuring smile and a hug—Egwene was so relieved to see another friendly face that she returned the hug with barely a thought that Nynaeve was behaving as if she were comforting children—but as they walked on, Nynaeve gave her thick braid a sharp tug from time to time, too.

Very few men came into that part of the Tower, and Egwene saw only two: Warders walking side by side in conversation, one with his sword on his hip, the other with his on his back. One was short and slender, even slight, the other almost as wide as he was tall, yet both moved with a dangerous grace. The color-shifting Warder cloaks made them queasy-making to watch for long, parts of them sometimes seeming to fade into the walls beyond. She saw Nynaeve looking at them, and shook her head. *She has to do something about Lan. If any of us can do anything about anyone after today.*

The antechamber of the Amyrlin Seat's study was grand enough for any palace, though the chairs scattered about for those who might wait were plain, but Egwene had eyes only for Leane Sedai. The Keeper wore her narrow stole of office, blue to show she had been raised from the Blue Ajah, and her face could have been carved from smooth, brownish stone. There was no one else there.

"Did they give any trouble?" The Keeper's clipped way of talking gave no hint now of either anger or sympathy.

"No, Aes Sedai," Theodrin and the apple-cheeked Accepted said together.

"This one had to be pulled by the scruff of her neck, Aes Sedai," Faolain said, indicating Egwene. The Accepted sounded indignant. "She balks as if she has forgotten what the discipline of the White Tower is."

"To lead," Leane said, "is neither to push nor to pull. Go to Marris Sedai, Faolain, and ask her to allow you to contemplate on this while raking the paths in the Spring Garden." She dismissed Faolain and the other two Accepted, and they dropped deep curtsies. From the depth of hers, Faolain shot a furious look at Egwene.

The Keeper paid no attention to the Accepted's leaving. Instead, she studied the remaining women, tapping a forefinger against her lips, till Egwene had the feeling they had all been measured to the inch and weighed to the ounce.

Nynaeve's eyes took on a dangerous sparkle, and she had a tight grip on her braid.

Finally Leane raised a hand toward the doors to the Amyrlin's study. The Great Serpent bit its own tail, a pace across, on the dark wood of each. "Enter," she said.

Nynaeve stepped forward promptly and opened one of the doors. That was enough to get Egwene moving. Elayne held her hand tightly, and she gripped Elayne's just as hard. Leane followed them in and took a place to one side, halfway between the three of them and the table in the center of the room.

The Amyrlin Seat sat behind the table, examining papers. She did not look up. Once Nynaeve opened her mouth, but closed it again, at a sharp look from the Keeper. The three of them stood in a line in front of the Amyrlin's table and waited. Egwene tried not to fidget. Long minutes went by—it seemed like hours—before the Amyrlin raised her head, but when those blue eyes fixed them each in turn, Egwene decided she could have waited longer. The Amyrlin's gaze was like two icicles boring into her heart. The room was cool, but a trickle of sweat began to run down her back.

"So!" the Amyrlin said finally. "Our runaways return."

"We did not run away, Mother." Nynaeve was obviously straining for calm, but her voice shook with emotion. Anger, Egwene knew. That strong will was all too often accompanied by anger. "Liandrin told us we were to go with her, and—" The loud crack of the Amyrlin's hand slapping the table cut her off.

"Do not invoke Liandrin's name here, child!" the Amyrlin snapped. Leane watched them with a stern serenity.

"Mother, Liandrin is Black Ajah," Elayne burst out.

"That is known, child. Suspected, at least, and as good as known. Liandrin left the Tower some months ago, and twelve other—*women*—went with her. None has been seen since. Before they left, they tried to break into the storeroom where the *angreal* and *sa'angreal* are kept, and did manage to enter that where the smaller *ter'angreal* are stored. They stole a number of those, including several we do not know the use of."

Nynaeve stared at the Amyrlin in horror, and Elayne suddenly rubbed her arms as if she were cold. Egwene knew she was shivering, too. Many times she had imagined returning to confront Liandrin and accuse her, to see her condemned to some punishment—except that she had never managed to imagine any punishment strong enough to suit that doll-faced Aes Sedai's crimes. She had even pictured returning to find Liandrin already fled—in terror of her return, it was usually. But she had never imagined anything like this. If Liandrin and the others—she had not really wanted to believe there were others—had stolen those remnants of the Age of Legends, there was no telling what they could do with them. *Thank the Light they did not get any sa'angreal*, she thought. The other was bad enough.

Sa'angreal were like *angreal*, allowing an Aes Sedai to channel more of the Power than she safely could unaided, but far more powerful than *angreal*, and rare. *Ter'angreal* were something different. Existing in greater numbers than either *angreal* or *sa'angreal*, though still not common, they used the One Power rather than helping to channel it, and no one truly understood them. Many would work only for someone who could channel, needing the actual channeling of the Power, while others did what they did for anyone. Where all the *angreal* and *sa'angreal* Egwene had ever heard of were small, *ter'angreal* could seemingly be any size. Each had apparently been made for a specific purpose by those Aes Sedai of three thousand years ago, to do a certain thing, and Aes Sedai since had died trying to learn what; died, or had the ability to channel burned out of them. There were sisters of the Brown Ajah who had made *ter'angreal* their life's study.

Some were in use, if likely not for the purposes they had been made. The stout white rod that the Accepted held while taking the Three Oaths on being raised to Aes Sedai was a *ter'angreal*, binding them to the oaths as surely as if they had been bred in the bone. Another *ter'angreal* was the site of the final test before a novice was raised to the Accepted. There were others, including many no one could make work at all, and many others that seemed to have no practical use.

Why did they take things no one knows how to use? Egwene wondered. *Or maybe the Black Ajah* does *know.* That possibility made her stomach churn. That might be as bad as *sa'angreal* in Darkfriend hands.

"Theft," the Amyrlin went on in tones as cold as her eyes, "was the least of what they did. Three sisters died that night, as well as two Warders, seven guards, and nine of the servants. Murder, done to hide their thieving and their flight. It may not be proof that they were—*Black Ajah*"—the words grated from her mouth—"but I cannot believe otherwise. When there are fish heads and blood in the water, you don't need to see the silverpike to know they are there."

"Then why are we being treated as criminals?" Nynaeve demanded. "We were tricked by a woman of the—of the Black Ajah. That should be enough to clear us of any wrongdoing."

The Amyrlin barked a mirthless laugh. "You think so, do you, child? It may be your salvation that no one in the Tower but Verin, Leane, and I even suspects you had anything to do with Liandrin. If that were known, much less the little demonstration you put on for the Whitecloaks—no need to look so surprised; Verin told me everything—if it were known you had gone off with Liandrin, the Hall might very well vote for stilling the three of you before you could take a breath."

"That is not fair!" Nynaeve said. Leane stirred, but Nynaeve went on. "It is not right! It—!"

The Amyrlin stood up. That was all, but it cut Nynaeve short.

Egwene thought she was wise to keep quiet. She had always believed Nynaeve was as strong, as strong-willed, as anyone could be. Until she met the woman wearing the striped stole. *Please keep your temper, Nynaeve. We might as well be children—babes—facing our mother, and this Mother can do far worse than beat us.*

It seemed to her a way out was being offered in what the Amyrlin had said, but she was not sure what way. "Mother, forgive me for speaking, but what do you intend to do to us?"

"Do to you, child? I intend to punish you and Elayne for leaving the Tower without permission, and Nynaeve for leaving the city without permission. First, you will each be called to Sheriam Sedai's study, where I've told her to switch you till you wish you had a cushion to sit on for the next week. I have already had this announced to the novices and the Accepted."

Egwene blinked in surprise. Elayne gave an audible grunt, stiffened her back, and muttered something under her breath. Nynaeve was the only one who seemed to take it without shock. Punishment, whether extra labors or something else, was always between the Mistress of Novices and whoever was called to her. Those were usually novices, but included the Accepted who stepped far enough beyond the bounds. *Sheriam always keeps it between you and her*, Egwene thought bleakly. *She can't have told everyone. But better than being imprisoned. Better than being stilled.*

"The announcement is part of the punishment, of course," the Amyrlin went on, as if she had read Egwene's mind. "I have also had it announced that you are all three assigned to the kitchens, to work with the scullions, until further notice. And I have let it be whispered about that 'further notice' might just mean the rest of your natural lives. Do I hear objections to any of this?"

"No, Mother," Egwene said quickly. Nynaeve would hate scrubbing pots even more than the other. *It could be worse, Nynaeve. Light, it could be so much worse.* Nynaeve's nostrils had flared, but she gave her head a tight shake.

"And you, Elayne?" the Amyrlin said. "The Daughter-Heir of Andor is used to gentler treatment."

"I want to be Aes Sedai, Mother," Elayne said in a firm voice.

The Amyrlin fingered a paper in front of her on the table and seemed to study it for a moment. When she raised her head, her smile was not at all pleasant. "If any of you had been silly enough to answer otherwise, I had something to add to your tally that would have had you cursing your mother for ever letting your father steal that first kiss. Letting yourselves be winkled out of the Tower like thoughtless children. Even an infant would never have fallen into that trap. I will teach you to think before you act, or else I'll use you to chink cracks in the water gates!"

Egwene found herself offering silent thanks. A prickle ran over her skin as the Amyrlin continued.

"Now, as to what else I intend to do with you. It seems you have all increased your ability to channel remarkably since you left the Tower. You have learned much. Including some things," she added sharply, "that I intend to see you unlearn!"

Nynaeve surprised Egwene by saying, "I know we have done . . . things . . . we should not have, Mother. I assure you, we will do our best to live as if we had taken the Three Oaths."

The Amyrlin grunted. "See that you do," she said dryly. "If I could, I'd put the Oath Rod in your hands tonight, but as that is reserved for being raised to Aes Sedai, I must trust to your good sense—if you have any—to keep you whole. As it is, you, Egwene, and you, Elayne, are to be raised to the Accepted."

Elayne gasped, and Egwene stammered a shocked, "Thank you, Mother." Leane shifted where she stood. Egwene did not think the Keeper looked best pleased. Not surprised—she had obviously known it was coming—but not pleased, either.

"Do not thank me. Your abilities have gone too far for you to remain novices. Some will think you should not have the ring, not after what you've done, but the sight of you up to your elbows in greasy pots should mute the criticism. And lest *you* start thinking it's some sort of reward, remember that the first few weeks as one of the Accepted are used to pick the rotting fish out of the basket of good ones. Your worst day as a novice will seem a fond dream compared to the least of your studies over the next weeks. I suspect that some of the sisters who teach you will make your trials even worse than they strictly must be, but I don't believe you will complain. Will you?"

I can learn, Egwene thought. *Choose my own studies. I can learn about the dreams, learn now to . . .*

The Amyrlin's smile cut off her train of thought. That smile said nothing the sisters could do to them would be worse than it needed to be, if it left them alive. Nynaeve's face was a mixture of deep sympathy and horrified remembrance of her own first weeks as one of the Accepted. The combination was enough to make Egwene swallow hard. "No, Mother," she said faintly. Elayne's reply was a hoarse whisper.

"Then that's done. Your mother was not at all pleased by your disappearance, Elayne."

"She knows?" Elayne squeaked.

Leane sniffed, and the Amyrlin arched an eyebrow, saying, "I could hardly keep it from her. You missed her by less than a month, which may be as well for you. You might not have survived that meeting. She was mad enough to chew through an oar, at you, at me, at the White Tower."

"I can imagine, Mother," Elayne said faintly.

"I don't think you can, child. You may have ended a tradition that began before there *was* an Andor. A custom stronger than most laws. Morgase refused to take Elaida back with her. For the first time ever, the Queen of Andor does not have an Aes Sedai advisor. She demanded your immediate return to Caemlyn as soon as you were found. I convinced her it would be safer for you to train here a little longer. She was ready to remove your two brothers from their training with the Warders, too. They talked their way out of that themselves. I still do not know how."

Elayne seemed to be looking inward, perhaps seeing Morgase in all her anger. She shivered. "Gawyn is my brother," she said absently. "Galad is not."

"Do not be childish," the Amyrlin told her. "Sharing the same father makes Galad your brother, too, whether or not you like him. I will not allow childishness out of you, girl. A measure of stupidity can be tolerated in a novice; it is not allowed in one of the Accepted."

"Yes, Mother," Elayne said glumly.

"The Queen left a letter for you with Sheriam. Aside from giving you the rough side of her tongue, I believe she states her intention of bringing you home as soon as it is safe for you. She is sure that in a few more months at most you will be able to channel without risking killing yourself."

"But I want to learn, Mother." The iron had returned to Elayne's voice. "I want to be Aes Sedai."

The Amyrlin's smile was even grimmer than her last. "As well that you do, child, because I have no intention of letting Morgase have you. You have the potential to be stronger than any Aes Sedai in a thousand years, and I will not let you go until you achieve the shawl as well as the ring. Not if I have to grind you into sausage to do it. *I will not let you go.* Do I make myself clear?"

"Yes, Mother." Elayne sounded uneasy, and Egwene did not blame her. Caught between Morgase and the White Tower like a towel between two dogs, caught between the Queen of Andor and the Amyrlin Seat. If Egwene had ever

envied Elayne her wealth and the throne she would one day
occupy, at that moment she surely did not.

The Amyrlin said briskly, "Leane, take Elayne down to
Sheriam's study. I have a few words yet to say to these other
two. Words I do not think they will enjoy hearing."

Egwene exchanged startled looks with Nynaeve; for a
moment, worry dissolved the tension between them. *What
does she have to say to us and not to Elayne?* she wondered. *I do not care, so long as she does not try to stop me
learning. But why not Elayne, too?*

Elayne grimaced at the mention of the Mistress of
Novices's study, but she drew herself up as Leane came to
her side. "As you command, Mother," she said formally,
lowering herself in a perfect curtsy, skirts sweeping wide,
"so shall I obey." She followed Leane out with her head
held high.

CHAPTER
14

The Bite of the Thorns

The Amyrlin Seat did not speak at once—she walked to the tall, arched windows and looked out across the balcony at the garden below, hands clasped tightly behind her. Minutes went by before she spoke, still with her back to the two of them.

"I have kept the worst of it from getting out, but how long will that last? The servants do not know of the stolen *ter'angreal*, and they do not connect the deaths with Liandrin and the others leaving. It was not easy to manage that, gossip being what it is. They believe the deaths were the work of Darkfriends. And so they were. Rumors are reaching the city, too. That Darkfriends got into the Tower, that they did murder. There was no way to stop that. It does our reputation no good, but at least it is better than the truth. At least none outside the Tower, and few inside, know Aes Sedai were killed. Darkfriends in the White Tower. Faugh! I've spent my life denying that. I will not let them be here. I will hook them, and gut them, and hang them out in the sun to dry."

Nynaeve gave Egwene an uncertain look—half as uncertain as Egwene felt—then took a deep breath. "Mother, are we to be punished more? Beyond what you've already sentenced us to?"

The Amyrlin looked over her shoulder at them; her eyes were lost in shadow. "Punished more? You might well say that. Some will say I've given you a gift, raising you. Now feel the real bite of that rose's thorns." She strode briskly back to her chair and sat down, then seemed to lose her urgency again. Or to gain uncertainty.

To see the Amyrlin look uncertain made Egwene's stomach clench. The Amyrlin Seat was always sure, always serenely centered on her path. The Amyrlin was strength personified. For all her own raw power, the woman on the other side of the table had the knowledge and experience to wind her around a spindle. To see her suddenly wavering— like a girl who knew she had to dive head first into a pond without any idea of how deep it was or whether there were rocks or mud on the bottom—to see that, chilled Egwene right to her core. *What does she mean, the real bite of the thorns? Light, what does she mean to do to us?*

Fingering a carved black box on the table in front of her, the Amyrlin peered at it as if looking at something beyond. "It is a question of who I can trust," she said softly. "I should be able to trust Leane and Sheriam, at least. But do I dare? Verin?" Her shoulders shook with a quick, silent laugh. "I already trust Verin with more than my life, but how far can I take it? Moiraine?" She was silent for a moment. "I have always believed I could trust Moiraine."

Egwene shifted uneasily. How much did the Amyrlin know? It was not the kind of thing she could ask, not of the Amyrlin Seat. *Do you know that a young man from my village, a man I used to think I'd marry one day, is the Dragon Reborn? Do you know two of your Aes Sedai are helping him?* At least she was sure the Amyrlin did not know she had dreamed of him last night, running from Moiraine. She thought she was sure. She kept silent.

"What are you talking about?" Nynaeve demanded. The Amyrlin looked up at her, and she moderated her tone as she added, "Forgive me, Mother, but are we to be punished more? I do not understand this talk of trust. If you want my opinion, Moiraine is not to be trusted."

"That is your opinion, is it?" the Amyrlin said. "A year out of your village, and you think you know enough of the world to choose which Aes Sedai to trust, and which not? A master sailor who's barely learned to hoist a sail!"

"She did not mean anything, Mother," Egwene said, but she knew Nynaeve meant exactly what she had said. She shot a warning glance at Nynaeve. Nynaeve gave her braid a sharp tug, but she kept her mouth shut.

"Well, who is to say," the Amyrlin mused. "Trust is as slippery as a basket of eels, sometimes. The point is, you

162   THE DRAGON REBORN

two are what I have to work with, thin reeds though you
may be."

Nynaeve's mouth tightened, though her voice stayed
level. "Thin reeds, Mother?"

The Amyrlin went on as if she had not spoken. "Liandrin
tried to stuff you headfirst into a weir, and it may well be
she left because she learned you were returning, and could
unmask her, so I have to believe you aren't—Black Ajah. I
would rather eat scales and entrails," she muttered, "but I
suppose I'll have to get used to saying that name."

Egwene gaped in shock—*Black Ajah? Us? Light!*—but
Nynaeve barked, "We certainly are not! How dare you say
such a thing? How dare you even suggest it?"

"If you doubt me, child, go ahead!" the Amyrlin said in
a hard voice. "You may have an Aes Sedai's power sometimes, but you are not yet Aes Sedai, not by miles. Well?
Speak, if you have more to say. I promise to leave you
weeping for forgiveness! 'Thin reed'? I'll break you like a
reed! I've no patience left."

Nynaeve's mouth worked. Finally, though, she gave herself a shake, and drew a calming breath. When she spoke
her voice still had an edge, but a small one. "Forgive me,
Mother. But you should not—We are not—We would not
do such a thing."

With a compressed smile, the Amyrlin leaned back in
her chair. "So you can keep your temper, when you want
to. I had to know that." Egwene wondered how much of it
had been a test; there was a tightness around the Amyrlin's
eyes that suggested her patience might well be exhausted.
"I wish I could have found a way to raise you to the shawl,
Daughter. Verin says you are already as strong as any
woman in the Tower."

"The shawl!" Nynaeve gasped. "Aes Sedai? Me?"

The Amyrlin gestured slightly as if tossing something
away, but she looked regretful to lose it. "No point wishing for what can't be. I could hardly raise you to full sister
and send you to scrub pots at the same time. And Verin
also says you still cannot channel consciously unless you
are furious. I was ready to sever you from the True Source
if you even looked like embracing *saidar*. The final tests for
the shawl require you to channel while maintaining utter

calm under pressure. Extreme pressure. Even I cannot—
and would not—set that requirement aside."

Nynaeve seemed stunned. She was staring at the Amyrlin
with her mouth hanging open.

"I don't understand, Mother," Egwene said after a moment.

"I suppose you don't, at that. You are the only two in the
Tower I can be absolutely sure are not Black Ajah." The
Amyrlin's mouth still twisted around those words. "Liandrin and her twelve went, but did all of them go? Or did
they leave some of their number behind, like a stub in shallow water that you don't see till it puts a hole in your boat?
It may be I'll not find that out until it is too late, but I will
not let Liandrin and the others get away with what they did.
Not the theft, and especially not the murders. No one kills
my people and walks away unscathed. And I'll not let thirteen trained Aes Sedai serve the Shadow. I mean to find
them, and still them!"

"I don't see what that has to do with us," Nynaeve said
slowly. She did not look as if she liked what she was thinking.

"Just this, child. You two are to be my hounds, hunting
the Black Ajah. No one will believe it of you, not a pair of
half-trained Accepted I humiliated publicly."

"That is crazy!" Nynaeve's eyes had opened wide by the
time the Amyrlin reached the words "Black Ajah," and her
knuckles were white from her grip on her braid. She bit her
words off and spat them: "They are all full Aes Sedai. Egwene
hasn't even been raised to Accepted yet, and you know I cannot channel enough to light a candle unless I am angry, not
of my own free will. What chance would we have?"

Egwene nodded agreement. Her tongue had stuck to the
roof of her mouth. *Hunt the Black Ajah? I'd rather hunt a
bear with a switch! She's just trying to scare us, to punish
us more. She has to be!* If that was what the Amyrlin was
trying, she was succeeding all too well.

The Amyrlin was nodding, too. "Every word you say is
true. But each of you is more than a match for Liandrin in
sheer power, and she is the strongest of them. Yet they are
trained, and you are not, and you, Nynaeve, do have limitations, as yet. But when you don't have an oar, child, any
plank will do to paddle the boat ashore."

"But I would be useless," Egwene blurted. Her voice came out as a squeak, but she was too afraid to be ashamed. *She means it! Oh, Light, she means it! Liandrin gave me to the Seanchan, and now she wants me to hunt* thirteen *like her?* "My studies, my lessons, working in the kitchens. Anaiya Sedai will surely want to continue testing me to see if I am a Dreamer. I'll barely have time left over to sleep and eat. How can I hunt anything?"

"You will have to find the time," the Amyrlin said, cool and serene once more, as if hunting the Black Ajah were no more than sweeping a floor. "As one of the Accepted, you choose your own studies, within limits, and the times for them. And the rules are a little easier for Accepted. A little easier. They must be found, child."

Egwene looked to Nynaeve, but what Nynaeve said was, "Why is Elayne not part of this? It can't be because you think she is Black Ajah. Is it because she is Daughter-Heir of Andor?"

"A full net on the first cast, child. I would make her one of you if I could, but at the moment Morgase gives me enough problems as it is. When I have her combed and curried and prodded back on the proper path, perhaps Elayne will join you. Perhaps then."

"Then leave Egwene out, too," Nynaeve said. "She is barely old enough to be a woman. I will do your hunting for you." Egwene made a sound of protest—*I am* a woman!— but the Amyrlin spoke before her.

"I am not setting you out as bait, child. If I had a hundred of you, I would still not be happy, but there are only you two, so two I will have."

"Nynaeve," Egwene said, "I do not understand you. Do you mean you want to do this?"

"It isn't that I want to," Nynaeve said wearily, "but I'd rather hunt them than sit wondering if the Aes Sedai teaching me is really a Darkfriend. And whatever they are up to, I do not want to wait until they're ready to find out what it is."

The decision Egwene came to twisted her stomach. "Then I will do it, too. I don't want to sit wondering and waiting any more than you do." Nynaeve opened her mouth, and Egwene felt a flash of anger; it was such a relief after fear. "And don't you dare say I'm too young again. At least I can channel when I want to. Most of the time. I am not a little girl anymore, Nynaeve."

Nynaeve stood there, jerking on her braid and not saying a word. Finally the stiffness drained out of her. "You are not, are you? I have said myself you are a woman, but I suppose I did not really believe it, inside. Girl, I—No, woman. Woman, I hope you realize you've climbed into a pickling cauldron with me, and the fire may be lit."

"I know it." Egwene was proud that her voice hardly shook at all.

The Amyrlin smiled as if pleased, but there was something in her blue eyes that made Egwene suspect she had known what their decisions would be all along. For an instant, she felt those puppeteer's strings on her arms and legs again.

"Verin. . . ." The Amyrlin hesitated, then muttered half to herself. "If I must trust someone, it might as well be her. She knows as much as I already, and maybe more." Her voice strengthened. "Verin will give you all that is known of Liandrin and the others, and also a list of the *ter'angreal* that were taken, and what they will do. Those that we know. As for any of the Black Ajah still in the Tower. . . . Listen, watch, and be careful of your questions. Be like mice. If you have even a suspicion, report it to me. I will keep an eye on you myself. No one will think that strange, given what you're being punished for. You can make your reports when I look in on you. Remember, they have killed before. They could easily kill again."

"That's all very well," Nynaeve said, "but we will still be Accepted, and it is Aes Sedai we're after. Any full sister can tell us to go about our business, or send us off to do her laundry, and we will have no choice but to obey. There are places Accepted are not supposed to go, things we're not supposed to do. Light, if we were sure a sister was Black Ajah, she could tell the guards to lock us in our rooms and keep us there, and they would do it. They certainly would not take the word of an Accepted over that of an Aes Sedai."

"For the most part," the Amyrlin said, "you must work within the limitations of the Accepted. The idea is for no one to suspect you. But. . . ." She opened the black box on her table, hesitated and looked at the other two women as if still unsure she wanted to do this, then took out a number of stiff, folded papers. Sorting through them carefully, she hesitated again, then chose out two. The remainder she shoved back into the box, and handed those two to Egwene and Nynaeve. "Keep these well hidden. They are for an emergency only."

Egwene unfolded her thick paper. It held writing in a neat, round hand, and was sealed at the bottom with the White Flame of Tar Valon.

What the bearer does is done at my order and by my authority. Obey, and keep silent, at my command.

> Siuan Sanche
> Watcher of the Seals
> Flame of Tar Valon
> The Amyrlin Seat

"I could do anything with this," Nynaeve said in a wondering voice. "Order the guards to march. Command the Warders." She gave a little laugh. "I could make a Warder dance, with this."

"Until I found out about it," the Amyrlin agreed dryly. "Unless you had a very convincing reason, I'd make you wish Liandrin had caught you."

"I didn't mean to do any of that," Nynaeve said hastily. "I just meant that it gives more authority than I had imagined."

"You may need every shred of it. But just you remember, child. A Darkfriend won't heed that any more than a Whitecloak would. They would both likely kill you just for having it. If that paper is a shield . . . well, paper shields are flimsy, and this one may have a target painted on it."

"Yes, Mother," Egwene and Nynaeve said together. Egwene folded her paper up and tucked it into her belt pouch, resolving not to take it out again unless she absolutely had to. *And how will I know when that is?*

"What about Mat?" Nynaeve asked. "He's very sick, Mother, and he does not have much time left."

"I will send word to you," the Amyrlin said curtly.

"But, Mother—"

"I will send word to you! Now, off with you, children. The hope of the Tower rests in your hands. Go to your rooms and get some rest. Remember, you have appointments with Sheriam, and with the pots."

CHAPTER
15

The Gray Man

Outside the Amyrlin Seat's study, Egwene and Nynaeve found the corridors empty except for an occasional serving woman, hurrying about her duties on soft-slippered feet. Egwene was grateful for their presence. The halls suddenly seemed like caverns, for all the tapestries and stonework. Dangerous caverns.

Nynaeve strode along purposefully, tugging at her braid fitfully again, and Egwene hurried to keep up. She did not want to be left alone.

"If the Black Ajah *is* still here, Nynaeve, and if they even suspect what we're doing. . . . I hope you didn't mean what you said about acting as if we are already bound by the Three Oaths. I don't intend to let them kill me, not if I can stop it by channeling."

"If any of them are still here, Egwene, they will know what we are doing as soon as they see us." Despite what she was saying, Nynaeve sounded preoccupied. "Or at least they will see us as a threat, and that's much the same thing as far as what they will do."

"How will they see us as a threat? Nobody is threatened by someone they can order about. Nobody is threatened by someone who has to scrub pots and turn the spits three times a day. That's why the Amyrlin is putting us to work in the kitchens. Part of the reason, anyway."

"Perhaps the Amyrlin did not think it through," Nynaeve said absently. "Or perhaps she did, and means something different for us than what she claims. Think, Egwene. Liandrin would not have tried to put us out of the way unless she thought we were a threat to her. I can't imagine how, or to what, but I cannot see how it could have changed, either. If there are any Black Ajah still here, they will surely see us the same way, whether they suspect what we're doing or not."

Egwene swallowed. "I hadn't thought of that. Light, I wish I were invisible. Nynaeve, if they are still after us, I will risk being stilled before I let Darkfriends kill me, or maybe worse. And I won't believe you will let them take you, either, no matter what you told the Amyrlin."

"I meant it." For a moment Nynaeve seemed to rouse from her thoughts. Her steps slowed. A pale-haired novice carrying a tray rushed past. "I meant every word, Egwene." Nynaeve went on when the novice was out of hearing. "There are other ways to defend ourselves. If there were not, Aes Sedai would be killed every time they left the Tower. We just have to reason those ways out, and use them."

"I know several ways already, and so do you."

"They are dangerous." Egwene opened her mouth to say they were only dangerous to whoever attacked her, but Nynaeve plowed on over her. "You can come to like them too much. When I let out all my anger at those Whitecloaks this morning. . . . It felt too good. It is too dangerous." She shivered and quickened her pace again, and Egwene had to step lively to catch up.

"You sound like Sheriam. You never have before. You have pushed every limit they've put on you. Why would you accept limits now, when we might have to ignore them to stay alive?"

"What good if it ends with us being put out of the Tower? Stilled or not, what good then?" Nynaeve's voice dropped as if she were speaking to herself. "I can do it. I must, if I'm to stay here long enough to learn, and I must learn if I'm to—" Suddenly she seemed to realize she was speaking aloud. She shot a hard look at Egwene, and her voice firmed. "Let me think. Please, be quiet and let me think."

Egwene held her tongue, but inside she bubbled with unasked questions. What special reason did Nynaeve have for wanting to learn more of what the White Tower could teach? What was it she wanted to do? Why was Nynaeve keeping it secret from her? *Secrets. We've learned to keep too many secrets since coming to the Tower. The Amyrlin is keeping secrets from us, too. Light, what is she going to do about Mat?*

Nynaeve accompanied her all the way back to the novices' quarters, not turning aside to the Accepted's quarters. The galleries were still empty, and they met no one as they climbed the spiraling ramps.

As they came up on Elayne's room, Nynaeve stopped, knocked once, and immediately opened the door and put her head inside. Then she was letting the white door swing shut and striding toward the next, Egwene's room. "She isn't here yet," she said. "I need to talk to both of you."

Egwene caught her shoulders and pulled her to an abrupt halt. "What—?" Something tugged at her hair, stung her ear. A black blur streaked in front of her face to clang against the wall, and in the next breath Nynaeve was bearing her to the gallery floor, behind the railing.

Wide-eyed and sprawling, Egwene stared at what lay on the stone in front of her door, where it had fallen. A bolt from a crossbow. A few dark strands from her hair were tangled in the four heavy prongs, meant for punching through armor. She raised a trembling hand to touch her ear, to touch the tiniest nick, damp with a bead of blood. *If I had not stopped just then. . . . If I hadn't. . . .* The quarrel would have gone right through her head, and would probably have killed Nynaeve, too. "Blood and ashes!" she gasped. "Blood and bloody ashes!"

"Watch your language," Nynaeve admonished, but her heart was not in it. She lay peering between the white stone balusters toward the far side of the galleries. A glow surrounded her, to Egwene's eyes. She had embraced *saidar.*

Hastily, Egwene tried to reach out for the One Power, too, but at first haste defeated her. Haste, and images that kept intruding on the emptiness, images of her head being ripped apart like a rotten melon by a heavy quarrel that went on to bury itself in Nynaeve. She took a deep breath and tried again, and finally the rose floated in nothingness, opened to the True Source, and the Power filled her.

She rolled onto her stomach to peer through the railing beside Nynaeve. "Do you see anything? Do you see him? I'll put a lightning bolt through him!" She could feel it building, pressing on her to loose it. "It *is* a man, isn't it?" She could not imagine a man coming into the novices' quarters, but it was impossible to picture a woman carrying a crossbow through the Tower.

"I don't know." Quiet anger filled Nynaeve's voice; her anger was always at its worst when she grew quiet with it. "I thought I saw—Yes! There!" Egwene felt the Power pulse in the other woman, and then Nynaeve was unhurriedly getting to her feet, brushing at her dress as if there were nothing more to worry about.

Egwene stared at her. "What? What did you do? Nynaeve?"

"'Of the Five Powers,'" Nynaeve said in a lecturing tone, faintly mocking, "'Air, sometimes called Wind, is thought by many to be of the least use. This is far from true.'" She finished with a tight laugh. "I told you there were other ways to defend ourselves. I used Air, to hold him with air. If it is a he; I could not see him clearly. A trick the Amyrlin showed me once, though I doubt she expected me to see how it was done. Well, are you going to lie there all day?"

Egwene scrambled up to hurry after her around the gallery. Before long a man did come into sight around the curve, dressed in plain brown breeches and coat. He stood facing the other way, balanced on the ball of one foot, with the other hanging in midair as if he had been caught in the middle of running. The man would feel as if he were buried in thick jelly, yet it was nothing but air stiffened around him. Egwene remembered the Amyrlin's trick, too, but she did not think she could duplicate it. Nynaeve only had to see a thing done once to know how to do it herself. When she could manage to channel at all, of course.

They came closer, and Egwene's melding with the Power vanished in shock. The hilt of a dagger stood out from the man's chest. His face sagged, and death had already filmed his half-closed eyes. He crumpled to the gallery floor as Nynaeve loosed the trap that had held him.

He was an average-appearing man, of average height and average build, with features so ordinary Egwene did not think she would have noticed him in a group of three. She only studied him a moment, though, before realizing that something was missing. A crossbow.

She gave a start and looked about wildly. "There had to be another one, Nynaeve. Somebody took the crossbow. And somebody stabbed him. He could be out there ready to shoot at us again."

"Calm yourself," Nynaeve said, but she peered both ways along the gallery, jerking at her braid. "Just be calm, and we will figure out what to—" Her words cut off at the sound of steps on the ramp leading up to their level.

Egwene's heart pounded, seemingly in her throat. Eyes fastened on the head of the ramp, she desperately strove to touch *saidar* again, but for her that required calm, and her heartbeats shattered calm.

Sheriam Sedai stopped at the top of the ramp, frowning at what she saw. "What in the name of the Light has happened here?" She hurried forward, her serenity gone for once.

"We found him," Nynaeve said as the Mistress of Novices knelt beside the corpse.

Sheriam put a hand to the man's chest, and jerked it back twice as fast, hissing. Steeling herself visibly, she touched him again, and maintained the Touch longer. "Dead," she muttered. "As dead as it is possible to be, and more." When she straightened, she pulled a handkerchief from her sleeve and wiped her fingers. "You found him? Here? Like this?"

Egwene nodded, sure that if she spoke, Sheriam would hear the lie in her voice.

"We did," Nynaeve said firmly.

Sheriam shook her head. "A man—a dead man, at that!—in the novices' quarters would be scandal enough, but this . . . !"

"What makes him different?" Nynaeve asked. "And how could he be *more* than dead?"

Sheriam took a deep breath, and gave them each a searching look. "He is one of the Soulless. A Gray Man." Absently, she wiped her fingers again, her eyes going back to the body. Worried eyes.

"The Soulless?" Egwene said, a tremor in her voice, at the same time that Nynaeve said, "A Gray Man?"

Sheriam glanced at them, a look as penetrating as it was brief. "Not a part of your studies, yet, but you seem to have gone beyond the rules in a great many ways. And considering you found this. . . ." She gestured to the corpse. "The Soulless, the Gray Men, give up their souls to serve the Dark One as assassins. They are not really alive, after that. Not quite dead, but not truly alive. And despite the name, some Gray Men are women. A very few. Even among Darkfriends, only a handful of women are stupid enough to make that sacrifice. You can look right at them and hardly notice them, until it is too late. He was as much as dead while he walked. Now, only my eyes tell me that what is lying there ever lived at all." She gave them another long look. "No Gray Man has dared enter Tar Valon since the Trolloc Wars."

"What will you do?" Egwene asked. Sheriam's brows rose, and she quickly added, "If I may ask, Sheriam Sedai."

The Aes Sedai hesitated. "I suppose you may, since you had the bad luck to find him. It will be up to the Amyrlin Seat, but with everything that has happened, I believe she will want to keep this as quiet as is possible. We do not need more rumors. You will speak of this to none but me, or to the Amyrlin, should she mention it first."

"Yes, Aes Sedai," Egwene said fervently. Nynaeve's voice was cooler.

Sheriam appeared to take their obedience for granted. She gave no sign of having heard them. Her attention was all on the dead man. The Gray Man. The Soulless. "There will be no hiding the fact that a man was killed here." The glow of the One Power suddenly surrounded her, and just as abruptly, a long, low dome covered the body on the floor, grayish and so opaque that it was hard to see there was a body under it. "But this will keep anyone else from touching him who can discover his nature. I must have this removed before the novices come back."

Her tilted green eyes regarded them as if she had just re-membered their presence. "You two go, now. To your room, I think, Nynaeve. Considering what you are already facing, if it became known you were involved in this, even on the edge of it. . . . Go."

Egwene curtsied, and tugged at Nynaeve's sleeve, but Nynaeve said, "Why did you come up here, Sheriam Se-dai?"

For a moment Sheriam looked startled, but on the instant she frowned. Fists on her hips, she regarded Nynaeve with all the firmness of her office. "Does the Mistress of Novices now need an excuse for coming to the novices' quarters, Accepted?" she said softly. "Do Accepted now question Aes Sedai? The Amyrlin means to make something of you two, but whether she does or not, I will teach you manners, at least. Now, the pair of you, go, before I haul you both down to my study, and not for the appointment the Amyrlin Seat has already set for you."

A sudden thought came to Egwene. "Forgive me, Sheriam Sedai," she said quickly, "but I must fetch my cloak. I feel cold." She rushed away, around the gallery before the Aes Sedai could speak.

If Sheriam found that crossbow bolt in front of her door, there would be too many questions. No pretending they had only found the man, that he had no connection to her, then. But when she reached the door to her room, the heavy bolt was gone. Only the jagged chip in the stone beside the door said it had ever been there.

Egwene's skin crawled. *How could anyone take it without one of us seeing. . . . Another Gray Man!* She had embraced *saidar* before she knew it, only the sweet flow of the Power inside her telling her what she had done. Even so, it was one of the hardest things she had ever done, opening that door and going into her room. There was no one there. She snatched the white cloak off its peg and ran out, anyway, and she did not release *saidar* until she was halfway back to the others.

Something more had passed between the women while she was gone. Nynaeve was attempting to appear meek, and succeeding only in looking as if she had a sour stomach. Sheriam had her fists on her hips and was tapping her foot irritably, and the stare she was giving Nynaeve, like green millstones ready to start grinding barley flour, took in Egwene equally.

"Forgive me, Sheriam Sedai," she said hastily, dropping a curtsy and settling her cloak on her shoulders at the same time. "This . . . finding a dead man—a . . . a Gray Man!—it made me cold. If we may go now?"

At Sheriam's tight nod of dismissal, Nynaeve made a bare curtsy. Egwene seized her arm and hustled her away.

"Are you trying to *make* more trouble for us?" she demanded when they were two levels down. And safely out of earshot of Sheriam, she hoped. "What else did you say to her, to make her glare like that? More questions, I suppose? I hope you learned something worth making her mad at us."

"She would not say anything," Nynaeve muttered. "We must ask questions if we are to do any good, Egwene. We will have to take a few chances, or we'll never learn anything."

Egwene sighed. "Well, be a little more circumspect." From the set of Nynaeve's face, the other woman had no intention of going easy or avoiding risks. Egwene sighed again. "The crossbow bolt was gone, Nynaeve. It must have been another Gray Man who took it."

"So that is why you. . . . Light!" Nynaeve frowned and gave a sharp tug to her braid.

After a time Egwene said, "What was that she did to cover the . . . the body?" She did not want to think of it as a Gray Man; that reminded her there was another one out there. She did not want to think of anything at all, right then.

"Air," Nynaeve replied. "She used Air. A neat trick, and I think I see how to make something useful with it."

The use of the One Power was divided into the Five Powers: Earth, Air, Fire, Water, and Spirit. Different Talents required different combinations of the Five Powers. "I don't understand some of the ways the Five Powers are combined. Take Healing. I can see why it requires Spirit, and maybe Air, but why Water?"

Nynaeve rounded on her. "What are you babbling about? Have you forgotten what we're doing?" She looked around. They had reached the Accepted's quarters, a stack of galleries lower than the novices' quarters, surrounding a garden rather than a court. There was no one in sight except for another Accepted, hurrying along on another level, but she lowered her voice. "Have you forgotten the Black Ajah?"

"I am trying to forget it," Egwene said fiercely. "For a little while, anyway. I am trying to forget that we just left a dead man. I'm trying to forget that he almost killed me, and that he has a companion who might try it again." She touched her ear; the drop of blood had dried, but the nick still hurt. "We are lucky we aren't both dead right now."

Nynaeve's face softened, but when she spoke her voice held something of the time when she had been the Wisdom of Emond's Field, saying words that had to be said for someone's own good. "Remember that body, Egwene. Remember that he tried to kill you. Kill us. Remember the Black Ajah. Remember them all the time. Because if you forget, just once, the next time, it may be you lying dead."

"I know," Egwene sighed. "But I do not have to like it."

"Did you notice what Sheriam did not mention?"

"No. What?"

"She never wondered who stabbed him. Now, come on. My room is just down here, and you can put your feet up while we talk."

CHAPTER
16

Hunters Three

Nynaeve's room was considerably larger than the
novice rooms. She had a real bed, not one built
into the wall, two ladder-back armchairs instead
of a stool, and a wardrobe for her clothes. The furnishings
were all plain, suitable for a middling successful farmer's
house, but compared to the novices, the Accepted lived
in luxury. There was even a small rug, woven with scrolls
of yellow and red on blue. The room was not empty when
Egwene and Nynaeve entered.

Elayne stood in front of the fireplace, arms crossed
beneath her breasts and eyes red at least partly from anger. Two tall young men sprawled in the chairs, all arms
and legs. One, with his dark green coat undone to show a
snowy shirt, shared Elayne's blue eyes and red-gold hair,
and his grinning face marked him plainly as her brother.
The other, Nynaeve's age and with his gray coat neatly buttoned, was slender and dark of hair and eye. He rose, all
sure confidence and lithely muscled grace, when Egwene
and Nynaeve came in. He was, Egwene thought not for the
first time, the most handsome man she had ever seen. His
name was Galad.

"It is good to see you again," he said, taking her hand. "I
have worried much over you. We have worried much."

Her pulse quickened, and she took back her hand before he should feel it. "Thank you, Galad," she murmured.
Light, but he's beautiful. She told herself to stop thinking that way. It was not easy. She found herself smoothing her dress, wishing he were seeing her in silk instead of
this plain white wool, perhaps even one of those Domani

dresses Min had told her of, the ones that clung and seemed
so thin you thought they must be transparent even though
they were not. She flushed furiously and banished the image from her mind, willed him to look away from her face.
It did not help that half the women in the Tower, from scul-
lery maids to Aes Sedai themselves, looked at him as if they
had the same thoughts. It did not help that his smile seemed
for her alone. In fact, his smile made it worse. *Light, if he
even suspected what I was thinking, I'd die!*

The golden-haired young man leaned forward in his
chair. "The question is, where have you been? Elayne
dodges my questions as if she has a pocket full of figs and
doesn't want me to have any."

"I have told you, Gawyn," Elayne said in a tight voice, "it
is none of your affair. I came here," she added to Nynaeve,
"because I did not want to be alone. They saw me, and followed. They would not take no for an answer."

"Wouldn't they," Nynaeve said flatly.

"But it is our affair, sister," Galad said. "Your safety is
very much our affair." He looked at Egwene, and she felt
her heart jump. "The safety of all of you is very important
to me. To us."

"I am not your sister," Elayne snapped.

"If you want company," Gawyn told Elayne with a
smile, "we can do as well as any. And after what we went
through just to be here, we deserve some explanation of
where you've been. I would rather let Galad thump me all
over the practice yard all day than face Mother again for a
single minute. I'd rather have Coulin mad at me." Coulin
was Master of Arms, and kept a tight discipline among the
young men who came to train at the White Tower whether
they aspired to become Warders or just to learn from them.

"Deny the connection if you will," Galad told Elayne
gravely, "but it is still there. And Mother put your safety in
our hands."

Gawyn grimaced. "She'll have our hides, Elayne, if anything happens to you. We had to talk fast, or she'd have
hauled us back home with her. I have never heard of a queen
sending her own sons to the headsman, but Mother sounded
ready to make an exception if we don't bring you home
safely."

"I am sure," Elayne said, "that your fast talk was all for

me. None of it was meant to let you stay here studying with the Warders." Gawyn's face reddened.

"Your safety was our first concern." Galad sounded as if he meant it, and Egwene was sure he did. "We managed to convince Mother that if you did return here, you would need someone to look after you."

"Look after me!" Elayne exclaimed, but Galad went on smoothly.

"The White Tower has become a dangerous place. There have been deaths—murders—with no real explanations. Even some Aes Sedai have been killed, though they have tried to keep that quiet. And I have heard rumors of the Black Ajah, spoken in the Tower itself. By Mother's command, when it is safe for you to leave your training, we are to return you to Caemlyn."

For answer, Elayne lifted her chin and half turned away from him.

Gawyn ran a hand through his hair in frustration. "Light, Nynaeve, Galad and I are not villains. All we want to do is help. We would do it anyway, but Mother commanded it, so there's no chance of you talking us out of it."

"Morgase's commands carry no weight in Tar Valon," Nynaeve said in a level voice. "As for your offer of help, I will remember it. Should we need help, you will be among the first to hear of it. For now, I wish you to leave." She gestured pointedly to the door, but he ignored her.

"That is all very well, but Mother will want to know Elayne has come back. And why she ran off without a word, and what she was doing these months. Light, Elayne! The whole Tower was in a turmoil. Mother was half-crazed with fear. I thought she'd tear the Tower down with her bare hands." Elayne's face took on a measure of guilt, and Gawyn pressed his advantage. "You owe her that much, Elayne. You owe me that much. Burn me, you're being as stubborn as stone. You've been gone for months, and all I know about it is that you've run afoul of Sheriam. And the only reasons I know that much are because you've been crying and you won't sit down." Elayne's indignant stare said he had squandered whatever momentary advantage he might have had.

"Enough," Nynaeve said. Galad and Gawyn opened their mouths. She raised her voice. "I said enough!" She glared at them until it was clear their silence would hold, then went on. "Elayne *owes* the two of you nothing. Since she chooses to tell you nothing, that is that. Now, this is my room, not the common room of an inn, and I want you out of it."

"But, Elayne—" Gawyn began at the same time that Galad said, "We only want—"

Nynaeve spoke loudly enough to drown them out. "I doubt you asked permission to enter the Accepted's quarters." They stared at her, looking surprised. "I thought not. You will be out of my room, out of my sight, before I count three, or I will write a note to the Master of Arms about this. Coulin Gaidin has a much stronger arm than Sheriam Sedai, and you may be assured that I will be there to see he makes a proper job of it."

"Nynaeve, you wouldn't—" Gawyn began worriedly, but Galad motioned him to silence and stepped closer to Nynaeve.

Her face kept its stern expression, but she unconsciously smoothed the front of her dress as he smiled down at her. Egwene was not surprised. She did not think she had met a woman outside the Red Ajah who would not be affected by Galad's smile.

"I apologize, Nynaeve, for our forcing ourselves on you unwanted," he said smoothly. "We will go, of course. But remember that we are here if you need us. And whatever caused you to run away, we can help with that, as well."

Nynaeve returned his smile. "One," she said.

Galad blinked, his smile fading. Calmly, he turned to Egwene. Gawyn got up and started for the door. "Egwene," Galad said, "you know that you, especially, can call on me at any time, for anything. I hope you know that."

"Two," Nynaeve said.

Galad gave her an irritated look. "We will talk again," he told Egwene, bowing over her hand. With a last smile, he took an unhurried step toward the door.

"Thrrrrrrrrr"—Gawyn darted through the door, and even Galad's graceful stride quickened markedly—"ree," Nynaeve finished as the door banged shut behind them.

Elayne clapped her hands delightedly. "Oh, well done," she said. "Very well done. I did not even know men were forbidden the Accepted's quarters, too."

"They aren't," Nynaeve said dryly, "but those louts did

not know it, either." Elayne clapped her hands again and laughed. "I'd have let them just leave," Nynaeve added, "if Galad had not made such a show of taking his time about it. That young man has too fair a face for his own good." Egwene almost laughed at that; Galad was no more than a year younger that Nynaeve, if that, and Nynaeve was straightening her dress again.

"Galad!" Elayne sniffed. "He'll bother us again, and I do not know whether your trick will work more than once. He does what he sees as right no matter who it hurts, even himself."

"Then I will think of something else," Nynaeve said. "We can't afford to have them looking over our shoulders all the time. Elayne, if you wish, I can make a salve that will soothe you."

Elayne shook her head, then lay down across the bed with her chin in her hands. "If Sheriam found out, we would no doubt both have yet another visit to her study to look forward to. You have not said very much, Egwene. Cat caught your tongue?" Her expression became grimmer. "Or perhaps Galad has?"

Egwene blushed in spite of herself. "I simply did not choose to argue with them," she said in as dignified a tone as she could manage.

"Of course," Elayne said grudgingly. "I will admit that Galad is good-looking. But he is horrid, too. He *always* does right, as he sees it I know that does not sound horrid, but it is. He has never disobeyed Mother, not in the smallest thing that I know of. He will not tell a lie, even a small one, or break a rule. If he turns you in for breaking one, there isn't the slightest spite in it—he seems sad you could not live up to his standards, if anything—but that doesn't change the fact that he *will* turn you in."

"That sounds—uncomfortable," Egwene said carefully, "but not horrid. I cannot imagine Galad doing anything horrid."

Elayne shook her head, as if in disbelief that Egwene found it so hard to see what was clear to her. "If you want to pay attention to someone, try Gawyn. He is nice enough—most of the time—and he's besotted with you."

"Gawyn! He has never looked at me twice."

"Of course not, you fool, the way you stare at Galad

until your eyes look ready to fall out of your face."
Egwene's cheeks felt hot, but she was afraid it might well
be true. "Galad saved his life when Gawyn was a child,"
Elayne went on. "Gawyn will never admit he is interested
in a woman if Galad is interested in her, but I have heard
him talk about you, and I know. He never could hide things
from me."

"That is nice to know," Egwene said, then laughed at
Elayne's grin. "Perhaps I can get him to say some of those
things to me instead of you."

"You could choose Green Ajah, you know. Green sisters
sometimes marry. Gawyn truly is besotted, and you would
be good for him. Besides, I would like to have you for a
sister."

"If you two are finished with girlish chatter," Nynaeve
cut in, "there are important matters to talk about."

"Yes," Elayne said, "such as what the Amyrlin Seat had
to say to you after I left."

"I would rather not talk about that," Egwene said awkwardly. She did not like lying to Elayne. "She did not say
anything that was pleasant."

Elayne gave a sniff of disbelief. "Most people think I get
off easier than the others because I am Daughter-Heir of
Andor. The truth is that if anything, I catch it harder than
the rest because I'm Daughter-Heir. Neither of you did anything I did not, and if the Amyrlin had harsh words for you,
she would have twice as harsh for me. Now, what did she
say?"

"You must keep this just between us three," Nynaeve
said. "The Black Ajah—"

"Nynaeve!" Egwene exclaimed. "The Amyrlin said
Elayne was to be left out of it!"

"The Black Ajah!" Elayne almost shouted, scrambling
up to kneel in the middle of the bed. "You cannot leave me
out after telling me this much. I won't be left out."

"I never meant for you to be," Nynaeve assured her.
Egwene could only stare at her in amazement. "Egwene, it
was you and I who Liandrin saw as a threat. It was you and
I who were just nearly killed—"

"Nearly killed?" Elayne whispered.

"—perhaps because we are still a threat, and perhaps because they already know that we were closeted alone with

the Amyrlin, and even what she told us. We need someone
with us who they do not know about, and if she isn't known
to the Amyrlin, either, so much the better. I am not sure we
can trust the Amyrlin much further than the Black Ajah.
She means to use us for her own ends. I mean to see she
doesn't use us up. Can you understand that?"

Egwene nodded reluctantly. Just the same, she said, "It
will be dangerous, Elayne, as dangerous as anything we
faced in Falme. Maybe more so. You do not have to be part
of it, this time."

"I know that," Elayne said quietly. She paused, then went
on. "When Andor goes to war, the First Prince of the Sword
commands the army, but the Queen rides with them, too.
Seven hundred years ago, at the Battle of Cuallin Dhen,
the Andormen were being routed when Queen Modrellein
rode, alone and unarmed, carrying the Lion banner into
the midst of the Tairen army. The Andormen rallied and
attacked once more, to save her, and won the battle. That
is the kind of courage expected of the Queen of Andor. If
I have not learned to control my fear yet, I must before I
take my mother's place on the Lion Throne." Suddenly her
somber mood vanished in a giggle. "Besides, do you think I
would pass up an adventure so I could scrub pots?"

"You will do that anyway," Nynaeve told her, "and hope
that everyone thinks that is all you are doing. Now listen
carefully."

Elayne listened, and her mouth slowly dropped open as
Nynaeve unfolded what the Amyrlin Seat had told them,
and the task she had laid on them, and the attempt on their
lives. She shivered over the Gray Man, and read the docu-
ment the Amyrlin had given Nynaeve with a look of wonder, then returned it, murmuring, "I wish I could have that
when I face Mother next." By the time Nynaeve finished,
though, her face was a picture of indignation.

"Why, that's like being told to go up in the hills and find
lions, only you do not know whether there are any lions,
but if there are, they may be hunting you, and they may be
disguised as bushes. Oh, and if you find any lions, try not to
let them eat you before you can tell where they are."

"If you are afraid," Nynaeve said, "you can still stand
aside. It will be too late, once you've begun."

Elayne tossed her head back. "Of course I am afraid. I am

not a fool. But not afraid enough to quit before I have even started."

"There is something else, too," Nynaeve said. "I am afraid the Amyrlin may mean to let Mat die."

"But an Aes Sedai is supposed to Heal anyone who asks." The Daughter-Heir seemed caught between indignation and disbelief. "Why would she let Mat die? I cannot believe it! I will not!"

"Nor can I!" Egwene gasped. *She could not have meant that! The Amyrlin* couldn't *let him die!* "All the way here Verin said that the Amyrlin would see he was Healed."

Nynaeve shook her head. "Verin said the Amyrlin would 'see to him.' That is not the same thing. And the Amyrlin avoided saying yes or no when I asked her. Maybe she has not made her mind up."

"But *why*?" Elayne asked.

"Because the White Tower does what it does for its own reasons." Nynaeve's voice made Egwene shiver. "I do not know why. Whether they help Mat live or let him die depends on what serves their ends. None of the Three Oaths says they have to Heal him. Mat is just a tool, in the Amyrlin's eyes. So are we. She will use us to hunt the Black Ajah, but if you break a tool so it cannot be fixed, you don't weep over it. You just get another one. Both of you had best remember that."

"What are we going to do about him?" Egwene asked. "What can we do?"

Nynaeve went to her wardrobe and rummaged in the back of it. When she came out, she had a striped cloth bag of herbs. "With my medicines—and luck—perhaps I can Heal him myself."

"Verin could not," Elayne said. "Moiraine and Verin together could not, and Moiraine had an *angreal*. Nynaeve, if you draw too much of the One Power, you could burn yourself to a cinder. Or just still yourself, if you are lucky. If you can call that luck."

Nynaeve shrugged. "They keep telling me I have the potential to be the most powerful Aes Sedai in a thousand years. Perhaps it is time to find out whether they are right." She gave a tug to her braid.

It was plain that however brave Nynaeve's words, she was afraid. *But she won't let Mat die even if it means risking death herself.* "They keep saying we're all three so power-ful—or will be. Maybe, if we all try together, we can divide the flow among us."

"We have never tried working together," Nynaeve said slowly. "I am not sure I know how to combine our abilities. Trying could be almost as dangerous as drawing too much of the Power."

"Oh, if we are going to do it," Elayne said, climbing off the bed, "let's do it. The longer we talk of it, the more frightened I will become. Mat is in the guest rooms. I do not know which one, but Sheriam told me that much."

As if to put period to her words, the door banged open, and an Aes Sedai entered as though it were her room, and they the interlopers.

Egwene made her curtsy deep, to hide the dismay on her face.

CHAPTER
17

The Red Sister

Elaida was a handsome woman rather than beautiful, and the sternness on her face added maturity to her ageless Aes Sedai features. She did not look old, yet Egwene could never imagine Elaida as having been young. Except for the most formal occasions, few Aes Sedai wore the vine-embroidered shawl with the white teardrop Flame of Tar Valon large on the wearer's back, but Elaida wore hers, the long red fringe announcing her Ajah. Red slashed her dress of cream-colored silk, too, and red slippers peeked under the edge of her skirts as she moved into the room. Her dark eyes watched them as a bird's eyes watched worms.

"So all of you are together. Somehow, that does not surprise me." Her voice made no more pretense than her bearing did; she was a woman of power, and ready to wield it if she decided it was necessary, a woman who knew more than those she spoke to. It was much the same for a queen as for a novice.

"Forgive me, Elaida Sedai," Nynaeve said, dropping another curtsy, "but I was about to go out. I have much to catch up in my studies. If you will forgive—"

"Your studies can wait," Elaida said. "They have waited long enough already, after all." She plucked the cloth bag out of Nynaeve's hands and undid the strings, but after one glance inside she tossed it on the floor. "Herbs. You are not a village Wisdom any longer, child. Trying to hold on to the past will only hold you back."

"Elaida Sedai," Elayne said, "I—"

"Be silent, novice." Elaida's voice was cold and soft, as silk wrapped around steel is soft. "You may have broken a bond between Tar Valon and Caemlyn that has lasted a thousand years. You will speak when spoken to." Elayne's eyes examined the floor in front of her toes. Spots of color burned in her cheeks. Guilt, or anger? Egwene was not sure.

Ignoring them all, Elaida sat down in one of the chairs, carefully arranging her skirts. She made no gesture for the rest of them to sit. Nynaeve's face tightened, and she began giving sharp little tugs to her braid. Egwene hoped she would keep her temper well enough not to take the other chair without permission.

When Elaida had settled herself to her own satisfaction, she studied them for a time in silence, her face unreadable. At last she said, "Did you know that we have the Black Ajah among us?"

Egwene exchanged startled glances with Nynaeve and Elayne.

"We were told," Nynaeve said cautiously. "Elaida Sedai," she added after a pause.

Elaida arched an eyebrow. "Yes. I thought that you might know of it." Egwene gave a start at her tone, implying so much more than it said, and Nynaeve opened her mouth angrily, but the Aes Sedai's flat stare stilled tongues. "The two of you," Elaida went on in a casual tone, "vanish, taking with you the Daughter-Heir of Andor—the girl who *may* become Queen of Andor one day, if I do not strip off her hide and sell it to a glove maker—vanish without permission, without a word, without a trace."

"I was not carried off," Elayne said to the floor. "I went of my own will."

"Will you obey me, child?" A glow surrounded Elaida. The Aes Sedai's glare was fixed on Elayne. "Must I teach you, here and now?"

Elayne raised her head, and there was no mistaking what was in her face. Anger. For a long moment she met Elaida's stare.

Egwene's fingernails dug into her palms. It was maddening. She, or Elayne, or Nynaeve, could destroy Elaida where she sat. If they caught Elaida by surprise, at least; she was fully trained, after all. *And if we do anything but take whatever she wants to feed us, we throw away everything. Don't throw it away now, Elayne.*

Elayne's head dropped. "Forgive me, Elaida Sedai," she mumbled. "I—forgot myself."

The glow winked out of existence, and Elaida sniffed audibly. "You have learned bad habits, wherever these two took you. You cannot afford bad habits, child. You will be the first Queen of Andor ever to be Aes Sedai. The first queen anywhere to be Aes Sedai in over a thousand years. You will be one of the strongest of us since the Breaking of the World, perhaps strong enough to be the first ruler since the Breaking to openly tell the world she is Aes Sedai. Do not risk all of that, child, because you can still lose it all. I have invested too much time to see that. Do you understand me?"

"I think so, Elaida Sedai," Elayne said. She sounded as if she did not understand at all. No more did Egwene.

Elaida abandoned the subject. "You may be in grave danger. All three of you. You disappear and return, and in the interval, Liandrin and her . . . companions leave us. There will inevitably be comparisons. We are sure Liandrin and those who went with her are Darkfriends. Black Ajah. I would not see the same charge leveled at Elayne, and to protect her, it seems I must protect all of you. Tell me why you ran away, and what you have been doing these months, and I will do what I can for you." Her eyes fastened on Egwene like grappling hooks.

Egwene floundered for an answer that the Aes Sedai would accept. It was said that Elaida could hear a lie, sometimes. "It . . . it was Mat. He is very sick." She tried to choose her words carefully, to say nothing that was not true, yet give an impression far from truth. *Aes Sedai do it all the time.* "We went to. . . . We brought him back to be Healed. If we hadn't, he would die. The Amyrlin is going to Heal him." *I hope.* She made herself continue to meet the Red Aes Sedai's gaze, willed herself not to shift her feet guiltily. From Elaida's face, there was no way to tell whether she believed a word.

"That is enough, Egwene," Nynaeve said. Elaida's penetrating look shifted to her, but she gave no sign of being affected by it. She met the Aes Sedai's eyes without blinking. "Forgive me for interrupting, Elaida Sedai," she said smoothly, "but the Amyrlin Seat said our transgressions were to be put behind us and forgotten. As part of making a new beginning, we are not even to speak of them. The Amyrlin said it should be as if they never happened."

"She said that, did she?" Still nothing in Elaida's voice or on her face told whether she believed or not. "Interesting. You can hardly forget entirely when your punishment has been announced to the entire Tower. Unprecedented, that. Unheard of, for less than stilling. I can see why you are eager to put it all behind you. I understand you are to be raised to the Accepted, Elayne. And Egwene. That is hardly punishment."

Elayne glanced at the Aes Sedai as though for permission to speak. "The Mother said we were ready," she said. A touch of defiance entered her voice. "I have learned, Elaida Sedai, and grown. She would not have named me to be raised if I had not."

"Learned," Elaida said musingly. "And grown. Perhaps you have." There was no hint in her tone whether she thought this was good. Her gaze shifted back to Egwene and Nynaeve, searching. "You returned with this Mat, a youth from your village. There was another young man from your village. Rand al'Thor."

Egwene felt as if an icy hand had suddenly gripped her stomach.

"I hope he is well," Nynaeve said levelly, but her hand was a fist gripping her braid. "We have not seen him in some time."

"An interesting young man." Elaida studied them as she spoke. "I met him only once, but I found him—most interesting. I believe he must be *ta'veren*. Yes. The answers to many questions may rest in him. This Emond's Field of yours must be an unusual place to produce the two of you. And Rand al'Thor."

"It is just a village," Nynaeve said. "Just a village like any other."

"Yes. Of course." Elaida smiled, a cold quirk of her lips that twisted Egwene's stomach. "Tell me about him. The Amyrlin has not commanded you to be silent about him also, has she?"

Nynaeve gave her braid a tug. Elayne studied the carpet as if something important were hidden in it, and Egwene racked her brain for an answer. *She can hear lies, they say. Light, if she can really hear a lie. . . .* The moment stretched on, until finally Nynaeve opened her mouth.

At that instant the door opened again. Sheriam regarded the room with a measure of surprise. "It is well I find you here, Elayne. I want all three of you. I had not expected you, Elaida."

Elaida stood, arranging her shawl. "We are all curious about these girls. Why they ran away. What adventures they had while gone. They say the Mother has commanded them not to speak of it."

"As well not to," Sheriam said. "They are to be punished, and that should be an end to it. I have always felt that when punishment is done, the fault that caused it should be erased."

For a long moment the two Aes Sedai stood looking at each other, no expression on either smooth face. Then Elaida said, "Of course. Perhaps I will speak to them another time. About other matters." The look she gave to the three women in white seemed to Egwene to carry a warning, and then she was slipping past Sheriam.

Holding the door open, the Mistress of Novices watched the other Aes Sedai go down the gallery. Her face was still unreadable.

Egwene let out a long breath, and heard echoes from Nynaeve and Elayne.

"She threatened me," Elayne said incredulously, and half to herself. "She threatened me with stilling, if I don't stop being—*willful*!"

"You mistook her," Sheriam said. "If being willful were a stilling offense, the list of the stilled would have more names on it than you could learn. Few meek women ever achieve the ring and the shawl. That is not to say, of course, that you must not learn to act meekly when it is required."

"Yes, Sheriam Sedai," they all three said almost as one, and Sheriam smiled.

"You see? You can give the appearance of meekness, at least. And you will have plenty of opportunity to practice before you earn your way back into the Amyrlin's good graces. And mine. Mine will be harder to achieve."

"Yes, Sheriam Sedai," Egwene said, but this time only Elayne spoke with her.

Nynaeve said, "What of . . . the body, Sheriam Sedai? The . . . the Soulless? Have you discovered who killed him? Or why he entered the Tower?"

Sheriam's mouth tightened. "You take one step forward, Nynaeve, and then a step back. Since from Elayne's lack of surprise, you have obviously told her of it—*after I told you not to speak of the matter!*—then there are exactly seven people in the Tower who know a man was killed today in the novices' quarters, and two of them are men who know no more than that. Except that they are to keep their mouths shut. If an order from the Mistress of Novices carries no weight with you—and if that is so, I will correct you— perhaps you will obey one from the Amyrlin Seat. You are to speak of this to no one except the Mother or me. The Amyrlin will not have more rumors piled on those we must already contend with. Do I make myself clear?"

The firmness of her voice produced a chorus of "Yes, Sheriam Sedai"—but Nynaeve refused to stop at that. "Seven, you said, Sheriam Sedai. Plus whoever killed him. And maybe they had help getting into the Tower."

"That is no concern of yours." Sheriam's level gaze in- cluded them all. "I will ask whatever questions must be asked about this man. You will forget you know anything at all about a dead man. If I discover you are doing anything else. . . . Well, there are worse things than scrubbing pots to occupy your attention. And I will not accept any excuses. Do I hear any more questions?"

"No, Sheriam Sedai." This time, Nynaeve joined in, to Egwene's relief. Not that she felt very much relief. She- riam's watchful eye would make it doubly hard to carry out a search for the Black Ajah. For a moment she felt like laughing hysterically. *If the Black Ajah doesn't catch us, Sheriam will.* The urge to laugh vanished. *If Sheriam isn't Black Ajah herself.* She wished she could make that thought go away.

Sheriam nodded. "Very well, then. You will come with me."

"To where?" Nynaeve asked, and added, "Sheriam Se- dai," only an instant before the Aes Sedai's eyes narrowed.

"Have you forgotten," Sheriam said in a tight voice, "that in the Tower, Healing is always done in the presence of those who bring their sick to us?"

Egwene thought that the Mistress of Novices's stock of patience with them was about used up, but before she could stop herself, she burst out, "Then she *is* going to Heal him!"

"The Amyrlin Seat herself, among others, will see to him." Sheriam's face held no more expression than her voice. "Did you have reason to doubt it?" Egwene could only shake her head. "Then you waste your friend's life standing here. The Amyrlin Seat is not to be kept waiting." Yet despite her words, Egwene had the feeling the Aes Sedai was in no hurry at all.

CHAPTER 18

Healing

Lamps on iron wall brackets lit the passages deep beneath the Tower, where Sheriam took them. The few doors they passed were shut tight, some locked, some so cunningly worked that they remained unseen until Egwene was right on top of them. Dark openings marked most of the crossing hallways, while down others she could only see the dim glow of distant lights spaced far apart. She saw no other people. These were not places even Aes Sedai often came. The air was neither cool nor warm, but she shivered anyway, and at the same time felt sweat trickling down her back.

It was down here, in the depths of the White Tower, that novices went through their last test before being raised to Accepted. Or put out of the Tower, if they failed. Down here, Accepted took the Three Oaths after passing their final test. No one, she realized, had ever told her what happened to an Accepted who failed. Down here, somewhere, was the room where the Tower's few *angreal* and *sa'angreal* were kept, and the places where the *ter'angreal* were stored. The Black Ajah had struck at those storerooms. And if some of the Black Ajah were lying in wait in one of those dark side corridors, if Sheriam were leading them not to Mat, but to. . . .

She gave a squeak when the Aes Sedai stopped suddenly, then colored when the others looked at her curiously. "I was thinking about the Black Ajah," she said weakly.

"Do not think of it," Sheriam said, and for once she sounded like the Sheriam of old, kindly if firm. "The Black

Ajah will not be your worry for years to come. You have what the rest of us do not: time before you must deal with it. Much time, yet. When we enter, stay against the wall and keep silent. You are allowed here as a benevolence, to attend, not to distract or interfere." She opened a door covered in gray metal worked to look like stone.

The square room within was spacious, its pale stone walls bare. The only furnishing was a long stone table draped with a white cloth, in the middle of the room. Mat lay on that table, fully clothed save for coat and boots, eyes closed and face so gaunt that Egwene wanted to cry. His labored breathing made a hoarse whistle. The Shadar Logoth dagger hung sheathed at his belt, the ruby capping its hilt seeming to gather light, so it glowed like some fierce red eye despite the illumination of a dozen lamps, magnified by the pale walls and white-tiled floor.

The Amyrlin Seat stood at Mat's head, and Leane at his feet. Four Aes Sedai stood down one side of the table, and three down the other. Sheriam joined the three. One of them was Verin. Egwene recognized Serafelle, another Brown sister, and Alanna Mosvani, of the Green Ajah, and Anaiya, of the Blue, which was Moiraine's Ajah.

Alanna and Anaiya had each taught her some of her lessons in opening herself to the True Source, in how to surrender to *saidar* in order to control it. And between her first arrival in the White Tower and her departure, Anaiya must have tested her fifty times to see if she was a Dreamer. The tests had shown nothing one way or the other, but plainfaced, kindly Anaiya, with that warm smile that was her only beauty, had kept calling her back for more tests, as implacable as a boulder rolling downhill.

The rest were unknown to her, except for one cool-eyed woman she thought was a White. The Amyrlin and the Keeper wore their stoles, of course, but none of the others had anything to mark them out except Great Serpent rings and ageless Aes Sedai faces. None of them acknowledged the presence of Egwene and the other two by so much as a glance.

Despite the outward calm of the women around the table, Egwene thought she saw signs of uncertainty. A tightness to Anaiya's mouth. A slight frown on Alanna's darkly beautiful face. The cool-eyed woman kept smoothing her pale blue dress over her thighs without seeming to realize what she was doing.

An Aes Sedai Egwene did not know set a plain, polished wooden box, long and narrow, on the table and opened it. From its nest in the red silk lining, the Amyrlin took out a white, fluted wand the length of her forearm. It could have been bone, or ivory, but was neither. No one alive knew what it was made of.

Egwene had never seen the wand before, but she recognized it from a lecture Anaiya had given the novices. One of the few *sa'angreal*, and perhaps the most powerful, that the Tower possessed. *Sa'angreal* had no power of their own, of course—they were merely devices for focusing and magnifying what an Aes Sedai could channel—but with that wand, a strong Aes Sedai might be able to crumple the walls of Tar Valon.

Egwene clutched Nynaeve's hand on one side and Elayne's on the other. *Light! They're not sure they can Heal him, even with a* sa'angreal—*with that sa'angreal! What chance would we have had? We'd probably have killed him, and ourselves, too. Light!*

"I will meld the flows," the Amyrlin said. "Be careful. The Power needed to break the bond with the dagger and Heal its damage is very close to what could kill him. I will focus. Attend." She held the wand straight out in front of her in both hands, above Mat's face. Still unconscious, he shook his head and tightened a fist on the dagger's hilt, muttering something that sounded like a denial.

A glow appeared around each Aes Sedai, that soft, white light that only a woman who could channel could see. Slowly the lights spread, until that which seemed to emanate from one woman touched that which came from the woman beside her, merged with it, till there was only one light, a light that, to Egwene's eyes, diminished the lamps to nothing. And in that brightness was a stronger light still. A bar of bone-white fire. The *sa'angreal*.

Egwene fought the urge to open herself to *saidar* and add her flow to the tide. It was a pull so strong she was about to be jerked off her feet. Elayne tightened her hold on her hand. Nynaeve took a step toward the table, then stopped with an angry shake of her head. *Light*, Egwene thought, *I could do it*. But she did not know what it was she could do.

Light, it's so strong. It's so—wonderful. Elayne's hand was trembling.

On the table, Mat thrashed in the middle of the glow, jerking this way, then that, muttering incomprehensibly. But he did not loosen his hold on the dagger, and his eyes remained closed. Slowly, ever so slowly, he began to arch his back, muscles straining till he shook. Still he fought and bucked, until finally only his heels and his shoulders touched the table. His hand on the dagger sprang open and, quivering, crept back from the hilt; was forced, fighting, from the hilt. His lips skinned away from his teeth in a snarl, a grimace of pain, and his breath came in forced grunts.

"They are killing him," Egwene whispered. "The Amyrlin is killing him! We have to do something."

Just as softly, Nynaeve said, "If we stop them—if we could stop them—he'll die. I do not think I could handle half that much of the Power." She paused as if she had just heard her own words—that she could channel half of what ten full Aes Sedai did with a *sa'angreal*—and her voice grew even fainter. "Light help me, I want to."

She fell silent abruptly. Did she mean that she wanted to help Mat, or that she wanted to channel that flow of Power? Egwene could feel that urge in herself, like a song that compelled her to dance.

"We must trust them," Nynaeve said in an intense whisper, finally. "He has no other chance."

Suddenly Mat shouted, loud and strong. *"Muad'drin tia dar allende caba'drin rhadiem!"* Arched and struggling, eyes squeezed shut, he bellowed the words clearly. *"Los Valdar Cuebiyari! Los! Carai an Caldazar! Al Caldazar!"*

Egwene frowned. She had learned enough to recognize the Old Tongue, if not to understand more than a few words. *Carai an Caldazar! Al Caldazar!* "For the honor of the Red Eagle! For the Red Eagle!" Ancient battle cries of Manetheren, a nation that had vanished during the Trolloc Wars. A nation that had stood where the Two Rivers was now. That much, she knew; but in some way it seemed for a moment that she should understand the rest, too, as if the meaning were just out of sight, and all she had to do was turn her head to know.

With a loud pop of tearing leather, the golden-sheathed dagger rose from Mat's belt, hung a foot above his straining body. The ruby glittered, seemed to send off crimson sparks, as if it, too, fought the Healing.

Mat's eyes opened, and he glared at the women standing around him. *"Mia ayende, Aes Sedai! Caballein misain ye! Inde muagdhe Aes Sedai misain ye! Mia ayende!"* And he began to scream, a roar of rage that went on and on, till Egwene wondered that he had breath left in him.

Hurriedly Anaiya bent to lift a dark metal box from under the table, moving as if it were heavy. When she set it beside Mat and opened the lid, only a small space was revealed within sides at least two inches thick. Anaiya bent again for a set of tongs such as a goodwife might use in her kitchen, and grasped the floating dagger in them as carefully as if it were a poisonous snake.

Mat's scream grew frantic. The ruby shone furiously, flashing blood-red.

The Aes Sedai thrust the dagger into the box and snapped the lid down, letting out a loud sigh as it clicked shut. "A filthy thing," she said.

As soon as the dagger was hidden, Mat's shriek cut off, and he collapsed as if muscle and bone had turned to water. An instant later the glow surrounding Aes Sedai and table winked out.

"Done," the Amyrlin said hoarsely, as if she had been the one screaming. "It is done."

Some of the Aes Sedai sagged visibly, and sweat beaded on more than one brow. Anaiya pulled a plain linen handkerchief from her sleeve and wiped her face openly. The cool-eyed White dabbed almost surreptitiously at her cheeks with a bit of Lugard lace.

"Fascinating," Verin said. "That the Old Blood could flow so strongly in anyone today." She and Serafelle put their heads together, talking softly, but with many gestures.

"Is he Healed?" Nynaeve said. "Will he . . . live?"

Mat lay as if sleeping, but his face still had that hollow-cheeked gauntness. Egwene had never heard of a Healing that did not cure *everything. Unless just separating him from the dagger took* all *of the Power they used. Light!*

"Brendas," the Amyrlin said, "will you see that he is taken back to his room?"

"As you command, Mother," the cool-eyed woman said, her curtsy as emotionless as she herself seemed. When she left to summon bearers, several of the other Aes Sedai left, too, including Anaiya. Verin and Serafelle followed, still talking to one another too quietly for Egwene to make out what they said.

"Is Mat all right?" Nynaeve demanded. Sheriam raised her eyebrows.

The Amyrlin Seat turned toward them. "He is as well as he can be," she said coldly. "Only time will tell. Carrying something with Shadar Logoth's taint for so long . . . who knows what effect it will have on him? Perhaps none, perhaps much. We will see. But the bond with the dagger is broken. Now he needs rest, and as much food as can be gotten into him. He should live."

"What was that he was shouting, Mother?" Elayne asked, then hastily added, "If I may ask."

"He was ordering soldiers." The Amyrlin gave the young man lying on the table a quizzical look. He had not moved since collapsing, but Egwene thought his breathing seemed easier, the rise and fall of his chest more rhythmic. "In a battle two thousand years gone, I would say. The Old Blood comes again."

"It was not all about a battle," Nynaeve said. "I heard him say Aes Sedai. That was no battle. Mother," she added belatedly.

For a moment the Amyrlin seemed to consider, perhaps what to say, perhaps whether to say anything. "For a time," she said finally, "I believe the past and the present were one. He was there, and he was here, and he knew who we were. He commanded us to release him." She paused again. "'I am a free man, Aes Sedai. I am no Aes Sedai meat.' That is what he said."

Leane sniffed loudly, and some of the other Aes Sedai muttered angrily under their breath.

"But, Mother," Egwene said, "he could not have meant it as it sounds. Manetheren was allied with Tar Valon."

"Manetheren was an ally, child," the Amyrlin told her, "but who can know the heart of a man? Not even he himself, I suspect. A man is the easiest animal to put on a leash, and the hardest to keep leashed. Even when he chooses it himself."

"Mother," Sheriam said, "it is late. The cooks will be waiting for these helpers."

"Mother," Egwene asked anxiously, "could we not stay with Mat? If he may still die. . . ."

The Amyrlin's look was level, her face without expression. "You have chores to do, child."

It was not scrubbing pots she meant. Egwene was sure of that. "Yes, Mother." She curtsied, her skirts brushing Nynaeve's and Elayne's as they made theirs. One last time she looked at Mat, then followed Sheriam out. Mat had still not moved.

CHAPTER
19

Awakening

Mat opened his eyes slowly and stared up at the white plaster ceiling, wondering where he was and how he had come there. An intricate fringe of gilded leaves bordered the ceiling, and the mattress under his back felt plumped full of feathers. Somewhere rich, then. Somewhere with money. But his head was empty of the where and the how, and a lot more besides.

He had been dreaming, and bits of those dreams still tumbled together with memories in his head. He could not separate one from the other. Wild flights and fights, strange people from across the ocean, Ways and Portal Stones and pieces of other lives, things right out of a gleeman's tales, these had to be dreams. At least, he thought they must be. But Loial was no dream, and he was an Ogier. Chunks of conversations drifted around in his thoughts, talks with his father, with friends, with Moiraine, and a beautiful woman, and a ship captain, and a well-dressed man who spoke to him like a father giving sage advice. Those were probably real. But it was all bits and fragments. Drifting.

"Muad'drin tia dar allende caba'drin rhadiem," he murmured. The words were only sounds, yet they sparked— something.

The packed lines of spearmen stretched a mile or more to either side below him, dotted with the pennants and banners of towns and cities and minor Houses. The river secured his flank on the left, the bogs and mires on the right. From the hillside he watched the spearmen struggle against the mass of Trollocs trying to break through, ten times the humans' number. Spears pierced black Trolloc mail, and spiked axes

carved bloody gaps in the human ranks. Screams and bel-
lows harried the air. The sun burned hot overhead in a
cloudless sky, and shimmers of heat rose above the battle
line. Arrows still rained down from the enemy, slaying Trol-
loc and human alike. He had called his archers back, but
the Dreadlords did not care so long as they broke his line.
On the ridge behind him, the Heart Guard awaited his com-
mand, horses stamping impatiently. Armor on men and
horses alike shone silver in the sunlight; neither men nor
animals could stand the heat much longer.

They must win here or die. He was known as a gambler;
it was time to toss the dice. In a voice that carried over the
tumult below, he gave the order as he swung up into his
saddle. "Footmen prepare to pass cavalry forward!" His
bannerman rode close beside him, the Red Eagle banner
flapping over his head, as the command was repeated up
and down the line.

Below, the spearmen suddenly moved, sidestepping with
good discipline, narrowing their formations, opening wide
gaps between. Gaps into which the Trollocs poured, roar-
ing bestial cries, like a black, oozing tide of death.

He drew his sword, raised it high. "Forward the Heart
Guard!" He dug his heels in, and his mount leaped down the
slope. Behind him, hooves thundered in the charge. "For-
ward!" He was first to strike into the Trollocs, his sword
rising and falling, his bannerman close behind. "For the
honor of the Red Eagle!" The Heart Guard pounded into
the gaps between the spearmen, smashing the tide, hurl-
ing it back. "The Red Eagle!" Half-human faces snarled at
him, oddly curved swords sought him, but he cut his way
ever deeper. Win or die. "Manetheren!"

Mat's hand trembled as he raised it to his forehead. *"Los*
Valdar Cuebiyari," he muttered. He was almost sure he knew
what it meant—"Forward the Heart Guard," or maybe "The
Heart Guard will advance"—but that could not be. Moiraine
had told him a few words of the Old Tongue, and those were
all he knew of it. The rest might as well be magpie chatter.

"Crazy," he said roughly. "It probably isn't even the Old
Tongue at all. Just gibberish. That Aes Sedai is crazy. It was
only a dream."

Aes Sedai. Moiraine. He suddenly became aware of his
too-thin wrist and bony hand, and looked at them. He had

been sick. Something to do with a dagger. A dagger with
a ruby in the hilt, and a long-dead, tainted city called Shadar Logoth. It was all foggy and distant, and made no real
sense, but he knew it was no dream. Egwene and Nynaeve
had been taking him to Tar Valon to be Healed. He remembered that much.

He tried to sit up, and fell back, as weak as a newborn
lamb. Laboriously, he pulled himself up and shoved the
single woolen blanket aside. His clothes were gone, perhaps
into the vine-carved wardrobe standing against the wall.
For the moment he did not care about clothes. He struggled
to his feet, tottered across the flowered carpet to cling to
a high-backed armchair, and lurched from the chair to the
table, gilded scrolls on its legs and edges.

Beeswax candles, four to each tall stand and small mirrors behind the flames, lit the room brightly. A larger mirror on the wall above the highly polished washstand threw
his reflection back at him, gaunt and wasted, cheeks hollow
and dark eyes sunken, hair sweat-matted, bent like an old
man and wavering like pasture grass in a breeze. He made
himself stand straight, but it was not much improvement.

A large, covered tray sat on the table in front of his hands,
and his nose caught the smells of food. He twitched aside
the cloth, revealing two large silver pitchers and dishes of
thin green porcelain. He had heard that the Sea Folk charged
its weight in silver for that porcelain. He had expected beef
tea, or sweetbreads, the kinds of things invalids had pushed
on them. Instead, one plate held slices of a beef roast piled
thickly, with brown mustard and horseradish. On others there
were roasted potatoes, sweetbeans with onions, cabbage, and
butterpeas. Pickles, and a wedge of yellow cheese. Thick
slices of crusty bread, and a dish of butter. One pitcher was
filled with milk and still beaded with condensation on the
outside, the other with what smelled like spiced wine. There
was enough of everything for four men. His mouth watered,
and his stomach growled at him.

First I find out where I am. But he rolled up a slice of
beef and dipped it in the mustard before pushing himself
away from the table toward the three tall, narrow windows.

Wooden shutters carved in lacy patterns covered them,
but through the holes he could see that it was night outside.
Lights from other windows made dots in the blackness. For

a moment he sagged against the white stone windowsill in frustration, but then he began to think.

You can turn the worst that comes to your advantage if you only think, his father always said, and certainly Abell Cauthon was the best horse trader in the Two Rivers. When it seemed somebody had taken advantage of Mat's father, it always turned out they had gotten the greasy end of the stick. Not that Abell Cauthon ever did anything dishonest, but even Taren Ferry folk never got the best of him, and everybody knew how close to the bone they cut. All because he thought about things from every side that there was.

Tar Valon. It had to be Tar Valon. This room belonged in a palace. The flowered Domani carpet alone probably cost as much as a farm. More, he did not think he was sick any longer, and from what he had been told, Tar Valon was his only chance to get well. He had never actually felt sick, not that he remembered, not even when Verin—another name swam out of the haze—had told someone nearby that he was dying. Now he felt weak as a babe and hungry as a starving wolf, but somehow, he was sure the Healing had been done. *I feel—whole and well, that's all. I've been Healed.* He grimaced at the shutters.

Healed. That meant they had used the One Power on him. The notion sent goose bumps marching across his skin, but he had known it would be done. "Better than dying," he told himself. Some of the stories he had heard about Aes Sedai came back. "It has to be better than dying. Even Nynaeve thought I was going to die. Anyway, it's done, and worrying about it now won't help anything." He realized he had finished the slice of beef and was licking its juice from his fingers.

Unsteadily, he made his way back to the table. There was a stool underneath. He pulled it out and sat down. Not bothering with knife or fork, he made another roll of beef. How could he turn being in Tar Valon—*In the White Tower. It has to be*—to his advantage?

Tar Valon meant Aes Sedai. That was certainly no reason to stay even an hour. Exactly the opposite. What he remembered of his time with Moiraine, and later with Verin, was not much to go on. He could not recall either of them doing anything really terrible, but then he could not recall a great deal of that time at all. Anyway, whatever Aes Sedai did, they did for their own reasons.

"And those aren't always the reasons you think they are," he mumbled around a mouthful of potato, then swallowed. "An Aes Sedai never lies, but the truth an Aes Sedai tells you isn't always the truth you think it is. That's one thing I have to remember: I can't be sure about them even when I think I know." It was not a cheering conclusion. He filled his mouth with butterpeas.

Thinking about Aes Sedai made him remember a little about them. The seven Ajahs: Blue, Red, Brown, Green, Yellow, White, and Gray. The Reds were the worst. *Except for that Black Ajah they all claim doesn't exist.* But the Red Ajah should be no threat to him. They were only interested in men who could channel.

Rand. Burn me, how could I forget that? Where is he? Is he all right? He sighed regretfully, and spread butter on a piece of still-warm bread. *I wonder if he's gone mad yet.*

Even if he knew the answers, he could do nothing to help Rand. He was not sure he would if he could. Rand could channel, and Mat had grown up with stories of men channeling, stories to frighten children. Stories that frightened adults, too, because some of them were all too true. Discovering what Rand could do had been like finding out his best friend tortured small animals and killed babies. Once you finally made yourself believe it, it was hard to call him a friend any longer.

"I have to look out for myself," he said angrily. He upended the wine pitcher over his silver cup and was surprised to find it empty. He filled the cup with milk, instead. "Egwene and Nynaeve want to be Aes Sedai." He had not really remembered that until he said it aloud. "Rand is following Moiraine around and calling himself the Dragon Reborn. The Light knows what Perrin is up to. He's been acting crazy ever since his eyes turned funny. I have to look out for myself." *Burn me, I have to! I'm the last one of us who's still sane. There's only me.*

Tar Valon. Well, it was supposed to be the wealthiest city in the world, and it was the center of trade between the Borderlands and the south, the center of Aes Sedai power. He did not think he could get an Aes Sedai to gamble with him. Or trust the fall of the dice or the turn of the cards if he did. But there had to be merchants, and others with silver and gold. The city itself would be worth a few days. He knew he had traveled far since leaving the Two Rivers, but aside from a few vague memories of Caemlyn and Cairhien, he could remember nothing of any great cities. He had always wanted to see a great city.

"But not one full of Aes Sedai," he muttered sourly, scraping up the last of the butterpeas. He gulped them down and went back for another helping of beef.

Idly, he wondered if the Aes Sedai might let him have the ruby from the Shadar Logoth dagger. He remembered the dagger in only the fuzziest way, but even that was like remembering a terrible injury. His insides knotted up, and sharp pain dug at his temples. Yet the ruby was clear in his mind, as big as his thumbnail, dark as a drop of blood, glittering like some crimson eye. Surely he had more claim to it than they did, and it had to be worth as much as a dozen farms back home.

They'll probably say it is tainted, too. And likely it was. Still he spun a little fancy of trading the ruby to some of the Coplins for their best land. Most of that family— troublemakers from the cradle, where they were not thieves and liars as well—deserved whatever happened to them and more. But he really did not believe the Aes Sedai would give it back to him, did not relish the notion of carrying it as far as Emond's Field if they did. And the thought of owning the largest farm in the Two Rivers was no longer as exciting as it once had been. Once that had been his biggest ambition, that, and to be known as his father's equal as a horse trader. Now it seemed such a small thing to want. A cramped thing, with the whole wide world just waiting out there.

First off, he decided, he would find Egwene and Nynaeve. *Maybe they've come to their senses. Maybe they've given up this foolishness about becoming Aes Sedai.* He did not think they would have, but he could not go without seeing them. He would go; that was sure. A visit with them, a day to see the city, perhaps a game with the dice to pad out his purse, and then he would be off for somewhere where there were no Aes Sedai. Before he returned home—*I will go home one day. One day, I will*—he meant to see something of the world, and without any Aes Sedai making him dance to her tune.

Rummaging around the tray for something more to eat, he was shocked to realize nothing was left but smears and a few crumbs of bread and cheese. The pitchers were both empty. He squinted down at his stomach in wonder. He should have been stuffed to the ears with all that in him, but he felt as if he had hardly eaten at all. He scraped the last bits of cheese together between thumb and forefinger. Halfway to his mouth, his hand froze.

I blew the Horn of Valere. Softly he whistled a bit of tune, then cut it short when the words came to him:

> I'm down at the bottom of the well.
> It's night, and the rain is coming down.
> The sides are falling in,
> and there's no rope to climb.
> I'm down at the bottom of the well.

"There had better be a bloody rope to climb," he whispered. He let the cheese crumbs fall on the tray. For the moment he felt sick again. Determinedly he tried to think, tried to penetrate the fog that shrouded everything in his head.

Verin had been bringing the Horn to Tar Valon, but he could not remember if she knew he was the one who had blown it. She had never said anything to make him think so. He was sure of that. He thought he was. *So what if she does know? What if they all do? Unless Verin did something with it I don't know about, they have the Horn. They don't need me.* But who could say what Aes Sedai thought they needed?

"If they ask," he said grimly, "I never even touched it. If they know. . . . If they know, I'll . . . I'll handle that when it comes. Burn me, they can't want anything from me. They can't!"

A soft knock on the door brought him swaying to his feet, ready to run. If there had been any place to run to, and if he could have managed more than three steps. But there was not, and he could not.

The door opened.

CHAPTER
20

Visitations

The woman who came in, dressed all in white silk and silver, shut the door behind her and leaned back against it to study him with the darkest eyes Mat had ever seen. She was so beautiful he almost forgot to breathe, with hair as black as night held by a finely woven silver band, and as graceful in repose as another woman would be dancing. He halfway thought that he knew her, but he rejected the idea out of hand. No man could ever forget a woman like her.

"You may be passable, I suppose, once you fill out again," she said, "but for now, perhaps you could put on something."

For an instant Mat continued to stare at her; then suddenly he realized he was standing there naked. Face scarlet, he shambled to the bed, pulled the blanket around himself like a cloak, and more fell than sat down on the edge of the mattress. "I'm sorry for . . . I mean, I . . . that is, I didn't expect . . . I . . . I . . . ." He drew a deep breath. "I apologize for your finding me this way."

He could still feel the heat in his cheeks. For a moment he wished that Rand, whatever he had become, or even Perrin were there to advise him. They always seemed to get on well with women. Even girls who knew that Rand was all but promised to Egwene used to stare at him, and they seemed to think Perrin's slow ways were gentle and attractive. However hard he tried, he always managed to make a fool of himself in front of girls. As he had just done.

"I would not have visited you in this way, Mat, except that I was here in the . . . in the White Tower—" She smiled as if the name amused her—"for another purpose, and I

wanted to see all of you." Mat's face reddened again, and he
tugged the blanket around him tighter, but she seemed not
to have been teasing him. More graceful than a swan, she
glided to the table. "You are hungry. That's to be expected,
the way they do things. Make sure you eat all they give you.
You will be surprised at how quickly you put weight back
and regain strength."

"Pardon," Mat said diffidently, "but do I know you?
Meaning no offense, but you seem . . . familiar." She looked
at him until he began to shift uneasily. A woman like her
would expect to be remembered.

"You may have seen me," she said finally. "Somewhere.
Call me Selene." Her head tilted slightly; she appeared to
be waiting for him to recognize the name.

It tugged at the edges of memory. He thought he must
have heard it before, but he could not say when or where.
"Are you an Aes Sedai, Selene?"

"No." The word was soft but surprisingly emphatic.

For the first time, he studied her, able now to see more
than her beauty. She was almost as tall as he was, slender
and, he suspected from the way she moved, strong. He was
not sure of her age—a year or two older than he, or maybe
as much as ten—but her cheeks were smooth. Her necklace
of smooth white stones and woven silver matched her wide
belt, but she did not wear a Great Serpent ring. The absence
should not have surprised him—no Aes Sedai would ever
say right out that she was not—yet it did. There was an air
about her—a self-confidence, a surety in her own power to
match any queen's, and something more—that he associated with Aes Sedai.

"You aren't by any chance a novice, are you?" He had
heard that novices wore white, but he could not really believe it of her. *She makes Elayne look like a cringer.* Elayne.
Another name drifting into his head.

"Hardly that," Selene said with a wry twist to her mouth.
"Let us just say that I am someone whose interests coincide
with yours. These . . . Aes Sedai mean to use you, but you
will like it, in the main, I think. And accept it. There is no
need to convince you to seek out glory."

"Use me?" The memory returned to him of thinking that,
but about Rand, that the Aes Sedai meant to use Rand, not
him. *They've no bloody use for me. Light, they can't have!*

"What do you mean? I'm no one important. I am no use to anyone but myself. What kind of glory?"

"I knew that would pull you. You, above all."

Her smile made his head spin. He scrubbed a hand through his hair. The blanket slipped, and he caught it hastily before it could fall. "Now listen, they are not interested in me." *What about me sounding the Horn?* "I am just a farmer." *Maybe they think I'm tied to Rand in some way. No, Verin said. . . .* He was not sure what Verin had said, or Moiraine, but he thought most Aes Sedai knew nothing at all about Rand. He wanted to keep it that way, at least until he was a long way gone. "Just a simple country man. I only want to see a little of the world and go back to my da's farm." *What does she mean, glory?*

Selene shook her head as if she had heard his thoughts. "You are more important than you yet know. Certainly more important than these so-called Aes Sedai know. You *can* have glory, if you know enough not to trust them."

"You certainly sound as if you don't trust them." *So-called?* A thought came to him, but he could not manage to say it. "Are you a . . . ? Are you . . . ?" It was not the kind of thing you accused someone of.

"A Darkfriend?" Selene said mockingly. She sounded amused, not angered. She sounded contemptuous. "One of those pathetic followers of Ba'alzamon who think he will give them immortality and power? I follow no one. There is one man I could stand beside, but I do not follow."

Mat laughed nervously. "Of course not." *Blood and ashes, a Darkfriend wouldn't name herself Darkfriend. Probably has a poisoned knife, if she is.* He had a vague memory of a woman dressed as one nobly born, a Darkfriend with a deadly dagger in her slender hand. "That wasn't what I meant at all. You look. . . . You look like a queen. That's what I meant. Are you a Lady?"

"Mat, Mat, you must learn to trust me. Oh, I will use you, too—you have too suspicious a nature, especially since carrying that dagger, for me to deny it—but my use will gain you wealth, and power, and glory. I will not compel you. I have always believed men perform better if convinced rather than forced. These Aes Sedai do not even realize how important you are, and he will try to dissuade or kill you, but I can give you what you desire."

"He?" Mat said sharply. *Kill me? Light, it's Rand they were after, not me. How does she know about the dagger? I suppose the whole Tower knows.* "Who wants to kill me?"

Selene's mouth tightened as if she had said too much. "You know what you want, Mat, and I know it every bit as well as you. You must choose who you will trust to gain it for you. I admit I will use you. These Aes Sedai will never do that. I will lead you to wealth and glory. They will keep you tied to a leash until you die."

"You say a lot," Mat said, "but how do I know any of it is true? How do I know I can trust you any more than I can them?"

"By listening to what they tell you, and what they do not. Will they tell you your father came to Tar Valon?"

"My da was here?"

"A man named Abell Cauthon, and another named Tam al'Thor. They made nuisances of themselves until they gained an audience, I have heard, wanting to know where you and your friends were. And Siuan Sanche sent them back to the Two Rivers with empty hands, not even letting them know you were alive. Will they tell you that, unless you ask? Perhaps not even then, for you might try to run away back home."

"My da thinks I am dead?" Mat said slowly.

"He can be told you live. I can see to it. Think on who to trust, Mat Cauthon. Will they tell you that even now Rand al'Thor is trying to escape, and the one called Moiraine is hunting him? Will they tell you that the Black Ajah infests their precious White Tower? Will they even tell you how they mean to use you?"

"Rand is trying to escape? But—" Maybe she knew Rand had proclaimed himself the Dragon Reborn, and maybe she did not, but he would not tell her. *The Black Ajah! Blood and bloody ashes!* "Who are you, Selene? If you're not Aes Sedai, what are you?"

Her smile hid secrets. "Just remember that there is another choice. You need not be a puppet for the White Tower or prey for Ba'alzamon's Darkfriends. The world is more complex than you can imagine. Do as these Aes Sedai wish for the present, but remember your choices. Will you do that?"

"I don't see that I have much choice at all," he said glumly. "I suppose I will."

Selene's look sharpened. Friendliness sloughed off her voice like an old snake skin. "Suppose? I did not come to you like this, talk in this way, for suppose, Matrim Cauthon." She stretched out a slim hand.

Her hand was empty, and she stood halfway across the room, but he leaned back, away from her hand, as if she were right on top of him with a dagger. He did not know why, really, except that there was a threat in her eyes, and he was sure it was real. His skin began to tingle, and his headache returned.

Suddenly tingle and pain vanished together, and Selene's head whipped around as if listening to something beyond the walls. A tiny frown appeared on her face, and she lowered her hand. The frown vanished. "We will talk again, Mat. I have much to say to you. Remember your choices. Remember that there are many hands that would kill you. I alone guarantee you life, and all you seek, if you do as I say." She slipped out of the door as silently and gracefully as she had entered.

Mat let out a long breath. Sweat ran down his face. *Who in the Light is she?* A Darkfriend, perhaps. Except that she had sounded as contemptuous of Ba'alzamon as she was of Aes Sedai. Darkfriends spoke of Ba'alzamon the way anyone else might speak of the Creator. And she had not asked him to conceal her visit from the Aes Sedai.

Right, he thought sourly. *Pardon me, Aes Sedai, but this woman came to see me. She wasn't Aes Sedai, but I think maybe she started to use the One Power on me, and she said she wasn't a Darkfriend, but she did say you mean to use me, and the Black Ajah's in your Tower. Oh, and she said I'm important. I don't know how. You don't mind if I leave now, do you?*

Going was beginning to be a better idea by the minute. He slid awkwardly off the bed and made his way unsteadily to the wardrobe, still clutching his blanket around him. His boots were on the floor inside, and his cloak hung from a peg, under his belt, with pouch and sheathed belt knife. It was just a country knife, with a stout blade, but it could do as much as any fine dagger. The rest of his clothes—two sturdy wool coats, three pairs of breeches, half a dozen linen shirts and smallclothes—had been brushed or washed as required, and neatly folded on the shelves that took up one side of the wardrobe. He felt the pouch hanging from the belt, but it was empty. Its contents lay jumbled on a shelf with what had been emptied from his pockets.

He brushed aside a redhawk's feather, a smooth, striped rock he had liked the colors of, his razor, and his bone-handled pocketknife, and freed his wash-leather purse from some coils of spare bowstring. When he tugged it open, he found his memory had been all too good in this instance.

"Two silver marks and a handful of copper," he muttered. "I won't get far on that." Once it would have seemed a small fortune to him, but that had been before he left Emond's Field.

He stooped to peer back into the shelf. *Where are they?* He began to be afraid the Aes Sedai might have thrown them out, the way his mother would if she had ever found them. *Where . . . ?* He felt a surge of relief. Way in the back, behind his tinderbox and ball of twine for snares and the like, were his two leather dice cups.

They rattled as he pulled them out, but he still popped off the tight-fitting round caps. Everything was as it should be. Five dice carved with symbols, for crowns, and five marked with spots. The spotted dice would do for a number of games, but more men seemed to play crowns than anything else. With these, his two marks would become enough to take him far away from Tar Valon. *Away from Aes Sedai and Selene, both.*

A peremptory knock was followed immediately by the door opening. He whirled around. The Amyrlin Seat and the Keeper of the Chronicles were entering. He would have recognized them even without the Amyrlin's broad, striped stole, and the Keeper's narrower blue stole. He had seen them once and only once, a long way from Tar Valon, but he could not forget the two most powerful women among the Aes Sedai.

The Amyrlin's eyebrows rose at the sight of him standing there with the blanket hanging from his shoulders and his purse and dice cups in his hands. "I don't think you will need those for a while yet, my son," she said dryly. "Put them up and get back to bed before you fall on your face."

He hesitated, his back stiffening, but his knees chose that moment to wobble, and the two Aes Sedai were looking at him, dark eyes and blue alike appearing to read his every rebellious thought. He did as he was told, holding the blanket around him with both hands. He lay down straight as a board, not sure what else he could do.

"How are you feeling?" the Amyrlin asked briskly as she put a hand on his head. Goose bumps covered his skin. Had she done something with the One Power, or was it being touched by an Aes Sedai that made him feel a chill?

"I'm fine," he told her. "Why, I am ready to be on my way. Just let me say goodbye to Egwene and Nynaeve, and I'll be out of your hair. I mean, I will go . . . uh, Mother." Moiraine and Verin had not seemed to care much how he talked, but this was the Amyrlin Seat, after all.

"Nonsense," the Amyrlin said. She pulled the high-backed chair around, closer to the bed, and sat, addressing Leane. "Men always seem to refuse to admit they are sick until they're sick enough to make twice as much work for women. Then they claim they're well too soon, with the same result."

The Keeper glanced at Mat and nodded. "Yes, Mother, yet this one cannot claim he is well when he can barely stand up. At least he has eaten everything on his tray."

"I'd be surprised if he had left enough crumbs to interest a finch. And still hungry, unless I miss my guess."

"I could have someone bring him a pie, Mother. Or some cakes."

"No, I think he has had as much as he can hold for now. If he brings it all back up, it won't do him any good."

Mat scowled. It seemed to him that when you got sick, you became invisible to women unless they were actually talking to you. And then they took at least ten years off your age. Nynaeve, his mother, his sisters, the Amyrlin Seat, they all did it.

"I'm not hungry at all," he announced. "I am fine. If you will let me put my clothes on, I'll show you how well I am. I will be out of here before you know it." They were both looking at him, now. He cleared his throat. "Uh . . . Mother."

The Amyrlin snorted. "You've eaten a meal for five, and you will eat three or four like it every day for days yet, or else you will starve to death. You've just been Healed from a link to the evil that killed every man, woman, and child in Aridhol, and no less strong for near two thousand years waiting for you to pick it up. It was killing you just as surely as it killed them. That is not like having a fish spine stuck in your thumb, boy. We very nearly killed you ourselves trying to save you."

"I am not hungry," he maintained. His stomach growled loudly to give him the lie.

"I read you aright the first time I saw you," the Amyrlin said. "I knew right then you'd bolt like a startled fisher-bird if you ever thought someone was trying to hold you. As well I took precautions."

He eyed them warily. "Precautions?" They looked back, all serenity. He felt as if their eyes were pinning him to the bed.

"Your name and description are on their way to the bridge guards," the Amyrlin said, "and the dockmasters. I'll not try to hold you inside the Tower, but you will not leave Tar Valon until you are well. Should you try to hide in the city, hunger will drive you back here eventually, or if it doesn't, we will find you before you starve."

"Why do you want to keep me here so badly?" he demanded. He heard Selene's voice. *They want to use you.* "Why should you care whether I starve or not? I can feed myself."

The Amyrlin gave a small laugh with little amusement in it. "With two silver marks and a handful of copper, my son? Your dice would need to be very lucky indeed to buy all the food you'll need in the next few days. We do not Heal people, then let them waste our efforts by dying while they still need care. In addition to which, you may yet need more Healing."

"More? You said you had Healed me. Why should I need more?"

"My son, you carried that dagger for months. I believe we dug every trace of it out of you, but if we missed even the smallest speck, it could still be fatal. And who knows what effect your having it in your possession so long may have? Half a year from now, a year, and you may wish you had an Aes Sedai to hand to Heal you again."

"You want me to stay here a year?" he said incredulously, and loudly. Leane shifted her feet and eyed him sharply, but the Amyrlin's calm features were unruffled.

"Perhaps not so long as that, my son. Long enough to be

certain, though. Surely you want as much. Would you set sail in a boat when you didn't know whether the caulking would hold, or whether a plank might be rotten?"

"I never had much to do with boats," Mat muttered. It might be true. Aes Sedai never lied, but there were too many mights and mays in it for him. "I've been gone from home a long time, Mother. My da and my mother probably think I am dead."

"If you wish to write a letter to them, I will see that it is carried to Emond's Field."

Mat waited for more, but no more came. "Thank you, Mother." He essayed a small laugh. "I'm half surprised my da did not come looking for me. He's the kind of man who would." He was not sure, but he thought there was a small hesitation before the Amyrlin answered.

"He did come. Leane spoke to him."

The Keeper took it up immediately. "We did not know where you were then, Mat. I told him so, and he left before the heavy snows. I gave him some gold to make the journey home easier."

"No doubt," the Amyrlin said, "he will be pleased to hear from you. And your mother will, certainly. Give me the letter when you have written it, and I will see to it."

They had told him, but he had had to ask. *And they didn't mention Rand's da. Maybe because they didn't think I would care, and maybe because. . . . Burn me, I don't know. Who can tell with Aes Sedai?* "I was traveling with a friend, Mother. Rand al'Thor. You remember him. Do you know if he is all right? I'll bet his da is worried, too."

"As far as I know," the Amyrlin said smoothly, "the boy is well enough, but who can say? I have seen him only once, the time I saw you, in Fal Dara." She turned to the Keeper. "Perhaps he could do with a small piece of pie, Leane. And something for his throat, if he is going to do all this talking. Will you see that it is brought to him?"

The tall Aes Sedai left with a murmured, "As you command, Mother."

When the Amyrlin turned back to Mat, she was smiling, but her eyes were blue ice. "There are things it would be dangerous for you to talk about, perhaps even in front of Leane. A flapping tongue has killed more men than sudden storms ever did."

"Dangerous, Mother?" His mouth felt suddenly parched, but he resisted the urge to lick his lips. *Light, how much does she know about Rand? If only Moiraine didn't keep so many secrets.* "Mother, I don't know anything dangerous. I can hardly remember half of what I do know."

"Do you remember the Horn?"

"What horn is that, Mother?"

She was on her feet and looming over him so fast he hardly saw her move. "You play games with me, boy, and I will make you weep for your mother to come running. I have no time for games, and neither do you. Now, do—you—remember?"

Clutching the blanket tightly around him, he had to swallow before he could say, "I remember, Mother."

She seemed to relax, just a little, and Mat shrugged his shoulders queasily. He felt as if he had just been allowed to lift them off a chopping block.

"Good. That is good, Mat." She sat back down slowly, studying him. "Do you know that you are linked to the Horn?" He mouthed the word "linked" silently, shocked, and she nodded. "I did not think you knew. You were first to blow the Horn of Valere after it was found. For you, it will summon dead heroes back from the grave. For anyone else, it is only a horn—so long as you live."

He took a deep breath. "So long as I live," he said in a dull voice, and the Amyrlin nodded. "You could have let me die." She nodded again. "Then you could have had anyone you want blow it, and it would have worked for them." Another nod. "Blood and ashes! You mean me to blow it for you. When the Last Battle comes, you mean me to call heroes back from the grave to fight the Dark One for you. Blood and bloody ashes!"

She put an elbow on the arm of the chair and propped her chin on her hand. Her eyes never left him. "Would you prefer the alternative?"

He frowned, then remembered what the alternative was. If someone else had to sound the Horn. . . . "You want me to blow the Horn? Then I'll blow the Horn. I never said I would not, did I?"

The Amyrlin gave an exasperated sigh. "You remind me of my uncle Huan. No one could ever pin him down. He liked to gamble, too, and he'd much rather have fun than work. He died pulling children out of a burning house. He wouldn't stop going back as long as there was one left inside. Are you like him, Mat? Will you be there when the flames are high?"

He could not meet her eyes. He studied his fingers as they plucked irritably at his blanket. "I'm no hero. I do what I have to do, but I am no hero."

"Most of those we call heroes only did what they had to do. I suppose it will have to be enough. For now. You must not speak to anyone but me of the Horn, my son. Or of your link to it."

For now? he thought. *It's all you are going to bloody get, now or ever.* "I don't mean to bloody tell everybo—" She arched an eyebrow, and he made his voice smooth again. "I do not want to tell anyone. I wish nobody knew. Why do you want to keep it such a secret? Don't you trust your Aes Sedai?"

For a long moment he thought he had gone too far. Her face hardened, and her look could have carved axe handles.

"If I could make it so that only you and I knew," she said coldly, "I would. The more people know a thing, the more the knowledge spreads, even with the best will. Most of the world believes the Horn of Valere is only legend, and those who know better believe one of the Hunters has yet to find it. But Shayol Ghul knows it has been found, and that means at least some Darkfriends know. But they do not know where it is, and, if the Light shines on us, they do not know you sounded it. Do you really want Darkfriends coming after you? Halfmen, or other Shadowspawn? They want the Horn. You must know that. It will work as well for the Shadow as for the Light. But if it is to work for them, they must take you, or kill you. Do you want to risk that?"

Mat wished he had another blanket, and maybe a goose-down comforter. The room suddenly felt very cold. "Are you telling me Darkfriends could come after me here? I thought the White Tower could keep Darkfriends out." He remembered what Selene had said about the Black Ajah, and wondered what the Amyrlin would say to that.

"A good reason to stay, wouldn't you say?" She got to her feet, smoothing her skirts. "Rest, my son. Soon you will feel much better. Rest." She closed the door softly behind her.

For a long time Mat lay staring up at the ceiling. He barely noticed when a serving woman came with his piece of pie and another pitcher of milk, taking the tray of empty dishes when she went. His stomach rumbled loudly at the warm smell of apples and spices, but he paid that no mind, either. The Amyrlin thought she held him like a sheep in a pen. And Selene. . . . *Who in the Light is she? What does she want?* Selene had been right about some things; but the Amyrlin had told him she meant to use him, and how. In a way. There were too many holes in what she had said to suit him, too many holes she could slip something deadly through. The Amyrlin wanted something, and Selene wanted something, and he was the rope they were tugging between them. He thought he would rather face Trollocs than be caught between those two.

There had to be a way out of Tar Valon, a way out of both their grasps. Once he was beyond the river, he could keep out of Aes Sedai hands, and Selene's, and Darkfriends', too. He was sure of it. There had to be a way. All he had to do was think about it from every angle.

The pie grew cold on the table.

CHAPTER
21

A World of Dreams

Egwene scrubbed her hands with a hand towel as she hurried down the dimly lit corridor. She had washed them twice, but they still felt greasy. She had not thought there could be so many pots in the world. And today had been bake day, so buckets of ashes had had to be hauled from the ovens. And the hearths cleaned. And the tables rubbed bone-white with fine sand, and the floors scrubbed on hands and knees. Ash and grease stained her white dress. Her back ached, and she wanted to be in her bed, but Verin had come to the kitchens, supposedly for a meal to eat in her rooms, and whispered a summons to her in passing.

Verin had her quarters above the library, in corridors used only by a few other Brown sisters. There was a dusty air to the halls there, as if the women who lived along them were too busy with other things to bother having the servants clean very often, and the passages took odd turns and twists, sometimes dipping or rising unexpectedly. The tapestries were few, their colorful weavings dulled, apparently cleaned as seldom as everything else here. Many of the lamps were unlit, plunging much of the hall into gloom. Egwene thought she had it to herself, except for a flash of white ahead, perhaps a novice or a servant scurrying about some task. Her shoes, clicking on bare black and white floor tiles, made echoes. It was not a comforting place for one thinking of the Black Ajah.

She found what Verin had told her to look for. A dark paneled door at the top of a rise, beside a dusty tapestry of a king on horseback receiving the surrender of another king. Verin had named the pair of them—men dead hundreds of years before Artur Hawkwing was born; Verin always seemed to know such things—but Egwene could not remember their names, or the long-vanished countries they had ruled. It was the only wall hanging she had seen that matched Verin's description, though.

Minus the sound of her own footsteps, the hallway seemed even emptier than before, and more threatening. She rapped on the door, and entered hurriedly on the heels of an absentminded "Who is it? Come in."

One step into the room, she stopped and stared. Shelves lined the walls, except for one door that must lead to inner rooms and except for where maps hung, often in layers, and what seemed to be charts of the night sky. She recognized the names of some constellations—the Plowman and the Haywain, the Archer and the Five Sisters—but others were unfamiliar. Books and papers and scrolls covered nearly every flat surface, with all sorts of odd things interspersed among the piles, and sometimes on top of them. Strange shapes of glass or metal, spheres and tubes interlinked, and circles held inside circles, stood among bones and skulls of every shape and description. What appeared to be a stuffed brown owl, not much bigger than Egwene's hand, stood on what seemed to be a bleached white lizard's skull, but could not be, for the skull was longer than her arm and had crooked teeth as big as her fingers. Candlesticks had been stuck about in a haphazard fashion, giving good light here and shadows there, although seeming in danger of setting fire to papers in some places. The owl blinked at her, and she jumped.

"Ah, yes," Verin said. She was seated behind a table as cluttered as everything else in the room, a torn page held carefully in her hands. "It is you. Yes." She noticed Egwene's sideways glance at the owl, and said absently, "He keeps down mice. They chew paper." Her gesture took in the entire room, and reminded her of the page she held. "Fascinating, this. Rosel of Essam claimed more than a hundred pages survived the Breaking, and she should have known, since she wrote barely two hundred years afterwards, but only this one piece still exists, so far as I know. Perhaps only this very copy.

Rosel wrote that it held secrets the world could not face, and she would not speak of them plainly. I have read this page a thousand times, trying to decipher what she meant."

The tiny owl blinked at Egwene again. She tried not to look at it. "What does it say, Verin Sedai?"

Verin blinked, very much as the owl had. "What does it say? It is a direct translation, mind, and reads almost like a bard reciting in High Chant. Listen. 'Heart of the Dark. Ba'alzamon. Name hidden within name shrouded by name. Secret buried within secret cloaked by secret. Betrayer of Hope. Ishamael betrays all hope. Truth burns and sears. Hope fails before truth. A lie is our shield. Who can stand against the Heart of the Dark? Who can face the Betrayer of Hope? Soul of shadow, Soul of the Shadow, he is—'" She stopped with a sigh. "It ends there. What do you make of it?"

"I don't know," Egwene said. "I do not like it."

"Well, why should you, child? Like it, or understand it? I have studied it nearly forty years, and I do neither." Verin carefully placed the page inside a silk-lined folder of stiff leather, then casually stuffed the folder into a stack of papers. "But you did not come for that." She rummaged across the table, muttering to herself, several times barely catching a pile of books or manuscripts before it toppled. Finally she came up with a handful of pages covered in a thin, spidery hand and tied with nubby string. "Here, child. Everything that is known about Liandrin and the women who went with her. Names, ages, Ajahs, where they were born. Everything I could find in the records. Even how they performed in their studies. What we know of the *ter'angreal* they took, too, which isn't much. Only descriptions, for the most part. I do not know whether any of this will help. I saw nothing of any use in this."

"Perhaps one of us will see something." A sudden wave of suspicion took Egwene by surprise. *If she didn't leave something out.* The Amyrlin seemed to trust Verin only because she had to. What if Verin was Black Ajah herself? She gave herself a shake. She had traveled all the way from Toman Head to Tar Valon with Verin, and she refused to believe this plump scholar could be a Darkfriend. "I trust you, Verin Sedai." *Can I, really?*

The Aes Sedai blinked at her again, then dismissed whatever thought had come to her with a shake of her head. "That list I gave you may be important, or it may be so much waste of paper, but it isn't the only reason I summoned you." She started moving things on the table, making some shaky stacks taller to clear a space. "I understand from Anaiya that you might become a Dreamer. The last was Corianin Nedeal, four hundred and seventy-three years ago, and from what I can make of the records, she barely deserved the name. It would be quite interesting, if you do."

"She tested me, Verin Sedai, but she couldn't be sure that any of my dreams foretold the future."

"That is only part of what a Dreamer does, child. Perhaps the least part. Anaiya believes in bringing girls along too slowly, in my opinion. Look here." With one finger, Verin drew a number of parallel lines across the area she had cleared, lines clear in dust atop the old beeswax. "Let these represent worlds that might exist if different choices had been made, if major turning points in the Pattern had gone another way."

"The worlds reached by the Portal Stones," Egwene said, to show she had listened to Verin's lectures on the journey from Toman Head. What could this possibly have to do with whether or not she was a Dreamer?

"Very good. But the Pattern may be even more complex than that, child. The Wheel weaves our lives to make the Pattern of an Age, but the Ages themselves are woven into the Age Lace, the Great Pattern. Who can know if this is even the tenth part of the weaving, though? Some in the Age of Legends apparently believe that there were still other worlds—even harder to reach than the worlds of the Portal Stones, if that can be believed—lying like this." She drew more lines, cross-hatching the first set. For a moment she stared at them. "The warp and the woof of the weave. Perhaps the Wheel of Time weaves a still greater Pattern from worlds." Straightening, she dusted her hands. "Well, that is neither here nor there. In all of these worlds, whatever their other variations, a few things are constant. One is that the Dark One is imprisoned in all of them."

In spite of herself, Egwene stepped closer to peer at the lines Verin had drawn. "In all of them? How can that be?

Are you saying there is a Father of Lies for each world?"
The thought of so many Dark Ones made her shiver.

"No, child. There is one Creator, who exists everywhere
at once for all of these worlds. In the same way, there is
only one Dark One, who also exists in all of these worlds at
once. If he is freed from the prison the Creator made in one
world, he is freed on all. So long as he is kept prisoner in
one, he remains imprisoned on all."

"That does not seem to make sense," Egwene protested.

"Paradox, child. The Dark One is the embodiment of
paradox and chaos, the destroyer of reason and logic, the
breaker of balance, the unmaker of order."

The owl suddenly took flight on silent wings, landing
atop a large white skull on a shelf behind the Aes Sedai.
It peered down at the two women, blinking. Egwene had
noticed the skull when she came in, with its curled horns
and snout, and vaguely wondered what sort of ram had so
big a head. Now she took in the roundness of it, the high
forehead. Not a ram's skull. A Trolloc.

She drew a shuddering breath. "Verin Sedai, what does
this have to do with being a Dreamer? The Dark One is
bound in Shayol Ghul, and I do not want to even think of
him escaping." *But the seals on his prison are weakening.
Even novices know that, now.*

"Do with being a Dreamer? Why, nothing, child. Except that we must all confront the Dark One in one way or
another. He is prisoned now, but the Pattern did not bring
Rand al'Thor into the world for no purpose. The Dragon
Reborn will face the Lord of the Grave; that much is sure.
If Rand survives that long, of course. The Dark One will try
to distort the Pattern, if he can. Well, we have gone rather
far afield, haven't we?"

"Forgive me, Verin Sedai, but if this"—Egwene indicated the lines drawn in the dust—"has nothing to do with
being a Dreamer, why are you telling me about it?"

Verin stared at her as if she were deliberately being dense.
"Nothing? Of course it has something to do with it, child.
The point is that there is a third constant besides the Creator
and the Dark One. There is a world that lies *within* each of
these others, inside all of them at the same time. Or perhaps
surrounding them. Writers in the Age of Legends called

it *Tel'aran'rhiod*, "the Unseen World." Perhaps "the World of Dreams" is a better translation. Many people—ordinary folk who could not think of channeling—sometimes glimpse *Tel'aran'rhiod* in their dreams, and even catch glimmers of these other worlds through it. Think of some of the peculiar things you have seen in your dreams. But a Dreamer, child—a true Dreamer—can enter *Tel'aran'rhiod*."

Egwene tried to swallow, but a lump in her throat stopped her. *Enter it?* "I . . . I don't think I am a Dreamer, Verin Sedai. Anaiya Sedai's tests—"

Verin cut her off. "—prove nothing one way or the other. And Anaiya still believes that you may very well be one."

"I suppose I will learn whether I am or not eventually," Egwene mumbled. *Light, I want to be, don't I? I want to learn! I want it all.*

"You have no time to wait, child. The Amyrlin has entrusted a great task to you and Nynaeve. You must reach out for any tool you might be able to use." Verin dug a red wooden box from under the welter on her table. The box was large enough to hold sheets of paper, but when the Aes Sedai opened the lid a crack, all she pulled out was a ring carved from stone, all flecks and stripes of blue and brown and red, and too large to be a finger ring. "Here, child."

Egwene shifted the papers to take it, and her eyes widened in surprise. The ring certainly looked like stone, but it felt harder than steel and heavier than lead. And the circle of it was twisted. If she ran a finger along one edge, it would go around twice, inside as well as out; it only had one edge. She moved her finger along that edge twice, just to convince herself.

"Corianin Nedeal," Verin said, "had that *ter'angreal* in her possession for most of her life. You will keep it, now."

Egwene almost dropped the ring. *A* ter'angreal? *I am to keep a* ter'angreal?

Verin seemed not to notice her shock. "According to her, it eases the passage to *Tel'aran'rhiod*. She claimed it would work for those without Talent as well as for Aes Sedai, so long as you are touching it when you sleep. There are dangers, of course. *Tel'aran'rhiod* is not like other dreams. What happens there is real; you are actually there instead of just glimpsing it." She pushed back the sleeve of her dress, revealing a faded scar the length of her forearm. "I tried it myself, once, some years ago. Anaiya's Healing did not work as well as it should have. Remember that." The Aes Sedai let her sleeve cover the scar again.

"I will be careful, Verin Sedai." *Real? My dreams are bad enough as they are. I want no dreams that leave scars! I'll put it in a sack and stick it in a dark corner and leave it there. I'll—*But she wanted to learn. She wanted to be Aes Sedai, and no Aes Sedai had been a Dreamer in nearly five hundred years. "I'll be very careful." She slipped the ring into her pouch and tugged the drawstrings tight, then picked up the papers Verin had given her.

"Remember to keep it hidden, child. No novice, or even an Accepted, should have a thing like that in her possession. But it may prove useful to you. Keep it hidden."

"Yes, Verin Sedai." Remembering Verin's scar, she almost wished another Aes Sedai would come along and take it from her right then.

"Good, child. Now, off with you. It grows late, and you must be up early to help with breakfast. Sleep well."

Verin sat looking at the door for a time after it closed behind Egwene. The owl hooted softly behind her. Pulling the red box to her, she opened the lid all the way and frowned at what nearly filled the space.

Page upon page, covered with a precise hand, the black ink barely faded after nearly five hundred years. Corianin Nedeal's notes, everything she had learned in fifty years of studying that peculiar *ter'angreal*. A secretive woman, Corianin. She had kept by far the greater part of her knowledge from everyone, trusting it only to these pages. Only chance and a habit of rummaging through old papers in the library had led Verin to them. As far as she could discover, no Aes Sedai besides herself knew of the *ter'angreal*; Corianin had managed to erase its existence from the records.

Once again she considered burning the manuscript, just as she had considered giving it to Egwene. But destroying knowledge, any knowledge, was anathema to her. And for the other. . . . *No. It is best by far to leave things as they*

are. What will happen, will happen. She let the lid drop
shut. *Now where did I put that page?*

Frowning, she began to search the stacks of books and
papers for the leather folder. Egwene was already out of her
mind.

CHAPTER

22

The Price of the Ring

E gwene had only gone a short distance from Verin's
rooms when Sheriam met her. The Mistress of Novices wore a preoccupied frown.

"If someone hadn't remembered Verin speaking to you, I
might not have found you." The Aes Sedai sounded mildly
irritated. "Come along, child. You are holding everything
up! What are those papers?"

Egwene clutched them a little tighter. She tried to make
her voice both meek and respectful. "Verin Sedai thinks I
should study them, Aes Sedai." What would she do if Sheriam asked to see them? What excuse could she give for
refusing, what explanation for pages telling all about thirteen women of the Black Ajah and the *ter'angreal* they had
stolen?

But Sheriam seemed to have dismissed the papers from
her mind as soon as she asked. "Never mind that. You are
wanted, and everyone is waiting." She took Egwene's arm
and forced her to walk faster.

"Wanted, Sheriam Sedai? Waiting for what?"

Sheriam shook her head with exasperation. "Did you forget that you are to be raised to the Accepted? When you
come to my study tomorrow, you will be wearing the ring,
though I doubt it will soothe you very much."

Egwene tried to stop short, but the Aes Sedai hurried her
on, taking a narrow set of stairs that curled down through
the library walls. "Tonight? Already? But I am half-asleep,
Aes Sedai, and dirty, and. . . . I thought I would have days
yet. To get ready. To prepare."

"The hour waits on no woman," Sheriam said. "The

Wheel weaves as the Wheel wills, *when* the Wheel wills. Besides, how would you prepare? You already know the things you must. More than your friend Nynaeve did." She pushed Egwene through a tiny door at the foot of the stairs and hurried her across another hall to a ramp curving down and down.

"I listened to the lectures," Egwene protested, "and I remember them, but . . . can't I have a night's sleep first?" The winding ramp seemed to have no end.

"The Amyrlin Seat decided there was no point in waiting." Sheriam gave Egwene a sidelong smile. "Her exact words were, 'Once you decide to gut a fish, there's no use waiting till it rots.' Elayne has already been through the arches by this time, and the Amyrlin means you to go through tonight as well. Not that I can see the point of such a hurry," she added, half to herself, "but when the Amyrlin commands, we obey."

Egwene let herself be pulled down the ramp in silence, a knot forming in her belly. Nynaeve had been far from forthcoming about what had happened when she was raised to the Accepted. She would not speak of it at all, except for a grimaced 'I hate Aes Sedai!' Egwene was trembling by the time the ramp finally ended at a broad hallway, far below the Tower in the rock of the island.

The hall was plain and undecorated, the pale rock through which it had been hewn smoothed but left otherwise untouched, and there was only one set of dark wooden doors, as tall and wide as fortress gates and as plain, although of smoothly finished and finely fitted planks, at the very end. Those great doors were so well balanced, though, that Sheriam easily pushed one open, and pulled Egwene through after her, into a great, domed chamber.

"Not before time!" Elaida snapped. She stood to one side in her red-fringed shawl, beside a table on which sat three large silver chalices.

Lamps on tall stands illumined the chamber, and what sat centered under the dome. Three rounded, silver arches, just tall enough to walk under, sitting on a thick silver ring with their ends touching where they joined it. An Aes Sedai sat cross-legged on the bare rock before each of the spots where arches joined ring, all three wearing their shawls.

Alanna was the sister of the Green Ajah, but she did not know the Yellow sister, or the White.

Surrounded by the glow of *saidar* embraced, the three Aes Sedai stared fixedly at the arches, and within the silver structure an answering glow flickered and grew. That structure was a *ter'angreal*, and whatever it had been made for in the Age of Legends, now novices passed through it to become Accepted. Inside it, Egwene would have to face her fears. Three times. The white light within the arches no longer flickered; it stayed within them as if confined, but it filled the space, made it opaque.

"Be easy, Elaida," Sheriam said calmly. "We will be done soon." She turned to Egwene. "Novices are given three chances at this. You may refuse twice to enter, but at the third refusal, you are sent away from the Tower forever. That is how it is done usually, and you certainly have the right to refuse, but I do not think the Amyrlin Seat will be pleased with you if you do."

"She should not be given this chance." There was iron in Elaida's voice, and her face was scarcely softer. "I do not care what her potential is. She should be put out of the Tower. Or failing that, set to scrubbing floors for the next ten years."

Sheriam gave the Red sister a sharp look. "You were not so adamant about Elayne. You demanded to be part of this, Elaida—perhaps because of Elayne—and you will do your part for this girl as well, as you are supposed to, or you will leave and I will find another."

The two Aes Sedai stared at one another until Egwene would not have been surprised to see the glow of the One Power surround them. Finally Elaida gave a toss of her head and sniffed loudly.

"If it must be done, let us do it. Give the miserable girl her chance to refuse and be done with it. It is late."

"I won't refuse." Egwene's voice quavered, but she steadied it and held her head high. "I want to go on."

"Good," Sheriam said. "Good. Now I will tell you two things no woman hears until she stands where you do. Once you begin, you must go on to the end. Refuse at any point, and you will be put out of the Tower just as if you had refused to begin for the third time. Second. To seek, to strive, is to know danger." She sounded as if she had said this many times. There was a light of sympathy in her eyes, but her face was almost as stern as Elaida's. The sympathy frightened Egwene more than the sternness. "Some women have entered, and never come out. When the *ter'angreal* was allowed to grow quiet, they—were—not—there. And they were never seen again. If you will survive, you must be steadfast. Falter, fail, and. . . ." Sheriam's face drove the unspoken words home; Egwene shivered. "This is your last chance. Refuse now, and it counts only as the first. You may still try twice more. If you accept now, there is no turning back. It is no shame to refuse. I could not do it, my first time. Choose."

They never came out? Egwene swallowed hard. *I want to be Aes Sedai. And first I have to become Accepted.* "I accept."

Sheriam nodded. "Then ready yourself."

Egwene blinked, then remembered. She had to enter unclothed. She bent to set down the tied bundle of papers Verin had given her—and hesitated. If she left them there, Sheriam or Elaida either one could go through them while she was inside the *ter'angreal.* They could find that smaller *ter'angreal* in her pouch. If she refused to go on, she could hide them away, perhaps leave them with Nynaeve. Her breath caught. *I cannot refuse now. I've already begun.*

"Have you already chosen to refuse, child?" Sheriam asked, frowning. "Knowing what that will mean, now?"

"No, Aes Sedai," Egwene said quickly. Hastily she undressed and folded her clothes, then set them on top of the pouch and the papers. It would have to do.

Beside the *ter'angreal,* Alanna suddenly spoke. "There is some sort of—resonance." She never took her eyes from the arches. "An echo, almost. I do not know from where."

"Is there a problem?" Sheriam asked sharply. She sounded surprised, too. "I will not send a woman in there if there is any problem."

Egwene looked yearningly at her piled clothes. *Please, yes, Light, a problem. Something that will let me hide those papers without refusing to enter.*

"No," Alanna said. "It is like having a biteme buzz 'round your head when you're trying to think, but it does not inter-fere. I would not have mentioned it, only it has never happened before that I ever heard." She shook her head. "It is gone now."

"Perhaps," Elaida said dryly, "others thought such a small thing was not worth mentioning."

"Let us go on." Sheriam's tone would not put up with any more distractions. "Come."

With a last glance at her clothes and the hidden papers, Egwene followed her toward the arches. The stone felt like ice under her bare feet.

"Whom do you bring with you, Sister?" Elaida intoned.

Continuing her measured pace, Sheriam replied, "One who comes as a candidate for Acceptance, Sister." The three Aes Sedai around the *ter'angreal* did not move.

"Is she ready?"

"She is ready to leave behind what she was, and, passing through her fears, gain Acceptance."

"Does she know her fears?"

"She has never faced them, but now is willing."

"Then let her face what she fears." Even in its formality, there was a note of satisfaction in Elaida's voice.

"The first time," Sheriam said, "is for what was. The way back will come but once. Be steadfast."

Egwene took a deep breath and stepped forward, through the arch and into the glow. Light swallowed her whole.

"Jaim Dawtry dropped by. There's odd news down from Baerlon with the peddler."

Egwene raised her head from the cradle she was rocking. Rand was standing in the doorway. For an instant her head spun. She looked from Rand—*my husband*—to the child in the cradle—*my daughter*—and back again, in wonder.

The way back will come but once. Be steadfast.

It was not her own thought, but a disembodied voice that could have been inside her head or out, male or female, yet emotionless and unknowable. Somehow, it did not seem strange to her.

The moment of wonder passed, and the only thing to wonder about was why she had thought anything seemed out of round. Of course Rand was her husband—her handsome, loving husband—and Joiya was her daughter—the most beautiful, sweetest little girl in the Two Rivers. Tam,

Rand's father, was out with the sheep, supposedly so Rand could work on the barn but really so he could have more time to play with Joiya. This afternoon Egwene's mother and father would come out from the village. And probably Nynaeve, to see if motherhood was interfering with Egwene's studies to replace Nynaeve as Wisdom one day.

"What kind of news?" she asked. She took up rocking the cradle again, and Rand came over to grin down at the tiny child wrapped in swaddling clothes. Egwene laughed softly to herself. He was so taken with his daughter that he did not hear what people said to him half the time. "Rand? What kind of news? Rand?"

"What?" His grin faded. "Strange news. War. There's some big war, taking up most of the world, so Jaim claims." That was strange news; word of wars seldom reached the Two Rivers till the wars were long done. "He says everybody is fighting some folk called the Shawkin, or the Sanchan, or something like that. I never heard of them."

Egwene knew—she thought she knew—Whatever it was, was gone.

"Are you all right?" he asked. "It's nothing to upset us here, my heart. Wars never touch the Two Rivers. We are too far from everywhere for anyone to care."

"I'm not upset. Did Jaim say anything else?"

"Nothing you can believe. He sounded like a Coplin. He said the peddler told him these people use Aes Sedai in battle, but then he claimed they offer a thousand gold marks to anyone who turns an Aes Sedai over to them. And they kill anybody who hides one. It makes no sense. Well, it's nothing to trouble us. It is all a long way from here."

Aes Sedai. Egwene touched her head. *The way back comes but once. Be steadfast.*

She noticed Rand had a hand to his own head. "The headaches?" she asked.

He nodded, his eyes suddenly tight. "That powder Nynaeve gave me doesn't seem to be working the last few days."

She hesitated. These headaches of his worried her. They grew worse every time they came, now. And worst of all was something she had not noticed at first, something she almost wished she never had noticed. When Rand's head hurt, strange things happened soon after. Lightning out of a clear sky, smashing to bits that huge oak stump he had been working two days to root out where he and Tam were clearing new field. Storms that Nynaeve did not hear coming when she listened to the wind. Wildfires in the forest. And the deeper his pain grew, the worse what followed. No one else had connected these things to Rand, not even Nynaeve, and Egwene was grateful for that. She did not want to think about what it might mean.

That is plain stupid foolish, she told herself. *I must know if I am going to help him.* Because she had a secret of her own, one that frightened her even as she tried to puzzle out what it meant. Nynaeve was teaching her the herbs, teaching Egwene to follow her as Wisdom, one day. Nynaeve's cures often worked in near miraculous fashion, wounds healed with barely a scar, sick folk brought back from the edge of the grave. But three times now, Egwene had cured someone Nynaeve had given up for dead. Three times she had sat to hold a hand through the last hour, and seen the person get up from a deathbed. Nynaeve had questioned her closely on what she had done, what herbs she had used, in what blending. Thus far, she had not found the courage to admit that she had done nothing. *I must have done something. Once might be chance, but three times. . . . I have to figure it out. I have to learn.* That set off a buzz in her head, as though the words were echoing inside her skull. *If I could do something for them, I can help my husband.*

"Let me try, Rand," she said. And as she stood, through the open door, she saw a silver arch standing in front of the house, an arch filled with white light. *The way back will come but once. Be steadfast.* She took two steps toward the door before she could stop herself.

She halted, looked back at Joiya gurgling in her cradle, at Rand still pressing hand to his head and looking at her as if wondering where she was going. "No," she said. "No, this is what I want. This is what I want! Why can't I have this, too?" She did not understand her own words. Of course, this was what she wanted, and she had it.

"What is it you want, Egwene?" Rand asked. "If it's anything I can get, you know I will. If I can't get it, I'll make it."

The way back will come but once. Be steadfast.

She took another step, into the doorway. The silver arch

beckoned her. Something waited on the other side. Something she wanted more than anything else in the world. Something she had to do.

"Egwene, I—"

There was a thump behind her. She looked over her shoulder to see Rand on his knees, bowed and head cradled in his hands. The pain had never hit him so hard. *What will come after this?*

"Ah, Light!" he panted. "Light! Hurts! Light, it hurts worse than ever! Egwene?"

Be steadfast.

It was waiting. Something she had to do. Had to. She took a step. It was hard, harder than anything she had ever done in her life. Outside, toward the arch. Behind her, Joiya was laughing.

"Egwene? Egwene, I can't—" He cut off with a loud groan.

Steadfast.

She stiffened her back and kept walking, but she could not keep the tears from rolling down her cheeks. Rand's groans built to a scream, drowning Joiya's laughter. From the corner of her eye, Egwene saw Tam coming, running as hard as he could.

He can't help, she thought, and tears became wracking sobs. *There is nothing he can do. But I could. I could.*

She stepped into the light, and was consumed.

Trembling and sobbing, Egwene stepped out of the arch, the same by which she had entered, memory cascading back with Sheriam's face confronting her. Cold clear water washed away her tears as Elaida slowly emptied a silver chalice over her head. Her weeping went on; she did not think it would ever end.

"You are washed clean," Elaida pronounced, "of what sin you may have done, and of those done against you. You are washed clean of what crime you may have committed, and of those committed against you. You come to us washed clean and pure, in heart and soul."

Light, Egwene thought as the water ran down her body, *let it be so. Can water wash away what I did?* "Her name was Joiya," she told Sheriam between sobs. "Joiya. Nothing can be worth what I just . . . what I. . . ."

"There is a price to become Aes Sedai," Sheriam replied, but the sympathy was back in her eyes, stronger than before. "There is always a price."

"Was it real? Did I dream it?" Weeping swallowed what she wanted to say. *Did I leave him to die? Did I leave my baby?*

Sheriam put an arm around her shoulders, began guiding her around the circle of arches. "Every woman I have ever watched come out of there has asked that question. The answer is, no one knows. It has been speculated that perhaps some of those who do not come back chose to stay because they found a happier place, and lived out their lives there." Her voice hardened. "If it is real, and they stayed from choice, then I hope the lives they live are far from happy. I have no sympathy for any who run from their responsibilities." The edge on her tone softened slightly. "Myself, I believe it is not real. But the danger is. Remember that." She stopped in front of the next glow-filled arch. "Are you ready?"

Shifting her feet, Egwene nodded, and Sheriam took her arm away.

"The second time is for what is. The way back will come but once. Be steadfast."

Egwene trembled. *Whatever happens, it cannot be worse than the last. It cannot be.* She stepped into the glow.

She stared down at her dress, blue silk sewn with pearls, all dusty and torn. Her head came up, and she took in the ruins of a great palace around her. The Royal Palace of Andor, in Caemlyn. She knew that, and wanted to scream.

The way back will come but once. Be steadfast.

The world was not the way she wanted it, no way that she could think of without wanting to cry, but all her tears had been cried away long ago, and the world was as it was. Ruin was what she expected to see.

Careless of making more rips in her dress but as careful of sound as a mouse, she climbed one of the piles of rubble and peered into the curving streets of the Inner City. As far as she could see in every direction lay ruin and desolation, buildings that looked as if they had been torn apart by madmen, thick plumes of smoke rising from the fires still burning. There were people in the streets, bands of armed men prowling, searching. And Trollocs. The men shied away from the Trollocs, and the Trollocs snarled at them and laughed, harsh guttural laughter. But they knew each other, worked together.

A Myrddraal came striding down the street, its black cloak swaying gently with its steps even when the wind gusted to drive dust and rubbish past it. Men and Trollocs alike cowered under its eyeless stare. "Hunt!" Its voice sounded like something long dead crumbling. "Do not stand there shivering! Find him!"

Egwene slipped back down the pile of jumbled stones as silently as she could.

The way back will come but once. Be steadfast.

She stopped, afraid the whisper had come from Shadowspawn. In some way, though, she was sure it had not. Glancing back over her shoulder, half fearful of seeing the Myrddraal standing where she had just been, she hurried onward and into the ruined palace, climbing over fallen timbers, squeezing between heavy blocks of collapsed masonry as she made her way. Once she stepped on a woman's arm, sticking out from under a mound of plaster and bricks that had been an interior wall and perhaps part of the floor above. She noticed the arm as little as she noticed the Great Serpent ring on one finger. She had trained herself not to see the dead buried in the refuse heap Trollocs and Darkfriends had made of Caemlyn. She could do nothing for the dead.

Forcing her way through a narrow gap where part of the ceiling had fallen, she found herself in a room half buried under what had stood above it. Rand lay with a heavy beam pinning him across the waist, his legs hidden beneath the stone blocks that filled half the room. Dust and sweat coated his face. He opened his eyes when she came near him.

"You came back." He forced the words out in a hoarse rasp. "I was afraid—No matter. You have to help me."

She sank wearily to the floor. "I could lift that beam easily with Air, but as soon as it moves, everything else will come down on top of you. On top of both of us. I cannot manage all of it, Rand."

His laugh was bitter and painful, and cut off almost as soon as it began. Fresh sweat glistened on his face, and he spoke with an effort. "I could shift the beam myself. You know that. I could shift that and the stones above, all of them. But I have to let go of myself to do it, and I can't trust that. I cannot trust—" He stopped, wheezing for breath.

"I do not understand," she said slowly. "Let go of yourself? What can't you trust?" *The way back will come but once. Be steadfast.* She rubbed her hands roughly over her ears.

"The madness, Egwene. I am—actually—holding it—at bay." His gasping laugh made her skin prickle. "But it takes everything I have just to do that. If I let go, even a little, even for an instant, the madness will have me. I won't care what I do then. You have to help me."

"How, Rand! I've tried everything I know. Tell me how, and I will do it."

His hand flopped out, fell just short of a dagger lying in the dust bare-bladed. "The dagger," he whispered. His hand made a painful journey back to his chest. "Here. In the heart. Kill me."

She stared at him, at the dagger, as if they were both poisonous serpents. "No! Rand, I will not. I cannot! How could you ask such a thing?"

Slowly his hand crept back toward the dagger. His fingers came short again. He strained, moaning, brushed it with a fingertip. Before he could try again, she kicked it away from him. He collapsed with a sob.

"Tell me why," she demanded. "Why would you ask me to—to murder you? I will Heal you, I will do anything to get you out of there, but I cannot kill you. Why?"

"They can turn me, Egwene." His breathing was so tortured, she wished she could weep. "If they take me— the Myrddraal—the Dreadlords—they can turn me to the Shadow. If madness has me, I cannot fight them. I won't know what they are doing till it is too late. If there is even a spark of life left when they find me, they can still do it. Please, Egwene. For the love of the Light. Kill me."

"I—I can't, Rand. Light help me, I cannot!"

The way back will come but once. Be steadfast.

She looked over her shoulder, and a silver arch filled with white light took up most of the open space among the rubble.

"Egwene, help me."

Be steadfast.

She stood and took a step toward the arch. It was right there in front of her. One more step, and. . . .

"Please, Egwene. Help me. I can't reach it. For the love of the Light, Egwene, help me!"

"I cannot kill you," she whispered. "I can't. Forgive me." She stepped forward.

"HELP ME, EGWENE!"

Light burned her to ash.

Staggering, she stepped out of the arch, neither noticing her nakedness nor caring. A shudder ran through her, and she covered her mouth with both hands. "I couldn't, Rand," she whispered. "I couldn't. Please forgive me." *Light help him. Please, Light help Rand.*

Cold water poured over her head.

"You are washed clean of false pride," Elaida intoned. "You are washed clean of false ambition. You come to us washed clean, in heart and soul."

As the Red sister turned away, Sheriam gently took Egwene's shoulders and guided her toward the last arch. "One more, child. One more, and it is done."

"He said they could turn him to the Shadow," Egwene mumbled. "He said the Myrddraal and the Dreadlords could force him."

Sheriam missed a step, and looked around quickly. Elaida was almost back to the table. The Aes Sedai surrounding the *ter'angreal* stared at it, seeming lost to anything else. "An unpleasant thing to talk of, child," Sheriam said finally, and softly. "Come. One more."

"Can they?" Egwene insisted.

"Custom," Sheriam said, "is not to speak of what happens within the *ter'angreal.* A woman's fears are her own."

"Can they?"

Sheriam sighed, glanced at the other Aes Sedai again, then dropped her voice to a whisper and spoke swiftly. "This is something known only to a few, child, even in the Tower.

You should not learn it now, if ever, but I will tell you. There is—a weakness in being able to channel. That we learn to open ourselves to the True Source means that we can be—opened to other things." Egwene shuddered. "Calm yourself, child. It is not so easily done. It is a thing not done, so far as I know—Light send it has not been done!—since the Trolloc Wars. It took thirteen Dreadlords—Darkfriends who could channel—weaving the flows through thirteen Myrddraal. You see? Not easily done. There are no Dreadlords today. This is a secret of the Tower, child. If others knew, we could never convince them they were safe. Only one who can channel can be turned in this way. The weakness of our strength. Everyone else is as safe as a fortress; only their own deeds and will can turn them to the Shadow."

"Thirteen," Egwene said in a tiny voice. "The same number who left the Tower. Liandrin, and twelve more."

Sheriam's face hardened. "That is nothing for you to dwell on. You will forget it." Her voice climbed to a normal volume. "The third time is for what will be. The way back will come but once. Be steadfast."

Egwene stared at the glowing arch, stared at some far distance beyond it. *Liandrin and twelve others. Thirteen Darkfriends who can channel. Light help us all.* She stepped into the light. It filled her. It shone through her. It burned her to the bone, seared her to the soul. She flashed incandescent in the light. *Light help me!* There was nothing but the light. And the pain.

Egwene stared into the standing mirror, and was not sure whether she was more surprised by the ageless smoothness of her face or the striped stole that hung around her neck. The stole of the Amyrlin Seat.

The way back will come but once. Be steadfast.

Thirteen.

She swayed, caught at the mirror and almost toppled it and herself to the blue-tiled floor of her dressing chamber. *Something is wrong,* she thought. The wrongness had nothing to do with her sudden dizziness, or at least that was not what felt wrong. It was something else. But she had no idea what.

There was an Aes Sedai at her elbow, a woman with

Sheriam's high cheekbones but dark hair and concerned brown eyes, and the hand-wide stole of the Keeper on her shoulders. Not Sheriam, though. Egwene had never seen her before; she was sure she knew her as well as she knew herself. Haltingly, she put a name to the woman. Beldeine.

"Are you ill, Mother?"

Her stole is green. That means she was raised from the Green Ajah. The Keeper always comes from the same Ajah as the Amyrlin she serves. Which means if I'm the Amyrlin—if?—then I was Green Ajah, too. That thought shook her. Not that she had been Green Ajah, but that she had to reason it out. *Light, something is wrong with me.*

The way back will come bu. . . . The voice in her head trailed away to finish in a buzz.

Thirteen Darkfriends.

"I am well, Beldeine," Egwene said. The name felt strange on her tongue; it felt as if she had been saying it for years. "We mustn't keep them waiting." *Keep who waiting?* She did not know, except that she felt infinitely sad about ending that wait, endlessly reluctant.

"They will be growing impatient, Mother." There was a hesitation in Beldeine's voice, as if she felt the same reluctance as Egwene, but for a different reason. Unless Egwene missed her guess, behind that outer calm, Beldeine was terrified.

"In that case, we had best be about it."

Beldeine nodded, then took a deep breath before crossing the carpet to where her staff of office, topped with the snowdrop White Flame of Tar Valon, stood propped beside the door. "I suppose we must, Mother." She took up the staff and opened the door for Egwene, then hurried ahead so that they made a procession of two, Keeper of the Chronicles leading the Amyrlin Seat.

Egwene noticed little of the corridors they took. All her attention was directed inward. *What is the matter with me? Why can't I remember? Why is so much of what I . . . almost remember wrong?* She touched the seven-striped stole on her shoulders. *Why am I half sure I'm still a novice?*

The way back will come but on—This time it ended abruptly.

Thirteen of the Black Ajah.

She stumbled at that. It was a frightening thought, but it

chilled her to the marrow beyond fear. It felt—personal. She wanted to scream, to run and hide. She felt as if they were after her. *Nonsense. The Black Ajah has been destroyed.* That seemed an odd thought, too. Part of her remembered something called the Great Purge. Part of her was sure no such thing had happened.

Eyes fixed ahead, Beldeine had not noticed her stumble. Egwene had to lengthen her stride to catch up. *This woman is scared to her toenails. What in the Light is she taking me to?*

Beldeine stopped before tall, paired doors, their dark wood each inlaid with a large silver Flame of Tar Valon. She wiped her hands on her dress, as if they were suddenly sweaty, before opening one door and leading Egwene up a straight ramp of the same silver-streaked white stone that made Tar Valon's walls. Even here it seemed to shine.

The ramp let into a large, circular room under a domed ceiling at least thirty paces high. A raised platform ran around the outer edge of the room, fronted by steps except where this ramp and two others came out, spaced equally around the circle. The Flame of Tar Valon lay centered in the floor, surrounded by widening spirals of color, the colors of the seven Ajahs. At the opposite side of the room from where the ramp entered, a high-backed chair stood, heavy and ornately carved in vines and leaves, painted in the colors of all the Ajahs.

Beldeine rapped her staff sharply on the floor. There was a tremor in her voice. "She comes. The Watcher of the Seals. The Flame of Tar Valon. The Amyrlin Seat. She comes."

With a rustle of skirts, shawled women on the platform got up from their chairs. Twenty-one chairs in groupings of three, each triad painted and cushioned in the same color as the fringe on the shawls of the women who stood before them.

The Hall of the Tower, Egwene thought as she crossed the floor to her chair. The Amyrlin Seat's chair. *That's all it is. The Hall of the Tower, and the Sitters for the Ajahs. I've been here thousands of times.* But she could not remember one of them. *What am I doing in the Hall of the Tower? Light, they'll skin me alive when they see. . . .* She was not sure what it was they would see, only that she prayed they did not.

The way back will come but—
The way back will—
The way—
The Black Ajah waits. That, at least, was whole. It came
from everywhere. Why did no one else seem to hear it?

Settling in the chair of the Amyrlin Seat—the chair that
was also the Amyrlin Seat—she realized she had no idea
what to do next. The other Aes Sedai had seated themselves
when she did, all but Beldeine, who stood beside her with
the staff, swallowing nervously. They all seemed to be
waiting on her.

"Begin," she said finally.

It seemed to be enough. One of the Red Sitters stood.
Egwene was shocked to recognize Elaida. At the same
time she knew that Elaida was foremost of the Sitters for
the Red, and her own bitterest enemy. The look on Elaida's
face as she stared across the chamber made Egwene shiver
inside. It was stern and cold—and triumphant. It promised
things best not thought of.

"Bring him in," Elaida said loudly.

From one of the ramps—not the one Egwene had entered
by—came the crunch of boots on stone. People appeared.
A dozen Aes Sedai surrounding three men, two of them
burly guards with the white teardrops of the Flame of Tar
Valon on their chests, tugging the chains in which the third
stumbled as if dazed.

Egwene jerked forward in her chair. The chained man
was Rand. Eyes half-closed, head sagging, he seemed
nearly asleep, moving only as the chains directed.

"This man," Elaida proclaimed, "has named himself
the Dragon Reborn." There was a buzz of distaste, not as
if the listeners were surprised, but as though it were not
something they wanted to hear. "This man has channeled
the One Power." The buzz was louder now, disgusted and
tinged with fear. "There is only one penalty for this, known
and recognized in every nation, but pronounced only here,
in Tar Valon, in the Hall of the Tower. I call on the Amyrlin
Seat to pronounce the sentence of gentling on this man."

Elaida's eyes glittered at Egwene. *Rand. What do I do?*
Light, what do I do?

"Why do you hesitate?" Elaida demanded. "The sentence

has been set down for three thousand years. Why do you hesitate, Egwene al'Vere?"

One of the Green Sitters was on her feet, anger bright through her calm. "Shame, Elaida! Show respect for the Amyrlin Seat! Show respect for the Mother!"

"Respect," Elaida answered coldly, "can be lost as well as won. Well, Egwene? Can it be you show your weakness, your unfitness for your office, at last? Can it be you will not pronounce sentence on this man?"

Rand tried to lift his head and failed.

Egwene struggled to her feet, head spinning, trying to remember she was the Amyrlin Seat with the power to command all these women, screaming that she was a novice, that she did not belong here, that something was dreadfully wrong. "No," she said shakily. "No, I cannot! I will not—"

"She betrays herself!" Elaida's shout drowned out Egwene's attempt to speak. "She condemns herself out of her own mouth! Take her!"

As Egwene opened her mouth, Beldeine moved beside her. Then the Keeper's staff struck her head.

Blackness.

First there was pain in her head. There was something hard under her back, and cold. Next came the voices. Murmurs.

"Is she still unconscious?" It was a rasp, a file on bone.

"Do not worry," a woman said from far, far away. She sounded uneasy, afraid, and trying not to show either. "She will be dealt with before she knows what is happening to her. Then she is ours, to do with as we will. Perhaps we will give her to you for sport."

"After you make your own use of her."

"Of course."

The distant voices moved further away.

Her hand brushed against her leg, touched bare, pebbly flesh. She opened her eyes a crack. She was naked, bruised, lying on a rough wooden table, in what seemed to be a disused storeroom. Splinters stuck her back. There was a metallic taste of blood in her mouth.

A cluster of Aes Sedai stood to one side of the room, talking among themselves, voices low yet urgent. The pain in her head made thinking difficult, but it seemed important to count them. Thirteen.

Another group, black-cloaked and hooded men, joined the Aes Sedai, who seemed caught between cowering and trying to dominate with their presence. One of the men turned his head to look toward the table. The dead white face within the hood had no eyes.

Egwene had no need to count the Myrddraal. She knew. Thirteen Myrddraal, and thirteen Aes Sedai. Without another thought, she screamed in pure terror. Yet even in the midst of fear that tried to split her bones, she reached out for the True Source, clawed desperately for *saidar*.

"She's awake!"

"She cannot be! Not yet!"

"Shield her! Quickly! Quickly! Cut her off from the Source!"

"It's too late! She is too strong!"

"Seize her! Hurry!"

Hands reached for her arms and legs. Pasty pale hands like slugs under rocks, ordered by minds behind pale, eyeless faces. If those hands touched her flesh, she knew she would go mad. The Power filled her.

Flames burst from Myrddraal skin, ripping through black cloth as if they were solid daggers of fire. Shrieking Halfmen crisped and burned like oiled paper. Fist-sized chunks of stone tore themselves free of the walls and whizzed across the room, producing shrieks and grunts as they thudded into flesh. The air stirred, shifted, howled into a whirlwind.

Slowly, painfully, Egwene pushed herself off the table. The wind whipped her hair and made her stagger, but she continued to drive it as she stumbled toward the door. An Aes Sedai loomed in front of her, a woman bruised and bleeding, surrounded by the glow of the Power. A woman with death in her dark eyes.

Egwene's mind put a name to the face. Gyldan. Elaida's closest confidante, always whispering together in corners, closeting themselves in the night. Egwene's mouth tightened. Disdaining stones and wind, she balled up her fist and punched Gyldan between the eyes as hard as she could. The Red sister—the *Black* sister—crumpled as if her bones had melted.

Rubbing her knuckles, Egwene staggered out into the hall. *Thank you, Perrin*, she thought, *for showing me how to do that. But you didn't tell me how much it hurts when you do.*

Shoving the door shut against the wind, she channeled. Stones around the doorway shivered, cracked, settled against the wood. It would not hold them for long, but anything that slowed pursuit for even a minute was worth doing. Minutes might mean life. Gathering her strength, she forced herself to break into a run. It wobbled, but at least it was a run.

She must find some clothes, she decided. A woman clothed had more authority than the same woman naked, and she was going to need every bit of authority. They would look for her first in her rooms, but she had a spare dress and shoes in her study—and another stole—and that lay not far off.

It was unnerving, trotting through empty hallways. The White Tower no longer held the numbers it once had, but there was usually someone about. The loudest sound was the slap of her bare soles on the tiles.

She hurried through the antechamber of her study to the inner room, and at last she found someone. Beldeine was sitting on the floor, head in her hands, weeping.

Egwene stopped warily, as Beldeine raised reddened eyes to meet hers. No glow of *saidar* surrounded the Keeper, but Egwene was still cautious. And confident. She could not see her own glow, of course, but the power—the Power—surging through her was enough. Especially when added to her secret.

Beldeine scrubbed a hand across tearstained cheeks. "I had to. You must understand. I had to. They. . . . They. . . ." She took a deep, shuddering breath; it all came out in a rush. "Three nights ago they took me while I slept and stilled me." Her voice rose to a near shriek. "They *stilled* me! I cannot channel any longer!"

"Light," Egwene breathed. The rush of *saidar* cushioned her against the shock. "The Light help and comfort you, my daughter. Why didn't you tell me? I would have. . . ." She let it trail away, knowing there was nothing she could do.

"What would you have done? What? Nothing! There's nothing you can do. But they said they could give it back to

me, with the power of . . . the power of the Dark One." Her
eyes squeezed shut, leaking tears. "They hurt me, Mother,
and they made me. . . . Oh, Light, they hurt me! Elaida told
me they would make me whole again, make me able to
channel again, if I obeyed. That's why I. . . . I had to!"

"So Elaida *is* Black Ajah," Egwene said grimly. A narrow wardrobe stood against the wall, and in it hung a green
silk dress, kept for when she had no time to return to her
rooms. A striped stole hung beside the dress. She began to
dress herself, quickly. "What have they done with Rand?
Where have they taken him? Answer me, Beldeine! Where
is Rand al'Thor?"

Beldeine huddled, lips trembling, eyes turned bleakly
inward, but finally she roused herself enough to say, "The
Traitor's Court, Mother. They took him to the Traitor's
Court."

Shivers assaulted Egwene. Shivers of fear. Shivers of
rage. Elaida had not waited, not even an hour. The Traitor's
Court was used for only three purposes: executions, the
stilling of an Aes Sedai, or the gentling of a man who could
channel. But all of the three took an order from the Amyrlin Seat. *So who wears the stole out there?* Elaida, she was
sure. *But how could she make them accept her so quickly,
with me not tried, not sentenced? There cannot be another
Amyrlin until I've been stripped of stole and staff. And
they'll not find that easy to do. Light! Rand!* She started for
the door.

"What can you do, Mother?" Beldeine cried. "What can
you do?" It was not clear whether she meant for Rand or for
herself.

"More than anyone suspects," Egwene said. "I never held
the Oath Rod, Beldeine." Beldeine's gasp followed her from
the room.

Egwene's memory still played hide-and-seek with her.
She knew no woman could achieve the shawl and the ring
without pledging the Three Oaths with the Oath Rod firmly
in hand, the *ter'angreal* sealing her to keep those oaths as
if they had been engraved on her bones at birth. No woman
became Aes Sedai without being bound to them. Yet she
knew that somehow, in some fashion she could not begin to
dredge up, she had done just that.

Her shoes clicked swiftly as she ran. At least she knew

now why the halls were empty. Every Aes Sedai, except perhaps those she had left in the storeroom, every Accepted, every novice, even all the servants, would be gathered in the Traitor's Court, according to custom, to watch the will of Tar Valon made fact.

And the Warders would be ringing the courtyard against the possibility that someone might try to free the man to be gentled. The remnants of Guaire Amalasan's armies had attempted it, at the end of what some called the War of the Second Dragon, just before Artur Hawkwing's rise had given Tar Valon other things to worry it, and so had Raolin Darksbane's followers, long years earlier. Whether Rand had any followers or not, she could not remember, but Warders remembered such things, and guarded against them.

If Elaida, or another, truly did wear the stole of the Amyrlin, the Warders might well not admit her to the Traitor's Court. She knew she could force a way in. It would need to be done quickly; there was no point if Rand was gentled while she was still wrapping Warders in Air. Even Warders would break if she loosed the lightnings on them, and balefire, and broke the ground under their feet. *Balefire?* she wondered. But it would also do no good if she broke Tar Valon's power to save Rand. She had to save both.

Well short of the ways that led to the Traitor's Court, she turned aside and climbed, up stairs and ramps that grew narrower and tighter the higher she went, until she thrust open a trapdoor and climbed out onto a sloping tower top, a roof of nearly white tiles. From there, she could see across other roofs, past other towers, into the broad open well of the Traitor's Court.

The court was crowded except for a cleared space in the middle. People filled the windows overlooking it, crowded the balconies and even the rooftops, but she could make out the lone man, small at that distance, swaying in his chains in the center of the cleared space. Rand. Twelve Aes Sedai surrounded him, and another—who Egwene knew had to be wearing a seven-striped stole, even though she could not distinguish it—stood before Rand. *Elaida.* The words she must be saying crept into Egwene's head.

This man, abandoned of the Light, has touched saidin, *the male half of the True Source. Thus do we hold him.*

*Most abominably has this man channeled the One Power,
knowing that* saidin *is tainted by the Dark One, tainted for
men's pride, tainted for men's sin. Thus do we chain him.*

Forcefully, Egwene pushed the rest of it out of her
thoughts. *Thirteen Aes Sedai. Twelve sisters and the Amyrlin, the traditional number for gentling. The same number
as for. . . .* She rid herself of that, too. She had no time for
anything but what she was there to do. If she could only
manage to reason out how.

At that distance, she thought she could manage to lift
him with Air. Pick him right out of the circle of Aes Sedai
and float him straight to her. Maybe. Even if she could find
the strength, even if she did not drop him to his death halfway, it would be a slow process, with him a helpless target
for archers, and the glow of *saidar* pointing out her own
position for any Aes Sedai who looked. Any Myrddraal, for
that matter.

"Light," she muttered, "there's no other way short of
starting a war inside the White Tower. And I may do that
anyway." She gathered the Power, separated skeins, directed flows.

The way back will come but once. Be steadfast.

It had been so long since she last heard those words that
she gave a start, slipped on the smooth tiles, barely caught
herself short of the edge. The ground lay a hundred paces
down. She looked over her shoulder.

There on the tower top, tilted to sit flat against the sloping tiles, was a silver arch filled with a glowing light. The
arch flickered and wavered; streaks of angry red and yellow
darted through the white light.

The way back will come but once. Be steadfast.

The archway thinned to transparency, grew solid again.

Frantic, Egwene gazed toward the Traitor's Court. There
had to be time. There had to be. All she needed was a few
minutes, perhaps ten, and luck.

Voices bored into her head, not the disembodied, unknowable voice that warned her to be steadfast, but women's
voices she almost believed she knew.

*—can't hold much longer. If she does not come out
now—*

Hold! Hold, burn you, or I'll gut you all like sturgeons!

—going wild, Mother! We can't—

The voices faded to a drone, the drone to silence, but the unknowable spoke again.

The way back will come but once. Be steadfast.

There is a price to be Aes Sedai.

The Black Ajah waits.

With a scream of rage, of loss, Egwene threw herself at the arch as it shimmered like a heat haze. She almost wished she would miss and plunge to her death.

Light plucked her apart fiber by fiber, sliced the fibers to hairs, split the hairs to wisps of nothing. All drifted apart on the light. Forever.

CHAPTER
23

Sealed

Light pulled her apart fiber by fiber, sliced the fibers to hairs that drifted apart, burning. Drifting and burning, forever. Forever.

Egwene stepped out of the silver arch cold and stiff with anger. She wanted the iciness of anger to counter the searing of memory. Her body remembered burning, but other memories scored and scorched more deeply. Anger cold as death.

"Is that all there is for me?" she demanded. "To abandon him again and again. To betray him, fail him, again and again? Is that what there is for me?"

Suddenly she realized that all was not as it should be. The Amyrlin was there now, as Egwene had been taught she would be, and a shawled sister from each Ajah, but they all stared at her worriedly. Two Aes Sedai now sat at each place around the *ter'angreal*, sweat running down their faces. The *ter'angreal* hummed, almost vibrated, and violent streaks of color tore the white light inside the arches.

The glow of *saidar* briefly enveloped Sheriam as she put a hand on Egwene's head, sending a new chill through her. "She is well." The Mistress of Novices sounded relieved. "She is unharmed." As if she had not expected it.

Tension seemed to go out of the other Aes Sedai facing Egwene. Elaida let out a long breath, then hurried away for the last chalice. Only the Aes Sedai around the *ter'angreal* did not relax. The hum had lessened, and the light began the flickering that signaled the *ter'angreal* was settling toward quiescence, but those Aes Sedai looked as if they were fighting it every inch of the way.

"What . . . ? What happened?" Egwene asked.

"Be silent," Sheriam said, but gently. "For now, be silent. You are well—that is the main thing—and we must complete the ceremony." Elaida came, close to running, and handed the final silver chalice to the Amyrlin.

Egwene hesitated only a moment before kneeling. *What happened?*

The Amyrlin emptied the chalice slowly over Egwene's head. "You are washed clean of Egwene al'Vere from Emond's Field. You are washed clean of all ties that bind you to the world. You come to us washed clean, in heart and soul. You are Egwene al'Vere, Accepted of the White Tower." The last drop splashed onto Egwene's hair. "You are sealed to us, now."

The last words seemed to have a special meaning, just between Egwene and the Amyrlin. The Amyrlin thrust the chalice at one of the other Aes Sedai and produced a gold ring in the shape of a serpent biting its own tail. Despite herself, Egwene trembled as she raised her left hand, trembled again as the Amyrlin slipped the Great Serpent ring onto the third finger. When she became Aes Sedai, she could wear the ring on the finger she chose, or not at all if it was necessary to hide who she was, but the Accepted wore it there.

Unsmiling, the Amyrlin pulled her to her feet. "Welcome, Daughter," she said, kissing her cheek. Egwene was surprised to feel a thrill. Not child, but daughter. Always before she had been child. The Amyrlin kissed her other cheek. "Welcome."

Stepping back, the Amyrlin regarded her critically, but spoke to Sheriam. "Get her dry and into some clothes, then be certain she is well. Certain, you understand."

"I am certain, Mother." Sheriam sounded surprised. "You saw me delve her."

The Amyrlin grunted, and her eyes shifted to the *ter'angreal*. "I mean to know what went wrong tonight." She strode away in the direction of her glare, skirts swaying purposefully. Most of the other Aes Sedai joined her around the *ter'angreal*, now only a silver structure of arches on a ring.

"The Mother is worried about you," Sheriam said as she

drew Egwene to one side, to where there was a thick towel
for her hair, and another for the rest of her.

"How much reason did she have?" Egwene asked. *The
Amyrlin wants nothing to happen to her hound till the deer
is pulled down.*

Sheriam did not answer. She merely frowned slightly,
then waited until Egwene was dry before handing her a
white dress banded at the bottom with seven rings.

She slipped into that dress with a flash of disappointment.
She was one of the Accepted, with the ring on her finger
and the bands on her dress. *Why don't I feel any different?*

Elaida came over, her arms filled with Egwene's novice
dress and shoes, her belt and pouch. And the papers Verin
had given her. In Elaida's hands.

Egwene made herself wait for the Aes Sedai to hand the
bundle to her rather than snatch them away. "Thank you,
Aes Sedai." She tried to eye the papers surreptitiously; she
could not tell if they had been disturbed. The string was still
tied. *How would I know if she's read all of them?* Squeezing
her pouch under cover of the novice dress, she felt the peculiar ring, the *ter'angreal,* inside. *At least that's still here.
Light, she could have taken that, and I don't know that I
would have minded. Yes, I would. I think I would.*

Elaida's face was as cold as her voice. "I did not want you
to be brought forward tonight. Not because I feared what happened; no one could foresee that. But because of what you
are. A wilder." Egwene tried to protest, but Elaida kept on, as
implacable as a mountain glacier. "Oh, I know you learned to
channel under Aes Sedai teaching, but you are still a wilder.
A wilder in spirit, a wilder in ways. You have vast potential,
else you would never have survived in there tonight, but potential changes nothing. I do not believe you will ever be part
of the White Tower, not in the way the rest of us are, no matter
on which finger you wear your ring. It would have been better
for you had you settled for learning enough to stay alive, and
gone back to your sleepy village. Far better." Turning on her
heel, she stalked away, out of the chamber.

If she isn't Black Ajah, Egwene thought sourly, *she's
the next thing to it.* Aloud, she muttered to Sheriam, "You
could have said something. You could have helped me."

"I would have helped a novice, child," Sheriam replied
calmly, and Egwene winced. She was back to "child" again.

"I try to protect novices where they need it, since they cannot protect themselves. You are Accepted, now. It is time for you to learn to protect yourself."

Egwene studied Sheriam's eyes, wondering if she had imagined an emphasis on that last sentence. Sheriam had had as much opportunity as Elaida to read the list of names, to decide that Egwene was mixed in with the Black Ajah. *Light, you're becoming suspicious of everybody. Better that than dead, or captured by thirteen of them and. . . .* Hastily, she stopped that line of thought; she did not want it in her head. "Sheriam, what did happen tonight?" she asked. "And don't put me off." Sheriam's eyebrows rose almost to her scalp, it seemed, and she hastily amended her question. "Sheriam Sedai, I mean. Forgive me, Sheriam Sedai."

"Remember you aren't Aes Sedai yet, child." Despite the steel in her voice, a smile touched Sheriam's lips, yet it vanished as she went on. "I do not know what happened. Except that I very much fear you almost died."

"Who knows what happens to those who do not come out of a *ter'angreal*?" Alanna said as she joined them. The Green sister was known for her temper and her sense of humor, and some said she could flash from one to the other and back again before you could blink, but the look she gave Egwene was almost diffident. "Child, I should have stopped this when I had the chance, when I first noticed that—reverberation. It came back. That is what happened. It came back a thousandfold. Ten thousand. The *ter'angreal* almost seemed to be trying to shut off the flow from *saidar*—or melt itself through the floor. You have my apologies, though words are not enough. Not for what almost happened to you. I say this, and by the First Oath you know it is true. To show my feelings, I will ask the Mother to let me share your time in the kitchens. And, yes, your visit to Sheriam, too. Had I done as I should, you would not have been in danger of your life, and I will atone for it."

Sheriam's laugh was scandalized. "She will never allow that, Alanna. A sister in the kitchens, much less. . . . It is unheard of. It's impossible! You did what you believed right. There is no fault to you."

"It was not your fault, Alanna Sedai," Egwene said. *Why is Alanna doing this? Unless maybe to convince me she* didn't *have anything to do with whatever went wrong. And maybe so she can keep an eye on me all the time*. It was that image, a proud Aes Sedai up to her elbows in greasy pots three times a day just to watch someone, that convinced her she was letting her imagination run away with her. But it was also unthinkable that Alanna should do as she said she would. In any case, the Green sister certainly had had no chance to see the list of names while tending the *ter'angreal*. *But if Nynaeve is right, she wouldn't need to see those names to want to kill me if she is Black Ajah. Stop that!* "Really, it wasn't."

"Had I done as I should," Alanna maintained, "it would never have happened. The only time I have ever seen anything like it was once years ago when we tried to use a *ter'angreal* in the same room with another that may have been in some way related to it. It is extremely rare to find two such as that. The pair of them melted, and every sister within a hundred paces had such a headache for a week that she couldn't channel a spark. What's the matter, child?"

Egwene's hand had tightened around her pouch till the twisted stone ring impressed itself on her palm through the thick cloth. Was it warm? *Light, I did it myself.* "Nothing, Alanna Sedai. Aes Sedai, you did nothing wrong. You have no reason to share my punishments. None at all. None!"

"A bit vehement," Sheriam observed, "but true." Alanna only shook her head.

"Aes Sedai," Egwene said slowly, "what does it mean to be Green Ajah?" Sheriam's eyes opened wider with amusement, and Alanna grinned openly.

"Just with the ring on your finger," the Green sister said, "and already trying to decide which Ajah to choose? First, you must love men. I don't mean be in love with them, but love them. Not like a Blue, who merely likes men, so long as they share her causes and do not get in her way. And certainly not like a Red, who despises them as if every one of them were responsible for the Breaking." Alviarin, the White sister who had come with the Amyrlin, gave them a cool look and moved on. "And not like a White," Alanna said with a laugh, "who has no room in her life for any passions at all."

"That was not what I meant, Alanna Sedai. I want to know what it *means* to be a Green sister." She was not sure Alanna would understand, because she was not certain she herself understood what she wanted to know, but Alanna nodded slowly as if she did.

"Browns seek knowledge, Blues meddle in causes, and Whites consider the questions of truth with implacable logic. We all do some of it all, of course. But to be a Green means to stand ready." A note of pride entered Alanna's voice. "In the Trolloc Wars, we were often called the Battle Ajah. All Aes Sedai helped where and when they could, but the Green Ajah alone was always with the armies, in almost every battle. We were the counter to the Dreadlords. The Battle Ajah. And now we stand ready, for the Trollocs to come south again, for Tarmon Gai'don, the Last Battle. We will be there. That is what it means to be a Green."

"Thank you, Aes Sedai," Egwene said. *That is what I was? Or what I will be? Light, I wish I knew if it was real, if it had anything at all to do with here and now.*

The Amyrlin joined them, and they swept deep curtsies to her. "Are you well, Daughter?" she asked Egwene. Her eyes flicked to the corner of the papers sticking out from under the novice dress in Egwene's hands, then back to Egwene's face immediately. "I will know the why of what occurred tonight before I am done."

Egwene's cheeks reddened. "I am well, Mother."

Alanna surprised her by asking the Amyrlin just what she had said she would.

"I never heard of such a thing," the Amyrlin barked. "The owner doesn't muck out with the bilge boys even if he has run the boat on a mudflat." She glanced at Egwene, and worry tightened her eyes. And anger. "I share your concern, Alanna. Whatever this child has done, it did not deserve that. Very well. If it will assuage your feelings, you may visit Sheriam. But it is to be strictly between you two. I'll not have Aes Sedai held up to ridicule, even inside the Tower."

Egwene opened her mouth to confess all and let them take the ring—*I don't want the bloody thing, really*—but Alanna forestalled her.

"And the other, Mother?"

"Do not be ridiculous, Daughter." The Amyrlin was angry, and sounded more so by the word. "You'd be a laughingstock inside the day, except for those who decided you were mad. And don't think it would not follow you. Tales like that have a way of traveling. You would find stories told of the *scullion Aes Sedai* from Tear to Maradon. And that would reflect on every sister. No. If you need to rid yourself of some feeling of guilt and cannot handle it as a grown woman would, very well. I have told you that you may visit Sheriam. Accompany her tonight when you leave here. That will give you the rest of the night to decide if it was of any help. And tomorrow you can start finding out what went wrong here tonight!"

"Yes, Mother." Alanna's voice was perfectly neutral.

The desire to confess had died in Egwene. Alanna had shown only one brief flash of disappointment, when she realized the Amyrlin would not allow her to join Egwene in the kitchens. *She doesn't want to be punished any more than any sensible person does. She did want an excuse to be in my company. Light, she couldn't have deliberately caused the* ter'angreal *to go wild; I did that. Can she be Black Ajah?*

Wrapped in thought, Egwene heard a throat cleared, then again, more roughly. Her eyes focused. The Amyrlin was staring right into her, and when she spoke, she bit off each word.

"Since you seem to be asleep standing up, child, I suggest you go to bed." For one instant her glance flashed to the nearly concealed papers in Egwene's hands. "You have much work to do tomorrow, and for many days thereafter." Her eyes held Egwene's a moment longer, and then she was striding away before any of them could curtsy.

Sheriam rounded on Alanna as soon as the Amyrlin was out of earshot. The Green Aes Sedai glowered and took it in silence. "You *are* mad, Alanna! A fool, and doubly a fool if you think I will go lightly on you just because we were novices together. Are you taken by the Dragon, to—?" Suddenly Sheriam became aware of Egwene, and the target of her anger shifted. "Did I not hear the Amyrlin Seat order you to your bed, Accepted? If you breathe a word of this, you will wish I had buried you in a field to manure the ground. And I will see you in my study in the morning, when the bell rings First and not one breath later. Now, go!"

Egwene went, her head spinning. *Is there anybody I can trust? The Amyrlin? She sent us off chasing thirteen of the Black Ajah and forgot to mention that thirteen is just the number needed to turn a woman who can channel to the Shadow against her will. Who can I trust?*

She did not want to be alone, could not stand the thought of it, and so she hurried to the Accepted's quarters, thinking that tomorrow she would be moving there herself, and immediately after knocking pushed open Nynaeve's door. She could trust her with anything. Her and Elayne.

But Nynaeve was seated in one of the two chairs, with Elayne's head buried in her lap. Elayne's shoulders shook to the sound of weeping, the softer weeping that comes after no energy is left for deeper sobs but the emotion still burns. Dampness shone on Nynaeve's cheeks, too. The Great Serpent gleaming on her hand, smoothing Elayne's hair, matched the ring on the hand Elayne used to clutch at Nynaeve's skirt.

Elayne lifted a face red and swollen from long crying, sniffing through her sobs when she saw Egwene. "I could not be that awful, Egwene. I just couldn't!"

The accident with the *ter'angreal*, Egwene's fear that someone might have read the papers Verin had given her, her suspicions of everyone in that chamber, all these had been terrible, but they had buffered her in a rough, ungentle way from what had happened inside the *ter'angreal*. They had come from outside; the other was inside. Elayne's words stripped the buffer away, and what was inside hit Egwene as if the ceiling had collapsed. Rand her husband, and Joiya her baby. Rand pinned and begging her to kill him. Rand chained to be gentled.

Before she was aware of moving, she was on her knees beside Elayne, all the tears that should have fallen earlier coming out in a flood. "I couldn't help him, Nynaeve," she sobbed. "I just left him there."

Nynaeve flinched as if struck, but the next moment her arms were around both Egwene and Elayne, hugging them, rocking them. "Hush," she crooned softly. "It eases with time. It eases, a little. One day we will make them pay our price. Hush. Hush."

CHAPTER
24

Scouting and Discoveries

Sunlight through the carved shutters, creeping across the bed, woke Mat. For a moment, he only lay there, frowning. He had not reasoned out any plan for escaping from Tar Valon before sleep had overtaken him, but neither had he given up. Too much memory still lay covered with fog, but he would not give up.

Two serving women came bustling with hot water and a tray heavy with food, laughing and telling him how much better he looked already, and how soon he would be back on his feet if he did what the Aes Sedai told him. He answered them curtly, trying not to sound bitter. *Let them think I mean to go along.* His stomach rumbled at the smells from the tray.

When they left, he tossed aside his blanket and hopped out of bed, pausing only to stuff half a slice of ham into his mouth before pouring out water to wash and shave. Staring into the mirror above the washstand, he paused in lathering his face. He did look better.

His cheeks were still hollow, but not quite as hollow as they had been. The dark circles had vanished from under his eyes, which no longer seemed set so deep in his head. It was as if every bite he had eaten the night before had gone into putting meat on his bones. He even felt stronger.

"At this rate," he muttered, "I will be gone before they know it." But he was still surprised when, after shaving, he sat down and consumed every scrap of ham, turnip, and pear on the tray.

He was sure they expected him to climb back into bed once he had eaten, but instead, he dressed. Stamping his feet to settle them in his boots, he eyed his spare clothes and decided to leave them, for now. *I have to know what I'm doing, first. And if I have to leave them. . . .* He tucked the dice cups into his pouch. With those, he could get all the clothes he needed.

Opening the door, he peeked out. More doors paneled in pale, golden wood lined the hall, with colorful tapestries between, and a runner of blue carpet ran down the white-tiled floor. But there was no one out there. No guard. He tossed his cloak over one shoulder and hurried out. Now to find a way outside.

It took some little wandering, down stairs and along corridors and across open courts, before he found what he wanted, a doorway to the outside, and he saw people before then: serving women and white-clad novices hurrying about their chores, the novices running even harder than the servants; a handful of roughly dressed male servants carrying large chests and other heavy loads; Accepted in their banded dresses. Even a few Aes Sedai.

The Aes Sedai did not seem to notice him as they strode along, intent on whatever purpose, or else they gave him no more than a passing glance. His were country clothes, but well made; he did not look a vagabond, and the serving men showed that men were allowed in this part of the Tower. He suspected they might take him for another servant, and that was just as well with him, so long as no one asked him to lift anything.

He did feel some regret that none of the women he saw was Egwene or Nynaeve, or even Elayne. *She's a pretty one, even if she does have her nose in the air half the time. And she could tell me how to find Egwene and the Wisdom. I cannot go without saying goodbye. Light, I don't suppose one of them would turn me in, just because they are becoming Aes Sedai themselves? Burn me, for a fool! They'd never do that. Anyway, I will risk it.*

But once out-of-doors, under a bright morning sky with only a few drifting white clouds, he put the women from his mind for the time. He was looking across a wide, flag-stoned yard with a plain stone fountain in the middle and a barracks on the other side that was made of gray stone. It looked almost like a huge boulder among the few trees growing out of rimmed holes in the flagstones close by.

Guardsmen in their shirtsleeves sat in front of the long, low building, tending weapons and armor and harness. Guardsmen were what he wanted, now.

He sauntered across the yard and watched the soldiers as if he had nothing better to do. As they worked they talked and laughed among themselves like men after the harvest. Now and again one of them looked curiously at Mat as he strolled among them, but none challenged his right to be there. From time to time he asked a casual question. And finally he got the answer he sought.

"Bridge guard?" said a stocky, dark-haired man no more than five years older than Mat. His words had a heavy Illianer accent. Young he might have been, but a thin white scar crossed his left cheek, and the hands oiling his sword moved with familiarity and competence. He squinted up at Mat before returning to his task. "I do be on the bridge guard, and back there again this even. Why do you ask?"

"I was just wondering what conditions were like on the other side of the river." *I might as well find that out, too.* "Good for traveling? It can't be muddy, unless you have had more rain than I know about."

"Which side of the river?" the guardsman asked placidly. His eyes did not lift from the oiled rag he was running along his blade.

"Uh . . . east. The east side."

"No mud. Whitecloaks." The man leaned to one side to spit, but his voice did not change. "Whitecloaks do be poking their noses into every village for ten miles. They have no hurt anyone yet, but them just being there do upset the folk. Fortune prick me if I do no think they wish to provoke us, for they do look as if they would attack if they could. No good for anyone who do want to travel."

"What about west, then?"

"The same." The guardsman raised his eyes to Mat's. "But you will no be crossing, lad, east or west. Your name do be Matrim Cauthon, or Fortune abandon me. Last night a sister, herself in person, did come to the bridge where I did stand guard. She did drill your features at us till each could speak them back to her. A guest, she did say, and no to be harmed. But no to be allowed out of the city, either, if you must be tied hand and foot to keep you from it." His eyes narrowed. "Is it that you did steal something from them?" he asked doubtfully. "You do no have the look of those the sisters do guest."

"I didn't steal anything!" Mat said indignantly. *Burn me, I didn't even get a chance to work around to it easy. They must all know me.* "I'm no thief!"

"No, it is no that I do see in your face. No thievery. But you do have the look of the fellow who did try to sell me the Horn of Valere three days gone. So he did claim it did be, all bent and battered as it did be. Do you have a Horn of Valere to sell? Or mayhap it do be the Dragon's sword?"

Mat gave a jump at the mention of the Horn, but he managed to keep his voice level. "I was sick." Others of the guardsmen were looking at him now. *Light, they'll all know I am not supposed to leave, now.* He forced a laugh. "The sisters Healed me." Some of the guardsmen frowned at him. Perhaps they thought other men should show more respect than to call the Aes Sedai sisters. "I guess the Aes Sedai don't want me to go before I have all my strength back." He tried willing the men, all of those watching him now, to accept that. *Just a man who was Healed. Nothing more. No reason to trouble yourself about him any further.*

The Illianer nodded. "You do have the look of sickness in your face, too. Perhaps that do be the reason. But never did I hear of so much effort to keep one sick man in the city."

"That's the reason," Mat said firmly. They were all still looking at him. "Well, I need to be going. They said I have to take walks. Lots of long walks. To build up strength, you know."

He felt their eyes following him as he left, and he scowled. He had simply meant to find out how well his description had been passed around. If only the officers among the bridge guards had had it, he might have been able to slip by. He had always been good at slipping into places unseen. And out. It was a talent you developed when your mother always suspected you were up to some mischief and you had two sisters to tell on you. *And now I've made sure half a barracks full of guardsmen will know me. Blood and bloody ashes!*

Much of the Tower grounds were gardens full of trees, leatherleaf and paperbark and elms, and he soon found himself walking along a wide, twisting graveled path. It could have led through countryside, if not for the towers visible over the treetops. And the white bulk of the Tower itself, behind him but pressing on him as if he carried it on his shoulders. If there were ways out of the Tower grounds that were not watched, this seemed the place to find them. If they existed.

A girl in novice white appeared ahead on the path, striding purposefully toward him. Wrapped in her own thoughts, she did not see him at first. When she came close enough for him to make out her big, dark eyes and the way her hair was braided, he grinned suddenly. He knew this girl—memory drifting up from shrouded depths—though he would never have expected to find her here. He had never expected to see her again at all. He grinned to himself. *Good luck to balance bad.* As he remembered, she had quite an eye for the boys.

"Else," he called to her. "Else Grinwell. You remember me, don't you? Mat Cauthon. A friend and I visited your father's farm. Remember? Have you decided to become Aes Sedai, then?"

She stopped short, staring at him. "What are you doing up and out?" she said coldly.

"You know about that, do you?" He moved closer to her, but she stepped back, keeping her distance. He stopped. "It's not catching. I was Healed, Else." Those large, dark eyes seemed more knowing than he remembered, and not nearly so warm, but he supposed studying to be an Aes Sedai could do that. "What is the matter, Else? You look like you don't know me."

"I know you," she said. Her manner was not as he remembered, either; he thought she could give Elayne lessons now. "I have . . . work to be about. Let me by."

He grimaced. The path was broad enough for six to walk abreast without crowding. "I told you it isn't catching."

"Let me by!"

Muttering to himself, he stepped to one edge of the gravel. She went past him along the other side, watching to make sure he did not come closer. Once by, she quickened her steps, glancing over her shoulder at him until she was out of sight around a bend.

Wanted to make sure I didn't follow her, he thought sourly. *First the guardsmen, and now Else. My luck is not in, today.*

He started off again, and soon heard a ferocious clatter from one side ahead, like dozens of sticks being beat together. Curious, he turned off toward it, into the trees.

A little way brought him to a large expanse of bare ground, the earth beaten hard, at least fifty paces across and nearly twice as long. At intervals around it under the trees stood wooden stands holding quarterstaffs, and practice swords made of strips of wood bound loosely together, and a few real swords and axes and spears.

Spaced across the open ground, pairs of men, most stripped to the waist, flailed at each other with more practice swords. Some moved so smoothly it almost seemed they danced with one another, flowing from stance to stance, stroke to counterstroke in continuous motion. There was nothing quickly apparent aside from skill to mark them from the others, but Mat was sure he was watching Warders.

Those who did not move so smoothly were all younger, each pair under the watchful eyes of an older man who seemed to radiate a dangerous grace even standing still. *Warders and students*, Mat decided.

He was not the only audience. Not ten paces from him, half a dozen women with ageless Aes Sedai faces and as many more in the banded white dresses of the Accepted stood watching one pair of students, bare to the waist and slick with sweat, under the guidance of a Warder shaped much like a block of stone. The Warder used a short-stemmed pipe in one hand, trailing tabac smoke, to direct his pupils.

Sitting down cross-legged under a leatherleaf, Mat rooted three large pebbles out of the ground and began to juggle them idly. He did not feel weak, exactly, but it was good to sit. If there was a way out of the Tower grounds, it would not go away while he took a short rest.

Before he had been there five minutes he knew who it was the Aes Sedai and Accepted were watching. One of the blocky Warder's pupils was a tall, lithe young man who moved like a cat. *And almost as pretty as a girl*, Mat thought wryly. Every woman was staring at the tall fellow with sparkling eyes, even the Aes Sedai.

The tall man handled his practice sword almost as deftly as the Warders, now and then earning an approving gravelly comment from his teacher. It was not that his opponent, a youth more Mat's age, with red-gold hair, was unskilled. Far from it, as much as Mat could see, though he had never claimed to know anything about swords. The golden-haired man met every lightning attack, turning it away before the bound strips could strike him, and even launched an occasional attack of his own. But the handsome fellow countered those attacks and flowed back into his own in the space of a heartbeat.

Mat shifted the pebbles to one hand, but kept them spinning in the air. He did not think he would care to face either of them. Certainly not with a sword.

"Break!" The Warder's voice sounded like rocks emptying out of a bucket. Chests heaving, the two men let their practice swords fall to their sides. Sweat matted their hair. "You can rest till I finish my pipe. But rest fast; I am almost in the dottle."

Now that they had stopped dancing about, Mat got a good look at the youth with the red-gold hair and let the pebbles drop. *Burn me, I'll bet my whole purse that's Elayne's brother. And the other one's Galad, or I'll eat my boots.* On the journey from Toman Head it had seemed half of Elayne's conversation had been of Gawyn's virtues and Galad's vices. Oh, Gawyn had some vices according to Elayne, but they were small; to Mat they sounded like the sort of things no one but a sister would consider vices at all. As for Galad, once Elayne was pinned down, he sounded like what every mother said she wanted her son to be. Mat did not think he wanted to spend much time in Galad's company. Egwene blushed whenever Galad was mentioned, though she seemed to think no one noticed.

A ripple seemed to pass through the watching women when Gawyn and Galad stopped, and they appeared on the point of stepping forward almost as one. But Gawyn caught sight of Mat, said something quietly to Galad, and the two of them walked by the women. The Aes Sedai and Accepted turned to follow with their eyes. Mat scrambled to his feet as the pair approached.

"You are Mat Cauthon, are you not?" Gawyn said with a grin. "I was sure I recognized you from Egwene's description. And Elayne's. I understand you were sick. Are you better now?"

"I'm fine," Mat said. He wondered if he was supposed to call Gawyn "my Lord" or something of the sort. He had refused to call Elayne "my Lady"—not that she had demanded it, actually—and he decided he would not do her brother better.

"Did you come to the practice yard to learn the sword?" Galad asked.

Mat shook his head. "I was only out walking. I don't know much about swords. I think I'll put my trust in a good bow, or a good quarterstaff. I know how to use those."

"If you spend much time around Nynaeve," Galad said, "you'll need bow, quarterstaff, *and* sword to protect yourself. And I don't know whether that would be enough."

Gawyn looked at him wonderingly. "Galad, you just very nearly made a joke."

"I do have a sense of humor, Gawyn," Galad said with a frown. "You only think I do not because I do not care to mock people."

With a shake of his head, Gawyn turned back to Mat. "You should learn something of the sword. Everyone can do with that sort of knowledge these days. Your friend—Rand al'Thor—carried a most unusual sword. What do you hear of him?"

"I haven't seen Rand in a long time," Mat said quickly. Just for a moment, when he had mentioned Rand, Gawyn's look had gained intensity. *Light, does he know about Rand? He couldn't. If he did, he'd be denouncing me for a Darkfriend just for being Rand's friend. But he knows something.* "Swords aren't the be-all and end-all, you know. I could do fairly well against either of you, I think, if you had a sword and I had my quarterstaff."

Gawyn's cough was obviously meant to swallow a laugh. Much too politely, he said, "You must be very good." Galad's face was frankly disbelieving.

Perhaps it was that they both clearly thought he was making a wild boast. Perhaps it was because he had mishandled questioning the guardsman. Perhaps it was because Else, who had such an eye for the boys, wanted nothing to do with him, and all those women were staring at Galad like cats watching a jug of cream. Aes Sedai and Accepted or not, they were still women. All these explanations ran through Mat's head, but he rejected them angrily, especially the last. He was going to do it because it would be fun. And it might earn some coin. His luck would not even have to be back.

"I will wager," he said, "two silver marks to two from each of you that I can beat both of you at once, just the way I said. You can't have fairer odds than that. There are two of you, and one of me, so two to one are fair odds." He almost laughed aloud at the consternation on their faces.

"Mat," Gawyn said, "there's no need to make wagers. You have been sick. Perhaps we will try this some time when you are stronger."

"It would be far from a fair wager," Galad said. "I'll not take your wager, now or later. You are from the same village as Egwene, are you not? I . . . I would not have her angry with me."

"What does she have to do with it? Thump me once with one of your swords, and I will hand over a silver mark to each of you. If I thump you till you quit, you give me two each. Don't you think you can do it?"

"This is ridiculous," Galad said. "You would have no chance against one trained swordsman, let alone two. I'll not take such advantage."

"Do you think that?" asked a gravel voice. The blocky Warder joined them, thick black eyebrows pulled down in a scowl. "You think you two are good enough with your swords to take a boy with a stick?"

"It would not be fair, Hammar Gaidin," Galad said.

"He has been sick," Gawyn added. "There is no need for this."

"To the yard," Hammar grated with a jerk of his head back over his shoulder. Galad and Gawyn gave Mat regretful looks, then obeyed. The Warder eyed Mat up and down doubtfully. "Are you sure you're up to this, lad? Now I take a close look at you, you ought to be in a sickbed."

"I am already out of one," Mat said, "and I'm up to it. I have to be. I don't want to lose my two marks."

Hammar's heavy brows rose in surprise. "You mean to hold to that wager, lad?"

"I need the money." Mat laughed.

His laughter cut off abruptly as he turned toward the nearest stand that held quarterstaffs and his knees almost buckled. He stiffened them so quickly he thought anyone who noticed would think he had just stumbled. At the stand he took his time choosing out a staff, nearly two inches thick and almost a foot taller than he was. *I have to win this. I opened my fool mouth, and now I have to win. I can't afford to lose those two marks. Without those to build on, it will take forever to win the money I need.*

When he turned back, the quarterstaff in both hands before him, Gawyn and Galad were already waiting out where they had been practicing. *I have to win.* "Luck," he muttered. "Time to toss the dice."

Hammar gave him an odd look. "You speak the Old Tongue, lad?"

Mat stared back at him for a moment, not speaking. He felt cold to the bone. With an effort, he made his feet start out onto the practice yard. "Remember the wager," he said loudly. "Two silver marks from each of you against two from me."

A buzz rose from the Accepted as they realized what was happening. The Aes Sedai watched in silence. Disapproving silence.

Gawyn and Galad split apart, one to either side of him, keeping their distance, neither with his sword more than half-raised.

"No wager," Gawyn said. "There's no wager."

At the same time, Galad said, "I'll not take your money like this."

"I mean to take yours," Mat said.

"Done!" Hammar roared. "If they have not the nerve to cover your wager, lad, I'll pay the score myself."

"Very well," Gawyn said. "If you insist on it—done!"

Galad hesitated a moment more before growling, "Done, then. Let us put an end to this farce."

The moment's warning was all Mat needed. As Galad rushed at him, he slid his hands along the quarterstaff and pivoted. The end of the staff thudded into the tall man's ribs, bringing a grunt and a stumble. Mat let the staff bounce off Galad and spun, carrying it on around just as Gawyn came within range. The staff dipped, darted under Gawyn's practice sword, and clipped his ankle out from under him. As Gawyn fell, Mat completed the spin in time to catch Galad across his upraised wrist, sending his practice sword flying. As if his wrist did not pain him at all, Galad threw himself into a smooth, rolling dive and came up with his sword in both hands.

Ignoring him for the moment, Mat half turned, twisting his wrists to whip the length of the staff back beside him. Gawyn, just starting to rise, took the blow on the side of his head with a loud thump only partly softened by the padding of hair. He went down in a heap.

Mat was only vaguely aware of an Aes Sedai rushing out to tend Elayne's fallen brother. *I hope he's all right. He should be. I've hit myself harder than that falling off a fence.* He still had Galad to deal with, and from the way Galad was poised on the balls of his feet, sword raised precisely, he had begun to take Mat seriously.

Mat's legs chose that moment to tremble. *Light, I can't weaken now.* But he could feel it creeping back in, the wobbly feeling, the hunger as if he had not eaten for days. *If I wait for him to come to me, I'll fall on my face.* It was hard to keep his knees straight as he started forward. *Luck, stay with me.*

From the first blow, he knew that luck, or skill, or whatever had brought him this far, was still there. Galad managed to turn that one with a sharp clack, and the next, and the next, and the next, but strain stiffened his face. That smooth swordsman, almost as good as the Warders, fought with every ounce of his skill to keep Mat's staff from him. He did not attack; it was all he could do to defend. He moved continually to the side, trying not to be forced back, and Mat pressed him, staff a blur. And Galad stepped back, stepped back again, wooden blade a thin shield against the quarterstaff.

Hunger gnawed at Mat as if he had swallowed weasels. Sweat rolled down into his eyes, and his strength began to fade as if it leached out with the sweat. *Not yet. I can't fall yet. I have to win. Now.* With a roar, he threw all his reserves into one last surge.

The quarterstaff flickered past Galad's sword and in quick succession struck knee, wrist, and ribs and finally thrust into Galad's stomach like a spear. With a groan, Galad folded over, fighting not to fall. The staff quivered in Mat's hands, on the point of a final crushing thrust to the throat. Galad sank to the ground.

Mat almost dropped the quarterstaff when he realized

what he had been about to do. *Win, not kill. Light, what was I thinking?* Reflexively he grounded the butt of the staff, and as soon he did, he had to clutch at it to hold himself erect. Hunger hollowed him like a knife reaming marrow from a bone. Suddenly he realized that not only the Aes Sedai and Accepted were watching. All practice, all learning, had stopped. Warders and students alike stood watching him.

Hammar moved to stand beside Galad, still groaning on the ground and trying to push himself up. The Warder raised his voice to shout, "Who was the greatest blademaster of all time?"

From the throats of dozens of students came a massed bellow. "Jearom, Gaidin!"

"Yes!" Hammar shouted, turning to make sure all heard. "During his lifetime, Jearom fought over ten thousand times, in battle and single combat. He was defeated once. By a farmer with a quarterstaff! Remember that. Remember what you just saw." He lowered his eyes to Galad, and lowered his voice as well. "If you cannot get up by now, lad, it is finished." He raised a hand, and the Aes Sedai and Accepted rushed to surround Galad.

Mat slid down the staff to his knees. None of the Aes Sedai even glanced his way. One of the Accepted did, a plump girl he might have liked to ask for a dance if she were not going to be an Aes Sedai. She frowned at him, sniffed, and turned back to peering at what the Aes Sedai were doing around Galad.

Gawyn was on his feet, Mat noted with relief. He pulled himself up as Gawyn came over. *Mustn't let them know. I'll never get out of here if they decide to nurse me from sunup to sunup.* Blood darkened the red-gold hair on the side of Gawyn's head, but there was neither cut nor bruise apparent.

He pushed two silver marks into Mat's hand with a dry "I think I will listen next time." He noticed Mat's glance, touched his head. "They Healed it, but it was not bad. Elayne has given me worse more than once. You are good with that."

"Not as good as my da. He's won the quarterstaff at Bel Tine every year as long as I can remember, except once or twice when Rand's da did." That interested look came back into Gawyn's eyes, and Mat wished he had never mentioned Tam al'Thor. The Aes Sedai and the Accepted were all still clustered around Galad. "I . . . I must have hurt him badly. I did not mean to do that."

Gawyn glanced that way—there was nothing to be seen but two rings of women's backs, Accepted's white dresses making the outer ring as they peered over the shoulders of crouching Aes Sedai—and laughed. "You did not kill him—I heard him groaning—so he should be on his feet by now, but they are not going to let this chance pass, now they have their hands on him. Light, four of them are Green Ajah!" Mat gave him a confused look—*Green Ajah? What does that have to do with anything?*—and Gawyn shook his head. "It doesn't matter. Just rest assured that the worst Galad has to worry about is finding himself Warder to a Green Aes Sedai before his head clears." He laughed. "No, they would not do that. But I will wager you those two marks of mine in your hand that some of them wish they could."

"Not your marks," Mat said, shoving them in his coat pocket, "mine." The explanation had made little sense to him. Except that Galad was well. All he knew of what passed between Warders and Aes Sedai were the pieces he remembered of Lan and Moiraine, and there was nothing there like what Gawyn seemed to be suggesting. "Do you think they'd mind if I collected my wager from him?"

"They very likely would," Hammar said dryly as he joined them. "You are not very popular with those particular Aes Sedai right now." He snorted. "You'd think even Green Aes Sedai would be better than girls just loose from their mother's apron strings. He isn't *that* good-looking."

"He is not," Mat agreed.

Gawyn grinned at both of them, until Hammar glared at him. "Here," the Warder said, pushing two more silver coins into Mat's hand. "I will collect from Galad later. Where are you from, lad?"

"Manetheren." Mat froze when he heard the name come out of his mouth. "I mean, I'm from the Two Rivers. I have heard too many old stories." They just looked at him without saying anything. "I. . . . I think I will go back and see if I can find something to eat." Not even the Midmorning bell had rung yet, but they nodded as if it made sense.

He kept the quarterstaff—no one had told him to put it back—and walked slowly until the trees hid him from the practice yard. When they did, he leaned on the staff as though it were the only thing holding him up. He was not sure it was not.

He thought that if he parted his coat, he would see a hole where his stomach should have been, a hole growing larger as it pulled the rest of him in. But he hardly thought of hunger. He kept hearing voices in his head. *You speak the Old Tongue, lad? Manetheren.* It made him shiver. *Light help me, I keep digging myself deeper. I have to get out of here. But how?* He hobbled back toward the Tower proper like an old, old man. *How?*

CHAPTER
25

Questions

E gwene lay across Nynaeve's bed, chin in her hands,
watching Nynaeve pace back and forth. Elayne
sprawled in front of the fireplace, which was still full
of the ashes of last night's fire. Yet again Elayne was studying the list of names Verin had produced, patiently reading every word one more time. The other pages, the list of
ter'angreal, sat on the table; after one shocked reading they
had not discussed that one further, though they had talked
of everything else. And argued, too.

Egwene stifled a yawn. It was only the middle of the
morning, but none of them had gotten much sleep. They
had had to be up early. For the kitchens, and breakfast. For
other things that she refused to think about. The little sleep
she herself had managed had been filled with unpleasant
dreams. *Maybe Anaiya could help me understand them,
those that need understanding, but. . . . But what if she is
Black Ajah?* After staring at every woman in that chamber
last night, wondering which was Black Ajah, she was finding trust for anyone but her two companions hard to come
by. But she did wish she had some way of interpreting those
dreams.

The nightmares about what had happened inside the
ter'angreal last night were easy enough to understand, though
they had made her wake up weeping. She had dreamed of
the Seanchan, too, of women in dresses with lightning bolts
woven on their breasts, collaring a long line of women who
wore Great Serpent rings, forcing them to call lightning
against the White Tower. That had started her awake in a
cold sweat, but that had to be just a nightmare, too. And

the dream about Whitecloaks binding her father's hands. A nightmare brought on by homesickness, she supposed. But the others. . . .

She glanced at the other two women again. Elayne was still reading. Nynaeve still paced with that steady tread.

There had been a dream of Rand, reaching for a sword that seemed to be made of crystal, never seeing the fine net dropping over him. And one of him kneeling in a chamber where a parched wind blew dust across the floor, and creatures like the one on the Dragon banner, but much smaller, floated on that wind, and settled into his skin. There had been a dream of him walking down into a great hole in a black mountain, a hole filled with a reddish glare as from vast fires below, and even a dream of him confronting Seanchan.

About that last, she was uncertain, but she knew the others had to mean something. Back when she had been sure she could trust Anaiya, back before she had left the Tower, before she learned the reality of the Black Ajah, a little cautious questioning of the Aes Sedai—done, oh, so carefully, so Anaiya would think it no more than the curiosity she showed about other things—had revealed that a Dreamer's dreams about *ta'veren* were almost always significant, and the more strongly *ta'veren*, the more "almost always" became "certainly."

But Mat and Perrin were *ta'veren*, too, and she had also dreamed of them. Odd dreams, even more difficult to understand than the dreams of Rand. Perrin with a falcon on his shoulder, and Perrin with a hawk. Only the hawk held a leash in her talons—Egwene was somehow convinced both hawk and falcon were female—and the hawk was trying to fasten it around Perrin's neck. That made her shiver even now; she did not like dreams about leashes. And that dream of Perrin—with a beard!—leading a huge pack of wolves that stretched as far as the eye could see. Those about Mat had been even nastier. Mat, placing his own left eye on a balance scale. Mat, hanging by his neck from a tree limb. There had been a dream of Mat and Seanchan, too, but she was willing to dismiss that as a nightmare. It had to have been just a nightmare. Just like the one about Mat speaking the Old Tongue. That had to come from what she had heard during his Healing.

She sighed, and the sigh turned into another yawn. She and the others had gone to his room after breakfast to see how he was, but he had not been there.

He is probably well enough to go dancing. Light, now I will probably dream about him dancing with Seanchan! No more dreams, she told herself firmly. *Not now. I will think about them when I am not so tired.* She thought of the kitchens, of the midday meal soon to come, and then supper, and breakfast again tomorrow, and pots and cleaning and scrubbing going on forever. *If I am ever not tired again.* Shifting her position on the bed, she looked at her friends again. Elayne still had her eyes on the list of names. Nynaeve's steps had slowed. *Any moment now, Nynaeve will say it again. Any moment.*

Nynaeve came to a halt, staring down at Elayne. "Put those away. We have been over them twenty times, and there isn't a word that helps. Verin gave us rubbish. The question is, was it all she had, or did she give us rubbish on purpose?"

As expected. Maybe half an hour till she says it again. Egwene frowned down at her hands, glad she could not see them clearly. The Great Serpent ring looked—out of place—on hands all wrinkled from long immersion in hot, soapy water.

"Knowing their names helps," Elayne said, still reading. "Knowing what they look like helps."

"You know very well what I mean," Nynaeve snapped.

Egwene sighed and folded her arms in front of her, rested her chin on them. When she had come out of Sheriam's study that morning, with the sun still not even a glint on the horizon, Nynaeve had been waiting with a candle in the cold, dark hall. She had not been seeing very clearly, but she was sure Nynaeve had looked ready to chew stone. And knowing chewing stones would not change anything in the next few minutes. That was why she was so irritable. *She's as touchy about her pride as any man I ever met. But she should not take it out on Elayne and me. Light, if Elayne can stand it, she should be able to. She isn't the Wisdom anymore.*

Elayne hardly appeared to notice whether Nynaeve was irritable or not. She frowned into the distance thoughtfully. "Liandrin was the only Red. All the other Ajahs lost two each."

"Oh, do be quiet, child," Nynaeve said.

Elayne wiggled her left hand to display her Great Serpent ring, gave Nynaeve a meaningful look, and went right on. "No two were born in the same city, and no more than two in any one country. Amico Nagoyin was the youngest, some fifteen years older than Egwene and I. Joiya Byir could be our great-grandmother's great-grandmother."

Egwene did not like it that one of the Black Ajah shared her daughter's name. *Fool girl! People sometimes have the same name, and you never had a daughter. It wasn't real!*

"And what does that tell us?" Nynaeve's voice was too calm; she was ready to explode like a wagon full of fireworks. "What secrets have you found in it that I missed? I am getting old and blind, after all!"

"It tells us it is all too neat," Elayne said calmly. "What chance that thirteen women chosen solely because they were Darkfriends would be so neatly arrayed across age, across nations, across Ajahs? Shouldn't there be perhaps three Reds, or four born in Cairhien, or just two the same age, if it was all chance? They had women to choose from or they could not have chosen so random a pattern. There are still Black Ajah in the Tower, or elsewhere we don't know about. It must mean that."

Nynaeve gave her braid one ferocious tug. "Light! I think you may be right. You did find secrets I couldn't. Light, I was hoping they all went with Liandrin."

"We do not even know that she is their leader," Elayne said. "She could have been ordered to . . . to *dispose* of us." Her mouth twisted. "I am afraid I can only think of one reason for them to go to such lengths to spread everything out so, to avoid any pattern except a lack of pattern. I think it means there *is* a pattern of some kind to the Black Ajah."

"If there's a pattern," Nynaeve said firmly, "we will find it. Elayne, if watching your mother run her court taught you to think like this, I'm glad you watched closely." Elayne's answering smile made a dimple in her cheek.

Egwene eyed the older woman carefully. It seemed Nynaeve was finally ready to stop being a bear with a sore tooth. She raised her head. "Unless they want us to think they're hiding a pattern, so we will waste our time hunting for it when there isn't one. I am not saying there isn't; I am only saying we do not know yet. Let's look for it, but I think we ought to look at other things, too, don't you?"

"So you finally decided to rouse," Nynaeve said. "I thought you had gone to sleep." But she was still smiling.

"She is right," Elayne said disgustedly. "I have built a bridge out of straw. Worse than straw. Wishes. Maybe you are right, too, Nynaeve. What use is this—this rubbish?" She snatched one paper out of the stack in front of her. "Rianna has black hair with a white streak above her left ear. If I am close enough to see that, it's closer than I want to be." She grabbed another page. "Chesmal Emry is one of the most talented Healers anyone has seen in years. Light, could you imagine being Healed by one of the Black Ajah?" A third sheet. "Marillin Gemalphin is fond of cats and goes out of her way to help injured animals. Cats! Paah!" She scrabbled all the pages together, crumpling them in her fists. "It *is* useless rubbish."

Nynaeve knelt beside her and gently pried her hands from around the papers. "Perhaps, and perhaps not." She smoothed the pages carefully on her breast. "You found in them something for us to look for. Perhaps we will find more, if we are persistent. And there is the other list." Both her eyes and Elayne's darted to Egwene, brown and blue alike frowning worriedly.

Egwene avoided looking at the table where the other sheets lay. She did not want to think about them, but she could not avoid it. The list of *ter'angreal* had etched itself into her mind.

Item. A rod of clear crystal, smooth and perfectly clear, one foot long and one inch in diameter. Use unknown. Last study made by Corianin Nedeal. Item. A figurine of an unclothed woman in alabaster, one hand tall. Use unknown. Last study made by Corianin Nedeal. Item. A disc, apparently of simple iron yet untouched by rust, three inches in diameter, finely engraved on both sides with a tight spiral. Use unknown. Last study made by Corianin Nedeal. Item. Too many items, and more than half the "use unknowns" last studied by Corianin Nedeal. Thirteen of them, to be exact.

Egwene shivered. *It's getting so I do not even like to think of that number.*

The knowns on the list were fewer, not all of any apparent real use, but hardly more comforting, as she saw it. A wooden carving of a hedgehog, no bigger than the last joint of a man's thumb. Such a simple thing, and surely harmless. Any woman who tried to channel through it went to sleep. Half a day of peaceful, dreamless sleep, but it was too close not to make her skin crawl. Three more had to do with sleep in some way. It was almost a relief to read of a fluted rod of black stone, a full pace in length, that produced balefire, with the notation DANGEROUS AND ALMOST IMPOSSIBLE TO CONTROL writ so strong in Verin's hand that it tore the paper in two places. Egwene still had no idea what balefire was, but though it surely sounded dangerous if anything ever did, it just as surely had nothing to do Corianin Nedeal or dreams.

Nynaeve carried the smoothed-out pages to the table and set them down. She hesitated before spreading the others out and running her finger down one page, then the next. "Here's one Mat would enjoy," she said in a voice much too light and airy. "Item. A carved cluster of six spotted dice, joined at the corners, less than two inches across. Use unknown, save that channeling through it seems to suspend chance in some way, or twist it." She began to read aloud. "'Tossed coins presented the same face every time, and in one test landed balanced on edge one hundred times in a row. One thousand tosses of the dice produced five crowns one thousand times.'" She gave a forced laugh. "Mat would love that."

Egwene sighed and got to her feet, walked stiffly to the fireplace. Elayne scrambled up, watching as silently as Nynaeve. Pushing her sleeve as far up her arm as it would go, Egwene reached carefully up the chimney. Her fingers touched wool on the smoke shelf, and she pulled out a wadded, singed stocking with a hard lump in the toe. She brushed a smear of soot from her arm, then took the stocking to the table and shook it out. The twisted ring of striped, flecked stone spun across the tabletop and fell flat atop a page of the *ter'angreal* list. For a few moments they just stared at it.

"Perhaps," Nynaeve said finally, "Verin simply missed the fact that so many of them were last studied by Corianin." She did not sound as if she really believed it.

Elayne nodded, but doubtfully. "I saw her walking in the

rain once, soaking wet, and took a cloak to her. She was so wrapped up in whatever she was thinking, I do not believe she knew it was raining until I put the cloak around her shoulders. She could have missed it."

"Maybe," Egwene said. "If she did not, she had to know I'd notice as soon as I read the list. I do not know. Sometimes I think Verin notices more than she lets on. I just do not know."

"So there's Verin to suspect," Elayne sighed. "If she is Black Ajah, then they know exactly what we are doing. And Alanna." She gave Egwene an uncertain, sidelong look.

Egwene had told them everything. Except what happened inside the *ter'angreal* during her testing; she could not bring herself to talk about that, any more than Nynaeve or Elayne could tell of their testings. Everything that happened in the testing chamber, what Sheriam had said about the terrible weakness conferred by the ability to channel, every word Verin had said, whether it seemed important or not. The one part they had had trouble accepting was Alanna; Aes Sedai just did not do things like that. No one in her right mind did anything like that, but Aes Sedai least of all.

Egwene glowered at them, almost hearing them say it. "Aes Sedai are not supposed to lie, either, but Verin and the Mother seem awfully close with what they tell us. There are not *supposed* to be Black Ajah."

"I like Alanna." Nynaeve tugged her braid, then shrugged. "Oh, very well. Perha—That is, she did behave oddly."

"Thank you," Egwene said, and Nynaeve gave her an acknowledging nod as if she had heard no sarcasm.

"In any case, the Amyrlin knows of it, and she can keep an eye on Alanna far more easily than we can."

"What about Elaida and Sheriam?" Egwene asked.

"I have never been able to like Elaida," Elayne said, "but I cannot truly believe she is Black Ajah. And Sheriam? It's impossible."

Nynaeve snorted. "It should be impossible for any of them. When we do find them, there is nothing says they'll all be women we do not like. But I don't mean to put suspicion—not this kind of suspicion!—on any woman. We need more to go on than that they might have seen something they shouldn't." Egwene nodded agreement as quickly as Elayne, and Nynaeve went on: "We will tell the Amyrlin that much, and put no more weight to it than it deserves. If she ever looks in on us as she said she would. If you are with us when she comes, Elayne, remember she does not know about you."

"I am not likely to forget it," Elayne said fervently. "But we should have some other way to get word to her. My mother would have planned it better."

"Not if she could not trust her messengers," Nynaeve said. "We will wait. Unless you two think one of us should have a talk with Verin? No one would think that remarkable."

Elayne hesitated, then gave her head a small shake. Egwene was quicker and more vigorous with hers; slip of the mind or not, Verin had left out too much to be trusted.

"Good." Nynaeve sounded more than satisfied. "I am just as pleased we cannot talk to the Amyrlin when we choose. This way we make our own decisions, act when and as we decide, without her directing our every step." Her hand ran down the pages listing stolen *ter'angreal* as if she were reading it again, then closed on the striped stone ring. "And the first decision concerns this. It's the first thing we have seen that has any real connection to Liandrin and the others." She frowned at the ring, then took a deep breath. "I am going to sleep with it tonight."

Egwene did not hesitate before taking the ring out of Nynaeve's hand. She wanted to hesitate—she wanted to keep her hands by her sides—but she did not, and she was pleased. "I am the one they say might be a Dreamer. I do not know whether that gives me any advantage, but Verin said it's dangerous using this. Whichever of us uses it, she needs any advantage she can find."

Nynaeve gripped her braid and opened her mouth as if to protest. When she finally spoke, though, it was to say, "Are you sure, Egwene? We do not even know if you *are* a Dreamer, and I can channel more strongly than you. I still think I—" Egwene cut her off.

"You can channel more strongly if you are angry. Can you be sure you'll be angry in a dream? Will you have time to become angry before you need to channel? Light, we don't even know that anyone can channel in a dream.

If one of us has to do it—and you are right; it is the only connection we have—it should be me. Maybe I really am a Dreamer. Besides, Verin did give it to me."

Nynaeve looked as if she wanted to argue, but at last she gave a grudging nod. "Very well. But Elayne and I will be there. I do not know what we can do, but if anything goes wrong, perhaps we can wake you up, or. . . . We will be there." Elayne nodded, too.

Now that she had their agreement, Egwene felt a queasiness in the pit of her stomach. *I talked them into it. I wish I did not want them to talk me out of it.* She became aware of a woman standing in the doorway, a woman in novice white, with her hair in long braids.

"Did no one ever teach you to knock, Else?" Nynaeve said.

Egwene hid the stone ring inside her fist. She had the strangest feeling that Else had been staring at it.

"I have a message for you," Else said calmly. Her eyes studied the table, with all the papers scattered on it, then the three women around it. "From the Amyrlin."

Egwene exchanged wondering looks with Nynaeve and Elayne.

"Well, what is it?" Nynaeve demanded.

Else arched an eyebrow in amusement. "The belongings left behind by Liandrin and the others were put in the third storeroom on the right from the main stairs in the second basement under the library." She glanced at the papers on the table again and left, neither hurrying nor moving slowly.

Egwene felt as if she could not breathe. *We're afraid to trust anybody, and the Amyrlin decides to trust Else Grinwell of all women?*

"That fool girl cannot be trusted not to blab to anyone who'll listen!" Nynaeve started for the door.

Egwene grabbed up her skirts and darted past her at a run. Her shoes skidded on the tiles of the gallery, but she caught a glimpse of white vanishing down the nearest ramp and dashed after it. *She must be running, too, to be so far ahead already. Why is she running?* The flash of white was already disappearing down another ramp. Egwene followed.

A woman turned to face her at the foot of the ramp, and Egwene stopped in confusion. Whoever she was, this was certainly not Else. All in silver and white silk, she sparked feelings Egwene had never had before. She was taller, more beautiful by far, and the look in her black eyes made Egwene feel small, scrawny, and none too clean. *She can probably channel more of the Power than I can, too. Light, she is probably smarter than all three of us put together on top of it. It isn't fair for one woman to*—Abruptly she realized the way her thoughts were going. Her cheeks reddened, and she gave herself a shake. She had never felt—less—than any other woman before, and she was not about to start now.

"Bold," the woman said. "You are bold to go running about so, alone, where so many murders have been done." She sounded almost pleased.

Egwene drew herself up and straightened her dress hurriedly, hoping the other woman would not notice, knowing she did, wishing the woman had not seen her running like a child. *Stop that!* "Pardon, but I am looking for a novice who came this way, I think. She has large, dark eyes and dark hair in braids. She's plump, and pretty in a way. Did you see which way she went?"

The tall woman looked her up and down in an amused way. Egwene could not be sure, but she thought the woman might have glanced a moment at the clenched fist by her side, where she still held the stone ring. "I do not think you will catch up to her. I saw her, and she was running quite fast. I suspect she is far away from here by now."

"Aes Sedai," Egwene began, but she was given no chance to ask which way Else had gone. Something that might have been anger, or annoyance, flashed through those black eyes.

"I have taken up enough time with you for now. I have more important matters to see to. Leave me." She gestured back the way Egwene had come.

So strong was the command in her voice that Egwene turned and was three steps up the ramp before she realized what she was doing. Bristling, she spun back. *Aes Sedai or no, I*—

The gallery was empty.

Frowning, she dismissed the nearest doors—no one lived in those rooms, except possibly mice—and ran down the ramp, peered both ways, followed the curve of the gallery with her eyes all the way around. She even peered over the rail, down into the small Garden of the Accepted, and studied the other galleries, higher as well as lower. She saw two Accepted in their banded dresses, one Faolain and the other a woman she knew by sight if not name. But there was no woman in silver and white anywhere.

CHAPTER
26

Behind a Lock

S haking her head, Egwene walked back to the doors
she had dismissed. *She had to go somewhere.* Inside
the first, the few furnishings were shapeless mounds
under dusty cloths, and the air seemed stale, as if the door
had not been opened in some time. She grimaced; there
were mouse tracks in the dust on the floor. But no others.
Two more doors, opened hastily, showed the same thing. It
was no surprise. There were many more empty rooms than
occupied in the Accepted's galleries.

When she pulled her head out of the third room, Nynaeve
and Elayne were coming down the ramp behind her with no
particular haste.

"Is she hiding?" Nynaeve asked in surprise. "In there?"

"I lost her." Egwene peered both ways along the curving
gallery again. *Where did she go?* She did not mean Else.

"If I had thought Else could outrun you," Elayne said
with a smile, "I'd have chased her, too, but she has always
looked too plump for running to me." Her smile was worried, though.

"We will have to find her later," Nynaeve said, "and
make sure she knows to keep her mouth shut. How could
the Amyrlin trust that girl?"

"I thought I was right on top of her," Egwene said slowly,
"but it was someone else. Nynaeve, I turned my back for
a moment, and she was gone. Not Else—I never even saw
her!—the woman I thought was Else at first. She was just—
gone, and I don't know where."

Elayne's breath caught. "One of the Soulless?" She

looked around hastily, but the gallery was still empty except for the three of them.

"Not her," Egwene said firmly. "She—" *I am not going to tell them she made me feel six years old, with a torn dress, a dirty face, and a runny nose.* "She was no Gray Man. She was tall and striking, with black eyes and black hair. You'd notice her in a crowd of a thousand. I have never seen her before, but I think she is Aes Sedai. She must be."

Nynaeve waited, as though for more, then said impatiently, "If you see her again, point her out to me. If you think there's cause. We've no time to stand here talking. I mean to see what is in that storeroom before Else has a chance to tell the wrong person about it. Maybe they were careless. Let's not give them a chance to correct it, if they were."

As she fell in beside Nynaeve, with Elayne on the other side, Egwene realized she still had the stone ring—*Corianin Nedeal's* ter'angreal—clutched in her fist. Reluctantly, she tucked it into her pouch and pulled the drawstrings tight. *As long as I don't go to sleep with the bloody—But that's what I am planning, isn't it?*

But that was for tonight, and no use worrying about it now. As they made their way through the Tower, she kept an eye out for the woman in silver and white. She was not sure why she was relieved not to see her. *I am a grown woman, and quite capable, thank you.* Still, she was just as glad that no one they encountered looked even remotely like her. The more she thought of the woman, the more she felt there was something—wrong—about her. *Light, I am starting to see the Black Ajah under my bed. Only, maybe they* are *under the bed.*

The library stood a little apart from the tall, thick shaft of the White Tower proper, its pale stone heavily streaked with blue, and it looked much like crashing waves frozen at their climax. Those waves loomed as large as a palace in the morning light, and Egwene knew they certainly contained as many rooms as one, but all those rooms—those below the odd corridors in the upper levels, where Verin had her chambers—were filled with shelves, and the shelves filled with books, manuscripts, papers, scrolls, maps, and charts, collected from every nation over the course of three thou-

sand years. Not even the great libraries in Tear and Cairhien
held so many.

The librarians—Brown sisters all—guarded those shelves,
and guarded the doors as closely, to make sure not a scrap
of paper left unless they knew who took it and why. But it
was not to one of the guarded entrances that Nynaeve led
Egwene and Elayne.

Around the foundations of the library, lying flat to the
ground in the shade of tall pecan trees, were other doors,
both large and small. Laborers sometimes needed access to
the storerooms beneath, and the librarians did not approve
of sweating men tracking through their preserve. Nynaeve
pulled up one of those, no bigger than the front door of a
farmhouse, and motioned the others down a steep flight of
stairs descending into darkness. When she let it down behind them, all light vanished.

Egwene opened herself to *saidar*—it came so smoothly
that she barely realized what she was doing—and channeled a trickle of the Power that flooded through her. For
a moment the mere feel of that rush surging within her
threatened to overwhelm other sensations. A small ball
of bluish-white light appeared, balanced in the air above
her hand. She took a deep breath and reminded herself of
why she was walking stiffly. It was a link to the rest of the
world. The feel of her linen shift against her skin returned,
of woolen stockings, and her dress. With a small pang of
regret, she banished the desire to pull in more, to let *saidar*
absorb her.

Elayne made a glowing sphere for herself at the same
time, and the pair provided more light than two lanterns
would have. "It feels so—wonderful, doesn't it?" she murmured.

"Be careful," Egwene said.

"I am." Elayne sighed. "It just feels. . . . I will be careful."

"This way," Nynaeve told them sharply and brushed by
to lead them down. She did not go too far ahead. She was
not angry, and had to use the light the other two provided.

The dusty side corridor by which they had entered, lined
with wooden doors set in gray stone walls, took nearly a
hundred paces to reach the much wider main hall that ran

the length of the library. Their lights showed footprints overlaying footprints in the dust, most from the large boots men would wear and most themselves faded by dust. The ceiling was higher here, and some of the doors nearly large enough for a barn. The main stairs at the end, half the width of the hall, were where large things were brought down. Another flight beside them led deeper. Nynaeve took it without a pause.

Egwene followed quickly. The bluish light washed out Elayne's face, but Egwene thought it still looked paler than it should. *We could scream our lungs out down here, and no one would hear a whimper.*

She felt a lightning bolt form, or the potential for one, and nearly stumbled. She had never before channeled two flows at once; it did not seem difficult at all.

The main hall of the second basement was much like the first level, wide and dusty but with a lower ceiling. Nynaeve hurried to the third door on the right and stopped.

The door was not large, but its rough wooden planks somehow gave an impression of thickness. A round iron lock hung from a length of stout chain that was drawn tight through two thick staples, one in the door, the other cemented into the wall. Lock and chain alike had the look of newness; there was almost no dust on them.

"A lock!" Nynaeve jerked at it; the chain had no give, and neither did the lock. "Did either of you see a lock anywhere else?" She pulled it again, then flung it against the door hard enough to bounce. The bang echoed down the hall. "I did not see one other locked door!" She pounded a fist on the rough wood. "Not one!"

"Calm yourself," Elayne said. "There is no need to throw a tantrum. I could open the lock myself, if I could see how the inside of it works. We will open it some way."

"I do not want to calm myself," Nynaeve snapped. "I want to be furious! I want . . . !"

Letting the rest of the tirade fade from her awareness, Egwene touched the chain. She had learned more things than how to make lightning bolts since leaving Tar Valon. One was an affinity for metal. That came from Earth, one of the Five Powers few women had much strength in—the other was Fire—but she had it, and she could feel the chain, feel *inside* the chain, feel the tiniest bits of the cold metal, the patterns they made. The Power within her quivered in time to the vibrations of those patterns.

"Move out of my way, Egwene."

She looked around and saw Nynaeve wrapped in the glow of *saidar* and holding a prybar so close in color to the blue-white of the light that it was nearly invisible. Nynaeve frowned at the chain, muttered something about leverage, and the prybar was suddenly twice as long.

"Move, Egwene."

Egwene moved.

Thrusting the end of the prybar through the chain, Nynaeve braced it, then heaved with all her strength. The chain snapped like thread, Nynaeve gasped and stumbled halfway across the hall in surprise, and the prybar clattered to the floor. Straightening, Nynaeve stared from the bar to the chain in amazement. The prybar vanished.

"I think I did something to the chain," Egwene said. *And I wish I knew what.*

"You could have said something," Nynaeve muttered. She pulled the rest of the chain from the staples and threw open the door. "Well? Are you going to stand there all day?"

The dusty room inside was perhaps ten paces square, but it held only a heap of large bags made of heavy brown cloth, each stuffed full, tagged, and sealed with the Flame of Tar Valon. Egwene did not have to count them to know there were thirteen.

She moved her ball of light to the wall and fastened it there; she was not certain how she did it, but when she took her hand away, the light remained. *I keep learning how to do things without knowing what they are*, she thought nervously.

Elayne frowned at her as if considering, then hung her light on the wall, too. Watching, Egwene thought she saw what it was she had done. *She learned it from me, but I just learned it from her.* She shivered.

Nynaeve went straight to tumbling the bags apart and reading the tags. "Rianna. Joiya Byir. These are what we are after." She examined the seal on one bag, then broke the wax and unwound the binding cords. "At least we know no one's been here before us."

Egwene chose a bag and broke the seal without reading the name on the tag. She did not really want to know whose possessions she was searching. When she upended them onto the dusty floor, they proved to be mainly old clothes and shoes, with a few ripped and crumpled papers of the sort that might hide under the wardrobe of a woman who was not too assiduous in seeing her rooms cleaned. "I don't see anything useful here. A cloak that would not do for rags. A torn half of a map of some city. Tear, it says in the corner. Three stockings that need darning." She stuck her finger through the hole in a velvet slipper that had no mate and waggled it at the others. "This one left no clues behind."

"Amico did not leave anything, either," Elayne said glumly, tossing clothes aside with both hands. "It might as well be rags. Wait, here's a book. Whoever bundled these up must have been in a hurry to toss in a book. *Customs and Ceremonies of the Tairen Court.* The cover is torn off, but the librarians will want it anyway." The librarians certainly would. No one threw away books, no matter how badly damaged.

"Tear," Nynaeve said in a flat voice. Kneeling amid the clutter from the bag she was searching, she retrieved a scrap of paper she had already thrown away. "A list of trading ships on the Erinin, with the dates they sailed from Tar Valon and the dates they were expected to arrive in Tear."

"It could be coincidence," Egwene said slowly.

"Perhaps," Nynaeve said. She folded the paper and tucked it up her sleeve, then broke the seal on another bag.

When they finally finished, every bag searched twice and discarded rubbish heaped around the edges of the room, Egwene sat down on one of the empty bags, so engrossed that she barely noticed her own wince. Drawing up her knees, she studied the little collection they had made, all laid in a row.

"It is too much," Elayne said. "There is too much of it."

"Too much," Nynaeve agreed.

There was a second book, a tattered, leather-bound volume entitled *Observations on a Visit to Tear,* with half its pages falling out. Caught in the lining of a badly torn cloak in Chesmal Emry's bag, where it might have slipped through a rip in one of the pockets of the cloak, had been another list of trading vessels. It said no more than the names, but they were all on the other list, too, and according to that, those vessels all had sailed in the early morn-

ing after the night Liandrin and the others left the Tower.
There was a hastily sketched plan of some large building,
with one room faintly noted as "Heart of the Stone," and
a page with the names of five inns, the word "Tear" heading the page badly smudged but barely readable. There
was. . . .

"There's something from everyone," Egwene muttered.
"Every one of them left something pointing to a journey
to Tear. How could anyone miss seeing it, if they looked?
Why did the Amyrlin say nothing of this?"

"The Amyrlin," Nynaeve said bitterly, "keeps her own
counsel, and what matter if we burn for it!" She drew a
deep breath, and sneezed from the dust they had stirred up.
"What worries me is that I am looking at bait."

"Bait?" Egwene said. But she saw it as soon as she spoke.

Nynaeve nodded. "Bait. A trap. Or maybe a diversion.
But trap or diversion, it's so obvious no one could be taken
in by it."

"Unless they do not care whether whoever found this saw
the trap or not." Uncertainty tinged Elayne's voice. "Or perhaps they meant it to be so obvious that whoever found it
would dismiss Tear immediately."

Egwene wished she could not believe that the Black Ajah
could be as sure of themselves as that. She realized she was
gripping her pouch in her fingers, running her thumb along
the twisted curve of the stone ring inside. "Perhaps they
meant to taunt whoever found it," she said softly. "Perhaps
they thought whoever found this would rush headlong after
them, in anger and pride." *Did they know* we *would find it?
Do they see us that way?*

"Burn me!" Nynaeve growled. It was a shock; Nynaeve
never used such language.

For a time they simply stared in silence at the array.

"What do we do now?" Elayne asked finally.

Egwene squeezed the ring hard. Dreaming was closely
linked to Foretelling; the future, and events in other places,
could appear in a Dreamer's dreams. "Maybe we will know
after tonight."

Nynaeve looked at her, silent and expressionless, then
chose out a dark skirt that seemed not to have too many
holes and rips, and began bundling in it the things they had
found. "For now," she said, "we will take this back to my

room and hide it. I think we just have time, if we don't want
to be late to the kitchens."

Late, Egwene thought. The longer she held the ring
through her pouch, the greater the urgency she felt. *We're
already a step behind, but maybe we won't be too late.*

CHAPTER
27

Tel'aran'rhiod

The room Egwene had been given, on the same gallery with Nynaeve and Elayne, was little different from Nynaeve's. Her bed was a trifle wider, her table a little smaller. Her bit of rug had flowers instead of scrolls. That was all. After the novices' quarters, it seemed like a room in a palace, but when the three of them gathered there late that night, Egwene wished she were back on the novice galleries, with no ring on her finger and no bands on her dress. The others looked as nervous as she felt.

They had worked in the kitchens for two more meals, and in between tried to puzzle out the meaning of what they had found in the storeroom. Was it a trap, or an attempt to divert the search? Did the Amyrlin know of the things, and if she did, why had she not mentioned them? Talking provided no answers, and the Amyrlin never appeared so they could ask her.

Verin had come into the kitchens after the midday meal, blinking as if she were not sure why she was there. When she saw Egwene and the other two on their knees among the cauldrons and kettles, she looked surprised for a moment, then walked over and asked, loud enough for anyone to hear, "Have you found anything?"

Elayne, with her head and shoulders inside a huge soup kettle, banged her head on the rim backing out. Her blue eyes seemed to take up her entire face.

"Nothing but grease and sweat, Aes Sedai," Nynaeve said. The tug she gave her braid left a smear of greasy soap suds on her dark hair, and she grimaced.

Verin nodded as if that were the answer she had been seeking. "Well, keep looking." She peered around the kitchen again, frowning as though puzzled to find herself there, and left.

Alanna came to the kitchens after midday, too, collecting a bowl of big green gooseberries and a pitcher of wine, and Elaida, then Sheriam, appeared after supper, and Anaiya, too.

Alanna had asked Egwene if she wanted to know more of the Green Ajah, inquired when they were going to get on with their studies. Just because the Accepted chose their own lessons and pace did not mean they were not supposed to do any at all. The first few weeks would be bad, of course, but they had to choose, or the choosing would be done for them.

Elaida merely stood for a time, stern-faced and staring at them, hands on her hips, and Sheriam did the same in almost the identical pose. Anaiya stood the same way, but her look was more concerned. Until she saw them glancing at her. Then her face became a match for Elaida's and Sheriam's before her.

None of those visits meant anything that Egwene could see. The Mistress of Novices certainly had reason to check on them, as well as on the novices working in the kitchens, and Elaida had reason to keep an eye on the Daughter-Heir of Andor. Egwene tried not to think of the Aes Sedai's interest in Rand. As for Alanna, she was not the only Aes Sedai who came for a tray to take back to her rooms rather than eat with the others. Half the sisters in the Tower were too busy for meals, too busy to take the time to summon a servant to fetch a tray. And Anaiya . . . ? Anaiya could well be concerned for her Dreamer. Not that she would do anything to ease a punishment set by the Amyrlin Seat herself. That could have been Anaiya's reason for coming. It could have been.

Hanging her dress in the wardrobe, Egwene told herself once again that even Verin's slip could have been perfectly ordinary; the Brown sister was often absentminded. *If it was a slip.* Sitting on the edge of her bed, she pulled up her shift and began rolling down her stockings. She was almost beginning to dislike white as much as she did gray.

Nynaeve stood in front of the fireplace with Egwene's

pouch in one hand, tugging her braid. Elayne sat by the table, making nervous conversation.

"Green Ajah," the golden-haired woman said for what Egwene thought must be the twentieth time since midday. "I might choose Green Ajah myself, Egwene. Then I can have three or four Warders, perhaps marry one of them. Who better for Prince Consort of Andor than a Warder? Unless it is. . . ." She trailed off, blushing.

Egwene felt a pang of jealousy she thought she had put down long ago, and sympathy mixed with it. *Light, how can I be jealous when I cannot look at Galad without shivering and feeling as if I am melting, both at the same time? Rand was mine, but no more. I wish I could give him to you, Elayne, but he is not for either of us, I think. It may be all well and good for the Daughter-Heir to marry a commoner, as long as he's an Andorman, but not to marry the Dragon Reborn.* She let the stockings fall on the floor, telling herself there were more important things to worry about tonight than neatness. "I am ready, Nynaeve."

Nynaeve handed her the pouch, and a long, thin strip of leather. "Perhaps it will work for more than one at once. I could . . . go with you, perhaps."

Emptying the stone ring onto her palm, Egwene threaded the leather strip through it, then tied it around her neck. The stripes and flecks of blue and brown and red seemed more vivid against the white of her shift. "And leave Elayne to watch over the both of us alone? When the Black Ajah may know us?"

"I can do it," Elayne said stoutly. "Or let me go with you, and Nynaeve can keep guard. She is the strongest of us, when she's angry, and if there is need for a guard, you can be sure she will be."

Egwene shook her head. "What if it won't work for two? What if two of us trying makes it not work at all? We would not even know till we woke up, and then we've wasted the night. We cannot waste even one if we are to catch up. We're too far behind them already." They were valid reasons, and she believed them, but there was another, closer to her heart. "Besides, I'll feel better knowing both of you are watching over me, in case. . . ."

She did not want to say it. In case someone came while she was asleep. The Gray Men. The Black Ajah. Any one of the things that had turned the White Tower from a place of safety to a dark woods full of pits and snares. Something coming in while she lay there helpless. Their faces showed they understood.

As she stretched herself out on the bed and plumped a feather pillow behind her head, Elayne moved the chairs, one to either side of the bed. Nynaeve snuffed the candles one by one, then, in the dark, sat in one of the chairs. Elayne took the other.

Egwene closed her eyes and tried to think sleepy thoughts, but she was too conscious of the thing lying between her breasts. Far more conscious than of any soreness remaining from her visit to Sheriam's study. The ring seemed to weigh as much as a brick, now, and thoughts of home and quiet pools of water all slid apart with remembrance of it. Of *Tel'aran'rhiod.* The Unseen World. The World of Dreams. Waiting just the other side of sleep.

Nynaeve began to hum softly. Egwene recognized a nameless, wordless tune her mother used to hum to her when she was little. When she was lying in bed, in her own room, with a fluffy pillow, and warm blankets, and the mingled smells of rose oil and baking from her mother, and. . . . *Rand, are you all right? Perrin? Who was she?* Sleep came.

She stood among rolling hills quilted with wildflowers and dotted with small thickets of leafy trees in the hollows and on the crests. Butterflies floated above the blossoms, wings flashing yellow and blue and green, and two larks sang to each other nearby. Just enough fluffy white clouds drifted in a soft blue sky, and the breeze held that delicate balance between cool and warm that came only a few special days in spring. It was a day too perfect to be anything but a dream.

She looked at her dress, and laughed delightedly. Exactly her favorite shade of sky-blue silk, slashed with white in the skirt—that changed to green as she frowned momentarily— sewn with rows of tiny pearls down the sleeves and across the bosom. She stuck out a foot just to peek at the toe of a velvet slipper. The only jarring note was the twisted ring of multicolored stone hanging around her neck on a leather cord.

She took the ring in her hand and gasped. It felt as light

as a feather. If she tossed it up, she was sure it would drift away like thistledown. Somehow, she did not feel afraid of it any longer. She tucked it inside the neck of her dress to get it out of the way.

"So this is Verin's *Tel'aran'rhiod*," she said. "Corianin Nedeal's World of Dreams. It does not look dangerous to me." But Verin had said it was. Black Ajah or not, Egwene did not see how any Aes Sedai could tell a lie right out. *She could be mistaken.* But she did not believe Verin was.

Just to see if she could, she opened herself to the One Power. *Saidar* filled her. Even here, it was present. She channeled the flow lightly, delicately, directed it into the breeze, swirling butterflies into fluttering spirals of color, into circles linked with circles.

Abruptly she let it go. The butterflies settled back, unconcerned by their brief adventure. Myrddraal and some other Shadowspawn could sense someone channeling. Looking around, she could not imagine such things in that place, but just because she could not imagine them did not mean they were not there. And the Black Ajah had all those *ter'angreal* studied by Corianin Nedeal. It was a sickening reminder of why she was there.

"At least I know I can channel," she muttered. "I'm not learning anything standing here. Perhaps if I look around. . . ." She took a step . . .

. . . and was standing in the dank, dark hallway of an inn. She was an innkeeper's daughter; she was sure it was an inn. There was not a sound, and all the doors along the hall were shut tight. Just as she wondered who was behind the plain wooden door in front of her, it swung silently open.

The room within was bare, and cold wind moaned through open windows, stirring old ash on the hearth. A big dog lay curled up on the floor, shaggy tail across its nose, between the door and a thick pillar of rough-cut, black stone that stood in the middle of the floor. A large, shaggy-haired young man sat leaning back against the pillar in only his smallclothes, head lolling as if asleep. A massive black chain ran around the pillar and across his chest, the ends gripped in his clenched hands. Asleep or not, his heavy muscles strained to hold that chain tight, to prison himself against the pillar.

"Perrin?" she said wonderingly. She stepped into the room. "Perrin, what's the matter with you? Perrin!" The dog uncurled itself and stood.

It was not a dog, but a wolf, all black and gray, lips curling back from glistening white teeth, yellow eyes regarding her as they might have a mouse. A mouse it meant to eat.

Egwene stepped back hastily into the hall in spite of herself. "Perrin! Wake up! There's a wolf!" Verin had said what happened here was real, and showed the scar to prove it. The wolf's teeth looked as big as knives. "Perrin, wake up! Tell it I'm a friend!" She embraced *saidar*. The wolf stalked nearer.

Perrin's head came up; his eyes opened drowsily. Two sets of yellow eyes regarded her. The wolf gathered himself. "Hopper," Perrin shouted, "no! Egwene!"

The door swung shut before her face, and total darkness enveloped her.

She could not see, but she felt sweat beading on her forehead. Not from heat. *Light, where am I? I don't like this place. I want to wake up!*

A whirring sound, and she jumped before she recognized a cricket. A frog gave a bass croak in the darkness, and a chorus answered it. As her eyes adapted, she dimly made out trees all around her. Clouds blanketed the stars, and the moon was a thin sliver.

Off to her right through the woods was another glow, flickering. A campfire.

She considered a moment before moving. Wanting to wake up had not been enough to take her way from *Tel'aran'rhiod*, and she still had not found out anything useful. And she had not been hurt in any way. *So far*, she thought, shivering. But she had no idea who—or what—was at that campfire. *It could be Myrddraal. Besides, I'm not dressed for running around in the forest.* It was the last thought that decided her; she prided herself on knowing when she was being foolish.

Taking a deep breath, she gathered up her silken skirts and crept closer. She might not have Nynaeve's skill at woodcraft, but she knew enough to avoid stepping on dead twigs. At last she peered carefully around the trunk of an old oak at the campfire.

The only one there was a tall young man, sitting and staring into the flames. Rand. Those flames did not burn wood. They did not burn anything that she could see. The fire danced above a bare patch of ground. She did not think they even scorched the soil.

Before she could move, Rand raised his head. She was surprised to see he was smoking a pipe, a thin ribbon of tabac smoke lifting from the bowl. He looked tired, so very tired.

"Who's out there?" he demanded loudly. "You've rustled enough leaves to wake the dead, so you might as well show yourself."

Egwene's lips compressed, but she stepped out. *I did not!* "It's me, Rand. Do not be afraid. It is a dream. I must be in your dreams."

He was on his feet so suddenly that she stopped dead. He seemed in some way larger than she remembered. And a touch dangerous. Perhaps more than a touch. His blue-gray eyes seemed to burn like frozen fire.

"Do you think I don't know it is a dream?" he sneered. "I know that makes it no less real." He stared angrily out into the darkness as if looking for someone. "How long will you try?" he shouted at the night. "How many faces will you send? My mother, my father, now her! Pretty girls won't tempt me with a kiss, not even one I know! I deny you, Father of Lies! I deny you!"

"Rand," she said uncertainly. "It's Egwene. I am Egwene."

There was a sword in his hands, suddenly, out of nowhere. Its blade was worked out of a single flame, slightly curved and graven with a heron. "My mother gave me honeycake," he said in a tight voice, "with the smell of poison rank on it. My father had a knife for my ribs. She—she offered kisses, and more." Sweat slicked his face; his stare seemed enough to set her afire. "What do you bring?"

"You are going to listen to me, Rand al'Thor, if I have to sit on you." She gathered *saidar*, channeled the flows to make the air hold him in a net.

The sword spun in his hands, roaring like an open furnace.

She grunted and staggered; it felt as if a rope stretched too tight had broken and snapped back into her.

Rand laughed. "I learn, you see. When it works. . . ." He grimaced and started toward her. "I could stand any face but that one. Not her face, burn you!" The sword flashed out.

Egwene fled.

She was not sure what it was she did, or how, but she found herself back among the rolling hills under a sunny sky, with larks singing and butterflies playing. She drew a deep, shuddering breath.

I've learned. . . . What? That the Dark One is still after Rand? I knew that already. That maybe the Dark One wants to kill him? That's different. Unless maybe he's gone mad already, and does not know what he is saying. Light, why couldn't I help him? Oh, Light, Rand!

She took another long breath to calm herself. "The only way to help him is to gentle him," she muttered. "As well go ahead and kill him." Her stomach twisted and knotted. "I'll never do that. Never!"

A redbird had perched on a cloudberry bush nearby, crest lifting as it tilted its head to watch her cautiously. She addressed the bird. "Well, I am not helping anything standing here talking to myself, am I? Or talking to you, either."

The redbird took wing as she stepped toward the bush. It was still a flash of crimson as she took the next step, vanished into a thicket as she took a third.

She stopped and fished the stone ring on its cord out of the front of her dress. Why was it not changing? Everything had changed so fast up till now that she could hardly catch her breath. Why not now? Unless there was some answer right here? She looked around uncertainly. The wildflowers taunted her, and the larksong mocked her. This place seemed too much of her own making.

Determined, she tightened her hand around the *ter'angreal*. "Take me where I need to be." She shut her eyes and concentrated on the ring. It was stone, after all; Earth should give her some feeling for it. "Do it. Take me where I need to be." Once again she embraced *saidar*, fed a trickle of the One Power into the ring. She knew it did not need any flow of Power directed at it to work, and she did not try to do anything to it. Only to give it more of the Power to use. "Take me to where I can find an answer. I need to know what the Black Ajah wants. Take me to the answer."

"Well, you've found your way at last, child. All sorts of answers here."

Egwene's eyes snapped open. She stood in a great hall, its vast domed ceiling supported by a forest of massive redstone columns. And hanging in midair was a sword of crystal, gleaming and sparkling as it slowly revolved. She was not certain, but she thought it might be the sword Rand had been reaching for in that dream. That other dream. This all felt so real, she had to keep reminding herself it was a dream, too.

An old woman stepped out of the shadows of the column, bent and hobbling with a stick. Ugly did not begin to describe her. She had a bony, pointed chin, an even bonier, sharper nose, and it seemed there were more warts growing hairs on her face than there was face.

"Who are you?" Egwene said. The only people she had seen so far in *Tel'aran'rhiod* were those she already knew, but she did not think she could have forgotten this poor old woman.

"Just poor old Silvie, my Lady," the old woman cackled. At the same time she managed a stoop that might have been meant for a curtsy, or possibly a cringe. "You know poor old Silvie, my Lady. Served your family faithfully all these years. Does this old face still frighten you? Don't let it, my Lady. It serves me, when I need it, as good as a prettier."

"Of course, it does," Egwene said. "It's a strong face. A good face." She hoped the woman believed it. Whoever this Silvie was, she seemed to think she knew Egwene. Perhaps she knew answers, too. "Silvie, you said something about finding answers here."

"Oh, you've come to the right place for answers, my Lady. The Heart of the Stone is full of answers. And secrets. The High Lords would not be pleased to see us here, my Lady. Oh, no. None but the High Lords enter here. And servants, of course." She gave a sly, screeching laugh. "The High Lords don't sweep and mop. But who sees a servant?"

"What kind of secrets?"

But Silvie was hobbling toward the crystal sword. "Plots," she said as if to herself. "All of them pretending to serve the Great Lord, and all the while plotting and planning to regain what they lost. Each one thinking he or she is the only one plotting. Ishamael is a fool!"

"What?" Egwene said sharply. "What did you say about Ishamael?"

The old woman turned to present a crooked, ingratiating smile. "Just a thing poor folks say, my Lady. It turns the Forsaken's power, calling them fools. Makes you feel good, and safe. Even the Shadow can't take being called a fool. Try it, my Lady. Say, Ba'alzamon is a fool!"

Egwene's lips twitched on the edge of a smile. "Ba'alzamon is a fool! You are right, Silvie." It actually did feel good, laughing at the Dark One. The old woman chuckled. The sword revolved just beyond her shoulder. "Silvie, what is that?"

"*Callandor*, my Lady. You know that, don't you? The Sword That Cannot Be Touched." Abruptly she swung her stick behind her; a foot from the sword, the stick stopped with a dull *thwack* and bounded back. Silvie grinned wider. "The Sword That Is Not a Sword, though there's precious few knows what it is. But none can touch it save one. They saw to that, who put it here. The Dragon Reborn will hold *Callandor* one day, and prove to the world he's the Dragon by doing it. The first proof, anyway. Lews Therin come back for all the world to see, and grovel before. Ah, the High Lords don't like having it here. They like nothing to do with the Power. They'd rid themselves of it, if they could. If they could. I suppose there's others would take it, if they could. What wouldn't one of the Forsaken give, to hold *Callandor*?"

Egwene stared at the sparkling sword. If the Prophecies of the Dragon were true, if Rand was the Dragon as Moiraine claimed, he would wield it one day, though from the rest of what she knew of the Prophecies concerning *Callandor*, she could not see how it could ever come to be. *But if there's a way to take it, maybe the Black Ajah knows how. If they know it, I can figure it out.*

Cautiously, she reached out with the Power, probing at whatever held and shielded the sword. Her probe touched—something—and stopped. She could sense which of the Five Powers had been used here. Air, and Fire, and Spirit. She could trace the intricate weave made by *saidar*, set with a strength that amazed her. There were gaps in that weave, spaces where her probe should slide through. When she tried, it was like fighting the strongest part of the weave head on. It hit her then, what she was trying to force a way through, and she let her probe vanish. Half that wall had been woven using *saidar*; the other half, the part she could not sense or touch, had been made with *saidin*. That was not it, exactly—the wall was all of one piece—but it was close enough. *A stone wall stops a blind woman as surely as one who can see it.*

Footsteps echoed in the distance. Boots.

Egwene could not tell how many there were, or from which direction they were coming, but Silvie gave a start and immediately stared off among the columns. "He's coming to stare at it again," she muttered. "Awake or asleep, he wants. . . ." She seemed to remember Egwene, and put on a worried smile. "You must leave, now, my Lady. He mustn't find you here, or even know you've been."

Egwene was already backing in among the columns, and Silvie followed, flapping her hands and waving her stick. "I am going, Silvie. I just have to remember the way." She fingered the stone ring. "Take me back to the hills." Nothing happened. She channeled a hairlike flow to the ring. "Take me back to the hills." The redstone columns still surrounded her. The boots were closer, close enough not to be swallowed in their own echoes anymore.

"You don't know the way out," Sylvie said flatly, then went on in a near whisper, ingratiating and mocking at once, an old retainer who felt she could take liberties. "Oh, my Lady, this is a dangerous place to come into, if you don't know the way out. Come, let poor old Silvie take you out. Poor old Silvie will tuck you safe in your bed, my Lady." She wrapped both arms around Egwene, urging her further from the sword. Not that Egwene needed much urging. The boots had stopped; he—whoever he was—was probably gazing at *Callandor.*

"Just show me the way," Egwene whispered back. "Or tell me. There's no need to push." The old woman's fingers had somehow gotten tangled around the stone ring. "Don't touch that, Silvie."

"Safe in your bed."

Pain annihilated the world.

With a throat-wrenching shriek, Egwene sat up in the dark, sweat rolling down her face. For a moment she had no idea where she was, and did not care. "Oh, Light," she moaned, "that hurt. Oh, Light, that hurt!" She ran her hands over herself, sure her skin must be scored or wealed to make such a burning, but she could not find a mark.

"We are here," Nynaeve's voice said from the darkness. "We're here, Egwene."

Egwene threw herself toward the voice and wrapped her arms around Nynaeve's neck in sheer relief. "Oh, Light, I'm back. Light, I'm back."

"Elayne," Nynaeve said.

In a few moments one of the candles was giving a small light. Elayne paused with the candle in hand and the spill she had lit with flint and steel in the other. Then she smiled, and every candle in the room burst into flame. She stopped at the washstand and came back to the bed with a cool, damp cloth to wash Egwene's face.

"Was it bad?" she asked worriedly. "You never stirred. You never mumbled. We did not know whether to wake you or not."

Hurriedly, Egwene fumbled the leather cord from around her neck and hurled it and the stone ring across the room. "Next time," she panted, "we decide on a time, and you wake me after it. Wake me if you have to stick my head in a basin of water!" She had not realized that she had decided there would be a next time. *Would you put your head in a bear's mouth just to show you weren't afraid? Would you do it twice just because you'd done it once and didn't die?*

Yet it was more than a matter of proving to herself that she was not afraid. She was afraid, and knew it. But so long as the Black Ajah had those *ter'angreal* Corianin had studied, she would have to keep going back. She was sure the answer to why they wanted them lay in *Tel'aran'rhiod*. If she could find answers about the Black Ajah there— perhaps other answers, too, if half what she had been told about Dreaming were true—she had to go back. "But not tonight," she said softly. "Not yet."

"What happened?" Nynaeve asked. "What did you . . . dream?"

Egwene lay back on the bed and told them. Of it all, the only thing she left out was about Perrin talking to the wolf. She left the wolf out altogether. She felt a little guilty about keeping secrets from Elayne and Nynaeve, but it was Perrin's secret to tell, when and if he chose, not hers. The rest she gave them word for word, describing everything. When she was done, she felt emptied.

"Aside from being tired," Elayne said, "did he look hurt? Egwene, I cannot believe he would ever hurt you. I cannot believe he would."

"Rand," Nynaeve said dryly, "will have to look after himself awhile longer." Elayne blushed; she looked pretty doing it. Egwene realized that Elayne looked pretty doing anything, even crying, or scrubbing pots. *"Callandor,"* Nynaeve continued. "The Heart of the Stone. That was marked on the plan. I think we know where the Black Ajah is."

Elayne had regained her poise. "It does not change the trap," she said. "If it is not a diversion, it is a trap."

Nynaeve smiled grimly. "The best way to catch whoever set a trap is to spring it and wait for him to come. Or her, in this instance."

"You mean go to Tear?" Egwene said, and Nynaeve nodded.

"The Amyrlin has cut us loose, it seems. We make our own decisions, remember? At least we know the Black Ajah is in Tear, and we know who to look for there. Here, all we can do is sit and stew in our own suspicions of everybody, wonder if there is another Gray Man out there. I would rather be the hound than the rabbit."

"I have to write to my mother," Elayne said. When she saw the looks they gave her, her voice became defensive. "I have already vanished once without her knowing where I was. If I do it again. . . . You do not know Mother's temper. She could send Gareth Bryne and the whole army against Tar Valon. Or hunting after us."

"You could stay here," Egwene said.

"No. I will not let you two go alone. And I won't stay here wondering if the sister teaching me is a Darkfriend, or if the next Gray Man will come after me." She gave a small laugh. "I will not work in the kitchens while you two are off adventuring, either. I just have to tell my mother than I am out of the Tower on the Amyrlin's orders, so she won't become furious if she hears rumors. I do not have to tell her where we are going, or why."

"You surely had better not," Nynaeve said. "She very likely would come after you if she knew about the Black Ajah. For that matter, you can't know how many hands your

letter will pass through before it reaches her, or what eyes
might read it. Best not to say anything you don't mind anyone knowing."

"That's another thing." Elayne sighed. "The Amyrlin
does not know I am one of you. I have to find some way to
send it with no chance of her seeing it."

"I will have to think on that." Nynaeve's brows furrowed.
"Perhaps once we're on our way. You could leave it at Aringill on the way downriver, if we have time to find someone
there going to Caemlyn. A sight of one of those papers the
Amyrlin gave us might convince somebody. We will have
to hope they work on ship captains, too, unless one of you
has more coin than I have." Elayne shook her head dole-
fully.

Egwene did not even bother. What money they had
possessed had all gone on the journey from Toman Head,
except for a few coppers each. "When. . . ." She had to stop
and clear her throat. "When do we leave? Tonight?"

Nynaeve looked as if she were considering it for a moment, but then she shook her head. "You need sleep, after. . . ." Her gesture took in the stone ring lying where it
had bounced off the wall. "We will give the Amyrlin one
more chance to seek us out. When we finish with breakfast,
you both pack what you want to take, but keep it light. We
have to leave the Tower without anyone noticing, remember.
If the Amyrlin doesn't reach us by midday, I mean to be on
a trading ship, shoving that paper down the captain's throat
if need be, before Prime sounds. How does that sound to
you two?"

"It sounds excellent," Elayne said firmly, and Egwene
said, "Tonight or tomorrow, the sooner the better, as far
as I can see." She wished she sounded as confident as
Elayne.

"Then we had best get some sleep."

"Nynaeve," Egwene said in a small voice, "I. . . . I don't
want to be alone tonight." It pained her to make that admis-
sion.

"I don't, either," Elayne said. "I keep thinking about the
Soulless. I do not know why, but they frighten me even
more than the Black Ajah."

"I suppose," Nynaeve said slowly, "I don't really want
to be alone, myself." She eyed the bed where Egwene lay.

"That looks big enough for three, if everybody keeps her elbows to herself."

Later, when they were shifting about trying to find a way to lie that did not feel so crowded, Nynaeve suddenly laughed.

"What is it?" Egwene asked. "You are not that ticklish."

"I just thought of someone who'd be happy to carry Elayne's letter for her. Happy to leave Tar Valon, too. In fact, I'd bet on it."

CHAPTER
28

A Way Out

Clad only in his breeches, Mat was just finishing
a snack after breakfast—some ham, three apples,
bread, and butter—when the door of his room
opened, and Nynaeve, Egwene, and Elayne filed in, all
smiling at him brightly. He got up for a shirt, then stub-
bornly sat down again. They could at least have knocked.
In any case, it was good to see their faces. At first, it was.

"Well, you do look better," Egwene said.

"As if you had had a month of good food and rest,"
Elayne said.

Nynaeve pressed a hand to his forehead. He flinched before he recalled that she had done much the same for at
least five years, back home. *She was just the Wisdom then*,
he thought. *She wasn't wearing that ring.*

She had noticed his flinch. She gave him a tight smile.
"You look ready to be up and about, to me. Are you tired of
being cooped up, yet? You never could stand two days in a
row indoors."

He eyed the last apple core reluctantly, then dropped it
back on the plate. Almost, he started to lick the juice off
his fingers, but they were all three looking at him. And still
smiling. He realized he was trying to decide which of them
was prettiest, and could not. Had they been anybody but
who—and what—they were, he would have asked any and
all of them to dance a jig or a reel. He had danced with
Egwene often enough, back home, and even once with
Nynaeve, but that seemed a long time ago.

"'One pretty woman means fun at the dance. Two pretty
women mean trouble in the house. Three pretty women

mean run for the hills.'" He gave Nynaeve an even tighter smile than her own. "My da used to say that. You're up to something, Nynaeve. You are all smiling like cats staring at a finch caught in a thornbush, and I think I am the finch."

The smiles flickered and vanished. He noticed their hands and wondered why they all looked as if they had been washing dishes. The Daughter-Heir of Andor surely never washed a dish, and he had as hard a time imagining Nynaeve at it, even knowing she had done her own back in Emond's Field. They all three wore Great Serpent rings, now. That was new. And not a particularly pleasant surprise. *Light, it had to happen sometime. It's none of my business, and that is all there is to it. None of my business. It just isn't.*

Egwene shook her head, but it seemed as much for the other two women as for him. "I told you we should ask him straight out. He's stubborn as any mule when he wants to be, and tricksome as a cat. You are, Mat. You know it, so stop frowning."

He put his grin back quickly.

"Hush, Egwene," Nynaeve said. "Mat, just because we want to ask you a favor does not mean we don't care how you feel. We do care, and you know that, unless you're being even more wool-headed than usual. Are you well? You look remarkably well compared to how I last saw you. It really does look more like a month than two days."

"I'm ready to run ten miles and dance a jig at the end of it." His stomach growled, reminding him how long it was to midday yet, but he ignored it, and hoped they had not noticed. He almost did feel as if he had had a month of rest and food. And had had one meal in the last day. "What favor?" he asked suspiciously. Nynaeve did not ask favors, in his recollection; Nynaeve told people what to do and expected to see it done.

"I want you to carry a letter for me," Elayne said before Nynaeve could speak. "To my mother, in Caemlyn." She smiled, making a dimple in her cheek. "I would appreciate it so very much, Mat." The morning light through the windows seemed to pick out highlights in her hair.

I wonder if she likes to dance. He pushed the thought right out of his head. "That does not sound too very hard, but it's a long trip. What do I get out of it?" From the look on her face, he did not think that dimple had failed her very often.

She drew herself up, slim and proud, He could almost see a

throne behind her. "Are you a loyal subject of Andor? Do you not wish to serve the Lion Throne, and your Daughter-Heir?"

Mat snickered.

"I told you that would not work either," Egwene said. "Not with him."

Elayne had a wry twist to her mouth. "I thought it worth a try. It always works on the Guards, in Caemlyn. You said if I smiled—" She cut off short, very obviously not looking at him.

What did you say, Egwene, he thought, furious. *That I'm a fool for any girl who smiles at me?* He kept his outward calm, though, and managed to maintain his grin.

"I wish asking were enough," Egwene said, "but you do not do favors, do you, Mat? Have you ever done anything without being coaxed, wheedled, or bullied?"

He only smiled at her. "I will dance with both of you, Egwene, but I won't run errands." For an instant he thought she was going to stick out her tongue at him.

"If we can go back to what we planned in the first place," Nynaeve said in a too-calm voice. The other two nodded, and she turned her attentions on him. For the first time since coming in, she looked like the Wisdom of old, with a stare that could pin you in your tracks and her braid ready to lash like a cat's tail.

"You are even ruder than I remembered, Matrim Cauthon. With you sick so long—and Egwene, and Elayne, and I taking care of you like a babe in swaddling—I had almost forgotten. Even so, I would think you'd have a little gratitude in you. You've talked about seeing the world, seeing great cities. Well, what better city than Caemlyn? Do what you want, show your gratitude, and help someone all at the same time." She produced a folded parchment from inside her cloak and set it on the table. It was sealed with a lily, in golden yellow wax. "You cannot ask for more than that."

He eyed the paper regretfully. He barely remembered passing through Caemlyn, once, with Rand. It was a shame to stop them now, but he thought it best. *If you want the fun of the jig, you have to pay the harper sooner or later.* And the way Nynaeve was now, the longer he kept from paying, the worse it would be. "Nynaeve, I can't."

"What do you mean, you cannot? Are you a fly on the wall, or a man? A chance to do a favor for the Daughter-

Heir of Andor, to see Caemlyn, to meet Queen Morgase herself in all probability, and you cannot? I really do not know what more you could possibly want. Don't you skitter away like grease on a griddle this time, Matrim Cauthon! Or has your heart changed so you like seeing these all around you?" She waved her left hand in his face, practically hitting him in the nose with her ring.

"Please, Mat?" Elayne said, and Egwene was staring at him as if he had grown horns like a Trolloc.

He squirmed on his chair. "It is not that I don't want to. I cannot! The Amyrlin's made it so I can't get off the bloo— the island. Change that, and I will carry your letter in my teeth, Elayne."

Looks passed between them. He sometimes wondered if women could read each other's minds. They certainly seemed to read his when he least wanted it. But this time, whatever they had decided silently among themselves, they had not read his thoughts.

"Explain," Nynaeve said curtly. "Why would the Amyrlin want to keep you here?"

He shrugged, and looked her straight in the eye, and gave her his best rueful grin. "It's because I was sick. Because it went on so long. She said she would not let me go until she was sure I wouldn't go off somewhere and die. Not that I'm going to, of course. Die, I mean."

Nynaeve frowned, and jerked her braid, and suddenly took his head between her hands; a chill ran through him. *Light, the Power!* Before the thought was done, she had released him.

"What . . . ? What did you do to me, Nynaeve?"

"Not a tenth part of what you deserve, in all likelihood," she said. "You are as healthy as a bull. Weaker than you look, but healthy."

"I told you I was," he said uneasily. He tried to get his grin back. "Nynaeve, she looked like you. The Amyrlin, I mean. Managing to loom even if she is a foot too short for it, and bullying. . . ." The way her eyebrows climbed, he decided that was not a road to go down any further. As long as he kept them away from the Horn. He wondered if they knew. "Well. Anyway, I think they want to keep me here because of that dagger. I mean, until they figure out exactly how it did what it did. You know how Aes Sedai are." He gave a small laugh. They all just looked at him. *Maybe I shouldn't have said that. Burn me! They want to be bloody Aes Sedai. Burn me, I'm going on too long. I wish Nynaeve would stop staring at me like that. Keep it short.* "The Amyrlin made it so I cannot cross a bridge or board a ship without an order from her. You see? It's not that I do not want to help. I just can't."

"But you will if we can get you out of Tar Valon?" Nynaeve said intently.

"You get me out of Tar Valon, and I'll carry Elayne to her mother on my back."

Elayne's eyebrows went up, this time, and Egwene shook her head, mouthing his name with a sharp look in her eyes. Women had no sense of humor, sometimes.

Nynaeve motioned the two of them to follow her to the windows, where they turned their backs to him and talked so softly he could catch only a murmur. He thought he heard Egwene say something about only needing one if they stayed together. Watching, he wondered if they really thought they could get around the Amyrlin's order. *If they can do that, I will carry their bloody letter. I really will carry it in my teeth.*

Without thinking, he picked up an apple core and bit off the end. One chew, and he hastily spit the mouthful of bitter seeds back onto the plate.

When they came back to the table, Egwene handed him a thick, folded paper. He eyed them suspiciously before opening it out. As he read, he began humming to himself without knowing it.

What the bearer does is done at my order and by my authority. Obey, and keep silent, at my command.

                                    Siuan Sanche
                                    Watcher of the Seals
                                    Flame of Tar Valon
                                    The Amyrlin Seat

And sealed at the bottom with the Flame of Tar Valon in a circle of white wax as hard as stone.

He realized he was humming "A Pocket Full of Gold" and stopped. "Is this real? You didn't . . . ? How did you get this?"

"She did not forge it, if that is what you mean," Elayne said.

"Never you mind how we got it," Nynaeve said. "It is real. That is all that need concern you. I would not show it around, were I you, or the Amyrlin will take it back, but it will get you past the guards and onto a ship. You said you'd take the letter, if we did that."

"You can consider it in Morgase's hands right now." He did not want to stop reading the paper, but he folded it back up anyway, and laid it on top of Elayne's letter. "You wouldn't happen to have a little coin to go with this, would you? Some silver? A gold mark or two? I have almost enough for my passage, but I hear things are growing expensive downriver."

Nynaeve shook her head. "Don't you have money? You gambled with Hurin almost every night until you grew too sick to hold the dice. Why should things be more expensive downriver?"

"We gambled for coppers, Nynaeve, and he would not even do that after a while. It doesn't matter. I will manage. Don't you listen to what people say? There's civil war in Cairhien, and I hear it is bad in Tear, too. I've heard a room at an inn in Aringill costs more than a good horse back home."

"We have been busy," she said sharply, and exchanged worried looks with Egwene and Elayne that set him wondering again.

"It doesn't matter. I can make out." There had to be gaming in the inns near the docks. A night with the dice would put him aboard a ship in the morning with a full purse.

"Just you deliver that letter to Queen Morgase, Mat," Nynaeve said. "And do not let anyone know you have it."

"I'll take it to her. I said I would, didn't I? You would think I didn't keep my promises." The looks he got from Nynaeve and Egwene reminded him of a few he had not kept. "I will do it. Blood and—I will do it!"

They stayed awhile longer, talking of home for the most part. Egwene and Elayne sat on the bed, and Nynaeve took the armchair, while he kept his stool. Talk of Emond's Field made him homesick, and it seemed to make Nynaeve and Egwene sad, as if they were speaking of something they would never see again. He was sure their eyes moistened, but when he tried to change the subject, they brought it back ing.

Elayne talked to him of Caemlyn, of what to expect at
the Royal Palace and who to speak to, and a little of the city.
Sometimes she held herself in a way that made him all but
see a crown on her head. A man would have to be a fool to
let himself get involved with a woman like her. When they
rose to leave, he was sorry to see them go.

He stood, suddenly feeling awkward. "Look, you have
done me a favor here." He touched the Amyrlin's paper, on
the table. "A big favor. I know you're all going to be Aes
Sedai"—he stumbled a little on that—"and you will be a
queen one day, Elayne, but if you ever need help, if there
is ever anything I can do, I will come. You can count on it.
Did I say something funny?"

Elayne had a hand over her mouth, and Egwene was
struggling openly with a laugh. "No, Mat," Nynaeve said
smoothly, but her lips twitched. "Just something I have
observed about men."

"You would have to be a woman to understand," Elayne
said.

"Journey well and safely, Mat," Egwene said. "And remember, if a woman does need a hero, she needs him today,
not tomorrow." The laughter bubbled out of her.

He stared at the door closing behind them. Women, he
decided for at least the hundredth time, were odd.

Then his eye fell on Elayne's letter, and the folded paper
lying atop it. The Amyrlin's blessed, not-to-be-understood,
but welcome-as-a-fire-in-winter paper. He danced a little
caper in the middle of the flowered carpet. Caemlyn to
see, and a queen to meet. *Your own words will free me of
you, Amyrlin. And get me away from Selene, too.*

"You'll never catch me," he laughed, and meant it for
both of them. "You'll never catch Mat Cauthon."

CHAPTER
29

A Trap to Spring

I n a corner the spit dog was lying at its ease. Glaring
at it, Nynaeve mopped sweat from her forehead with
her hand and leaned her back into doing the work he
should have done. *I'd not have put it past them to shove me
in his wicker wheel instead of letting me turn this Light-
forsaken handle! Aes Sedai! Burn them all!* It was a measure of her upset that she used such language, and another
that she did not even notice she had done it. She did not
think the fire in the long, gray stone fireplace would seem
any hotter if she crawled into it. She was sure the brindle
dog was grinning at her.

Elayne was skimming grease out of the dripping pan
under the roasts with a long-handled wooden spoon, while
Egwene used its twin to baste the meat. The great kitchen
went on about its midday routine around them. Even the
novices had grown so used to seeing Accepted there that
they hardly even glanced at the three women. Not that the
cooks allowed the novices to dawdle for gawking. Work
built character, so the Aes Sedai said, and the cooks saw
to it that the novices built strong character. And the three
Accepted, too.

Laras, the Mistress of the Kitchens—she was really the
chief cook, but so many had used the other for so long that
it might as well have been her title—came over to examine
the roasts. And the women sweating over them. She was
more than merely stout, with layers of chins, and a spotless
white apron that could have made three novice dresses. She
carried her own long-handled wooden spoon like a scep-
ter. It was not for stirring, that spoon. It was for directing

those under her, and smacking those who were not building character quickly enough to suit her. She studied the roasts, sniffed disparagingly, and turned her frown on the three Accepted.

Nynaeve met Laras' look with a level look of her own and kept turning the spit. The massive woman's face never altered. Nynaeve had tried smiling, but that did nothing to change Laras' expression. Stopping work to speak to her, quite civilly, had been a disaster. It was bad enough being bullied and chivied by Aes Sedai. She had to put up with that, however much it rankled and burned, if she was to learn how to use her abilities. Not that she liked what she could do—it was one thing to know Aes Sedai were not Darkfriends for channeling the Power, but quite another to know she herself could channel—yet she had to learn if she was to get back at Moiraine; hating Moiraine for what she had done to Egwene and the other Emond's Fielders, pulling their lives apart and manipulating them all for Aes Sedai purposes, was nearly all that kept her going. But to be treated as a lazy, none-too-bright child by this Laras, to be forced to curtsy and scurry for this woman she could have put in her place with a few well-chosen words back home— that made her grind her teeth almost as much as did the thought of Moiraine. *Maybe if I just do not look at her. . . . No! I will be burned if I'll drop my eyes before this . . . this cow!*

Laras sniffed more loudly and walked away. She rolled from side to side as she crossed the freshly mopped gray tiles.

Still bending with spoon and greasepot, Elayne glowered after her. "If that woman strikes me but once more, I shall have Gareth Bryne arrest her and—"

"Be quiet," Egwene whispered. She did not stop basting the roasts, and she never looked at Elayne. "She has ears like a—"

Laras turned back as if she had indeed heard, her frown deepening, and her mouth opened wide. Before a sound emerged, the Amyrlin Seat entered the kitchen like a whirlwind. Even the striped stole on her shoulders seemed to bristle. For once, Leane was nowhere to be seen.

At last, Nynaeve thought grimly. *And not beforetime, either!*

But the Amyrlin did not glance her way. The Amyrlin did not say a word to anyone. Running her hand across a tabletop scrubbed bone-white, she looked at her fingers and grimaced as if at filth. Laras was at her side in an instant, all smiles, but the Amyrlin's flat stare made her swallow them in silence.

The Amyrlin stalked about the kitchen. She stared at the women slicing oatcake. She glared at the women peeling vegetables. She sneered into the soup kettles, then at the women tending them; the women became engrossed in studying the surface of the soup. Her frown set the girls carrying plates and bowls out to the dining hall to a run. Her glower put the novices darting like mice sighting a cat. By the time she had made her way half around the kitchen, every woman there was working twice as fast as she had been. By the time she completed her circuit, Laras was the only one even daring to glance at her.

The Amyrlin stopped in front of the roasting spit, fists on her hips, and looked at Laras. She only looked, expressionless, blue eyes cold and hard.

The large woman gulped, and her chins wobbled as she smoothed her apron. The Amyrlin did not blink. Laras' eyes dropped, and she shifted heavily from foot to foot. "If the Mother will pardon me," she said in a faint voice. Making something that might have been meant for a curtsy, she rushed away, so forgetting herself that she joined the women at one of the soup kettles and began stirring with her own spoon.

Nynaeve smiled, keeping her head down to hide it. Egwene and Elayne kept working, too, but they also kept glancing at the Amyrlin, standing with her back to them not two paces away.

The Amyrlin was spreading her stare across the entire kitchen from where she stood. "If they are this easily cowed," she muttered softly, "perhaps they really have been getting away with too much for too long."

Easily cowed indeed, Nynaeve thought. *Pitiful excuses for women. All she did was look at them!* The Amyrlin glanced over a stole-covered shoulder, caught her eye for an instant. Suddenly Nynaeve realized she was turning the spit faster. She told herself she had to pretend to be cowed like everyone else.

The Amyrlin's gaze fell on Elayne, and abruptly she spoke, nearly loud enough to rattle the copper pots and pans hanging on the walls. "There are some words I will not tolerate in a young woman's mouth, Elayne of House Trakand. If you let them in, I will see them scrubbed out!" Everyone in the kitchen jumped.

Elayne looked confused, and indignation crept across Egwene's face.

Nynaeve shook her head, small frantic shakes. *No, girl! Hold your tongue! Don't you see what she is doing?*

But Egwene did open her mouth, with a respectful if determined, "Mother, she did not—"

"Silence!" The Amyrlin's roar produced another ripple of jumps. "Laras! Can you find something to teach two girls to speak when they should and say what they should, *Mistress* of the Kitchens? Can you manage that?"

Laras came waddling faster than Nynaeve had ever seen the woman move before, darting at Elayne and Egwene to seize an ear of each, all the while repeating, "Yes, Mother. Immediately, Mother. As you command, Mother." She hurried the two young women out of the kitchen as if eager to escape the Amyrlin's stare.

The Amyrlin was now close enough to Nynaeve to touch her, but still looking over the kitchen. A young cook, turning with a mixing bowl in her hands, chanced to catch the Amyrlin's eye. She gave a great squeak as she scuttled away across the floor.

"I did not mean for Egwene to be caught in that." The Amyrlin barely moved her lips. It looked as if she were muttering to herself, and from the expression on her face, no one in the kitchen wanted to hear what she was saying. Nynaeve could just make out the words. "But perhaps it will teach her to think before she speaks."

Nynaeve turned the spit and kept her head down, trying to look as if she were also muttering under her breath if anyone looked. "I thought you were going to keep a close eye on us, Mother. So we could report what we find."

"If I come stare at you every day, Daughter, some would grow suspicious." The Amyrlin kept up her study of the kitchen. Most of the women seemed to be avoiding even looking in her direction for fear of incurring her wrath. "I planned to have you brought to my study after the mid-

day meal. To scold you for not choosing your studies, so
I implied to Leane. But there is news that could not wait.
Sheriam found another Gray Man. A woman. Dead as last
week's fish, and not a mark on her. She was laid out as
if resting, right in the middle of Sheriam's bed. Not very
pleasant for Sheriam."

Nynaeve stiffened, and the spit halted for a moment before she put it back to revolving. "Sheriam had a chance to
see the lists Verin gave to Egwene. So did Elaida. I make
no accusations, but they had the chance. And Egwene said
Alanna . . . behaved oddly, too."

"She told you of that, did she? Alanna is Arafellin.
They have strange ideas about honor and debts in Arafel."
She shrugged dismissively, but said, "I suppose I can
keep an eye on her. Have you learned anything useful yet,
child?"

"Some," Nynaeve muttered grimly. *What about keeping
an eye on Sheriam? Maybe she didn't just find that Gray
Man. The Amyrlin could watch Elaida, too, for that matter. So Alanna really did.* . . . "I do not understand why you
trust Else Grinwell, but your message was helpful."

In short, quick sentences, Nynaeve told of the things
they had found in the storeroom under the library, making it seem only she and Egwene had gone, and added the
conclusions they had reached concerning them. She did
not mention Egwene's dream—or whatever it had been;
Egwene insisted it had been real—of *Tel'aran'rhiod*. Nor
did she speak of the *ter'angreal* Verin had given Egwene.
She could not make herself entirely trust the woman wearing the seven-striped stole—or any woman who could wear
the shawl, for that matter—and it seemed best to keep some
things in reserve.

When she was done, the Amyrlin was silent so long that
Nynaeve began to think the woman had not heard. She was
about to repeat herself, a little louder, when the Amyrlin
finally spoke, still hardly moving her lips.

"I sent no message, Daughter. The things Liandrin and
the others left were searched thoroughly, and burned after
nothing was found. No one would use Black Ajah leavings.
As for Else Grinwell. . . . I remember the girl. She could
have learned, had she applied herself, but all she wanted
was to smile at the men at the Warders' practice yard. Else

Grinwell was put on a trading vessel and sent back to her mother ten days ago."

Nynaeve tried to swallow the lump that had formed in her throat. The Amyrlin's words made her think of bullies taunting smaller children. The bullies were always so contemptuous of the littler children, always so sure the small ones were too stupid to realize what was happening, that they made little effort to disguise their snares. That the Black Ajah was so contemptuous of her made her blood boil. That they could set this snare filled her stomach with ice. *Light, if Else was sent away. . . . Light, anybody I talk to could be Liandrin, or any of the others. Light!*

The spit had stopped. Hastily she started it turning once more. No one seemed to have noticed, though. They were all still doing their best not to look at the Amyrlin.

"And what do you mean to do about this . . . so-obvious trap?" the Amyrlin said softly, still staring over the kitchen, away from Nynaeve. "Do you mean to fall into this one, too?"

Nynaeve's face reddened. "I know this trap for a trap. Mother. And the best way to catch whoever set a trap is to spring it and wait for him—or her—to come." It sounded weaker than it had when she had said it to Egwene and Elayne, after what the Amyrlin had just told her, but she still meant it.

"Perhaps so, child. Perhaps it is the way to find them. If they do not come and find you held tightly in their net." She gave a vexed sigh. "I will put gold in your room for the journey. And I will let it be whispered about that I have sent you out to a farm to hoe cabbages. Will Elayne be going with you?"

Nynaeve forgot herself enough to stare at the Amyrlin, then hurriedly put her eyes back on her hands. Her knuckles were white on the spit handle. "You scheming old. . . . Why all the pretense, if you knew? Your sly plots have had us squirming nearly as much as the Black Ajah has. Why?" The Amyrlin's face had tightened, enough to make her force a more respectful tone. "If I may ask, Mother."

The Amyrlin snorted. "Putting Morgase back on the proper path whether she wants to go or not will be hard enough without her thinking I've sent her daughter to sea in a leaky skiff. This way I can say straight out that it was none of my doing. It may be a bit hard on Elayne, when she finally has to face her mother, but I have three hounds, now, not two. I told you I'd have a hundred if I could." She adjusted her stole on her shoulders. "This has gone on long enough. If I stay this close to you, it may be noticed. Have you anything more to tell me? Or to ask? Make it quick, Daughter."

"What is *Callandor*, Mother?" Nynaeve asked.

This time it was the Amyrlin who forgot herself, half turning toward Nynaeve before jerking herself back. "They cannot be allowed to have that." Her whisper was barely audible, as if meant for her own ears alone. "They cannot possibly take it, but. . . ." She took a deep breath, and her soft words firmed enough to be clear to Nynaeve, if to no one two paces further away. "No more than a dozen women in the Tower know what *Callandor* is, and perhaps as many outside. The High Lords of Tear know, but they never speak of it except when a Lord of the Land is told on being raised. The Sword That Cannot Be Touched is a *sa'angreal*, girl. Only two more powerful were ever made, and thank the Light, neither of those was ever used. With *Callandor* in your hands, child, you could level a city at one blow. If you die keeping that out of the Black Ajah's hands—you, and Egwene, and Elayne, all three—you'll have done a service to the whole world, and cheap at the price."

"How could they take it?" Nynaeve asked. "I thought only the Dragon Reborn could touch *Callandor*."

The Amyrlin gave her a sideways look sharp enough to carve the roasts on the spit. "They could be after something else," she said after a moment. "They stole *ter'angreal* here. The Stone of Tear holds nearly as many *ter'angreal* as the Tower."

"I thought the High Lords hated anything to do with the One Power," Nynaeve whispered incredulously.

"Oh, they do hate it, child. Hate it, and fear it. When they find a Tairen girl who can channel, they bundle her onto a ship for Tar Valon before the day is done, with hardly time to speak goodbyes to her family." The Amyrlin's murmur was bitter with memory. "Yet they hold one of the most powerful focuses of the Power the world has ever seen, inside their precious Stone. It is my belief that is why they have collected so many *ter'angreal*—and indeed, anything

to do with the Power—over the years, as if by doing so
they can diminish the existence of the thing they cannot
rid themselves of, the thing that reminds them of their own
doom every time they enter the Heart of the Stone. Their
fortress that has broken a hundred armies will fall as one
of the signs the Dragon is Reborn. Not even the only sign;
just one. How that must rankle their proud hearts. Their
downfall will not even be the one great sign of the world's
change. They cannot even ignore it by staying out of the
Heart. That is where Lords of the Land are raised to High
Lords, and where they must perform what they call the Rite
of the Guarding four times a year, claiming that they guard
the whole world against the Dragon by holding *Callandor*.
It must bite at their souls like a bellyful of live silverpike,
and no more than they deserve." She gave herself a shake,
as if realizing she had said far more than she had intended.
"Is that all, child?"

"Yes, Mother," Nynaeve said. *Light, it always comes back
to Rand, doesn't it? Always back to the Dragon Reborn.* It
was still an effort to think of him that way. "That's all."

The Amyrlin shifted her stole again, frowning at the
frenzied scurry in the kitchen. "I'll have to set this aright.
I needed to speak to you without delay, but Laras is a good
woman, and she manages the kitchen and the larders well."

Nynaeve sniffed, and addressed her hands on the spit
handle. "Laras is a sour lump of lard, and too handy with
that spoon by half." She thought she had muttered it under
her breath, but she heard the Amyrlin chuckle wryly.

"You are a fine judge of character, child. You must have
done well as the Wisdom of your village. It was Laras who
went to Sheriam and demanded to know how long you
three are to be kept to the dirtiest and hardest work, without
a turn at lighter. She said she would not be a party to breaking any woman's health or spirit, no matter what I said. A
fine judge of character, child."

Laras came back into the kitchen doorway then, hesitat-
ing to enter her own domain. The Amyrlin went to meet
her, smiles replacing her frowns and stares.

"It all looks very well to me, Laras." The Amyrlin's
words came loud enough for the entire kitchen to hear. "I
see nothing out of place, and everything as it should be.

You are to be commended. I think I will make Mistress of the Kitchens a formal title."

The stout woman's face fluttered from uneasiness to shock to beaming pleasure. By the time the Amyrlin swept out of the kitchen, Laras was all smiles. Her frown returned, though, as she looked from the Amyrlin's departing back to her workers. The kitchen seemed to leap into motion. Laras' grim stare settled on Nynaeve.

Turning the spit again, Nynaeve tried smiling at the big woman.

Laras' frown deepened, and she began tapping her spoon on her thigh, apparently forgetting that for once it had been used for its intended purpose. It left smears of soup on the white of her apron.

I will smile at her if it kills me, Nynaeve thought, though she had to grit her teeth to do it.

Egwene and Elayne appeared, twisting their faces and scrubbing their mouths with their sleeves. At a stare from Laras, they dashed to the spit and resumed their labors.

"Soap," Elayne muttered thickly, "tastes horrid!"

Egwene trembled as she spooned juice from the dripping pan over the roasts. "Nynaeve, if you tell me the Amyrlin told us to stay here, I will scream. I might run away for real."

"We leave after the washing up is done," she told them, "just as quickly as we can fetch our belongings from our rooms." She wished she could share the eagerness that flashed in their eyes. *Light send we aren't walking into a trap we can't get out of. Light send it so.*

CHAPTER
30

The First Toss

After Nynaeve and the others left him, Mat spent most of the day in his room, except for one brief excursion. He was planning. And eating. He ate nearly everything the serving women brought him, and asked for more. They were more than happy to oblige. It was bread and cheese and fruit he asked for, and he piled winter-wrinkled apples and pears, wedges of cheese and loaves of bread inside the wardrobe, leaving empty trays for them to take away.

At midday he had to endure a visit from an Aes Sedai— Anaiya, he seemed to remember her name was. She put her hands on his head and sent cold chills through him. It was the One Power, he decided, not simply being touched by an Aes Sedai. She was a plain woman despite her smooth cheeks and Aes Sedai serenity.

"You seem much better," she told him, smiling. Her smile made him think of his mother. "Even hungrier than I expected, so I hear, but better. I am informed you are trying to eat the larders bare. Believe me when I say we will see you have all the food you need. You do not have to worry that we'll let you miss a meal before you are fully well again."

He gave the grin he used on his mother when he especially wanted her to believe him. "I know you won't. And I do feel better. I thought I might see some of the city this afternoon. If you have no objections, of course. Maybe visit an inn tonight. There's nothing like a night of common-room talk to pick one's spirits up."

He thought her lips twitched on the edge of a bigger smile. "No one will try to stop you, Mat. But do not try to

leave the city. It will only upset the guards, and bring you
nothing but a trip back here under escort."

"I would not do that, Aes Sedai. The Amyrlin Seat said
I'd starve to death in a few days if I left."

She nodded as if she did not believe a word he said. "Of
course." As she turned from him, her eyes fell on the quarterstaff he had brought from the practice yard, propped in
the corner of the room. "You do not need to protect yourself
from us, Mat. You are as safe here as you could be anywhere. Almost certainly safer."

"Oh, I know that, Aes Sedai. I do." After she left he
frowned at the door, wondering if he had managed to convince her of anything.

It was more evening than afternoon when he left the room
for what he hoped was the final time. The sky was purpling,
and the setting sun painted clouds to the west in shades of
red. Once he had his cloak around him, and the big leather
scrip he had found on his one earlier foray dangling from
his shoulder and bulging with the bread and cheese and
fruit he had squirreled away, one look in the mirror told
him there was no hiding what he intended. He tied the rest
of his clothes up in a roll with the blanket from the bed and
slung that across his shoulders, too. The quarterstaff did for
a walking staff. He left nothing behind. His coat pockets
held all his smaller belongings, and his belt pouch held the
most important. The Amyrlin Seat's paper. Elayne's letter.
And his dice cups.

He saw Aes Sedai as he made his way out of the Tower,
and some of them noticed him, though most merely flickered an eyebrow, and none spoke to him. Anaiya was one.
She gave him an amused smile and a rueful shake of her
head. He returned a shrug and the guiltiest grin he could
manage, and she went silently on, still shaking her head.
The guards at the Tower gates simply looked at him.

It was not until he was across the big square and into the
streets of the city that relief finally surged up in him. And
triumph. *If you can't hide what you are going to do, do it
so everybody thinks you are a fool. Then they stand around
waiting to see you fall on your face. Those Aes Sedai will
be waiting for the guards to bring me back. When I do
not return by morning, then they'll start a search. Not too
frantic at first, because they'll think I have gone to ground*

somewhere in the city. By the time they realize I haven't, this rabbit will be a long way downriver from the hounds.

With as light a heart as he could remember having in years, or so it seemed, he began to hum "We're Over the Border Again," heading toward the harbor where vessels would be sailing down to Tear and all the villages along the Erinin between. He would not be going so far as that, of course. Aringill, where he would take to land again for the rest of the trip to Caemlyn, was only halfway downriver.

I'll deliver your bloody letter. The nerve of her, thinking I'd say I would, then not. I will deliver the bloody thing if it kills me.

Twilight was beginning to cover Tar Valon, but there was still enough light to grace the fantastical buildings, and the oddly shaped towers connected by high bridges spanning open air over hundred-pace drops. People yet filled the streets, in so many different kinds of clothing that he thought every nation must be represented. Along the major avenues, pairs of lamplighters used their ladders to light lanterns atop tall poles. But in the part of Tar Valon he sought, the only light was what spilled from windows.

Ogier had built the great buildings and towers of Tar Valon, but other, newer parts had grown under the hands of men. Newer meaning two thousand years in some cases. Down near Southharbor, men's hands had tried to match, if not duplicate, the fanciful Ogier work. Inns where ships' crews caroused bore enough stonework for palaces. Statues in niches and cupolas on rooftops, ornately worked cornices and intricately carved friezes, all decorated chandlers' shops and merchant houses. Bridges arched across the streets here, too, but the streets were cobblestone, not great paving blocks, and many of the bridges were wood instead of stone, sometimes as low as the second stories of the buildings they joined, and never higher than four.

The dark streets hummed with as much life as any in Tar Valon. Traders off their vessels and those who bought what the vessels carried, people who traveled the River Erinin and people who worked it, all filled the taverns and the common rooms of the inns, in company with those who sought the money such folk carried, by fair means or murky. Raucous music filled the streets from bittern and flute, harp and hammered dulcimer. The first inn Mat entered had three dice games in progress, men crouched in circles near the common-room walls and shouting the wins and losses.

He only meant to gamble an hour or so before finding a ship, just long enough to add a few coins to his purse, but he won. He had always won more than he lost, as far as he could remember, and there had been times with Hurin, and in Shienar, when six or eight tosses in a row won for him. Tonight, every toss won. Every toss.

From the looks some of the men gave him, he was glad he had left his own dice in his pouch. Those looks made him decide to move on. With surprise he realized that he had nearly thirty silver marks in his purse now, but he had not won so much from any one man that they would not all be glad to see him go.

Except for one dark sailor with tight curls—one of the Sea Folk, someone had said, though Mat wondered what one of the Atha'an Miere was doing so far from the sea—who followed him down the darkened street, arguing for a chance to make good his losses. He wanted to reach the docks—thirty silver marks was more than enough—but the sailor argued on, and he had only used half his hour, so he gave in, and with the man entered the next tavern they passed.

He won again, and it was as if a fever gripped him. He won every throw. From tavern to inn to tavern he went, never staying long enough to anger anyone with the amount of his winnings. And he still won every toss. He exchanged silver for gold with a money changer. He played at crowns, and fives, and maiden's ruin. He played games with five dice, and with four, and three, and even only two. He played games he did not know before he squatted in the circle, or took a place at the table. And he won. Somewhere during the night, the dark sailor—Raab, he had said his name was—staggered away, exhausted but with a full purse; he had decided to put his wagers on Mat. Mat visited another money changer—or perhaps two; the fever seemed to cloud his brain as badly as his memories of the past were clouded—and made his way to another game. Winning.

And so he found himself, he did not know how many hours later, in a tavern filled with tabac smoke—The Tremalking Splice, he thought it was called—staring down at five dice, each showing a deeply carved crown. Most of the patrons here seemed interested only in drinking as much as they could, but the rattle of dice and shouts of players from another game in the far corner were almost submerged by a woman singing to a quick tune from a hammered dulcimer.

> I'll dance with a girl with eyes of brown,
> or a girl with eyes of green,
> I'll dance with a girl with any color eyes,
> but yours are the prettiest I've seen.
> I'll kiss a girl with hair of black,
> or a girl with hair of gold,
> I'll kiss a girl with any color hair,
> but it's you I want to hold.

The singer had named the song as "What He Said to Me." Mat remembered the tune as "Will You Dance With Me," with different words, but at that moment all he could think of were those dice.

"The king again," one of the men squatting with Mat muttered. It was the fifth time in a row Mat had thrown the king.

He had won the bet of a gold mark, not even caring by this time that his Andoran mark outweighed the other man's Illianer coin, but he scooped the dice into the leather cup, rattled it hard, and spun them across the floor again. Five crowns. *Light, it can't be. Nobody ever threw the king six times running. Nobody.*

"The Dark One's own luck," another man growled. He was a bulky fellow, his dark hair tied at the nape of his neck with a black ribbon, with heavy shoulders, scars on his face, and a nose that had been broken more than once.

Mat was scarcely aware of moving before he had the bulky man by the collar, hauling him to his feet, slamming him back against the wall. "Don't you say that!" he snarled. "Don't you ever say that!" The man blinked down at him in astonishment; he was a full head taller than Mat.

"Just a saying," somebody behind him was muttering. "Light, it's just a saying."

Mat released his grip on the scar-faced man's coat and backed away. "I. . . . I . . . I don't like anybody saying things like that about me. I'm no Darkfriend!" *Burn me, not the Dark One's luck. Not that! Oh, Light, did that bloody dagger really do something to me?*

"Nobody said you was," the broken-nosed man muttered. He seemed to be getting over his surprise, and trying to decide whether to be angry.

Gathering his belongings from where he had piled them behind him, Mat walked out of the tavern, leaving the coins where they lay. It was not that he was afraid of the big man. He had forgotten the man, and the coins, too. All he wanted was to be outside, in fresh air, where he could think.

In the street, he leaned against the wall of the tavern not far from the door, breathing the coolness in. The dark streets of Southharbor were all but empty, now. Music and laughter still floated from the inns and taverns, but few people made their way through the night. Holding the quarterstaff upright in front of him with both hands, he lowered his head to his fists and tried to think at the puzzle from every side.

He knew he was lucky. He could remember always being lucky. But somehow, his memories from Emond's Field did not show him as lucky as he had been since leaving. Certainly he had gotten away with a great deal, but he could remember also being caught in pranks he had been sure would succeed. His mother had always seemed to know what he was up to, and Nynaeve able to see through whatever defenses he put up. But it was not just since leaving the Two Rivers that he had become lucky. The luck had come once he took the dagger from Shadar Logoth. He remembered playing at dice back home with a sharp-eyed, skinny man who worked for a merchant come down from Baerlon to buy tabac. He remembered the strapping his father had given him, too, on learning Mat owed the man a silver mark and four pence.

"But I'm free of the bloody dagger," he mumbled. "Those bloody Aes Sedai said I was." He wondered how much he had won tonight.

When he dug into his coat pockets, he found them filled with loose coins, crowns and marks, both silver and gold that glittered and glinted in the light from nearby windows. He had two purses now, it seemed, and both fat. He undid the strings, and found more gold. And still more stuffed into his belt pouch between and around and on top of his dice cups, crumpling Elayne's letter and the Amyrlin's paper. He had a memory of tossing silver pence to serving girls because they had pretty smiles or pretty eyes or pretty ankles, and because silver pence were not worth keeping.

Not worth keeping? Maybe they weren't. Light, I'm rich! I am bloody rich! Maybe it was something the Aes Sedai did. Something they did Healing me. By accident, maybe. That could be it. Better that the other. Those bloody Aes Sedai must have done it to me.

A big man moved out from the tavern, the door already swinging shut to cut off the light that might have shown his face.

Mat pressed his back close against the wall, stuffed the purses back into his coat, and firmed his grip on the quarterstaff. Wherever his luck tonight had come from, he did not mean to lose all that gold to a footpad.

The man turned toward him, peered, then gave a start. "C-cool night," he said drunkenly. He staggered closer, and Mat saw that most of his size was fat. "I have to. . . . I have to. . . ." Stumbling, the fat man moved on up the street, talking to himself disjointedly.

"Fool!" Mat muttered, but he was not sure whether he meant it for the fat man or for himself. "Time to find a ship to take me away from here." He squinted at the black sky, trying to estimate how long till dawn. Two, maybe three hours, he thought. "Past time." His stomach growled at him; he dimly recalled eating in some of the inns, but he did not remember what. The fever of the dice had had him by the throat. A hand pushed into the scrip found only crumbs. "Way past time. Or one of them will come pick me up with her fingers and stick me in her pouch." He pushed away from the wall and started for the docks, where the ships would be.

At first he thought the faint sounds behind him were echoes of his boots on the cobblestones. Then he realized someone was following him. And trying to be stealthy. *Well*, these *are footpads, for sure.*

Hefting the quarterstaff, he briefly considered turning to confront them. But it was dark, and the footing on cobblestones uncertain, and he had no idea how many there were. *Just because you did well against Gawyn and Galad doesn't make you a bloody hero out of a story.*

He turned down a narrower, twisting side street, trying to walk on tiptoe and move quickly at the same time. Every

window was dark here, and most shuttered. He was almost
to the end when he saw movement ahead, two men peering
into the side street from where it let out onto another. And
he heard slow footsteps behind him, soft scrapes of boot
leather on stone.

In an instant he ducked into the shadowy corner where
one building stuck out further than the next. It seemed the
best he could do for the moment. Gripping the quarterstaff
nervously, he waited.

A man appeared from back the way he had come, crouching as he eased himself ahead one slow step at a time, and
then another man. Each carried a knife in his hand and
moved as if stalking.

Mat tensed. If they came just a few steps closer before
they noticed him hiding in the deeper shadows of the corner, he could take them by surprise. He wished his stomach would stop fluttering. Those knives were a great deal
shorter than the practice swords, but they were steel, not
wood.

One of the men squinted toward the far end of the narrow
street and suddenly straightened, shouting, "Didn't he come
your way, then?"

"I have seen nothing but the shadows," came the answer
in a heavy accent. "I wish to be out of this. There are the
strange things moving this night."

Not four paces from Mat, the two men exchanged looks,
sheathed their knives, and trotted back the way they had
come.

He let out a long, slow breath. *Luck. Burn me if it's not
good for more than dice.*

He could no longer see the men at the mouth of the street,
but he knew they were still out on the next street somewhere. And more behind him the other way.

One of the buildings he was crouched against stood only
a single story high here, and the roof looked flat enough.
And a white stone frieze carved in huge grape leaves ran up
the joining of the two buildings.

Easing his quarterstaff up till one end rested on the edge
of the roof, he gave it a hard shove. It landed with a clatter
on the roof tiles. Not waiting to see if anyone had heard, he
scrambled up the frieze, the big leaves giving easy toeholds
even for a man in boots. In seconds he had the staff back

in hand and was trotting across the roof, trusting to luck for his footing.

Three more times he climbed, each time gaining one story. The slightly sloping, tiled roofs ran some distance at that level, and there was a breeze at that height, prickling the hair on the back of his neck with its chill and almost making him think he was being followed. *Stop that, fool! They're three streets away by now, looking for somebody else with a fat purse, and bad luck to them.*

His boots slipped on the tiles, and he decided it might be a good idea to think about getting back down into the street himself. Cautiously, he moved to the edge of the roof and peered down. An empty street lay a good forty feet or more below him, with three taverns and an inn spilling light and music onto the cobblestones. But off to his right was a stone bridge running from the top floor of his building to the one on the other side.

The bridge looked awfully narrow, running through darkness untouched by the tavern lights, arcing over a long fall to hard cobblestones, but he tossed the quarterstaff down and made himself follow before he could think about it too much. His boots thumped onto the bridge, and he let himself roll the way he had as a boy falling out of a tree. He fetched up against the waist-high railing.

"Bad habits pay off in the long run," he told himself as he got to his feet and picked up the staff.

The window at the other end of the bridge was tightly shuttered and lightless. He did not think whoever lived in there would appreciate a stranger appearing in the middle of the night. He could see lots of stonework, but if there was as much as a fingerhold in reach of the bridge, the night hid it. *Well, stranger or no stranger, inside I go.*

He turned from the railing and suddenly became aware of a man sharing the bridge with him. A man with a dagger in his hand.

Mat grabbed at the hand as the knife darted toward his throat. He barely caught the fellow's wrist with his fingers, and then the quarterstaff between them tangled itself in his legs, tripping him to fall back against the railing, to fall half over it pulling the other man on top of him. Balanced there on the small of his back, teetering with his assailant's bared teeth in his face, he was as aware of the long drop under

his head as he was of the blade catching faint moonlight
as it edged toward his throat. His finger grip on the man's
wrist was slipping, and his other hand was caught with the
quarterstaff between their bodies. Only seconds had passed
since he first saw the man, and in seconds more, he was going to die with a knife in his throat.

"Time to toss the dice," he said. He thought the other
man looked confused for an instant, but an instant was all
he had. With a heave of his legs, Mat flipped them both off
into the empty air.

For a stretched-out moment he seemed to have no weight.
Air whistled past his ears and ruffled his hair. He thought
he heard the other man scream, or start to. The impact
knocked all the air out of his lungs and made silver-black
flecks dance across his blurring vision.

When he could breathe again—and see—he realized
he was lying on top of the man who had attacked him, his
fall cushioned by the other's body. "Luck," he whispered.
Slowly he climbed to his feet, cursing the bruise the quarterstaff had put across his ribs.

He expected the other man to be dead—not many could
survive a thirty-foot fall to cobblestones with another's
weight on top of him—but what he had not expected was
to see the fellow's dagger driven to the hilt into his own
heart. Such an ordinary-looking man to have tried to kill
him. Mat did not think he would even have noticed him in
a crowded room.

"You had bad luck, fellow," he told the corpse shakily.

Suddenly, everything that had happened rushed back in
on him. The footpads in the twisting street. The scramble
over the rooftops. This fellow. The fall. His eyes rose to
the bridge overhead, and a fit of trembling hit him. *I must
have been crazy. A little adventure is one thing, but Rogosh
Eagle-eye wouldn't ask for this.*

He realized he was standing over a dead man with a dagger in his chest, just waiting for someone to come along and
run shouting for city guards with the Flame of Tar Valon on
their chests. The Amyrlin's paper might get him away from
them, but maybe not before she found out. He could still
end up back in the White Tower, without that paper, and
possibly not even allowed outside the Tower grounds.

He knew he should be on his way to the docks right then,

and on the first vessel sailing if it was a rotten tub full of
old fish, but his knees were shaking hard enough in reaction
that he could hardly walk. What he wanted was to sit down
for just a minute. Just a minute to steady his knees, and then
he was headed for the docks.

The taverns were closer, but he started toward the inn.
The common room of an inn was a friendly place, where
a man could rest a minute and not worry about who might
be sneaking up behind him. Enough light came out through
the windows for him to make out the sign. A woman with
her hair in braids, holding what he thought was an olive
branch, and the words "The Woman of Tanchico."

CHAPTER
31

The Woman of Tanchico

T he common room of the inn was brightly lit, the tables not near a quarter full so late. A few white-aproned serving women with mugs of ale or wine passed among the men, and a low murmur of talk ran under the sound of a harp being strummed and plucked. The patrons, some with pipes clenched in their teeth and one pair hunched over a stones board, had the look of ship's officers and minor merchants from the smaller houses, their coats well cut and of fine wool, but with none of the gold or silver or embroidery that richer men might have had. And for once there was no clack and rattle of dice to be heard. Fires blazed on the long hearths at the ends of the room, but even without those there would have been a warm feeling about the place.

The harper stood on a tabletop, reciting "Mara and the Three Foolish Kings," to the music of his harp. His instrument, all worked in gold and silver, was fit for a palace. Mat knew him. He had saved Mat's life, once.

The harper was a lean man who would have been tall except for a stoop, and he moved with a limp when he shifted his footing on the tabletop. Even here inside, he wore his cloak, all covered with fluttering patches in a hundred colors. He always wanted everyone to know he was a gleeman. His long mustaches and bushy eyebrows were as snow-white as the thick hair on his head, and his blue eyes held a look of sorrow as he recited. The look was as unexpected as the man. Mat had never known Thom Merrilin to be a sorrowful man.

He took a table, setting his things on the floor by his stool, and ordered two mugs. The pretty young serving girl's big brown eyes twinkled at him.

"Two, young master? You do not look such a hard-drinking man as that." Her voice held a mischievous edge of laughter.

After rummaging a bit, he brought out two silver pennies from his pocket. One more than paid for the wine, but he slipped her another for her eyes. "My friend will be joining me."

He knew Thom had seen him. The old gleeman had nearly stopped the story dead when Mat came in. That was new, too. Few things startled Thom enough for him to let it show, and nothing short of Trollocs had ever made him stop a story in the middle that Mat knew. When the girl brought the wine and his coppers in change, he let the pewter mugs sit and listened to the end of the story.

"'It was as we have said it should be,' said King Madel, trying to untangle a fish from his long beard." Thom's voice seemed almost to echo inside a great hall, not an ordinary common room. His plucked harp sounded the three kings' final foolishness. "'It was as we said it would be,' announced Orander. And, feet slipping in the mud, he sat down with a great splash. 'It was as we said it must be,' proclaimed Kadar as he searched, up to his elbows in the river, for his crown. 'The woman knows not whereof she speaks. She is the fool!' Madel and Orander agreed with him loudly. And with that, Mara had had enough. 'I've given them all the chances they deserve and more,' she murmured to herself. Slipping Kadar's crown into her bag with the first two, she climbed back onto her cart, clucked to her mare, and drove straight back to her village. And when Mara had told them all that happened, the people of Heape would have no king at all." He strummed the major theme of the kings' foolishness once more, this time sliding to a crescendo that sounded even more like laughter, made a sweeping bow, and nearly fell off the table.

Men laughed and stamped their feet, though likely every one of them had heard the story many times before, and called for more. The story of Mara was always well received, except perhaps by kings.

Thom nearly fell again climbing down from the table, and he was more unsteady in his walk than a somewhat stiff

leg could account for as he came to where Mat was sitting.
Casually putting his harp on the table, he dropped onto a
stool in front of the second mug and gave Mat a flat stare.
His eyes had always been sharp as awls, but they seemed to
be having trouble focusing.

"Common," he muttered. His voice was still deep, but
it no longer seemed to reverberate. "The tale is a hundred
times better in Plain Chant, and a thousand in High, but
they want Common." Without another word, he buried his
face in his wine.

Mat could not recall ever seeing Thom finish playing that
harp without immediately putting it away in its hard leather
case. He had never seen him the worse for drink. It was a
relief to hear the gleeman complaining about his listeners;
Thom never thought their standards were as high as his. At
least something of him had not changed.

The serving girl was back, with no twinkle in her eyes.
"Oh, Thom," she said softly, then rounded on Mat. "If I'd
known he was the friend you awaited, I'd not have brought
you wine for him if you gave a hundred silver pence."

"I did not know he was drunk," Mat protested.

But her attention was back on Thom, her voice gentle
again. "Thom, you need some rest. They'll keep you telling
stories all night and all day, if you let them."

Another woman appeared on Thom's other side, lifting
her apron off over her head. She was older than the first, but
no less pretty. The two might have been sisters. "A beautiful
story, I've always thought, Thom, and you tell it beautifully.
Come, I've slipped a warming pan into your bed, and you
can tell me all about the court in Caemlyn."

Thom peered into the mug as if surprised to find it
empty, then blew out his long mustaches and looked from
one woman to the other. "Pretty Mada. Pretty Saal. Did I
ever tell you that two pretty women have loved me in my
life? That is more than most men can claim."

"You've told us all about it, Thom," the older woman said
sadly. The younger glared at Mat as if this were all his fault.

"Two," Thom murmured. "Morgase had a temper, but I
thought I could ignore that, so it ended with her wanting to
kill me. Dena, I killed. As good as. Not much difference.
Two chances I've had, more than most, and I threw them
both away."

"I will take care of him," Mat said. Mada and Saal were both glaring at him, now. He gave them his best smile, but it did not work. His stomach muttered loudly. "Don't I smell chicken roasting? Bring me three or four." The two women blinked and exchanged startled looks when he added, "Do you want something to eat, too, Thom?"

"I could do with more of this fine Andoran wine." The gleeman raised his cup hopefully.

"No more wine for you tonight, Thom." The older woman would have taken his cup if he had let her.

Almost on top of the first woman, the younger said, in a mixture of firmness and pleading, "You'll have some chicken, Thom. It is very good."

Neither would leave until the gleeman agreed to eat something, and when they did go, they gave Mat such a combination of stares and sniffs that he could only shake his head. *Burn me, you would think I was encouraging him to drink more! Women! But pretty eyes on the pair of them.*

"Rand said you were alive," he told Thom when Mada and Saal were out of hearing. "Moiraine always said she thought you were. But I heard you were in Cairhien, and meaning to go on to Tear."

"Rand is still well, then?" Thom's eyes sharpened to almost the keenness Mat remembered. "I am not sure I expected that. Moiraine is still with him, is she? A fine-looking woman. A fine woman, if she were not Aes Sedai. Meddle with that sort, and you get more than your fingers burned."

"Why wouldn't you expect Rand to be all right?" Mat asked carefully. "Do you know of something that could harm him?"

"Know? I don't know anything, boy. I suspect more than is healthy for me, but I know nothing."

Mat abandoned that line of talk. *No use firming his suspicions. No use letting him know I know more than's healthy myself.*

The older woman—Thom called her Mada—came back with three chickens with crisp, brown skins, giving the white-haired man a worried look, and Mat a warning one, before she left. Mat ripped off a leg and set to as he talked. Thom frowned into his cup and never looked at the birds.

"Why are you here in Tar Valon, Thom? It's the last place

I'd have expected to see you, the way you feel about Aes Sedai. I heard you were coining money in Cairhien."

"Cairhien," the old gleeman muttered, the sharpness fading from his eyes again. "Such trouble it causes killing a man, even when he deserves killing." He made a flourish with one hand and was holding a knife. Thom always had knives secreted about him. Drunk he might have been, but he held the blade steady enough. "Kill a man who needs killing, and sometimes others pay for it. The question is, was it worth doing anyway? There's always a balance, you know. Good and evil. Light and Shadow. We would not be human if there wasn't a balance."

"Put that away," Mat growled around a mouthful. "I don't want to talk about killing." *Light, that fellow is still lying right out there in the street. Burn me, I ought to be on a ship by now.* "I just asked why you're in Tar Valon. If you had to leave Cairhien because you killed someone, I do not want to know about it. Blood and ashes, if you can't pull your wits out of the wine enough to talk straight, I'll leave now."

With a sour look, Thom made the knife disappear. "Why am I in Tar Valon? I'm here because it is the worst place I could be, except maybe Caemlyn. It's what I deserve, boy. Some of the Red Ajah still remember me. I saw Elaida in the street the other day. If she knew I was here, she would peel my hide off in strips, and then she would stop being pleasant."

"I never knew you to feel sorry for yourself," Mat said disgustedly. "Do you mean to drown yourself in wine?"

"What do you know of it, boy?" Thom snarled. "Put a few years on you, see something of life, maybe love a woman or two, and then you'll know. Perhaps you will, if you have the brains to learn. Aaaah! You want to know why I'm in Tar Valon? Why are you in Tar Valon? I remember you shivering when you found out Moiraine was Aes Sedai. You nearly soiled yourself every time anybody even mentioned the Power. What are you doing in Tar Valon, with Aes Sedai on every side?"

"I am leaving Tar Valon. That's what I am doing here. Leaving!" Mat grimaced. The gleeman had saved his life, and maybe more. A Fade had been involved. That was why Thom's right leg did not work as well as it should. *There*

could not be enough wine on a ship to keep him this drunk.
"I am going to Caemlyn, Thom. If you need to risk your
fool life for some reason, why not come with me?"

"Caemlyn?" Thom said musingly.

"Caemlyn, Thom. Elaida will likely be going back there
sooner or later, so you'd have her to worry about. And from
what I remember, if Morgase puts her hands on you, you
will wish Elaida had you."

"Caemlyn. Yes. Caemlyn would fit my mood like a
glove." The gleeman glanced at the chicken platter and gave
a start. "What did you do, boy? Stuff them up your sleeve?"
There was nothing left of the three birds but bones and carcasses with only a few strips of flesh remaining.

"Sometimes I get hungry," Mat muttered. It was an effort
not to lick his fingers. "Are you coming with me, or not?"

"Oh, I will come, boy." As Thom pushed himself to his
feet, he did not seem as unsteady as he had been. "You wait
here—and try not to eat the table—while I get my things
and say some goodbyes." He limped away, not staggering
once.

Mat drank a little of his wine and stripped off a few
shreds that were left on the chicken carcasses, wondering if
he had time to order another, but Thom was back quickly.
His harp and flute in their dark leather cases hung on his
back with a tied blanketroll. He carried a plain walking
staff as tall as he was. The two serving women followed
on either side. Mat decided they were sisters. Identical big
brown eyes looked up at the gleeman with identical expressions. Thom was kissing first Saal, then Mada, and patting
cheeks as he headed for the door, jerking his head for Mat
to follow. He was outside before Mat could finish collecting
his own belongings and pick up his quarterstaff.

The younger of the two women, Saal, stopped Mat as he
reached the door. "Whatever you said to him, I forgive you
for the wine, even if it is taking him away. I've not seen him
this alive in weeks." She pressed something into his hand,
and when he glanced at it, his eyes widened in confusion.
She had given him a silver Tar Valon mark. "For whatever it
was you said. Besides, whoever is feeding you is not doing
a good job of it, but you still have pretty eyes." She laughed
at the expression on his face.

Mat was laughing, too, in spite of himself, as he went out

into the street, rolling the silver coin across the backs of his fingers. *So I have pretty eyes, do I?* His laughter shut off like the last drip from a wine barrel: Thom was there, but not the corpse. The windows of the taverns down the street put enough light across the cobblestones for him to be sure of it. The city guard would not have carried a dead man away without asking questions, at those taverns and at The Woman of Tanchico, too.

"What are you staring at, boy?" Thom asked. "No Trollocs in those shadows."

"Footpads," Mat muttered. "I was thinking about footpads."

"No street thieves or strong-arms in Tar Valon, either, boy. When the guards take a footpad—not that many try that game here; the word spreads—but when they do, they haul him to the Tower, and whatever it is the Aes Sedai do to him, the fellow leaves Tar Valon the next day as wide-eyed as a goosed girl. I understand they're even harder on women caught thieving. No, the only way you'll have your money stolen here is somebody selling you polished brass for gold or using shaved dice. There are no footpads."

Mat turned on his heel and strode past Thom, heading toward the docks, quarterstaff thumping off the cobblestones as if he could push himself ahead faster. "We're going to be on the first ship sailing, whatever it is. The first, Thom."

Thom's stick clicked hurriedly after him. "Slow down, boy. What's your hurry? There are plenty of ships, sailing day and night. Slow down. There aren't any footpads."

"The first bloody ship, Thom! If it's sinking, we'll be on it!" *If they weren't footpads, what were they? They had to be thieves. What else could they be?*

CHAPTER
32

The First Ship

Southharbor itself, the great Ogier-made basin, was huge and round, surrounded by high walls of the same silver-streaked white stone as the rest of Tar Valon. One long wharf, most of it roofed, ran all the way around, except where the wide water gates stood open to give access to the river. Vessels of every size lined the wharf, most moored by the stern, and despite the hour dockmen in coarse, sleeveless shirts hurried about loading and unloading bales and chests, crates and barrels, with ropes and booms, or on their backs. Lamps hanging from the roof beams lit the wharfs and made a band of light around the black water in the middle of the harbor. Small open boats scuttled through the darkness, the square lanterns atop their tall sternposts making it seem as if fireflies skittered across the harbor. They were small only compared to the ships, though; some had as many as six pairs of long oars.

When Mat led a still-muttering Thom under an arch of polished redstone and down broad steps to the wharf, crewmen on one three-masted ship were unfastening the mooring lines not twenty paces away. The vessel was larger than most Mat could see, between fifteen and twenty spans from sharp bow to squared stern, with a flat, railed deck almost level with the wharf. The important thing was that it was casting off. *The first ship that sails.*

A gray-haired man came up the wharf: three lines of hemp rope sewn down the sleeves of his dark coat marked him as a dockmaster. His wide shoulders suggested that he might have begun as a dockman hauling rope instead of wearing it. He glanced casually in Mat's direction, and stopped, surprise on his leathery face. "Your bundles say what you're planning, lad, but you might as well forget it. The sister showed me a drawing of you. You'll board no ship in Southharbor, lad. Go back up those stairs so I don't have to tell a man off to watch you."

"What under the Light . . . ?" Thom murmured.

"That's all changed," Mat said firmly. The ship was casting off the last mooring line; the furled triangular sails still made thick, pale bundles on the long, slanted booms, but men were readying the sweeps. He pulled the Amyrlin's paper out of his pouch and thrust it in the dockmaster's face. "As you can see, I'm on the business of the Tower, at the order of the Amyrlin Seat herself. And I have to leave on that very vessel there."

The dockmaster read the words, then read them again. "I never saw such a thing in my life. Why would the Tower say you couldn't go, then give you . . . *that*?"

"Ask the Amyrlin, if you want," Mat told him in a weary voice that said he did not think anyone could possibly be stupid enough to do that, "but she'll have my hide, and yours, if I do not sail on that ship."

"You'll never make it," the dockmaster said, but he was already cupping his hands to his mouth. "Aboard the *Gray Gull* there! Stop! The Light burn you, stop!"

The shirtless fellow at the tiller looked back, then spoke to a tall companion in a dark coat with puffy sleeves. The tall man never took his eyes off the crewmen just dipping the sweeps into the water. "Give way together," he called, and sweepblades curled up froth.

"I'll make it," Mat snapped. *The first ship I said, and the first ship I meant!* "Come on, Thom!"

Without waiting to see if the gleeman followed, he ran down the wharf, dodging around men and barrows stacked with cargo. The gap between the *Gray Gull*'s stern and the wharf widened as the sweeps bit deeper. Hefting his quarterstaff, he hurled it ahead of him toward the ship like a spear, took one more step, and jumped as hard as he could.

The dark water passing beneath his feet looked icy, but in a heartbeat he had cleared the ship's rail and was rolling across the deck. As he scrambled to his feet, he heard a grunt and a curse behind him.

Thom Merrilin hoisted himself up on the railing with another curse, and climbed over onto the deck. "I lost my stick," he muttered. "I'll want another." Rubbing his right leg, he peered down at the still widening strip of water behind the vessel and shivered. "I had a bath today already." The shirtless steersman stared wide-eyed from him to Mat and back again, clutching the tiller as if wondering whether he could use it to defend himself from madmen.

The tall man seemed nearly as stunned. His pale blue eyes bulged, and his mouth worked soundlessly for a moment. His dark beard, cut to a point, seemed to quiver with rage, and his narrow face grew purple. "By the Stone!" he bellowed finally. "What is the meaning of this? I've no room on this vessel for as much as a ship's cat, and I'd not take vagabonds who leap onto my decks if I did. Sanor! Vasa! Heave this rubbish over the side!" Two extremely large men, barefoot and stripped to the waist, straightened from coiling lines and started toward the stern. The men at the sweeps continued their work, bending to lift the blades, taking three long steps along the deck, then straightening and walking backwards, hauling the ship ahead on their blades.

Mat waved the Amyrlin's paper toward the bearded man—the captain, he supposed—with one hand, and fished a gold crown out of his pouch with the other, taking care even in his haste that the fellow saw there were more where that came from. Tossing the heavy coin to the man, he spoke quickly, still waving the paper. "For the inconvenience of our boarding as we did, Captain. More to come for passage. On business of the White Tower. Personal command of the Amyrlin Seat. Imperative we sail immediately. To Aringill, in Andor. Utmost urgency. The blessings of the White Tower on all who aid us; the Tower's wrath on any who impede us."

Certain the man had seen the Flame of Tar Valon seal by that time—and little more, Mat hoped—he folded the paper again and thrust it back out of sight. Eyeing the two big men uneasily as they came up on either side of the captain— *Burn me, they both have arms like Perrin's!*—he wished he had his quarterstaff in hand. He could see it lying where it had landed, further down the deck. He tried to look sure and confident, the sort of man others had better not trifle with, a man with the power of the White Tower behind him. *A long way behind me, I hope.*

The captain looked at Mat doubtfully, and even more so at Thom in his gleeman's cloak and none too steady afoot, but he motioned Sanor and Vasa to stop where they were. "I would not anger the Tower. Burn my soul, for the time being the river trade takes me from Tear to this den of. . . . I come too often to anger . . . anyone." A tight smile appeared on his face. "But I spoke the truth. By the Stone, I did! Six cabins I have for passengers, and all full. You can sleep on deck and eat with the crew for another gold crown. Each."

"That is ridiculous!" Thom snapped. "I don't care what the war has done downriver, that is ridiculous!" The two large sailors shifted their bare feet.

"It is the price," the captain said firmly. "I do not want to anger anyone, but I'd as soon not have any business you can be on aboard my vessel. Like letting a man pay you so he can coat you with hot tar, mixing in *that* business. You pay the price, or you go over the side, and the Amyrlin Seat herself can dry you off. And I'll keep this for the trouble you've given me, thank you." He stuffed the gold crown Mat has tossed him into a pocket of his puffy-sleeved coat.

"How much for one of the cabins?" Mat asked. "To ourselves. You can put whoever is in it now with someone else." He did not want to sleep out in the cold night. *And if you don't overwhelm a fellow like this, he'll steal your breeches and say he is doing you a favor.* His stomach rumbled loudly. "And we eat what you eat, not with the crew. And plenty of it!"

"Mat," Thom said, "I'm the one who is supposed to be drunk here." He turned to the captain, flourishing his patch-covered cloak as well as he could with blanketroll and instrument cases hung about him. "As you may have noticed, Captain, I am a gleeman." Even in the open air, his voice suddenly seemed to echo. "For the price of our passages, I would be more than glad to entertain your passengers and your crew—"

"My crew is aboard to work, gleeman, not be entertained." The captain stroked his pointed beard; his pale eyes priced Mat's plain coat to the copper. "So you want a cabin, do you?" He barked a laugh. "And my meals? Well, you can have my cabin and my meals. For five gold crowns from each of you! Andoran weight!" Those were the heaviest. He began to laugh so hard his words came out in wheezes. Flanking him, Sanor and Vasa grinned wide grins. "For ten crowns, you can take my cabin, and my meals, and I'll move in with the passengers and eat with the crew. Burn my soul, I will! By the Stone, I swear it! For ten gold crowns. . . ." Laughter choked off anything else.

He was still laughing and gasping for breath and wiping tears from his eyes when Mat pulled out one of his two purses, but laughter stopped by the time Mat had counted five crowns into his hands. The captain blinked in disbelief; the two big crewmen looked poleaxed.

"Andoran weight, you said?" Mat asked. It was hard to judge without scales, but he laid seven more on the pile. Two actually were Andoran, and he thought the others made up the weight. *Close enough, for this fellow.* After a moment, he added another two gold Tairen crowns. "For whoever you'll be pushing out of the cabin they paid for." He did not think the passengers would see a copper of it, but it sometimes paid to appear generous. "Unless you mean to share with them? No, of course not. They ought to have something for having to crowd in with others. There's no need for you to eat with your crew, Captain. You are welcome to share Thom's meals and mine in your cabin." Thom stared at him as hard as the others did.

"Are you . . . ?" The bearded man's voice was a hoarse whisper. "Are you . . . by any chance . . . a young lord in disguise?"

"I am no lord." Mat laughed. He had reason to laugh. The *Gray Gull* was well out into the darkness of the harbor, now, with the wharf a band of light pointing up the black gap, not far ahead now, where the water gates let out onto the river. The sweeps drove the vessel toward that gap quickly. Men were already swinging the long, slanting booms around preparatory to unlashing the sails. And with gold in his hands, the captain no longer seemed ready to throw anyone overboard. "If you don't mind, Captain, could we see our cabin? Your cabin, I mean. It's late, and I for one want a few hours' sleep." His stomach spoke to him. "And supper!"

As the vessel put its bow into the blackness, the bearded man himself led the way down a ladder to a short, narrow passage lined with doors set close together. While the captain cleared his things from his cabin—it ran the width of the stern, with its bed and all of its furnishings built into the walls except two chairs and a few chests—and saw that Mat and Thom were settled, Mat learned a great deal, beginning with the fact that the man would not be pushing any passengers out of their quarters. He had too much respect for the coin they had paid, if not for them, to allow that. The captain would take his first's cabin, and that officer would take the second's bed, pushing each lower man down till the deckmaster would end sleeping up in the bow with the crew.

Mat did not think that information could be very useful, but he listened to everything the man said. It was always best to know not only where you were going, but who you were dealing with, or they might just take your coat and boots and leave you to walk home through the rain in bare feet.

The captain was a Tairen named Huan Mallia, and he spoke with great volubility once he had worked out Mat and Thom to his own satisfaction. He was not nobly born, he said, not him, but he would not have anyone think he was a fool. A young man with more gold than any young man should have by right might be a thief, if everyone did not know thieves never escaped Tar Valon with their haul. A young man dressed like a farmboy but with the air and confidence of the lord he denied being—"By the Stone, I'll not say you are, if you say you are not." Mallia winked and chuckled and tugged the point of his beard. A young man carrying a paper bearing the Amyrlin Seat's seal and bound for Andor. There was no secret that Queen Morgase had visited Tar Valon, though her reason certainly was. It was obvious to Mallia something was afoot between Caemlyn and Tar Valon. And Mat and Thom were messengers—for Morgase, he thought, by Mat's accent. Anything he could do to help in so great an enterprise would be his pleasure, not that he meant to poke where he was not wanted.

Mat exchanged startled looks with Thom, who was stowing his instrument cases under a table built out from one wall. The room had two small windows on either side, and a pair of lamps in jointed brackets for light. "That's nonsense," Mat said.

"Of course," Mallia replied. He straightened from pulling clothes out of a chest at the foot of the bed and smiled. "Of course." A cupboard in the wall seemed to hold charts of the river he would need. "I'll say no more."

But he did mean to poke, though he attempted to disguise it, and he rambled while he tried to pry. Mat listened, and answered the questions with grunts or shrugs or a word or two, while Thom said less than that. The gleeman kept shaking his head while unburdening himself of his possessions.

Mallia had been a river man all his life, though he dreamed of sailing on the sea. He hardly spoke of a country beside Tear without contempt; Andor was the only one to escape, and the praise he finally managed was grudging despite his obvious efforts. "Good horses in Andor, I've heard. Not bad. Not as good as Tairen stock, but good enough. You make good steel, and iron goods, bronze and copper—I've traded for them often enough, though you charge a weighty price—but then you have those mines in the Mountains of Mist. Gold mines, too. We have to earn our gold, in Tear."

Mayene received his greatest contempt. "Even less a country than Murandy is. One city and a few leagues of land. They underprice the oil from our good Tairen olives just because their ships know how to find the oilfish shoals. They've no right to be a country at all."

He hated Illian. "One day we'll loot Illian bare, tear down every town and village, and sow their filthy ground with salt." Mallia's beard almost bristled with outrage at how filthy the Illian land was. "Even their olives are putrid! One day we'll carry every last Illianer pig off in chains! That is what the High Lord Samon says."

Mat wondered what the man thought Tear would do with all those people if they actually fulfilled this scheme. The Illianers would have to be fed, and they would surely do no work in chains. It made no sense to him, but Mallia's eyes shone when he spoke of it.

Only fools let themselves be ruled by a king or a queen, by one man or woman. "Except Queen Morgase, of course," he put in hastily. "She is a fine woman, so I've heard. Beautiful, I'm told." All those fools bowing to one fool. The High Lords ruled Tear together, reaching decisions in concert, and that was how things should be. The High Lords knew what was right and good and true. Especially the High Lord Samon. No man could go wrong obeying the High Lords. Especially the High Lord Samon.

Beyond kings and queens, beyond even Illian, lay a bigger hatred Mallia attempted to keep hidden, but he talked so much in trying to find out what they were up to, and grew so carried away by the sound of his own voice, that he let more slip than he intended.

They must travel a great deal, serving a great Queen like Morgase. They must have seen many lands. He dreamed of the sea because then he could see lands he had only heard of, because then he could find the Mayener oilfish shoals, could out-trade the Sea Folk and the filthy Illianers. And the sea was far from Tar Valon. They must understand that, forced as they were to travel among odd places and people, places and people they could not have stomached if they were not serving Queen Morgase.

"I never liked docking there, never knowing who might be using the Power." He almost spat the last word. Since he had heard the High Lord Samon speak, though. . . . "Burn my soul, it makes me feel like hullworms are burrowing into my belly just looking at their White Tower, now, knowing what they plan."

The High Lord Samon said the Aes Sedai meant to rule the world. Samon said they meant to crush every nation, put their foot on every man's throat. Samon said Tear could no longer hold the Power out of its own lands and believe that was enough. Samon said Tear had its rightful day of glory coming, but Tar Valon stood between Tear and glory.

"There's no hope for it. Sooner or later they will have to be hunted down and killed, every last Aes Sedai. The High Lord Samon says the others might be saved—the young ones, the novices, the Accepted—if they're brought to the Stone, but the rest must be eradicated. That's what the High Lord Samon says. The White Tower must be destroyed."

For a moment Mallia stood in the middle of his cabin, arms full of clothes and books and rolled charts, hair almost brushing the deck beams overhead, staring at nothing with pale blue eyes while the White Tower tumbled into ruin. Then he gave a start as if realizing what he had just said. His pointed beard waggled uncertainly.

"That is . . . that's what he says. I . . . I think that may be going too far, myself. The High Lord Samon. . . . He speaks so that he carries a man beyond his own beliefs. If Caemlyn can make covenants with the Tower, why, so can Tear." He shivered and did not seem to know it. "That is what I say."

"As you say," Mat told him, and felt mischief bubble inside. "I think your suggestion is the right one, Captain. But don't stop with a few Accepted, though. Ask a dozen Aes Sedai to come, or two. Think what the Stone of Tear would be like with two dozen Aes Sedai in it."

Mallia shuddered. "I will send a man for my money chest," he said stiffly, and stalked out.

Mat frowned at the closed door. "I think I shouldn't have said that."

"I don't know why you might think that," Thom said dryly. "Next you could try telling the Lord Captain Commander of the Whitecloaks he should marry the Amyrlin Seat." His brows drew down, like white caterpillars. "High Lord Samon. I never heard of any High Lord Samon."

It was Mat's turn to be dry. "Well, even you cannot know everything about all the kings and queens and nobles there are, Thom. One or two might just have escaped your notice."

"I know the names of the kings and queens, boy, and the names of all the High Lords of Tear, too. I suppose they could have raised a Lord of the Land, but I'd think I would have heard of the old High Lord dying. If you had settled for booting some poor fellows out of their cabin instead of taking the captain's, we'd each have a bed to ourselves, narrow and hard as it might be. Now we have to share Mallia's. I hope you don't snore, boy. I cannot abide snoring."

Mat ground his teeth. As he recalled, Thom had a snore like a woodrasp working on an oak knot. He had forgotten that.

It was one of the two large men—Sanor or Vasa; he did not give his name—who came to pull the captain's iron-bound money chest from under the bed. He never said a word, only made sketchy bows, and frowned at them when he thought they were not looking, and left.

Mat was beginning to wonder if the luck that had been with him all night had deserted him at last. He was going to have to put up with Thom's snoring, and truth to tell, it might not have been the best luck in the world to jump onto

this particular ship waving a paper signed by the Amyrlin
Seat and sealed with the Flame of Tar Valon. On impulse he
pulled out one of his cylindrical leather dice cups, popped
off the tight-fitting lid, and upended the dice onto the table.

They were spotted dice, and five single pips stared up at
him. The Dark One's Eyes, that was called in some games.
It was a losing toss in those, a winning in other games. *But
what game am I playing?* He scooped the dice up, tossed
them again. Five pips. Another toss, and again the Dark
One's Eyes winked at him.

"If you used those dice to win all that gold," Thom said
quietly, "no wonder you had to leave by the first ship sailing." He had stripped down to his shirt, and had that half
over his head when he spoke. His knees were knobby and
his legs seemed all sinew and stringy muscle, the right a
little shrunken. "Boy, a twelve-year-old girl would cut your
heart out if she knew you were using dice like that against
her."

"It isn't the dice," Mat muttered. "It's the luck." *Aes Sedai
luck? Or the Dark One's luck?* He pushed the dice back into
the cup and capped it.

"I suppose," Thom said, climbing into the bed, "you
aren't going to tell me where all that gold came from, then."

"I won it. Tonight. With their dice."

"Uh-huh. And I suppose you're not going to explain that
paper you were waving around—I saw the seal, boy!—or
all that talk about White Tower business, or why the dockmaster had your description from an Aes Sedai, either."

"I am carrying a letter to Morgase for Elayne, Thom,"
Mat said a good deal more patiently than he felt. "Nynaeve
gave me the paper. I don't know where she got it."

"Well, if you are not going to tell me, I am going to sleep.
Blow out the lamps, will you?" Thom rolled on his side and
pulled a pillow over his head.

Even after Mat had stripped off down to his smallclothes
and crawled under the blankets—after blowing out the
lamps—he could not sleep, though Mallia had done well
by himself with a good feather mattress. He had been
right about Thom's snoring, and that pillow muffled nothing. It sounded as if Thom were cutting wood cross-grain
with a rusty saw. And he could not stop thinking. How
had Nynaeve and Egwene, and Elayne, gotten that paper

from the Amyrlin? They had to be involved with the Amyrlin Seat herself—in some plot, one of those White Tower machinations—but now that he thought about it, they had to be holding something back from the Amyrlin, too.

"'Please carry a letter to my mother, Mat,'" he said softly, in a high-pitched, mocking voice. "Fool! The Amyrlin would have sent a Warder with any letter from the Daughter-Heir to the Queen. Blind fool, wanting to get out of the Tower so bad I couldn't see it." Thom's snore seemed to trumpet agreement.

Most of all, though, he thought about luck, and footpads.

The first bump of something against the stern barely registered on him. He paid no attention to a thump and scuffle from the deck overhead, or the tread of boots. The vessel itself made enough noises, and there had to be someone on deck for the ship to make its way downriver. But stealthy footsteps in the passageway leading to his door merged with thoughts of footpads and made his ears prick up.

He nudged Thom in the ribs with an elbow. "Wake up," he said softly. "There's somebody outside in the hall." He was already easing himself off the bed, hoping the cabin floor—*Deck, floor, whatever it bloody is!*—would not creak under his feet. Thom grunted, smacked his lips, and resumed snoring.

There was no time to worry about Thom. The footsteps were right outside. Taking up his quarterstaff, Mat placed himself in front of the door and waited.

The door swung open slowly, and two cloaked men, one behind the other, were faintly outlined by dim moonlight through the hatch at the top of the ladder they had crept down. The moonlight was enough to glint off bare knife blades. Both men gasped; they obviously had not expected to find anyone waiting for them.

Mat thrust with the quarterstaff, catching the first man hard right under where his ribs joined together. He heard his father's voice as he struck. *It's a killing blow, Mat. Don't ever use it unless it's your life.* But those knives made it for his life; there was no room in the cabin for swinging a staff.

Even as the man made a choking sound and folded toward the deck, fighting vainly for breath, Mat stepped forward and drove the end of the quarterstaff over him into the second man's throat with a loud crunch. That fellow dropped his knife to clutch at his throat, and fell on top of his companion, both of them scraping their boots across the deck, death rattles already sounding in their throats.

Mat stood there, staring down at them. *Two men. No, burn me, three! I don't think I ever hurt another human being before, and now I've killed three men in one night. Light!*

Silence filled the dark passageway, and he heard the thump of boots on the deck overhead. The crewmen all went barefoot.

Trying not to think about what he was doing, Mat ripped the cloak from one of the dead men and settled it around his shoulders, hiding the pale linen of his smallclothes. On bare feet he padded down the passage and climbed the ladder, barely sticking his eyes above the hatch coping.

Pale moonlight reflected off the taut sails, but night still covered the deck with shadows, and there was no sound except the rush of water along the vessel's sides. Only one man at the tiller, the hood of his cloak pulled up against the chill, seemed to be on deck. The man shifted, and boot leather scuffed on the deck planks.

Holding the quarterstaff low and hoping it would not be noticed, Mat climbed on up. "He's dead," he muttered in a low, rough whisper.

"I hope he squealed when you cut his throat." The heavily accented voice was one Mat remembered calling from the mouth of a twisting street in Tar Valon. "This boy, he causes us too much of the trouble, Wait! Who are you?"

Mat swung the staff with all his strength. The thick wood smashed into the man's head, the hood of his cloak only partly muffling a sound like a melon hitting the floor.

The man fell across the tiller, shoving it over, and the vessel lurched, staggering Mat. Out of the corner of his eye he saw a shape rising out of the shadows by the railing, and the gleam of a blade, and he knew he would never get his staff around before it struck home. Something else that shone streaked through the night and merged with the dim shape with a dull *thunk*. The rising motion became a fall, and a man sprawled almost at Mat's feet.

A babble of voices rose belowdecks as the ship swung again, the tiller shifting with the first man's weight.

Thom limped from the hatch in cloak and smallclothes, raising the shutter on a bull's-eye lantern. "You were lucky, boy. One of those below had this lantern. Could have set the ship on fire, lying there." The light showed a knife hilt sticking up from the chest of a man with dead, staring eyes. Mat had never seen him before; he was sure he would have remembered someone with that many scars on his face. Thom kicked a dagger away from the dead man's outflung hand, then bent to retrieve his own knife, wiping the blade on the corpse's cloak. "Very lucky, boy. Very lucky indeed."

There was a rope tied to the stern rail. Thom stepped over to it, shining the light down astern, and Mat joined him. At the other end of the rope was one of the small boats from Southharbor, its square lantern extinguished. Two more men stood among the pulled-in oars.

"The Great Lord take me, it's him!" one of them gasped. The other darted forward to work frantically at the knot holding the rope.

"You want to kill these two as well?" Thom asked, his voice booming as it did when he performed.

"No, Thom," Mat said quietly. "No."

The men in the boat must have heard the question and not the answer, for they abandoned the attempt to free their boat and leaped over the side with great splashes. The sound of them thrashing away across the river was loud.

"Fools," Thom muttered. "The river narrows somewhat after Tar Valon, but it must still be half a mile or more wide here. They'll never make it in the dark."

"By the Stone!" came a shout from the hatch. "What happens here? There are dead men in the passageway! What's Vasa doing lying on the tiller? He'll run us onto a mudbank!" Naked save for linen underbreeches, Mallia dashed to the tiller, hauling the dead man off roughly as he pulled the long lever to put the course straight again. "That isn't Vasa! Burn my soul, who are all these dead men?" Others were clambering on deck now, barefoot crewmen and frightened passengers wrapped in cloaks and blankets.

Shielding his actions with his body, Thom slipped his knife under the rope and severed it in one stroke. The small boat began falling back into the darkness. "River brigands, Captain," he said. "Young Mat and I have saved your vessel from river brigands. They might have cut everyone's throat if not for us. Perhaps you should reconsider your passage fee."

"Brigands!" Mallia exclaimed. "There are plenty of those down around Cairhien, but I never heard of it this far north!" The huddled passengers began to mutter about brigands and having their throats cut.

Mat walked stiffly to the hatch. Behind him, he heard Mallia. "He's a cold one. I never heard that Andor employed assassins, but burn my soul, he is a cold one."

Mat stumbled down the ladder, stepped over the two bodies in the passage, and slammed the door of the captain's cabin behind him. He made it halfway to the bed before the shaking hit him, and then all he could do was sink down on his knees. *Light, what game am I playing in? I have to know the game if I'm going to win. Light, what game?*

Playing "Rose of the Morning" softly on his flute, Rand peered into his campfire, where a rabbit was roasting on a stick slanting over the flames. A night wind made the flames flicker; he barely noticed the smell of the rabbit, though a vagrant thought did come that he needed to find more salt in the next village or town. "Rose of the Morning" was one of the tunes he had played at those weddings.

How many days ago was that? Were there really so many, or did I imagine it? Every woman in the village deciding to marry at once? What was its name? Am I going mad already?

Sweat beaded on his face, but he played on, barely loud enough to be heard, staring into the fire. Moiraine had told him he was *ta'veren*. Everyone said he was *ta'veren*. Maybe he really was. People like that—changed—things around them. A *ta'veren* might have *caused* all those weddings. But that was too close to something he did not want to think about.

They say I'm the Dragon Reborn, too. They all say it. The living say it, and the dead. That doesn't make it true. I had to let them proclaim me. Duty. I had no choice, but that does not make it true.

He could not seem to stop playing that one tune. It made him think of Egwene. He had thought once that he would marry Egwene. A long time ago, that seemed. That was gone, now. She had come in his dreams, though. *It might have been her. Her face. It was her face.*

Only, there had been so many faces, faces he knew. Tam, and his mother, and Mat, and Perrin. All trying to kill him. It had not really been them, of course. Only their faces, on Shadowspawn. He thought it had not really been them. Even in his dreams it seemed the Shadowspawn walked. Were they only dreams? Some dreams were real, he knew. And others were only dreams, nightmares, or hopes. But how to tell the difference? Min had walked his dreams one night—and tried to plant a knife in his back. He was still surprised at how much that had pained him. He had been careless, let her come close, let down his guard. Around Min, he had not felt any need to be on his guard in so long, despite the things she saw when she looked at him. Being with her had been like having balm soothed into his wounds.

And then she tried to kill me! The music rose to a discordant screech, but he pulled it back to softness. *Not her. Shadowspawn with her face. Least of them all would Min hurt me.* He could not understand why he thought that, but he was sure it was true.

So many faces in his dreams. Selene had come, cool and mysterious and so lovely his mouth went dry just thinking of her, offering him glory as she had—so long ago, it seemed—but now it was the sword she said he had to take. And with the sword would come Selene. *Callandor.* That was always in his dreams. Always. And taunting faces. Hands, pushing Egwene, and Nynaeve, and Elayne into cages, snaring them in nets, hurting them. Why should he weep more for Elayne than for the other two?

His head spun. His head hurt as much as his side, and sweat rolled down his face, and he softly played "Rose of the Morning" through the night, fearing to sleep. Fearing to dream.

CHAPTER
33

Within the Weave

From his saddle, Perrin frowned down at the flat stone half hidden in weeds by the roadside. This road of hard-packed dirt, already called the Lugard Road now they were near the Manetherendrelle and the border of Murandy, had been paved once, long in the past, so Moiraine had said two days earlier, and bits of paving stone still worked their way to the surface from time to time. This one had an odd marking on it.

If dogs had been able to make footprints on stone, he would have said it was the print of a large hound. There were no hound's footprints in any of the bare ground he could see, where softer dirt on the verge might take one, and no smell of any dog's trail. Just a faint trace in the air of something burned, almost the sulphurous smell left by setting off fireworks. There was a town ahead, where the road struck the river; maybe some children had sneaked out here with some of the Illuminators' handiwork.

A long way yet for children to sneak. But he had seen farms. It could have been farm children. *Whatever it is, it has nothing to do with that marking. Horses don't fly, and dogs don't make footprints on stone. I'm getting too tired to think straight.*

Yawning, he dug his heels into Stepper's ribs, and the dun broke into a gallop after the others. Moiraine had been pushing them hard since leaving Jarra, and there was no waiting for anyone who stopped for even a moment. When the Aes Sedai put her mind on something, she was as hard as cold hammered iron. Loial had given up reading as he rode six days earlier, after looking up to find himself left a mile behind and everyone else almost out of sight over the next hill.

Perrin slowed Stepper alongside the Ogier's big horse, behind Moiraine's white mare, and yawned again. Lan was up ahead somewhere, scouting. The sun behind them stood no more than an hour above the treetops, but the Warder had said they would reach a town called Remen, on the Manetherendrelle, before dark. Perrin was not sure he wanted to see what awaited them there. He did not know what it might be, but the days since Jarra had made him wary.

"I don't see why you can't sleep," Loial told him. "I am so tired by the time she lets us halt for the night, I fall asleep before I can lie down."

Perrin only shook his head. There was no way to explain to Loial that he did not dare sleep soundly, that even his lightest sleep was full of troubled dreams. Like that odd one with Egwene and Hopper in it. *Well, no wonder I dream about her. Light, I wonder how she is. Safe in the Tower by now, and learning how to be Aes Sedai. Verin will look after her, and after Mat, too.* He did not think anyone needed to look after Nynaeve; around Nynaeve, to his mind, other people needed someone to look after them.

He did not want to think about Hopper. He was succeeding in keeping live wolves out of his head, although at the price of feeling as if he had been hammered-and-drawn by a hasty hand; he did not want to think a dead wolf might be creeping in. He shook himself and forced his eyes wide open. Not even Hopper.

There had been more reasons than bad dreams not to sleep well. They had found other signs left by Rand's passage. Between Jarra and the River Boern there had been none Perrin could see, but when they crossed the Boern by a stone bridge arching from one fifty-foot river cliff to another, they had left behind a town called Sidon all in ashes. Every building. Only a few stone walls and chimneys still stood among the ruins.

Bedraggled townspeople said a lantern dropped in a barn had started it, and then the fire seemed to run wild, and everything went wrong. Half the buckets that could be found had holes in them. Every last burning wall had fallen outward instead of in, setting houses to either side alight. Flaming timbers from the inn had somehow tumbled as far as the main well in the square, so no one could draw more water from it to fight the fires, and houses had fallen right on top of three other wells. Even the wind had seemed to shift, fanning the flames in every direction.

There had been no need to ask Moiraine if Rand's presence had caused it; her face, like cold iron, was answer enough. The Pattern shaped itself around Rand, and chance ran wild.

Beyond Sidon they had ridden through four small towns where only Lan's tracking told them Rand was still ahead. Rand was afoot, now, and had been for some time. They had found his horse back beyond Jarra, dead, looking as if it had been mauled by wolves, or dogs run wild. It had been hard for Perrin not to reach out, then, especially when Moiraine looked up from the horse to frown at him. Luckily, Lan had found the tracks of Rand's boots, running from where the dead horse lay. One boot heel had a three-cornered gouge from a rock; it made his prints plain. But afoot or mounted, he seemed to be staying ahead of them.

In the four villages after Sidon, the biggest excitement anyone could remember was seeing Loial ride in, and discovering that he was an Ogier, for real and for true. They were so caught up with that, that they barely even noticed Perrin's eyes, and when they did. . . . Well, if Ogier were real, then men could very well have any color eyes at all.

But after those came a little place named Willar, and it was celebrating. The spring on the village common was flowing again, after a year of hauling water a mile from a stream when all efforts at digging wells had failed and half the people had moved away. Willar would not die after all. Three more untouched villages had been followed in quick succession, all in one day, by Samaha, where every well in town had gone dry just the night before, and people were muttering about the Dark One; then Tallan, where all the old arguments the village had ever known had bubbled to the surface like overflowing cesspits a morning earlier, and it had taken three murders to shock everyone back to his senses; and finally Fyall, where the crops this spring looked to be the poorest anyone could remember, but the Mayor, digging a new privy behind his house, had found rotted leather sacks full of gold, so none would go hungry. No one in Fyall recognized the fat coins, with a woman's face on one side and an eagle on the other; Moiraine said they had been minted in Manetheren.

Perrin had finally asked her about it, as they sat around their campfire one night. "After Jarra, I thought. . . . They were all so happy, with their weddings. Even the White-cloaks were only made to look like fools. Fyall was all right—Rand couldn't have had anything to do with their crops; they were failing before he ever came, and that gold was surely good, with their need—but all this other. . . . That town burning, and the wells failing, and. . . . That is evil, Moiraine. I can't believe Rand is evil. The Pattern may be shaping itself around him, but how can the Pattern be that evil? It makes no sense, and things have to make sense. If you make a tool with no sense to it, it's wasted metal. The Pattern wouldn't make waste."

Lan gave him a wry look, and vanished into the darkness to make a circuit around their campsite. Loial, already stretched out in his blankets, lifted his head to listen, ears pricking forward.

Moiraine was silent for a time, warming her hands. Finally she spoke while staring into the flames. "The Creator is good, Perrin. The Father of Lies is evil. The Pattern of Age, the Age Lace itself, is neither. The Pattern is what is. The Wheel of Time weaves all lives into the Pattern, all actions. A pattern that is all one color is no pattern. For the Pattern of an Age, good and ill are the warp and the woof."

Even riding through late-afternoon sunshine three days later, Perrin felt the chill he had had on first hearing her say those words. He wanted to believe the Pattern was good. He wanted to believe that when men did evil things, they were going against the Pattern, distorting it. To him the Pattern was a fine and intricate creation made by a master smith. That it mixed pot metal and worse in with good steel with never a care was a cold thought.

"I care," he muttered softly. "Light, I do care." Moiraine glanced back at him, and he fell silent. He was not sure what the Aes Sedai cared about, beyond Rand.

A few minutes later Lan appeared from ahead and swung his black warhorse in beside Moiraine's mare. "Remen lies just over the next hill," he said. "They have had an eventful day or two, it seems."

Loial's ears twitched once. "Rand?"

The Warder shook his head. "I do not know. Perhaps Moiraine can say, when she sees." The Aes Sedai gave him a searching look, then heeled her white mare to a quicker step.

They topped the hill, and Remen lay spread out below them, hard against the river. The Manetherendrelle stretched more than half a mile wide here, and there was no bridge, though two crowded, bargelike ferries crept across, propelled by long oars, and one nearly empty was returning. Three more shared long stone docks with nearly a dozen river traders' vessels, some with one mast, some with two. A few bulky gray stone warehouses separated the docks from the town itself, where the buildings seemed mostly of stone, as well, though roofed in tiles of every color from yellow to red to purple, and the streets ran every which way around a central square.

Moiraine pulled up the deep hood of her cloak to hide her face before they rode down.

As usual, the people in the streets stared at Loial, but this time Perrin heard awed murmurs of "Ogier." Loial sat straighter in his saddle than he had in some time, and his ears stood straight, and a smile just curled the ends of his wide mouth. He was obviously trying not to let on that he was pleased, but he looked like a cat having its ears scratched.

Remen looked like any of a dozen towns to Perrin—it was full of man-made aromas and man smell; with a strong smell of the river, of course—and he was wondering what Lan could have meant when the hair on the back of his neck stirred as he scented something—wrong. As soon as his nose took it in, it was gone like a horsehair dropped onto hot coals, but he remembered it. He had smelled the same smell at Jarra, and it had vanished the same way, then. It was not a Twisted One or a Neverborn—*Trolloc, burn me, not a Twisted One! Not a Neverborn! A Myrddraal, a Fade, a Halfman, anything but a Neverborn!*—not a Trolloc or a Fade, yet the stench had been every bit as sharp, every bit as vile. But whatever gave off that scent left no lasting trail, it seemed.

They rode into the town square. One of the big paving blocks had been pried up, right in the middle of the square, so a gibbet could be erected. A single thick timber rose out of the dirt, supporting a braced crosspiece from which hung an iron cage, the bottom of it four paces high. A tall man dressed all in grays and browns sat in the cage, holding his knees under his chin. He had no room to do otherwise. Three small boys were pitching stones at him. The man looked straight ahead, not flinching when a stone made it between the bars. More than one trickle of blood stained his face. The townspeople walking by paid no more mind to what the boys were doing than the man did, though every last one of them looked at the cage, most of them with approval, and some with fear.

Moiraine made a sound in her throat that might have been disgust.

"There is more," Lan said. "Come. I've already arranged rooms at an inn. I think you will find it interesting."

Perrin looked back over his shoulder at the caged man as he rode after them. There was something familiar about the man, but he could not place it.

"They shouldn't do that." Loial's rumble sounded halfway to a snarl. "The children, I mean. The grown-ups should stop them."

"They should," Perrin agreed, barely paying attention. *Why is he familiar?*

The sign over the door of the inn Lan led them to, nearer the river, read Wayland's Forge, which Perrin took for a good omen, though there seemed to be nothing of the smithy about the place except the leather-aproned man with a hammer painted on the sign. It was a large, purple-roofed, three-story building of squared and polished gray stones, with large windows and scroll-carved doors, and it had a prosperous look. Stablemen came running to take the horses, bowing even more deeply after Lan tossed them coins.

Inside, Perrin stared at the people. The men and women at the tables were all dressed in their feastday clothes, it seemed to him, with more embroidered coats, more lace on dresses, more colored ribbons and fringed scarves, than he had seen in a long time. Only four men sitting at one table wore plain coats, and they were the only ones who did not look up expectantly when Perrin and the others walked in. The four men kept on talking softly. He could make out a little of what they were saying, about the virtues of ice

peppers over furs as cargo and what the troubles in Saldaea
might have done to prices. Captains of trading ships, he decided. The others seemed to be local folk. Even the serving
women appeared to be wearing their best, their long aprons
covering embroidered dresses with bits of lace at the neck.

The kitchen was working heavily; he could smell mutton,
lamb, chicken, and beef, as well as some sort of vegetables.
And a spicy cake that made him forget meat for a moment.

The innkeeper himself met them just inside, a plump,
bald-headed man with shining brown eyes in a smooth
pink face, bowing and dry-washing his hands. If he had not
come to them, Perrin would never have taken him for the
landlord, for instead of the expected white apron, he wore a
coat like everyone else, all white-and-green embroidery on
stout blue wool that had the man sweating with its weight.

Why are they all wearing clothes for festival? Perrin
wondered.

"Ah, Master Andra," the innkeeper said, addressing
Lan. "And an Ogier, just as you said. Not that I doubted, of
course. Not with all that's happened, and never your word,
master. Why not an Ogier? Ah, friend Ogier, to be having
you in the house gives me more pleasure than you can be
knowing. 'Tis a fine thing, and a fitting cap to it all. Ah,
and mistress. . . ." His eyes took in the deep blue silk of her
dress and the rich wool of her cloak, dusty from travel but
still fine. "Forgive me, Lady, please." His bow bent him
like a horseshoe. "Master Andra did not make your station
clear, Lady. I meant no disrespect. You are even more welcome than friend Ogier here, of course, Lady. Please, take
no offense at Gainor Furlan's poor tongue."

"I take none." Moiraine's voice calmly accepted the title
Furlan gave her. It was far from the first time the Aes Sedai had gone under another name, or pretended to be something she was not. It was not the first Perrin had heard Lan
name himself Andra, either. The deep hood still hid Moiraine's smooth Aes Sedai features, and she held her cloak
around her with one hand as if taken with a chill. Not the
hand on which she wore her Great Serpent ring. "You have
had strange occurrences in the town, innkeeper, so I understand. Nothing to trouble travelers, I trust."

"Ah, Lady, you might be calling them strange indeed.
Your own radiant presence is more than enough to honor

this humble house, Lady, and bringing an Ogier with you, but we have Hunters in Remen, too. Right here in Wayland's Forge, they are. Hunters for the Horn of Valere, set out from Illian for adventure. And adventure they found, Lady, here in Remen, or just a mile or two upriver, fighting wild Aielmen, of all things. Can you imagine black-veiled Aiel savages in Altara, Lady?"

Aiel. Now Perrin knew what was familiar about the man in the cage. He had seen an Aiel, once, one of those fierce, nearly legendary denizens of the harsh land called the Waste. The man had looked a good deal like Rand, taller than most, with gray eyes and reddish hair, and he had been dressed like the man in the cage, all in browns and grays that would fade into rock or brush, with soft boots laced to his knees. Perrin could almost hear Min's voice again. *An Aielman in a cage. A turning point in your life, or something important that will happen.*

"Why do you have . . . ?" He stopped to clear his throat so he would not sound so hoarse. "How did an Aiel come to be caged in your town square?"

"Ah, young master, that is a story to. . . ." Furlan trailed off, eyeing him up and down, taking in his plain country clothes and the longbow in his hands, pausing over the axe at his belt opposite his quiver. The plump man gave a start when his study reached Perrin's face, as if, with a Lady and an Ogier present, he had just now noticed Perrin's yellow eyes. "He would be your servant, Master Andra?" he asked cautiously.

"Answer him," was all Lan said.

"Ah. Ah, of course, Master Andra. But here's who can tell it better than myself. 'Tis Lord Orban, himself. 'Tis he we have gathered to hear."

A dark-haired, youngish man in a red coat, with a bandage wound around his temples, was making his way down the stairs at the side of the common room using padded crutches, the left leg of his breeches cut away so more bandages could strap his calf from ankle to knee. The townspeople murmured as if seeing something wondrous. The ship captains went on with their quiet talking; they had come 'round to furs.

Furlan might have thought the man in the red coat could tell the story better, but he went ahead himself. "Lord Or-

ban and Lord Gann faced twenty wild Aielmen with only
ten retainers. Ah, fierce was the fighting and hard, with
many wounds given and received. Six good retainers died,
and every man took hurts, Lord Orban and Lord Gann
worst of all, but every Aiel they slew, save those who fled,
and one they took prisoner. 'Tis that one you see out there
in the square, where he'll not be troubling the countryside
anymore with his savage ways, no more than the dead ones
will."

"You have had trouble from Aiel in this district?" Moiraine
asked.

Perrin was wondering the same thing, with no little consternation. If some people still occasionally used "black-
veiled Aiel" as a term for someone violent, it was testimony
to the impression the Aiel War had left, but that was twenty
years in the past, now, and the Aiel had never come out of
the Waste before or since. *But I saw one this side of the
Spine of the World, and now I've seen two.*

The innkeeper rubbed at his bald head. "Ah. Ah, no,
Lady, not exactly. But we would have had, you can be sure,
with twenty savages loose. Why, everyone remembers
how they killed and looted and burned their way across
Cairhien. Men from this very village marched to the Battle
of the Shining Walls, when the nations gathered to throw
them back. I myself suffered from a twisted back at the
time and so could not go, but I remember well, as we all do.
How they came here, so far from their own land, or why, I
do not know, but Lord Orban and Lord Gann saved us from
them." There was a murmur of agreement from the folk in
feastday clothes.

Orban himself came stumping across the common room,
not seeming to see anyone but the innkeeper. Perrin could
smell stale wine before he was even close. "Where's that old
woman taken herself off to with her herbs, Furlan?" Orban
demanded roughly. "Gann's wounds are paining him, and
my head feels about to split open."

Furlan almost bent his head to the floor. "Ah, Mother
Leich will be back in the morning, Lord Orban. A birthing, Lord. But she said she'd stitched and poulticed your
wounds, and Lord Gann's, so there'd be no worrying. Ah,
Lord Orban, I'm sure she'll be seeing to you first thing on
the morrow."

The bandaged man muttered something under his breath—
under his breath to any ears but Perrin's—about waiting on
a farmwife "throwing her litter" and something else about
being "sewn up like a sack of meal." He shifted sullen, angry eyes, and for the first time appeared to see the newcomers. Perrin, he dismissed immediately, which did not
surprise Perrin at all. His eyes widened a little at Loial—
He's seen Ogier, Perrin thought, *but he never thought to
see one here*—narrowed a bit at Lan—*He knows a fighting
man when he sees one, and he does not like seeing one*—
and brightened as he stooped to peer inside Moiraine's
hood, though he was not close enough to see her face.

Perrin decided not to think anything at all about that, not
concerning an Aes Sedai, and he hoped neither Moiraine
nor Lan thought anything of it, either. A light in the Warder's
eyes told him he had missed on that hope, at least.

"Twelve of you fought twenty Aiel?" Lan asked in a flat
voice.

Orban straightened, wincing. In an elaborately casual
tone, he said, "Aye, you must expect things such as that
when you seek the Horn of Valere. It was not the first such
encounter for Gann and me, nor will it be the last before we
find the Horn. If the Light shines on us." He sounded as if
the Light could not possibly do anything else. "Not all our
fights have been with Aiel, of course, but there are always
those who would stop Hunters, if they could. Gann and I,
we do not stop easily." Another approving murmur came
from the townspeople. Orban stood a little straighter.

"You lost six, and took one prisoner." From Lan's voice,
it was not clear if that was a good exchange or a poor one.

"Aye," Orban said, "we slew the rest, save those who ran.
No doubt they're hiding their dead now; I've heard they
do that. The Whitecloaks are out searching for them, but
they'll never find them."

"There are Whitecloaks here?" Perrin asked sharply.

Orban glanced at him, and dismissed him once more.
The man addressed Lan again. "Whitecloaks always put
their noses in where they are not wanted or needed. Incom-
petent louts, all of them. Aye, they'll ride all over the countryside for days, but I doubt they'll find as much as their
own shadows."

"I suppose they won't," Lan said.

The bandaged man frowned as if unsure exactly what Lan meant, then rounded on the innkeeper again. "You find that old woman, hear! My head is splitting." With a last glance at Lan, he hobbled away, climbing back up the stairs one at a time, followed by murmurs of admiration for a Hunter of the Horn who had slain Aielmen.

"This is an eventful town." Loial's deep voice drew every eye to him. Except for the ship captains, who seemed to be discussing rope, as near as Perrin could make out. "Everywhere I go, you humans are doing things, hurrying and scurrying, having things happen to you. How can you stand so much excitement?"

"Ah, friend Ogier," Furlan said, "'tis the way of us humans to want excitement. How much I regret not being able to march to the Shining Walls. Why, let me tell you—"

"Our rooms." Moiraine did not raise her voice, but her words cut the innkeeper short like a sharp knife. "Andra did arrange rooms, did he not?"

"Ah, Lady, forgive me. Yes, Master Andra did indeed hire rooms. Forgive me, please. 'Tis all the excitement, makes my head empty itself. Please forgive me, Lady. This way, if you please. If you'll please to follow me." Bowing and scraping, apologizing and babbling without pause, Furlan led them up the stairs.

At the top, Perrin paused to look back. He heard the murmurs of "Lady" and "Ogier" down there, could feel all those eyes, but it seemed to him that he felt one pair of eyes in particular, someone staring not at Moiraine and Loial, but at him.

He picked her out immediately. For one thing, she stood apart from the others, and for another she was the only woman in the room not wearing at least a little lace. Her dark gray, almost black, dress was as plain as the ship captains' clothes, with wide sleeves and narrow skirts, and never a frill or stitch of fancy-work. The dress was divided for riding, he saw when she moved, and she wore soft boots that peeked out under the hem. She was young—no older than he was, perhaps—and tall for a woman, with black hair to her shoulders. A nose that just missed being too large and too bold, a generous mouth, high cheekbones, and dark, slightly tilted eyes. He could not quite decide whether she was beautiful or not.

As soon as he looked down, she turned to address one of the serving women and did not glance at the stairs again, but he was sure he had been right. She had been staring at him.

CHAPTER

34

A Different Dance

Furlan burbled on as he showed them to their rooms, though Perrin did not really listen. He was too busy wondering if the black-haired girl knew what yellow eyes meant. *Burn me, she* was *looking at me.* Then he heard the innkeeper say the words "proclaiming the Dragon in Ghealdan," and he thought his ears would go to sharp points like Loial's.

Moiraine stopped dead in the doorway to her room. "There is another false Dragon, innkeeper? In Ghealdan?" The hood of her cloak still hid her face, but she sounded shaken to her toes. Even listening for the man's reply, Perrin could not help staring at her; he smelled something close to fear.

"Ah, Lady, never you fear. 'Tis a hundred leagues to Ghealdan, and none will trouble you here, not with Master Andra about, and Lord Orban and Lord Gann. Why—"

"Answer her!" Lan said harshly. "Is there a false Dragon in Ghealdan?"

"Ah. Ah, no, Master Andra, not precisely. I said there's a man proclaiming the Dragon in Ghealdan, so we heard a few days gone. Preaching his coming, you might say. Talking about that fellow over in Tarabon we've heard about. Though some do say 'tis Arad Doman, not Tarabon. A long way from here, in any case. Why, any other day, I expect we'd talk more of that than anything else, except maybe the wild tales about Hawkwing's army come back—" Lan's cold eyes might as well have been knife blades from the way Furlan swallowed and scrubbed his hands faster. "I

only know what I hear, Master Andra. 'Tis said the fellow
has a stare can pin you where you stand, and he talks all
sorts of rubbish about the Dragon coming to save us, and
we all have to follow, and even the beasts will fight for the
Dragon. I don't know whether they've arrested him yet or
not. 'Tis likely; the Ghealdanin would not put up long with
that kind of talk."

Masema, Perrin thought wonderingly. *It's bloody
Masema.*

"You are right, innkeeper," Lan said. "This fellow isn't
likely to trouble us here. I knew a fellow once who liked to
make wild speeches. You remember him, Lady Alys, don't
you? Masema?"

Moiraine gave a start. "Masema. Yes. Of course. I had
put him out of my mind." Her voice firmed. "When next I
see Masema, he will wish someone had peeled his hide to
make boots." She slammed the door behind her so hard that
the crash echoed down the hallway.

"Keep a quiet!" came a muffled shout from the far end.
"My head is splitting!"

"Ah." Furlan washed his hands in one direction, then
rubbed them in the other. "Ah. Forgive me, Master Andra,
but Lady Alys is a fierce-sounding woman."

"Only with those who displease her," Lan said blandly.
"Her bite is far worse than her bark."

"Ah. Ah. Ah. Your rooms are this way. Ah, friend Ogier,
when Master Andra told me you were coming, I had an old
Ogier bed brought from the attic where it has been gathering dust these three hundred years or more. Why, 'tis. . . ."

Perrin let the words wash over him, hearing them no
more than a river rock hears the water. The black-haired
young woman worried him. And the caged Aiel.

Once in his own room—a small one in the back; Lan
had done nothing to disabuse the innkeeper of the notion
that Perrin was a servant—he moved mechanically, still
wrapped in thought. He unstrung his bow and propped it
in the corner—keeping it strung too long ruined bow and
string alike—set down his blanketroll and saddlebags beside the washstand and threw his cloak across them. He
hung his belts with quiver and axe from pegs on the wall,
and nearly lay down on the bed before a jaw-cracking yawn
reminded him how dangerous that might be. The bed was

narrow, and the mattress appeared to be all lumps; it looked more inviting than any bed he could remember. He sat on the three-legged stool, instead, and thought. Always he liked to think things through.

After a time, Loial rapped on the door and put his head in. The Ogier's ears practically quivered with excitement, and his grin very nearly split his broad face in two. "Perrin, you will not believe it! My bed is sung wood! Why, it must be well over a thousand years old. No Treesinger has sung a piece so large in at least that long. I myself would not care to try it, and I have the talent more strongly than most, now. Well, to be truthful, there are not many of us with the talent at all, anymore. But I *am* among the best of those who can sing wood."

"That is very interesting," Perrin said. *An Aiel in a cage. That is what Min said. Why was that girl staring at me?*

"I thought it was." Loial sounded a little put out that he did not share the Ogier's excitement, but all Perrin wanted to do was think. "Supper is ready below, Perrin. They have prepared their finest in case the Hunters want anything, but we can have some."

"You go on, Loial. I'm not hungry." The smells of cooking meat floating up from the kitchen did not interest him. He hardly noticed Loial going.

Hands on his knees, yawning now and again, he tried to work it out. It seemed like one of those puzzles Master Luhhan made, the metal pieces appearing to be linked inextricably. But there was always a trick to make the iron loops and whirls come apart, and there had to be here, too.

The girl had been looking at him. His eyes might explain that, except that the innkeeper had ignored them, and no one else had even noticed. They had an Ogier to look at, and Hunters of the Horn in the house, and a Lady visiting, and an Aiel caged in the square. Nothing as small as the color of a man's eyes could seize their attention; nothing about a servant could compete with the rest. *So why did she pick me to stare at?*

And the Aiel in the cage. What Min saw was always important. But how? What was he supposed to do? *I could have stopped those children throwing rocks. I should have.* It was no use telling himself the adults would certainly have told him to go on about his business, that he was a stranger in Remen and the Aiel was none of his concern. *I should have tried.*

No answers came to him, so he went back to the beginning and patiently worked through it once more, then again, and again. Still he found nothing except regret for what he had not done.

It came to him after a time that night had finally fallen. The room was dark except for a little moonlight through the lone window. He thought about the tallow candle and the tinderbox he had seen on the mantel over the narrow fireplace, but there was more than enough light for his eyes. *I have to do something, don't I?*

He buckled on his axe, then paused. He had done it without thinking; wearing the thing had become as natural as breathing. He did not like that. But he left the belt around his waist, and went out.

Light from the stairs made the hallway seem almost bright after his room. Talk and laughter drifted up from the common room, and cooking smells from the kitchen. He strode toward the front of the inn, to Moiraine's room, knocked once, and went in. And stopped, his face burning.

Moiraine pulled the pale blue robe that hung from her shoulders around herself. "You wish something?" she asked coolly. She had a silver-backed hairbrush in one hand, and her dark hair, spilling down her neck in dark waves, glistened as if she had been brushing it. Her room was far finer than his, with polished wooden paneling on the walls and silver-chased lamps and a warm fire on the wide brick hearth. The air smelled of rose-scented soap.

"I. . . . I thought Lan was here," he managed to get out. "You two always have your heads together, and I thought he'd. . . . I thought. . . ."

"What do you want, Perrin?"

He took a deep breath. "Is this Rand's doing? I know Lan followed him here, and it all seems odd—the Hunters, and Aiel—but did he do it?"

"I do not think so. I will know more when Lan tells me what he discovers tonight. With luck, what he finds will help with the choice I must make."

"A choice?"

"Rand could have crossed the river and be on his way to Tear cross-country. Or he could have taken ship downriver

to Illian, meaning to board another there for Tear. The journey is leagues longer that way, but days faster."

"I don't think we are going to catch him, Moiraine. I
don't know how he's doing it, but even afoot he is staying
ahead of us. If Lan is right, he is still half a day ahead."

"I could almost suspect he had learned to Travel," Moiraine said with a small frown, "except that if he had, he
would have gone straight to Tear. No, he has the blood of
long walkers and strong runners in him. But we may take
the river anyway. If I cannot catch him, I will be in Tear
close behind him. Or waiting for him."

Perrin shifted his feet uneasily; there was cold prom-
ise in her voice. "You told me once that you could sense a
Darkfriend, one who was far gone into the Shadow, at least.
Lan, too. Have you sensed anything like that here?"

She gave a loud sniff and turned back to a tall standing
mirror with finely made silver-work set in the legs. Holding
her robe closed with one hand, she ran the brush through
her hair with the other. "Very few humans are so far gone
as that, Perrin, even among the worst Darkfriends." The
brush halted in midstroke. "Why do you ask?"

"There was a girl down in the common room staring at
me. Not at you and Loial, like everybody else. At me."

The brush resumed motion, and a smile briefly touched
Moiraine's lips. "You sometimes forget, Perrin, that you
are a good-looking young man. Some girls admire a pair
of shoulders." He grunted and shuffled his feet. "Was there
something else, Perrin?"

"Uh . . . no." She could not help with Min's viewing, not
beyond telling him what he already knew, that it was important. And he did not want to tell her what Min had seen.
Or that Min had seen anything, for that matter.

Back out in the hall with the door closed, he leaned
against the wall for a moment. *Light, just walking in on
her like that, and her. . . .* She was a pretty woman. *And
likely old enough to be my mother, or more.* He thought
Mat would probably have asked her down to the common
room to dance. *No, he wouldn't. Even Mat isn't fool enough
to try charming an Aes Sedai.* Moiraine did dance. He had
danced with her once himself. And nearly fallen over his
own feet with every other step. *Stop thinking about her like
a village girl just because you saw. . . . She's bloody Aes*

Sedai! You have that Aiel to worry about. He gave himself
a shake and went downstairs.

The common room was full as it could be, with every
chair taken, and stools and benches brought in, and those
who had nowhere to sit standing along the walls. He did
not see the black-haired girl, and no one else looked at him
twice as he hurriedly crossed the room.

Orban occupied a table to himself, his bandaged leg
propped up on a chair with a cushion, with a soft slipper
on that foot, a silver goblet in his hand, the serving women
keeping it filled with wine. "Aye," he was saying to the
whole room, "we knew the Aiel for fierce fighters, Gann
and I, but there was no time to hesitate. I drew my sword,
and dug my heels into Lion's ribs. . . ."

Perrin gave a start before he realized the man meant his
horse was named Lion. *Wouldn't put it past him to say he
was riding a lion.* He felt a little ashamed; just because he
did not like the man was no reason to suppose the Hunter
would take his boasting that far. He hurried on outside
without looking back.

The street in front of the inn was as crowded as inside,
with people who could not find a place in the common
room peering in through the windows, and twice as many
huddling around the doors to listen to Orban's tale. No one
glanced at Perrin twice, though his passage brought muttered complaints from those jostled a little further from the
door.

Everyone who was out in the night must have been at the
inn, for he saw no one as he walked to the square. Sometimes the shadow of a person moved across a lighted window, but that was all. He had the feel of being watched,
though, and looked around uneasily. Nothing but night-
cloaked streets dotted with glowing windows. Around the
square, most of the windows were dark except a few on upper floors.

The gibbet stood as he remembered, the man—the
Aiel—still in the cage, hanging higher than he could reach.
The Aiel seemed to be awake—at least his head was up—
but he never looked down at Perrin. The stones the children
had been throwing were scattered beneath the cage.

The cage hung from a thick rope tied to a ring on one of
the upper bars and running through a heavy pulley on the

crosspiece down to a pair of stubs, waist-high from the bottom of the upright on either side. The excess rope lay in a careless tangle of coils at the foot of the gibbet.

Perrin looked around again, searching the dark square. He still had the feel of being watched, but he still saw nothing. He listened, and heard nothing. He smelled chimney smoke and cooking from the houses, and man-sweat and old blood from the man in the cage. There was no fear scent from him.

His weight, and then there's the cage, he thought as he moved closer to the gibbet. He did not know when he had decided to do this, or even if he really had decided, but he knew he was going to do it.

Hooking a leg around the heavy upright, he heaved on the rope, hoisting the cage enough to gain a little slack. The way the rope jerked told him the man in the cage had finally moved, but he was in too much of a hurry to stop and tell him what he was doing. The slack let him unwind the rope from around the stubs. Still bracing himself with his leg around the upright, he quickly lowered the cage hand over hand to the paving blocks.

The Aiel was looking at him now, studying him silently. Perrin said nothing. When he got a good look at the cage, his mouth tightened. If a thing was made, even a thing like this, it should be made well. The entire front of the cage was a door, on rude hinges made by a hasty hand, held by a good iron lock on a chain as badly wrought as the cage. He fumbled the chain around until he found the worst link, then jammed the thick spike on his axe through it. A sharp twist of his wrist forced the link open. In seconds he separated the chain, rattled it free, and swung open the front of the cage.

The Aiel sat there, knees yet under his chin, staring at him.

"Well?" Perrin whispered hoarsely. "I opened it, but I'm not going to bloody carry you." He looked hastily around the night-dark square. Still nothing moved, but he still had the feel of eyes watching.

"You are strong, wetlander." The Aiel did not move beyond working his shoulders. "It took three men to hoist me up there. And now you bring me down. Why?"

"I don't like seeing people in cages," Perrin whispered.

He wanted to go. The cage was open, and those eyes were watching. But the Aiel was not moving. *If you do a thing, do it right.* "Will you get out of there before somebody comes?"

The Aiel grasped the frontmost overhead bar of the cage, heaved himself out and to his feet in one motion, then half hung there, supporting himself with his grip on the bar. He would have been nearly a head taller than Perrin, standing straight. He glanced at Perrin's eyes—Perrin knew how they must shine, burnished gold in the moonlight—but he did not mention them. "I have been in there since yesterday, wetlander." He sounded like Lan. Not that their voices or accents were anything alike, but the Aiel had that same unruffled coolness, that same calm sureness. "It will take a moment for my legs to work. I am Gaul, of the Imran sept of the Shaarad Aiel, wetlander. I am *Shae'en M'taal*, a Stone Dog. My water is yours."

"Well, I am Perrin Aybara. Of the Two Rivers. I'm a blacksmith." The man was out of the cage; he could go now. Only, if anyone came along before Gaul could walk, he would be right back into the cage unless they killed him, and either way would waste Perrin's work. "If I had thought, I'd have brought a waterbottle, or a skin. Why do you call me 'wetlander'?"

Gaul gestured toward the river; even Perrin's eyes could not be sure in the moonlight, but he thought the Aiel looked uneasy for the first time. "Three days ago, I watched a girl sporting in a huge pool of water. It must have been twenty paces across. She . . . pulled herself out into it." He made an awkward swimming gesture with one hand. "A brave girl. Crossing these . . . rivers . . . has nearly unmanned me. I never thought there could be such a thing as too much water, but I never thought there was so much water in the world as you wetlanders have."

Perrin shook his head. He knew the Aiel Waste held little water—it was one of the few things he knew about the Waste or the Aiel—but he had not thought it could be scarce enough to cause this reaction. "You're a long way from home, Gaul. Why are you here?"

"We search," Gaul said slowly. "We look for He Who Comes With the Dawn."

Perrin had heard that name before, under circumstances

that made him sure who it meant. *Light, it always comes back to Rand. I am tied to him like a mean horse for shoeing.* "You are looking in the wrong direction, Gaul. I'm looking for him, too, and he is on his way to Tear."

"Tear?" The Aiel sounded surprised. "Why . . . ? But it must be. Prophecy says when the Stone of Tear falls, we will leave the Three-fold Land at last." That was the Aiel name for the Waste. "It says we will be changed, and find again what was ours, and was lost."

"That may be. I don't know your prophecies, Gaul. Are you about ready to leave? Somebody could come any minute."

"It is too late to run," Gaul said, and a deep voice shouted, "The savage is loose!" Ten or a dozen white-cloaked men came running across the square, drawing swords, their conical helmets shining in the moonlight. Children of the Light.

As if he had all the time in the world, Gaul calmly lifted a dark cloth from his shoulders and wrapped it around his head, finishing with a thick black veil that hid his face except for his eyes. "Do you like to dance, Perrin Aybara?" he asked. With that, he darted away from the cage. Straight at the oncoming Whitecloaks.

For an instant they were caught by surprise, but an instant was apparently all the Aiel needed. He kicked the sword out of the grip of the first to reach him, then his stiffened hand struck like a dagger at the Whitecloak's throat, and he slid around the soldier as he fell. The next man's arm made a loud snap as Gaul broke it. He pushed that man under the feet of a third, and kicked a fourth in the face. It *was* like a dance, from one to the next without stopping or slowing, though the tripped fellow was climbing back to his feet, and the one with the broken arm had shifted his sword. Gaul danced on in the midst of them.

Perrin had only an amazed moment himself, for not all the Whitecloaks had put their attentions on the Aiel. Barely in time, he gripped the axe haft with both hands to block a sword thrust, swung . . . and wanted to cry out as the half-moon blade tore the man's throat. But he had no time for crying out, none for regrets; more Whitecloaks followed before the first fell. He hated the gaping wounds the axe made, hated the way it chopped through mail to rend flesh beneath, split helmet and skull with almost equal ease. He hated it all. But he did not want to die.

Time seemed to compress and stretch out, both at once. His body felt as if he fought for hours, and breath rasped raw in his throat. Men seemed to move as though floating through jelly. They seemed to leap in an instant from where they started to where they fell. Sweat rolled down his face, yet he felt as cold as quenching water. He fought for his life, and he could not have said whether it lasted seconds or all night.

When he finally stood, panting and nearly stunned, looking at a dozen white-cloaked men lying on the paving blocks of the square, the moon appeared not to have moved at all. Some of the men groaned; others lay silent and still. Gaul stood among them, still veiled, still empty-handed. Most of the men down were his work. Perrin wished they all were, and felt ashamed. The smell of blood and death was sharp and bitter.

"You do not dance the spears badly, Perrin Aybara."

Head spinning, Perrin muttered, "I don't see how twelve men fought twenty of you and won, even if two of them are Hunters."

"Is that what they say?" Gaul laughed softly. "Sarien and I were careless, being so long in these soft lands, and the wind was from the wrong direction, so we smelled nothing. We walked into them before we knew it. Well, Sarien is dead, and I was caged like a fool, so perhaps we paid enough. It is time for running now, wetlander. Tear; I will remember it." At last he lowered the black veil. "May you always find water and shade, Perrin Aybara." Turning, he ran into the night.

Perrin started to run, too, then realized he had a bloody axe in his hands. Hastily he wiped the curved blade on a dead man's cloak. *He's dead, burn me, and there's blood on it already.* He made himself put the haft back through the loop on his belt before he broke into a trot.

At his second step he saw her, a slim shape at the edge of the square, in dark, narrow skirts. She turned to run; he could see they were divided for riding. She darted back into the street and vanished.

Lan met him before he reached the place where she had been standing. The Warder took in the cage sitting empty beneath the gibbet, the shadowed white mounds that caught the moonlight, and he tossed his head as if he were about to erupt. In a voice as tight and hard as a new wheel rim, he said, "Is this your work, blacksmith? The Light burn me! Is there anyone who can connect it to you?"

"A girl," Perrin said. "I think she saw. I don't want you to hurt her, Lan! Plenty of others could have seen, too. There are lighted windows all around."

The Warder grabbed Perrin's coat sleeve and gave him a push toward the inn. "I saw a girl running, but I thought. . . . No matter. You dig the Ogier out and haul him down to the stable. After this, we need to get our horses to the docks as quickly as possible. The Light alone knows if there is a ship sailing tonight, or what I'll have to pay to hire one if there isn't. Don't ask questions, blacksmith! Do it! Run!"

CHAPTER
35

The Falcon

The Warder's long legs outdistanced Perrin's, and by the time he pushed through the throng outside the inn doors, Lan was already striding up the stairs, not seeming in any particular hurry. Perrin made himself walk as slowly. From the doorway behind him came grumbles about people pushing ahead of other people.

"Again?" Orban was saying, holding his silver cup up to be refilled. "Aye, very well. They lay in ambush close beside the road we traveled, and an ambush I did not expect so close to Remen. Screaming, they rushed upon us from the crowding brush. In a breath they were in our midst, their spears stabbing, slaying two of my best men and one of Gann's immediately. Aye, I knew Aiel when I saw them, and. . . ."

Perrin hurried up the stairs. *Well, Orban knows them now.*

Voices came from behind Moiraine's door. He did not want to hear what she had to say about this. He hurried past to stick his head into Loial's room.

The Ogier bed was a low, massive thing, twice as long and half as wide as any human bed Perrin had ever seen. It took up much of the room, and that was as large and as fine as Moiraine's. Perrin vaguely remembered Loial saying something about it being sung wood, and at any other time he might have stopped to admire those flowing curves that made it seem as if the bed had somehow grown where it stood. Ogier really must have stopped in Remen at some time in the past, for the innkeeper had also found a wooden armchair that fit Loial, and filled it with cushions. The Ogier was comfortably sitting on them in his shirt and breeches, idly scratching a bare ankle with a toenail as he wrote in a large, cloth-bound book on an arm of the chair.

"We're leaving!" Perrin said.

Loial gave a jump, nearly upsetting his ink bottle and almost dropping the book. "Leaving? We only just arrived," he rumbled.

"Yes, leaving. Meet us at the stable as quickly as you can. And don't let anyone see you go. I think there's a back stair that runs down by the kitchen." The smell of food at his end of the hall had been too strong for there not to be.

The Ogier gave one regretful look at the bed, then started tugging on his high boots. "But why?"

"The Whitecloaks," Perrin said. "I'll tell you more later." He ducked back out before Loial could ask any more.

He had not unpacked. Once he had belted on his quiver, slung his cloak around him, tossed blanketroll and saddlebags on his shoulder, and picked up his bow, there was no sign he had ever been there. Not a wrinkle in the folded blankets at the foot of the bed, not a splash of water in the cracked basin on the washstand. Even the tallow candle still had a fresh wick, he realized. *I must have known I would not be staying. I don't seem to leave any mark behind me, of late.*

As he had suspected, a narrow stair at the back led down to a hall that ran out past the kitchen. He peered cautiously into the kitchen. A spit dog trotted in his big wicker wheel, turning a long spit that held a haunch of lamb, a large piece of beef, five chickens, and a goose. Fragrant steam rose from a soup cauldron hanging from a sturdy crane over a second hearth. But there was not a cook to be seen, nor any living soul except the dog. Thankful for Orban's lies, he hurried on into the night.

The stable was a large structure of the same stone as the inn, though only the stone faces around the big doors had been polished. A single lantern hanging from a stall-post gave a dim light. Stepper and the other horses stood in stalls near the doors; Loial's big mount nearly filled his. The smell of hay and horses was familiar and comforting. Perrin was the first to arrive.

There was only one stableman on duty, a narrow-faced fellow in a dirty shirt, with lanky gray hair, who demanded to know who Perrin was to order four horses saddled, and who was his master, and what he was doing all bundled up to travel in the middle of the night, and did Master Furlan know he was sneaking off like this, and what did he have hidden in those saddlebags, and what was wrong with his eyes, was he sick?

A coin flipped through the air from behind Perrin, glinting gold in the lantern light. The stableman snagged it with one hand and bit it.

"Saddle them," Lan said. His voice was soft, as cold iron is soft, and the stableman bobbed a bow and scurried to make the horses ready.

Moiraine and Loial came into the stable just as they could take up their reins, and then they were all leading their horses behind Lan, off down a street that ran behind the stable toward the river. The soft clop of the horses' hooves on the paving blocks attracted only a slat-ribbed dog that barked once and ran away as they went by.

"This brings back memories, doesn't it, Perrin?" Loial said, quietly for him.

"Keep your voice down," Perrin whispered. "What memories?"

"Why, it is like old times." The Ogier had managed to mute his voice; he sounded like a bumblebee only the size of a dog instead of a horse. "Sneaking away in the night, with enemies behind us, and maybe enemies ahead, and danger in the air, and the cold tang of adventure."

Perrin frowned at Loial over Stepper's saddle. It was easy enough; his eyes cleared the saddle, and Loial stood head and shoulders and chest above it on the other side. "What are you talking about? I believe you are coming to like danger! Loial, you must be crazy!"

"I am only fixing the mood in my head," Loial said, sounding formal. Or perhaps defensive. "For my book. I have to put it all in. I believe I am coming to like it. Adventuring. Of course, I am." His ears gave two violent twitches. "I have to like it if I wish to write of it."

Perrin shook his head.

At the stone wharves the bargelike ferries lay snugged

for the night, still and dark, as did most of the ships. Lantern lights and people moved around on the dock alongside a two-masted vessel, though, and on the deck as well. The main smells were tar and rope, with strong hints of fish, though something back in the nearest warehouse gave off sharp, spicy aromas that the others nearly submerged.

Lan located the captain, a short, slight man with an odd way of holding his head tilted to one side while he listened. The bargaining was over soon enough, and booms and sling rigged to hoist the horses aboard. Perrin kept a close eye on the horses, talking to them; horses had little tolerance for the unusual, such as being lifted into the air, but even the Warder's stallion seemed soothed by his murmurs.

Lan gave gold to the captain, and silver to two sailors who ran barefoot to a warehouse for sacks of oats. More crewmen tethered the horses between the masts in a sort of small pen made of rope, all the while muttering about the mess they would have to clean. Perrin did not think anyone was supposed to overhear, but his ears caught the words. The men were just not used to horses.

In short order the *Snow Goose* was ready to sail, only a little ahead of what the captain—his name was Jaim Adarra—had intended. Lan led Moiraine below as the lines were cast off, and Loial followed yawning. Perrin stayed at the railing near the bow, though the Ogier's every yawn had summoned one of his own. He wondered if the *Snow Goose* could outrun wolves down the river, outrun dreams. Men began readying the sweeps to push the vessel away from the wharf.

As the last line was tossed ashore and seized by a dockman, a girl in narrow, divided skirts burst out of the shadows between two warehouses, a bundle in her arms and a dark cloak streaming behind her. She leaped onto the deck just as the men at the sweeps began pushing off.

Adarra bustled from his place by the tiller, but she calmly set down her bundle and said briskly, "I will take passage downriver . . . oh . . . say, as far as he is going." She nodded toward Perrin without looking at him. "I've no objections to sleeping on deck. Cold and wet do not bother me."

A few minutes of bargaining followed. She passed over three silver marks, frowned at the coppers she got back, then stuffed them into her purse and came forward to stand beside Perrin.

She had an herbal scent to her, light and fresh and clean. Those dark, tilted eyes regarded him over high cheekbones, then turned to look back toward shore. She was about his own age, he decided; he could not decide if her nose fit her face, or dominated it. *You are a fool, Perrin Aybara. Why care what she looks like?*

The gap to the wharf was a good twenty paces, now; the sweeps dug in, cutting white furrows in black water. For a moment he considered tossing her over the side.

"Well," she said after a moment, "I never expected my travels to take me back to Illian so soon as this." Her voice was high, and she had a flat way of speaking, but it was not unpleasant. "You *are* going to Illian, are you not?" He tightened his mouth. "Don't sulk," she said. "You left quite a mess back there, you and that Aielman between you. The uproar was just beginning when I left."

"You did not tell them?" he said in surprise.

"The townsfolk think the Aielman chewed through the chain, or broke it with his bare hands. They had not decided which when I left." She made a sound suspiciously like a giggle. "Orban was quite loud in his disgust that his wounds would keep him from hunting down the Aielman personally."

Perrin snorted. "If he ever sees an Aiel again, he'll bloody soil himself." He cleared his throat and muttered, "Sorry."

"I do not know about that," she said, as if his remark had been nothing out of the way. "I saw him in Jehannah during the winter. He fought four men together, killed two and made the other two yield. Of course, he started the fight, so that takes something away from it, but they knew what they were doing. He did not pick a fight with men who could not defend themselves. Still, he is a fool. He has these peculiar ideas about the Great Blackwood. What some call the Forest of Shadows. Have you ever heard of it?"

He eyed her sideways. She spoke of fighting and killing as calmly as another woman might speak of baking. He had never heard of any Great Blackwood, but the Forest of Shadows lay just south of the Two Rivers. "Are you following me? You were staring at me, back at the inn. Why? And why didn't you tell them what you saw?"

"An Ogier," she said, staring at the river, "is obviously an Ogier, and the others were not much more difficult to figure out. I managed a much better look inside *Lady Alys*'s hood than Orban did, and her face makes that stone-faced fellow a Warder. The Light burn me if I'd want that one angry with me. Does he always look like that, or did he eat a rock for his last meal? Anyway, that left only you. I do not like things I cannot account for."

Once again he considered tossing her over the side. Seriously, this time. But Remen was now only a blotch of light well behind them in the darkness, and no telling how far it was to shore.

She seemed to take his silence as an urging to go on. "So there I have an"—she looked around, then dropped her voice, though the closest crewman was working a sweep ten feet away—"an Aes Sedai, a Warder, an Ogier—and you. A countryman, by first look at you." Her tilted eyes rose to study his yellow ones intently—he refused to look away—and she smiled. "Only you free a caged Aielman, hold a long talk with him, then help him chop a dozen Whitecloaks into sausage. I assume you do this regularly; you certainly looked as if it were nothing out of the ordinary for you. I scent something strange in a party of travelers such as yours, and strange trails are what Hunters look for."

He blinked; there was no mistaking that emphasis. "A Hunter? You? You cannot be a Hunter. You're a girl."

Her smile became so innocent that he almost walked away from her. She stepped back, made a flourish with each hand, and was holding two knives as neatly as old Thom Merrilin could have done it. One of the men at the sweeps made a choking sound, and two others stumbled; sweeps thrashed and tangled, and the *Snow Goose* lurched a little before the captain's shouts set things right. By that time, the black-haired girl had made the knives disappear again.

"Nimble fingers and nimble wits will take you a good deal further than a sword and muscles. Sharp eyes help, as well, but fortunately, I have these things."

"And modesty, as well," Perrin murmured. She did not seem to notice.

"I took the oath and received the blessing in the Great Square of Tammaz, in Illian. Perhaps I *was* the youngest, but in that crowd, with all the trumpets and drums and

cymbals and shouting. . . . A six-year-old could have taken
the oath, and none would have noticed. There were over a
thousand of us, perhaps two, and every one with an idea
of where to find the Horn of Valere. I have mine—it still
may be the right one—but no Hunter can afford to pass
up a strange trail. The Horn will certainly lie at the end
of a strange trail, and I have never seen one any stranger
than the trail you four make. Where are you bound? Illian?
Somewhere else?"

"What was your idea?" he asked. "About where the Horn
is?" *Safe in Tar Valon, I hope, and the Light send I never
see it again.* "You think it's in Ghealdan?"

She frowned at him—he had the feeling she did not give
up a scent once she had raised it, but he was ready to offer
her as many side trails as she would take—then said, "Have
you ever heard of Manetheren?"

He nearly choked. "I have heard of it," he said cautiously.

"Every queen of Manetheren was an Aes Sedai, and
the king the Warder bound to her. I can't imagine a place
like that, but that is what the books say. It was a large
land—most of Andor and Ghealdan and more besides—
but the capital, the city itself, was in the Mountains of Mist.
That is where I think the Horn is. Unless you four lead
me to it."

His hackles stirred. She was lecturing him as if he were
an untaught village lout. "You'll not find the Horn or Manetheren. The city was destroyed during the Trolloc Wars,
when the last queen drew too much of the One Power to
destroy the Dreadlords who had killed her husband." Moiraine had told him the names of that king and queen, but he
did not remember them.

"Not in Manetheren, farmboy," she said calmly, "though
a land such as that would make a good hiding place. But
there were other nations, other cities, in the Mountains of
Mist, so old that not even Aes Sedai remember them. And
think of all those stories about it being bad luck to enter
the mountains. What better place for the Horn to be hidden
than in one of those forgotten cities."

"I have heard stories of something being hidden in the
mountains." Would she believe him? He had never been
good at lying. "The stories did not say what, but it's supposed to be the greatest treasure in the world, so maybe it

is the Horn. But the Mountains of Mist stretch for hundreds of leagues. If you are going to find it, you should not waste time following us. You'll need it all to find the Horn before Orban and Gann."

"I told you, those two have some strange idea the Horn is hidden in the Great Blackwood." She smiled up at him. Her mouth was not too big at all, when she smiled. "And I told you a Hunter has to follow strange trails. You are lucky Orban and Gann were injured fighting all those Aielmen, or they might well be aboard, too. At least I will not get in your way, or try to take over, or pick a fight with the Warder."

He growled disgustedly. "We are just travelers on our way to Illian, girl. What is your name? If I have to share this ship with you for days yet, I can't keep calling you girl."

"I call myself Mandarb." He could not stop the guffaw that burst out of him. Those tilted eyes regarded him with heat. "I will teach you something, farmboy." Her voice remained level. Barely. "In the Old Tongue, Mandarb means 'blade.' It is a name worthy of a Hunter of the Horn!"

He managed to get his laughter under control, and hardly wheezed at all as he pointed to the rope pen between the masts. "You see that black stallion? His name is Mandarb."

The heat went out of her eyes, and spots of color bloomed on her cheeks. "Oh. I was born Zarine Bashere, but Zarine is no name for a Hunter. In the stories, Hunters have names like Rogosh Eagle-eye."

She looked so crestfallen that he hastened to say, "I like the name Zarine. It suits you." The heat flashed back into her eyes, and for a moment he thought she was about to produce one of her knives again. "It is late, Zarine. I want some sleep."

He turned his back to start for the hatch that led belowdeck, prickles running across his shoulders. Crewmen still padded up the deck and back, working the sweeps. *Fool. A girl would not stick a knife in me. Not with all these people watching. Would she?* Just as he reached the hatch, she called to him.

"Farmboy! Perhaps I will call myself Faile. My father used to call me that, when I was little. It means 'falcon.'"

He stiffened and almost missed the first step of the ladder. *Coincidence.* He made himself go down without looking back toward her. *It has to be.* The passageway was dark, but enough moonlight filtered down behind him for him to make his way. Someone was snoring loudly in one of the cabins. *Min, why did you have to go seeing things?*

CHAPTER
36

Daughter of the Night

R ealizing that he had no way of knowing which
cabin was supposed to be his, he put his head into
several. They were dark, and all of them had two
men asleep in the narrow beds built against each side, all
but one, which held Loial, sitting on the floor between the
beds—and barely fitting—scribbling in his cloth-bound
book of notes by the light of a gimballed lantern. The Ogier
wanted to talk about the events of the day, but Perrin, jaws
creaking with the effort of holding his yawns in, thought the
ship must have run far enough downriver by now to make
it safe to sleep. Safe to dream. Even if they tried, wolves
could not long keep pace with the sweeps and the current.

Finally he found a windowless cabin with no one in it at
all, which suited him just as well. He wanted to be alone.
A coincidence in the name, that's all, he thought as he lit
the lantern mounted on the wall. *Anyway, her real name
is Zarine.* But the girl with the high cheekbones and dark,
tilted eyes was not uppermost in his thoughts. He put his
bow and other belongings on one cramped bed, tossed his
cloak over them, and sat on the other to tug off his boots.

Elyas Machera had found a way to live with what he was,
a man somehow linked with wolves, and he had not gone
mad. Thinking back, Perrin was sure Elyas had been living
that way for years before he ever met the man. *He wants to
be that way. He accepts it, anyway.* That was no solution.
Perrin did not want to live that way, did not want to accept.
*But if you have the bar stock to make a knife, you accept it
and make a knife, even if you'd like a woodaxe. No! My life
is more than iron to be hammered into shape.*

Cautiously, he reached out with his mind, feeling for wolves, and found—nothing. Oh, there was a dim impression of wolves somewhere in the distance, but it faded even as he touched it. For the first time in so long, he was alone. Blessedly alone.

Blowing out the lantern, he lay down, for the first time in days. *How in the Light will Loial manage in one of these?* Those all but sleepless nights rolled over him, exhaustion slacking his muscles. It came to him that he had managed to put the Aiel out of his head. And the Whitecloaks. *Light-forsaken axe! Burn me, I wish I had never seen it,* was his last thought before sleep.

Thick gray fog surrounded him, dense enough low down that he could not see his own boots, and so heavy on every side that he could not make out anything ten paces away. There was surely nothing nearer. Anything at all might lie within it. The mist did not feel right; there was no dampness to it. He put a hand to his belt, seeking the comfort of knowing he could defend himself, and gave a start. His axe was not there.

Something moved in the fog, a swirling in the grayness. Something coming his way.

He tensed, wondering if it was better to run or stand and fight with his bare hands, wondering if there was anything to fight.

The billowing furrow boring through the fog resolved itself into a wolf, its shaggy form almost one with the heavy mist.

Hopper?

The wolf hesitated, then came to stand beside him. It was Hopper—he was certain—but something about the wolf's stance, something in the yellow eyes that looked up briefly to meet his, demanded silence, in mind as well as body. Those eyes demanded that he follow, too.

He laid a hand on the wolf's back, and as he did, Hopper started forward. He let himself be led. The fur under his hand was thick and shaggy. It felt real.

The fog began to thicken, until only his hand told him Hopper was still there, until a glance down did not even show him his own chest. Just gray mist. He might as well have been wrapped in new-sheared wool for all he could see. It struck him that he had heard nothing, either. Not even the sound of his own footsteps. He wiggled his toes, and was relieved to feel the boots on his feet.

The gray became darker, and he and the wolf walked through pitch-blackness. He could not see his hand when he touched his nose. He could not see his nose, for that matter. He tried closing his eyes for a moment, and could not tell any difference. There was still no sound. His hand felt the rough hair of Hopper's back, but he was not sure he could feel anything under his boots.

Suddenly Hopper stopped, forcing him to halt, too. He looked around . . . and snapped his eyes shut. He could tell a difference, now. And feel something, too, a queasy twisting of his stomach. He made himself open his eyes and look down.

What he saw could not have been there, not unless he and Hopper were standing in midair. He could see nothing of the wolf or himself, as if neither had bodies at all—that thought nearly tied his stomach into knots—but below him, as clear as if lit by a thousand lamps, stretched a vast array of mirrors, seemingly hanging in blackness though as level as if they stood on a vast floor. They stretched as far as he could see in every direction, but right beneath his feet, there was a clear space. And people in it. Suddenly he could hear their voices as well as if he had been standing among them.

"Great Lord," one of the men muttered, "where is this place?" He looked around once, flinching at his image cast back at him many thousandfold, and held his eyes forward after that. The others huddled around him seemed even more afraid. "I was asleep in Tar Valon, Great Lord. I *am* asleep in Tar Valon! Where is this place? Have I gone mad?"

Some of the men around him wore ornate coats full of embroidery, others plainer garb, while some seemed to be naked, or in their smallclothes.

"I, too, sleep," a naked man nearly screamed. "In Tear. I remember lying down with my wife!"

"And I do sleep in Illian," a man in red and gold said, sounding shaken. "I know that I do sleep, but that cannot be. I know that I do dream, but that does be impossible. Where does this be, Great Lord? Are you really come to me?"

The dark-haired man who faced them was garbed in black, with silver lace at his throat and wrists. Now and again he put a hand to his chest, as if it hurt him. There was light everywhere down there, coming from nowhere, but this man below Perrin seemed cloaked in shadow. Darkness rolled around him, caressed him.

"Silence!" The black-clothed man did not speak loudly, but he had no need to. For the space of that word, he had raised his head; his eyes and mouth were holes boring into a raging forge-fire, all flame and fiery glow.

Perrin knew him, then. Ba'alzamon. He was staring down at Ba'alzamon himself. Fear struck through him like hammered spikes. He would have run, but he could not feel his feet.

Hopper shifted. He felt the thick fur under his hand and gripped it hard. Something real. Something more real, he hoped, than what he saw. But he knew that both were real.

The men huddling together cowered.

"You have been given tasks," Ba'alzamon said. "Some of these tasks you have carried out. At others, you have failed." Now and again his eyes and mouth vanished in flame again, and the mirrors flashed with reflected fire. "Those who have been marked for death must die. Those who have been marked for taking must bow to me. To fail the Great Lord of the Dark cannot be forgiven." Fire shone through his eyes, and the darkness around him roiled and spun. "You." His finger pointed out the man who had spoken of Tar Valon, a fellow dressed like a merchant, in plainly cut clothes of the finest cloth. The others shied away from him as if he had blackbile fever, leaving him to cower alone. "You allowed the boy to escape Tar Valon."

The man screamed, and began to quiver like a file struck against an anvil. He seemed to become less solid, and his scream thinned with him.

"You all dream," Ba'alzamon said, "but what happens in this dream is real." The shrieking man was only a bundle of mist shaped like a man, his scream far distant, and then even the mist was gone. "I fear he will never wake." He laughed, and his mouth roared flame. "The rest of you will not fail me again. Begone! Wake, and obey!" The other men vanished.

For a moment Ba'alzamon stood alone, then suddenly there was a woman with him, clad all in white and silver.

Shock hit Perrin. He could never forget a woman so beautiful. She was the woman from his dream, the one who had urged him to glory.

An ornate silver throne appeared behind her, and she sat, carefully arranging her silken skirts. "You make free use of my domain," she said.

"Your domain?" Ba'alzamon said. "You claim it yours, then? Do you no longer serve the Great Lord of the Dark?" The darkness around him thickened for an instant, seemed to boil.

"I serve," she said quickly. "I have served the Lord of the Twilight long. Long did I lie imprisoned for my service, in an endless, dreamless sleep. Only Gray Men and Myrddraal are denied dreams. Even Trollocs can dream. Dreams were always mine, to use and walk. Now I am free again, and I will use what is mine."

"What is yours," Ba'alzamon said. The blackness swirling 'round him seemed mirthful. "You always thought yourself greater than you were, Lanfear."

The name cut at Perrin like a newly honed knife. One of the Forsaken had been in his dreams. Moiraine had been right. Some of them were free.

The woman in white was on her feet, the throne gone. "I am as great as I am. What have your plans come to? Three thousand years and more of whispering in ears and pulling the strings of throned puppets like an Aes Sedai!" Her voice invested the name with all scorn. "Three thousand years, and yet Lews Therin walks the world again, and these Aes Sedai all but have him leashed. Can you control him? Can you turn him? He was mine before ever that straw-haired chit Ilyena saw him! He will be mine again!"

"Do you serve yourself now, Lanfear?" Ba'alzamon's voice was soft, but flame raged continuously in his eyes and mouth. "Have you abandoned your oaths to the Great Lord of the Dark?" For an instant the darkness nearly obliterated him, only the glowing fires showing through. "They are not so easily broken as the oaths to the Light you forsook, proclaiming your new master in the very Hall of the Servants. Your master claims you forever, Lanfear. Will you serve, or do you choose an eternity of pain, of endless dying without release?"

"I serve." Despite her words, she stood tall and defiant. "I serve the Great Lord of the Dark and none other. Forever!"

The vast array of mirror began to vanish as if black waves rolled in over it, ever closer to the center. The tide rolled over Ba'alzamon and Lanfear. There was only blackness.

Perrin felt Hopper move, and he was more than glad to follow, guided only by the feel of fur under his hand. It was not until he was moving that he realized he could. He tried to puzzle out what he had seen, without any success. Ba'alzamon and Lanfear. His tongue stuck to the roof of his mouth. For some reason, Lanfear frightened him more than Ba'alzamon did. Perhaps because she had been in his dreams in the mountains. *Light! One of the Forsaken in my dreams! Light!* And unless he had missed something, she had defied the Dark One. He had been told and taught that the Shadow could have no power over you if you denied it; but how could a Darkfriend—not just a Darkfriend; one of the Forsaken!—defy the Shadow? *I must be mad, like Simion's brother. These dreams have driven me mad!*

Slowly the blackness became fog again, and the fog gradually thinned until he walked out of it with Hopper onto a grassy hillside bright with daylight. Birds began to sing from a thicket at the foot of the hill. He looked back. A hilly plain dotted with clumps of trees stretched to the horizon. There was no sign of fog anywhere. The big, grizzled wolf stood watching him.

"What was that?" he demanded, struggling in his mind to turn the question to thoughts the wolf could understand. "Why did you show it to me? What was it?"

Emotions and images flooded his thoughts, and his mind put words to them. *What you must see. Be careful, Young Bull. This place is dangerous. Be wary as a cub hunting porcupine.* That came as something closer to Small Thorny Back, but his mind named the animal the way he knew it as a man. *You are too young, too new.*

"Was it real?"

All is real, what is seen, and what is not seen. That seemed to be all the answer Hopper was going to give.

"Hopper, how are you here? I saw you die. I felt you die!"

All are here. All brothers and sisters that are, all that

were, all that will be. Perrin knew that wolves did not smile, not the way humans did, but for an instant he had the impression that Hopper was grinning. *Here, I soar like the eagle.* The wolf gathered himself and leaped, up into the air. Up and up it carried him, until he dwindled to a speck in the sky, and a last thought came. *To soar.*

Perrin stared after him with his mouth hanging open. *He did it.* His eyes burned suddenly, and he cleared his throat and scrubbed at his nose. *I will be crying like a girl, next.* Without thinking, he looked around to see if anyone had seen him, and that quickly everything changed.

He was standing on a rise, with shadowy, indistinct dips and swells all around him. They seemed to fade into the distance too soon. Rand stood below him. Rand, and a ragged circle of Myrddraal and men and women his eyes seemed to slide right past. Dogs howled somewhere in the distance, and Perrin knew they were hunting something. Myrddraal scent and the stink of burned sulphur filled the air. Perrin's hackles rose.

The circle of Myrddraal and people came closer to Rand, all walking as if asleep. And Rand began to kill them. Balls of fire flew from his hands and consumed two. Lightning flashed from above to shrivel others. Bars of light like white-hot steel flew from his fists to more. And the survivors continued to walk slowly closer, as if none of them saw what was happening. One by one they died, until none were left, and Rand sank down on his knees, panting. Perrin was not sure whether he was laughing or crying; it seemed to be some of each.

Shapes appeared over the rises, more people coming, more Myrddraal, all intent on Rand.

Perrin cupped his hands to his mouth. "Rand! Rand, there are more coming!"

Rand looked up at him from his crouch, snarling, sweat slicking his face.

"Rand, they're—!"

"Burn you!" Rand howled.

Light burned Perrin's eyes, and pain seared everything.

Groaning, he rolled into a ball on the narrow bed, the light still burning behind his eyelids. His chest hurt. He raised a hand to it and winced when he felt a burn under his shirt, a spot no bigger than a silver penny.

Bit by bit he forced his knotted muscles to let him straighten his legs and lie flat in the dark cabin. *Moiraine. I have to tell Moiraine this time. Just have to wait till the pain goes away.*

But as the pain began to fade, exhaustion took him. He barely had a thought that he must get up before sleep pulled him down again.

When he opened his eyes again, he lay staring at the beams overhead. Light at the top and bottom of the door told him morning had come. He put a hand to his chest to convince himself he had imagined it, imagined it so well that he had actually felt a burn. . . .

His fingers found the burn. *I didn't imagine it, then.* He had dim memories of a few other dreams, fading even as he recalled them. Ordinary dreams. He even felt as if he had had a good night's sleep. *And could use another one right now.* But it meant he could sleep. *As long as there are no wolves around, anyway.*

He remembered making a decision in that brief waking after the dream with Hopper, and after a moment he decided it had been a good one.

It took knocking on five doors and being cursed at twice—the inhabitants of two cabins had gone on deck—before he found Moiraine. She was fully dressed, but sitting on one of the narrow beds cross-legged, reading in her book of notes by lantern light. Back near the beginning, he saw, notes that must have been made even before she had come to Emond's Field. Lan's things were neatly placed on the other bed.

"I had a dream," he told her, and proceeded to tell her of it. All of it. He even pulled up his shirt to show her the small circle on his chest, red, with wavy red lines radiating from it. He had kept things from her before, and he suspected he would again, but this might be too important to hold back. The pin was the smallest part of a pair of scissors, and the easiest made, but without it, the scissors cut no cloth. When he was done, he stood there waiting.

She had watched him without expression, except that those dark eyes had examined every word as it came out of his mouth, weighed it, measured it, held it up to the light.

Now she sat the same way, only it was he who was examined, weighed, and held up to the light.

"Well, is it important?" he demanded finally. "I think it was one of those wolf dreams you told me about—I'm sure it was; it must have been!—but that doesn't make what I saw real. Only, you said maybe some of the Forsaken are free, and he called her Lanfear, and. . . . Is it important, or am I standing here making a fool out of myself?"

"There are women," she said slowly, "who would do their best to gentle you if they heard what I just did." His lungs seemed to freeze; he could not breathe. "I am not accusing you of being able to channel," she went on, and the ice inside him melted, "or even of being able to learn. An attempt at gentling would not harm you, beyond the rough treatment the Red Ajah would give you before they realized their error. Such men are so rare, even the Reds with all their hunting have not found more than three in the last ten years. Before the outbreak of false Dragons, at least. What I am trying to make clear to you is that I do not think you will suddenly begin wielding the Power. You do not have to be afraid of that."

"Well, thank you very much for that," he said bitterly. "You did not have to scare me to death just so you could tell me there was no need to be frightened!"

"Oh, you do have reason to be frightened. Or at least careful, as the wolf suggested. Red sisters, or others, might kill you before they discovered there was nothing to gentle in you."

"Light! Light burn me!" He stared at her with a frown. "You're trying to lead me around by the nose, Moiraine, but I am no calf, and there's no ring in my nose. The Red Ajah or any other would not think of gentling unless there was something real in what I dreamed. Does it mean the Forsaken are loose?"

"I told you before that they might be. Some of them. Your . . . dreams are nothing I expected, Perrin. Dreamers have written of wolves, but I did not expect this."

"Well, I think it was real. I think I saw something that really happened, something I wasn't supposed to see." *What you must see.* "I think Lanfear is loose at the very least. What are you going to do?"

"I am going to Illian. And then I will go to Tear, and

hope to reach it before Rand. We had need to leave Remen too quickly for Lan to learn whether he crossed the river or went down it. We should know before we reach Illian, though. We will find sign if he has gone this way." She glanced at her book as if she wanted to resume her reading.

"Is that all you are going to do? With Lanfear loose, and the Light alone knows how many of the others?"

"Do not question me," she said coldly. "You do not know which questions to ask, and you would comprehend less than half the answers if I gave them. Which I will not."

He shifted his feet under her gaze until it became clear she would say no more on the matter. His shirt rubbed painfully at the burn on his chest. It did not seem a bad hurt—*Not for being struck by lightning it doesn't!*—but how he had come by it was another matter. "Uh. . . . Will you Heal this?"

"Are you no longer uneasy about the One Power being used on you, then, Perrin? No, I will not Heal it. It is not serious, and it will remind you of the need to be careful." Careful about pressing her, he knew, as well as about dreams or letting others know of them. "If there is nothing else, Perrin?"

He started for the door, then stopped. "There is one thing. If you knew a woman's name was Zarine, would you think it meant anything about her?"

"Why under the Light do you ask this question?"

"A girl," he said awkwardly. "A young woman. I met her last night. She's one of the other passengers." He would let her discover for herself that Zarine knew she was Aes Sedai. And seemed to think following them would lead her to the Horn of Valere. He would not keep back anything he thought was important, but if Moiraine could be secretive, so could he.

"Zarine. It is a Saldaean name. No woman would name her daughter that unless she expected her to be a great beauty. And a heartbreaker. One to lie on cushions in palaces, surrounded by servants and suitors." She smiled, briefly but with great amusement. "Perhaps you have another reason to be careful, Perrin, if there is a Zarine as a passenger with us."

"I intend to be careful," he told her. At least he knew why

Zarine did not like her name. Hardly fitting for a Hunter of the Horn. *As long as she doesn't call herself "falcon."*

When he went on deck, Lan was there, looking over Mandarb. And Zarine was sitting on a coil of rope near the railing, sharpening one of her knives and watching him. The big, triangular sails were set and taut, and the *Snow Goose* flew downriver.

Zarine's eyes followed Perrin as he walked by her to stand in the bow. The water curled to either side of the prow like earth turning around a good plow. He wondered about dreams and Aielmen, Min's viewings and falcons. His chest hurt. Life had *never* been as tangled as this.

Rand sat up out of his exhausted sleep, gasping, the cloak he had used as a blanket falling away. His side ached, the old wound from Falme throbbing. His fire had burned down to coals with only a few wavering flames, but it was still enough to make the shadows move. *That was Perrin. It was! It was* him, *not a dream. Somehow. I almost killed him! Light, I have to be careful!*

Shivering, he picked up a length of oak branch and started to shove it into the coals. The trees were scattered in these Murandian hills, still close to the Manetherendrelle, but he had found just enough fallen branches for his fire, the wood just old enough to be properly cured but not rotten. Before the wood touched the coals, he stopped. There were horses coming, ten or a dozen of them, walking slowly. *I have to be careful. I cannot make another mistake.*

The horses swung toward his failing fire, entered the dim light, and stopped. The shadows obscured their riders, but most seemed to be rough-faced men wearing round helmets and long leather jerkins sewn all over with metal discs like fish scales. One was a woman with graying hair and a no-nonsense look on her face. Her dark dress was plain wool, but the finest weave, and adorned with a silver pin in the shape of a lion. A merchant, she seemed to him; he had seen her sort among those who came to buy tabac and wool in the Two Rivers. A merchant and her guards.

I have to be careful, he thought as he stood. *No mistakes.*

"You have chosen a good campsite, young man," she said. "I have often used it on my way to Remen. There is a small spring nearby. I trust you have no objection to my sharing it?" Her guards were already dismounting, hitching at their sword belts and loosening saddle girths.

"None," Rand told her. *Careful.* Two steps brought him close enough, and he leaped into the air, spinning— Thistledown Floats on the Whirlwind—heron-mark blade carved from fire coming into his hands to take her head off before surprise could even form on her face. *She was the most dangerous.*

He alighted as the woman's head rolled from the crupper of her horse. The guards yelled and clawed for their swords, screamed as they realized his blade burned. He danced among them in the forms Lan had taught him, and knew he could have killed all ten with ordinary steel, but the blade he wielded was part of him. The last man fell, and it had been so like practicing the forms that he had already begun the sheathing called Folding the Fan before he remembered he wore no scabbard and this blade would have turned it to ash at a touch if he had.

Letting the sword vanish, he turned to examine the horses. Most had run away, but some not far, and the woman's tall gelding stood with rolling eyes, whickering uneasily. Her headless corpse, lying on the ground, had maintained its grip on the reins, and held the animal's head down.

Rand pulled them free, pausing only to gather his few belongings before swinging into the saddle. *I have to be careful,* he thought as he looked over the dead. *No mistakes.*

The Power still filled him, the flow from *saidin* sweeter than honey, ranker than rotted meat. Abruptly he channeled—not really understanding what it was he did, or how, only that it seemed right; and it worked, lifting the corpses. He set them in a line, facing him, kneeling, faces in the dirt. For those who had faces left. Kneeling to him.

"If I *am* the Dragon Reborn," he told them, "that is the way it is supposed to be, isn't it?" Letting go of *saidin* was hard, but he did it. *If I hold it too much, how will I keep the madness away?* He laughed bitterly. *Or is it too late for that?*

Frowning, he peered at the line. He had been sure there were only ten men, but eleven men knelt in that line, one of them without armor of any sort but with a dagger still gripped in his hand.

"You chose the wrong company," Rand told that man.

Wheeling the gelding, he dug in his heels and set the animal to a dead gallop into the night. It was a long way to Tear, yet, but he meant to get there by the straightest way, if he had to kill horses or steal them. *I will put an end to it. The taunting. The baiting. I will end it! Callandor.* It called to him.

CHAPTER

37

Fires in Cairhien

E gwene returned a graceful nod to the respectful bow
of the ship's crewman who padded past her, barefoot, on his way to pull a rope that already seemed
taut, possibly shifting a trifle the way one of the big square
sails set. As he trotted back toward where the round-faced
captain stood by the tillerman, he bowed again, and she
nodded once more before returning her attentions to the
forested Cairhien shore, separated from the *Blue Crane* by
less than twenty spans of water.

A village was sliding past, or what had been a village
once. Half the houses were only smoldering piles of rubble with chimneys sticking starkly out of the ruins. On
the other houses, doors swung with the wind, and pieces
of furniture, bits of clothing and houseware littered the dirt
street, tumbled about as if thrown. Nothing living moved
in the village except for one half-starved dog that ignored the passing ship as it trotted out of sight behind the
toppled walls of what appeared to have been an inn. She
could never see such a sight without a queasiness settling
in her belly, but she tried to maintain the dispassionate
serenity she thought an Aes Sedai might have. It did not
help much. Beyond the village, a thick plume of smoke
was rising into the sky. Three or four miles off, she estimated.

This was not the first such plume of smoke she had seen
since the Erinin began to flow along the border of Cairhien,
nor the first such village. At least this time there were no
bodies in sight. Captain Ellisor sometimes had to sail close

to the Cairhienin shore because of mudflats—he said they shifted in this part of the river—but however close he came, she had not seen a single living person.

The village and the smoke plume slipped away behind the ship, but already another column of smoke was coming into view ahead, further from the river. The forest was thinning, ash and leatherleaf and black elder giving way to willow and whitewood and wateroak, and some she did not recognize.

The wind caught her cloak, but she let it stream, feeling the cold cleanness of the air, feeling the freedom of wearing brown instead of any sort of white, though it had not been her first choice. Yet dress and cloak were of the best wool, well cut and well sewn.

Another sailor trotted by, bowing as he went. She vowed to learn at least some of what it was they were doing; she did not like feeling ignorant. Wearing her Great Serpent ring on her right hand made for a good deal of bowing with a captain and crew born mainly in Tar Valon.

She had won that argument with Nynaeve, though Nynaeve had been sure she herself was the only one of the three of them old enough for people to believe she was Aes Sedai. But Nynaeve had been wrong. Egwene was ready to admit that both she and Elayne had received startled looks on boarding the *Blue Crane* that afternoon at Southharbor, and Captain Ellisor's eyebrows had climbed almost to where his hair would have begun had he had any, but he had been all smiles and bows.

"An honor, Aes Sedai. Three Aes Sedai to travel on my vessel? An honor indeed. I promise you a quick journey as far as you wish. And no trouble with Cairhienin brigands. I no longer put in on that side of the river. Unless you wish it, of course, Aes Sedai. Andoran soldiers do hold a few towns on the Cairhienin side. An honor, Aes Sedai."

His eyebrows had shot up again when they asked for just one cabin among them—not even Nynaeve wanted to be alone at night if she did not have to be. Each could have a cabin to herself at no extra charge, he told them; he had no other passengers, his cargo was aboard, and if Aes Sedai had urgent business downriver, he would not wait even an hour for anyone else who might want passage. They said again that one cabin would be sufficient.

He was startled, and it had been plain from his face that he did not understand, but Chin Ellisor, born and bred in Tar Valon, was not one to question Aes Sedai once they made their intentions clear. If two of them seemed very young, well, some Aes Sedai were young.

The abandoned ruins vanished behind Egwene. The column of smoke drew closer, and there was a hint of another much further still from the riverbank. The forest was turning to low, grassy hills dotted with thickets. Trees that made flowers in the spring had them, tiny white blossoms on snowberry and bright red sugarberry. One tree she did not know was covered in round white flowers bigger than her two hands together. Occasionally a climbing wild-rose put swaths of yellow or white through branches thick with the green of leaves and the red of new growth. It was all too sharp a contrast to the ashes and rubble to be entirely pleasant.

Egwene wished she had an Aes Sedai to question herself right then. One she could trust. Brushing her pouch with her fingers, she could barely feel the twisted stone ring of the *ter'angreal* inside.

She had tried it every night but two since leaving Tar Valon, and it had not worked the same way twice. Oh, she always found herself in *Tel'aran'rhiod*, but the only thing she saw that might have been any use was the Heart of the Stone again, each time without Silvie to tell her things. There was certainly nothing about the Black Ajah.

Her own dreams, without the *ter'angreal*, had been filled with images that seemed almost like glimpses of the Unseen World. Rand holding a sword that blazed like the sun, till she could hardly see that it was a sword, could hardly make out that it was him at all. Rand threatened in a dozen ways, none of them the least bit real. In one dream he had been on a huge stones board, the black and white stones as big as boulders, and him dodging the monstrous hands that moved them and seemed to try to crush him under them. It could have meant something. It very probably did, but beyond the fact that Rand was in danger from someone, or two someones—she thought that much was clear—beyond that, she simply did not know.

I cannot help him, now. I have my own duty. I don't even know where he is, except that it is probably five hundred leagues from here.

She had dreamed of Perrin with a wolf, and with a falcon, and a hawk—and the falcon and the hawk fighting—of Perrin running from someone deadly, and Perrin stepping willingly over the edge of a towering cliff while saying, "It must be done. I must learn to fly before I reach the bottom." There had been one dream of an Aiel, and she thought that had to do with Perrin, too, but she was not sure. And a dream of Min, springing a steel trap but somehow walking through it without so much as seeing it. There had been dreams of Mat, too. Of Mat with dice spinning 'round him—she felt she knew where that one came from—of Mat being followed by a man who was not there—she still did not understand that; there was a man following, or maybe more than one, but in some way there was no one there—of Mat riding desperately toward something unseen in the distance that he had to reach, and Mat with a woman who seemed to be tossing fireworks about. An Illuminator, she assumed, but that made no more sense than anything else.

She had had so many dreams that she was beginning to doubt them all. Maybe it had to do with using the *ter'angreal* so often, or maybe with just carrying it. Maybe she was finally learning what a Dreamer did. Frantic dreams, hectic dreams. Men and women breaking out of a cage, then putting on crowns. A woman playing with puppets, and another dream where the strings on puppets led to the hands of larger puppets, and their strings led to still greater puppets, on and on until the last strings vanished into unimaginable heights. Kings dying, queens weeping, battles raging. Whitecloaks ravaging the Two Rivers. She had even dreamed of the Seanchan again. More than once. Those she shut away in a dark corner; she would not let herself think of them. Her mother and father, every night.

She was certain what that meant, at least, or thought she was. *It means I'm off hunting the Black Ajah, and I do not know what my dreams mean or how to make the fool* ter'angreal *do what it should, and I'm frightened, and. . . . And homesick.* For an instant she thought how good it would be to have her mother send her up to bed knowing everything would be better in the morning. *Only mother can't solve my problems for me anymore, and father can't promise to chase away monsters and make me believe it. I have to do it myself now.*

How far in the past all that was, now. She did not want it back, not really, but it had been a warm time, and it seemed so long ago. It would be wonderful just to see them again, to hear their voices. *When I wear this ring on the finger I choose by right.*

She had finally let Nynaeve and Elayne each try sleeping one night with the stone ring—surprised at how reluctant she had been to let it out of her own hands—and they had awakened to speak of what was surely *Tel'aran'rhiod*, but neither had seen more than a glimpse of the Heart of the Stone, nothing that was of any use.

The thick column of smoke now lay abreast of the *Blue Crane*. Perhaps five or six miles from the river, she thought. The other was only a smudge on the horizon. It could almost have been a cloud, but she was sure it was not. Small thickets grew tight along the riverbank in some places, and between them the grass came right down to the water except where an undercut bank had fallen in.

Elayne came on deck and joined her at the rail, the wind whipping her dark cloak as well. She wore sturdy wool, too. That had been one argument Nynaeve won. Their clothes. Egwene had maintained that Aes Sedai always wore the best, even when they traveled—she had been thinking of the silks she wore in *Tel'aran'rhiod*—but Nynaeve pointed out that even with as much gold as the Amyrlin had left in the back of her wardrobe, and it was a fat purse, they still had no idea how much things would cost downriver. The servants said Mat had been right about the civil war in Cairhien, and what it had done to prices. To Egwene's surprise, Elayne had pointed out that Brown sisters wore wool more often than silk. Elayne had been so eager to be away from the kitchen, Egwene thought, she would have worn rags.

I wonder how Mat is doing? No doubt trying to dice with the captain for whatever ship he's traveling on.

"Terrible," Elayne murmured. "It is so terrible."

"What is?" Egwene said absently. *I hope he isn't showing that paper we gave him around too freely.*

Elayne gave her a startled look, and then a frown. "That!" She gestured toward the distant smoke. "How can you ignore it?"

"I can ignore it because I do not want to think of what the people are going through, because I cannot do anything about it, and because we have to reach Tear. Because what we're hunting is in Tear." She was surprised at her own vehemence. *I can't do anything about it. And the Black Ajah is in Tear.*

The more she thought of it, the more certain she became that they would have to find a way into the Heart of the Stone. Perhaps no one but the High Lords of Tear were allowed into it, but she was becoming convinced that the key to springing the Black Ajah's trap and thwarting them lay in the Heart of the Stone.

"I know all of that, Egwene, but it does not stop me feeling for the Cairhienin."

"I have heard lectures about the wars Andor fought with Cairhien," Egwene said dryly. "Bennae Sedai says you and Cairhien have fought more often than any two nations except Tear and Illian."

The other woman gave her a sidelong look. Elayne had never gotten used to Egwene's refusal to admit she was Andoran herself. At least, lines on maps said the Two Rivers was part of Andor, and Elayne believed the maps.

"We have fought wars against them, Egwene, but since the damage they suffered in the Aiel War, Andor has sold them nearly as much grain as Tear has. The trade has stopped, now. With every Cairhienin House fighting every other for the Sun Throne, who would buy the grain, or see it distributed to the people? If the fighting is as bad as what we've seen on the banks. . . . Well. You cannot feed a people for twenty years and feel nothing for them when they must be starving."

"A Gray Man," Egwene said, and Elayne jumped, trying to look in every direction at once. The glow of *saidar* surrounded her.

"Where?"

Egwene took a slower look around the decks, but to make

sure no one was close enough to overhear. Captain Ellisor still stood in the stern, by the shirtless man holding the long tiller. Another sailor was up in the very bow, scanning the waters ahead for signs of submerged mudbanks, and two more padded about the deck, now and again adjusting a rope to the sails. The rest of the crew were all below. One of the pair stopped to check the lashings on the rowboat tied upside down on the deck; she waited for him to go on before speaking.

"Fool!" she muttered softly. "Me, Elayne, not you, so don't glower at me like that." She continued in a whisper. "A Gray Man is after Mat, Elayne. That must be what that dream meant, but I never saw it. I *am* a fool!"

The glow around Elayne vanished. "Do not be so hard on yourself," she whispered back. "Perhaps it does mean that, but I did not see it, and neither did Nynaeve." She paused; red-gold curls swung as she shook her head. "But it doesn't make sense, Egwene. Why would a Gray Man be after Mat? There is nothing in my letter to my mother that could harm us in the slightest."

"I do not know why." Egwene frowned. "There has to be a reason. I am sure that is what that dream means."

"Even if you are right, Egwene, there is nothing you can do about it."

"I know that," Egwene said bitterly. She did not even know whether he was ahead of them or behind. Ahead, she suspected; Mat would have left without any delay. "Either way," she muttered to herself, "it does no good. I finally know what one of my dreams means, and it doesn't help a hemstitch worth!"

"But if you know one meaning," Elayne told her, "perhaps now you will know others. If we sit down and talk them over, perhaps—"

The *Blue Crane* gave a shuddering lurch, throwing Elayne to the deck and Egwene on top of her. When Egwene struggled to her feet, the shoreline no longer slid by. The vessel had halted, with the bow raised and the deck canted to one side. The sails flapped noisily in the wind.

Chin Ellisor pushed himself to his feet and ran for the bow, leaving the tillerman to rise on his own. "You blind worm of a farmer!" he roared toward the man in the bow, who was clinging to the rail to keep from falling the rest of the way over. "You dirt-grubbing get of a goat! Haven't you been on the river long enough yet to recognize how the water ruffles over a mudflat?" He seized the man on the rail by the shoulders and pulled him back onto the deck, but only to shove him out of the way so he could peer down over the bow himself. "If you've put a hole in my hull, I will use your guts for caulking!"

The other crewmen were clambering to their feet, now, and more came scrambling up from below. They all ran to cluster around the captain.

Nynaeve appeared at the head of the ladder that led down to the passenger cabins, still straightening her skirts. With a sharp tug at her braid, she frowned at the knot of men in the bow, then strode to Egwene and Elayne. "He ran us onto something, did he? After all his talk of knowing the river as well as he knows his wife. The woman probably never receives as much as a smile from him." She jerked the thick braid again and went forward, pushing her way through the sailors to reach the captain. They were all intent on the water below.

There was no point in joining her. *He will have us off faster if he's left to it.* Nynaeve was probably telling him how to do the work. Elayne seemed to feel the same way, from the rueful shake of the head she gave as she watched the captain and crewmen all turn their attention respectfully from whatever was under the bow to Nynaeve.

A ripple of agitation ran through the men, and grew stronger. For a moment the captain's hands could be seen, waving in protest over the other men's heads, and then Nynaeve was striding away from them—they made way, bowing now—with Ellisor hurrying beside her and mopping his round face with a large red handkerchief. His anxious voice became audible as they drew near.

". . . a good fifteen miles to the next village on the Andor side, Aes Sedai, and at least five or six miles downriver on the Cairhien side! Andoran soldiers hold it, it is true, but they do not hold the miles from here to there!" He wiped at his face as if he were dripping sweat.

"A sunken ship," Nynaeve told the other two women. "The work of river brigands, the captain thinks. He means to try backing off it with the sweeps, but he does not seem to think that will work."

"We were running fast when we hit, Aes Sedai. I wanted to make good speed for you." Ellisor rubbed even harder at his face. He was afraid the Aes Sedai would blame him, Egwene realized. "We are stuck hard. But I do not think we are taking water, Aes Sedai. There is no need to worry. Another ship will be along. Two sets of sweeps will surely get us free. There is no need for you to be put ashore, Aes Sedai. I do swear it, by the Light."

"You were thinking of leaving the ship?" Egwene asked. "Do you think that is wise?"

"Of course, it's—!" Nynaeve stopped and frowned at her. Egwene returned the frown with a level stare. Nynaeve went on in a calmer tone, if still a tight one. "The captain says it may be an hour before another ship comes along. One with enough sweeps to make a difference. Or a day. Or two, maybe. I do not think we can afford to waste a day or two waiting. We can be in this village—what did you call it, Captain? Jurene?—we can walk to Jurene in two hours or less. If Captain Ellisor frees his vessel as quickly as he hopes, we can reboard then. He says he will stop to see if we are there. If he does not get free, though, we can take ship from Jurene. We may even find a vessel waiting. The captain says traders do stop there, because of the An-doran soldiers." She drew a deep breath, but her voice grew tighter. "Have I explained my reasoning fully enough? Do you need more?"

"It is clear to me," Elayne put in quickly before Egwene could speak. "And it sounds a good idea. You think it is a good idea, too, don't you, Egwene?"

Egwene gave a grudging nod. "I suppose it is."

"But, Aes Sedai," Ellisor protested, "at least go to the Andor bank. The war, Aes Sedai. Brigands, and every sort of ruffian, and the soldiers not much better. The very wreck under our bow shows the sort of men they are."

"We have not seen a living soul on the Cairhien side," Nynaeve said, "and in any case, we are far from defense-less, Captain. And I will not walk fifteen miles when I can walk six."

"Of course, Aes Sedai." Ellisor really was sweating, now. "I did not mean to suggest. . . . Of course you are not defenseless, Aes Sedai. I did not mean to suggest it." He wiped his face furiously, but it still glistened.

Nynaeve opened her mouth, glanced at Egwene, and seemed to change what she had intended to say. "I am going below for my things," she told the air halfway between Egwene and Elayne, then turned on Ellisor. "Captain, make your rowboat ready." He bowed and scurried away even before she turned for the hatch, and was shouting for men to put the boat over the side before she was below.

"If one of you says 'up,'" Elayne murmured, "the other says 'down.' If you do not stop it, we may not reach Tear."

"We will reach Tear," Egwene said. "And sooner once Nynaeve realizes she is not the Wisdom any longer. We are all"—she did not say Accepted; there were too many men hurrying about—"on the same level, now." Elayne sighed.

In short order the rowboat had ferried them ashore, and they were standing on the bank with walking staffs in hand, their belongings in bundles on their backs, and hung about them in pouches and scripts. Rolling grassland and scattered copses surrounded them, though the hills were forested a few miles in from the river. The sweeps on the *Blue Crane* were cutting up froth, but failing to budge the vessel. Egwene turned and started south without another glance. And before Nynaeve could take the lead.

When the others caught up to her, Elayne gave her a reproving look. Nynaeve walked staring straight ahead. Elayne told Nynaeve what Egwene had said about Mat and a Gray Man, but the older woman listened in silence and only said, "He'll have to look after himself," without pausing in her stride. After a time, the Daughter-Heir gave up trying to make the other two talk, and they all walked in silence.

Clumps of trees close along the riverbank soon hid the *Blue Crane*, thick growths of wateroak and willow. They did not go through the copses, small as they were, for anything at all might be hiding in the shadows under their branches. A few low bushes grew scattered between the thickets here close to the river, but they were too sparse to hide a child much less a brigand, and they were widely spaced.

"If we do see brigands," Egwene announced, "I am going to defend myself. There is no Amyrlin looking over our shoulders here."

Nynaeve's mouth thinned. "If need be," she told the air in front of her, "we can frighten off any brigands the way we did those Whitecloaks. If we can find no other way."

"I wish you would not talk of brigands," Elayne said. "I would like to reach this village without—"

A figure in brown and gray rose from behind a bush standing by itself almost in front of them.

CHAPTER
38

Maidens of the Spear

Egwene embraced *saidar* before the scream was well out of her mouth, and she saw the glow around Elayne, too. For an instant she wondered if Ellisor had heard their screams and would send help; the *Blue Crane* could not be more than a mile upriver. Then she was dismissing the need for help, already weaving flows of Air and Fire into lightning. She could almost still hear their yelling.

Nynaeve was simply standing there with her arms crossed beneath her breasts and a firm expression on her face, but Egwene was not sure whether that was because she was not angry enough to touch the True Source, or because she had already seen what Egwene was just now seeing. The person facing them was a woman no older than Egwene herself, if somewhat taller.

She did not let go of *saidar*. Men were sometimes silly enough to think a woman was harmless merely because she was a woman; Egwene had no such illusions. In a corner of her mind she noted that Elayne was no longer surrounded by the glow. The Daughter-Heir must still harbor foolish notions. *She was never a Seanchan prisoner.*

Egwene did not think many men would be stupid enough to think the woman in front of them was not dangerous, even though her hands were empty and she wore no visible weapon. Blue-green eyes and reddish hair cut short except for a narrow tail that hung to her shoulders; soft, laced knee-boots and close-fitting coat and breeches all in the shades of earth and rock. Such coloring and clothing had been described to her once; this woman was Aiel.

Looking at her, Egwene felt a sudden odd affinity for the woman. She could not understand it. *She looks like Rand's cousin, that's why.* Yet even that feeling—almost of kinship—could not stifle her curiosity. *What under the Light are Aiel doing here? They never leave the Waste; not since the Aiel War.* She had heard all of her life how deadly Aiel were—these Maidens of the Spear no less than the members of the male warrior societies—but she felt no particular fear and, indeed, some irritation at having been afraid. With *saidar* feeding the One Power into her, she had no need to fear anyone. *Except maybe a fully trained sister,* she admitted. *But certainly not one woman, even if she is Aiel.*

"My name is Aviendha," the Aiel woman said, "of the Nine Valleys sept of the Taardad Aiel." Her face was as flat and expressionless as her voice. "I am *Far Dareis Mai*, a Maiden of the Spear." She paused a moment, studying them. "You have not the look in your faces, but we saw the rings. In your lands, you have women much like our Wise Ones, the women called Aes Sedai. Are you women of the White Tower, or not?"

For a moment Egwene did feel unease. *We?* She looked around them carefully, but saw no one behind any bush within twenty paces.

If there were others, they had to be in the next thicket, more than two hundred paces ahead, or in the last one, twice that distance behind. Too far to threaten. *Unless they have bows.* But they would have to be good with them. Back home, in the competitions at Bel Tine and Sunday, only the best bowmen shot at any distance much beyond two hundred paces.

But she still felt better knowing she could hurl a lightning bolt at anyone who tried such a shot.

"We are women of the White Tower," Nynaeve said calmly. She was very obvious in not looking around for other Aiel. Even Elayne was peering about. "Whether you would consider any of us wise is another matter," Nynaeve went on. "What do you want of us?"

Aviendha smiled. She was really quite lovely, Egwene realized; the grim expression had masked it. "You talk as the Wise Ones do. To the point, and small suffering of fools." Her smile faded, but her voice remained calm. "One of us lies gravely hurt, perhaps dying. The Wise Ones often heal those who would surely die without them, and I have heard Aes Sedai can do more. Will you aid her?"

Egwene almost shook her head in confusion. *A friend of hers is dying? She sounds as if she is asking if we'll lend her a cup of barley flour!*

"I will help her if I can," Nynaeve said slowly. "I cannot make promises, Aviendha. She may die despite anything I can do."

"Death comes for us all," the Aiel said. "We can only choose how to face it when it comes. I will take you to her."

Two women in Aiel garb stood up no more than ten paces away, one out of a little fold in the ground that Egwene would not have supposed could hide a dog, and the other in grass that reached only halfway to her knees. They lowered their black veils as they stood—that gave her another jolt; she was sure Elayne had told her the Aiel only hid their faces when they might have to do killing—and settled the cloth that had wrapped their heads about their shoulders. One had the same reddish hair as Aviendha, with gray eyes, the other dark blue eyes and hair like fire. Neither was any older than Egwene or Elayne, and both looked ready to use the short spears in their hands.

The woman with fiery hair handed Aviendha weapons; a long, heavy-bladed knife to belt at her waist, and a bristling quiver for the other side; a dark, curved bow that had the dull shine of horn, in a case to fasten on her back; and four short spears with long points to grip in her left hand along with a small, round hide buckler. Aviendha wore them as naturally as a woman in Emond's Field would wear a scarf, just as her companions did. "Come," she said, and started for the thicket they had already passed.

Egwene finally released *saidar*. She suspected all three of the Aiel could stab her with those spears before she could do anything about it, if that was what they wanted, but though they were wary, she did not think they would. *And what if Nynaeve can't Heal their friend? I wish she would ask before she makes these decisions that involve all of us!*

As they headed for the trees, the Aiel scanned the land around them as if they expected the empty landscape to hold enemies as adept at hiding as themselves. Aviendha strode ahead, and Nynaeve kept up with her.

"I am Elayne of House Trakand," Egwene's friend said as if making conversation, "Daughter-Heir to Morgase, Queen of Andor."

Egwene stumbled. *Light, is she mad? I know Andor fought them in the Aiel War. It might be twenty years, but they say Aiel have long memories.*

But the flame-haired Aiel closest to her only said, "I am Bain, of the Black Rock sept of the Shaarad Aiel."

"I am Chiad," the shorter, blonder woman on her other side said, "of the Stones River sept of the Goshien Aiel."

Bain and Chiad glanced at Egwene; their expressions did not change, but she had the feeling they thought she was showing bad manners.

"I am Egwene al'Vere," she told them. They seemed to expect more, so she added, "Daughter of Marin al'Vere, of Emond's Field, in the Two Rivers." That seemed to satisfy them, in a way, but she would have bet they understood it no more than she did all these septs and clans. *It must mean families, in some way.*

"You are first-sisters?" Bain seemed to be taking in all three of them.

Egwene thought they must mean sisters as it was used for Aes Sedai, and said "Yes," just as Elayne said "No."

Chiad and Bain exchanged a very quick look that suggested they were talking to women who might not be completely whole in their minds.

"First-sister," Elayne told Egwene as if she were lecturing, "means women who have the same mother. Second-sister means their mothers are sisters." She turned her words to the Aiel. "We neither of us know a great deal of your people. I ask you to excuse our ignorance. I sometimes think of Egwene as a first-sister, but we are not blood kin."

"Then why do you not speak the words before your Wise Ones?" Chiad asked. "Bain and I became first-sisters."

Egwene blinked. "How can you *become* first-sisters? Either you have the same mother, or you do not. I do not mean to offend. Most of what I know about the Maidens of the Spear comes from the little Elayne has told me. I know you fight in battle and don't care for men, but no more than that." Elayne nodded; the way she had described the Maidens to Egwene had sounded much like a cross between female Warders and the Red Ajah.

That look flashed back across the Aiel's faces, as if they were not certain how much sense Egwene and Elayne had.

"We do not care for men?" Chiad murmured as if puzzled.

Bain knotted her brow in thought. "What you say comes near truth, yet misses it completely. When we wed the spear, we pledge to be bound to no man or child. Some do give up the spear, for a man or a child"—her expression said she herself did not understand this—"but once given up, the spear cannot be taken back."

"Or if she is chosen to go to Rhuidean," Chiad put in. "A Wise One cannot be wedded to the spear."

Bain looked at her as if she had announced the sky was blue, or that rain fell from clouds. The glance she gave Egwene and Elayne said perhaps they did not know these things. "Yes, that is true. Though some try to struggle against it."

"Yes, they do." Chiad sounded as though she and Bain were sharing something between them.

"But I have gone far from the trail of my explanation," Bain went on. "The Maidens do not dance the spears with one another even when our clans do, but the Shaarad Aiel and the Goshien Aiel have held blood feud between them over four hundred years, so Chiad and I felt our wedding pledge was not enough. We went to speak the words before the Wise Ones of our clans—she risking her life in my hold, and I in hers—to bond us as first-sisters. As is proper for first-sisters who are Maidens, we guard each other's backs, and neither will let a man come to her without the other. I would not say we do not care for men." Chiad nodded, with just the hint of a smile. "Have I made the truth clear to you, Egwene?"

"Yes," Egwene said faintly. She glanced at Elayne and saw the bewilderment in her blue eyes she knew must be in her own. *Not Red Ajah. Green, maybe. A cross between Warders and Green Ajah, and I do not understand another thing out of that.* "The truth is quite clear to me, now, Bain. Thank you."

"If the two of you feel you are first-sisters," Chiad said, "you should go to your Wise Ones and speak the words. But you are Wise Ones, though young. I do not know how it would be done in that case."

Egwene did not know whether to laugh or blush. She kept
having an image of her and Elayne sharing the same man.
*No, that is only for first-sisters who are Maidens of the
Spear. Isn't it?* Elayne did have spots of color in her cheeks,
and Egwene was sure she was thinking of Rand. *But we do
not share him, Elayne. We can neither of us have him.*

Elayne cleared her throat. "I do not think there is a need
for that, Chiad. Egwene and I already guard each other's
backs."

"How can that be?" Chiad asked slowly. "You are not
wedded to the spear. And you are Wise Ones. Who would
lift a hand against a Wise One? This confuses me. What
need have you for guarding of backs?"

Egwene was spared having to come up with an answer
by their arrival at the copse. There were two more Aiel under the trees, deep into the thicket, but next to the river.
Jolien, of the Salt Flat sept of the Nakai Aiel, a blue-eyed
woman with red-gold hair nearly the color of Elayne's, was
watching over Dailin, of Aviendha's sept and clan. Sweat
matted Dailin's hair, making it a darker red, and she only
opened her gray eyes once, when they first came near, then
closed them again. Her coat and shirt lay beside her, and
red stained the bandages wrapped around her middle.

"She took a sword," Aviendha said. "Some of those fools
that the oath-breaking treekillers call soldiers thought we
were another handful of the bandits who infest this land.
We had to kill them to convince them otherwise, but Dailin. . . . Can you heal her, Aes Sedai?"

Nynaeve went to her knees beside the injured woman and
lifted the bandages enough to peer under them. She winced
at what she saw. "Have you moved her since she was hurt?
There is scabbing, but it has been broken."

"She wanted to die near water," Aviendha said. She
glanced once at the river, then quickly away again. Egwene
thought she might have shivered, too.

"Fools!" Nynaeve began rummaging in her pouch of
herbs. "You could have killed her moving her with an injury like that. She wanted to die near water!" she said disgustedly. "Just because you carry weapons like men doesn't
mean you have to think like them." She pulled a deep
wooden cup out of the bag and pushed it at Chiad. "Fill
that. I need water to mix these so she can drink them."

Chiad and Bain stepped to the river's edge and returned together. Their faces never changed, but Egwene thought they had almost expected the river to reach up and grab them.

"If we had not brought her here to the . . . river, Aes Sedai," Aviendha said, "we would never have found you, and she would have died anyway."

Nynaeve snorted and began sifting powdered herbs into the cup of water, muttering to herself. "Corenroot helps make blood, and dogwort for knitting flesh, and healall, of course, and. . . ." Her mutters trailed off into whispers too low to hear. Aviendha was frowning at her.

"The Wise Ones use herbs, Aes Sedai, but I had not heard that Aes Sedai used them."

"I use what I use!" Nynaeve snapped and went back to sorting through her powders and whispering to herself.

"She truly does sound like a Wise One," Chiad told Bain softly, and the other woman gave a tight nod.

Dailin was the only Aiel without her weapons in hand, and they all looked ready to use them in a heartbeat. *Nynaeve surely isn't soothing anyone*, Egwene thought. *Get them talking about something. Anything. Nobody feels like fighting if they're talking of something peaceful.*

"Do not be offended," she said carefully, "but I notice you are all uneasy about the river. It does not grow violent unless there is a storm. You could swim in it if you wanted, though the current is strong away from the banks." Elayne shook her head.

The Aiel looked blank; Aviendha said, "I saw a man—a Shienaran—do this swimming . . . once."

"I don't understand," Egwene said. "I know there isn't much water in the Waste, but you said you were 'Stones River sept,' Jolien. Surely you have swum in the Stones River?" Elayne looked at her as if she were mad.

"Swim," Jolien said awkwardly. "It means . . . to get in the water? All that water? With nothing to hold on to." She shuddered. "Aes Sedai, before I crossed the Dragonwall, I had never seen flowing water I could not step across. The Stones River. . . . Some claim it had water in it once, but that is only boasting. There are only the stones. The oldest records of the Wise Ones and the clan chief say there was never anything but stones since the first day our sept broke

off from the High Plain sept and claimed that land. Swim!"
She gripped her spears as if to fight the very word. Chiad
and Bain moved a pace further from the riverbank.

Egwene sighed. And colored when she met Elayne's eye.
*Well, I am not a Daughter-Heir, to know all these things. I
will learn them, though.* As she looked around at the Aiel
women, she realized that far from soothing them, she had
put them even more on edge. *If they try anything, I will hold
them with Air.* She had no idea whether she could seize four
people at once, but she opened herself to *saidar,* wove the
flows in Air and held them ready. The Power pulsed in her
with eagerness to be used. No glow surrounded Elayne, and
she wondered why. Elayne looked right at her and shook
her head.

"I would never harm an Aes Sedai," Aviendha said
abruptly. "I would have you know that. Whether Dailin
lives or dies, it makes no difference in that. I would never
use this"—she lifted one short spear a trifle—"against any
woman. And you are Aes Sedai." Egwene had the sudden
feeling that the woman was trying to soothe *them.*

"I knew that," Elayne said, as if talking to Aviendha,
but her eyes told Egwene the words were for her. "No one
knows much of your people, but I was taught that Aiel
never harm women unless they are—what did you call it?—
wedded to the spear."

Bain seemed to think Elayne was failing to see truth
clearly again. "That is not exactly the way of it, Elayne. If
a woman not wedded came at me with weapons, I would drub
her until she knew better of it. A man. . . . A man might
think a woman of your lands was wedded if she bore weapons; I do not know. Men can be strange."

"Of course," Elayne said. "But so long as we do not attack you with weapons, you will not try to harm us." All
four Aiel looked shocked, and she gave Egwene a quick significant look.

Egwene held on to *saidar* anyway. Just because Elayne had
been taught something did not mean it was true, even if the
Aiel said the same thing. And *saidar* felt . . . good in her.

Nynaeve lifted up Dailin's head and began pouring her
mixture into the woman's mouth. "Drink," she said firmly.
"I know it tastes bad, but drink it all." Dailin swallowed,
choked, and swallowed again.

"Not even then, Aes Sedai," Aviendha told Elayne. She kept her eyes on Dailin and Nynaeve, though. "It is said that once, before the Breaking of the World, we served the Aes Sedai, though no story says how. We failed in that service. Perhaps that is the sin that sent us to the Three-fold Land; I do not know. No one knows what the sin was, except maybe the Wise Ones, or the clan chiefs, and they do not say. It is said if we fail the Aes Sedai again, they will destroy us."

"Drink it all," Nynaeve muttered. "Swords! Swords and muscles and no brains!"

"*We* are not going to destroy you," Elayne said firmly, and Aviendha nodded.

"As you say, Aes Sedai. But the old stories are all clear on one point. We must never fight Aes Sedai. If you bring your lightnings and your balefire against me, I will dance with them, but I will not harm you."

"Stabbing people," Nynaeve growled. She lowered Dailin's head, and laid a hand on the woman's brow. Dailin's eyes had closed again. "Stabbing women!" Aviendha shifted her feet and frowned again, and she was not alone among the Aiel.

"Balefire," Egwene said. "Aviendha, what is balefire?"

The Aiel woman turned her frown on her. "Do you not know, Aes Sedai? In the old stories, Aes Sedai wielded it. The stories make it a fearsome thing, but I know no more. It is said we have forgotten much that we once knew."

"Perhaps the White Tower has forgotten much, too," Egwene said. *I knew of it in that . . . dream, or whatever it was. It was as real as* Tel'aran'rhiod. *I'd gamble with Mat on that.*

"No right!" Nynaeve snapped. "No one has a right to tear bodies so! It is not right!"

"Is she angry?" Aviendha asked uneasily. Chiad and Bain and Jolien exchanged worried looks.

"It is all right," Elayne said.

"It is better than all right," Egwene added. "She *is* getting angry, and it is much better than all right."

The glow of *saidar* surrounded Nynaeve suddenly—Egwene leaned forward, trying to see, and so did Elayne—and Dailin started up with a scream, eyes wide open. In an instant, Nynaeve was easing her back down, and the glow faded. Dailin's eyes slid shut, and she lay there panting.

I saw it, Egwene thought. *I . . . think I did.* She was not
sure she had even been able to make out all the many flows,
much less the way Nynaeve had woven them together. What
Nynaeve had done in those few seconds had seemed like
weaving four carpets at once while blindfolded.

Nynaeve used the bloody bandages to wipe Dailin's stomach, smearing away bright red new blood and black crusts
of dried old. There was no wound, no scar, only healthy
skin considerably paler than Dailin's face.

With a grimace, Nynaeve took the bloody cloths, stood
up, and threw them into the river. "Wash the rest of that off
of her," she said, "and put some clothes back on her. She's
cold. And be ready to feed her. She will be hungry." She
knelt by the water to wash her hands.

CHAPTER
39

Threads in the Pattern

Jolien put an unsteady hand to where the wound had
been in Dailin's middle; when she touched smooth
skin, she gasped as if she had not believed her own
eyes.

Nynaeve straightened, drying her hands on her cloak.
Egwene had to admit that good wool did better for a towel
than silk or velvet. "I said wash her and get some clothes on
her," Nynaeve snapped.

"Yes, Wise One," Jolien said quickly, and she, Chiad, and
Bain all leaped to obey.

A short laugh burst from Aviendha, a laugh almost at the
edge of tears. "I have heard that a Wise One in the Jagged
Spire sept is said to be able to do this, and one in the Four
Holes sept, but I always thought it was boasting." She drew
a deep breath, regaining her composure. "Aes Sedai, I owe
you a debt. My water is yours, and the shade of my septhold
will welcome you. Dailin is my second-sister." She saw
Nynaeve's uncomprehending look and added, "She is my
mother's sister's daughter. Close blood, Aes Sedai. I owe a
blood debt."

"If I have any blood to spill," Nynaeve said dryly, "I will
spill it myself. If you wish to repay me, tell me if there is a
ship at Jurene. The next village south of here?"

"The village where the soldiers fly the White Lion
banner?" Aviendha said. "There was a ship there when I
scouted yesterday. The old stories mention ships, but it was
strange to see one."

"The Light send it is still there." Nynaeve began putting
away her folded papers of powdered herbs. "I have done

what I can for the girl, Aviendha, and we must go on. All that she needs now is food and rest. And try not to let people stick swords in her."

"What comes, comes, Aes Sedai," the Aiel woman replied.

"Aviendha," Egwene said, "feeling as you do about rivers, how do you cross them? I am sure there is at least one river nearly as big as the Erinin between here and the Waste."

"The Alguenya," Elayne said. "Unless you went around it."

"You have many rivers, but some have things called bridges where we had need to cross, and others we could wade. For the rest, Jolien remembered that wood floats." She slapped the trunk of a tall whitewood. "These are big, but they float as well as a branch. We found dead ones and made ourselves a . . . ship . . . a little ship, of two or three lashed together to cross the big river." She said it matter-of-factly.

Egwene stared in wonder. If she were as afraid of something as the Aiel obviously were of rivers, could she make herself face it the way they did? She did not think so. *What about the Black Ajah*, a small voice asked. *Have you stopped being afraid of them? That is different*, she told it. *There's no bravery in that. I either hunt them, or else I sit like a rabbit waiting for a hawk.* She quoted the old saying to herself. *"It is better to be the hammer than the nail."*

"We had best be on our way," Nynaeve said.

"In a moment," Elayne told her. "Aviendha, why have you come all this way and put up with such hardship?"

Aviendha shook her head disgustedly. "We have not come far at all; we were among the last to set out. The Wise Ones nipped at me like wild dogs circling a calf, saying I had other duties." Suddenly she grinned, gesturing to the other Aiel. "These stayed back to taunt me in my misery, so they said, but I do not think the Wise Ones would have let me go if they had not been there to companion me."

"We seek the one foretold," Bain said. She was holding a sleeping Dailin so Chiad could slip a shirt of brown linen onto her. "He Who Comes With the Dawn."

"He will lead us out of the Three-fold Land," Chiad added. "The prophecies say he was born of *Far Dareis Mai*."

Elayne looked startled. "I thought you said the Maidens of the Spear were not allowed to have children. I am sure I was taught that." Bain and Chiad exchanged those looks again, as if Elayne had come near truth and yet missed it once more.

"If a Maiden bears a child," Aviendha explained carefully, "she gives the child to the Wise Ones of her sept, and they pass the child to another woman in such a way that none knows whose child it is." She, too, sounded as if she were explaining that stone is hard. "Every woman wants to foster such a child in the hope she may raise He Who Comes With the Dawn."

"Or she may give up the spear and wed the man," Chiad said, and Bain added, "There are sometimes reasons one must give up the spear."

Aviendha gave them a level look, but continued as if they had not spoken. "Except that now the Wise Ones say he is to be found here, beyond the Dragonwall. 'Blood of our blood mixed with the old blood, raised by an ancient blood not ours.' I do not understand it, but the Wise Ones spoke in such a way as to leave no doubts." She paused, obviously choosing her words. "You have asked many questions, Aes Sedai. I wish to ask one. You must understand that we look for omens and signs. Why do three Aes Sedai walk a land where the only hand without a knife in it is a hand too weak with hunger to grasp the hilt? Where do you go?"

"Tear," Nynaeve said briskly, "unless we stay here talking until the Heart of the Stone crumbles to dust." Elayne began adjusting the cord of her bundle and the strap of her scrip for walking, and after a moment Egwene did the same.

The Aiel women were looking at one another, Jolien frozen in the act of closing Dailin's gray-brown coat. "Tear?" Aviendha said in a cautious tone. "Three Aes Sedai walking through a troubled land on their way to Tear. This is a strange thing. Why do you go to Tear, Aes Sedai?"

Egwene glanced at Nynaeve. *Light, a moment ago they were laughing, and now they're as tense as they ever were.*

"We hunt some evil women," Nynaeve said carefully. "Darkfriends."

"Shadowrunners." Jolien twisted her mouth around the word as if she had bitten into a rotten apple.

"Shadowrunners in Tear," Bain said, and as if part of the same sentence Chiad added, "And three Aes Sedai seeking the Heart of the Stone."

"I did not say we were going to the Heart of the Stone," Nynaeve said sharply. "I merely said I did not want to stay here till it falls to dust. Egwene, Elayne, are you ready?" She started out of the thicket without waiting for an answer, walking staff thumping the ground and long strides carrying her south.

Egwene and Elayne made hasty goodbyes before following after her. The four Aiel on their feet stood watching them go.

When the two of them were a little way beyond the trees, Egwene said, "My heart almost stopped when you named yourself. Weren't you afraid they might try to kill you, or to take you prisoner? The Aiel War was not *that* long ago, and whatever they said about not harming women who don't carry spears, they looked ready enough to use those spears on anything, to me."

Elayne shook her head ruefully. "I have just learned how much I do not know about the Aiel, but I was taught that they do not think of the Aiel War as a war at all. From the way they behaved toward me, I think maybe that much of what I learned is truth. Or maybe it was because they think I am Aes Sedai."

"I know they are strange, Elayne, but *no* one can call three years of battles anything but a war. I do not care how much they fight among themselves, a war is a war."

"Not to them. Thousands of Aiel crossed the Spine of the World, but apparently they saw themselves more like thief-takers, or headsmen, come after King Laman of Cairhien for the crime of cutting down *Avendoraldera*. To the Aiel, it was not a war; it was an execution."

Avendoraldera, according to one of Verin's lectures, had been an offshoot of the Tree of Life itself, brought to Cairhien some five hundred years ago as an unprecedented offer of peace from the Aiel, given along with the right to cross the Waste, a right otherwise given to none but peddlers, gleemen, and the Tuatha'an. Much of Cairhien's wealth had been built on the trade in ivory and perfumes and spices and, most of all, silk, from the lands beyond the Waste. Not even Verin had any idea of how the Aiel had come by a sapling of *Avendesora*—for one thing, the old books were clear that it made no seed; for another, no one knew where the Tree of Life was, except for a few stories that were clearly wrong, but surely the Tree of Life could have nothing to do with the Aiel—or of why the Aiel had called the Cairhienin the Watersharers, or insisted their trains of merchant wagons fly a banner bearing the trefoil leaf of *Avendesora*.

Egwene supposed, grudgingly, that she could understand why they had started a war—even if they did not think it was one—after King Laman cut down their gift to make a throne unlike any other in the world. Laman's Sin, she had heard it called. According to Verin, not only had Cairhien's trade across the Waste ended with the war, but those Cairhienin who ventured into the Waste now vanished. Verin claimed they were said to be "sold as animals" in the lands beyond the Waste, but not even she understood how a man or a woman could be sold.

"Egwene," Elayne said, "you know who He Who Comes With the Dawn must be, don't you?"

Staring at Nynaeve's back still well ahead of them, Egwene shook her head—*Does she mean to race us to Jurene?*—then almost stopped walking. "You do not mean—?"

Elayne nodded. "I think so. I do not know much of the Prophecies of the Dragon, but I have heard a few lines. One I remember is, 'On the slopes of Dragonmount shall he be born, born of a maiden wedded to no man.' Egwene, Rand does look like an Aiel. Well, he looks like the pictures I have seen of Tigraine, too, but she vanished before he was born, and I hardly think she could have been his mother anyway. I think Rand's mother was a Maiden of the Spear."

Egwene frowned in thought as she hurried along, running everything she knew of Rand's birth through her head. He had been raised by Tam al'Thor after Kari al'Thor died, but if what Moiraine said was true, they could not be his real mother and father. Nynaeve had sometimes seemed to know some secret about Rand's birth. *But I will bet I couldn't pry it out of her with a fork!*

They caught up to Nynaeve, Egwene glowering as she thought, Nynaeve staring straight ahead toward Jurene and that ship, and Elayne frowning at the pair of them as if they were two children sulking over who should have the larger piece of cake.

After a time of silent strides, Elayne said, "You handled that very well, Nynaeve. The Healing, and the rest, too. I do not think they ever doubted you were Aes Sedai. Or that we all were, because of the way you bore yourself."

"You did do a good job," Egwene said after a minute. "That was the first time I have ever really watched what is done during a Healing. It makes making lightning look like mixing oatcake."

A surprised smile appeared on Nynaeve's face. "Thank you," she murmured, and reached over to give Egwene's hair a little tug the way she had when Egwene was a little girl.

I am not a little girl any longer. The moment passed as quickly as it had come, and they went on in silence once more. Elayne sighed loudly.

They covered another mile, or a little more, swiftly, despite swinging in from the river to go around the thickets along the bank. Nynaeve insisted on staying well clear of the trees. Egwene thought it was silly to think more Aiel would be hiding in the copses, but the swing inland did not add much distance to what they had to cover; none of the growths were very big.

Elayne watched the trees, though, and she was the one who suddenly screamed, "Look out!"

Egwene jerked her head around; men were stepping out from among the trees, slings whirling 'round their heads. She reached for *saidar*, and something struck her head, and darkness drank everything.

Egwene could feel herself swaying, feel something moving under her. Her head seemed to be nothing but pain. She tried to raise a hand to her temples, but something dug into her wrists, and her hands did not move.

"—better than lying there all day waiting for dark," a man's rough voice said. "Who knows if another ship would come by close in? And I don't trust that boat. It leaks."

"You do better hope Adden does believe you did see those rings before you did decide," another man said. "He does want fat cargoes, not women, I think." the first man muttered something coarse about what Adden could do with his leaky boat, and the cargoes, too.

Her eyes opened. Silver-flecked spots danced across her vision; she thought she might be going to throw up on the ground swaying past under her head. She was tied across the back of a horse, her wrists and ankles joined by a rope running under its belly, her hair hanging down.

It was still daylight. She craned her neck to look around. So many rough-dressed men on horses surrounded her that she could not see whether Nynaeve and Elayne had been captured, as well. Some of the men wore bits of armor—a battered helmet, or a dented breastplate, or a jerkin sewn all over with metal scales—but most wore only coats that had not been cleaned in months, if ever. From the smell, the men had not cleaned themselves in months, either. They all wore swords, at their waists or on their backs.

Rage hit her, and fear, but most of all white-hot anger. *I won't be a prisoner. I won't be bound! I won't!* She reached for *saidar* and the pain nearly lifted the top of her head; she barely stifled a moan.

The horse paused for a moment of shouts and the creak of rusty hinges, then went ahead a little further, and the men began to dismount. As they moved apart, she could see something of where they were. A log palisade surrounded them, built atop a large, round earthen mound, and men with bows stood guard on a wooden walk built just high enough for them to see over the rough-hewn ends of the logs. One low, windowless log house seemed to be built into the mounded dirt under the wall. There was no other structure beyond a few lean-to sheds. Aside from the men and horses that had just entered, the rest of the open space was filled with cook fires, and tethered horses, and more unwashed men. There must have been at least a hundred. Caged goats and pigs and chickens filled the air with squeals and grunts and clucks that blended with coarse shouts and laughter to make a din that pierced her head.

Her eyes found Nynaeve and Elayne, bound head down across saddleless horses as she was. Neither seemed to be stirring; the very end of Nynaeve's braid dragged across the dirt as her horse stirred. A small hope faded; that one of them might be free, to help whoever was held escape. *Light, I cannot stand to be a prisoner again. Not again.* Gingerly, she tried reaching for *saidar* again. The pain was not so bad this time—merely as if someone had dropped a rock on her head—but it shattered the emptiness before she could even think of a rose.

"One of them's awake!" a man's panicked voice shouted.

Egwene tried to hang limp and look unthreatening. *How in the Light could I look threatening tied up like a sack of meal! Burn me, I have to buy time. I have to!* "I will not harm you," she told the sweaty-faced fellow who came running toward her. Or she tried to tell him. She was not sure how much she had actually said before something crashed into her head again and darkness rolled over her in a wave of nausea.

Waking was easier the next time. Her head still hurt, but not as much as it had, though her thoughts did seem to spin dizzily. *At least my stomach isn't. . . . Light, I'd better not think of that.* There was a taste of sour wine and something bitter in her mouth. Strips of lamplight showed through horizontal cracks in a crudely made wall, but she lay in darkness, on her back. On dirt, she thought. The door did not seem to fit well either, but it looked all too sturdy.

She pushed herself to her hands and knees, and was surprised to find she was not tied in any way. Except for that one wall of unpeeled logs, the others all seemed to be of rough stone. The light through the cracks was enough to show her Nynaeve and Elayne lying sprawled on the dirt. There was blood on the Daughter-Heir's face. Neither of them moved except for the rise and fall of their chests as they breathed. Egwene hesitated between trying to wake them immediately and seeing what lay on the other side of that wall. *Just a peek*, she told herself. *I might as well see what we have guarding us before I wake them.*

She told herself it was not because she was afraid she might be unable to waken them. As she put her eye to one of the cracks near the door, she thought of the blood on Elayne's face and tried to remember exactly what it was Nynaeve had done for Dailin.

The next room was large—it had to be all the rest of the log building she had seen—and windowless, but brightly lit with gold and silver lamps hanging from spikes driven into the walls and the logs that made the high ceiling. There was no fireplace. On the packed dirt floor farmhouse tables and chairs mingled with chests covered in gilt-work and inlaid with ivory. A carpet woven in peacocks lay beside a huge canopied bed, piled deep with filthy blankets and comforters, with elaborately carved and gilded posts.

A dozen men stood or sat around the room, but all eyes were on one large, fair-haired man who might have been handsome if his face were cleaner. He stood staring down at the top of a table with fluted legs and gilded scrollwork, one hand on his sword hilt, a finger of the other pushing something she could not make out in small circles on the tabletop.

The outer door opened, revealing night outside, and a lanky man with his left ear gone came in. "He has no come, yet," he said roughly. He was missing two fingers on his left hand, too. "I do no like dealing with that kind."

The big, fair-haired man paid him no mind, only kept moving whatever it was on the table. "Three Aes Sedai," he murmured, then laughed. "Good prices for Aes Sedai, if you have the belly to deal with the right buyer. If you're ready to risk having your belly ripped out through your mouth should you try selling him a pig in a sack. Not so safe as slitting the crew's throats on a trader's ship, eh, Coke? Not so easy, wouldn't you say?"

There was a nervous stir among the other men, and the one addressed, a stocky fellow with shifty eyes, leaned forward anxiously. "They *are* Aes Sedai, Adden." She recognized that voice; the man who had made the coarse suggestions. "They must be, Adden. The rings prove it, I tell you!" Adden picked up something from the table, a small circle that glinted gold in the lamplight.

Egwene gasped and felt at her fingers. *They took my ring!*

"I do no like it," muttered the lanky man with the missing ear. "Aes Sedai. Any one of them could kill us all. Fortune prick me! You do be a stone-carved fool, Coke, and I ought to carve your throat. What if one of them do wake before he does come?"

"They'll not wake for hours." That was a fat man with a hoarse voice and a gap-toothed sneer. "My granny taught me of that stuff we fed them. They'll sleep till sunrise, and he'll come long afore then."

Egwene worked her mouth around the sour wine taste and the bitterness. *Whatever it was, your granny lied to you. She should have strangled you in your cradle!* Before this "he" came, this man who thought he could buy Aes Sedai—*like a bloody Seanchan!*—she would have Nynaeve and Elayne on their feet. She crawled to Nynaeve.

As near as she could tell, Nynaeve seemed to be sleeping, so she began with the simple expedient of shaking her. To her surprise, Nynaeve's eyes shot open.

"Wha—?"

She got a hand over Nynaeve's mouth in time to stop the word. "We are being held prisoner," she whispered. "There are a dozen men on the other side of that wall, and more outside. A great many more. They gave us something to make us sleep, but it wasn't very successful. Do you remember, yet?"

Nynaeve pulled Egwene's hand aside. "I remember." Her voice was soft and grim. She grimaced and twisted her mouth, then suddenly barked a nearly silent laugh. "Sleepwell root. The fools gave us sleepwell root mixed in wine. Wine near gone to vinegar, it tastes like. Quick, do you remember anything of what I taught you? What does sleepwell root do?"

"It clears headaches so you can sleep," Egwene said just as softly. And nearly as grimly, until she heard what she was saying. "It makes you a little drowsy, but that is all." The fat man had not listened well to what his granny told him. "All they did was help clear the pain of being hit in the head."

"Exactly," Nynaeve said. "And once we wake Elayne, we'll give them a thanking they won't forget." She rose, only to crouch beside the golden-haired woman.

"I think I saw more than a hundred of them outside when they brought us in," Egwene whispered to Nynaeve's back. "I am sure you won't mind if I use the Power as a weapon this time. And someone is apparently coming to *buy* us. I mean to do something to that fellow that will make him walk in the Light till the day he dies!" Nynaeve was still crouched over Elayne, but neither of them was moving. "What is the matter?"

"She is hurt badly, Egwene. I think her skull is broken, and she is barely breathing. Egwene, she is dying as surely as Dailin was."

"Can't you do something?" Egwene tried to remember all the flows Nynaeve had woven to Heal the Aiel woman, but she could recall no more than every third thread. "You have to!"

"They took my herbs," Nynaeve muttered fiercely, her voice trembling. "I can't! Not without the herbs!" Egwene was shocked to realize Nynaeve was on the point of tears. "Burn them all, I can't do it without—!" Suddenly she seized Elayne's shoulders as if she meant to lift the unconscious woman and shake her. "Burn you, girl," she rasped, "I did not bring you all this way to die! I should have left you scrubbing pots! I should have tied you up in a sack for Mat to carry to your mother! I will not let you die on me! Do you hear me? I won't allow it!" *Saidar* suddenly shone around her, and Elayne's eyes and mouth opened wide together.

Egwene got her hands over Elayne's mouth just in time to muffle any sound, she thought, but as she touched her, the eddies of Nynaeve's Healing caught her like a straw on the edge of a whirlpool. Cold froze her to the bone, meeting heat that seared outward as if it meant to crisp her flesh; the world vanished in a sensation of rushing, falling, flying, spinning.

When it finally ended, she was breathing hard and staring down at Elayne, who stared back over the hands she still had pressed over her mouth. The last of Egwene's headache was gone. Even the backwash of what Nynaeve had done had apparently been enough for that. The murmur of voices from the other room was no louder; if Elayne had made any noise—or if she had—Adden and the others had not noticed.

Nynaeve was on her hands and knees, head down and shaking. "Light!" she muttered. "Doing it that way . . . was like peeling off . . . my own skin. Oh, Light!" She peered at Elayne. "How do you feel, girl?" Egwene pulled her hands away.

"Tired," Elayne murmured. "And hungry. Where are we? There were some men with slings. . . ."

Hastily Egwene told her what had happened. Elayne's face began to darken a long way before she was done.

"And now," Nynaeve added in a voice like iron, "we are going to show these louts what it means to meddle with us." *Saidar* shone around her once more.

Elayne was unsteady getting to her feet, but the glow surrounded her, as well. Egwene reached out to the True Source almost gleefully.

When they looked through the cracks again, to see exactly what they had to deal with, there were three Myrddraal in the room.

Dead-black garb hanging unnaturally still, they stood by the table, and every man but Adden had moved as far from them as he could, till they all had their backs against the walls and their eyes on the dirt floor. Across the table from the Myrddraal, Adden faced those eyeless stares, but sweat made runnels in the dirt on his face.

The Fade picked up a ring from the table. Egwene saw now that it was a much heavier circle of gold than the Great Serpent rings.

Face pressed against the crack between two logs, Nynaeve gasped softly and fumbled at the neck of her dress.

"Three *Aes Sedai*," the Halfman hissed, its amusement sounding like dead things powdering to dust, "and one carried this." The ring made a heavy thud as the Myrddraal tossed it back on the table.

"They are the ones I seek," another of them rasped. "You will be well rewarded, human."

"We must take them by surprise," Nynaeve said softly. "What kind of lock holds this door?"

Egwene could just see the lock on the outside of the door, an iron thing on a chain heavy enough to hold an enraged bull. "Be ready," she said.

She thinned one flow of Earth to finer than a hair, hoping the Halfmen could not sense so small a channeling, and wove it into the iron chain, into the tiniest bits of it.

One of the Myrddraal lifted its head. Another leaned across the table toward Adden. "I itch, human. Are you sure they sleep?" Adden swallowed hard and nodded his head.

The third Myrddraal turned to stare at the door to the room where Egwene and the others crouched.

The chain fell to the floor, the Myrddraal staring at it snarled, and the outer door swung open, black-veiled death flowing in from the night.

The room erupted in screams and shouts as men clawed for their swords to fight stabbing Aiel spears. The Myrddraal drew blades blacker than their garb and fought for their lives, too. Egwene had once seen six cats all fighting each other; this was that a hundredfold. And yet in seconds, silence reigned. Or almost silence.

Every human not wearing a black veil lay dead with a spear through him; one pinned Adden to the wall. Two Aiel lay still, as well, amid the jumble of overturned furniture and dead. The three Myrddraal stood back-to-back in the center of the room, black swords in their hands. One was clutching his side as if wounded, though he gave no other sign of it. Another had a long gash down its pale face; it did not bleed. Around them circled the five veiled Aiel still alive, crouching. From outside came screams and clashes of metal that said more Aiel still fought in the night, but in the room was a softer sound.

As they circled, the Aiel drummed their spears against their small hide bucklers. *Thrum-thrum-THRUM-thrum . . . thrum-thrum-THRUM-thrum . . . thrum-thrum-THRUM-thrum*. The Myrddraal turned with them, and their eyeless faces seemed uncertain, uneasy that the fear their gaze struck into every human heart did not seem to touch these.

"Dance with me, Shadowman," one of the Aiel called suddenly, tauntingly. He sounded like a young man.

"Dance with me, Eyeless." That was a woman.

"Dance with me."

"Dance with me."

"I think," Nynaeve said, straightening, "that it is time." She threw open the door, and the three women wrapped in the glow of *saidar* stepped out.

It seemed as though, for the Myrddraal, the Aiel had ceased to exist, and for the Aiel, the Myrddraal. The Aiel stared at Egwene and the others above their veils as if not quite sure what they were seeing; she heard one of the women gasp loudly. The Myrddraal's eyeless stare was different. Egwene could almost feel the Halfmen's knowledge of their own deaths in it; Halfmen knew women embracing the True

Source when they saw them. She was sure she could feel a
desire for her death, too, if theirs could buy hers, and an even
stronger desire to strip the soul out of her flesh and make
both playthings for the Shadow, a desire to. . . .

She had just stepped into the room, yet it seemed she
had been meeting that stare for hours. "I'll take no more of
this," she growled, and unleashed a flow of Fire.

Flames burst out of all three Myrddraal, sprouting in
every direction, and they shrieked like splintered bones
jamming a meat-grinder. Yet she had forgotten she was not
alone, that Elayne and Nynaeve were with her. Even as the
flames consumed the Halfmen, the very air seemed suddenly to push them together in midair, crushing them into
a ball of fire and blackness that grew smaller and smaller.
Their screams dug at Egwene's spine, and *something* shot
out from Nynaeve's hands—a thin bar of white light that
made noonday sun seem dark, a bar of fire that made molten metal seem cold, connecting her hands to the Myrddraal. And they ceased to exist as if they had never been.
Nynaeve gave a startled jump, and the glow around her
vanished.

"What . . . what was that?" Elayne asked.

Nynaeve shook her head; she looked as stunned as Elayne
sounded. "I don't know. I . . . I was so angry, so afraid, at
what they wanted to. . . . I do not know what it was."

Balefire, Egwene thought. She did not know how she
knew, but she was certain of it. Reluctantly, she made herself release *saidar*; made it release her. She did not know
which was harder. *And I did not see a thing of what she
did!*

The Aiel unveiled themselves, then. A trifle hastily,
Egwene thought, as if to tell her and the other two they were
no longer ready to fight. Three of the Aiel were male, one
an older man with more than touches of gray in his dark red
hair. They were tall, these Aielmen, and young or old, they
had that calm sureness in their eyes, that dangerous grace
of motion Egwene associated with Warders; death rode on
their shoulders, and they knew it was there and were not
afraid. One of the women was Aviendha. The screams and
shouts outside were dying away.

Nynaeve started toward the fallen Aiel.

"There is no need, Aes Sedai," the older man said. "They took Shadowman steel."

Nynaeve still bent to check each, pulling their veils away so she could peel back eyelids and feel throats for a pulse. When she straightened from the second, her face was white. It was Dailin. "Burn you! Burn you!" It was not clear whether she meant Dailin, or the man with gray in his hair, or Aviendha, or all Aiel. "I did not Heal her so she could die like this!"

"Death comes to us all," Aviendha began, but when Nynaeve rounded on her, she fell silent. The Aiel exchanged glances, as if not certain whether Nynaeve might do to them what had been done to the Myrddraal. It was not fear in their eyes, only awareness.

"Shadowman steel kills," Aviendha said, "it does not wound." The older man looked at her, a slight surprise in his eyes—Egwene decided that, like Lan, for this man that flicker of the eyelids was the equivalent of another man's open astonishment—and Aviendha said, "They know little of some things, Rhuarc."

"I am sorry," Elayne said in a clear voice, "that we interrupted your . . . dance. Perhaps we should not have interfered."

Egwene gave her a startled look, then saw what she was doing. *Put them at ease, and give Nynaeve a chance to cool down.* "You were handling things quite well," she said. "Perhaps we offended by putting our noses in."

The graying man—Rhuarc—gave a deep chuckle. "Aes Sedai, I for one am glad of . . . whatever it was you did." For a moment he looked not entirely sure of that, but in the next he had his good temper back. He had a good smile, and a strong, square face; he was handsome, if a little old. "We could have killed them, but three Shadowmen. . . . They would have killed two or three of us, certainly, perhaps all, and I cannot say we would have finished them all. For the young, death is an enemy they wish to try their strength against. For those of us a little older, she is an old friend, an old lover, but one we are not eager to meet again soon."

Nynaeve seemed to relax with his speech, as if meeting an Aiel who did not seem anxious to die had leached the

tension out of her. "I should thank you," she said, "and I do.
I will admit I am surprised to see you, though. Aviendha,
did you expect to find us here? How?"

"I followed you." The Aiel woman seemed unembar-
rassed. "To see what you would do. I saw the men take you,
but I was too far back to help. I was sure you must see me
if I came too close, so I stayed a hundred paces behind. By
the time I saw you could not help yourselves, it was too late
to try alone."

"I am sure you did what you could," Egwene said faintly.
*She was just a hundred paces behind us? Light, the brig-
ands never saw anything.*

Aviendha took her words as urging to tell more. "I knew
where Coram must be, and he knew where Dhael and
Luaine were, and they knew. . . ." She paused, frowning at
the older man. "I did not expect to find any clan chief, much
less my own, among those who came. Who leads the Taardad Aiel, Rhuarc, with you here?"

Rhuarc shrugged as if it were of no account. "The sept
chiefs will take their turns, and try to decide if they truly
wish to go to Rhuidean when I die. I would not have come,
except that Amys and Bair and Melaine and Seana stalked
me like ridgecats after a wild goat. The dreams said I must
go. They asked if I truly wanted to die old and fat in a bed."

Aviendha laughed as if at a great joke. "I have heard it
said that a man caught between his wife and a Wise One
often wishes for a dozen old enemies to fight instead. A
man caught between a wife and three Wise Ones, and the
wife a Wise One herself, must consider trying to slay Sightblinder."

"The thought came to me." He frowned down at something on the floor; three Great Serpent rings, Egwene saw,
and a much heavier golden ring made for a man's large finger. "It still does. All things must change, but I would not
be a part of that change if I could set myself aside from it.
Three Aes Sedai, traveling to Tear." The other Aiel glanced
at one another as if they did not want Egwene and her companions to notice.

"You spoke of dreams," Egwene said. "Do your Wise
Ones know what their dreams mean?"

"Some do. If you would know more than that, you must
speak to them. Perhaps they will tell an Aes Sedai. They

do not tell men, except what the dreams say we must do."
He sounded tired, suddenly. "And that is usually what we
would avoid, if we could."

He stooped to pick up the man's ring. On it, a crane flew
above a lance and crown; Egwene knew it now. She had
seen it often before, dangling about Nynaeve's neck on a
leather cord. Nynaeve stepped on the other rings to snatch
it out of his hand; her face was flushed, with anger and too
many other emotions for Egwene to read. Rhuarc made no
move to take it back, but went on in the same weary tone.

"And one of them carries a ring I have heard of as a boy.
The ring of Malkieri kings. They rode with the Shienarans
against the Aiel in my father's time. They were good in the
dance of the spears. But Malkier fell to the Blight. It is said
only a child king survived, and he courts the death that took
his land as other men court beautiful women. Truly, this is a
strange thing, Aes Sedai. Of all the strange sights I thought
I might see when Melaine harried me out of my own hold
and over the Dragonwall, none has been so strange as this.
The path you set me is one I never thought my feet would
follow."

"I set no paths for you," Nynaeve said sharply. "All I
want is to continue my journey. These men had horses. We
will take three of them and be on our way."

"In the night, Aes Sedai?" Rhuarc said. "Is your journey
so urgent that you would travel these dangerous lands in the
dark?"

Nynaeve struggled visibly before saying, "No." In a
firmer tone she added, "But I mean to leave with the sunrise."

The Aiel carried the dead outside the palisade, but neither Egwene nor her companions wanted to use the filthy
bed Adden had slept in. They picked up their rings and slept
under the sky in their cloaks and the blankets the Aiel gave
them.

When dawn pearled the sky to the east, the Aiel produced a breakfast of tough, dried meat—Egwene hesitated
over that until Aviendha told her it was goat—flatbread that
was almost as difficult to chew as the stringy meat, and a
blue-veined white cheese that had a tart taste and was hard
enough to make Elayne murmur that the Aiel must practice
by chewing rocks. But the Daughter-Heir ate as much as

Egwene and Nynaeve together. The Aiel turned the horses loose—they did not ride unless they had to, Aviendha explained, sounding as if she herself would as soon run on blistered feet—after choosing out the three best for Egwene and the others. They were all tall and nearly as big as warhorses, with proud necks and fierce eyes. A black stallion for Nynaeve, a roan mare for Elayne, and a gray mare for Egwene.

She chose to call the gray Mist, in the hope that a gentle name might soothe her, and indeed, Mist did seem to step lightly as they rode south, just as the sun lifted a red rim above the horizon.

The Aiel accompanied them afoot, all those who had survived the fight. Three more had died aside from the two the Myrddraal killed. They were nineteen, altogether, now. They loped along easily alongside the horses. At first, Egwene tried holding Mist to a slow walk, but the Aiel thought this very funny.

"I will race you ten miles," Aviendha said, "and we shall see who wins, your horse or I."

"I will race you twenty!" Rhuarc called, laughing.

Egwene thought they might actually be serious, and when she and the others let their horses walk at a quicker pace, the Aiel certainly showed no sign of falling back.

When the thatched rooftops of Jurene came in sight, Rhuarc said, "Fare you well, Aes Sedai. May you always find water and shade. Perhaps we will meet again before the change comes." He sounded grim. As the Aiel curved away to the south, Aviendha and Chiad and Bain each raised a hand in farewell. They did not seem to be slowing down now that they no longer ran with the horses; if anything, they ran a little faster. Egwene had a suspicion they meant to maintain that pace until they reached wherever it was they were going.

"What did he mean by that?" she asked. "'Perhaps we will meet again before the change'?" Elayne shook her head.

"It does not matter what he meant," Nynaeve said. "I am just as glad they came last night, but I am glad to have them gone, too. I hope there is a ship here."

Jurene itself was a small place, all wooden houses and none more than a single story, but the White Lion banner

of Andor flew over it on a tall staff, and fifty of the Queen's
Guards held it, in red coats with long white collars beneath
shining breastplates. They had been placed there, their captain said, to make a safe haven for refugees who wished to
flee to Andor, but fewer such came every day. Most went
to villages further downriver, now, nearer Aringill. It was
a good thing the three women had come when they did,
as he expected to receive orders returning his company to
Andor any day. The few inhabitants of Jurene would likely
go with them, leaving what remained for brigands and the
Cairhienin soldiers of warring Houses.

Elayne kept her face hidden in the hood of her sturdy
wool cloak, but none of the soldiers seemed to associate
the girl with red-gold hair with their Daughter-Heir. Some
asked her to stay; Egwene was not sure whether Elayne was
pleased or shocked. She herself told the men who asked
her that she had no time for them. It was nice, in an odd
way, to be asked; she certainly had no wish to kiss any of
these fellows, but it was pleasant to be reminded that some
men, at least, thought she was as pretty as Elayne. Nynaeve
slapped one man's face. That almost made Egwene laugh,
and Elayne smiled openly; Egwene thought Nynaeve had
been pinched, and despite the glare on her face, she did not
look entirely displeased, either.

They were not wearing their rings. It had not taken much
effort on Nynaeve's part to convince them that one place
they did not want to be taken for Aes Sedai was Tear, especially if the Black Ajah was there. Egwene had hers in
her pouch with the stone *ter'angreal*; she touched it often
to remind herself they were still there. Nynaeve wore hers
on the cord that held Lan's heavy ring between her breasts.

There was a ship in Jurene, tied to the single stone dock
sticking into the Erinin. Not the ship Aviendha had seen, it
seemed, but still a ship. Egwene was dismayed when she
saw it. Twice as wide as the *Blue Crane*, the *Darter* belied
its name with a bluff bow as round as its captain.

That worthy fellow blinked at Nynaeve and scratched his
ear when she asked if his vessel was fast. "Fast? I am full
of fancy wood from Shienar and rugs from Kandor. What
need to be fast with a cargo like that? Prices only go up.
Yes, I suppose there are faster ships behind me, but they'll
not put in here. I would not have stopped myself if I hadn't

found worms in the meat. Fool notion that they'd have meat to sell in Cairhien. The *Blue Crane*? Aye, I saw Ellisor hung up on something upriver this morning. He'll not get off soon, I'm thinking. That's what a fast ship brings you."

Nynave paid their fares—and twice as much again for the horses—with such a look on her face that neither Egwene nor Elayne spoke to her until long after the *Darter* had wallowed away from Jurene.

CHAPTER

40

A Hero in the Night

Leaning on the rail, Mat watched the walled town of
Aringill come closer as the sweeps worked the *Gray
Gull* in toward the long, tarred-timber docks. Pro-
tected by high stone wing-walls that thrust out into the river,
those docks swarmed with people, and more were leaving the ships of various sizes that lay tied all along them.
Some of the people pushed barrows, or pulled sledges or
tall-wheeled carts, all piled high with furniture and chests
lashed in place, but most carried bundles on their backs, if
that. Not everyone bustled. Many men and women huddled
together uncertainly, and children clung crying to their
legs. Soldiers in red coats and shiny breastplates kept trying
to make them move off the docks into the town, but most
seemed too frightened to move.

Mat turned and shaded his eyes to peer at the river they
were leaving. The Erinin was busier here than he had seen
it south of Tar Valon, with nearly a dozen vessels under way
in sight, ranging from a long, sharp-prowed splinter darting
upriver against the current, pushed by two triangular sails,
to a wide, bluff-bowed ship with square sails, still wallow-
ing along well to the north.

Nearly half the ships he could see had nothing to do with
the river trade, though. Two broad-beamed craft with empty
decks were lumbering across the river, toward a smaller
town on the far bank, while three others labored back
toward Aringill, their decks packed with people like barrels
of fish. The setting sun, still its own height above the horizon, shadowed a banner flying over that other town. That
shore was Cairhien, but he did not need to see the banner to

know it was the White Lion of Andor. There had been talk enough in the few Andoran villages where the *Gray Gull* had stopped briefly.

He shook his head. Politics did not interest him. *As long as they don't try telling me again I'm an Andorman just because of some map. Burn me, they might even try to make me fight in their bloody army, if this Cairhien business spreads. Following orders. Light!* With a shiver, he turned back to Aringill. Barefoot men on the *Gray Gull* were readying ropes to toss to others on the docks.

Captain Mallia was eyeing him from back by the tiller. The fellow had never given up his efforts to ingratiate himself with them, his attempts to learn what their important mission was. Mat had finally shown him the sealed letter and told him that he was carrying it from the Daughter-Heir to the Queen. A personal message from a daughter to her mother; no more. Mallia had only seemed to hear the words "Queen Morgase."

Mat grinned to himself. A deep coat pocket held two purses fatter than when he had boarded the vessel; he had enough loose coin to more than fill another two. His luck had not been quite so good as on that first, strange night when the dice and everything else had seemed to go crazy, but still it was good enough. After the third night, Mallia had given up trying to show his friendliness by gambling, but his money chest was already lighter by then. It would be lighter still after Aringill. Mallia had need to restock his food—Mat glanced at the people milling on the docks—if he could, here, at any price.

The grin faded as his thoughts went back to the letter. A little work with a hot knife blade, and the golden lily seal had been lifted. He had found nothing: Elayne was studying hard and making progress and eager to learn. She was a dutiful daughter, and the Amyrlin Seat had punished her for running away and told her never to speak of it again, so her mother would understand why she could not say more. She said she had been raised to the Accepted, and was that not wonderful, so soon, and she was being trusted with greater duties now, and would have to leave Tar Valon for just a short time on the service of the Amyrlin herself. Her mother was not to worry.

It was all very well for her to tell Morgase not to worry. It was him she had landed in the soup kettle. This silly letter had to be the reason those men had come after him, but even Thom had been able to make nothing of it, though he muttered about "ciphers" and "codes" and "the Game of Houses."

Mat had the letter safe in the lining of his coat, now, its seal replaced, and he was willing to bet no one would ever know. If someone wanted it badly enough to kill him for it, they might try again. *I told you I'd deliver it, Nynaeve, and I bloody will, no matter who tries to stop me.* Even so, he would have words to say the next time he saw those three irritating women—*If I ever do. Light, I never thought of that*—words he did not think they would enjoy hearing.

As the crewmen hurled their lines onto the dock, Thom came on deck, his instrument cases on his back and his bundle in one hand. Even with a limp he strutted to the rail, giving the tail of his cloak little flourishes to make the colored patches flutter, and blowing out his long, white mustaches importantly.

"Nobody is watching, Thom," Mat said. "I don't think they would even see a gleeman unless he had food in his hands."

Thom stared at the docks. "Light! I had heard it was bad, but I did not expect this! Poor fools. Half of them look as if they are starving. It may cost us one of your purses for a room tonight. And the other for a meal, if you intend to keep on the way you've been going. Nearly made me ill to watch you. You try eating that way where those people down there can see you, and you may have your brains battered out."

Mat only smiled at him.

Mallia came stumping down the deck, tugging the point of his beard, as the *Gray Gull* was warped into her berth. Crewmen ran to set a gangplank, and Sanor stood guard on it, heavy arms folded across his chest, in case the throng on the docks tried to board. None of them did.

"So you will be leaving me here," Mallia told Mat. The captain's smile was not as ready as it might have been. "Are you certain there is nothing I can do to help further? Burn my soul, I never saw such a rabble! Those soldiers ought to clear the docks—with the sword, if need be!—so decent traders can do business. Perhaps Sanor can make a path through this scum to your inn for you."

So you'll know where we are staying? Not bloody likely. "I had thought of eating before I went ashore, and maybe a game of dice to pass the time." Mallia's face went white. "But I think I would like a steady floor under me for my next meal. So we will leave you now, Captain. It has been an enjoyable voyage."

While relief still battled consternation on the captain's face, Mat picked up his things from the deck and, using the quarterstaff as a walking stick, made his way to the gangplank with Thom. Mallia followed as far as the head of the plank, murmuring regrets at their departure that jumped from real to insincere and back again. Mat was certain the man hated losing a chance to ingratiate himself with his High Lord Samon by learning details of a pact between Andor and Tar Valon.

As Mat and the gleeman pushed through the crowds, Thom muttered, "I know the man is far from likable, but why do you have to keep taunting him? Wasn't it enough that you ate every scrap of what he thought would feed him all the way to Tear?"

"I have not been eating it all for nearly two days." The hunger had simply been gone one morning, to his great relief. It had been as if Tar Valon had loosed its last hold on him. "I've been throwing most of it over the side, and a hard job it was making sure nobody saw." Among these drawn faces, many of them children's, it did not seem so funny anymore. "Mallia deserved taunting. What about that ship, yesterday? The one that was stuck on a mudbank or something. He could have stopped to help, but he would not go near it however much they shouted." There was a woman with long, dark hair ahead who might have been pretty if she had not looked so bone weary, peering into the face of every man who passed her as if looking for someone; a boy little taller than her waist and two girls shorter clung to her, all crying. "All that talk about river brigands and traps. It didn't look like any trap to me."

Thom dodged around a high-wheeled cart—a cage holding two squealing pigs was lashed atop the canvas-covered mound—and nearly tripped over a sledge being pulled, by a man and a woman. "And you go out of your way to help people, do you? Strange how that has escaped my eye."

"I'll help anyone who can pay," Mat said firmly. "Only fools in stories do something for nothing."

The two girls sobbed into their mother's skirts while the boy fought his tears. The woman's deep-set eyes rested on Mat for a moment, studying his face, before drifting on; they looked as if she wished she could weep, too. On impulse he dug a fistful of loose coins out of his pocket without looking to see what they were and pressed them into her hand. She gave a start of surprise, stared at the gold and silver in her hand with incomprehension that quickly turned to a smile, and opened her mouth, tears of gratitude filling her eyes.

"Buy them something to eat," he said quickly, and hurried on before she could speak. He noticed Thom looking at him. "What are you gawking at? Coin comes easily as long as I can find somebody who likes to dice." Thom nodded slowly, but Mat was not sure he had gotten his point across. *Bloody children's crying was getting on my nerves, that's all. Fool gleeman will probably expect me to give gold away to every waif that comes along, now. Fool!* For an uncomfortable moment, he was not certain whether the last had been meant for Thom or himself.

Taking himself in hand, he avoided looking at any face long enough to really see it until he found the one he wanted, at the foot of the dock. The helmetless soldier in red coat and breastplate, urging people into the town, had the grizzled look of a squadman, an experienced leader of ten or so. Squinting into the setting sun, he reminded Mat of Uno, though he had both his eyes. He looked almost as tired as the people he was chivying. "Move along," he was shouting in a hoarse voice. "You can't bloody stay here. Move along. Into the town with you."

Mat stationed himself squarely in front of the soldier and put on a smile. "Your pardon, Captain, but can you tell me where I might find a decent inn? And a stable with good horses to sell. We have a long way to go, come morning."

The soldier eyed him up and down, examined Thom and his gleeman's cloak, then shifted back to Mat. "Captain, is it? Well, boy, you'll have the Dark One's own luck if you find a stable to sleep in. Most of this lot are sleeping under hedges. And if you find a horse that hasn't been slaughtered for cooking, you'll likely have to fight the man who owns it to make him sell."

"Eating horse!" Thom muttered disgustedly. "Has it really become that bad on this side of the river? Isn't the Queen sending food?"

"It is bad, gleeman." The soldier looked as if he wanted to spit. "They're crossing over faster than the mills can grind flour, or wagons carry foodstuffs from the farms. Well, it will not last much longer. The order has come down. Tomorrow, we stop letting anyone across, and if they try, we send them back." He scowled at the people milling on the dock as if it were all their fault, then brought the same hard look to bear on Mat. "You are taking up space, traveler. Move along." His voice rose to a shout again, directed at everyone within hearing. "Move along! You cannot bloody stay here! Move along!"

Mat and Thom joined the thin stream of people, carts, and sledges flowing toward the gates in the town wall, and into Aringill.

The main streets were paved with flat gray stones, but they were crowded with so many people that it was difficult to see the stones under your own boots. Most appeared to be moving aimlessly, with nowhere to go, and those who had given up squatted dejectedly along the sides of the street, the lucky ones with bundled belongings in front of them or some cherished possession clutched in their arms. Mat saw three men holding clocks, and a dozen or more with silver goblets or platters. The women held children to their breasts, mainly. A babble filled the air, a low, wordless hum of worry. He pushed through the crowd with a frown on his face, searching for the sign that would mark an inn. The buildings were every sort, wood and brick and stone all cheek by jowl, with roofs of tile, or slate, or thatch.

"It does not sound like Morgase," Thom said after a time, half to himself. His bushy eyebrows were pulled down like a white arrow pointing to his nose.

"What does not sound like her?" Mat asked absently.

"Stopping the crossings. Sending people back. She always had a temper like lightning, but she always had a soft heart, too, for anyone poor or hungry." He shook his head.

Mat saw a sign, then—The Riverman, it said, and showed

a barefoot, shirtless fellow doing a jig—and turned that way, forcing an angle across the flow with the quarterstaff. "Well, it had to be her. Who else could it be? Forget Morgase, Thom. We've a long way to Caemlyn, yet. First let us see how much gold it takes to buy a bed for the night."

The common room of The Riverman looked as crowded as the street outside, and when the innkeeper heard what Mat wanted, he laughed till his chins shook. "I am sleeping four to a bed, now. If my own mother came to me, I could not give her a blanket by the fire."

"As you must have noticed," Thom said, his voice taking on that echoing quality, "I am a gleeman. Surely you can find at least pallets in a corner in return for me entertaining your patrons with stories and juggling, eating of fire, and sleight of hand." The innkeeper laughed in his face.

As Mat pulled him back into the street, Thom growled in his normal voice, "You never gave me a chance to ask after his stable. Surely I could have gotten us a place in the hayloft, at least."

"I have slept in enough stables and barns since leaving Emond's Field," Mat told him, "and under enough bushes, too. I want a bed."

But at the next four inns he found, the innkeeper gave him the same answer as the first; the last two almost threw him out bodily when he offered to dice for a bed. And when the owner of the fifth told him he could not give a pallet to the Queen herself—this at a place called The Good Queen—he sighed and asked, "What about your stable, then? Surely we can bed down in the hayloft for a price."

"My stable is for horses," the round-faced man said, "not that many are left in the city." He had been polishing a silver cup; now he opened one door of a shallow cupboard standing on top of a deep, drawered chest and placed it inside with others; none of them matched. A tooled-leather dice cup sat atop the chest, just beyond the arc of the cupboard's doors. "I do not put people in there to frighten the horses, and perhaps make off with them. Those who pay me for stabling their animals want them well tended, and I've two of my own in there, besides. There are no beds in my stable for you."

Mat eyed the dice cup thoughtfully. He pulled a gold Andoran crown out of his pocket and set it atop the chest. The next coin was a silver Tar Valon mark, then a gold one, and a gold Tairen crown. The innkeeper looked at the coins and licked his plump lips. Mat added two silver Illianer marks and another gold Andoran crown, and looked at the round-faced man. The innkeeper hesitated. Mat reached for the coins. The innkeeper's hand reached them first.

"Perhaps just the two of you would not disturb the horses too greatly."

Mat smiled at him. "Speaking of horses, what price for those two of yours? With saddles and bridles, of course."

"I will not sell my horses," the man said, clutching the coins to his chest.

Mat picked up the dice cup and rattled it. "Twice as much again against the horses, saddles, and bridles." He shook his coat pocket to make the loose coins rattle, too, to show he had more to cover the wager. "My one toss against the best of your two." He almost laughed as greed lit the innkeeper's entire face.

When Mat walked into the stable, the first thing he did was check along the half-dozen stalls with horses in them for a pair of brown geldings. They were nondescript animals, but they were his. They needed currying badly, but otherwise they seemed in good condition, especially considering that all the stablemen but one had run off. The innkeeper had been extremely disparaging of their complaints that they could no longer live on what he paid them, and he seemed to think it a crime that the one man who remained had actually had the audacity to say he was going home to bed just because he was tired from doing three men's work.

"Five sixes," Thom muttered behind him. The looks he cast around the stable did not seem as enthralled as they might, seeing that he had suggested it in the first place. Dust motes shone in the last light of the setting sun coming through the big doors, and the ropes used to hoist hay bales hung like vines from pulleys in the roof beams. The hayloft was dim in the gloom above. "When he threw four sixes and a five on his second toss, he thought you'd lost for sure, and so did I. You have not been winning every toss of late."

"I win enough." Mat was just as relieved not to be winning every throw. Luck was one thing, but remembering that night still sent shivers down his back. Still, for one moment as he shook that dice cup, he had all but known what the pips would be. As he tossed the quarterstaff up into the loft, thunder crashed in the sky. He scrambled up the ladder, calling back to Thom. "This was a good idea. I'd think you would be happy to be in out of the rain tonight."

Most of the hay was in bales stacked against the outer walls, but there was more than enough loose for him to make a bed with his cloak over it. Thom appeared at the top of the ladder as he was pulling two loaves of bread and a wedge of green-veined cheese from his leather scrip. The innkeeper—his name was Jeral Florry—had parted with the food for merely enough coin to have bought one of those horses in more peaceful days. They ate while rain began drumming on the roof, washing the food down with water from their waterbottles—Florry had had no wine at any price—and when they were done, Thom dug out his tinder-box and thumbed his long-stemmed pipe full of tabac and settled back for a smoke.

Mat was lying on his back, staring at the shadowed roof and wondering if the rain would break before morning—he wanted that letter out of his hands as quickly as possible—when he heard an axle creak into the stable. Rolling to the edge of the loft, he peered down. There was enough dusk left for him to see.

A slender woman was straightening from the shafts of the high-wheeled cart she had just dragged in out of the rain, pulling off her cloak and muttering to herself as she shook the wet from it. Her hair was plaited in a multitude of small braids, and her silk dress—he thought it was a pale green—was elaborately embroidered across her breasts. The dress had been fine, once, but now it was tattered and stained. She knuckled her back, still talking to herself in a low voice, and hurried to the stable doors to peer out into the rain. Just as hurriedly, she ducked out to pull the big doors shut, enclosing the stable in darkness. There was a rustling below, a clink and a slosh, and suddenly a small flare of light bloomed into a lantern in her hands. She looked around, found a hook on a stall post, hung the lantern, and went to dig under the roped canvas covering her cart.

"She did that quickly," Thom said softly around his pipe. "She could have set fire to the stable striking flint and steel in the dark like that."

The woman came out with the end of a loaf of bread,

which she gnawed as if it were hard and her hunger did not care.

"Is there any of that cheese left?" Mat whispered. Thom shook his head.

The woman began sniffing at the air, and Mat realized she probably smelled Thom's tabac smoke. He was about to stand and announce their presence when one of the stable doors opened again.

The woman crouched, ready to run, as four men walked in out of the rain, doffing their wet cloaks to reveal pale coats with wide sleeves and embroidery across the chest, and baggy breeches embroidered down the legs. Their clothes might be fancy, but they were all big men, and their faces were grim.

"So, Aludra," a man in a yellow coat said, "you did not run so fast as you thought to, eh?" He had a strange accent, to Mat's ear.

"Tammuz," the woman said as if it were a curse. "It is not enough that you cause me to be cast out of the Guild with your blundering, you great ox-brain you, but now you chase after me as well." She had the same odd way of speaking as the man. "Do you think that I am glad to see you?"

The one called Tammuz laughed. "You are a very large fool, Aludra, which I always knew. Had you merely gone away, you could have lived a long life in some quiet place. But you could not forget the secrets in your head, eh? Did you believe we would not hear that you try to earn your way making what it is the right of the Guild alone to make?" Suddenly there was a knife in his hand. "It will be a great pleasure to cut your throat, Aludra."

Mat was not even aware that he had stood up until one of the doubled ropes dangling from the ceiling was in his hands and he had launched himself out of the loft. *Burn me for a bloody fool!*

He only had time for that one frantic thought, and then he was plowing through the cloaked men, sending them toppling like pins in a game of bowls. The ropes slipped through his hands, and he fell, tumbling across the straw-covered floor himself, coins spilling from his pockets, to end up against a stall. When he scrambled to his feet, the four men were already rising, too. And they all had knives in their hands, now. *Light-blind fool! Burn me! Burn me!*

"Mat!"

He looked up, and Thom tossed his quarterstaff down to him. He snagged it out of the air just in time to knock the blade out of Tammuz's fist and thump him a sharp crack on the side of the head. The man crumpled, but the other three were right behind, and for a hectic moment Mat had all he could do with a whirling staff to keep knife blades away from him, rapping knees and ankles and ribs until he could land a good blow on a head. When the last man fell, he stared at them a moment, then raised his glare to the woman. "Did you have to choose this stable to be murdered in?"

She slipped a slim-bladed dagger back into a sheath at her belt. "I would have helped you, but I feared that you might mistake me for one of these great buffoons if I came near with steel in my hand. And I chose this stable because the rain is wet and so am I, and no one was watching this place."

She was older than he had thought, at least ten or fifteen years older than he, but pretty still, with large, dark eyes and a small, full mouth that seemed on the point of a pout. *Or getting ready for a kiss.* He gave a small laugh and leaned on his staff. "Well, what is done is done. I suppose you were not trying to bring us trouble."

Thom was climbing down from the loft, awkwardly because of his leg, and Aludra looked from him to Mat. The gleeman had put his cloak back on; he seldom let anyone see him without it, especially for the first time. "This is like a story," she said. "I am rescued by a gleeman and a young hero"—she frowned at the men sprawled on the stable floor—"from these whose mothers were pigs!"

"Why did they want to kill you?" Mat asked. "He said something about secrets."

"The secrets," Thom said in very nearly his performing voice, "of making fireworks, unless I miss my guess. You are an Illuminator, are you not?" He made a courtly bow with an elaborate swirl of his cloak. "I am Thom Merrilin, a gleeman, as you have seen." Almost as an afterthought, he added, "And this is Mat, a young man with a knack for finding trouble."

"I was an Illuminator," Aludra said stiffly, "but this great pig Tammuz, he ruined a performance for the King of

Cairhien, and nearly he destroyed the chapter house, too. But me, I was Mistress of the Chapter House, so it was me that the Guild held responsible." Her voice became defensive. "I do not tell the secrets of the Guild, no matter what that Tammuz says, but I will not let myself starve while I can make fireworks. I am no more in the Guild, so the laws of the Guild, they do not apply to me now."

"Galldrian," Thom said, sounding almost as wooden as she had. "Well, he is a dead king now, and he'll see no more fireworks."

"The Guild," she said, sounding tired, "they all but blame me for this war in Cairhien, as if that one night of disaster, it made Galldrian die." Thom grimaced. "It seems I can no longer remain here," she went on. "Tammuz and these other oxen, they will wake soon. Perhaps this time they will tell the soldiers that I stole what I have made." She eyed Thom and then Mat, frowning in thought, and seemed to reach a decision. "I must reward you, but I have no money. However, I have something that is perhaps as good as gold. Maybe better. We shall see what you think."

Mat exchanged glances with Thom as she went to root under the canvas covering her cart. *I'll help anyone who can pay.* He thought a speculative light had appeared in Thom's blue eyes.

Aludra separated one bundle from a number like it, a short roll of heavy, oiled cloth almost as fat as her arms would go around. Setting it down on the straw, she undid the binding cords and unrolled the cloth across the floor. Four rows of pockets ran along the length of it, the pockets in each row larger than those in the one before. Each pocket held a wax-coated cylinder of paper just large enough for its end, trailing a dark cord, to stick out.

"Fireworks," Thom said. "I knew it. Aludra, you must not do this. You can sell those for enough to live ten days or more at a good inn, and eat well every day. Well, anywhere but here in Aringill."

Kneeling beside the long strip of oiled cloth, she sniffed at him. "Be quiet, you old one you." She made it sound not unkindly. "I am not allowed to show gratitude? You think I would give you this if I had no more for selling? Attend me closely."

Mat squatted beside her, fascinated. He had seen fireworks

twice in his life. Peddlers had brought them to Emond's Field, at great expense to the Village Council. When he was ten, he had tried to cut one open to see what was inside, and had caused an uproar. Bran al'Vere, the Mayor, had cuffed him; Doral Barran, who had been the Wisdom then, had switched him; and his father had strapped him when he got home. Nobody in the village would talk to him for a month, except for Rand and Perrin, and they mostly told him what a fool he had been. He reached out to touch one of the cylinders. Aludra slapped his hand away.

"Attend me first, I say! These smallest, they will make a loud bang, but no more." They were the size of his little finger. "These next, they make a bang and a bright light. The next, they make the bang, and the light, and many sparkles. The last"—these were fatter than his thumb—"make all of those things, but the sparkles, they are many colors. Almost like a nightflower, but not up in the sky."

Nightflower? Mat thought.

"You must be especially careful of these. You see, the fuse, it is very long." She saw his blank look, and waggled one of the long, dark cords at him. "This, this!"

"Where you put the fire," he muttered. "I know that." Thom made a sound in his throat and stroked his mustaches with a knuckle as if covering a smile.

Aludra grunted. "Where you put the fire. Yes. Do not stay close to any of them, but these largest, you run away from when you light the fuse. You comprehend me?" She briskly rolled up the long cloth. "You may sell these if you wish, or use them. Remember, you must never put this close to fire. Fire will make them all explode. So many as this at once, it could destroy a house, maybe." She hesitated over retying the cords, then added, "And there is one last thing, which you may have heard. Do not cut open any of these, as some great fools do to see what is inside. Sometimes when what is inside touches air, it will explode without the need of fire. You can lose fingers, or even a hand."

"I've heard that," Mat said dryly.

She frowned at him as if wondering whether he meant to do it anyway, then finally pushed the rolled bundle toward him. "Here. I must go now, before these sons of goats awaken." Glancing at the still open door, and the rain falling in the night beyond, she sighed. "Perhaps I will find somewhere else dry. I think I will go toward Lugard, to-morrow. These pigs, they will expect me to go to Caemlyn, yes?"

It was even further to Lugard than to Caemlyn, and Mat suddenly remembered that hard end of bread. And she had said she had no money. The fireworks would buy no meals until she found someone who could afford them. She had never even looked at the gold and silver that had spilled from his pockets when he fell; it glittered and sparkled among the straw in the lantern light. *Ah, Light, I cannot let her go hungry, I suppose.* He scooped up as much as he could reach quickly.

"Uh . . . Aludra? I have plenty, you can see. I thought perhaps. . . ." He held out the coins toward her. "I can always win more."

She paused with her cloak half around her shoulders, then smiled at Thom as she swept it the rest of the way on. "He is young yet, eh?"

"He is young," Thom agreed. "And not half so bad as he would like to think himself. Sometimes he is not."

Mat glowered at both of them and lowered his hand.

Lifting the shafts of her cart, Aludra got it turned around and started for the door, giving Tammuz a kick in the ribs as she passed. He groaned groggily.

"I would like to know something, Aludra," Thom said. "How did you light that lantern so quickly in the dark?"

Stopping short of the door, she smiled over her shoulder at him. "You wish me to tell you all of my secrets? I am grateful, but I am not in love. That secret, not even the Guild knows, for it is my discovery alone. I will tell you this much. When I know how to make it work properly, and work only when I want it to, sticks will make my fortune for me." Throwing her weight against the shafts, she pulled the cart into the rain, and the night swallowed her.

"Sticks?" Mat said. He wondered if she might not be a little strange in the head.

Tammuz groaned again.

"Best we do the same as she, boy," Thom said. "Else it's a choice between slitting four throats and maybe spending the next few days explaining ourselves to the Queen's Guards. These look the sort who'd set them on us out of spite. And they have enough to be spiteful for, I suppose."

One of Tammuz's companions twitched as if coming to, and muttered something incomprehensible.

By the time they had gathered everything and saddled the horses, Tammuz was up on his hands and knees with his head hanging, and the others were stirring and groaning, too.

Swinging into his saddle, Mat stared at the rain outside the open door, falling harder than ever. "A bloody hero," he said. "Thom, if I ever look like acting the hero again, you kick me."

"And what would you have done differently?"

Mat scowled at him, then pulled up his hood and spread the tail of his cloak over the fat roll tied behind the high cantle of his saddle. Even with oiled cloth, a little more protection from the rain could not hurt. "Just kick me!" He booted his horse in the ribs and galloped into the rainy night.

CHAPTER
41

A Hunter's Oath

As the *Snow Goose* moved toward the long stone docks of Illian, sails furled and propelled by its sweeps, Perrin stood near the stern watching great numbers of long-legged birds wading in the tall marsh grass that all but encircled the great harbor. He recognized the small white cranes, and could guess at their much larger blue brothers, but many of the crested birds—red-feathered or rosy, some with flat bills broader than a duck's—he did not know at all. A dozen sorts of gulls swooped and soared above the harbor itself, and a black bird with a long, sharp beak skimmed just above the water, its underbeak cutting a furrow. Ships three and four times as long as the *Snow Goose* lay anchored across the expanse of the harbor, waiting their turns at the docks, or for the tides to shift so they could sail beyond the long breakwater. Small fishing boats worked close to the marsh, and in the creeks winding through it, two or three men in each dragging nets on long poles swung out from either side of the boat.

The wind carried a sharp scent of salt, and did little to break the heat. The sun stood well over halfway down to the horizon, but it seemed like noon. The air felt damp; it was the only way he could think of it. Damp. His nose caught the smell of fresh fish from the boats, of old fish and mud from the marsh, and the sour stink of a large tanning yard that lay on a treeless island in the marsh grass.

Captain Adarra muttered something softly behind him, the tiller creaked, and the *Snow Goose* changed its course a trifle. Barefoot men at the sweeps moved as if not wanting to make a sound. Perrin did not glance at them beyond a flicker of his eye.

He peered at the tannery, instead, watching men scrape hides stretched on rows of wooden frames, and other men lift hides out of huge, sunken vats with long sticks. Sometimes they stacked the hides on barrows, wheeling them into the long, low building at the edge of the yard; sometimes the hides went back into the vats, with an addition of liquids poured from large stone crocks. They probably made more leather in a day than was made in Emond's Field in months, and he could see another tannery on another island beyond the first.

It was not that he had any real interest in ships or fishing boats or tanning yards, or even very much in the birds—though he did wonder what those pale red ones could be fishing for with their flat bills, and some of them looked good to eat unless he watched himself—but anything at all was better than watching the scene behind him on the deck of the *Snow Goose*. The axe at his belt was no defense against that. *A stone wall wouldn't be defense enough*, he thought.

Moiraine had been neither pleased nor displeased to discover that Zarine—*I'll not call her Faile, whatever she wants to name herself! She is no falcon!*—knew she was Aes Sedai, though she had been perhaps a little upset with him for not telling her. *A little upset. She called me a fool, but that was all. Then.* Moiraine did not seem to care one way or another about Zarine being a Hunter of the Horn. But once she learned the girl thought they would lead her to the Horn of Valere, once she learned he had known that, too, and not told her—Zarine had been more than forthcoming about both subjects with Moiraine, to his mind—then her cold dark stare had taken on a quality that made him feel as if he had been packed in a barrel of snow in the dead of winter. The Aes Sedai said nothing, but she stared too often and too hard for any comfort.

He looked over his shoulder and quickly returned to studying the shoreline. Zarine was sitting cross-legged on the deck near the horses tethered between the masts, her bundle and dark cloak beside her, her narrow, divided skirts neatly arrayed, pretending to study the rooftops and towers of the oncoming city. Moiraine was studying Illian, too, from just ahead of the men working the sweeps, but now and then she shot a hard look at the girl from under the deep hood of her fine gray wool cloak. *How can she stand wearing that?* His own coat was unbuttoned and his shirt unlaced at the neck.

Zarine met each Aes Sedai look with a smile, but every time Moiraine turned away, she swallowed and wiped her forehead.

Perrin rather admired her for managing that smile when Moiraine was watching. It was a good deal more than he could do. He had never seen the Aes Sedai truly lose her temper, but he himself was at the point of wishing she would shout, or rage, or anything but stare at him. *Light, maybe not* anything! Maybe the stare was bearable.

Lan sat further toward the bow than Moiraine—his color-shifting cloak was still in the saddlebags at his feet— outwardly absorbed in examining his sword blade, but making little effort to hide his amusement. Sometimes his lips appeared to quirk very close to a smile. Perrin was not certain; at times he thought it was only a shadow. Shadows could make a hammer seem to smile. Each woman obviously thought she was the object of that amusement, but the Warder did not appear to mind the tight-lipped frowns he received from both of them.

A few days earlier Perrin had heard Moiraine ask Lan, in a voice like ice, whether he saw something to laugh at. "I would never laugh at you, Moiraine Sedai," he had replied calmly, "but if you truly intend to send me to Myrelle, I must become used to smiling. I hear that Myrelle tells her Warders jokes. Gaidin must smile at their bondholder's quips; you have often given me quips to laugh at, have you not? Perhaps you would rather I stay with you after all." She had given him a look that would have nailed any other man to the mast, but the Warder never blinked. Lan made cold steel seem like tin.

The crew had taken to padding about their work in utter silence when Moiraine and Zarine were on deck together. Captain Adarra held his head tilted, and looked as if he were listening for something he did not want to hear. He passed his orders in whispers, instead of the shouts he had used at first. Everyone knew Moiraine was Aes Sedai, now, and everyone knew she was displeased. Perrin had let himself get into one shouting match with Zarine, and he was not sure which of them had said the words "Aes Sedai," but the whole crew knew. *Bloody woman!* He was uncertain whether he meant Moiraine or Zarine. *If she is the falcon, what is the hawk supposed to be? Am I going to be stuck with* two *women like her? Light! No! She is not a falcon, and that is an end to it!* The only good thing he could find in all this was that with an angry Aes Sedai to worry about, none of the crew looked twice at his eyes.

Loial was nowhere in sight, at the moment. The Ogier stayed in his stifling cabin whenever Moiraine and Zarine were topside together—working on his notes, he said. He only came on deck at night, to smoke his pipe. Perrin did not see how he could take the heat; even Moiraine and Zarine were better than being belowdecks.

He sighed and kept his eyes on Illian. The city the ship was approaching was large—as big as Cairhien or Caemlyn, the only two great cities he had ever seen—and it reared out of a huge marsh that stretched for miles like a plain of waving grass. Illian had no walls at all, but it seemed to be all towers and palaces. The buildings were all pale stone, except for some that appeared covered with white plaster, but the stone was white and gray and reddish and even faint shades of green. Rooftops of tile sparkled under the sun with a hundred different hues. The long docks held many ships, most dwarfing the *Snow Goose*, and bustled with the loading and unloading of cargo. There were shipyards at the far end of the city, where great ships stood in every stage from skeletons of thick wooden ribs to nearly ready to slide into the harbor.

Perhaps Illian was large enough to keep wolves at bay. They surely would not hunt in those marshes. The *Snow Goose* had outrun the wolves that had followed him from the mountains. He reached out for them gingerly, now, and felt—nothing. A curiously empty feeling, given that it was what he wanted. His dreams had been his own—for the most part—since that first night. Moiraine had asked about them in a cold voice, and he had told the truth. Twice he had found himself in that odd sort of wolf dream, and both times Hopper had appeared, chasing him away, telling him he was too young yet, too new. What Moiraine made of

that, he had no idea; she told him nothing, except to say he
had best be wary.

"That's as well by me," he growled. He was almost becoming used to Hopper being dead but not dead, in the wolf
dreams, at least. Behind him, he heard Captain Adarra
scuff his boots on the deck and mutter something, startled
that anyone would speak aloud.

Lines were hurled ashore from the ship. While they
were still being made fast to stone posts along the docks,
the slightly built captain leaped into motion, whispering
fiercely to his crew. He had booms rigged to lift the horses
onto the wharf almost as quickly as the gangplank was laid
in place. Lan's black warhorse kicked and nearly broke the
boom hoisting him. Loial's huge, hairy-fetlocked mount
needed two.

"An honor," Adarra whispered to Moiraine with a bow
as she stepped onto the wide plank leading to the dock. "An
honor to have served you, Aes Sedai." She strode ashore
without looking at him, her face hidden in her deep hood.

Loial did not appear until everyone else was on the dock,
and the horses, too. The Ogier came thumping up the gangplank trying to don his long coat while carrying his big saddlebags and striped blanketroll, and his cloak over one arm.
"I did not know we had arrived," he rumbled breathlessly.
"I was rereading my. . . ." He trailed off with a glance at
Moiraine. She appeared to be absorbed in watching Lan
saddle Aldieb, but the Ogier's ears flickered like a nervous
cat's.

His notes, Perrin thought. *One of these days I have to see
what he is saying about all this.* Something tickled the back
of his neck, and he jumped a foot before he realized he was
smelling a clean, herbal scent through the spices and tar
and stinks of the docks.

Zarine wiggled her fingers, smiling at them. "If I can do
that with just a brush of my fingers, farmboy, I wonder how
high you would jump if I—?"

He was growing a little tired of considering looks from
those dark, tilted eyes. *She may be pretty, but she looks at
me the way I'd look at a tool I'd never seen before, trying
to puzzle out how it was made, and what it is supposed to
be used for.*

"Zarine." Moiraine's voice was cool but unruffled.

"I am called Faile," Zarine said firmly, and for a moment, with her bold nose, she did look like a falcon.

"Zarine," Moiraine said firmly, "it is time for our ways to part. You will find better Hunting elsewhere, and safer."

"I think not," Zarine said just as firmly. "A Hunter must follow the trail she sees, and no Hunter would ignore the trail you four leave. And I am Faile." She spoiled it a bit by swallowing, but she did not blink as she met Moiraine's eyes.

"Are you certain?" Moiraine said softly. "Are you sure you will not change your mind . . . Falcon?"

"I will not. There is nothing you or your stone-faced Warder can do to stop me." Zarine hesitated, then added slowly, as if she had decided to be entirely truthful, "At least, there is nothing that you will do that can stop me. I know a little of Aes Sedai; I know, for all the stories, that there are things you will not do. And I do not believe stone-face would do what he must to make me give over."

"Are you sure enough of that to risk it?" Lan spoke quietly, and his face did not change, but Zarine swallowed again.

"There is no need to threaten her, Lan," Perrin said. He was surprised to realize he was glaring at the Warder.

Moiraine's glance silenced him and the Warder both. "You believe you know what an Aes Sedai will not do, do you?" she said more softly than before. Her smile was not pleasant. "If you wish to go with us, this is what you must do." Lan's eyelids flickered in surprise; the two women stared at each other like falcon and mouse, but Zarine was not the falcon, now. "You will swear by your Hunter's oath to do as I say, to heed me, and not to leave us. Once you know more than you should of what we do, I will not allow you to fall into the wrong hands. Know that for truth, girl. You will swear to act as one of us, and do nothing that will endanger our purpose. You will ask no questions of where we go or why; you will be satisfied with what I choose to tell you. All of this you will swear, or you will remain here in Illian. And you will not leave this marsh until I return to release you, if it takes the rest of your life. That *I* swear."

Zarine turned her head uneasily, watching Moiraine out of one eye. "I may accompany you if I swear?" The Aes Sedai nodded. "I will be one of you, the same as Loial or stone-face. But I can ask no questions. Are they allowed to ask questions?" Moiraine's face lost a little of its patience. Zarine stood up straighter and held her head high. "Very well, then. I swear, by the oath I took as a Hunter. If I break one, I will have broken both. I swear it!"

"Done," Moiraine said, touching the younger woman's forehead; Zarine shivered. "Since you brought her to us, Perrin, she is your responsibility."

"Mine!" he yelped.

"I am no one's responsibility but my own!" Zarine nearly shouted.

The Aes Sedai went serenely on as if they had never opened their mouths. "It seems you have found Min's falcon, *ta'veren*. I have tried to discourage her, but it appears she will perch on your shoulder whatever I do. The Pattern weaves a future for you, it seems. Yet remember this. If I must, I will snip your thread from the Pattern. And if the girl endangers what must be, you will share her fate."

"I did not ask for her to come along!" Perrin protested. Moiraine calmly mounted Aldieb, adjusting her cloak over the white mare's saddle. "I did not ask for her!" Loial shrugged at him and silently mouthed something. No doubt a saying about the dangers of angering Aes Sedai.

"You are *ta'veren*?" Zarine said disbelievingly. Her gaze ran over his sturdy country clothes and settled on his yellow eyes. "Well, perhaps. Whatever you are, she threatens you as easily as she does me. Who is Min? What does she mean, I will perch on your shoulder?" Her face tightened. "If you try making me your responsibility, I will carve your ears. Do you hear me?"

Grimacing, he slipped his unstrung bow under the saddle girths along Stepper's flank, and climbed into the saddle. Restive after days on the ship, the dun lived up to his name until Perrin calmed him with a firm hand on the reins and pats to his neck.

"None of that deserves an answer," he growled. *Min bloody told her! Burn you, Min! Burn you, too, Moiraine! And Zarine!* He could never remember Rand or Mat being bullied by women on every side. Or himself, before leaving Emond's Field. Nynaeve had been the only one. And Mistress Luhhan, of course; she ran him and Master Luhhan both, everywhere but in the smithy. And Egwene had had a way about her, though mostly with Rand. Mistress al'Vere, Egwene's mother, always had a smile, but things seemed to end up being done as she wanted, too. And the Women's Circle had looked over everybody's shoulder.

Grumbling to himself, he reached down and took Zarine by an arm; she gave a squawk and nearly dropped her bundle as he hoisted her up behind his saddle. Those divided skirts of hers made it easy for her to straddle Stepper. "Moiraine will have to buy you a horse," he muttered. "You cannot walk the whole way."

"You are strong, blacksmith," Zarine said, rubbing her arm, "but I am not a piece of iron." She shifted around, stuffing her bundle and her cloak between them. "I can buy my own horse, if I need one. The whole way where?"

Lan was already riding off the dock into the city, with Moiraine and Loial behind him. The Ogier looked back at Perrin.

"No questions, remember? And my name is Perrin, Zarine. Not 'big man,' or 'blacksmith,' or anything else. Perrin. Perrin Aybara."

"And mine is Faile, shaggy-hair."

With something close to a snarl, he booted Stepper after the others. Zarine had to throw her arms around his waist to keep from being tossed over the dun's crupper. He thought she was laughing.

CHAPTER

42

Easing the Badger

The hubbub of the city quickly submerged Zarine's laughter—if that was what it was—beneath all the clamor that Perrin remembered from Caemlyn and Cairhien. The sounds were different here, slower, and pitched differently, but they were the same, too. Boots and wheels and hooves on rough, uneven paving stones, cart and wagon axles squealing, music and song and laughter drifting from inns and taverns. Voices. A hum of voices like putting his head into a giant beehive. A great city, living.

From down a side street he heard the clang of hammer on anvil, and shifted his shoulders unconsciously. He missed the hammer and tongs in his hands, the white-hot metal giving off sparks as his blows shaped it. The smithy sounds faded behind, buried under the rumble of carts and wagons, and the babble of shopkeepers and people in the streets. Under all the smells of people and horses, cooking and baking, and a hundred scents he had found peculiar to cities lay the smell of marsh and salt water.

He was surprised the first time they came to a bridge inside the city—a low arch of stone over a waterway no more than thirty paces across—but by the third such bridge, he realized that Illian was crisscrossed by as many canals as streets, with men poling laden barges as often as plying whips to move heavy wagons. Sedan chairs wove through the crowds in the streets, and occasionally the lacquered coach of some wealthy merchant or a noble, with crest or House sign painted large on the doors. Many of the men wore peculiar beards that left their upper lip bare, while the women seemed to favor hats with wide brims and attached scarves that they wound around their necks.

Once they crossed a great square, many hides in extent, surrounded by huge columns of white marble at least fifteen spans tall and two spans thick, supporting nothing but a wreath of carved olive branches at the top of each. A huge, white palace stood at either end of the square, each all columned walks and airy balconies, slender towers and purple roofs. Each reflected the other exactly, at first glance, but then Perrin realized that one was just a fraction smaller in each dimension, its towers perhaps less than a pace shorter.

"The King's Palace," Zarine said against his back, "and the Great Hall of the Council. It is said the first King of Illian said the Council of Nine could have any palace they wished, just as long as they did not try to build one larger than his. So the Council copied the King's palace exactly, but two feet smaller in every measurement. That has been the way of Illian ever since. The King and the Council of Nine duel with each other, and the Assemblage struggles with both, and so while they carry on their battles, the people live much as they wish, with none to look over their shoulders too much. It is not a bad way to live, if you must be tied to one city. You would also like to know, I think, blacksmith, that this is the Square of Tammaz, where I took the Hunter's Oath. I think I will end up teaching you so much, no one will notice the hay in your hair."

Perrin held his tongue with an effort, resolving not to stare so openly again.

No one seemed to take Loial as anything much out of the ordinary. A few people looked at him twice, and some small children scampered along in their wake for a time, but it appeared that Ogier were not unknown in Illian. None of the folk seemed to notice the heat or the damp, either.

For once, Loial did not appear pleased with the people's acceptance. His long eyebrows drooped down on his cheeks, and his ears had wilted, though Perrin was not sure that was not just the air. His own shirt clung to him with a mixture of sweat and the damp air.

"Are you afraid you'll find other Ogier here, Loial?" he asked. He felt Zarine stir against his back and cursed his tongue. He meant to let the woman know even less than Moiraine apparently meant to tell her. That way, perhaps, she would grow bored enough to leave. *If Moiraine will let her go, now. Burn me, I don't want any bloody falcon perched on my shoulder, even if she is pretty.*

Loial nodded. "Our stonemasons sometimes come here." He spoke in a whisper not only for an Ogier, but for anyone. Even Perrin could barely hear. "From Stedding Shangtai, I mean. It was masons from our *stedding* who built part of Illian—the Palace of the Assemblage, the Great Hall of the Council, some of the others—and they always send to us when repairs need to be done. Perrin, if there are Ogier here, they will make me go back to the *stedding*. I should have thought of it before now. This place makes me uneasy, Perrin." His ears shifted nervously.

Perrin moved Stepper closer and reached up to pat Loial's shoulder. It was a long reach, above his head. Conscious of Zarine at his back, he chose his words carefully. "Loial, I do not believe Moiraine would let them take you. You have been with us a long time, and she seems to want you with us. She will not let them take you, Loial." *Why not?* he wondered suddenly. *She keeps me because she thinks I may be important to Rand, and maybe because she doesn't want me telling what I know to anyone. Maybe that's why she wants him to stay.*

"Of course, she would not," Loial said in a slightly stronger voice, and his ears perked up. "I am very useful, after all. She may need to travel the Ways again, and she could not without me." Zarine shifted against Perrin's back, and he shook his head, trying to catch Loial's eye. But Loial was not looking. He seemed to have just heard what he had said, and the tufts on his ears had fallen a little. "I do hope it's not that, Perrin." The Ogier looked at the city around them, and his ears went all the way back down. "I do not like this place, Perrin."

Moiraine rode closer to Lan and spoke softly, but Perrin managed to catch her words. "Something is wrong in this city." The Warder nodded.

Perrin felt an itch between his shoulders. The Aes Sedai had sounded grim. *First Loial, and now her. What don't I see?* The sun shone down on the sparkling roof tiles, made reflections from pale stone walls. Those buildings looked as if they might be cool, inside. The buildings were clean and bright, and so were the people. The people.

At first he saw nothing out of the ordinary. Men and women moving about their business, purposeful, but slower than he was used to further north. He thought it might be the heat, and the bright sun. Then he spotted a baker's lad trotting down the street with a big tray of fresh loaves balanced on his head; the young fellow wore a grimace on his face that was nearly a snarl. A woman in front of a weaver's shop looked as if she might bite the man holding up the bright-colored bolts for her inspection. A juggler on a corner ground his teeth and stared at the folk who tossed coins into the cap lying in front of him as if he hated them. Not everyone looked so, but it seemed to him that at least one face in five wore anger and hatred. And he did not think they were even aware of it.

"What is the matter?" Zarine asked. "You are tensing. It is like holding on to a rock."

"Something is wrong," he told her. "I do not know what, but something is wrong." Loial nodded sadly, and murmured about how they would make him go back.

The buildings around them began to change as they rode, crossing more bridges as they crossed Illian to its other side. The pale stone was as often undressed as polished, now. The towers and palaces vanished, to be replaced by inns and warehouses. Many of the men in the streets, and some of the women, had an oddly rolling gait; they all had the bare feet he associated with sailors. The smells of pitch and hemp were strong in the air, and the scent of wood, both freshly cut and cured, with sour mud overlying both. The canals' odors changed, too, making his nose wrinkle. *Chamber pots*, he thought. *Chamber pots and old privies.* It made him feel queasy.

"The Bridge of Flowers," Lan announced as they crossed yet another low bridge. He inhaled deeply. "And now we are in the Perfumed Quarter. The Illianers are a poetic people."

Zarine stifled a laugh against Perrin's back.

As if he were suddenly impatient with the slow pace of Illian, the Warder led them quickly through the streets to an inn, two stories of rough, green-veined stone topped with pale green tiles. Evening was coming on, the light growing softer as the sun settled. It gave a little relief from the heat, but not much. Boys seated on mounting blocks in front of the inn hopped up to take their horses. One black-haired lad about ten asked Loial if he were an Ogier, and when Loial said he was, the boy said, "I did think you did be," with a self-satisfied nod. He led Loial's big horse away, tossing the copper Loial had given him into the air and catching it.

Perrin frowned up at the inn sign for a moment before following the others in. A white-striped badger danced on its hind legs with a man carrying what seemed to be a silver shovel. Easing the Badger, it read. *It must be some story I never heard.*

The common room had sawdust on the floor, and tabac smoke filled the air. It also smelled of wine, and fish cooking in the kitchen, and a heavy, flowered perfume. The exposed beams of the high ceiling were rough-hewn and age-dark. This early in the evening, no more than a quarter of the stools and benches were filled, by men in workmen's plain coats and vests, some with the bare feet of sailors. All of them sat clustered as close as they could manage around one table where a pretty, dark-eyed girl, the wearer of the perfume, sang to the strumming of a twelve-string bittern and danced on the tabletop with swirls of her skirt. Her loose, white blouse had an extremely low neck. Perrin recognized the tune—"The Dancing Lass"—but the words the girl sang were different from what he knew.

> A Lugard girl, she came to town, to see what
> she could see.
> With a wink of her eye, and a smile on her lip,
> she snagged a boy or three, or three.
> With an ankle slim, and skin so pale,
> she caught the owner of a ship, a ship.
> With a soft little sigh, and a gay little laugh,
> she made her way so free. So free.

She launched into another verse, and when Perrin realized what she was singing, his face grew hot. He had thought nothing could shock him after seeing Tinker girls dance, but that had only hinted at things. This girl was singing them right out.

Zarine was nodding in time to the music and grinning. Her grin widened when she looked at him. "Why, farmboy,

I do not think I ever knew a man your age who could still blush."

He glared at her and barely stopped himself from saying something he knew would be stupid. *This bloody woman has me jumping before I can think. Light, I'll wager she thinks I never even kissed a girl!* He tried not to listen to any more of what the girl was singing. If he could not get the red out of his face, Zarine was sure to make more of it.

A flash of startlement had passed across the face of the proprietress when they entered. A large, round woman with her hair in a thick roll at the back of her neck and a smell of strong soap about her, she suppressed her surprise quickly, though, and hurried to Moiraine.

"Mistress Mari," she said, "I did never think to see you here today." She hesitated, eyeing Perrin and Zarine, glanced once at Loial, but not in the searching way she looked at them. Her eyes actually brightened at the sight of the Ogier, but her real attention was all on "Mistress Mari." She lowered her voice, "Have my pigeons no arrived safely?" Lan, she seemed to accept as a part of Moiraine.

"I am sure they have, Nieda," Moiraine said. "I have been away, but I am sure Adine has noted down everything you reported." She eyed the girl singing on the table with no outward disapproval, nor any other expression. "The Badger was considerably quieter when last I was here."

"Aye, Mistress Mari, it did be that. But the louts have no gotten over the winter yet, it does seem. I have no had a fight in the Badger in ten years, till the tail of this winter gone." She nodded toward the one man not sitting near the singer, a fellow even bigger than Perrin, standing against the wall with his thick arms folded, tapping his foot to the music. "Even Bili did have a hard time keeping them down, so I did hire the girl to take their minds from anger. From some place in Altara, she does come." She tilted her head, listening for a moment. "A fair voice, but I did sing it better—aye, and dance better, too—when I did be her age."

Perrin gaped at the thought of this huge woman capering on a table, singing that song—a bit of it came through; "I'll wear no shift at all. At all"—until Zarine fisted him hard in the short ribs. He grunted.

Nieda looked his way. "I'll mix you some honey and sulphur, lad, for that throat. You'll no want to take a chill before the weather warms, no with a pretty girl like that one on your arm."

Moiraine gave him a look that said he was interfering with her. "Strange that you should suffer fights," she said. "I well remember how your nephew stops such. Has something occurred to make people more irritable?"

Nieda mused for a moment. "Perhaps. It do be hard to say. The young lordlings do always come down to the docks for the wenching and carousing they can no get away with where the air does smell fresher. Perhaps they do come more often, now, since the hard of the winter. Perhaps. And others do snap at each other more, too. It did be a hard winter. That does make men angrier, and women as well. All that rain, and cold. Why, I did wake two mornings to find ice in my washbasin. No so hard as the last winter, of course, but that did be a winter for a thousand years. Almost enough to make me believe those travelers' tales of frozen water falling from the sky." She giggled to show how little she believed that. It was an odd sound from such a large woman.

Perrin shook his head. *She doesn't believe in snow?* But if she thought this weather was cool, he could believe it of her.

Moiraine bent her head in thought, her hood shadowing her face.

The girl on the table was beginning a new verse, and Perrin found himself listening in spite of himself. He had never heard of any woman doing anything remotely like what the girl was singing about, but it did sound interesting. He noticed Zarine watching him listen, and tried to pretend he had not been.

"What has occurred out of the ordinary in Illian of late?" Moiraine said finally.

"I do suppose you could call Lord Brend's ascension to the Council of Nine unusual," Nieda said. "Fortune prick me, I can no remember ever hearing his name before the winter, but he did come to the city—from somewhere near the Murandian border, it be rumored—and did be raised inside a week. It do be said he be a good man, and strongest of the Nine—they all do follow his lead, it be said, though he be newest and unknown—but sometimes I do have strange dreams of him."

Moiraine had opened her mouth—to tell Nieda she had meant in the last few nights, Perrin was sure—but she hesitated, and instead said, "What sort of strange dreams, Nieda?"

"Oh, foolishness, Mistress Mari. Just foolishness. You do truly wish to hear it? Dreams of Lord Brend in strange places, and walking bridges hanging in air. All fogged, these dreams do be, but near every night they do come. Did you ever hear of such? Foolishness, Fortune prick me! Yet, it do be odd. Bili does say he does dream the same dreams. I do think he does hear my dreams and copy them. Bili do be none too bright, sometimes, I do think."

"You may do him an injustice," Moiraine breathed.

Perrin stared at her dark hood. She had sounded shaken, even more shaken than when she thought a new false Dragon had risen in Ghealdan. He could not smell fear, but. . . . Moiraine was frightened. It was a far more terrifying thought than Moiraine angry. He could imagine her angry; he could not begin to conceive of her afraid.

"How I do maunder on," Nieda said, patting the rolled hair at the back of her neck. "As if my foolish dreams do be important." She giggled again. A quick giggle; this was not as foolish as believing in snow. "You do sound tired, Mistress Mari. I will show you to your rooms. And then a good meal of fresh-caught red-stripe."

Red-stripe? A fish, he thought it must be; he could smell fish cooking.

"Rooms," Moiraine said. "Yes. We will take rooms. The meal can wait. Ships. Nieda, what ships sail for Tear? Early on the morrow. I have that which I must do tonight." Lan glanced at her, frowning.

"For Tear, Mistress Mari?" Nieda laughed. "Why, none for Tear. The Nine did forbid any ship to sail for Tear a month gone now, nor any from Tear to call here, though I do think the Sea Folk pay it no mind. But there do be no Sea Folk ship in the harbor. It do be odd, that. The order of the Nine, I do mean, and the King silent on it, when he does always raise his voice if they but take a step without his lead. Or perhaps it be no that, exactly. All talk do be of war with Tear, but the boatmen and wagoneers who do carry supplies to the army do say the soldiers do all look north, to Murandy."

"The paths of the Shadow are tangled," Moiraine said in a tight voice. "We will do what we must. The rooms, Nieda. And then we will eat that meal."

Perrin's room was more comfortable than he expected, given the look of the rest of the Badger. The bed was wide, the mattress soft. The door was made of tilted slats, and when he opened the windows, a breeze crossed the room carrying the smells of the harbor. And something of the canals, too, but at least it was cooling. He hung his cloak on a peg along with his quiver and axe, and propped his bow in the corner. Everything else he left in the saddlebags and blanketroll. The night might not be restful.

If Moiraine had sounded afraid before, it had been nothing to when she said that something must be done tonight. For an instant then, fear scent had steamed from her as from a woman announcing that she was going to stick her hand in a hornets' nest and crush them with her bare fingers. *What in the Light is she up to? If Moiraine is frightened, I should be terrified.*

He was not, he realized. Not terrified, or even frightened. He felt . . . excited. Ready for something to happen, almost eager. Determined. He recognized the feelings. They were what wolves felt just before they fought. *Burn me, I'd rather be afraid!*

He was first back down to the common except for Loial. Nieda had arranged a large table for them, with ladder-back chairs instead of benches. She had even found a chair big enough for Loial. The girl across the room was singing a song about a rich merchant who, having just lost his team of horses in an improbable way, had for some reason decided to pull his carriage himself. The men listening around her roared with laughter. The windows showed darkness coming on more quickly than he had expected; the air smelled as if it might be making up to rain.

"This inn has an Ogier room," Loial said as Perrin sat down. "Apparently, every inn in Illian has one, in hopes of gaining Ogier custom when the stonemasons come. Nieda claims it is lucky, having an Ogier under the roof. I cannot think they get many. The masons always stay together when they go Outside to work. Humans are so hasty, and the Elders are always afraid tempers will flare and someone will put a long handle on his axe." He eyed the men around the singer as if he suspected them of it. His ears were drooping again.

The rich merchant was in the process of losing his carriage, to more laughter. "Did you find out whether any Ogier from Stedding Shangtai are in Illian?"

"There were, but Nieda said they left during the winter. She said they had not finished their work. I do not understand it. The masons would not have left work undone unless they were not paid, and Nieda said it was not that. One morning, they were just gone, though someone saw them walking down the Maredo Causeway in the night. Perrin, I do not like this city. I do not know why, but it makes me . . . uneasy."

"Ogier," Moiraine said, "are sensitive to some things." She still had her face hidden, but Nieda had apparently sent someone to buy her a light cloak of dark blue linen. The fear smell was gone from her, but her voice sounded under tight control. Lan held her chair for her; his eyes looked worried.

Zarine was the last down, running her fingers through just-washed hair. The herbal scent was stronger around her than before. She stared at the platter Nieda placed on the table and muttered under her breath. "I hate fish."

The stout woman had brought all the food on a small cart with shelves; it was dusty in places, as if it had been hastily brought out from the storeroom in Moiraine's honor. The dishes were Sea Folk porcelain, too, if chipped.

"Eat," Moiraine said, looking straight at Zarine. "Remember that any meal can be your last. You chose to travel with us, so tonight you will eat fish. Tomorrow, you may die."

Perrin did not recognize the nearly round white fish with red stripes, but they smelled good. He lifted two onto his plate with the serving fork, and grinned at Zarine around a mouthful. They tasted good, too, lightly spiced. *Eat your nasty fish, falcon*, he thought. He also thought that Zarine looked as if she might bite him.

"Do you wish me to stop the girl singing, Mistress Mari?" Nieda asked. She was setting bowls of peas and some sort of stiff yellow mush on the table. "So you can eat in quiet?"

Staring at her plate, Moiraine did not seem to hear.

Lan listened a moment—the merchant had already lost,

in succession, his carriage, his cloak, his boots, his gold, and
the rest of his clothes, and was now reduced to wrestling a
pig for its dinner—and shook his head. "She will not bother
us." He looked close to smiling for a moment, before he
glanced at Moiraine. Then the worry returned to his eyes.

"What is wrong?" Zarine said. She was ignoring the fish.
"I know something is. I have not see that much expression
on you, stone-face, since I met you."

"No questions!" Moiraine said sharply. "You will know
what I tell you and no more!"

"What *will* you tell me?" Zarine demanded.

The Aes Sedai smiled. "Eat your fish."

The meal went on in near silence after that, except for the
songs drifting across the room. There was one about a rich
man whose wife and daughters made a fool of him time and
again without ever deflating his self-importance, another
that concerned a young woman who decided to take a walk
without any clothes, and one that told of a blacksmith who
managed to shoe himself instead of the horse. Zarine nearly
choked laughing at that one, forgot herself enough to take
a bite of fish, and suddenly grimaced as if she had put mud
in her mouth.

I won't laugh at her, Perrin told himself. *However foolish she looks, I'll show her what manners are.* "They taste
good, don't they," he said. Zarine gave him a bitter look,
and Moiraine a frown for interrupting her thoughts, and
that was all the talk there was.

Nieda was clearing away the dishes and setting an array
of cheeses on the table when a stink of something vile lifted
the hackles on the back of Perrin's neck. It was a smell of
something that should not be, and he had smelled it twice
before. He peered about the common room uneasily.

The girl still sang to the knot of listeners, some men were
strolling across the floor from the door, and Bili still leaned
on the wall tapping his foot to the sounds of the bittern.
Nieda patted her rolled hair, gave the room a quick glance,
and turned to push the cart away.

He looked at his companions. Loial, unsurprisingly, had
pulled a book from his coat pocket and seemed to have
forgotten where he was. Zarine, absently rolling a piece of
white cheese into a ball, was eyeing first Perrin, then Moiraine, then him again, while trying to pretend she was not.

It was Lan and Moiraine he was really interested in, though. They could sense a Myrddraal, or a Trolloc, or any Shadow-spawn, before it came closer than a few hundred paces, but the Aes Sedai was staring distantly at the table in front of her, and the Warder was cutting a chunk of yellow cheese and watching her. Yet the smell of wrongness was there, as at Jarra and the edge of Remen, and this time it was not going away. It seemed to be coming from something within the common room.

He studied the room again. Bili against the wall, some men crossing the floor, the girl singing on the table, all the laughing men sitting around her. *Men crossing the floor?* He frowned at them. Six men with ordinary faces, walk-ing toward where he was sitting. Very ordinary faces. He was just starting to reinspect the men listening to the girl when suddenly it came to him that the stink of wrongness was rolling from the six. Abruptly they had daggers in their hands, as if they had realized he had seen them.

"They have knives!" he roared, and threw the cheese platter at them.

The common erupted into confusion, men shouting, the singer screaming, Nieda shouting for Bili, everything hap-pening at once. Lan leaped to his feet, and a ball of fire darted from Moiraine's hand, and Loial snatched up his chair like a club, and Zarine danced to one side, cursing. She had a knife in her hand, too, but Perrin was too busy to notice much of what anyone else did. Those men seemed to be looking straight at him, and his axe was hanging from a peg up in his room.

Seizing a chair, he ripped off a thick chair leg that ran up to make one side of the ladder-back, hurled the rest of the chair at the men, and set about him with his long bludgeon. They were trying to reach him with their naked steel, as if Lan and the others were only obstacles in their way. It was a tight tangle where all he could manage was to knock blades away from him, and his wilder swings threatened Lan and Loial and Zarine as much as any of his six attackers. From the corner of his eye he saw Moiraine standing to one side, frustration on her face; they were all so mixed together that she could do nothing without endangering friend as well as foe. None of the knife wielders as much as glanced at her; she was not between them and Perrin.

Panting, he managed to crack one of the ordinary-looking men across the head so hard that he heard bone splinter, and abruptly realized they were all down. It all seemed to him to have gone on for a quarter of an hour or more, but he saw that Bili was just halting, his large hands working as he stared at the six men sprawled dead on the floor. Bili had not even had time to reach the fight before it was done.

Lan wore a face even grimmer than usual; he began searching the bodies, thoroughly, but with a quickness that spoke of distaste. Loial still had his chair raised to swing; he gave a start and set it down with an embarrassed grin. Moiraine was staring at Perrin, and so was Zarine as she retrieved her knife from the chest of one of the dead men. That stench of wrongness was gone, as if it had died with them.

"Gray Men," the Aes Sedai said softly, "and after you."

"Gray Men?" Nieda laughed, both loud and nervously. "Why, Mistress Mari, next you'll say you do believe in boggles and bugbears and Fetches, and Old Grim riding with the black dogs in the Wild Hunt." Some of the men who had been listening to the songs laughed, too, though they looked as uneasily at Moiraine as at the dead men. The singer stared at Moiraine, as well, her eyes wide. Perrin remembered that one ball of fire, before everything grew too jumbled. One of the Gray Men had a somewhat charred look about him, and gave off a sickly sweet burned smell.

Moiraine turned from Perrin to the stout woman. "A man may walk in the Shadow," the Aes Sedai said calmly, "without being Shadowspawn."

"Oh, aye, Darkfriends." Nieda put her hands on generous hips and frowned at the corpses. Lan had finished his searching; he glanced at Moiraine and shook his head as if he had not really expected to find anything. "More likely thieves, though I did never hear of thieves bold enough to come right into an inn. I did never have even one killing in the Badger before. Bili! Clear these out, into a canal, and put down fresh sawdust. The back way, mind. I do no want the Watch putting their long noses into the Badger." Bili nodded as if eager to be useful after failing to take a hand earlier. He grabbed a dead man by the belt in either hand and carried them back toward the kitchen.

"Aes Sedai?" the dark-eyed singer said. "I did not mean to offend with my common songs." She was covering the exposed part of her bosom, which was most of it, with her hands. "I can sing others, if you would so like."

"Sing whatever you wish, girl," Moiraine told her. "The White Tower is not so isolated from the world as you seem to think, and I have heard rougher songs than you would sing." Even so, she did not look pleased that the common now knew she was Aes Sedai. She glanced at Lan, gathered the linen cloak around her, and started for the door.

The Warder moved quickly to intercept her, and they spoke quietly in front of the door, but Perrin could hear as well as if they whispered right next to him.

"Do you mean to go without me?" Lan said. "I pledged to keep you whole, Moiraine, when I took your bond."

"You have always known there were some dangers you are not equipped to handle, my Gaidin. I must go alone."

"Moiraine—"

She cut him off. "Heed me, Lan. Should I fail, you will know it, and you will be compelled to return to the White Tower. I would not change that even if I had time. I do not mean you to die in a vain attempt to avenge me. Take Perrin with you. It seems the Shadow has made his importance in the Pattern known to me, if not clear. I was a fool. Rand is so strongly *ta'veren* that I ignored what it must mean that he had two others close by him. With Perrin and Mat, the Amyrlin may still be able to affect the course of events. With Rand loose, she will have to. Tell her what has happened, my Gaidin."

"You speak as if you are already dead," Lan said roughly.

"The Wheel weaves as the Wheel wills, and the Shadow darkens the world. Heed me, Lan, and obey, as you swore to." With that, she was gone.

CHAPTER
43

Shadowbrothers

The dark-eyed girl climbed back on her table and started singing again, in an unsteady voice. The tune was one Perrin knew as "Mistress Aynora's Rooster," and though the words were different once more, to his disappointment—and embarrassment that he was disappointed—it actually was about a rooster. Mistress Luhhan herself would not have disapproved. *Light, I'm getting as bad as Mat.*

None of the listeners complained; some of the men did look a bit disgruntled, but they seemed to be as anxious about what Moiraine might approve as the singer was. No one wished to offend an Aes Sedai, even with her gone. Bili came back and hoisted two more Gray Men; a few of the men listening to the song glanced at the corpses and shook their heads. One of them spat on the sawdust.

Lan came to stand in front of Perrin. "How did you know them, blacksmith?" he asked quietly. "Their taint of evil is not strong enough for Moiraine or me to sense. Gray Men have walked past a hundred guards without being noticed, and Warders among them."

Very conscious of Zarine's eyes on him, Perrin tried to make his voice even softer than Lan's. "I . . . I smelled them. I've smelled them before, at Jarra and at Remen, but it always vanished. They were gone before we got there, both times." He was not sure whether Zarine had overheard or not; she was leaning forward trying to listen, and trying to appear not to at the same time.

"Following Rand, then. Following you, now, blacksmith." The Warder gave no visible sign of surprise. He raised his voice to a more normal level. "I am going to look around outside, blacksmith. Your eyes might see something I miss." Perrin nodded; it was a measure of the Warder's worry that he asked for help. "Ogier, your folk see better than most, too."

"Oh, ah," Loial said. "Well, I suppose I could take a look, too." His big, round eyes rolled sideways toward the two Gray Men still on the floor. "I would not think any more of them were out there. Would you?"

"What are we looking for, stone-face?" Zarine said.

Lan eyed her a moment, then shook his head as if he had decided not to say something. "Whatever we find, girl. I will know it when I see it."

Perrin thought about going upstairs for his axe, but the Warder made for the door, and he was not wearing his sword. *He hardly needs it*, Perrin thought grumpily. *He is almost as dangerous without it as with.* He held on to the chair leg as he followed. It was a relief to see that Zarine still had her knife in her hand.

Thick black clouds were roiling overhead. The street was as dark as late twilight, and empty of people who had apparently not waited to be caught in the rain. One fellow was running across a bridge down the street; he was the only person Perrin saw in any direction. The wind was picking up, blowing a rag along the uneven paving stones; another, caught under the edge of one of the mounting blocks, flapped with a small snapping sound. Thunder grumbled and rolled.

Perrin wrinkled his nose. There was a smell of fireworks on that wind. *No, not fireworks, exactly.* It was a burned sulphur sort of smell. Almost.

Zarine tapped the chair leg in his hands with her knife blade. "You really are strong, big man. You tore that chair apart as if it were made of twigs."

Perrin grunted. He realized he was standing straighter, and deliberately made himself slouch. *Fool girl!* Zarine laughed softly, and suddenly he did not know whether to straighten or stay as he was. *Fool!* This time he meant it for himself. *You're supposed to be looking. For what?* He did not see anything but the street, did not smell anything but the almost burned sulphur scent. And Zarine, of course.

Loial appeared to be wondering what it was he was looking

for, too. He scratched a tufted ear, peered one way down the street, then the other, then scratched the other ear. Then he stared up at the roof of the inn.

Lan appeared from the alleyway beside the inn and moved out into the street, eyes studying the darker shadows along the buildings.

"Maybe he missed seeing something," Perrin muttered, though he found it hard to believe, and turned toward the alley. *I am supposed to be looking, so I'll look. Maybe he did miss something.*

Lan had stopped a little way down the street, staring at the paving stones in front of his feet. The Warder started back toward the inn, walking quickly, but peering at the street ahead of him as if following something. Whatever it was led straight to one of the mounting blocks, almost beside the inn door. He stopped there, staring at the top of the gray stone block.

Perrin decided to abandon going down the alley—it stank as much as the canals in this part of Illian, for one thing— and walked over to Lan, instead. He saw what the Warder was staring at right away. Pressed into the top of the stone mounting block were two prints, as if a huge hound had rested its forepaws there. The smell that was almost burned sulphur was strongest here. *Dogs don't make footprints in stone. Light, they don't!* He could make out the trail Lan had followed, too. The hound had trotted up the street as far as the mounting block, then turned and gone back the way it had come. Leaving tracks in the stone as if they had been a plowed field. *They just don't!*

"Darkhound," Lan said, and Zarine gasped. Loial moaned softly. For an Ogier. "A Darkhound leaves no mark on dirt, blacksmith, not even on mud, but stone is another matter. There hasn't been a Darkhound seen south of the Mountains of Dhoom since the Trolloc Wars. This one was hunting for something, I'd say. And now that it has found it, it has gone to tell its master."

Me? Perrin thought. *Gray Men and Darkhounds hunting me? This is crazy!*

"Are you telling me Nieda was right?" Zarine demanded in a shaky voice. "Old Grim is really riding with the Wild Hunt? Light! I always thought it was just a story."

"Don't be a complete fool, girl," Lan said harshly. "If the

Dark One were free, we'd all be worse than dead by now."
He peered off down the street, the way the tracks went.
"But Darkhounds are real enough. Almost as dangerous as
Myrddraal, and harder to kill."

"Now you bring Fetches into it," Zarine muttered. "Gray
Men. Fetches. Darkhounds. You had better lead me to the
Horn of Valere, farmboy. What other surprises do you have
waiting for me?"

"No questions," Lan told her. "You still know little
enough that Moiraine will release you from your oath, if
you swear not to follow. I'll take that oath myself, and you
can go now. You would be wise to give it."

"You will not frighten me away, stone-face," Zarine said.
"I do not frighten easily." But she sounded frightened. And
smelled it, too.

"I have a question," Perrin said, "and I want an answer.
You didn't sense this Darkhound, Lan, and neither did Moiraine. Why not?"

The Warder was silent for a time. "The answer to that,
blacksmith," he said grimly at last, "may be more than you
or I, either one, want to know. I hope the answer does not
kill us all. You three get what sleep you can. I doubt we
will stay the night in Illian, and I fear we have hard riding
ahead."

"What are you going to do?" Perrin asked.

"I am going after Moiraine. To tell her about the Darkhound. She can't be angry with me for following for that,
not when she would not know it was there until it took her
throat."

The first big drops of rain splatted on the paving stones
as they went back inside. Bili had removed the last of the
dead Gray Men and was sweeping up the sawdust where
they had bled. The dark-eyed girl was singing a sad song
about a boy leaving his love. Mistress Luhhan would have
enjoyed it greatly.

Lan ran ahead of them, across the common room and up
the stairs, and by the time Perrin reached the second floor,
the Warder was already starting back down, buckling his
sword belt on, color-shifting cloak hanging over his arm as
if he hardly cared who saw it.

"If he is wearing that in a city. . . ." Loial's shaggy hair
almost brushed the ceiling as he shook his head. "I do not

know if I can sleep, but I will try. Dreams will be more pleasant than staying awake."

Not always, Loial, Perrin thought as the Ogier went on down the hall.

Zarine seemed to want to stay with him, but he told her to go to sleep and firmly shut the slatted door in her face. He stared at his own bed reluctantly as he stripped down to his underbreeches.

"I have to find out," he sighed, and crawled onto the bed. Rain drummed down outside, and thunder boomed. The breeze across his bed carried some of the rain's coolness, but he did not think he would need any of the blankets at the foot of the mattress. His last thought before sleep claimed him was that he had forgotten to light a candle again, though the room was dark. *Careless. Mustn't be careless. Carelessness ruins the work.*

Dreams tumbled through his head. Darkhounds chasing him; he never saw them, but he could hear their howling. Fades, and Gray Men. A tall, slender man flashed into them again and again, in richly embroidered coat and boots with gold fringe; most of the time he held what seemed to be a sword, shining like the sun, and laughed triumphantly. Sometimes the man sat on a throne, and kings and queens groveled before him. These felt strange, as if they were not really his dreams at all.

Then the dreams changed, and he knew he was in the wolf dream he sought. This time he had hoped for it.

He stood atop a high, flat-topped stone spire, the wind ruffling his hair, bringing a thousand dry scents and a faint hint of water hidden in the far distance. For an instant he thought he had the form of a wolf, and fumbled at his own body to make sure what he saw was really him. He wore his own coat and breeches and boots; he held his bow, and his quiver hung at his side. The axe was not there.

"Hopper! Hopper, where are you?" The wolf did not come.

Rugged mountains surrounded him, and other tall spires separated by arid flats and jumbled ridges, and sometimes a large plateau rising with sheer sides. Things grew, but nothing lush. Tough, short grass. Bushes wiry and covered with thorn, and other things that even seemed to have thorns on their fat leaves. Scattered, stunted trees, twisted by the wind. Yet wolves could find hunting even in this land.

As he peered at this rough land, a circle of darkness suddenly blanked out a part of the mountains; he could not have said whether the darkness was right in front of his face or halfway to the mountains, but he seemed to be seeing through it, and beyond. Mat, rattling a dice cup. His opponent stared at Mat with eyes of fire. Mat did not seem to see the man, but Perrin knew him.

"Mat!" he shouted. "It's Ba'alzamon! Light, Mat, you're dicing with Ba'alzamon!"

Mat made his toss, and as the dice spun, the vision faded, and the dark place was dry mountains again.

"Hopper!" Perrin turned slowly, looking in every direction. He even looked up in the sky—*He can fly, now*—where clouds promised a rain the ground far below the spire top would drink up as soon as it fell. "Hopper!"

A darkness formed among the clouds, a hole into somewhere else. Egwene and Nynaeve and Elayne stood looking at a huge metal cage, with a raised door held on a heavy spring. They stepped in and reached up together to loose the catch. The barred door snapped down behind them. A woman with her hair all in braids laughed at them, and another woman all in white laughed at her. The hole in the sky closed, and there were only clouds.

"Hopper, where are you?" he called. "I need you! Hopper!"

And the grizzled wolf was there, alighting on the spire top as if he had leaped from somewhere higher.

Dangerous. You have been warned, Young Bull. Too young. Too new yet.

"I need to know, Hopper. You said there were things I must see. I need to see more, know more." He hesitated, thinking of Mat, of Egwene and Nynaeve and Elayne. "The strange things I see here. Are they real?" Hopper's sending seemed slow, as if it were so simple the wolf could not understand the need to explain it, or how to. Finally, though, something came.

What is real is not real. What is not real is real. Flesh is a dream, and dreams have flesh.

"That doesn't tell me anything, Hopper. I do not understand." The wolf looked at him, as if he had said he did not understand that water was wet. "You said I had to see something, and you showed me Ba'alzamon, and Lanfear."

Heartfang. Moonhunter.

"Why did you show me, Hopper? Why did I have to see them?"

The Last Hunt comes. Sadness filled the sending, and a sense of inevitability. *What will be must be.*

"I do not understand! The Last Hunt? What Last Hunt? Hopper, Gray Men came to kill me tonight."

The Notdead hunt you?

"Yes! Gray Men! After me! And a Darkhound was right outside the inn! I want to know why they're after me."

Shadowbrothers! Hopper crouched, looking to either side as if he almost expected an attack. *Long since we have seen the Shadowbrothers. You must go, Young Bull. Great danger! Flee the Shadowbrothers!*

"Why are they after me, Hopper? You do know. I know you do!"

Flee, Young Bull. Hopper leaped, forepaws hitting Perrin's chest, knocking him back, over the edge. *Flee the Shadowbrothers.*

The wind rushed in his ears as he fell. Hopper and the edge of the spire top dwindled above him. "Why, Hopper?" he shouted. "I have to know why!"

The Last Hunt comes.

He was going to hit. He knew it. The ground below rushed up at him, and he tensed against the crushing impact that. . . .

He started awake, staring at the candle flickering on the small table beside the bed. Lightning flashes lit the window, and thunder rattled it. "What did he mean, the Last Hunt?" he mumbled. *I did not light any candle.*

"You talk to yourself. And thrash in your sleep."

He jumped, and cursed himself for not having noticed the herbal scent in the air. Zarine sat on a stool at the edge of the candlelight, elbow on her knee, chin on her fist, watching him.

"You are *ta'veren*," she said as if ticking off a point. "Stone-face thinks those odd eyes of yours can see things his can't. Gray Men want to kill you. You travel with an Aes

Sedai, a Warder, and an Ogier. You free caged Aiel and kill Whitecloaks. Who are you, farmboy, the Dragon Reborn?" Her voice said that was the most ridiculous thing she could think of, but he still shifted uneasily. "Whoever you are, big man," she added, "you could do with a little more hair on your chest."

He twisted around, cursing, and scrabbled one of the blankets over him to his neck. *Light, she keeps making me jump like a frog on a hot rock.* Zarine's face was at the edge of shadows. He could not see her clearly except when lightning shone through the window, the harsh illumination casting its own shadows across her strong nose and high cheekbones. Suddenly he remembered Min saying he should run from a beautiful woman. Once he had recognized Lanfear in that wolf dream, he had thought Min must mean her—he did not think it was possible for a woman to be any more beautiful than Lanfear—but she was just in a dream. Zarine was sitting there staring at him with those dark, tilted eyes, considering, weighing.

"What are you doing here?" he demanded. "What do you want? Who are you?"

She threw back her head and laughed. "I am Faile, farmboy, a Hunter of the Horn. Who do you think I am, the woman of your dreams? Why did you jump that way? You would think I had goosed you."

Before he could find words, the door crashed back against the wall, and Moiraine stood in the doorway, her face as pale and grim as death. "Your wolf dreams tell as truly as a Dreamer's, Perrin. The Forsaken *are* loose, and one of them rules in Illian."

CHAPTER

44

Hunted

Perrin climbed off the bed and started dressing, not caring whether Zarine was watching or not. He knew what he intended to do, but he asked Moiraine anyway. "Do we leave?"

"Unless you want to make closer acquaintance with Sammael," she said dryly. Thunder crashed overhead as if to punctuate her sentence, and lightning flashed. The Aes Sedai barely glanced at Zarine.

Stuffing his shirttail into his breeches, he suddenly wished he had his coat and cloak on. Naming which one of the Forsaken it was made the room seem cold. *Ba'alzamon isn't bad enough; we have to have the Forsaken loose, too. Light, does it even matter if we find Rand, now? Is it too late?* But he kept dressing, stamping his feet into his boots. It was that or give up, and Two Rivers folk were not known for giving up.

"Sammael?" Zarine said faintly. "One of the Forsaken rules . . . ? Light!"

"Do you still wish to follow?" Moiraine said softly. "I would not make you stay here, not now, but I will give you one last chance to swear to go another way than I."

Zarine hesitated, and Perrin paused with his coat half on. Surely no one would choose to go with people who had incurred the wrath of one of the Forsaken. Not now that she knew something of what they faced. *Not unless she has a very good reason.* For that matter, anyone who heard one of the Forsaken was loose should already be running for a Sea Folk ship and asking passage to the other side of the Aiel Waste, not sitting there thinking.

"No," Zarine said finally, and he began to relax. "No, I will not swear to go another way. Whether you lead me to the Horn of Valere or not, not even whoever does find the Horn will have a story such as this. I think this story will be told for the ages, Aes Sedai, and I will be part of it."

"No!" Perrin snapped. "That is not good enough. What do you want?"

"I have no time for this bickering," Moiraine broke in. "Any moment *Lord Brend* may learn that one of his Dark-hounds is dead. You can be sure he will know that means a Warder, and he will come looking for the Gaidin's Aes Sedai. Do you mean to sit here until he discovers where you are? Move, you foolish children! Move!" She vanished down the hall before he could open his mouth.

Zarine did not wait, either, running from the room without her candle. Perrin hastily gathered his things and dashed for the back stairs still buckling his axe belt around his waist. He caught up to Loial going down, the Ogier trying to stuff a wood-bound book into his saddlebags and put on his cloak at the same time. Perrin gave him a hand with the cloak while they both ran down the stairs, and Zarine caught the pair of them before they could dash out into the pouring rain.

Perrin hunched his shoulders against the wet and ran for the stable across the storm-darkened yard without waiting to pull up the hood of his cloak. *She has to have a reason. Being in a bloody story isn't reason enough for any but a madwoman!* The rain soaked his shaggy curls, laying them flat around his head, before he darted through the stable door.

Moiraine was there before them, in an oiled cloak still beaded with rain, and Nieda holding a lantern for Lan to finish saddling the horses. There was an extra, a bay gelding with an even stronger nose than Zarine's.

"I will send pigeons every day," the stout woman was saying. "No one will suspect me. Fortune prick me! Even Whitecloaks do speak well of me."

"Listen to me, woman!" Moiraine snapped. "This is not a Whitecloak or a Darkfriend I speak of. You will flee this city, and make anyone you care for flee with you. For a dozen years you have obeyed me. Obey me now!" Nieda nodded, but reluctantly, and Moiraine growled with exasperation.

"The bay is yours, girl," Lan said to Zarine. "Get on his back. If you do not know how to ride, you must learn by do- ing, or take my offer."

Putting one hand on the high pommel, she vaulted easily into the saddle. "I was on a horse once, stone-face, now that I think of it." She twisted around to tie her bundle behind her.

"What did you mean, Moiraine?" Perrin demanded as he tossed his saddlebag across Stepper's back. "You said he would find out where I am. He knows. The Gray Men!" Nieda giggled, and he wondered irritably how much she re- ally knew or believed among the things she said she did not believe in.

"Sammael did not send the Gray Men." Moiraine mounted Aldieb with a cool, straight-backed precision, almost as if there were no hurry. "The Darkhound was his, however. I believe it followed my trail. He would not have sent both. Someone wants you, but I do not think Sammael even knows you exist. Yet." Perrin stopped with one foot in the stirrup, staring at her, but she seemed more concerned with patting her mare's arching neck than with the questions on his face.

"As well I went after you," Lan said, and the Aes Sedai sniffed loudly.

"I could wish you were a woman, Gaidin. I would send you to the Tower as a novice to learn to obey!" He raised an eyebrow and touched the hilt of his sword, then swung into his saddle, and she sighed. "Perhaps it is as well you are disobedient. Sometimes it is well. Besides, I do not think Sheriam and Siuan Sanche together could teach you obedi- ence."

"I do not understand," Perrin said. *I seem to be saying that a great deal, and I'm tired of it. I want some answers I can understand.* He pulled himself the rest of the way up so Moiraine would not be looking down at him; she had enough advantage without that. "If he did not send the Gray Men, who did? If a Myrddraal, or another Forsaken. . . ." He stopped to swallow. *ANOTHER Forsaken! Light!* "If some- body else sent them, why did they not tell him? They're all Darkfriends, aren't they? And why me, Moiraine? Why me? Rand is the bloody Dragon Reborn!"

He heard the gasps from Zarine and Nieda, and only then

realized what he had said. Moiraine's stare seemed to skin him like the sharpest steel. *Hasty bloody tongue. When did I stop thinking before I speak?* It seemed to him it had happened when he first felt Zarine's eyes watching him. She was watching him now, with her mouth hanging open.

"You are sealed to us, now," Moiraine told the bold-faced woman. "There is no turning back for you. Ever." Zarine looked as if she wanted to say something and was afraid to, but the Aes Sedai had already turned her attention elsewhere. "Nieda, flee Illian tonight. In this hour! And hold your tongue even better than you have held it all these years. There are those who would cut it out for what you could say, before I could even find you." Her hard tone left doubts as to exactly how she meant that, and Nieda nodded vigorously as if she had heard it both ways.

"As for you, Perrin." The white mare moved closer, and he leaned back from the Aes Sedai despite all he could do. "There are many threads woven in the Pattern, and some are as black as the Shadow itself. Take care one of them does not strangle you." Her heels touched Aldieb's flanks, and the mare darted into the rain, Mandarb following close behind.

Burn you, Moiraine, Perrin thought as he rode after them. *Sometimes I do not know which side you are on.* He glanced at Zarine, riding beside him as if she had been born in a saddle. *And whose side are you on?*

Rain kept people off the streets and canals, so no visible eyes watched them go, but it made the footing uncertain for the horses on the uneven paving stones. By the time they reached the Maredo Causeway, a wide road of packed dirt stretching north through the marsh, the downpour had begun to slacken. Thunder still boomed, but the lightning flashed far behind them, perhaps out to sea.

Perrin felt a bit of luck was coming their way. The rain had stayed long enough to hide their departure, but now it seemed they would have a clear night for riding. He said as much, but Lan shook his head.

"Darkhounds like clear, moonlit nights best, blacksmith, rain the least. A good thunderstorm can keep them away completely." As if his words had bidden it, the rain faded to a faint drizzle. Perrin heard Loial groan behind him.

Causeway and marsh ended together, some two miles

or so from the city, but the road kept on, slowly bearing a little eastward. Cloud-dark evening faded into night, and the misting rain continued. Moiraine and Lan kept a steady, ground-eating pace. The horses' hooves splashed through puddles on the hard-packed dirt. The moon shone through gaps in the clouds. Low hills began to rise around them, and trees to appear more and more often. Perrin thought there must be forest ahead, but he was not sure how he liked the idea. Woods could hide them from pursuit; woods could let pursuit come close before they saw.

A thin howl rose far behind them. For a moment he thought it was a wolf; he surprised himself by nearly reaching out to the wolf before he could stop. The cry came again, and he knew it was no wolf. Others answered it, all miles behind, eerie wails holding blood and death, cries that spoke of nightmares. To his surprise, Lan and Moiraine slowed, the Aes Sedai studying the hills around them in the night.

"They are a long way," he said. "They'll not catch us if we keep on."

"The Darkhounds?" Zarine muttered. "Those are the Darkhounds? Are you sure it isn't the Wild Hunt, Aes Sedai?"

"But it is," Moiraine replied. "It is."

"You can never outrun the Darkhounds, blacksmith," Lan said, "not on the fastest horse. Always, you must face them and defeat them, or they will pull you down."

"I could have stayed in the *stedding*, you know," Loial said. "My mother would have had me married by now, but it would not have been a bad life. Plenty of books. I did not have to come Outside."

"There," Moiraine said, pointing to a tall, treeless mound well off to their right. There were no trees that Perrin could see for two hundred paces or more around it, either, and they were still sparse beyond that. "We must see them coming to have a chance."

The Darkhounds' dire cries rose again, closer, yet still far.

Lan quickened Mandarb's pace a little, now that Moiraine had chosen their ground. As they climbed, the horses' hooves clattered on rocks half-buried in the dirt and slicked

by the drizzle. To Perrin's eyes, most of them had too many
squared corners to be natural. At the top, they dismounted
around what seemed to be a low, rounded boulder. The
moon appeared through a gap in the clouds, and he found
himself looking at a weathered stone face two paces long.
A woman's face, he thought from the length of the hair. The
rain made her seem to be weeping.

Moiraine dismounted and stood looking off in the direction of the howls. She was a shadowed, hooded shape, rain
catching moonlight as it rolled down her oiled cloak.

Loial led his horse over to peer at the carving, then bent
closer and felt the features. "I think she was an Ogier," he
said at last. "But this is not an old *stedding*; I would feel it.
We all would. And we would be safe from Shadowspawn."

"What are you two staring at?" Zarine squinted at the
rock. "What is it? Her? Who?"

"Many nations have risen and fallen since the Breaking,"
Moiraine said without turning, "some leaving no more than
names on a yellowed page, or lines on a tattered map. Will
we leave as much behind?" The blood-drenched howls rose
again, still closer. Perrin tried to calculate their pace, and
thought Lan had been right; the horses could not have outrun them, after all. They would not have long to wait.

"Ogier," Lan said, "you and the girl hold the horses." Zarine protested, but he rode straight over to her. "Your knives
will not do much good here, girl." His sword blade gleamed
in the moonlight as he drew it. "Even this is a last resort.
It sounds like ten out there, not one. Your work is to keep
the horses from running when they smell the Darkhounds.
Even Mandarb does not like that smell."

If the Warder's sword was no good, then neither was the
axe. Perrin felt something near to relief at that, even if they
were Shadowspawn; he would not have to use the axe. He
drew the length of his unstrung bow from under Stepper's
saddle girths. "Maybe this will do some good."

"Try if you wish, blacksmith," Lan said. "They do not die
easily. Perhaps you will kill one."

Perrin drew a fresh bowstring from his pouch, trying to
shield it from the soft rain. The beeswax coating was thin,
and not much protection against prolonged damp. Setting
the bow slantwise between his legs, he bent it easily, fixing

the loops of the bowstring into the horn nocks at the ends of the bow. When he straightened, he could see the Darkhounds.

They ran like horses at a gallop, and as he caught sight of them, they gathered speed. They were only ten large shapes running in the night, sweeping through the scattered trees, yet he pulled a broadhead arrow from his quiver, nocked it but did not draw. He had been far from the best bowman in Emond's Field, but among the younger men, only Rand had been better.

At three hundred paces he would shoot, he decided. *Fool! You'd have a hard time hitting a target standing still at that distance. But if I wait, the way they are moving. . . .* Stepping up beside Moiraine, he raised his bow—*I just have to imagine that moving shadow is a big dog*—drew the goose-feather fletchings to his ear, and loosed. He was sure the shaft merged with the nearest shadow, but the only result was a snarl. *It is not going to work. They're coming too fast!* He was already drawing another arrow. *Why aren't you doing something, Moiraine?* He could see their eyes, shining like silver, their teeth gleaming like burnished steel. Black as the night itself and as big as small ponies, they sped toward him, silent now, seeking the kill. The wind carried a stink near to burned sulphur; the horses whickered fearfully, even Lan's warhorse. *Burn you, Aes Sedai, do something!* He loosed again; the frontmost Darkhound faltered and came on. *They can die!* He shot once more, and the lead Darkhound tumbled, staggered to its feet, then fell, yet even as it did he knew a moment of despair. One down, and the other nine had covered two thirds of the distance already; they seemed to be running even faster, like shadows flowing across the ground. *One more arrow. Time for one more, maybe, and then it's the axe. Burn you, Aes Sedai!* He drew again.

"Now," Moiraine said as his arrow left the bow. The air between her hands caught fire and streaked toward the Darkhounds, vanquishing night. The horses squealed and leaped against being held.

Perrin threw an arm across his eyes to shield them from a white-hot glare like burning, heat like a forge cracking open; sudden noon flared in the darkness, and was gone. When he uncovered his eyes, spots flickered across his vision, and the faint, fading image of that line of fire. Where the Darkhounds had been was nothing but night-covered ground and the soft rain; the only shadows that moved were cast by clouds crossing the moon.

I thought she'd throw fire at them, or call lightning, but this. . . . "What was that?" he asked hoarsely.

Moiraine was peering off toward Illian again, as if she could see through all those miles of darkness. "Perhaps he did not see," she said, almost to herself. "It is far, and if he was not watching, perhaps he did not notice."

"Who?" Zarine demanded. "Sammael?" Her voice shook a little. "You said he was in Illian. How could he see anything here? What did you do?"

"Something forbidden," Moiraine said coolly. "Forbidden by vows almost as strong as the Three Oaths." She took Aldieb's reins from the girl, and patted the mare's neck, calming her. "Something not used in nearly two thousand years. Something I might be stilled just for knowing."

"Perhaps . . . ?" Loial's voice was a faint boom. "Perhaps we should be going? There could be more."

"I think not," the Aes Sedai said, mounting. "He would not loose two packs at once, even if he has two; they would turn on each other instead of their prey. And I think we are not his main quarry, or he would have come himself. We were . . . an annoyance, I think"—her tone was calm, but it was clear she did not like being regarded so lightly—"and perhaps a little something extra to slip into his gamebag, if we were not too much trouble. Still, there is small good in remaining any nearer him than we must."

"Rand?" Perrin asked. He could almost feel Zarine leaning forward to listen. "If we are not what he hunts, is it Rand?"

"Perhaps," Moiraine said. "Or perhaps Mat. Remember that he is *ta'veren* also, and he blew the Horn of Valere."

Zarine made a strangled sound. "He *blew* it? Someone has *found* it already?"

The Aes Sedai ignored her, leaning out of her saddle to stare closely into Perrin's eyes, dark gleaming into burnished gold. "Once again events outpace me. I do not like that. And neither should you. If events outrun me, they may well trample you, and the rest of the world with you."

"We have many leagues to Tear yet," Lan said. "The

Ogier's suggestion is a good one." He was already in his saddle.

After a moment Moiraine straightened and touched the mare's ribs with her heels. She was halfway down the side of the mound before he could get his bow unstrung and take Stepper's reins from Loial. *Burn you, Moiraine! I'll find some answers somewhere!*

Leaning back against a fallen log, Mat enjoyed the warmth of the campfire—the rains had drifted south three days earlier, but he still felt damp—yet right at that moment, he was hardly aware of the dancing flames. He peered thoughtfully at the small, wax-covered cylinder in his hand. Thom was engrossed in tuning his harp, muttering to himself of rain and wet, never glancing Mat's way. Crickets chirped in the dark thicket around them. Caught between villages by sunset, they had chosen this copse away from the road. Two nights they had tried to buy a room for the night; twice a farmer had loosed his dogs on them.

Mat unsheathed his belt knife, and hesitated. *Luck. It only explodes sometimes, she said. Luck.* As carefully as he could, he slit along the length of the tube. It *was* a tube, and of paper, as he had thought—he had found bits of paper on the ground after fireworks were set off, back home— layers of paper, but all that filled the inside was something that looked like dirt, or maybe tiny gray-black pebbles and dust. He stirred them on his palm with one finger. *How in the Light could pebbles explode?*

"The Light burn me!" Thom roared. He thrust his harp into its case as if to protect it from what was in Mat's hand. "Are you trying to kill us, boy? Haven't you ever heard those things explode ten times as hard for air as for fire? Fireworks are the next thing to Aes Sedai work, boy."

"Maybe," Mat said, "but Aludra did not look like any Aes Sedai to me. I used to think that about Master al'Vere's clock—that it had to be Aes Sedai work—but once I got the back of the cabinet open, I saw it was full of little pieces of metal." He shifted uncomfortably at the memory. Mistress al'Vere had been the first to reach him that time, with the Wisdom and his father and the Mayor all right behind her, and none believing he just meant to look. *I could have put them all back together.* "I think Perrin could make one, if he saw those little wheels and springs and I don't know what all."

"You would be surprised, boy," Thom said dryly. "Even a bad clockmaker is a fairly rich man, and they earn it. But a clock does not explode in your face!"

"Neither did this. Well, it is useless, now." He tossed the handful of paper and little pebbles into the fire to a screech from Thom; the pebbles sparked and made tiny flashes, and there was a smell of acrid smoke.

"You *are* trying to kill us." Thom's voice was unsteady, and it rose in intensity and pitch as he spoke. "If I decide I want to die, I will go to the Royal Palace when we reach Caemlyn, and I'll pinch Morgase!" His long mustaches flailed. "Do not do that again!"

"It did not explode," Mat said, frowning at the fire. He fished into the oiled-cloth roll on the other side of the log and pulled out a firework of the next larger size. "I wonder why there was no bang."

"I do not care why there was no bang! Do not do it again!"

Mat glanced at him and laughed. "Stop shaking, Thom. There's no need to be afraid. I know what is inside them, now. At least, I know what it looks like, but. . . . Don't say it. I will not be cutting any more open, Thom. It is more fun to set them off, anyway."

"I am not afraid, you mud-footed swineherd," Thom said with elaborate dignity. "I am shaking with rage because I'm traveling with a goat-brained lout who might kill the pair of us because he cannot think past his own—"

"Ho, the fire!"

Mat exchanged glances with Thom as horses' hooves approached. It was late for anyone honest to be traveling. But the Queen's Guards kept the roads safe this close to Caemlyn, and the four who rode into the firelight certainly did not look like robbers. One was a woman. The men all wore long cloaks and seemed to be her retainers, while she was pretty and blue-eyed, in gold necklace and a gray silk dress and a velvet cloak with a wide hood. The men dismounted. One held her reins and another her stirrup, and she smiled at Mat, doffing her gloves as she came near the fire.

"I fear we are caught out late, young master," she said, "and I would trouble you for directions to an inn, if you know one."

He grinned and started to rise. He had made it as far as a crouch when he heard one of the men mutter something, and another produced a crossbow from under his cloak, already drawn, with a clip holding the bolt.

"Kill him, fool!" the woman shouted, and Mat tossed the firework into the flames and threw himself toward his quarterstaff. There was a loud bang and a flash of light— "Aes Sedai!" a man cried. "Fireworks, fool!" the woman shouted—and he rolled to his feet with the staff in his hand to see the crossbow bolt sticking out of the fallen log almost where he had been sitting, and the crossbowman falling with the hilt of one of Thom's knives adorning his chest.

It was all he had time to see, for the other two men darted past the fire at him, drawing swords. One of them suddenly stumbled to his knees, dropping his sword to claw at the knife in his back as he fell facedown. The last man did not see his companion fall; he obviously expected to be one of a pair, dividing their opponent's attention, as he thrust his blade at Mat's middle. Feeling almost contemptuous, Mat cracked the fellow's wrist with one end of his staff, sending the sword flying, and cracked his forehead with the other. The man's eyes rolled up in his head as he collapsed.

From the corner of his eye, Mat saw the woman walking toward him, and he stuck a finger at her like a knife. "Fine clothes you wear for a thief, woman! You sit down till I decide what to do with you, or I'll—"

She looked as surprised as Mat at the knife that suddenly bloomed in her throat, a red flower of spreading blood. He took a half step as if to catch her as she fell, knowing it was no good. Her long cloak settled over her, covering everything but her face, and the hilt of Thom's knife.

"Burn you," Mat muttered. "Burn you, Thom Merrilin! A woman! Light, we could have tied her up, given her to the Queen's Guards tomorrow in Caemlyn. Light, I might even have let her go. She'd rob nobody without these three, and the only one that lives will be days before he can see straight and months before he can hold a sword. Burn you, Thom, there was no need to kill her!"

The gleeman limped to where the woman lay, and kicked

back her cloak. The dagger had half fallen from her hand, its blade as wide as Mat's thumb and two hands long. "Would you rather I had waited till she nested that in your ribs, boy?" He retrieved his own knife, wiping the blade on her cloak.

Mat realized he was humming "She Wore a Mask That Hid Her Face," and stopped it. He bent down and hid hers with the hood of her cloak. "Best we move on," he said quietly. "I do not want to have to explain this if a patrol of the Guards happens by."

"With her in those clothes?" Thom said. "I should say not! They must have robbed a merchant's wife, or some noblewoman's carriage." His voice became gentler. "If we're going, boy, you had best see to saddling your horse."

Mat gave a start and pulled his eyes from the dead woman. "Yes, I had better, hadn't I?" He did not look at her again.

He had no such compunction about the men. As far as he was concerned, a man who decided to rob and kill deserved what he got when he lost the game. He did not dwell on them, but neither did he jerk his eyes away if they fell on one of the robbers. It was after he had saddled his gelding and tied his things on behind, while he was kicking dirt onto the fire, that he found himself looking at the man who had shot the crossbow. There was something familiar about those features, about the way the smothering fire made shadows across them. *Luck*, he told himself. *Always the luck.*

"The crossbowman was a good swimmer, Thom," he said as he climbed into the saddle.

"What foolery are you talking, now?" The gleeman was on his horse, too, and far more concerned with how his instrument cases rode behind his saddle than he was with the dead. "How could you know whether he could even swim at all?"

"He made it ashore from a small boat in the middle of the Erinin in the middle of the night. I guess that used up all his luck." He checked the lashings on the roll of fireworks again. *If that fool thought one of these was Aes Sedai, I wonder what he'd have thought if they* all *went off.*

"Are you sure, boy? The chances of it being the same man. . . . Why, even you wouldn't lay a wager against those odds."

"I am sure, Thom." *Elayne, I will wring your neck when I put my hands on you. And Egwene's and Nynaeve's, too.* "And I am sure I intend to have this bloody letter out of my hands an hour after we reach Caemlyn."

"I tell you, there is nothing in that letter, boy. I played *Daes Dae'mar* when I was younger than you, and I can recognize a code or a cipher even when I don't know what it says."

"Well, I never played your Great Game, Thom, your bloody Game of Houses, but I know when someone is chasing me, and they'd not be chasing this hard or this far for the gold in my pockets, not for less than a chest full of gold. It has to be the letter." *Burn me, pretty girls always get me in trouble.* "Do you feel like sleeping tonight, after this?"

"With the sleep of an innocent babe, boy. But if you want to ride, I'll ride."

The face of a pretty woman floated into Mat's head, with a dagger in her throat. *You had no luck, pretty woman.* "Then let's ride!" he said savagely.

CHAPTER
45

Caemlyn

Mat had vague memories of Caemlyn, but when they approached it in the early hours after sunrise, it seemed as if he had never been there before. They had not been alone on the road since first light, and other riders surrounded them now, and trains of merchants' wagons and folk afoot, all streaming toward the great city.

Built on rising hills, it was surely as large as Tar Valon, and outside the huge walls—a fifty-foot height of pale, grayish stone streaked with white and silver sparkling in the sun, spaced with tall, round towers with the Lion Banner of Andor waving atop them, white on red—outside those walls, it seemed as if another great city had been placed, wrapping around the walled city, all red brick and gray stone and white plastered walls, inns pushed in on houses of three and four stories so fine they must belong to wealthy merchants, shops with goods displayed on tables under awnings crowding against wide, windowless warehouses. Open markets under red and purple roof tiles lined the road on both sides, men and women already crying their wares, bargaining at the top of their voices, while penned calves and sheep and goats and pigs, caged geese and chickens and ducks, added to the din. He seemed to remember thinking Caemlyn was too noisy when he was here before; now it sounded like a heartbeat, pumping wealth.

The road led to arched gates twenty feet high, standing open under the watchful eye of red-coated Queen's Guards in their shining breastplates—they eyed Thom and him no more than anyone else, not even the quarterstaff slanted across his saddle in front of him; all they cared was that people keep moving, it seemed—and then they were within. Slender towers here rose even taller than those along the walls, and gleaming domes shone white and gold above streets teeming with people. Just inside the gates the road split into two parallel streets, separated by a wide strip of grass and trees. The hills of the city rose like steps toward a peak, which was surrounded by another wall, shining as white as Tar Valon's, with still more domes and towers within. That was the Inner City, Mat recalled, and atop those highest hills stood the Royal Palace.

"No point waiting," he told Thom. "I'll take the letter straight on." He looked at the sedan chairs and carriages making their way through the crowds, the shops with all their goods displayed. "A man could earn some gold in this city, Thom, once he found a game of dice, or cards." He was not quite so lucky at cards as at dice, but few except nobles and the wealthy played those games anyway. *Now that's who I should find a game with.*

Thom yawned at him and hitched at his gleeman's cloak as if it were a blanket. "We have ridden all night, boy. Let's at least find something to eat, first. The Queen's Blessing has good meals." He yawned again. "And good beds."

"I remember that," Mat said slowly. He did, in a way. The innkeeper was a fat man with graying hair, Master Gill. Moiraine had caught up to Rand and him there, when he had thought they were finally free of her. *She's off playing her game with Rand, now. Nothing to do with me. Not anymore.* "I will meet you there, Thom. I said I'd have this letter out of my hands an hour after I arrived, and I mean to. You go on."

Thom nodded and turned his horse aside, calling over his shoulder through a yawn. "Do not become lost, boy. It's a big city, Caemlyn."

And a rich one. Mat heeled his mount on up the crowded street. *Lost! I can find my bloody way.* The sickness appeared to have erased parts of his memory. He could look at an inn, its upper floors sticking out over the ground floor all the way around and its sign creaking in the breeze, and remember seeing it before, yet not recall another thing he could see from that spot. A hundred paces of street might abruptly spark in his memory, while the parts before and after remained as mysterious as dice still in the cup.

Even with the holes in his memory he was sure he had

never been to the Inner City or the Royal Palace—*I couldn't forget that!*—yet he did not need to remember the way. The streets of the New City—he remembered that name suddenly; it was the part of Caemlyn less than two thousand years old—ran every which way, but the main boulevards all led to the Inner City. The Guards at the gates made no effort to stop anyone.

Within those white walls were buildings that could almost have fit in Tar Valon. The curving streets topped hills to reveal thin towers, their tiled walls sparkling with a hundred colors in the sunlight, or to look down on parks laid out in patterns made to be viewed from above, or to show sweeping vistas across the entire city to the rolling plains and forests beyond. It did not really matter which streets he took here. They all spiraled in on what he sought, the Royal Palace of Andor.

In no time, he found himself crossing the huge oval plaza before the Palace, riding toward its tall, gilded gates. The pure white Palace of Andor would certainly not have been out of place among Tar Valon's wonders, with its slender towers and golden domes shining in the sun, its high balconies and intricate stonework. The gold leaf on one of those domes could have kept him in luxury for a year.

There were fewer people in the plaza than elsewhere, as if it were reserved for great occasions. A dozen of the Guards stood before the closed gates, bows slanted, all at exactly the same angle, across their gleaming breastplates, faces hidden by the steel bars of their burnished helmets' faceguards. A heavyset officer, with his red cloak thrown back to reveal a knot of gold braid on his shoulder, was walking up and down the line, eyeing each man as if he thought he might find rust or dust.

Mat drew rein and put on a smile. "Good morning to you, Captain."

The officer turned, staring at him through the bars of his face-guard with deep, beady eyes, like a pudgy rat in a cage. The man was older than he had expected—surely old enough to have more than one knot of rank—and fat rather than stocky. "What do you want, farmer?" he demanded roughly.

Mat drew a breath. *Make it good. Impress this fool so he doesn't keep me waiting all day. I don't want to have to flash the Amyrlin's paper around to keep from kicking my heels.* "I come from Tar Valon, from the White Tower, bearing a letter from—"

"*You* come from Tar Valon, farmer?" The fat officer's stomach shook as he laughed, but then his laughter cut off as if severed with a knife, and he glared. "We want no letters from Tar Valon, rogue, *if* you have such a thing! Our good Queen—may the Light illumine her!—will take no word from the White Tower until the Daughter-Heir is returned to her. I never heard of any messenger from the Tower wearing a countryman's coat and breeches. It is plain to me you are up to some trick, perhaps thinking you'll find a few coins if you come claiming to carry letters, but you will be lucky if you don't end in a prison cell! If you do come from Tar Valon, go back and tell the Tower to return the Daughter-Heir before we come and take her! If you're a trickster after silver, get out of my sight before I have you beaten within an inch of your life! Either way, you half-wit looby, be gone!"

Mat had been trying to edge a word in from the beginning of the man's speech. He said quickly, "The letter is from her, man. It is from—"

"Did I not tell you to be gone, ruffian?" the fat man bellowed. His face was growing nearly as red as his coat. "Take yourself out of my sight, you gutter scum! If you are not gone by the time I count ten, I will arrest you for littering the plaza with your presence! One! Two!"

"Can you count so high, you fat fool?" Mat snapped. "I tell you, Elayne sent—"

"Guards!" The officer's face was purple now. "Seize this man for a Darkfriend!"

Mat hesitated a moment, sure no one could take such a charge seriously, but the red-coated Guards dashed toward him, all dozen men in breastplates and helmets, and he wheeled his horse and galloped ahead of them, followed by the fat man's shouts. The gelding was no racer, but it outdistanced men afoot easily enough. People dodged out of his way along the curving streets, shaking fists after him and shouting as many curses as the officer had.

Fool, he thought, meaning the fat officer, then added another for himself. *All I had to do was say her bloody name in the beginning. "Elayne, the Daughter-Heir of Andor, sends this letter to her mother, Queen Morgase." Light, who could have thought they'd think that way about Tar Valon.* From what he remembered of his last visit, Aes Sedai and the White Tower had been close behind Queen Morgase in the Guards' affections. *Burn her, Elayne could have told me.* Reluctantly, he added, *I could have asked questions, too.*

Before he reached the arched gates that let out into the New City, he slowed to a walk. He did not think the Guards from the Palace could still be chasing him, and there was no point in attracting the eyes of those at the gate by galloping through, but they looked at him no more now than when he had first entered.

As he rode under the broad arch, he smiled and almost turned back. He had suddenly remembered something, and had an idea that appealed to him a good deal more than walking through the Palace gates. Even if that fat officer had not been watching the gates, he thought he would like it better.

He became lost twice while searching for The Queen's Blessing, but at last he found the sign with a man kneeling before a woman with red-gold hair and a crown of golden roses, her hand on his head. It was a broad stone building of three stories, with tall windows even up under the red roof tiles. He rode around back to the stableyard, where a horse-faced fellow, in a leather vest that could hardly be any tougher than his skin, took his horse's reins. He thought he remembered the fellow. *Yes. Ramey.*

"It has been a long time, Ramey." Mat tossed him a silver mark. "You remember me, don't you?"

"Can't say as I . . ." Ramey began, then caught the shine of silver where he had expected copper; he coughed, and his short nod turned into something that combined a knuckled forehead with a jerky bow. "Why, of course I do, young master. Forgive me. Slipped my mind. Mind no good for people. Good for horses. I know horses, I do. A fine animal, young master. I'll take good care of him, you can be sure." He delivered it all quickly, with no room for Mat to say a word, then hurried the gelding into the stable before he might have to come up with Mat's name.

With a sour grimace, Mat put the fat roll of fireworks under his arm and shouldered the rest of his belongings. *Fellow couldn't tell me from Hawkwing's toenails.* A bulky, muscular man was sitting on an upturned barrel beside the door to the kitchen, gently scratching the ear of a black-and-white cat crouched on his knee. The man studied Mat with heavy-lidded eyes, especially the quarterstaff across his shoulder, but he never stopped his scratching. Mat thought he remembered him, but he could not bring up a name. He said nothing as he went through the door, and neither did the man. *No reason they should remember me. Probably have bloody Aes Sedai coming for people every day.*

In the kitchen, two undercooks and three scullions were darting between stoves and roasting spits under the direction of a round woman with her hair in a bun and a long wooden spoon that she used to point out what she wanted done. Mat was sure he remembered the round woman. *Coline, and what a name for a woman that wide, but everybody called her Cook.*

"Well, Cook," he announced, "I am back, and not a year since I left."

She peered at him a moment, then nodded. "I remember you." He began to grin. "You were with that young prince, weren't you?" she went on. "The one who looked so like Tigraine, the Light illumine her memory. You're his serving man, aren't you? Is he coming back, then, the young prince?"

"No," he said curtly. *A prince! Light!* "I do not think he will be anytime soon, and I don't think you would like it if he did." She protested, saying what a fine, handsome young man the prince was—*Burn me, is there a woman anywhere who doesn't moon over Rand and make calf-eyes if you mention his bloody name? She'd bloody scream if she knew what he is doing now*—but he refused to let her get it out. "Is Master Gill about? And Thom Merrilin?"

"In the library," she said with a tight sniff. "You tell Basel Gill when you see him that I said those drains need cleaning. Today, mind." She caught sight of something one of the undercooks was doing to a beef roast and waddled over to her. "Not so much, child. You will make the meat too sweet if you put so much arrath on it." She seemed to have forgotten Mat already.

He shook his head as he went in search of this library he could not remember. He could not remember that Coline was married to Master Gill, either, but if he had ever heard a goodwife send instructions to her husband, that had been it. A pretty serving girl with big eyes giggled and directed him down a hall beside the common room.

When he stepped into the library, he stopped and stared. There had to be more than three hundred books on the shelves built on the walls, and more lying on the tables; he had never seen so many books in one place in his life. He noticed a leather-bound copy of *The Travels of Jain Farstrider* on a table near the door. He had always meant to read that—Rand and Perrin had always been telling him things out of it—but he never did seem to get around to reading the books he meant to read.

Pink-faced Basel Gill and Thom Merrilin were seated at one of the tables, facing each other across a stones board, pipes in their teeth trailing thin blue streamers of tabac smoke. A calico cat sat on the table beside a wooden dice cup, her tail curled over her feet, watching them play. The gleeman's cloak was nowhere in sight, so Mat supposed he had already gotten a room.

"You're done sooner than I expected, boy," Thom said around his pipestem. He tugged one long, white mustache as he considered where to place his next stone on the board's cross-hatchings. "Basel, you remember Mat Cauthon."

"I remember," the fat innkeeper said, peering at the board. "Sickly, the last time you were here, I recall. I hope you are better now, lad."

"I am better," Mat said. "Is that all you remember? That I was sick?"

Master Gill winced at Thom's move and took his pipe out of his mouth. "Considering who you left with, lad, and considering the way things are now, maybe it's best I remember no more than that."

"Aes Sedai not in such good odor now, are they?" Mat set his things in one big armchair, the quarterstaff propped against the back, and himself in another with one leg swinging over the arm. "The Guards at the Palace seemed to think the White Tower had stolen Elayne." Thom eyed the roll of fireworks uneasily, looked at his smoking pipe, and muttered to himself before going back to his study of the board.

"Hardly that," Gill said, "but the whole city knows she disappeared from the Tower. Thom says she's returned, but we've heard none of that here. Perhaps Morgase knows, but everyone down to a stableboy is stepping lightly so she doesn't snap off his head. Lord Gaebril has kept her from actually sending anyone to the headsman, but I'd not say she would not do it. And he has certainly not soothed her temper toward Tar Valon. If anything, I think he has made it worse."

"Morgase has a new advisor," Thom said in a dry voice. "Gareth Bryne did not like him, so Bryne has been retired to his estate to watch his sheep grow wool. Basel, are you going to place a stone or not?"

"In a moment, Thom. In a moment. I want to set it right." Gill clamped his teeth around his pipestem and frowned at the board, puffing up smoke.

"So the Queen has an advisor who doesn't like Tar Valon," Mat said. "Well, that explains the way the Guards acted when I said I came from there."

"If you told them that," Gill said, "you might be lucky you escaped without any broken bones. If it was any of the new men, at least. Gaebril has replaced half the Guards in Caemlyn with men of his choosing, and that is no mean feat considering how short a time he has been here. Some say Morgase may marry him." He started to put a stone on the board, then took it back with a shake of his head. "Times change. People change. Too much change for me. I suppose I am growing old."

"You seem to mean us both to grow old before you place a stone," Thom muttered. The cat stretched and slinked across the table for him to stroke her back. "Talking all day will not let you find a good move. Why don't you just admit defeat, Basel?"

"I never admit defeat," Gill said stoutly. "I'll beat you yet, Thom." He set a white stone on the intersection of two lines. "You will see." Thom snorted.

From what Mat could see of the board, he did not think Gill had much chance. "I will just have to avoid the Guards and put Elayne's letter right into Morgase's hands." *Especially if they're all like that fat fool. Light, I wonder if he's told them all I'm a Darkfriend?*

"You did not deliver it?" Thom barked. "I thought you were anxious to be rid of the thing."

"You have a letter from the Daughter-Heir?" Gill exclaimed. "Thom, why did you not tell me?"

"I am sorry, Basel," the gleeman muttered. He glared at Mat from under those bushy eyebrows and blew out his mustaches. "The boy thinks someone is out to kill him over it, so I thought I'd let him say what he wanted and no more. Seems he does not care any longer."

"What kind of letter?" Gill asked. "Is she coming home? And Lord Gawyn? I hope they are. I've actually heard talk of war with Tar Valon, as if anyone could be fool enough to go to war with Aes Sedai. If you ask me, it is all one with those mad rumors we've heard about Aes Sedai supporting a false Dragon somewhere in the west, and using the Power as a weapon. Not that I can see why that would make anyone want to go to war with them; just the opposite."

"Are you married to Coline?" Mat asked, and Master Gill gave a start.

"The Light preserve me from that! You would think the inn was hers now. If she was my wife . . . ! What does that have to do with the Daughter-Heir's letter?"

"Nothing," Mat said, "but you went on so long, I thought you must have forgotten your own questions." Gill made a choking sound, and Thom barked a laugh. Mat hurried on before the innkeeper could speak. "The letter is sealed; Elayne did not tell me what it says." Thom was eyeing him sideways and stroking his mustaches. *Does he think I'll admit we opened the thing?* "But I don't think she is coming home. She means to be Aes Sedai, if you ask me." He told them about his attempt to deliver the letter, smoothing over a few edges they had no need to know about.

"The new men," Gill said. "That officer sounds it, at least. I'll wager on it. No better than brigands, most of them, except the ones with a sly eye. You wait until this afternoon, lad, when the Guards on the gate will have changed. Say the Daughter-Heir's name right out, and just in case the new fellow is one of Gaebril's men, too, duck your head a little. A knuckle to your forehead, and you'll have no trouble."

"Burn me if I will. I pull wool and scratch gravel for nobody. Not to Morgase herself. This time, I'll not go near the Guards at all." *I would just as soon not know what word that fat fellow has spread.* They stared at him as if he were mad.

"How under the Light," Gill said, "do you mean to enter the Royal Palace without passing the Guards?" His eyes widened as if he were remembering something. "Light, you don't mean to. . . . Lad, you'd need the Dark One's own luck to escape with your life!"

"What are you going on about now, Basel? Mat, what fool thing do you intend to try?"

"I am lucky, Master Gill," Mat said. "You just have a good meal waiting when I come back." As he stood, he picked up the dice cup and spun the dice out beside the stones board for luck. The calico cat leaped down, hissing at him with her back arched. The five spotted dice came to rest, each showing a single pip. *The Dark One's Eyes.*

"That's the best toss or the worst," Gill said. "It depends on the game you are playing, doesn't it. Lad, I think you mean to play a dangerous game. Why don't you take that cup out into the common room and lose a few coppers? You look to me like a fellow who might like a little gamble. I will see the letter gets to the Palace safely."

"Coline wants you to clean the drains," Mat told him, and turned to Thom while the innkeeper was still blinking and muttering to himself. "It doesn't seem to make any odds whether I get an arrow in me trying to deliver that letter or a knife in my back waiting. It's six up, and a half dozen down. Just you have that meal waiting, Thom." He tossed a gold mark on the table in front of Gill. "Have my things put in a room, innkeeper. If it takes more coin, you will have it. Be careful of the big roll; it frightens Thom something awful."

As he stalked out, he heard Gill say to Thom, "I always thought that lad was a rascal. How does he come by gold?"

I always win, that's how, he thought grimly. *I just have to win once more, and I'm done with Elayne, and that's the last of the White Tower for me. Just once more.*

CHAPTER
46

A Message Out of the Shadow

Even as he returned to the Inner City on foot, Mat was far from certain that what he intended would actually work. It would, if what he had been told was true, but it was the truth of that he was not sure of. He avoided the oval plaza in front of the Palace, but wandered around the sides of the huge structure and its grounds, along streets that curved with the contours of the hills. The golden domes of the Palace glittered, mockingly out of reach. He had made his way almost all the way around, nearly back to the plaza, when he saw it. A steep slope thick with low flowers, rising from the street to a white wall of rough stone. Several leafy tree limbs stuck over the top of the wall, and he could see the tops of others beyond, in a garden of the Royal Palace.

A wall made to look like a cliff, he thought, *and a garden on the other side. Maybe Rand was telling the truth.*

A casual look both ways showed him he had the curving street to himself for the moment. He would have to hurry; the curves did not allow him to see very far; someone could come along any moment. He scrambled up the slope on all fours, careless of how his boots ripped holes in the banks of red and white blossoms. The rough stone of the wall gave plenty of fingerholds, and ridges and knobs provided toeholds even for a man in boots.

Careless of them to make it so easy, he thought as he climbed. For a moment the climbing took him back home with Rand and Perrin, to a journey they had made beyond the Sand Hills, into the edge of the Mountains of Mist. When they returned to Emond's Field, they had all caught

the fury from everyone who could lay hands on them—him
worst of all; everyone assumed it had been his idea—but for
three days they had climbed the cliffs, and slept under the
sky, and eaten eggs filched from redcrests' nests, and plump,
gray-winged grouse fetched with an arrow, or a stone from
a sling, and rabbits caught with snares, all the while laughing about how they were not afraid of the mountains' bad
luck and how they might find a treasure. He had brought
home an odd rock from that expedition, with the skull of a
good-sized fish somehow pressed into it, and a long, white
tail feather dropped by a snow eagle, and a piece of white
stone as big as his hand that looked almost as if it had been
carved into a man's ear. He thought it looked like an ear,
even if Rand and Perrin did not, and Tam al'Thor had said
it might be.

His fingers slipped out of a shallow groove, his balance
shifted and he lost the toehold under his left foot. With a
gasp, he barely caught hold of the top of the wall, and pulled
himself up the rest of the way. For a moment he lay there,
breathing hard. It would not have been that long a fall, but
enough to break his head. *Fool, letting my mind wander
like that. Nearly killed myself on those cliffs that way. That
was all a long time ago.* His mother had likely thrown all
those things out already, anyway. With one last look each
way to make sure no one had seen him—the curving length
of street below was still empty—he dropped inside the Palace grounds.

It was a large garden, with flagstoned walks through ex-
panses of grass among the trees, and grapevines thick on
arbors over the walks. And everywhere, flowers. White
blossoms covering the pear trees, and white and pink dot-
ting the apple trees. Roses in every color, and bright golden
sunburst, and purple Emond's Glory, and many he could
not identify. Some he was not sure could be real. One had
odd blossoms in scarlet and gold that looked almost like
birds, and another seemed no different from a sunflower except that its yellow flowers were two feet and more across
and stood on stalks as tall as an Ogier.

Boots crunched on flagstone, and he crouched low behind a bush against the wall as two guardsmen marched
past, their long, white collars hanging over their breastplates. They never glanced his way, and he grinned to him-

self. *Luck. With just a little luck, they'll never see me till I hand the bloody thing to Morgase.*

He slipped through the garden like a shadow, as if stalking rabbits, freezing by a bush or hard against a tree trunk when he heard boots. Two more pairs of soldiers strode by along the paths, the second close enough for him to have taken two steps and goosed them. As they vanished among the flowers and trees, he plucked a deep red starblaze and stuck the wavy-petaled flower in his hair with a grin. This was as much fun as stealing applecakes at Sunday, and easier. Women always kept a sharp watch on their baking; the fool soldiers never took their eyes off the flagstones.

It was not long before he found himself against the white wall of the Palace itself, and began sliding along it behind a row of flowering white roses on slatted frames, searching for a door. There were plenty of wide, arched windows just over his head, but he thought it might be a bit harder to explain being found climbing in through a window than walking down a hall. Two more soldiers appeared, and he froze; they would pass within three paces of him. He could hear voices from the window over his head, two men, just loud enough for him to make out the words.

"—on their way to Tear, Great Master." The man sounded frightened and obsequious.

"Let them ruin his plans, if they can." This voice was deeper and stronger, a man used to command. "It will serve him right if three untrained girls can foil him. He was always a fool, and he is still a fool. Is there any word of the boy? He is the one who can destroy us all."

"No, Great Master. He has vanished. But, Great Master, one of the girls is Morgase's nit."

Mat half turned, then caught himself. The soldiers were coming closer; they did not appear to have seen his start through the thickly woven rose stems. *Move, you fools! Get by so I can see who this man bloody is!* He had lost some of the conversation.

"—has been far too impatient since regaining his freedom," the deep voice was saying. "He never realized the best plans take time to mature. He wants the world in a day, and *Callandor* besides. The Great Lord take him! He may seize the girl and try to make some use of her. And that might strain my own plans."

"As you say, Great Master. Shall I order her brought out of Tear?"

"No. The fool would take it as a move against him, if he knew. And who can say what he chooses to watch aside from the sword? See that she dies quietly, Comar. Let her death attract no notice at all." His laughter was a rich rumble. "Those ignorant slatterns in their Tower will have a difficult time producing her after this disappearance. This may all be just as well. Let it be done quickly. Quickly, before he has time to take her himself."

The two soldiers were almost abreast of him; Mat tried to will their feet to move faster.

"Great Master," the other man said uncertainly, "that may be difficult. We know she is on her way to Tear, but the vessel she traveled on was found at Aringill, and all three of them had left it earlier. We do not know whether she has taken another ship, or is riding south. And it may not be easy to find her once she reaches Tear, Great Master. Perhaps if you—"

"Are there none but fools in the world, now?" the deep voice said harshly. "Do you think I could move in Tear without him knowing? I do not mean to fight him, not now, not yet. Bring me the girl's head, Comar. Bring me all three heads, or you will pray for me to take yours!"

"Yes, Great Master. It shall be as you say. Yes. Yes."

The soldiers crunched past, never looking to either side. Mat only waited for their backs to pass before leaping up to catch the broad stone windowsill and pull himself high enough to see through the window.

He barely noticed the fringed Tarabon carpet on the floor, worth a fat purse of silver. One of the broad, carved doors was swinging shut. A tall man, with wide shoulders and a deep chest straining the green silk of his silver-embroidered coat, was staring at the door with dark blue eyes. His black beard was close cut, with a streak of white over his chin. All in all, he looked a hard man, and one used to giving orders.

"Yes, Great Master," he said suddenly, and Mat almost lost his grip on the sill. He had thought this must be the man with the deep voice, but it was the cringing voice he heard. Not cringing now, but still the same. "It shall be as you say, Great Master," the man said bitterly. "I will cut the three wenches' heads off myself. As soon as I can find them!" He strode through the door, and Mat let himself back down.

For a moment he crouched there behind the rose frames. Someone in the Palace wanted Elayne dead, and had thrown in Egwene and Nynaeve as afterthoughts. *What under the Light are they doing, going to Tear?* It had to be them.

He pulled the Daughter-Heir's letter out of the lining of his coat and frowned at it. Maybe, with this in his hand, Morgase would believe him. He could describe one of the men. But the time for skulking was past; the big fellow could be off to Tear before he even found Morgase, and whatever she did then, there was no guarantee it could stop him.

Taking a deep breath, Mat wiggled between two of the rose frames at the cost of only a few pricks and snags from the thorns, and started down the flagstone path after the soldiers. He held Elayne's letter out in front of him so the golden lily seal was plainly visible, and went over in his mind exactly what he meant to say. When he had been sneaking about, guardsmen kept popping up like mushrooms after rain, but now he walked almost the length of the garden without seeing even one. He passed several doors. It would not be so good to enter the Palace without permission—the Guards might do nasty things first and listen after—but he was beginning to think about going through a door when it opened and a helmetless young officer with one golden knot on his shoulder strode out.

The man's hand immediately went to his sword hilt, and he had a foot of steel bared before Mat could push the letter toward him. "Elayne, the Daughter-Heir, sends this letter to her mother, Queen Morgase, Captain." He held the letter so the lily seal was prominent.

The officer's dark eyes flickered to either side, as if searching for other people, without really ever leaving Mat. "How did you come into this garden?" He did not draw his sword further, but he did not sheath it, either. "Elber is on the main gates. He's a fool, but he would never let anyone wander loose into the Palace."

"A fat man with eyes like a rat?" Mat cursed his tongue, but the officer gave a sharp nod; he almost smiled, too, but it did not seem to lessen his vigilance, or his suspicion. "He grew angry when he learned I had come from Tar Valon, and he wouldn't even give me a chance to show the letter or mention the Daughter-Heir's name. He said he would arrest me if I did not go, so I climbed the wall. I promised I would deliver this to Queen Morgase herself, you see, Captain. I promised it, and I always keep my promises. You see the seal?"

"That bloody garden wall again," the officer muttered. "It should be built three times high." He eyed Mat. "Guardsman-lieutenant, not captain. I am Guardsman-lieutenant Tallanvor. I recognize the Daughter-Heir's seal." His sword finally slid all the way back into the sheath. He stretched out a hand; not his sword hand. "Give me the letter, and I will take it to the Queen. After I show you out. Some would not be so gentle at finding you walking about loose."

"I promised to put it in her hands myself," Mat said. *Light, I never thought they might not let me give it to her.* "I did promise. To the Daughter-Heir."

Mat hardly realized Tallanvor's hand was moving before the officer's sword was resting against his neck. "I will take you to the Queen, countryman," Tallanvor said softly. "But know that I can take your head before you blink if you so much as think of harming her."

Mat put on his best grin. That slightly curved blade felt sharp on the side of his neck. "I am a loyal Andorman," he said, "and a faithful subject of the Queen, the Light illumine her. Why, if I had been here during the winter, I'd have followed Lord Gaebril for sure."

Tallanvor gave him a tight-mouthed stare, then finally took his sword away. Mat swallowed and stopped himself from touching his throat to see if he had been cut.

"Take the flower out of your hair," Tallanvor said as he sheathed his blade. "Do you think you came here courting?"

Mat snatched the starblaze blossom out of his hair and followed the officer. *Bloody fool, putting a flower in my hair. I have to stop playing the fool, now.*

It was not so much following, really, for Tallanvor kept an eye on him even while he led the way. The result was an odd sort of procession, with the officer to one side of him and ahead, but half turned in case Mat tried anything. For his part, Mat attempted to look as innocent as a babe splashing in his bathwater.

The colorful tapestries on the walls had earned their weavers silver, and so had the rugs on the white tile floors, even here in the halls. Gold and silver stood everywhere, plates and platters, bowls and cups, on chests and low cabinets of polished wood, as fine as anything he had seen in the Tower. Servants darted everywhere, in red livery with white collars and cuffs and the White Lion of Andor on their breasts. He found himself wondering if Morgase played at dice. *Wool-headed thought. Queens don't toss dice. But when I give her this letter and tell her somebody in her Palace means to kill Elayne, I'll wager she gives me a fat purse.* He indulged himself in a small fancy of being made a lord; surely the man who revealed a plot to murder the Daughter-Heir could expect some such reward.

Tallanvor led him down so many corridors and across so many courtyards that he was beginning to wonder if he could find his way out again without help, when suddenly one of the courts had more than servants in it. A columned walk surrounded the court, with a round pool in the middle with white and yellow fish swimming beneath lily pads and floating white water lilies. Men in colorful coats embroidered in gold or silver, women with wide dresses worked even more elaborately, stood attendance on a woman with red-gold hair who sat on the raised rim of the pool, trailing her fingers in the water and staring sadly at the fish that rose to her fingertips in hopes of food. A Great Serpent ring encircled the third finger of her left hand. A tall, dark man stood at her shoulder, the red silk of his coat almost hidden by the gold leaves and scrolls worked on it, but it was the woman who held Mat's eye.

He did not need the wreath of finely made golden roses in her hair, or the stole hanging over her dress of white slashed with red, the red length of the stole embroidered with the Lions of Andor, to know he was looking at Morgase, by the Grace of the Light, Queen of Andor, Defender of the Realm, Protector of the People, High Seat of House Trakand. She had Elayne's face and beauty, but it was what Elayne would have when she had ripened. Every other woman in the courtyard faded into the background by her very presence.

I'd dance a jig with her, and steal a kiss in the moonlight, too, no matter how old she is. He shook himself. *Remember exactly who she is!*

Tallanvor went to one knee, a fist pressed to the white stone of the courtyard. "My Queen, I bring a messenger who bears a letter from the Lady Elayne."

Mat eyed the man's posture, then contented himself with a deep bow. "From the Daughter-Heir . . . uh . . . my Queen." He held out the letter as he bowed, so the golden yellow wax of the seal was visible. *Once she reads it, and knows Elayne is all right, I will tell her.* Morgase turned her deep blue eyes on him. *Light! As soon as she's in a good mood.*

"You bring a letter from my scapegrace child?" Her voice was cold, but with an edge that spoke of heat ready to rise. "That must mean she is alive, at least! Where is she?"

"In Tar Valon, my Queen," he managed to get out. *Light, wouldn't I like to see a staring match between her and the Amyrlin.* On second thought, he decided he would rather not. "At least, she was when I left."

Morgase waved a hand impatiently, and Tallanvor rose to take the letter from Mat and hand it to her. For a moment she frowned at the lily seal, then broke it with a sharp twist of her wrists. She murmured to herself as she read, shaking her head at every other line. "She can say no more, can she?" she muttered. "We shall see whether she holds to that. . . ." Abruptly her face brightened. "Gaebril, she has been raised to the Accepted. Less than a year in the Tower, and raised already." The smile went as suddenly as it had come, and her mouth tightened. "When I put my hands on the wretched child, she will wish she were still a novice."

Light, Mat thought, *will nothing put her in a good mood?* He decided he was just going to have to say it out, but he wished she did not look as if she meant to cut someone's head off. "My Queen, by chance I overheard—"

"Be silent, boy," the dark man in the gold-encrusted coat said calmly. He was a handsome man, almost as good-looking as Galad and nearly as youthful-seeming, despite the white streaking his temples, but built on a bigger scale, with more than Rand's height and very nearly Perrin's shoulders. "We will hear what you have to say in a moment." He reached over Morgase's shoulder and plucked the letter out of her hand. Her glare turned on him—Mat could see her temper heating—but the dark man laid a strong hand on her shoulder, never taking his eyes off what he was reading, and Morgase's anger melted. "It seems she has left the Tower again," he said. "On the service of the Amyrlin Seat. The woman oversteps herself again, Morgase."

Mat had no trouble holding his tongue. *Luck.* It was stuck to the roof of his mouth. *Sometimes I don't know if it's good or bad.* The dark man was the owner of the deep voice, the "Great Master" who wanted Elayne's head. *She called him Gaebril. Her advisor wants to murder Elayne? Light!* And Morgase was staring up at him like an adoring dog with her master's hand on her shoulder.

Gaebril turned nearly black eyes on Mat. The man had a forceful gaze, and a look of knowing. "What can you tell us of this, boy?"

"Nothing ... uh ... my Lord." Mat cleared his throat; the man's stare was worse than the Amyrlin's. "I went to Tar Valon to see my sister. She's a novice. Else Grinwell. I'm Thom Grinwell, my Lord. The Lady Elayne learned I was meaning to see Caemlyn on my way back home—I'm from Comfrey, my Lord; a little village north of Baerlon; I'd never seen any place bigger than Baerlon before I went to Tar Valon—and she—the Lady Elayne, I mean—gave me that letter to bring." He thought Morgase had glanced at him when he said he came from north of Baerlon, but he knew there was a village called Comfrey there; he remembered hearing it mentioned.

Gaebril nodded, but he said, "Do you know where Elayne was going, boy? Or on what business? Speak the truth, and you have nothing to fear. Lie, and you will be put to the question."

Mat did not have to pretend a worried frown. "My Lord, I only saw the Daughter-Heir the once. She gave me the letter—and a gold mark!—and told me to bring it to the Queen. I know no more of what is in it than I've heard here." Gaebril appeared to consider it, with no sign on that dark face of whether he believed a word or not.

"No, Gaebril," Morgase said suddenly. "Too many have been put to the question. I can see the need as you have shown it to me, but not for this. Not a boy who only brought a letter whose contents he does not know."

"As my Queen commands, so shall it be," the dark man said. The tone was respectful, but he touched her cheek in a way that made color come to her face and her lips part as if she expected a kiss.

Morgase drew an unsteady breath. "Tell me, Thom Grinwell, did my daughter look well when you saw her?"

"Yes, my Queen. She smiled, and laughed, and showed a saucy tongue—I mean. . . ."

Morgase laughed softly at the look on his face. "Do not be afraid, young man. Elayne does have a saucy tongue, far too often for her own good. I am happy she is well." Those blue eyes studied him deeply. "A young man who has left his small village often finds it difficult to return to it. I think you will travel far before you see Comfrey again. Perhaps you will even return to Tar Valon. If you do, and if you see my daughter, tell her that what is said in anger is often repented. I will not remove her from the White Tower before time. Tell her that I often think of my own time there, and miss the quiet talks with Sheriam in her study. Tell her that I said that, Thom Grinwell."

Mat shrugged uncomfortably. "Yes, my Queen. But . . . uh . . . I do not mean to go to Tar Valon again. Once in any man's life is enough. My da needs me to help work the farm. My sisters will be stuck with the milking, with me gone."

Gaebril laughed, a deep rumble of amusement. "Are you anxious then to milk cows, boy? Perhaps you should see something of the world before it changes. Here!" He produced a purse and tossed it; Mat felt coins through the wash-leather when he caught it. "If Elayne can give you a gold mark for carrying her letter, I will give you ten for bringing it safely. See the world before you go back to your cows."

"Yes, my Lord." Mat lifted the purse and managed a weak grin. "Thank you, my Lord."

But the dark man had already waved him away and turned to Morgase with his fists on his hips. "I think the time has come, Morgase, to lance that festering sore on the border of Andor. By your marriage to Taringail Damodred, you have a claim to the Sun Throne. The Queen's Guards can make that claim as strong as any. Perhaps I can even aid them, in some small way. Hear me."

Tallanvor touched Mat on the arm, and they backed away, bowing. Mat did not think anyone noticed. Gaebril was still speaking, and every lord and lady seemed to hang on his words. Morgase was frowning as she listened, yet she nodded as much as any other.

CHAPTER
47

To Race the Shadow

From the small courtyard with its pool of fish, Tallanvor led Mat swiftly to the great court at the front of the Palace, behind the tall, gilded gates gleaming in the sun. It would be midday, soon. Mat felt an urge to be gone, a need to hurry. It was hard keeping his pace to the young officer's. Someone might wonder, if he started running, and maybe—just maybe—things had really been the way they seemed back there. Maybe Gaebril really did not suspect that he knew. *Maybe.* He remembered those nearly black eyes, seizing and holding like a pair of pitchfork tines through his head. *Light, maybe.* He forced himself to walk as if he had all the time in the world—*Just a haybrain country lout staring at the rugs and the gold. Just a mudfoot who'd never think anyone might put a knife in his back*—until Tallanvor let him through a sallyport in one of the gates, and followed him out.

The fat officer with the rat's eyes was still there with the Guards, and when he saw Mat his face went red again. Before he could open his mouth, though, Tallanvor spoke. "He has delivered a letter to the Queen from the Daughter-Heir. Be glad, Elber, that neither Morgase nor Gaebril knows you tried to keep it from them. Lord Gaebril was most interested in the Lady Elayne's missive."

Elber's face went from red to as white as his collar. He glared once at Mat, and scuttled back along the line of guardsmen, his beady eyes peering through the bars of their face-guards as if to determine whether any of them had seen his fear.

"Thank you," Mat told Tallanvor, and meant it. He had

forgotten all about the fat man until he was staring him in the face again. "Fare you well, Tallanvor."

He started across the oval plaza, trying not to walk too fast, and was surprised when Tallanvor walked along. *Light, is he Gaebril's man, or Morgase's?* He was just beginning to feel an itch between his shoulder blades, as if a knife might be about to go in—*He doesn't know, burn me! Gaebril doesn't suspect I know!*—when the young officer finally spoke.

"Did you spend long in Tar Valon? In the White Tower? Long enough to learn anything of it?"

"I was only there three days," Mat said cautiously. He would have made the time less—if he could have delivered the letter without admitting ever being in Tar Valon, he would have—but he did not think the man would believe he had gone all that way to see his sister and left the same day. *What under the Light is he after?* "I learned what I saw in that time. Nothing of any importance. They did not guide me around and tell me things. I was only there to see Else."

"You must have heard something, man. Who is Sheriam? Does talking to her in her study mean anything?"

Mat shook his head vigorously to keep relief from showing on his face. "I don't know who she is," he said truthfully. Perhaps he had heard Egwene, or perhaps Nynaeve, mention the name. An Aes Sedai, maybe? "Why should it mean anything?"

"I do not know," Tallanvor said softly. "There is too much I do not know. Sometimes I think she is trying to say something. . . ." He gave Mat a sharp look. "*Are* you a loyal Andorman, Thom Grinwell?"

"Of course I am." *Light, if I say that much more often, I may start believing it.* "What about you? Do you serve Morgase and Gaebril loyally?"

Tallanvor gave him a look as hard as the dice's mercy. "I serve Morgase, Thom Grinwell. Her, I serve to the death. Fare you well!" He turned and strode back toward the Palace with a hand gripping his sword hilt.

Watching him go, Mat muttered to himself. "I will wager this"—he gave Gaebril's wash-leather purse a toss—"that Gaebril says the same." Whatever games they played in the Palace, he wanted no place in any of them. And he meant to make sure Egwene and the others were out of them, too.

Fool women! Now I have to keep their bacon from burning instead of looking after my own! He did not start to run until the streets hid him from the Palace.

When he came dashing into The Queen's Blessing, nothing very much had changed in the library. Thom and the innkeeper still sat over the stones board—a different game, he saw from the positions of the stones, but no better for Gill—and the calico cat was back on the table, washing herself. A tray holding their unlit pipes and the remains of a meal for two sat near the cat, and his belongings were gone from the armchair. Each man had a wine cup at his elbow.

"I will be leaving, Master Gill," he said. "You can keep the coin and take a meal out of it. I'll stay long enough to eat, but then I am on the road to Tear."

"What is your hurry, boy?" Thom seemed to be watching the cat more than the board. "We only just arrived here."

"You delivered the Lady Elayne's letter, then?" the innkeeper said eagerly. "And kept your skin whole, it seems. Did you really climb over that wall like the other young man? No, that does not matter. Did the letter soothe Morgase? Do we still have to keep tiptoeing on eggs, man?"

"I suppose it soothed her," Mat said. "I think it did." He hesitated a moment, bouncing Gaebril's purse on his hand. It made a clinking sound. He had not looked to see if it really held ten gold marks; the weight was about right. "Master Gill, what can you tell me of Gaebril? Aside from the fact that he does not like Aes Sedai. You said he had not been in Caemlyn long?"

"Why do you want to know about him?" Thom asked. "Basel, are you going to place a stone or not?" The innkeeper sighed and stuck a black stone on the board, and the gleeman shook his head.

"Well, lad," Gill said, "there is not much to tell. He came out of the west during the winter. Somewhere out your way, I think. Maybe it was the Two Rivers. I've heard the mountains mentioned."

"We have no lords in the Two Rivers," Mat said. "Maybe there are some up around Baerlon. I do not know."

"That could be it, lad. I had never even heard of him before, but I do not keep up with the country lords. Came while Morgase was still in Tar Valon, he did, and half the city was afraid the Tower was going to make her disappear, too. The other half did not want her back. The riots started up again, the way they did last year at the tail of winter."

Mat shook his head. "I do not care about politics, Master Gill. It's Gaebril I want to know about." Thom frowned at him, and began cleaning the dottle from his long-stemmed pipe with a straw.

"It is Gaebril I am telling you about, lad," Gill said. "During the riots, he made himself leader of the faction supporting Morgase—got himself wounded in the fighting, I hear—and by the time she returned, he had it all suppressed. Gareth Bryne didn't like Gaebril's methods—he can be a very hard man—but Morgase was so pleased to find order restored that she named him to the post Elaida used to hold."

The innkeeper stopped. Mat waited for him to go on, but he did not. Thom thumbed his pipe full of tabac and walked over to light a spill at a small lamp kept for the purpose on the mantel above the fireplace.

"What else?" Mat asked. "The man has to have a reason for what he does. If he marries Morgase, would he be king when she dies? If Elayne were dead, too, I mean?"

Thom choked lighting his pipe, and Gill laughed. "Andor has a queen, lad. Always a queen. If Morgase and Elayne both died—the Light send it not so!—then Morgase's nearest female relative would take the throne. At least there's no question of who that is this time—a cousin, the Lady Dyelin—not like the Succession, after Tigraine vanished. It took two years before Morgase sat on the Lion Throne, then. Dyelin could keep Gaebril as her advisor, or marry him to cement the line—though she would not likely do that unless Morgase had had a child by him—but he would be the Prince Consort even then. No more than that. Thank the Light, Morgase is a young woman, yet. And Elayne is healthy. Light! The letter did not say she is ill, did it?"

"She is well." *For now, at least.* "Isn't there anything else you can tell me about him? You do not seem to like him. Why?"

The innkeeper frowned in thought, and scratched his chin, and shook his head. "I suppose I would not like him marrying Morgase, but I do not truly know why. He's said to be a fine man; the nobles all look to him. I do not like most of the men he's brought into the Guards. Too much has

changed since he came, but I cannot lay it all at his door.
There just seem to be too many people muttering in corners
since he came. You would think we were all Cairhienin, the
way they were before this civil war, all plotting and trying
to find advantage. I keep having bad dreams since Gaebril
came, and I am not the only one. Fool thing to worry about,
dreams. It is probably only worry about Elayne, and what
Morgase means to do concerning the White Tower, and
people acting like Cairhienin. I just do not know. Why are
you asking all these questions about Lord Gaebril?"

"Because he wants to kill Elayne," Mat said, "and Egwene
and Nynaeve with her." There was nothing useful in what
Gill had told him that he could see. *Burn me, I don't have to
know why he wants them dead. I just have to stop it.* Both
men were staring at him again. As if he were mad. Again.

"Are you coming down sick again?" Gill said suspiciously. "I remember you staring crossways at everyone the
last time. It's either that, or else you think this is some sort
of prank. You have the look of a prankster to me. If that is
it, it's a nasty one!"

Mat grimaced. "It is no bloody prank. I overheard him
telling some man called Comar to cut Elayne's head off.
And Egwene's and Nynaeve's while he was about it. A big
man, with a white stripe in his beard."

"That does sound like Lord Comar," Gill said slowly.
"He was a fine soldier, but it is said he left the Guard over
some matter of weighted dice. Not that anyone says it to his
face; Comar was one of the best blades in the Guards. You
really mean it, don't you?"

"I think he does, Basel," Thom said. "I very much think
he does."

"The Light shine on us! What did Morgase say? You did
tell her, didn't you? The Light burn you, you did tell her!"

"Of course, I did," Mat said bitterly. "With Gaebril standing right there, and her gazing at him like a lovesick lapdog!
I said, 'I may be a simple village man who just climbed
over your wall half an hour past, but I already happen to
know your trusted advisor there, the one you seem to be
in love with, intends to murder your daughter.' Light, man,
she'd have cut *my* head off!"

"She might have at that." Thom stared into the elaborate
carvings on the bowl of his pipe and tugged one mustache.

"Her temper was ever as sudden as lightning, and twice as dangerous."

"You know it better than most, Thom," Gill said absently. Staring at nothing, he scrubbed both hands through his graying hair. "There has to be something I can do. I haven't held a sword since the Aiel War, but. . . . Well, that would do no good. Get myself killed and do nothing by it. But I must do something!"

"Rumor." Thom rubbed the side of his nose; he seemed to be studying the stones board and talking to himself. "No one can keep rumors from reaching Morgase's ears, and if she hears it strongly enough, she will start to wonder. Rumor is the voice of the people, and the voice of the people often speaks truth. Morgase knows that. There is not a man alive I would back against her in the Game. Love or no love, once Morgase starts examining Gaebril closely, he'll not be able to hide as much as his childhood scars from her. And if she learns he means harm to Elayne"—he placed a stone on the board; it seemed an odd placement at first glance, but Mat saw that in three more moves, a third of Gill's stones would be trapped—"Lord Gaebril will have a most elaborate funeral."

"You and your Game of Houses," Gill muttered. "Still, it might work." A sudden smile appeared on his face. "I even know who to tell to start it. All I need do is mention to Gilda that I dreamed it, and in three days she'll have told serving girls in half the New City that it is a fact. She is the greatest gossip the Creator ever made."

"Just be certain it cannot be traced back to you, Basel."

"No fear of that, Thom. Why a week ago, a man told me one of my own bad dreams as a thing he'd heard from somebody who'd had it from someone else. Gilda must have eavesdropped on me telling it to Coline, but when I asked, he gave me a string of names that led all the way to the other side of Caemlyn and vanished. Why, I actually went over there and found the last man, just out of curiosity to see how many mouths had passed it, and he claimed it was his very own dream. No fear, Thom."

Mat did not really care what they did with their rumors—no rumors would help Egwene or the others—but one thing puzzled him. "Thom, you seem to be taking this all very calmly. I thought Morgase was the great love of your life."

The gleeman stared into the bowl of his pipe again. "Mat, a very wise woman once told me that time would heal my wounds, that time smoothed everything over. I didn't believe her. Only she was right."

"You mean you do not love Morgase anymore."

"Boy, it has been fifteen years since I left Caemlyn a half step ahead of the headsman's axe, with the ink of Morgase's signature still wet on the warrant. Sitting here listening to Basel natter on"—Gill protested, and Thom raised his voice—"natter on, I say, about Morgase and Gaebril, and how they might marry, I realized the passion faded a long time gone. Oh, I suppose I am still fond of her, perhaps I even love her a little, but it is not a grand passion anymore."

"And here I half thought you'd go running up to the Palace to warn her." He laughed, and was surprised when Thom joined him.

"I am not so big a fool as that, boy. Any fool knows men and women think differently at times, but the biggest difference is this. Men forget, but never forgive; women forgive, but never forget. Morgase might kiss my cheek and give me a cup of wine and say how she has missed me. And then she might just let the Guards haul me off to prison and the headsman. No. Morgase is one of the most capable women I've ever known, and that is saying something. I could almost pity Gaebril once she learns what he is up to. Tear, you say? Is there any chance of you waiting until tomorrow to leave? I could use a night's sleep."

"I mean to be as far toward Tear as I can before nightfall." Mat blinked. "Do you mean to come with me? I thought you meant to stay here."

"Did you not just hear me say I had decided *not* to have my head cut off? Tear sounds a safer place to me than Caemlyn, and suddenly that does not seem so bad. Besides, I like those girls." A knife appeared in his hand and was as suddenly gone again. "I'd not like anything to happen to them. But if you mean to reach Tear quickly, it's Aringill you want. A fast boat will have us there days sooner than horses, even if we rode them to death. And I don't say it just because my bottom has already taken on the shape of a saddle."

"Aringill, then. As long as it's fast."

"Well," Gill said, "I suppose if you are leaving, lad, I had better see about getting you that meal." He pushed back his chair and started for the door.

"Hold this for me, Master Gill," Mat said, and tossed him the wash-leather purse.

"What's this, lad? Coin?"

"Stakes. Gaebril doesn't know it, but he and I have a wager." The cat jumped down as Mat picked up the wooden dice cup and spun the dice out on the table. Five sixes. "And I always win."

CHAPTER
48

Following the Craft

As the *Darter* wallowed toward the docks of Tear, on the west bank of the River Erinin, Egwene did not see anything of the oncoming city. Slumped head down at the rail, she stared down at the waters of the Erinin rolling past the ship's fat hull, and the frontmost sweep on her side as it swung into her vision and back again, cutting white furrows in the river. It made her queasy, but she knew raising her head would only make the sickness worse. Looking at the shore would only make the slow, corkscrew motion of the *Darter* more apparent.

The vessel had moved in that twisting roll ever since Jurene. She did not care how it had sailed before then; she found herself wishing the *Darter* had sunk before reaching Jurene. She wished they had made the captain put in at Aringill so they could find another ship. She wished they had never gone near a ship. She wished a great many things, most of them just to take her mind off where she was.

The twisting was less now, under sweeps, than it had been under sail, but it had gone on too many days now for the change to make much difference to her. Her stomach seemed to be sloshing about inside her like milk in a stone jug. She gulped and tried to forget that image.

They had not done much in the way of planning on the *Darter*, she and Elayne and Nynaeve. Nynaeve could seldom go ten minutes without vomiting, and seeing that always made Egwene lose whatever food she had managed to get down. The increasing warmth as they went further downriver did not help. Nynaeve was below now, no doubt with Elayne holding a basin for her again.

Oh, Light, no! Don't think about that! Green fields. Meadows. Light, meadows do not heave like that. Hummingbirds. No, not hummingbirds! Larks. Larks singing.

"Mistress Joslyn? Mistress Joslyn!"

It took her a moment to recognize the name she had chosen to give Captain Canin, and the captain's voice. She raised her head slowly and fixed her eyes on his long face.

"We are docking, Mistress Joslyn. You've kept saying how eager you were to be ashore. Well, we're there." His voice did not hide his eagerness to be rid of his three passengers, two of whom did little more than sick up, as he called it, and moan all night.

Barefoot, shirtless sailors were tossing lines to men on the stone dock that thrust out into the river; the dockmen seemed to be wearing long leather vests in place of shirts. The sweeps had already been drawn in, except for a pair fending the ship off from coming against the dock too hard. The flat stones of the dock were wet; the air had a feel of rain not long gone, and that was a little soothing. The twisting motion had ceased some time since, she realized, but her stomach remembered. The sun was falling toward the west. She tried not to think of supper.

"Very good, Captain Canin," she said with all the dignity she could summon. *He'd not sound like that if I were wearing my ring, not even if I were sick on his boots.* She shuddered at the picture in her mind.

Her Great Serpent ring and the twisted ring of the *ter'angreal* hung on a leather cord about her neck, now. The stone ring felt cool against her skin—almost enough to counteract the damp warmth of the air—but aside from that, she had found that the more she used the *ter'angreal*, the more she wanted to touch it, without pouch or cloth between it and her.

Tel'aran'rhiod still showed her little of immediate use. Sometimes there had been glimpses of Rand, or Mat, or Perrin, and more in her own dreams without the *ter'angreal*, but nothing of which she could make any sense. The Seanchan, who she refused to think about. Nightmares of a Whitecloak putting Master Luhhan in the middle of a huge, toothed trap for bait. Why should Perrin have a falcon on his shoulder, and what was important about him choosing between that axe he wore now and a blacksmith's hammer?

What did it mean that Mat was dicing with the Dark One, and why did he keep shouting, "I am coming!" and why did she think in the dream that he was shouting at her? And Rand. He had been sneaking through utter darkness toward *Callandor*, while all around him six men and five women walked, some hunting him and some ignoring him, some trying to guide him toward the shining crystal sword and some trying to stop him from reaching it, appearing not to know where he was, or only to see him in flashes. One of the men had eyes of flame, and he wanted Rand dead with a desperation she could nearly taste. She thought she knew him. Ba'alzamon. But who were the others? Rand in that dry, dusty chamber again, with those small creatures settling into his skin. Rand confronting a horde of Seanchan. Rand confronting her, and the women with her, and one of *them* was a Seanchan. It was all too confusing. She had to stop thinking about Rand and the others and put her mind to what was right ahead of her. *What is the Black Ajah up to? Why don't I dream something about them? Light, why can't I learn to make it do what I want?*

"Have the horses put ashore, Captain," she told Canin. "I will tell Mistress Maryim and Mistress Caryla." That was Nynaeve—Maryim—and Elayne—Caryla.

"I have sent a man to tell them, Mistress Joslyn. And your animals will be on the dock as soon as my men can rig a boom."

He sounded very pleased to be rid of them. She thought about telling him not to hurry, but rejected it immediately. The *Darter*'s corkscrewing might have stopped, but she wanted dry land under her feet again. Now. Still, she stopped to pat Mist's nose and let the gray mare nuzzle her palm, to let Canin see she was in no great rush.

Nynaeve and Elayne appeared at the ladder from the cabins, laden with their bundles and saddlebags, and Elayne almost as laden with Nynaeve. When Nynaeve saw Egwene watching, she pushed herself away from the Daughter-Heir and walked unaided the rest of the way to where men were setting a narrow gangplank to the dock. Two crewmen came to fasten a wide canvas sling under Mist's belly, and Egwene hurried below for her own things. When she came back up, her mare was already on the dock and Elayne's roan dangled in the canvas sling halfway there.

For a moment after her feet were on the dock, all she felt was relief. This would not pitch and roll. Then she began to look at this city whose reaching had caused them such pains.

Stone warehouses backed the long docks themselves, and there seemed to be a great many ships, large and small, alongside the docks or anchored in the river. Hastily she avoided looking at the ships. Tear had been built on flat land, with barely a bump. Down muddy dirt streets between the warehouses, she could see houses and inns and taverns of wood and stone. Their roofs of slate or tile had oddly sharp corners, and some rose to a point. Beyond these, she could make out a high wall of dark gray stone, and behind it the tops of towers with balconies high around them and white-domed palaces. The domes had a squared shape to them, and the tower tops looked pointed, like some of the roofs outside the wall. All in all, Tear was easily as big as Caemlyn or Tar Valon, and if not so beautiful as either, it was still one of the great cities. Yet she found it hard to look at anything but the Stone of Tear.

She had heard of it in stories, heard that it was the greatest fortress in the world and the oldest, the first built after the Breaking of the World, yet nothing had prepared her for this sight. At first she thought it was a huge, gray stone hill or a small, barren mountain covering hundreds of hides, its length stretching from the Erinin west through the wall and into the city. Even after she saw the huge banner flapping from its greatest height—three white crescent moons slanting across a field half red, half gold; a banner waving at least three hundred paces above the river, yet large enough to be clearly seen at that height—even after she made out battlements and towers, it was difficult to believe the Stone of Tear had been built rather than carved out of a mountain already there.

"Made with the Power," Elayne murmured. She was staring at the Stone, too. "Flows of Earth woven to draw stone from the ground, Air to bring it from every corner of the world, and Earth and Fire to make it all in one piece, without seam or joint or mortar. Atuan Sedai says the Tower could not do it, today. Strange, given how the High Lords feel concerning the Power now."

"I think," Nynaeve said softly, eyeing the dockmen

moving around them, "that given that very thing, we should not mention certain other things aloud." Elayne appeared torn between indignation—she had spoken very softly—and agreement; the Daughter-Heir agreed with Nynaeve too often and too readily to suit Egwene.

Only when Nynaeve is right, she admitted to herself grudgingly. A woman who wore the ring, or was even associated with Tar Valon, would be watched here. The barefoot, leather-vested dockmen were not paying the three of them any mind as they hurried about, carrying bales or crates on their backs as often as on barrows. A strong odor of fish hung in the air; the next three docks had dozens of small fishing boats clustered around them, just like those in the drawing in the Amyrlin's study. Shirtless men and barefoot women were hoisting baskets of fish out of the boats, mounds of silver and bronze and green, and colors she had never suspected fish might be, such as bright red, and deep blue, and brilliant yellow, some with stripes or splotches of white and other colors.

She lowered her voice for Elayne's ear alone. "She is right, Caryla. Remember why you are Caryla." She did not want Nynaeve to hear such admissions. Her face did not change when she heard, but Egwene could feel satisfaction radiating from her like heat from a cook stove.

Nynaeve's black stallion was just being lowered to the dock; sailors had already carried their tack off the ship and simply dumped it on the wet stones of the dock. Nynaeve glanced at the horses and opened her mouth—Egwene was sure it was to tell them to saddle their animals—then closed it again, tight-lipped, as if it had cost her an effort. She gave her braid one hard tug. Before the sling was well out of the way, Nynaeve tossed the blue-striped saddle blanket across the black's back and hoisted her high-cantled saddle atop it. She did not even look at the other two women.

Egwene was not anxious to ride at that moment—the motion of a horse might be too close to the motion of the *Darter* for her stomach—but another look at those muddy streets convinced her. Her shoes were sturdy, but she would not enjoy having to clean mud off them, or having to hold her skirts up as she walked, either. She saddled Mist quickly and climbed onto her back, settling her skirts, before she could decide the mud might not be so bad after all.

A little needlework on the *Darter*—Elayne had done it all, this time; the Daughter-Heir sewed a very fine stitch—had divided all their dresses nicely for riding astride.

Nynaeve's face paled for a moment when she swung into her saddle and the stallion decided to frisk. She kept a tight-mouthed grip on herself and a firm hand on her reins and soon had him under control. By the time they had ridden slowly past the warehouses, she could speak. "We need to locate Liandrin and the others without them learning we are asking after them. They surely know we are coming—that someone is, at least—but I would like them not to know we are here until it is too late for them." She drew a deep breath. "I confess I have not thought of any way to do this. Yet. Do either of you have any suggestions?"

"A thief-taker," Elayne said without hesitation. Nynaeve frowned at her.

"You mean like Hurin?" Egwene said. "But Hurin was in the service of his king. Wouldn't any thief-taker here serve the High Lords?"

Elayne nodded, and for a moment Egwene envied the Daughter-Heir her stomach. "Yes, they would. But thief-takers are not like the Queen's Guards, or the Tairen Defenders of the Stone. They serve the ruler, but people who have been robbed sometimes pay them to retrieve what was stolen. And they also sometimes take money to find people. At least, they do in Caemlyn. I cannot think it is different here in Tear."

"Then we take rooms at an inn," Egwene said, "and ask the innkeeper to find us a thief-taker."

"Not an inn," Nynaeve said as firmly as she guided the stallion; she never seemed to let the animal get out of her control. After a moment she moderated her tone a little. "Liandrin, at least, knows us, and we have to assume the others do, too. They will surely be watching the inns for whoever followed the trail they sprinkled behind them. I mean to spring their trap in their faces, but not with us inside. We'll not stay at an inn."

Egwene refused to give her the satisfaction of asking.

"Where then?" Elayne's brow furrowed. "If I made myself known—and could make anyone believe it, in these clothes and with no escort—we would be welcomed by most of the noble Houses, and very likely in the Stone itself—there are good relations between Caemlyn and Tear—but there would be no keeping it quiet. The entire city would know before nightfall. I cannot think of anywhere else except an inn, Nynaeve. Unless you mean to go out to a farm in the country, but we will never find them from the country."

Nynaeve glanced at Egwene. "I will know when I see it. Let me look."

Elayne's frown swept from Nynaeve to Egwene and back again. "'Do not cut off your ears because you do not like your earrings,'" she muttered.

Egwene put her attention firmly on the street they were riding along. *I will be burned if I'll let her think I am even wondering!*

There were not a great many people out, not compared to the streets of Tar Valon. Perhaps the thick mud in the street discouraged them. Carts and wagons lurched past, most pulled by oxen with wide horns, the carter or wagoneer walking alongside with a long goad of some pale, ridged wood. No carriages or sedan chairs used these streets. The odor of fish hung in the air here, too, and no few of the men who hurried past carried huge baskets full of fish on their backs. The shops did not look prosperous; none displayed wares outside, and Egwene seldom saw anyone go in. The shops had signs—the tailor's needle and bolt of cloth, the cutler's knife and scissors, the weaver's loom, and the like—but the paint on most of them was peeling. The few inns had signs in as bad a state, and looked no busier. The small houses crowded between inns and shops often had tiles or slates missing from their roofs. This part of Tear, at least, was poor. And from what she saw on the faces, few of the people here cared to try any longer. They were moving, working, but most of them had given up. Few as much as glanced at three women riding where everyone else walked.

The men wore baggy breeches, usually tied at the ankle. Only a handful wore coats, long, dark garments that fit arms and chest tightly, then became looser below the waist. There were more men in low shoes than in boots, but most went barefoot in the mud. A good many wore no coat or shirt at all, and had their breeches held up by a broad sash, sometimes colored and often dirty. Some had wide, conical straw hats on their heads, and a few, cloth caps that sagged down one side of the face. The women's dresses had high necks, right up to their chins, and hems that stopped at the ankle. Many had short aprons in pale colors, sometimes two or three, each smaller than the one beneath it, and most wore the same straw hats as the men, but dyed to complement the aprons.

It was on a woman that she first saw how those who wore shoes dealt with the mud. The woman had small wooden platforms tied to the soles of her shoes, lifting them two hands out of the mud; she walked along as if her feet were planted firmly on the ground. Egwene saw others wearing the platforms after that, men as well as women. Some of the women went barefoot, but not as many as the men.

She was wondering which shop might sell those platforms, when Nynaeve suddenly turned her black down an alleyway between a long, narrow two-story house and a stone-walled potter's shop. Egwene exchanged glances with Elayne—the Daughter-Heir shrugged—and then they followed. Egwene did not know where Nynaeve was going or why—and she meant to have words with her about it—but she did not mean to become separated, either.

The alley suddenly let into a small yard behind the house, fenced in by the buildings around it. Nynaeve had already dismounted and tied her reins to a fig tree, where the stallion could not reach the green things sprouting in a vegetable patch that took up half the yard. A line of stones had been laid to make a path to the back door. Nynaeve strode to the door and knocked.

"What is it?" Egwene demanded in spite of herself. "Why are we stopping here?"

"Did you not see the herbs in the front windows?" Nynaeve knocked again.

"Herbs?" Elayne said.

"A Wisdom," Egwene told her as she got down from her saddle and tied Mist alongside the black. *Gaidin is no good name for a horse. Does she think I don't know who she means it for?* "Nynaeve has found herself a Wisdom, or Seeker, or whatever they call her here."

A woman opened the door just enough to look out suspiciously. At first Egwene thought she was stout, but then the woman opened the door the rest of the way. She was certainly well padded, but the way she moved spoke of muscle underneath. She looked as strong as Mistress Luhhan, and

some in Emond's Field claimed Alsbet Luhhan was almost
as strong as her husband. It was not true, but it was not far
wrong.

"How can I help you?" the woman said in an accent like
the Amyrlin's. Her gray hair was arranged in thick curls
that hung down the sides of her head, and her three aprons
were in shades of green, each slightly darker than the one
below, but even the topmost pale. "Which one of you needs
me?"

"I do," Nynaeve said. "I need something for a queasy
stomach. And perhaps one of my companions does, too.
That is, if we've come to the right place?"

"You're not Tairen," the woman said. "I should have
known that by your clothes, before you spoke. I'm called
Mother Guenna. I am called a Wise Woman, too, but I'm
old enough not to trust that to caulk a seam. You come, and
I will give you something for your stomach."

It was a neat kitchen, though not large, with copper pots
hanging on the wall, and dried herbs and sausages from
the ceiling. Several tall cupboards of pale wood had doors
carved with some sort of tall grass. The table had been
scrubbed almost white, and the backs of the chairs were
carved with flowers. A pot of fishy-smelling soup was sim-
mering atop the stone stove, and a kettle with a spout, just
beginning to steam. There was no fire on the stone hearth,
for which Egwene was more than grateful; the stove added
enough to the heat, though Mother Guenna seemed not
to notice it at all. Dishes lined the mantel, and more were
stacked neatly on shelves to either side. The floor looked as
if it had just been swept.

Mother Guenna closed the door after them, and as she
was crossing the kitchen to her cupboards, Nynaeve said,
"Which tea will you give me? Chainleaf? Or bluewort?"

"I would if I had any of either." Mother Guenna rooted in
the shelves a moment and came out with a stone jar. "Since
I've had no time to glean of late, I will give you a brew of
marshwhite leaves."

"I am not familiar with that," Nynaeve said slowly.

"It works as well as chainleaf, but it has a bite to the taste
some don't care for." The big woman sprinkled dried and
broken leaves into a blue teapot and carried it over to the
fireplace to add hot water. "Do you follow the craft, then?

Sit." She gestured to the table with a hand holding two blue-glazed cups she had taken from the mantel. "Sit, and we'll talk. Which one of you has the other stomach?"

"I am fine," Egwene said casually as she took a chair. "Are you queasy, Caryla?" The Daughter-Heir shook her head with perhaps a touch of exasperation.

"No matter." The gray-haired woman poured out a cup of dark liquid for Nynaeve, then sat across the table from her. "I made enough for two, but marshwhite tea keeps longer than salted fish. It works better the longer it sits, too, but it also grows more bitter. Makes a race between how much you need your stomach settled and what your tongue can stand. Drink, girl." After a moment, she filled the second cup and took a sip. "You see? It will not hurt you."

Nynaeve raised her own cup, making a small sound of displeasure at the first taste. When she lowered the cup again, though, her face was smooth. "It is just a little bitter perhaps. Tell me, Mother Guenna, will we have to put up with this rain and mud much longer?"

The older woman frowned, parceling displeasure among the three of them before she settled on Nynaeve. "I am not a Sea Folk Windfinder, girl," she said quietly. "If I could tell the weather, I'd sooner stick live silverpike down my dress than admit it. The Defenders take that sort of thing for next to Aes Sedai work. Now, do you follow the craft or not? You look as if you have been traveling. What is good for fatigue?" she barked suddenly.

"Flatwort tea," Nynaeve said calmly, "or andilay root. Since you ask questions, what would you do to ease birthing?"

Mother Guenna snorted. "Apply warm towels, child, and perhaps give her a little whitefennel if it was an especially hard birth. A woman needs no more than that, and a soothing hand. Can't you think of a question any country farmwife could not answer? What do you give for pains in the heart? The killing kind."

"Powdered gheandin blossom on the tongue," Nynaeve said crisply. "If a woman has biting pains in her belly and spits up blood, what do you do?"

They settled down as if testing each other, tossing questions and answers back and forth faster and faster. Sometimes the questioning lagged a moment when one spoke of a plant the other knew only by another name, but they picked up speed again, arguing the merits of tinctures against teas, salves against poultices, and when one was better than another. Slowly, all the quick questions began shifting toward the herbs and roots one knew that the other did not, digging for knowledge. Egwene began to grow irritable listening.

"After you give him the boneknit," Mother Guenna was saying, "you wrap the broken limb in toweling soaked in water where you've boiled blue goatflowers—only the blue, mind!"—Nynaeve nodded impatiently—"and as hot as he can stand it. One part blue goatflowers to ten of water, no weaker. Replace the towels as soon as they stop steaming, and keep it up all day. The bone will knit twice as fast as with boneknit alone, and twice as strong."

"I will remember that," Nynaeve said. "You mentioned using sheepstongue root for eye pain. I've never heard—"

Egwene could stand it no longer. "Maryim," she broke in, "do you really believe you'll ever need to know these things again? You are not a Wisdom any longer, or have you forgotten?"

"I have not forgotten anything," Nynaeve said sharply. "I remember a time when you were as eager to learn new things as I am."

"Mother Guenna," Elayne said blandly, "what do you do for two women who cannot stop arguing?"

The gray-haired woman pursed her lips and frowned at the table. "Usually, men or women, I tell them to stay away from each other. That is the best thing, and the easiest."

"Usually?" Elayne said. "What if there is a reason they cannot stay apart. Say they are sisters."

"I do have a way to make an arguer stop," the big woman said slowly. "It is not something I urge anyone to try, but some do come to me." Egwene thought there was a suspicion of a smile at the corners of her mouth. "I charge a silver mark each for women. Two for men, because men make more fuss. There are some will buy anything, if it costs enough."

"But what is the cure?" Elayne asked.

"I tell them they have to bring the other one here with them, the one they argue with. Both expect me to quiet the other's tongue." Despite herself, Egwene was listening. She noticed Nynaeve seemed to be paying sharp attention, as

well. "When they have paid me," Mother Guenna continued, flexing one hefty arm, "I take them out back and stick
their heads in my rain barrel till they agree to stop their
arguing."

Elayne burst out laughing.

"I think I may have done something very like that my-
self," Nynaeve said in a voice that was much too light.
Egwene hoped her own expression looked nothing like
Nynaeve's.

"I'd not be surprised if you have." Mother Guenna was
grinning openly now. "I tell them the next time I hear
they've been arguing, I will do it for free, but I'll use the
river. It is remarkable how often the cure works, for men
especially. And it is remarkable what it has done for my
reputation. For some reason, none of the people I cure this
way ever tells anyone else the details, so someone asks for
the cure every few months. If you've been fool enough to
eat mudfish, you do not go around telling people. I trust
none of you have any wish to spend a silver mark."

"I think not," Egwene said, and glared at Elayne when
she went off in peals of laughter again.

"Good," the gray-haired woman said. "Those I cure of
arguing have a tendency to avoid me like stingweed caught
in their nets, unless they actually take sick, and I am en-
joying your company. Most of those who come at present
want something to take away bad dreams, and they grow
sour when I have nothing to give them." For a moment she
slipped into a frown, rubbing her temples. "It is good to see
three faces that do not look as if there is nothing left but
to jump over the side and drown. If you are staying long
in Tear, you must come see me again. The girl called you
Maryim? I am Ailhuin. The next time, we'll talk over some
good Sea Folk tea instead of something that curdles your
tongue. Light, but I hate the taste of marshwhite; mudfish
would taste sweeter. In fact, if you have time to stay now,
I'll brew a pot of Tremalking black. Not long till supper,
either. It's just bread and soup and cheese, but you are welcome."

"That would be very nice, Ailhuin," Nynaeve said. "Actually. . . . Ailhuin, if you have a spare bedroom, I'd like to
hire it for the three of us."

The big woman looked at each of them without saying

anything. Getting to her feet, she tucked the pot of marsh-white tea away in the herb cupboard, then fetched a red teapot and a pouch from another. Only when she had brewed a pot of Tremalking black, put four clean cups and a bowl of honeycomb on the table along with pewter spoons, and reclaimed her chair did she speak.

"I've three empty bedrooms upstairs, now my daughters are all married. My husband, the Light shine on him, was lost in a storm in the Fingers of the Dragon near twenty years ago. There need be no talk of hiring, if I decide to let you have the rooms. If, Maryim." Stirring honey into her tea, she studied them again.

"What will make you decide?" Nynaeve asked quietly.

Ailhuin continued to stir, as if she had forgotten to drink. "Three young women, riding fine horses. I don't know much about horses, but those look as fine as what the lords and ladies ride, to me. You, Maryim, know enough of the craft that you ought to have hung herbs in your window already, or should be choosing where to do it. I've never heard of a woman practicing the craft too far from where she was born, but by your tongue, you are a long way." She glanced at Elayne. "Not many places with hair that color. Andor, I'd say, by your speech. Fool men are always talking about finding a yellow-haired Andor girl. What I want to know is why? Running away from something? Or running after something? Only, you don't look like thieves to me, and I never heard of three women chasing after a man together. So tell me why, and if I like it, the rooms are yours. If you want to pay something, you buy a bit of meat now and then. Meat is dear since the trade up to Cairhien fell away. But first the why, Maryim."

"We are chasing after something, Ailhuin," Nynaeve said. "Or rather, after some people." Egwene schooled herself to stillness and hoped she was doing as well as Elayne, who was sipping her tea as if she were listening to talk about dresses. Egwene did not believe Ailhuin Guenna's dark eyes missed a great deal. "They stole some things, Ailhuin," Nynaeve went on. "From my mother. And they did murder. We are here to see justice done."

"Burn my soul," the large woman said, "have you no menfolk? Men are not good for much beyond heavy hauling and getting in the way, most of the time—and kissing and such—but if there's a battle to be fought or a thief to catch, I say let them do it. Andor is as civilized as Tear. You are not Aiel."

"There was no one else but us," Nynaeve said. "Those who might have come in our place were killed."

The three murdered Aes Sedai, Egwene thought. *They could not have been Black Ajah. But if they had not been killed, the Amyrlin would not have been able to trust them. She's trying to keep to the bloody Three Oaths, but she is skirting it close.*

"Aaah," Ailhuin said sadly. "They killed your men? Brothers, or husbands, or fathers?" Spots of color bloomed in Nynaeve's cheeks, and the older woman mistook the emotion. "No, don't tell me, girl. I'll not pull up old grief. Let it lie on the bottom till it melts away. There, there, you calm yourself." It was an effort for Egwene not to growl with disgust.

"I must tell you this," Nynaeve said in a stiff voice. The red still colored her face. "These murderers and thieves are Darkfriends. They are women, but they are as dangerous as any swordsman, Ailhuin. If you wondered why we did not seek an inn, that is why. They may know we follow, and they may be watching for us."

Ailhuin waved it all away with a sniff. "Of the four most dangerous folk I know, two are women who never carry as much as a knife, and only one of the men is a swordsman. As for Darkfriends. . . . Maryim, when you are as old as I, you'll learn that false Dragons are dangerous, lionfish are dangerous, sharks are dangerous, and sudden storms out of the south; but Darkfriends are fools. Filthy fools, but fools. The Dark One is locked up where the Creator put him, and no Fetches or fangfish to scare children will get him out. Fools don't frighten me unless they're working the boat I'm riding. I suppose you don't have any proof you could take to the Defenders of the Stone? It would be just your word against theirs?"

What is a "Fetch"? Egwene wondered. *Or a "fangfish," for that matter.*

"We will have proof when we find them," Nynaeve said. "They will have the things they stole, and we can describe them. They are old things, and of little value to anyone but us, and our friends."

"You would be surprised what old things can be worth," Ailhuin said dryly. "Old Leuese Mulan pulled up three heartstone bowls and a cup in his nets last year, down in the Fingers of the Dragon. Now, instead of a fishing smack, he owns a ship trading up the river. Old fool did not even know what he had till I told him. Very likely there's more right where those came from, but Leuese couldn't even remember the exact spot. I do not know how he ever managed to get a fish into his net. Half the fishing boats in Tear were down there for months afterwards, dragging for *cuendillar*, not grunts or flatfish, and some had lords saying where to pull the nets. That's what old things can be worth, if they are old enough. Now, I've decided you do need a man in this, and I know just the one."

"Who?" Nynaeve said quickly. "If you mean a lord, one of the High Lords, remember we have no proof to offer till we find them."

Ailhuin laughed until she wheezed. "Girl, nobody from the Maule knows a High Lord, or any kind of lord. Mudfish don't school with silversides. I will bring you the dangerous man I know who isn't a swordsman, and the more dangerous of the two, at that. Juilin Sandar is a thief-catcher. The best of them. I do not know how it is in Andor, but here a thief-catcher will work for you or me as soon as for a lord or a merchant, and charge less at that. Juilin can find these women for you if they *can* be found, and bring your things back without you having to go near these Darkfriends."

Nynaeve agreed as if she were still not entirely sure, and Ailhuin tied those platforms to her shoes—clogs, she called them—and hurried out. Egwene watched her go, through one of the kitchen windows, past the horses and around the corner up the alley.

"You are learning how to be Aes Sedai, *Maryim*," she said as she turned from the window. "You manipulate people as well as Moiraine." Nynaeve's face went white.

Elayne stalked across the floor and slapped Egwene's face. Egwene was so shocked she could only stare. "You go too far," the golden-haired woman said sharply. "Too far. We must live together, or we will surely die together! Did you give Ailhuin your true name? Nynaeve told her what we could, that we seek Darkfriends, and that was risk enough, linking us with Darkfriends. She told her they were dangerous, murderers. Would you have had her say they are Black Ajah? In Tear? Would you risk everything on whether Ailhuin would keep *that* to herself?"

Egwene rubbed her cheek gingerly. Elayne had a strong arm. "I do not have to like doing it."

"I know," Elayne sighed. "Neither do I. But we *do* have to."

Egwene turned back to peering through the window at the horses. *I know we do. But I do not have to like it.*

CHAPTER
49

A Storm in Tear

Egwene finally returned to the table and her tea. She thought perhaps Elayne was right, that she had gone too far, but she could not bring herself to apologize, and they sat in silence.

When Ailhuin returned, she had a man with her, a lean fellow in his middle years who looked as if he had been carved from aged wood. Juilin Sandar took off his clogs by the door and hung his flat, conical straw hat on a peg. A sword-breaker, much like Hurin's but with short slots to either side of the long one, hung from a belt over his brown coat, and he carried a staff exactly as tall as he was, but not much thicker than his thumb and made of that pale wood, like ridged joints, that the ox-drivers used for their goads. His short-cut black hair lay flat on his head, and his quick, dark eyes seemed to note and record every detail of the room. And of everyone in it. Egwene would have bet he examined Nynaeve twice, and to her, at least, Nynaeve's lack of reaction was blatant; it was obvious she knew it, too.

Ailhuin motioned him to a place at the table, where he turned back the cuffs of his coat sleeves, bowed to each of them in turn, and sat with his staff propped against his shoulder, not speaking until the gray-haired woman had made a fresh pot of tea and everyone had sipped from their cups.

"Mother Guenna has told me of your problem," he said quietly as he set his cup down. "I will help you if I can, but the High Lords may have their own business to put me to, soon."

The big woman snorted. "Juilin, when did you begin

haggling like a shopkeeper trying to charge silk prices for linen? Do not claim you know when the High Lords will summon you before they do."

"I won't claim it," Sandar told her with a smile, "but I know when I've seen men on the rooftops in the night. Just out of the corner of my eye—they can hide like pipefish in reeds—but I have seen the movement. No one has reported a theft yet, but there are thieves working inside the walls, and you can buy your supper with that. Mark me. Before another week, I'll be summoned to the Stone because a band of thieves is breaking into merchants' houses, or even lords' manors. The Defenders may guard the streets, but when thieves need tracking they send for a thief-catcher, and me before any other. I am not trying to drive up my price, but whatever I do for these pretty women, I must do soon."

"I believe he speaks the truth," Ailhuin said reluctantly. "He'll tell you the moon is green and water white if he thinks it will bring him a kiss, but he lies less than most men about other things. He may be the most honest man ever born in the Maule." Elayne put a hand over her mouth, and Egwene struggled not to laugh. Nynaeve sat unmoved and obviously impatient.

Sandar grimaced at the gray-haired woman, then apparently decided to ignore what she had said. He smiled at Nynaeve. "I will admit that I'm curious about these thieves. I've known women thieves, and bands of thieves, but I never heard of a band of women thieves before. And I owe Mother Guenna favors." His eyes seemed to record Nynaeve all over again.

"What do you charge?" she asked sharply.

"To recover stolen goods," he said briskly, "I ask the tenth part of the value of what I recover. For finding someone, I ask a silver mark for each person. Mother Guenna says the things stolen have little value except to you, mistress, so I suggest you take that choice." He smiled again; he had very white teeth. "I would not take money from you at all, except that the brotherhood would frown on it, but I will take as little as I can. A copper or two, no more."

"I know a thief-taker," Elayne told him. "From Shienar. A very *respectful* man. He carries a sword as well as a sword-breaker. Why do you not?"

Sandar looked startled for a moment, and then upset with himself for being startled. He had not caught her hint, or else had decided to ignore it. "You are not Tairen. I have heard of Shienar, mistress, tales of Trollocs, and every man a warrior." His smile said these were tales for children.

"True stories," Egwene said. "Or true enough. I have been to Shienar."

He blinked at her, and went on. "I am not a lord, nor a wealthy merchant, nor even a soldier. The Defenders do not trouble foreigners much for carrying swords—unless they mean to stay long, of course—but I would be thrust into a cell under the Stone. There are laws, mistress." His hand rubbed along his staff, as if unconsciously. "I do as well as may be, without a sword." He focused his smile on Nynaeve once more. "Now, if you will describe these things—"

He stopped as she set her purse on the edge of the table and counted out thirteen silver marks. Egwene thought she had chosen the lightest coins; most were Tairen, only one Andoran. The Amyrlin had given them a great deal of gold, but even that would not last forever.

Nynaeve looked into the purse thoughtfully before tightening the strings and putting it back into her pouch. "There are thirteen women for you to find, Master Sandar, with as much silver again when you do. Find them, and we will recover our property ourselves."

"I will do that myself for less than this," he protested. "And there's no need for extra rewards. I charge what I charge. Have no fear I'll take a bribe."

"There is no fear of that," Ailhuin agreed. "I said he is honest. Just do not believe him if he says he loves you." Sandar glared at her.

"I pay the coin, Master Sandar," Nynaeve said firmly, "so I choose what I am buying. Will you find these women, and no more?" She waited for him to nod, reluctantly, before going on. "They may be together, or not. The first is a Taraboner. She is a little taller than I, with dark eyes and pale, honey-colored hair that she wears in many small braids after the Tarabon fashion. Some men might think her pretty, but she would not consider it a compliment. She has a mean, sulky mouth. The second is Kandori. She has long black hair with a white streak above her left ear, and. . . ."

She gave no names, and Sandar asked for none. Names

were so easily changed. His smile was gone now that the business was at hand. Thirteen women she described as he listened intently, and when she was done, Egwene was sure he could have recited them back word for word.

"Mother Guenna may have told you this," Nynaeve finished, "but I will repeat it. These women are more dangerous than you can believe. Over a dozen have died at their hands already, that I know of, and I would not be surprised if that was only a drop of the blood on their hands." Sandar and Ailhuin both blinked at that. "If they discover you are asking after them, you will die. If they take you, they will make you tell where we are, and Mother Guenna will probably die with us." The gray-haired woman looked disbelieving. "Believe it!" Nynaeve's stare demanded agreement. "Believe it, or I'll take back the silver and find another with more brains!"

"When I was young," Sandar said, voice serious, "a cutpurse put her knife in my ribs because I thought a pretty young girl wouldn't be as quick to stab as a man. I do not make that mistake anymore. I will behave as if these women are all Aes Sedai, and Black Ajah." Egwene almost choked, and he gave her a rueful grin as he scooped the coins into his own purse and stuck it behind his sash. "I did not mean to frighten you, mistress. There are no Aes Sedai in Tear. It may take a few days, unless they are together. Thirteen women together will be easy to find; apart, they will be harder. But either way, I will find them. And I will not frighten them away before you learn where they are."

When he had donned his straw hat and clogs and departed by the back door, Elayne said, "I hope he is not overconfident. Ailhuin, I heard what he said but. . . . He does understand that they are dangerous, does he not?"

"He has never been a fool except for a pair of eyes or a pretty ankle," the gray-haired woman said, "and that is a failing of every man. He is the best thief-catcher in Tear. Have no worry. He will find these Darkfriends of yours."

"It will rain again before morning." Nynaeve shivered, despite the warmth of the room. "I feel a storm gathering." Ailhuin only shook her head and set about filling bowls with fish soup for supper.

After they ate and cleaned up, Nynaeve and Ailhuin sat at the table talking of herbs and cures. Elayne worked on a small patch of embroidery she had begun on the shoulder of her cloak, tiny blue and white flowers, then read in a copy of *The Essays of Willim of Maneches* that Ailhuin had on her small shelf of books. Egwene tried reading, but neither the essays, nor *The Travels of Jain Farstrider*, nor the humorous tales of Aleria Elffin could hold her interest for more than a few pages. She fingered the stone *ter'angreal* through the bosom of her dress. *Where are they? What do they want in the Heart? None but the Dragon—none but Rand—can touch* Callandor, *so what do they want? What? What?*

As night deepened, Ailhuin showed them each to a bedroom on the second floor, but after she had gone to her own, they gathered in Egwene's by the light of a single lamp. Egwene had already undressed to her shift; the cord hung 'round her neck with the two rings. The striped stone felt far heavier than the gold. This was what they had done every night since leaving Tar Valon, with the sole exception of that night with the Aiel.

"Wake me after an hour," she told them.

Elayne frowned. "So short, this time?"

"Do you feel uneasy?" Nynaeve said. "Perhaps you are using it too often."

"We would still be in Tar Valon scrubbing pots and hoping to find a Black sister before a Gray Man found us if I had not," Egwene said sharply. *Light, Elayne's right. I am snapping like a sulky child.* She took a deep breath. "Perhaps I *am* uneasy. Maybe it is because we are so close to the Heart of the Stone, now. So close to *Callandor*. So close to the trap, whatever it is."

"Be careful," Elayne said, and Nynaeve said, more quietly, "Be very careful, Egwene. Please." She was tugging her braid in short jerks.

As Egwene lay down on the low-posted bed, with them on stools to either side, thunder rolled across the sky. Sleep came slowly.

It was the rolling hills again, as always at first, flowers and butterflies under spring sunshine, soft breezes and birds singing. She wore green silk, this time, with golden birds embroidered over her breasts, and green velvet slippers.

The *ter'angreal* seemed light enough to drift up out of her dress except for the weight of the Great Serpent ring holding it down.

By simple trial and error she had learned a little of the rules of *Tel'aran'rhiod*—even this World of Dreams, this Unseen World, had its rules, if odd ones; she was sure she did not know a tenth of them—and one way to make herself go where she wanted. Closing her eyes, she emptied her mind as she would have to embrace *saidar*. It was not as easy, because the rosebud kept trying to form, and she kept sensing the True Source, kept aching to embrace it, but she had to fill the emptiness with something else. She pictured the Heart of the Stone, as she had seen it in these dreams, formed it in every detail, perfect within the void. The huge, polished redstone columns. The age-worn stones of the floor. The dome, far overhead. The crystal sword, untouchable, slowly revolving hilt-down in midair. When it was so real she was sure she could reach out and touch it, she opened her eyes, and she was there, in the Heart of the Stone. Or the Heart of the Stone as it existed in *Tel'aran'rhiod*.

The columns were there, and *Callandor*. And around the sparkling sword, almost as dim and insubstantial as shadows, thirteen women sat cross-legged, staring at *Callandor* as it revolved. Honey-haired Liandrin turned her head, looking straight at Egwene with those big, dark eyes, and her rosebud mouth smiled.

Gasping, Egwene sat up in bed so fast she almost fell off the side.

"What is the matter?" Elayne demanded. "What happened? You look frightened."

"You only just closed your eyes," Nynaeve said softly. "This is the first time since the very beginning that you've come back without us waking you. Something did happen, didn't it?" She tugged her braid sharply. "Are you all right?"

How did I get back? Egwene wondered. *Light, I do not even know what I did.* She knew she was only trying to put off what she had to say. Unfastening the cord around her neck, she held the Great Serpent ring and the larger, twisted *ter'angreal* on her palm. "They are waiting for us," she said finally. There was no need to say who. "And I think they know we are in Tear."

Outside, the storm broke over the city.

Rain drumming on the deck over his head, Mat stared at the stones board on the table between him and Thom, but he could not really concentrate on the game, even with an Andoran silver mark riding on the outcome. Thunder crashed, and lightning flashed in the small windows. Four lamps lit the captain's cabin of the *Swift*. *Bloody ship may be as sleek as the bird, but it's still taking too bloody long.* The vessel gave a small jolt, then another; the motion seemed to change. *He had better not run us into the bloody mud! If he is not making the best time he can wring out of this buttertub, I will stuff that gold down his throat!* Yawning—he had not slept well since leaving Caemlyn; he could not stop worrying enough to sleep well—yawning, he set a white stone on the intersection of two lines; in three moves, he would capture nearly a fifth of Thom's black stones.

"You could be a good player, boy," the gleeman said around his pipe, placing his next stone, "if you put your mind to it." His tabac smelled like leaves and nuts.

Mat reached for another stone from the pile at his elbow, then blinked and let it lie. In the same three moves, Thom's stones would surround over a third of his. He had not seen it coming, and he could see no escape. "Do you ever lose a game? Have you ever lost a game?"

Thom removed his pipe and knuckled his mustaches. "Not in a long while. Morgase used to beat me about half the time. It is said good commanders of soldiers and good players of the Great Game are good at stones, as well. She is the one, and I've no doubt she could command a battle, too."

"Wouldn't you rather dice some more? Stones take too much time."

"I like a chance to win more than one toss in nine or ten," the white-haired man said dryly.

Mat bounded to his feet as the door banged open to admit Captain Derne. The square-faced man whipped his cloak from his shoulders, shaking the rain off and muttering curses to himself. "The Light sear my bones, I do not know why I ever let you hire *Swift*. You, demanding more flaming speed in the blackest night or the heaviest rain. More speed. Always more bloody speed! Could have run on a bloody mudflat a hundred times over by now!"

"You wanted the gold," Mat said harshly. "You said this heap of old boards was fast, Derne. When do we reach Tear?"

The captain smiled a tight smile. "We are tying off to the dock, now. And burn me for a bloody farmer if I carry anything that can flaming talk ever again! Now, where is the rest of my gold?"

Mat hurried to one of the small windows and peered out. In the harsh glare of lightning flashes he could see a wet stone dock, if not much else. He fished the second purse of gold from his pocket and tossed it to Derne. *Whoever heard of a riverman who didn't dice!* "About time," he growled. *Light send I'm not too late.*

He had stuffed all of his spare clothes and his blankets into the leather scrip, and he hung that on one side of him and the roll of fireworks on the other, from the cord he tied to it. His cloak covered it all, but gapped a little in the front. Better he got wet than the fireworks. He could dry out and be as good as new; a test with a bucket had shown fireworks could not. *I guess Rand's da was right.* Mat had always thought the Village Council would not set them off in the rain because they made a better show on clear nights.

"Aren't you about ready to sell those things?" Thom was settling his gleeman's cloak on his shoulders. It covered his leather-cased harp and flute, but his bundle of clothes and blankets he slung on his back outside the patch-covered cloak.

"Not until I figure out how they work, Thom. Besides, think what fun it will be when I set them all off."

The gleeman shuddered. "As long as you don't do it all at once, boy. As long as you don't throw them in the fireplace at supper. I'd not put it past you, the way you've been behaving with them. You're lucky the captain here did not throw us off the ship two days ago."

"He wouldn't." Mat laughed. "Not while that purse was in the offing. Eh, Derne?"

Derne was tossing the purse of gold in his hand. "I have not asked before this, but you've given me the gold, now, and you'll not take it back. What is this all about? All this flaming speed."

"A wager, Derne." Yawning, Mat picked up his quarter-staff, ready to go. "A wager."

"A wager!" Derne stared at the heavy purse. The other just like it was locked in his money chest. "There must be a flaming kingdom riding on it!"

"More than that," Mat said.

Rain bucketed down on the deck so hard that he could not see the gangplank except when lightning crackled above the city; the roar of the downpour barely let him hear himself think. He could see lights in windows up a street, though. There would be inns, up there. The captain had not come on deck to see them ashore, and none of the crew had stayed out in the rain, either. Mat and Thom made their way to the stone dock alone.

Mat cursed when his boots sank into the mud of the street, but there was nothing for it, so he kept on, striding along as fast as he could with his boots and the butt of his staff sticking at every step. The air smelled of fish, rank even with the rain. "We'll find an inn," he said, loudly, so he could be heard, "and then I will go out looking."

"In this weather?" Thom shouted back. Rain was rolling down his face, but he was more interested in keeping his instruments covered than his face.

"Comar could have left Caemlyn before us. If he had a good horse instead of the crowbaits we were riding, he could have set out downriver from Aringill maybe a full day ahead of us, and I don't know how much of that we caught up with that idiot Derne."

"It was a quick passage," Thom allowed. "*Swift* deserves its name."

"Be that as it may, Thom, rain or no rain, I have to find him before he finds Egwene and Nynaeve, and Elayne."

"A few more hours won't make much difference, boy. There are hundreds of inns in a city the size of Tear. There may be hundreds more outside the walls, some of them little places with no more than a dozen rooms to let, so tiny you could walk right by them and never know they were there." The gleeman hitched the hood of his cloak up more, muttering to himself. "It will take weeks to search them all.

But it will take Comar the same weeks. We can spend the night in out of the rain. You can wager whatever coin you have left that Comar won't be out in it."

Mat shook his head. *A tiny inn with a dozen rooms.* Before he left Emond's Field, the biggest building he had ever seen was the Winespring Inn. He doubted if Bran al'Vere had any more than a dozen rooms to let. Egwene had lived with her parents and her sisters in the rooms at the front of the second floor. *Burn me, sometimes I think we should never any of us have left Emond's Field.* But Rand surely had had to, and Egwene would probably have died if she had not gone to Tar Valon. *Now she might die because she did go.* He did not think he could settle for the farm again; the cows and the sheep certainly would not play dice. But Perrin still had a chance to go home. *Go home, Perrin,* he found himself thinking. *Go home while you still can.* He gave himself a shake. *Fool! Why would he want to?* He thought of bed, but pushed it away. *Not yet.*

Lightning streaked across the sky, three jagged bolts together, casting a stark light over a narrow house that seemed to have bunches of herbs hanging in the windows, and a shop, shut up tight, but a potter's from the sign with its bowls and plates. Yawning, he hunched his shoulders against the driving rain and tried to pull his boots out of the clinging mud more quickly.

"I think I can forget about this part of the city, Thom," he shouted. "All this mud, and that stink of fish. Can you see Nynaeve or Egwene—or Elayne!—choosing to stay here? Women like things neat and tidy, Thom, and smelling good."

"May be, boy," Thom muttered, then coughed. "You would be surprised what women will put up with. But it may be."

Holding his cloak to keep the roll of fireworks covered, Mat lengthened his stride. "Come on, Thom. I want to find Comar or the girls tonight, one or the other."

Thom limped after him, coughing now and again.

They strode through the wide gates in the city—unguarded, in the rain—and Mat was relieved to feel paving stones under his feet again. And not more than fifty paces up the street was an inn, the windows of the common room spilling light onto the street, music drifting out into the night. Even Thom covered that last fifty paces through the rain quickly, limp or no limp.

The White Crescent had a landlord whose girth made his long blue coat fit snugly below the waist as well as above, unlike those of most of the men in the low-backed chairs at the tables. Mat thought the landlord's baggy breeches, tied at the ankle above low shoes, had to be big enough for two ordinary men to fit inside, one in each leg. The serving women wore dark, high-necked dresses and short white aprons. There was a fellow playing a hammered dulcimer between the two stone fireplaces. Thom eyed the fellow critically and shook his head.

The rotund innkeeper, Cavan Lopar by name, was more than glad to give them rooms. He frowned at their muddy boots, but silver from Mat's pocket—the gold was running low—and Thom's patch-covered cloak smoothed his fat forehead. When Thom said he would perform for a small fee some nights, Lopar's chins waggled with pleasure. Of a big man with a white streak in his beard, he knew nothing, nor of three women meeting the descriptions Mat gave. Mat left everything but his cloak and his quarterstaff in his room, barely looking to see that it had a bed—sleep was enticing, but he refused to let himself think of it—then wolfed down a spicy fish stew and rushed back out into the rain. He was surprised that Thom came with him.

"I thought you wanted to be in where it's dry, Thom."

The gleeman patted the flute case he still had under his cloak. The rest of his things were up in his room. "People talk to a gleeman, boy. I may learn something you would not. I'd not like to see those girls harmed any more than you."

There was another inn a hundred paces down the rain-filled street on the other side, and another two hundred beyond that, and then more. Mat took them as he came to them, ducking in long enough for Thom to flourish his cloak and tell a story, then let someone buy him a cup of wine afterwards while Mat asked around after a tall man with a white streak in his close-cut black beard and three women. He won a few coins at dice, but he learned nothing, and neither did Thom. He was just glad the gleeman seemed to be taking only a few sips of wine at each inn; Thom had been close to abstemious on the boat, but Mat had not been certain he would not dive back into the wine once they reached Tear. By the time they had visited two dozen common rooms, Mat felt as if his eyelids had weights. The rain had lessened a bit, but it still fell steadily in big drops, and as the rain fell off the wind had freshened. The sky had the dark gray look of coming dawn.

"Boy," Thom muttered, "if we don't go back to The White Crescent, I am going to go to sleep here in the rain." He stopped to cough. "Do you realize you've marched right past three inns? Light, I am so tired I can't think. Do you have a scheme of where to go that you have not told me?"

Mat stared blearily up the street at a tall man in a cloak hurrying around a corner. *Light, I am tired. Rand is five hundred leagues from here, playing at being the bloody Dragon.* "What? Three inns?" They were standing almost in front of another, The Golden Cup according to the sign creaking in the wind. It looked nothing like a dice cup, but he decided to give it a try anyway. "One more, Thom. If we don't find them here, we'll go back and go to bed." Bed sounded better than a dice game with a hundred gold marks riding on the toss, but he made himself go in.

Two steps into the common room Mat saw him. The big man wore a green coat with blue stripes down puffy sleeves, but it was Comar, close-cut black beard with a white streak over his chin and all. He sat in one of the strangely low-backed chairs, at a table on the far side of the room, rattling a leather dice cup and smiling at the man across from him. That fellow wore a long coat and baggy breeches, and he was not smiling. He stared at the coins on the table as if wishing he had them back in his purse. Another dice cup sat at Comar's elbow.

Comar upended the leather cup in his hand, and began laughing almost before the dice stopped spinning. "Who is next?" he called loudly, pulling the wager to his side of the table. There was already a considerable pile of silver in front of him. He scooped the dice into the cup and rattled them. "Surely someone else wants to try his luck?" It seemed that no one did, but he kept rattling the cup and laughing.

The innkeeper was easy to pick out, though they did not seem to wear aprons in Tear. His coat was the same shade of deep blue as that of every other innkeeper Mat had spoken to. A plump man, though little more than half the size of Lopar and with half that fellow's number of chins, he was sitting at a table by himself, polishing a pewter mug furiously and glaring across the room toward Comar, though not when Comar was looking. Some of the other men gave the bearded man sidelong frowns, too. But not when he was looking.

Mat suppressed his first urge, which was to rush over to Comar, drub him over the head with his quarterstaff, and demand to know where Egwene and the others were. Something was wrong here. Comar was the first man he had seen wearing a sword, but the way the men looked at him was more than fear of a swordsman. Even the serving woman who brought Comar a fresh cup of wine—and was pinched for her trouble—had a nervous laugh for him.

Look at it from every side, Mat thought wearily. *Half the trouble I get into is from not doing that. I have to think.* Tiredness seemed to have stuffed his head with wool. He motioned to Thom, and they strolled over to the innkeeper, who eyed them suspiciously when they sat down. "Who is the man with the stripe in his beard?" Mat asked.

"Not from the city, are you?" the innkeeper said. "He is a foreigner, too. I've never seen him before tonight, but I know what he is. Some outlander who has come here and made his fortune in trade. A merchant rich enough to wear a sword. That is no reason for him to treat us like this."

"If you have never seen him before," Mat said, "how do you know he is a merchant?"

The innkeeper looked at him as if he were stupid. "His coat, man, and his sword. He cannot be a lord or a soldier if he's from off, so he has to be a rich merchant." He shook his head for the stupidity of foreigners. "They come to our places, to look down their noses at us, and fondle the girls under our very eyes, but he has no call to do this. If I go to the Maule, I don't gamble for some fisherman's coins. If I go to the Tavar, I do not dice with the farmers come to sell their crops." His polishing gained in ferocity. "Such luck, the man has. It must be how he made his fortune."

"He wins, does he?" Yawning, Mat wondered how he would do dicing with another man who had luck.

"Sometimes he loses," the innkeeper muttered, "when the stake is a few silver pennies. Sometimes. But let it reach a silver mark. . . . No less than a dozen times tonight, I have seen him win at Crowns with three crowns and two roses. And half again as often, at Top, it has been three sixes and two fives. He tosses nothing but sixes at Threes, and three sixes and a five every throw at Compass. If he has such luck, I say the Light shine on him, and well to him, but let him use it with other merchants, as is proper. How can a man have such luck?"

"Weighted dice," Thom said, then coughed. "When he wants to be sure of winning, he uses dice that always show the same face. He is smart enough not to have made it the highest toss—folk become suspicious if you always throw the king"—he raised an eyebrow at Mat—"just one that's all but impossible to beat, but he cannot change that they always show the same face."

"I have heard of such," the innkeeper said slowly. "Illianers use them, I hear." Then he shook his head. "But both men use the same cup and dice. It cannot be."

"Bring me two dice cups," Thom said, "and two sets of dice. Crowns or spots, it makes no difference, so long as they are the same."

The innkeeper frowned at him, but left—prudently taking the pewter cup with him—and came back with two leather cups. Thom rolled the five bone cubes from one onto the table in front of Mat. Whether with spots or symbols, every set of dice Mat had ever seen had been either bone or wood. These had spots. He picked them up, frowning at Thom. "Am I supposed to see something?"

Thom dumped the dice from the other cup into his hand, then, almost too quickly to follow, dropped them back in and twisted the cup over to rest upside down on the table before the dice could fall out. He kept his hand on top of the cup. "Put a mark on each of them, boy. Something small, but something you'll know for your mark."

Mat found himself exchanging puzzled glances with the innkeeper. Then they both looked at the cup upside down under Thom's hand. He knew Thom was up to something tricky—gleemen were always doing things that were impossible, like eating fire and pulling silk out of the air—but he did not see how Thom could do anything with him watching close. He unsheathed his belt knife and made a small scratch on each die, right across the circle of six spots.

"All right," he said, setting them back on the table. "Show me your trick."

Thom reached over and picked up the dice, then set them down again a foot away. "Look for your marks, boy."

Mat frowned. Thom's hand was still on the upended leather cup; the gleeman had not moved it or taken Mat's dice anywhere near it. He picked up the dice . . . and blinked. There was not a scratch on them. The innkeeper gasped.

Thom turned his free hand over, revealing five dice. "Your marks are on these. That is what Comar is doing. It is a child's trick, simple, though I'd never have thought he had the fingers for it."

"I do not think I want to play dice with you after all," Mat said slowly. The innkeeper was staring at the dice, but not as if he saw any solution. "Call the Watch, or whatever you call it here," Mat told him. "Have him arrested." *He'll kill nobody in a prison cell. Yet what if they are already dead?* He tried not to listen, but the thought persisted. *Then I'll see him dead, and Gaebril, whatever it takes! But they aren't, burn me! They can't be!*

The innkeeper was shaking his head. "Me? Me, denounce a merchant to the Defenders? They would not even look at his dice. He could say one word, and I would be in chains working the channeldredges in the Fingers of the Dragon. He could cut me down where I stood, and the Defenders would say I had earned it. Perhaps he will go away after a while."

Mat gave him a wry grimace. "If I expose him, will that be good enough? Will you call the Watch, or the Defenders or whoever, then?"

"You do not understand. You are a foreigner. Even if he is from off, he is a wealthy man, important."

"Wait here," Mat told Thom. "I do not mean to let him reach Egwene and the others, whatever it takes." He yawned as he scraped back his chair.

"Wait, boy," Thom called after him, soft yet urgent. The gleeman pushed himself up out of his chair. "Burn you, you don't know what you're putting your foot into!"

Mat waved for him to stay there and walked over to Comar. No one else had taken up the bearded man's challenge, and he eyed Mat with interest as Mat leaned his quarterstaff against the table and sat down.

Comar studied Mat's coat and grinned nastily. "You want to wager coppers, farmer? I do not waste my time with—" He cut off as Mat set an Andoran gold crown on the table and yawned at him, making no effort to cover his mouth. "You say little, farmer, though your manners could use improving, but gold has a voice of its own and no need of manners." He shook the leather cup in his hand and spilled the dice out. He was chuckling before they came to rest, showing three crowns and two roses. "You'll not beat that, farmer. Perhaps you have more gold hidden in those rags that you want to lose? What did you do? Rob your master?"

He reached for the dice, but Mat scooped them up ahead of him. Comar glared, but let him have the cup. If both tosses were the same, they would throw again until one man won. Mat smiled as he rattled the dice. He did not mean to give Comar a chance to change them. If they threw the same toss three or four times in a row—exactly the same, every time—even these Defenders would listen. The whole common room would see; they would have to back his word.

He spilled the dice onto the tabletop. They bounced oddly. He felt—something—shifting. It was as if his luck had gone wild. The room seemed to be writhing around him, tugging at the dice with threads. For some reason he wanted to look at the door, but he kept his eyes on the dice. They came to rest. Five crowns. Comar's eyes looked ready to pop out of his head.

"You lose," Mat said softly. If his luck was in to this extent, perhaps it was time to push it. A voice in the back of his head told him to think, but he was too tired to listen. "I think your luck is about used up, Comar. If you've harmed those girls, it's all gone."

"I have not even found . . ." Comar began, still staring at the dice, then jerked his head up. His face had gone white. "How do you know my name?"

He had not found them, yet. *Luck, sweet luck, stay with me.* "Go back to Caemlyn, Comar. Tell Gaebril you could not find them. Tell him they are dead. Tell him anything, but leave Tear tonight. If I see you again, I'll kill you."

"Who are you?" the big man said unsteadily. "Who—?" The next instant his sword was out and he was on his feet.

Mat shoved the table at him, overturning it, and grabbed for his quarterstaff. He had forgotten how big Comar was. The bearded man pushed the table right back at him. Mat fell over with his chair, holding a bare grasp on his staff, as Comar heaved the table out of the way and stabbed at him. Mat threw his feet against the man's middle to stop his rush, swung the staff awkwardly, just enough to deflect the sword. But the blow knocked the staff from his fingers, and he found himself gripping Comar's wrist, instead, with the man's blade a hand from his face. With a grunt he rolled backwards, heaving as hard as he could with his legs. Comar's eyes widened as he sailed over Mat to crash onto a table, face up. Mat scrambled for his staff, but when he had it, Comar had not moved.

The big man lay with his hips and legs sprawled across the top of the table, the rest of him hanging down with his head on the floor. The men who had been sitting at the table were on their feet a safe distance away, wringing their hands and eyeing each other nervously. A low, worried buzz filled the common room, not the noise Mat expected.

Comar's sword lay within easy reach of his hand. But he did not move. He stared at Mat, though, as Mat kicked the sword away and went to one knee beside him. *Light! I think his back is broken!* "I told you you should have gone, Comar. Your luck is all used up."

"Fool," the big man breathed. "Do you . . . think I . . . was the only . . . one hunting them? They won't . . . live till. . . ." His eyes stared at Mat, and his mouth was open, but he said no more. Nor ever would again.

Mat met the glazing stare, trying to will more words out of the dead man. *Who else, burn you? Who? Where are they? My luck. Burn me, what happened to my luck?* He became aware of the innkeeper pulling frantically at his arm.

"You must go. You must. Before the Defenders come. I will show them the dice. I will tell them it was an outlander, but a tall man. With red-colored hair, and gray eyes. No one will suffer. A man I dreamed of last night. No one real. No one will contradict me. He took coin from everyone with his dice. But you must go. You must!" Everyone else in the room was studiously looking another way.

Mat let himself be hauled away from the dead man and pushed outside. Thom was already waiting in the rain. He seized Mat's arm and limped down the street hurriedly, pulling Mat stumbling behind him. Mat's hood hung down his back; the rain soaked his hair and poured down his face, down his neck, but he did not notice. The gleeman kept looking over his shoulder, searching the street beyond Mat.

"Are you asleep, boy? You did not look asleep back there. Come on, boy. The Defenders will arrest any outlander within two streets, no matter what description that innkeeper gives."

"It's the luck," Mat mumbled. "I've figured it out. The dice. My luck works best when things are . . . random. Like dice. Not much good for cards. No good at stones. Too much pattern. It has to be random. Even finding Comar. I'd stopped visiting every inn. I walked into that one by chance. Thom, if I am going to find Egwene and the others in time, I have to look without any pattern."

"What are you talking about? The man is dead. If he already killed them. . . . Well, you've avenged them. If he hasn't, you saved them. Now will you bloody walk faster? The Defenders won't be long coming, and they are not so gentle as the Queen's Guards."

Mat shook his arm free and picked up his pace unsteadily, dragging the quarterstaff. "He let it slip that he hadn't located them, yet. But he said he was not the only one. Thom, I believe him. I was looking him in the eye, and he was telling the truth. I still have to find them, Thom. And now I don't even know who is after them. I have to find them."

Stifling a huge yawn with his fist, Thom pulled Mat's hood up against the rain. "Not tonight, boy. I need sleep, and so do you."

Wet. My hair's dripping in my face. His head seemed fuzzy. With a need for sleep, he realized after a moment. And he realized how tired he was, if he had to think just to know it. "All right, Thom. But I am going to look again as soon as it's light." Thom nodded and coughed, and they made their way back to The White Crescent through the rain.

Dawn was not long in coming, but Mat roused himself out of bed, and he and Thom set off trying to search every inn inside the walls of Tear. Mat let himself wander wherever the mood and the next turning took him, not looking for inns at all, and tossing a coin to decide whether to go in. For three days and nights he did this, and for three days and nights it rained without stopping, sometimes thundering, sometimes quiet, but always pouring down.

Thom's cough grew worse, so he had to stop playing the flute and telling stories, and he would not carry his harp out in that weather; he insisted on going along, however, and men still talked to a gleeman. Mat's luck with the dice seemed even better since he had begun this random wander, though he never stayed in one inn or tavern long enough to win more than a few coins. Neither of them heard anything useful. Rumors of war with Illian. Rumors of invading Mayene. Rumors of invasion from Andor, of the Sea Folk shutting off trade, of Artur Hawkwing's armies returning from the dead. Rumors the Dragon was coming. The men Mat gambled with were as gloomy about one rumor as the next; they seemed to him to hunt for the darkest rumors they could find and half believe them all. But he heard not a whisper that might lead him to Egwene and the others. Not one innkeeper had seen women matching their descriptions.

He began to have bad dreams, no doubt from all his worrying. Egwene and Nynaeve and Elayne, and some fellow with close-cropped white hair, wearing a coat with puffy, striped sleeves like Comar's, laughing and weaving a net around them. Only sometimes it was Moiraine he was weaving the net for, and sometimes he held a crystal sword instead, a sword that blazed like the sun as soon as he touched it. Sometimes it was Rand who held the sword. For some reason, he dreamed of Rand a good deal.

Mat was sure it was all because he was not getting enough sleep, not eating except when he happened to remember, but he would not stop. He had a wager to win, he told himself, and he meant to win this one if it killed him.

Chapter
50

The Hammer

The afternoon sun was hot as the ferry docked in Tear; puddles stood on the steaming stones of the dock, and the air seemed almost as damp to Perrin as Illian's had. The air smelled of pitch and wood and rope—he could see shipyards further south along the river—of spices and iron and barley, of perfumes and wines and a hundred different aromas he could not single out from the melange, most coming from the warehouses behind the docks. When the wind swirled momentarily out of the north, he caught the scents of fish, too, but those faded as the wind swung back. No smells of anything to hunt. His mind reached out to feel for wolves before he realized what he was doing and snapped his guards shut. He had done that too often of late. There had been no wolves, of course. Not in a city like this. He wished it did not feel so—alone.

As soon as the ramp at the end of the barge was lowered, he led Stepper up to the dock after Moiraine and Lan. The huge shape of the Stone of Tear lay off to their left, shadowed so that it looked like a mountain despite the great banner at its highest point. He did not want to look at the Stone, but it seemed impossible to look at the city without seeing it. *Is he here yet? Light, if he has already tried to get into* that, *he could be dead already.* And then it would all be for nothing.

"What are we meant to find here?" Zarine asked behind him. She had not stopped asking questions; she just did not ask them of the Aes Sedai or the Warder. "Illian showed us Gray Men and the Wild Hunt. What does Tear hold that— that someone wants to keep you from so badly?"

Perrin glanced around; none of the dockmen shuttling cargo about seemed to have heard. He was sure he would have smelled fear if they had. He bit back the sharp remark that hung on the end of his tongue. She had a quicker tongue, and a sharper.

"I wish you did not sound so eager," Loial rumbled. "You seem to think it will all be as easy as Illian, Faile."

"Easy?" Zarine muttered. "Easy! Loial, we were nearly killed twice in one night. Illian was enough for a Hunter's song in itself. What makes you call it easy?"

Perrin grimaced. He wished Loial had not decided to call Zarine by that name she had chosen; it was a constant reminder that Moiraine thought she was Min's falcon. And it did nothing to stop Perrin wondering if she was the beautiful woman Min had warned him against, too. *At least I've not run up against the hawk. Or a Tuatha'an with a sword! Now that would be the strangest of all, or I am a wool merchant!*

"Stop asking questions, Zarine," he said as he swung up into Stepper's saddle. "You will find out why we are here when Moiraine decides to tell you." He tried not to look at the Stone.

She turned those dark, tilted eyes on him. "I do not think you know why, blacksmith. I think that is why you will not tell me, because you cannot. Admit it, farmboy."

With a small sigh, he rode off the docks after Moiraine and Lan. Zarine did not dig at Loial in that cutting way when the Ogier refused to answer her questions. He thought she must be trying to browbeat him into using that name. He would not.

Moiraine had tied the oiled cloak behind her saddle, atop the innocuous-looking bundle that held the Dragon banner, and despite the heat had donned the blue linen cloak from Illian. Its deep, wide hood hid her face. Her Great Serpent ring was on a cord around her neck. Tear, she had said, did not forbid the presence of Aes Sedai, only channeling, but the Defenders of the Stone kept a close eye on any woman who wore the ring. She did not want to be watched on this visit to Tear.

Lan had stuffed his color-shifting cloak into his saddlebags two days earlier, when it had become apparent that whoever had sent the Darkhounds—*Sammael*, Perrin thought with a shiver, and tried not to think of the name at all—whoever had sent them had not sent any more pursuit. The Warder had made no concessions to the heat of Illian, and he made none to the lesser heat of Tear. His gray-green coat was buttoned up all the way.

Perrin wore his coat half undone, and the neck of his shirt untied. Tear might be a little cooler than Illian, but it was still as hot as summer in the Two Rivers, and as always after rain, the dampness of the air made the heat seem worse. His axe belt hung looped around the tall pommel of his saddle. It was handy there, if he needed it, and he felt better not wearing it.

He was surprised at the mud in the first streets they rode along. Only villages and smaller towns had dirt streets, that he had seen, and Tear was one of the great cities. But the people did not seem to mind, many going barefoot. A woman walking on little wooden platforms caught his attention for a time, and he wondered why they did not all wear them. Those baggy breeches on the men looked as if they might be cooler than the snug ones he wore, but he was sure he would feel a fool if he tried them. He made a picture in his head of himself wearing those breeches and one of those round straw hats, and chuckled at it.

"What do you find funny, Perrin?" Loial asked. His ears were drooping till their tufts were hidden in his hair, and he looked at the people in the street worriedly. "These folk look . . . defeated, Perrin. They did not look this way when I was here last. Even people who let their grove be cut down do not deserve to look like this."

As Perrin began to study faces instead of just looking at everything at once, he saw that Loial was right. Something had gone out of too many of those faces. Hope, maybe. Curiosity. They barely glanced at the party riding by, except to get out of the way of the horses. The Ogier, mounted on an animal as big as a draft horse, might as well have been Lan, or Perrin.

The streets changed, gaining wide stone paving, after they passed inside the gates of the high, gray city wall, past the hard, dark eyes of soldiers in breastplates over red coats with wide sleeves ending in narrow white cuffs, and rimmed, round helmets with a ridge over the top. Instead of the baggy breeches other men wore, theirs were tight, and

tucked into knee-high boots. The soldiers frowned at Lan's
sword and fingered their own, stared sharply at Perrin's axe
and his bow, but in a way, despite their frowns and sharp
looks, there was something beaten in their faces, too, as if
nothing were really worth the effort any longer.

The buildings were larger and taller inside the walls,
though most were made no differently from those outside.
The roofs looked a bit odd to Perrin, especially those that
came to points, but he had seen so many different kinds of
roof since leaving home that he only wondered what kind of
nails they used with their tiles. In some places, the people
did not use nails on their roof tiles at all.

Palaces and great buildings stood among the smaller and
more ordinary, seemingly placed haphazardly; a structure
of towers and squarish, white domes, surrounded on all
sides by wide streets, might have shops and inns and houses
on the other sides of those streets. A huge hall fronted by
squared columns of marble four paces on a side, with fifty
steps to climb to reach bronze doors five spans high, had a
bakery one side and a tailor on the other.

More men wore coats and breeches like the soldiers'
here, though in brighter colors and without armor, and
some even wore swords. None of them went barefoot, not
even those in baggy breeches. The women's dresses were
often longer, their necklines lower to bare shoulders and
even bosom, the cloth as likely to be silk as wool. The Sea
Folk traded a good deal of silk through Tear. As many sedan chairs and carriages drawn by teams of horses moved
through the streets as ox-carts and wagons. Yet too many of
the faces had that same look of having given up.

The inn Lan chose, the Star, had a weaver's shop on one
side and a smithy on the other, with narrow alleyways between. The smithy was of undressed gray stone, the weaver's and the inn of wood, though the Star stood four stories
tall and had small windows in its roof as well. The rattle of
looms was hard-pressed to compete with the clang of the
smith's hammer. They handed their horses over to stablemen, to be taken around back, and went inside the inn.
There were fish smells from the kitchen, baking and perhaps stewing, and the scent of roast mutton. The men in the
common room all wore the tight coats and loose breeches;
Perrin did not think richer men—somehow he was sure

the men in colorful coats with puffy sleeves and the bare-shouldered women in bright silk were all rich, or nobles—those folk would not put up with the noise. Perhaps that was why Lan had chosen it.

"How are we supposed to sleep with this racketing?" Zarine muttered.

"No questions?" he said with a smile. For a moment he thought she was going to stick out her tongue at him.

The innkeeper was a round-faced, balding man in a long, deep blue coat and those loose breeches, who bowed over hands clasped across his stout belly. His face had that look, a weary resignation. "The Light shine on you, mistresses, and welcome," he sighed. "The Light shine on you, masters, and welcome." He gave a small start at Perrin's yellow eyes, then passed wearily on to Loial. "The Light shine on you, friend Ogier, and welcome. It is a year or more since I have seen one of your kind in Tear. Some work or other at the Stone. They stayed in the Stone, of course, but I saw them in the street one day." He finished with another sigh, seemingly unable to summon any curiosity as to why another Ogier had come to Tear, or why any of them had come, for that matter.

The balding man, whose name was Jurah Haret, showed them to their rooms himself. Apparently Moiraine's silk dress and the way she kept her face hidden, taken with Lan's hard face and sword, made them a lady and her guard in his eyes, and so worthy of his personal attention. Perrin he obviously took as some kind of retainer, and Zarine he was plainly unsure of—to her visible disgust—and Loial was, after all, an Ogier. He called men to push beds together for Loial, and offered Moiraine a private room for her meals if she wished. She accepted graciously.

They kept together through it all, making a small procession through the upper halls until Haret bowed and sighed his way out of their presence, leaving them all where they had begun, outside Moiraine's room. The walls were white plaster, and Loial's head brushed the hall ceiling.

"Odious fellow," Zarine muttered, brushing furiously at the dust on her narrow skirts with both hands. "I believe he took me for your handmaid, Aes Sedai. I will not stand for that!"

"Watch your tongue," Lan said softly. "If you use that

name where folk can hear, you will regret it, girl." She looked as if she were going to argue, but his icy blue eyes stilled her tongue this time, if it did not cool her glare.

Moiraine ignored them. Staring off at nothing, she worked her cloak in her hands almost as if wiping them. Unaware what she was doing, in Perrin's opinion.

"How do we go about finding Rand?" he asked, but she did not appear to hear him. "Moiraine?"

"Remain close to the inn," she said after a moment. "Tear can be a dangerous city for those who do not know its ways. The Pattern can be torn, here." That last was soft, as if to herself. In a stronger voice she said, "Lan, let us see what we can discover without attracting attention. The rest of you, stay close to the inn!"

"'Stay close to the inn,'" Zarine mimicked as the Aes Sedai and the Warder disappeared down the stairs. But she said it quietly enough that they would not hear. "This Rand. He is the one you called the. . . ." If she looked like a falcon right then, it was a very uneasy falcon. "And we are in Tear, where the Heart of the Stone holds. . . . And the Prophecies say. . . . The Light burn me, *ta'veren*, is this a story I want to be in?"

"It is not a story, Zarine." For a moment Perrin felt almost as hopeless as the innkeeper had sounded. "The Wheel weaves us into the Pattern. You chose to tangle your thread with ours; it's too late to untangle it, now."

"Light!" she growled. "Now you sound like *her*!"

He left her there with Loial and went to put his things in his room—it had a low bed, comfortable but small, as city people seemed to think befitted a servant, a washstand, a stool, and a few pegs on the cracked plaster wall—and when he came out, they were both gone. The ring of hammer on anvil called to him.

So much in Tear looked odd that it was a relief to walk into the smithy. The ground floor was all one large room with no back wall except for two long doors that stood open on a yard for shoeing horses and oxen, complete with an ox sling. Hammers stood in their stands, tongs of various kinds and sizes hung on the exposed joists of the walls, buttresses and hoof knives and other farrier's tools lay neatly arranged on wooden benches with chisels and beak irons and swages and all the implements of the blacksmith's craft. Bins held lengths of iron and steel in various thicknesses. Five grinding wheels of different roughness stood about the hard dirt floor, six anvils, and three stone-sided forges with their bellows, though only one held glowing coals. Quenching barrels stood ready to hand.

The smith was plying his hammer on yellow-hot iron gripped in heavy tongs. He wore baggy breeches and had pale blue eyes, but the long leather vest over his bare chest and apron were not much different from those Perrin and Master Luhhan had worn back in Emond's Field, and his thick arms and shoulders spoke of years working metal. His dark hair had almost the same amount of gray that Perrin remembered in Master Luhhan's. More vests and aprons hung on the wall, as if the man had apprentices, but they were not in evidence now. The forge-fire smelled like home. The hot iron smelled like home.

The smith turned to thrust the piece he was working back into the coals, and Perrin stepped over to work the bellows for him. The man glanced at him, but said nothing. Perrin pulled the bellows handle up and down with slow, steady, even strokes, keeping the coals at the right heat. The smith went back to working the hot iron, on the rounded horn of the anvil, this time. Perrin thought he might be making a barrel scrape. The hammer rang with sharp, quick blows.

The man spoke without looking up from his work. "Apprentice?" was all he said.

"Yes," Perrin replied just as simply.

The smith worked on for a time. It *was* a barrel scrape, for cleaning the insides of wooden barrels. Now and again he eyed Perrin consideringly. Setting his hammer down, just for a moment, the smith picked up a short length of thick, square stock and pushed it into Perrin's hand, then picked up his hammer again and resumed work. "See what you can do with that," he said.

Without even thinking about it, Perrin stepped over to an anvil on the other side of the forge and tapped the stock against its edge. It made a nice ring. The steel had not been left long enough in the slowfurnace to pick up a great deal of carbon from the coal. He pushed it into the hot coals for almost its entire length, tasted the two water barrels to see which had been salted—the third was olive oil—then took off his coat and shirt and chose a leather vest that would fit his chest. Most of these Tairen fellows were not as large as he, but he found one that would do. Finding an apron was easier.

When he turned around, he saw the smith, still with his head down over his work, nodding and smiling to himself. But just because he knew his way around a smithy did not mean he had any skill at smithing. That was yet to be shown.

When he came back to the anvil with two hammers, a set of long-handled flat-tongs, and a sharp-topped hardy, the steel bar had heated to a dark red except for a small bit of what he had left out of the coals. He worked the bellows, watching the color of the metal lighten, until it reached a yellow just short of white. Then he pulled it out with the tongs, laid it on the anvil, and picked up the heavier of the two hammers. About ten pounds, he estimated, and with a longer handle than most people, who did not know metal working, thought was necessary. He held it near the end; hot metal gave off sparks, sometimes, and he had seen the scars on the hands of the smith from up at Roundhill, a careless fellow.

He did not want to make anything elaborate or fancy. Simple things seemed best at the moment. He began by rounding the edges of the bar, then hammered the middle out into a broad blade, almost as thick as the original at the butt, but a good hand and a half long. From time to time he returned the metal to the coals, to keep it at the pale yellow, and after a time he shifted to the lighter hammer, half the weight of the first. The piece beyond the blade, he thinned down, then bent it over the anvil horn in a curve down beside the blade. A wooden handle could be fixed onto that, eventually. Setting the sharp-chisel hardy in the anvil's hardy-hole, he laid the glowing metal atop it. One sharp blow of the hammer cut off the tool he had made. Or almost made. It would be a chamfer knife, for smoothing and leveling the tops of barrel staves after they were hopped together, among other things. When he was done. The other man's barrel scrape had made him think of it.

As soon as he had made the hot-cut, he tossed the glowing metal into the salted quenching barrel. Unsalted gave a harder quench, for the hardest metal, while the oil gave the softest, for good knives. And swords, he had heard, but he had never had any part in making anything like that.

When the metal had cooled enough, to a dull gray, he removed it from the water and took it to the grinding wheels. A little slow work with the footpedals ground a polish onto the blade. Carefully, he heated the blade portion again. This time the colors deepened, to straw, to bronze. When the bronze color began to run up the blade in waves, he set it aside to cool. The final edge could be sharpened then. Quenching again would destroy the tempering he had just done.

"A very neat bit of work," the smith said. "No wasted motion. You looking for work? My apprentices just walked away, all three of them, the worthless fools, and I've plenty you could do."

Perrin shook his head. "I do not know how long I will be in Tear. I'd like to work a little longer, if you do not mind. It has been a long time, and I miss it. Maybe I could do some of the work your apprentices would have done."

The smith snorted loudly. "You're a deal better than any of those louts, moping around and staring, muttering about their nightmares. As if everyone doesn't have nightmares, sometimes. Yes, you can work here, as long as you want. Light, I've orders for a dozen drawknives and three cooper's adzes, and a carpenter down the street needs a mortise hammer, and. . . . Too much to list it. Start with the draw-knives, and we will see how far we get before night."

Perrin lost himself in the work, for a time forgetting everything but the heat of the metal, the ring of his hammer, and the smell of the forge, but there came a time when he looked up and found the smith—Dermid Ajala, he had said his name was—taking off his vest, and the shoeing yard dark. All the light came from the forge and a pair of lamps. And Zarine was sitting on an anvil by one of the cold forges, watching him.

"So you really are a blacksmith, blacksmith," she said.

"He is that, mistress," Ajala said. "Apprentice, he says, but the work he did today amounts to his master's piece as far as I am concerned. Fine stroking, and better than steady." Perrin shifted his feet at the compliments, and the smith grinned at him. Zarine stared at both of them with a lack of comprehension.

Perrin went to replace the vest and apron on their peg, but once he had them off, he was suddenly conscious of Zarine's eyes on his back. It was if she were touching him; for a moment, the herbal scent of her seemed overwhelming.

He quickly pulled his shirt over his head, stuffed it raggedly into his breeches, and jerked on his coat. When he turned around, Zarine wore one of those small, secretive smiles that had always made him nervous.

"Is this what you mean to do, then?" she asked. "Did you come all this way to be a blacksmith again?" Ajala paused in the act of pulling the yard doors closed and listened.

Perrin picked up the heavy hammer he had used, a ten-pound head with a handle as long as his forearm. It felt good in his hands. It felt right. The smith had glanced at his eyes once and never even blinked; it was the work that was important, the skill with metal, not the color of a man's eyes. "No," he said sadly. "One day, I hope. But not yet." He started to hang the hammer back on the wall.

"Take it." Ajala cleared his throat. "I do not usually give away good hammers, but. . . . The work you've done today is worth more than the price of that hammer by far, and maybe it will help you to that 'one day.' Man, if I have ever seen anyone made to hold a smith's hammer, it is you. So take it. Keep it."

Perrin closed his hand around the haft. It did feel right. "Thank you," he said. "I cannot say what this means to me."

"Just remember the 'one day,' man. Just you remember it."

As they left, Zarine looked up at him and said, "Do you have any idea how strange men are, blacksmith? No. I did not think you did." She darted ahead, leaving him holding the hammer in one hand and scratching his head with the other.

No one in the common room looked at him twice, a golden-eyed man carrying a smith's hammer. He went up to his room, remembering for once to light a tallow candle. His quiver and the axe hung from the same peg on the plaster wall. He hefted the axe in one hand, the hammer in the other. By weight of metal, the axe, with its half-moon blade and thick spike, was a good five or six pounds lighter than the hammer, but it felt ten times heavier. Replacing the axe in the loop on its belt, he set the hammer on the floor beneath the peg, handle against the wall. Axe haft and hammer haft almost touched, two pieces of wood equally thick. Two pieces of metal, near enough the same weight. For a long time he sat on the stool staring at them. He was still staring when Lan put his head into the room.

"Come, blacksmith. We have things to talk over."

"I *am* a blacksmith," Perrin said, and the Warder frowned at him.

"Don't go winter-crazy on me now, blacksmith. If you cannot carry your weight any longer, you may drag us all down the mountain."

"I'll carry my weight," Perrin growled. "I will do what has to be done. What do you want?"

"You, blacksmith. Don't you listen? Come on, farmboy."

That name that Zarine so often called him pulled him to his feet angrily, now, but Lan was already turning away. Perrin hurried into the hall and followed him toward the front of the inn, meaning to tell the Warder he had had enough of this "blacksmith" and "farmboy," his name was Perrin Aybara. The Warder ducked into the inn's only private dining room, overlooking the street.

Perrin followed him. "Now listen, *Warder*, I—"

"You listen, Perrin," Moiraine said. "Be quiet and listen." Her face was smooth, but her eyes looked as grim as her voice sounded.

Perrin had not realized anyone was in the room except for himself and the Warder, standing with one arm up on the mantel of the unlit fireplace. Moiraine sat at the table in the middle of the floor, a simple piece, of black oak. None of the other chairs with their high, carved backs were occupied. Zarine was leaning against the wall at the other end of the room from Lan, scowling, and Loial had chosen to sit on the floor since none of the chairs really fit him.

"I'm glad you decided to join us, farmboy," Zarine said sarcastically. "Moiraine would not say anything till you came. She just looks at us as if she is deciding which of us is going to die. I—"

"Be quiet," Moiraine told her sharply. "One of the Forsaken is in Tear. The High Lord Samon is Be'lal." Perrin shivered.

Loial squeezed his eyes shut and groaned. "I could have remained in the *stedding*. I would probably have been very happy, married, whoever my mother chose. She is a fine woman, my mother, and she would not give me to a bad wife." His ears seemed to have hidden themselves completely in his shaggy hair.

"You can go back to Stedding Shangtai," Moiraine said. "Leave now, if you wish. I will not stop you."

Loial opened one eye. "I can go?"

"If you wish," she said.

"Oh." He opened the other eye, and scratched his cheek with blunt fingers the size of sausages. "I suppose. . . . I suppose . . . if I have a choice . . . that I will stay with all of you. I have taken a great many notes, but not nearly enough to complete my book, and I would not like to leave Perrin, and Rand—"

Moiraine cut him off in a cold voice. "Good, Loial. I am glad that you are staying. I will be glad to use any knowledge you have. But until this is done, I have no time to listen to your complaints!"

"I suppose," Zarine said in an unsteady voice, "that there is no chance of me leaving?" She looked at Moiraine, and shivered. "I thought not. Blacksmith, if I live through this, I will make you pay."

Perrin stared at her. *Me! The fool woman thinks it my fault? Did I ask her to come?* He opened his mouth, saw the look in Moiraine's eyes, and closed it again quickly. After a moment he said, "Is he after Rand? To stop him, or kill him?"

"I think not," she said quietly. Her voice was like cold steel. "I fear he means to let Rand enter the Heart of the Stone and take *Callandor*, then take it away from him. I fear he means to kill the Dragon Reborn with the very weapon that is meant to herald him."

"Do we run again?" Zarine said. "Like Illian? I never thought to run, but I never thought to find the Forsaken when I took the Hunter's oath."

"This time," Moiraine said, "we do not run. We dare not run. Worlds and time rest on Rand, on the Dragon Reborn. This time, we fight."

Perrin took a chair uneasily. "Moiraine, you are saying a lot of things right out that you told us we must not even think about. You *do* have this room warded against listening, don't you?" When she shook her head, he gripped the edge of the table hard enough to make the dark oak creak.

"I do not speak of a Myrddraal, Perrin. No one knows the strength of the Forsaken, except that Ishamael and Lanfear were the strongest, but the weakest of them could sense any warding I might set from a mile or more away. And rip all of us to shreds in seconds. Possibly without stirring from where he stood."

"You're saying he can tie you in knots," Perrin muttered. "Light! What are we supposed to do? How can we do anything?"

"Even the Forsaken cannot stand up to balefire," she said. He wondered if that was what she had used on the Darkhounds; it still made him uneasy, what he had seen, and what she had said then. "I have learned things in the last year, Perrin. I am . . . more dangerous than when I came to Emond's Field. If I can come close enough to Be'lal, I can destroy him. But if he sees me first, he can destroy us all, long before I have a chance." She turned her attention to Loial. "What can you tell me of Be'lal?"

Perrin blinked in confusion. *Loial?*

"Why are you asking him?" Zarine burst out angrily. "First you tell the blacksmith you mean us to fight one of the Forsaken!—who can kill us all before we can even think!—and now you ask Loial about him?" Loial murmured urgently, that name she used—"Faile! Faile!"—but she did not even slow. "I thought Aes Sedai knew everything. Light, at least I am smart enough not to say I will fight someone unless I know everything I can of him! You. . . ." She trailed off under Moiraine's stare, muttering.

"Ogier," the Aes Sedai said coolly, "have long memories, girl. It has been well over a hundred generations since the Breaking for humans, but less than thirty for Ogier. We still learn things from their stories that we did not know. Now tell me, Loial. What do you know of Be'lal. And briefly, for once. I want your long memory, not your long wind."

Loial cleared his throat, a sound much like firewood tumbling down a chute. "Be'lal." His ears flickered out of his hair like hummingbird wings, then snapped down again. "I do not know what can be in the stories about him you do not already know. He is not much mentioned, except in the razing of the Hall of the Servants just before Lews Therin Kinslayer and the Hundred Companions sealed him up with the Dark One. Jalanda son of Aried son of Coiam wrote that he was called the Envious, that he forsook the Light because he envied Lews Therin, and that he envied Ishamael and Lanfear, too. In *A Study of the War of the*

Shadow, Moilin daughter of Hamada daughter of Juendan called Be'lal the Netweaver, but I do not know why. She mentioned him playing a game of stones with Lews Therin and winning, and that he always boasted of it." He glanced at Moiraine and rumbled, "I am trying to be brief. I do not know anything important about him. Several writers say Be'lal and Sammael were both leaders in the fight against the Dark One before they forsook the Light, and both were masters of the sword. That is truly all I know. He may be mentioned in other books, other stories, but I have not read them. Be'lal is just not spoken of very often. I am sorry I could not tell you anything useful."

"Perhaps you have," Moiraine told him. "I did not know of the name, the Netweaver. Or that he envied the Dragon as well as his companions in the Shadow. That strengthens my belief that he wants *Callandor*. That must be the reason he has chosen to make himself a High Lord of Tear. And the Netweaver—a name for a schemer, a patient and cunning planner. You have done well, Loial." For a moment the Ogier's wide mouth curved up in a pleased smile, but then it curved down again.

"I will not pretend I am not afraid," Zarine said suddenly. "Only a fool would not be afraid of the Forsaken. But I swore I would be one of you, and I will. That is all that I wanted to say."

Perrin shook his head. *She* must *be crazy. I could wish I were not one of this party. I could wish I were back home working Master Luhhan's forge.* Aloud, he said, "If he is inside the Stone, if he is waiting there for Rand, we must go inside to reach him. How do we do that? Everyone keeps saying no one enters the Stone without the permission of the High Lords, and looking at it, I don't see any way but through the gates."

"You do not go in," Lan said. "Moiraine and I will be the only ones to enter. The more who go, the harder it will be. Whatever way in I find, I cannot believe it will be easy even for only two."

"Gaidin," Moiraine began in a firm voice, but the Warder cut her off with one just as firm.

"We go together, Moiraine. I will not stand aside this time." After a moment she nodded. Perrin thought he saw Lan relax. "The rest of you had better get some sleep," the

Warder went on. "I have to be out studying the Stone." He paused. "There is a thing that your news drove out of my head, Moiraine. A small thing, and I cannot see what it might mean. There are Aiel in Tear."

"Aiel!" Loial exclaimed. "Impossible! The entire city would be in a panic if one Aiel came through the gates."

"I did not say they were walking the streets, Ogier. The rooftops and chimneys of the city make as good hiding as the Waste. I saw no less than three, though apparently no one else in Tear has seen any of them. And if I saw three, you can be sure there are many times that I did not see."

"It means nothing to me," Moiraine said slowly. "Perrin, why are you frowning in that way?"

He had not known that he was frowning. "I was thinking about that Aiel in Remen. He said that when the Stone falls, the Aiel will leave the Three-fold Land. That's the Waste, isn't it? He said it was a prophecy."

"I have read every word of the Prophecies of the Dragon," Moiraine said softly, "in every translation, and there is no mention of the Aiel. We stagger blindly while Be'lal weaves his nets, and the Wheel weaves the Pattern around us. But are the Aiel the Wheel's weaving, or Be'lal's? Lan, you must find me the way into the Stone quickly. Us. Find us a way in quickly."

"As you command, Aes Sedai," he said, but his tone was more warm than formal. He vanished through the door. Moiraine frowned at the table, eyes clouded in thought.

Zarine came over to look down at Perrin, her head tilted to one side. "And what are you going to do, blacksmith? It seems they mean us to wait and watch while they go adventuring. Not that I will complain."

He doubted that last. "First," he told her, "I am going to have something to eat. And then I am going to think about a hammer." *And try to puzzle out how I feel about you. Falcon.*

CHAPTER
51

Bait for the Net

From the corner of her eye, Nynaeve thought she glimpsed a tall man with reddish hair, in a swirling brown cloak, well down the sunlit street, but as she turned to peer from under the wide brim of the blue straw hat Ailhuin had given her, an ox-drawn wagon was already lumbering between them. When it lurched on, the man was nowhere to be seen. She was almost certain that had been a wooden flute case on his back, and his clothes were certainly not Tairen. *It couldn't be Rand. Just because I keep dreaming about him does not mean he is going to come all the way from Almoth Plain.*

One of the barefoot men hurrying past, with the sickle-shaped tails of a dozen large fish sticking up from the basket on his back, suddenly tripped, catapulting silver-scaled fish over his head as he fell. He landed on hands and knees in the mud, staring at the fish that had come out of his basket. Every one of the long, sleek shapes stood upright, stuck nose down in the mud, forming a neat circle. Even a few passersby gaped at that. Slowly the man got to his feet, apparently unaware of the mud on him. Unslinging his basket, he began gathering the fish back into it, shaking his head and muttering to himself.

Nynaeve blinked, but her business was with this cow-faced brigand, facing her in the doorway of his shop with bloody cuts of meat hanging from hooks behind him. She gave her braid a tug and fixed the fellow with her eye.

"Very well," she said sharply, "I will take it, but if this is what you charge for so poor a cut, you'll not have more business from me."

He shrugged placidly as he took her coins, then wrapped the fatty mutton roast in a cloth she produced from the basket on her arm. She glared at him as she put the wrapped meat into the basket, but that did not affect him.

She whirled to stalk away—and nearly fell. She was still not used to these clogs; they kept sticking in the mud, and she could not see how the folk who wore them managed. She hoped this sunshine dried the ground soon, but she had a feeling that the mud was more or less permanent in the Maule.

Stepping gingerly, she started back toward Ailhuin's house, muttering under her breath. The prices were outrageous for everything, the quality inevitably poor, and almost no one seemed to care, not the people buying or those selling. It was a relief to pass a woman shouting at a shopkeeper, waving a bruised reddish-yellow fruit—Nynaeve did not know what; they had a good many fruits and vegetables she had never heard of, here—in each hand and calling for everyone to see what refuse the man sold, but the shopkeeper only stared at her wearily, not even bothering to argue back.

There was some excuse for the prices, she knew—Elayne had explained all about the grain being eaten by rats in the granaries because no one in Cairhien could buy, and how big the Cairhienin grain trade had become since the Aiel War—but nothing excused the way everyone seemed ready to lie down and die. She had seen hail ruin food crops in the Two Rivers, and grasshoppers eat them and blacktongue kill the sheep and redspot wither the tabac so there was nothing to sell when the merchants came down from Baerlon. She could remember two years in a row when there had been little to eat except turnip soup and old barley, and hunters had been lucky to bring home a scrawny rabbit, but Two Rivers folk picked themselves up when they were knocked down and went back to work. These people had had only one bad year, and their fisheries and their other trade seemed to be flourishing. She had no patience with them. The trouble was, she knew she should have a little patience. They were odd people with odd ways, and things she took for cringing, they seemed to see as a matter of course, even Ailhuin and Sandar. She should be able to summon up just a little patience.

If for them, why not for Egwene? She put that aside. The child behaved wretchedly, snapping at the most obvious suggestions, objecting to the most sensible things. Even when it was plain what they should do, Egwene wanted to be convinced. Nynaeve was not used to having to convince people, especially not people she had changed swaddling clothes for. The fact that she was only a matter of seven years older than Egwene was of no account.

It is all those bad dreams, she told herself. *I cannot understand what they mean, and now Elayne and I are having them, too, and I do not know what that means either, and Sandar won't say anything except that he is still looking, and I am so frustrated I . . . I could just spit!* She jerked her braid so hard it hurt. At least she had been able to convince Egwene not to use the *ter'angreal* again, to put the thing back in her pouch instead of wearing it next to her skin always. If the Black Ajah was in *Tel'aran'rhiod.* . . . She did not want to think about that possibility. *We* will *find them!*

"I will bring them down," she muttered. "Trying to sell me like a sheep! Hunting me like an animal! I am the hunter this time, not the rabbit! That Moiraine! If she had never come to Emond's Field, I could have taught Egwene enough. And Rand. . . . I could have . . . I could have done something." That she knew neither was true did not help; it made it worse. She hated Moiraine almost as much as she hated Liandrin and the Black Ajah, maybe as much as she hated the Seanchan.

She rounded a corner, and Juilin Sandar had to leap out of her way to keep from being trampled. Even used to them as he was, he nearly tripped over his own clogs, only his staff saving him from falling on his face in the mud. That pale, ridged wood was called bamboo, she had learned, and it was stronger than it looked.

"Mistress—uh—Mistress Maryim," Sandar said, regaining his balance. "I was . . . looking for you." He flashed her a nervous smile. "Are you angry? Why are you frowning at me that way?"

She smoothed her forehead. "I was not frowning at you, Master Sandar. The butcher. . . . It does not matter. Why are you looking for me?" Her breath caught. "Have you found them?"

He looked around as if he suspected the passersby of trying to listen. "Yes. Yes, you must come back with me. The others are waiting. The others. And Mother Guenna."

"Why are you so nervous? You did not let them discover your interest?" she said sharply. "What has frightened you?"

"No! No, mistress. I—I did not reveal myself." His eyes darted again, and he stepped closer, his voice dropping to a breathy, urgent whisper. "These women you seek, they are in the Stone! Guests of a High Lord! The High Lord Samon! Why did you call them thieves? The High Lord Samon!" he almost squeaked. There was sweat on his face.

Inside the Stone! With a High Lord! Light, how do we reach them now? She suppressed her impatience with an effort. "Be easy," she said soothingly. "Be at ease, Master Sandar. We can explain everything to your satisfaction." *I hope we can. Light, if he goes running to the Stone to tell this High Lord we are searching for them....* "Come with me to Mother Guenna's house. Joslyn, Caryla, and I will explain it all to you. Truly. Come."

He gave a short, uneasy nod, and walked alongside her, keeping his pace to what she could manage with the clogs. He looked as if he wanted to run.

At the Wise Woman's house, she hurried around to the back. No one ever used the front door, that she had seen, not even Mother Guenna herself. The horses were tied to a bamboo hitching rail, now—well away from Ailhuin's new figs as well as her vegetables—with their saddles and bridles stored inside. For once she did not stop to pat Gaidin's nose and tell him he was a good boy, and more sensible than his namesake. Sandar halted to scrape mud from his clogs with the butt of his staff, but she hurried inside.

Ailhuin Guenna was sitting in one of her high-backed chairs pulled out into the room, her arms at her sides. The gray-haired woman's eyes were bulging with anger and fear, and she struggled furiously without moving a muscle. Nynaeve did not need to sense the subtle weaving of Air to know what had happened. *Light, they've found us! Burn you, Sandar!*

Rage flooded her, washed away the walls inside that usually kept her from the Power, and as the basket fell from her hands, she was a white blossom on a blackthorn bush, opening to embrace *saidar*, opening. . . . It was as if she had run into another wall, a wall of clear glass; she could feel the True Source, but the wall stopped everything except the ache to be filled with the One Power.

The basket hit the floor, and as it bounced, the door behind her opened and Liandrin stepped in, followed by a black-haired woman with a white streak above her left ear. They wore long, colorful silk dresses cut to bare their shoulders, and the glow of *saidar* surrounded them.

Liandrin smoothed her red dress and smiled with that pouting rosebud mouth. Her doll's face was filled with amusement. "You see, do you not, wilder," she began, "you have no—"

Nynaeve hit her in the mouth as hard as she could. *Light, I have to get away.* She backhanded Rianna so hard the black-haired woman fell on her silk-covered rump with a grunt. *They must have the others, but if I can make it out the door, if I can get far enough away they can't shield me, I can do something.* She pushed Liandrin hard, shoving her away from the door. *Just let me escape their shielding, and I'll. . . .*

Blows hit her from every side, like fists and sticks, pummeling her. Neither Liandrin, blood trickling from a corner of her now-grim mouth, nor Rianna, her hair as disarrayed as her green dress, lifted a hand. Nynaeve could feel the flows of Air weaving about her as well as she could feel the blows themselves. She still struggled to reach the door, but she realized that she was on her knees, now, and the unseen blows would not stop, invisible sticks and fists striking at her back and her stomach, her head and her hips, her shoulders, her breasts, her legs, her head. Groaning, she fell onto her side and curled into a ball, trying to protect herself. *Oh, Light, I tried. Egwene! Elayne! I tried! I will not cry out! Burn you, you can beat me to death, but I won't cry!*

The blows stopped, but Nynaeve could not stop quivering. She felt bruised and battered from crown to toe.

Liandrin crouched beside her, arms around her knees, silk rustling against silk. She had wiped the blood away from her mouth. Her dark eyes were hard, and there was no amusement on her face now. "Perhaps you are too stupid to know when you are defeated, wilder. You fought almost as wildly as that other foolish girl, that Egwene. She almost went mad. You must all learn to submit. You *will* learn to submit."

Nynaeve shivered and reached for *saidar* again. It was not that she had any real hope, but she had to do something. Forcing through her pain, she reached out . . . and struck that invisible shield. Liandrin did have amusement back in her eyes, now, the grim mirth of a nasty child who pulls the wings off flies.

"We have no use for this one, at least," Rianna said, standing beside Ailhuin. "I will stop her heart." Ailhuin's eyes nearly came out of her head.

"No!" Liandrin's short, honey-colored braids swung as her head snapped around. "Always you kill too quickly, and only the Great Lord can make use of the dead." She smiled at the woman held to the chair by invisible bonds. "You saw the soldiers who came with us, old woman. You know who waits for us in the Stone. The High Lord Samon, he will not be pleased if you speak of what happened inside your house today. If you hold your tongue, you will live, perhaps to serve him again one day. If you speak, you will serve only the Great Lord of the Dark, from beyond the grave. Which do you choose?"

Suddenly Ailhuin could move her head. She shook her gray curls, working her mouth. "I. . . . I will hold my tongue," she said dejectedly, then gave Nynaeve an embarrassed, shamed look. "If I speak, what good will it do? A High Lord could have my head by raising an eyebrow. What good can I do you, girl? What good?"

"It is all right," Nynaeve said wearily. *Who could she tell? All she could do is die.* "I know you would help if you could." Rianna threw back her head and laughed. Ailhuin slumped, released completely, but she only sat there, staring at her hands in her lap.

Between them, Liandrin and Rianna pulled Nynaeve to her feet and pushed her toward the front of the house. "You give us any trouble," the black-haired woman said in a hard voice, "and I will make you peel off your own skin and dance in your bones."

Nynaeve almost laughed. *What trouble could I give?* She was shielded from the True Source. Her bruises ached so much she could barely stand. Anything she might do, they could handle like a child's tantrum. *But my bruises will*

*heal, burn you, and you'll make a slip yet! And when you
do. . . .*

There were others in the front room of the house. Two big
soldiers in rimmed, round helmets and shiny breastplates
over those puffy-sleeved red coats. The two men had sweat
on their faces, and their dark eyes rolled as if they were as
afraid as she. Amico Nagoyin was there, slender and pretty
with her long neck and pale skin, looking as innocent as a
girl gathering flowers. Joiya Byir had a friendly face despite
that smooth-cheeked calm of a woman who had worked
long with the Power, almost a grandmother's face in its
welcoming appearance, though her age had put no touch
of gray in her dark hair, any more than it had wrinkled
her skin. Her gray eyes looked more like those of the step-
mother in the stories, the one who murdered the children of
her husband's first wife. Both women shone with the Power.

Elayne stood between the two Black sisters, with a
bruised eye and a swollen cheek and a split lip, one sleeve
of her dress torn halfway off. "I am sorry, Nynaeve," she
said thickly, as if her jaw hurt. "We never saw them until it
was too late."

Egwene lay in a crumpled heap on the floor, her face
swollen with bruises, almost unrecognizable. As Nynaeve
and her escort came in, one of the big soldiers hoisted
Egwene over his shoulder. She dangled there as limply as a
half-empty barley sack.

"What did you do to her?" Nynaeve demanded. "Burn
you, what—!" Something unseen struck her across the
mouth hard enough to make her eyes go blank for a moment.

"Now, now," Joiya Byir said with a smile that her eyes
belied. "I will not stand for demands, or bad language." She
sounded like a grandmother, too. "You speak when you are
spoken to."

"I told you the girl, she would not stop fighting, yes?"
Liandrin said. "Let it be a lesson to you. If you try to cause
any trouble, you will be treated no more gently."

Nynaeve ached to do something for Egwene, but she let
herself be pushed out into the street. She made them push
her; it was a small way of fighting back, refusing to cooper-
ate, but it was all she had at the moment.

There were few people in the muddy street, as if everyone

had decided it was much better to be somewhere else, and
those few scurried by on the other side without a glance at
the shiny, black-lacquered coach standing behind a team of
six matched whites with tall white plumes on their bridles.
A coachman dressed like the soldiers, but without armor or
sword, sat on the seat, and another opened the door as they
appeared from the house. Before he did, Nynaeve saw the
sigil painted there. A silver-gauntleted fist clutching jagged
lightning bolts.

She supposed it was High Lord Samon's sign—*A Darkfriend, he must be, if he deals with the Black Ajah. The
Light burn him!*—but she was more interested in the man
who dropped to his knees in the mud at their appearance.
"Burn you, Sandar, why—?" She jumped as something that
felt like a stick of wood struck her across the shoulders.

Joiya Byir smiled chidingly and waggled a finger. "You
will be respectful, child. Or you might lose that tongue."

Liandrin laughed. Tangling a hand in Sandar's black
hair, she wrenched his head back. He stared up at her with
the eyes of a faithful hound—or of a cur expecting a kick.
"Do not be too hard on this man." She even made "man"
sound like "dog." "He had to be . . . persuaded . . . to serve.
But I am very good at persuading, no?" She laughed again.

Sandar turned a confused stare on Nynaeve. "I had to
do it, Mistress Maryim. I . . . had to." Liandrin twisted his
hair, and his eyes went back to her, the anxious hound's
once more.

Light! Nynaeve thought. *What did they do to him? What
are they going to do to us?*

She and Elayne were bundled roughly into the coach,
with Egwene slumped between them, her head lolling, and
Liandrin and Rianna climbed in and took the seat facing
forward. The glow of *saidar* still surrounded them. Where
the others went, Nynaeve did not much care at that moment.
She wanted to reach Egwene, to touch her, to comfort her
hurts, but she could not move a muscle below her neck except to writhe. Flows of Air bound the three of them like
layers of tightly wrapped blankets. The coach lurched into
motion, swaying hard in the mud despite its leather springs.

"If you have hurt her. . . ." *Light, I can see they've hurt
her. Why don't I say what I mean?* But it was almost as hard
to force the words out as it would have been to lift a hand.

"If you have killed her, I won't rest till you are all hunted down like wild dogs."

Rianna glared, but Liandrin only sniffed. "Do not be a complete fool, wilder. You are wanted alive. Dead bait will catch nothing."

Bait? For what? For who? "You are the fool, Liandrin! Do you think we are here alone? Only three of us, and not even full Aes Sedai? We are bait, Liandrin. And you have walked into the trap like a fat grouse."

"Do not tell her that!" Elayne said sharply, and Nynaeve blinked before she realized Elayne was helping her fabrication. "If you let your anger get the best of you, you will tell them what they must not hear. They must take us inside the Stone. They must—"

"Be quiet!" Nynaeve snapped. "You are letting *your* tongue run away with you!" Elayne managed to look abashed behind her bruises. *Let them chew on that*, Nynaeve thought.

But Liandrin only smiled. "Once your time as bait is done, you will tell us everything. You will want to. They say you will be very strong one day, but I will make sure you will always obey me, even before the Great Master Be'lal works his plans for you. He is sending for Myrddraal. Thirteen of them." Those rosebud lips laughed the final words.

Nynaeve felt her stomach twist. One of the Forsaken! Her brain numbed with shock. *The Dark One and all the Forsaken are bound in Shayol Ghul, bound by the Creator in the moment of creation.* But the catechism did not help; she knew too well how much of it was false. Then the rest of it came home to her. Thirteen Myrddraal. And thirteen sisters of the Black Ajah. She heard Elayne screaming before she realized she was screaming herself, jerking uselessly in those invisible bonds of Air. It was impossible to say which was louder, their despairing screams, or the laughter from Liandrin and Rianna.

CHAPTER
52

In Search of a Remedy

Slumped on the stool in the gleeman's room, Mat grimaced as Thom coughed again. *How are we going to keep looking if he's so bloody sick he can't walk?* He was ashamed as soon as he thought it. Thom had been as assiduous in searching as he had, pushing himself day and night, when he had to know he was coming down sick. Mat had been so absorbed in his hunt that he had paid too little attention to Thom's coughing. The change from constant rain to steamy heat had not helped it.

"Come on, Thom," he said. "Lopar says there's a Wise Woman not far. That is what they call a Wisdom here—a Wise Woman. Wouldn't Nynaeve like that!"

"I do not need . . . any foul-tasting . . . concoctions . . . poured down my throat, boy." Thom stuffed a fist through his mustaches in a vain attempt to stop his hacking. "You go ahead looking. Just give me . . . a few hours . . . on my bed . . . and I'll join you." The wracking wheezes doubled him over till his head was almost on his knees.

"So I am supposed to do all the work while you take your ease?" Mat said lightly. "How can I find anything without you? You learn most of what we hear." That was not exactly true; men talked as freely over dice as they did while buying a gleeman a cup of wine. More freely than they did with a gleeman hacking so hard they feared contagion. But he was beginning to think that Thom's cough was not going to go away by itself. *If the old goat dies on me, who will I play stones with?* he told himself roughly. "Anyway, your bloody coughing keeps me awake even in the next room."

Ignoring the white-haired man's protests, he pulled Thom

to his feet. He was shocked at how much of the gleeman's weight he had to support. Despite the damp heat, Thom insisted on his patch-covered cloak. Mat had his own coat unbuttoned completely and all three ties of his shirt undone, but he let the old goat have his way. No one in the common room even looked up as he half carried Thom out into the muggy afternoon.

The innkeeper had given simple directions, but when they reached the gate, and faced the mud of the Maule, Mat almost turned back to ask after another Wise Woman. There had to be more than one in a city this size. Thom's wheezing decided him. With a grimace Mat stepped off into the mud, half carrying the gleeman.

He had thought from the directions that they must have passed the Wise Woman's house on their way up from the dock that first night, and when he saw the long, narrow house with bunches of herbs hanging in the windows, right next to a potter's shop, he remembered it. Lopar had said something about going to the back door, but he had had enough of mud.

And the stink of fish, he thought, frowning at the barefoot men squelching by with their baskets on their backs. There were tracks of horses in the street, too, just beginning to be obliterated by feet and ox-carts. Horses pulling a wagon, or maybe a carriage. He had seen nothing but oxen drawing carts or wagons either one in Tear—the nobles and the merchants were proud of their fine stock, and never let one be put to anything like work—but he had not seen any carriages since leaving the walled city, either.

Dismissing horses and wheel tracks from his mind, he took Thom to the front door and knocked. After a time he knocked again. Then again.

He was on the point of giving up and returning to The White Crescent despite Thom coughing on his shoulder when he heard shuffling footsteps inside.

The door opened barely more than a crack, and a stout, gray-haired woman peered out. "What do you want?" she asked in a tired voice.

Mat put on his best grin. *Light, but I am getting sick myself at all these people who sound like there's no bloody hope.* "Mother Guenna? My name is Mat Cauthon. Cavan

Lopar told me you might do something for my friend's cough. I can pay well."

She studied them a moment, seemed to listen to Thom's wheezes, then sighed. "I suppose I can still do that, at least. You might as well come in." She swung the door open and was already plodding toward the back of the house before Mat moved.

Her accent sounded so much like the Amyrlin's that he shivered, but he followed, all but carrying Thom.

"I don't . . . need this," the gleeman wheezed. "Bloody mixtures . . . always taste like . . . dung!"

"Shut up, Thom."

Leading them all the way to the kitchen, the stout woman rummaged in one of the cupboards, taking out small stone pots and packets of herbs while muttering to herself.

Mat sat Thom down in one of the high-backed chairs, and glanced through the nearest window. There were three good horses tied out back; he was surprised the Wise Woman had more than one, or any for that matter. He had not seen anyone in Tear riding except nobles and the wealthy, and these animals looked as if they had cost more than a little silver. *Horses again. I don't care about bloody horses now!*

Mother Guenna brewed some sort of strong tea with a rank smell and forced it down Thom's throat, holding his nose when he tried to complain. Mat decided she had less fat on her than he had thought, from the way she held the gleeman's head steady in the crook of one arm while she poured the black liquid into him no matter how hard he tried to stop her.

When she took the cup away, Thom coughed and scrubbed at his mouth with equal vigor. "Gaaah! Woman . . . I don't know . . . whether you . . . mean to drown me . . . or kill me . . . with the taste! You ought . . . to be a bloody . . . blacksmith!"

"You will take the same twice a day till that hacking is gone," she said firmly. "And I have a salve that you'll rub on your chest every night." Some of the weariness left her voice as she confronted the gleeman, fists on her broad hips. "That salve stinks as bad as this tea tastes, but you will rub it on—thoroughly!—or I'll drag you upstairs like a scrawny carp in a net and tie you to a bed with that cloak of yours! I never had a gleeman come to me before, and I'll not let the first one that does cough himself to death."

Thom glowered and blew out his mustaches with a cough, but he seemed to take her threat seriously. At least, he did not say anything, but he looked as if he meant to throw her tea and her salve right back at her.

The more this Mother Guenna talked, the more she sounded like the Amyrlin to Mat. From the sour look on Thom's face, and the steady stare on hers, he decided he had better smooth matters over a little before the gleeman refused to take her medicines. And she decided to make him. "I knew a woman once who talked like you," he said. "All fish and nets and things. Sounded like you, too. The same accent, I mean. I suppose she's Tairen."

"Perhaps." The gray-haired woman suddenly sounded tired again, and she kept staring at the floor. "I knew some girls with the sound of your speech on their tongues, too. Two of them had it, anyway." She sighed heavily.

Mat felt his scalp prickle. *My luck can't be this good.* But he would not bet a copper on two other women with Two Rivers accents just happening to be in Tear. "Three girls? Young women? Named Egwene, and Nynaeve, and Elayne? That one has hair like the sun, and blue eyes."

She frowned at him. "Those were not the names they gave," she said slowly, "yet I suspected they did not give me their true names. But they had their reasons, I thought. One of them was a pretty girl with bright blue eyes and red-gold hair to her shoulders." She described Nynaeve with her braid to her waist and Egwene with her big, dark eyes and ready smile, too. Three pretty women as different from one another as they could be. "I see they are the ones you know," she finished. "I am sorry, boy."

"Why are you sorry? I have been trying to find them for days!" *Light, I walked right past this place the first night! Right past them! I wanted random. What could be more random than where a ship docks on a rainy night, and where you happen to look in a bloody lightning flash? Burn me! Burn me!* "Tell me where they are, Mother Guenna."

The gray-haired woman stared wearily at the stove where her spouted kettle was steaming. Her mouth worked, but she said nothing.

"Where are they?" Mat demanded. "It is important! They are in danger if I don't find them."

"You do not understand," she said softly. "You are an outlander. The High Lords. . . ."

"I do not care about any—" Mat blinked, and looked at Thom. The gleeman seemed to be frowning, but he was coughing so hard, Mat could not be sure. "What do the High Lords have to do with my friends?"

"You just do not—"

"Don't tell me I do not understand! I will pay for the information!"

Mother Guenna glared at him. "I do not take money for . . . !" She grimaced fiercely. "You ask me to tell you things I have been told not to speak of. Do you know what will happen to me if I do and you breathe my name? I will lose my tongue, to begin. Then I will lose other parts before the High Lords have what is left of me hung up to scream its last hours as a reminder to others to obey. And it will do those young women no good, not my telling or my dying!"

"I promise I will never mention your name to anyone. I swear it." *And I'll keep that oath, old woman, if you only tell me where they bloody are!* "Please? They are in danger."

She studied him for a long time; before she was done he had the feeling she knew every detail of him. "On that oath, I will tell you. I . . . liked them. But you can do nothing. You are too late, Matrim Cauthon. Too late by nearly three hours. They have been taken to the Stone. The High Lord Samon sent for them." She shook her head in worried puzzlement. "He sent . . . women who . . . could channel. I hold nothing against Aes Sedai myself, but that is against the law. The law the High Lords made. If they break every other law, they would not break that one. Why would a High Lord send Aes Sedai on his errands? Why would he want those girls at all?"

Mat almost burst out laughing. "Aes Sedai? Mother Guenna, you had my heart in my throat, and maybe my liver, too. If Aes Sedai came for them, there is nothing to worry about. All three of them are going to be Aes Sedai themselves. Not that I like it much, but that's what they—" His grin faded at the heavy way she shook her head.

"Boy, those girls fought like lionfish in a net. Whether they mean to be Aes Sedai or not, those who took them treated them like bilge pumpings. Friends do not give bruises like that."

He felt his face twisting. *Aes Sedai hurt them? What in the Light? The bloody Stone. It makes the Palace in Caemlyn look like walking into a barnyard! Burn me! I stood right out there in the rain and stared at this house! Burn me for a bloody Light-blinded fool!*

"If you break your hand," Mother Guenna said, "I will splint and poultice it, but if you damage my wall, I will strip your hide like a redfish!"

He blinked, then looked at his fist, at scraped knuckles. He did not even remember punching the wall.

The broad woman took his hand in a strong grip, but the fingers she used to probe were surprisingly gentle. "Nothing broken," she grunted after a while. Her eyes were just as gentle as she studied his face. "It seems you care for them. One of them, at least, I suppose it is. I am sorry, Mat Cauthon."

"Don't be," he told her. "At least I know where they are, now. All I have to do is get them out." He fished out his last two Andoran gold crowns and pressed them into her hand. "For Thom's medicines, and for letting me know about the girls." On impulse, he gave her a quick kiss on the cheek and a grin. "And that's for me."

Startled, she touched her cheek, not seeming to know whether to look at the coins or at him. "Get them out, you say. Just like that. Out of the Stone." Abruptly she stabbed him in the ribs with a finger as hard as a tree stub. "You remind me of my husband, Mat Cauthon. He was a headstrong fool who would sail into the teeth of a gale and laugh, too. I could almost think you'll manage it." Suddenly she saw his muddy boots, apparently for the first time. "It took me six months to teach him not to track mud into my house. If you do get those girls out, whichever of them you have your eye on will have a hard time training you to make you fit to be let inside."

"You are the only woman who could do that," he said with a grin that broadened at her glare. *Get them out. That's all I have to do. Bring them right out of the Stone of bloody Tear.* Thom coughed again. *He isn't going into the Stone like that. Only, how do I stop him?* "Mother Guenna, can I leave my friend here? I think he is too sick to go back to the inn."

"What?" Thom barked. He tried to push himself out of the chair, coughing so he could hardly speak. "I am no . . . such thing, boy! You think . . . walking into the Stone . . . will be like . . . walking into your mother's kitchen? You think you . . . would make it . . . as far as the gates . . . without me?" He hung on the back of the chair, his wheezing and hacking keeping him from rising more than half-way to his feet.

Mother Guenna put a hand on his shoulder and pushed him back down as easily as a child. The gleeman gave her a startled look. "I will take care of him, Mat Cauthon," she said.

"No!" Thom shouted. "You cannot . . . do this to me! You can't . . . leave me . . . with this old. . . ." Only her hand on his shoulder kept him from doubling over.

Mat grinned at the white-haired man. "I have enjoyed knowing you, Thom."

As he hurried out into the street, he found himself wondering why he had said that. *He isn't going to bloody die. That woman will keep him alive if she has to drag him kicking and screaming out of his grave by his mustaches. Yes, but who is going to keep me alive?*

Ahead of him, the Stone of Tear loomed over the city, impregnable, a fortress besieged a hundred times, a stone on which a hundred armies had broken their teeth. And he had to get inside, somehow. And bring out three women. Somehow.

With a laugh that made even the sullen folk in the street look at him, he headed back for The White Crescent, uncaring of mud or the damp heat. He could feel the dice tumbling inside his head.

CHAPTER

53

A Flow of the Spirit

Perrin shrugged into his coat as he walked back toward the Star through the evening shadows. A good tiredness soaked through his arms and shoulders; along with more common work, Master Ajala had had him make a large piece of ornamental work, all elaborate curves and scrolls, to go on some country lord's new gate. He had enjoyed making something so pretty.

"I thought his eyes would come out of his face, blacksmith, when you said you would not make that thing if it was for a High Lord."

He glanced sideways at Zarine, walking beside him, the shadows masking her face. Even for his eyes, the shadows were there, just fainter than they would have been for another's. They emphasized her high cheekbones, softened the strong curve of her nose. He just could not make up his mind about her. Even if Moiraine and Lan still insisted they stay close to the inn, he wished she could find something else to do besides watch him work. For some reason, he had found himself growing awkward whenever he thought of her tilted eyes on him. More than once he had fumbled with his hammer till Master Ajala frowned at him wonderingly. Girls had always been able to make him feel awkward especially when they smiled at him, but Zarine did not have to smile. Only look. He wondered again if she was the beautiful woman Min had warned him against. *Better if she is the falcon.* That thought surprised him so much that he stumbled.

"I did not want anything I make to get into the hands of one of the Forsaken." His eyes glowed golden as he looked at her. "If it was for a High Lord, how could I tell where it might end?" She shivered. "I did not mean to frighten you, Fai— Zarine."

She smiled broadly, no doubt thinking he could not see her. "You will fall yet, farmboy. Have you ever thought of wearing a beard?"

It is bad enough she's always mocking me, but half the time I do not even understand her!

As they reached the front door of the inn, Moiraine and Lan met them, coming the other way. Moiraine wore that linen cloak with the wide, deep hood that hid her face. Light from the common-room windows made yellow pools on the paving stones. Two or three carriages rumbled past, and there were perhaps a dozen people in sight, hurrying home for their suppers, but for the most part, shadows populated the street. The weaver's shop was closed tight. The silence was deafening.

"Rand is in Tear." The Aes Sedai's cool voice issued from the depths of her hood as from a cavern.

"Are you sure?" Perrin asked. "I have not heard of anything strange happening. No weddings, or wells drying up." He saw Zarine frown in confusion. Moiraine had not been forthcoming with her, and neither had he. Keeping Loial's tongue silent had been more difficult.

"Don't you listen to rumors, blacksmith?" the Warder said. "There have been marriages, as many in the last four days as in half a year before. And as many murders as in a whole year. A child fell from a tower balcony today. A hundred paces onto stone paving. She got up and ran to her mother without a bruise. The First of Mayene, a 'guest' in the Stone since before the winter, announced today that she will submit to the will of the High Lords, after saying yesterday she would see Mayene and all its ships burn before one Tairen country lord set foot in the city. They had not brought themselves to torture her, and that young woman has a will like iron, so you tell me if you think it might be Rand's doing. Blacksmith, from top to bottom, Tear bubbles like a cauldron."

"These things were not needed to tell me," Moiraine said. "Perrin, did you dream of Rand last night?"

"Yes," he admitted. "He was in the Heart of the Stone, holding that sword"—he felt Zarine shift beside him—"but

I have been worrying about that so much it is no wonder I dream of it. I had nothing but nightmares last night."

"A tall man?" Zarine said. "With reddish hair and gray eyes? Holding something that shines so brightly it hurts your eyes? In a place that is all great redstone columns? Blacksmith, tell me that was not your dream."

"You see," Moiraine said. "I have heard this dream spoken of a hundred times today. They all speak of nightmares— Be'lal apparently does not care to shield his dreams—but that one above all else." She laughed suddenly, like low, cool chimes. "People say he is the Dragon Reborn. They say he is coming. They whisper it fearfully in corners, but they say it."

"And what of Be'lal?" Perrin asked.

Moiraine's reply was cold-drawn steel. "I will deal with him tonight." There was no fear scent from her.

"*We* will deal with him tonight," Lan told her.

"Yes, my Gaidin. We will deal with him."

"And what do we do? Sit here and wait? I had enough waiting to last me a lifetime in the mountains, Moiraine."

"You and Loial—and Zarine—will go to Tar Valon," she told him. "Until this is done. It will be the safest place for you."

"Where is the Ogier?" Lan said. "I want all three of you on your way north as soon as possible."

"Upstairs, I suppose," Perrin said. "In his room, or maybe the dining room. There are lights in the windows up there. He is always working on those notes of his. I suppose he will have plenty to say in his book about us running away." He was surprised at the bitterness in his voice. *Light, fool, do you want to face one of the Forsaken? No. No, but I am tired of running. I remember not running, once. I remember fighting back, and it was better. Even if I thought I was going to die, it was better.*

"I will find him," Zarine announced. "I have no shame in admitting I will be glad enough to run from this fight. Men fight when they should run, and fools fight when they should run. But I had no need to say it twice." She strode ahead of them, her narrow, divided skirts making small whisking noises as they entered the inn.

Perrin glanced around the common room as they followed her toward the stairs in the back. There were fewer men at the tables than he expected. Some sat alone, with dull eyes, but where two or three sat together they talked in frightened whispers his ears could barely catch. Even so, he heard "Dragon" three times.

As he reached the top of the stairs, he heard another soft sound, a thump as of something falling in the private dining room. He peered that way along the hall. "Zarine?" There was no answer. He felt the hair on the back of his neck shift, and padded that way. "Zarine?" He pushed open the door. "Faile!"

She was lying on the floor near the table. As he started to rush into the room, Moiraine's commanding shout halted him.

"Stop, you fool! Stop, for your life!" She came along the hallway slowly, head turning as if she were listening for something, or searching for something. Lan followed with his hand on his sword—and a look in his eye as if he already knew steel would do no good. She came abreast of the door and stopped. "Move back, Perrin. Move back!"

In agony he stared at Zarine. At Faile. She lay there as if lifeless. Finally he made himself step back from the door, leaving it open, standing where he could see her. She looked as if she were dead. He could not see her chest stir. He wanted to howl. Frowning, he worked his hand, the one he had used to push the door into the room, opening and closing his fingers. It tingled sharply, as if he had struck his elbow. "Aren't you going to do anything, Moiraine? If you will not, I am going to her."

"Stand still or you will go nowhere," she said calmly. "What is that by her right hand? As if it dropped from her grip when she fell. I cannot make it out."

He glared at her, then peered into the room. "A hedgehog. It looks like a hedgehog carved out of wood. Moiraine, tell me what is going on! What has happened? Tell me!"

"A hedgehog," she murmured. "A hedgehog. Be silent, Perrin. I must think. I felt it trigger. I can sense the residues of the flows woven to set it. Spirit. Pure Spirit, and nothing else. Almost nothing uses pure flows of Spirit! Why does that hedgehog make me think of Spirit?"

"You felt what trigger, Moiraine? What was set? A trap?"

"Yes, a trap," she said, irritation making tiny cracks in her cool serenity. "A trap meant for me. I would have been

first into that room if Zarine had not rushed ahead. Lan and
I would surely have gone there to plan and wait for supper.
I will not wait on supper now. Be quiet, if you wish me
to help the girl at all. Lan! Bring me that innkeeper!" The
Warder flowed away down the stairs.

Moiraine paced up and down in the hall, sometimes stopping to peer through the door from the depths of her hood.
Perrin could see no sign that Zarine lived. Her breast did
not stir. He tried listening for her heartbeat, but even for his
ears it was impossible.

When Lan returned, shoving a frightened Jurah Haret
ahead of him by the scruff of his fat neck, the Aes Sedai
rounded on the balding man. "You promised to keep this
room for me, Master Haret." Her voice was as hard, as
precise, as a skinning knife. "To allow not even a serving
woman to enter to clean unless I was present. Who did you
let enter it, Master Haret? Tell me!"

Haret shook like a bowl of pudding. "O-only the t-two
Ladies, mistress. T-they w-wished to leave a surprise for
you. I swear, mistress. T-they showed it t-to me. A little
h-hedgehog. T-they said you w-would be surprised."

"I was surprised, innkeeper," she said softly. "Leave me!
And if you whisper a word of this, even in your sleep, I will
pull this inn down and leave only a hole in the ground."

"Y-yes, mistress," he whispered. "I swear it! I do swear!
"Go!"

The innkeeper fell to his knees in his haste to reach the
stairs, and went scrambling down with thumps that suggested he fell more than once as he ran.

"He knows I am here," Moiraine told the Warder, "and
he has found someone of the Black Ajah to set his trap, yet
perhaps he thinks I am caught in it. It was a tiny flash of the
Power, but perhaps he is strong enough to have sensed it."

"Then he will not suspect we are coming," Lan said quietly. He almost smiled.

Perrin stared at them, his teeth bared. "What about her?"
he demanded. "What was done to her, Moiraine? Is she
alive? I cannot see her breathe!"

"She is alive," Moiraine said slowly. "I cannot, I dare not,
go close enough to her to tell much beyond that, but she
is alive. She . . . sleeps, in a way. As a bear sleeps in the
winter. Her heart beats so slowly you could count minutes

between. Her breathing is the same. She sleeps." Even from within that hood, he could feel her eyes on him. "I fear she is not there, Perrin. Not in her body any longer."

"What do you mean she is not in her body? Light! You don't mean they . . . took her soul. Like the Gray Men!" Moiraine shook her head, and he drew a relieved breath. His chest hurt as if he had not breathed since she last spoke. "Then where is she, Moiraine?"

"I do not know," she said. "I have a suspicion, but I do not know."

"A suspicion, a hint, anything! Burn me, where?" Lan shifted at the roughness in his voice, but he knew he would try to break the Warder like iron over a hardy if the man tried to stop him. "Where?"

"I know very little, Perrin." Moiraine's voice was like cold, unfeeling music. "I have remembered the little I know of what connects a carved hedgehog with Spirit. The carving is a *ter'angreal* last studied by Corianin Nedeal, the last Dreamer the Tower had. The Talent called Dreaming is a thing of Spirit, Perrin. It is not a thing I have ever studied; my Talents lie in other ways. I believe that Zarine has been trapped inside a dream, perhaps even the World of Dreams, *Tel'aran'rhiod*. All that is her is inside that dream. All. A Dreamer sends only a part of herself. If Zarine does not return soon, her body will die. Perhaps she will live on in the dream. I do not know."

"There is too much you don't know," Perrin muttered. He peered into the room and wanted to cry. Zarine looked so small, lying there, so helpless. *Faile. I swear I will only call you Faile, ever again.* "Why don't you do something!"

"The trap has been sprung, Perrin, but it is a trap that will still catch anyone who steps into that room. I would not reach her side before it took me. And I have work I must do tonight."

"Burn you, Aes Sedai! Burn your work! This World of Dreams? Is it like the wolf dreams? You said these Dreamers sometimes saw wolves."

"I have told you what I can," she said sharply. "It is time for you to go. Lan and I must be on our way to the Stone. There can be no waiting, now."

"No." He said it quietly, but when Moiraine opened her mouth, he raised his voice. "No! I will not leave her!"

The Aes Sedai took a deep breath. "Very well, Perrin." Her voice was ice; calm, smooth, cold. "Remain if you wish. Perhaps you will survive this night. Lan!"

She and the Warder strode down the hall to their rooms. In moments they returned, Lan wearing his color-changing cloak, and vanished down the stairs without another word to him.

He stared through the open door at Faile. *I have to do something. If it is like the wolf dreams. . . .*

"Perrin," came Loial's deep rumble, "what is this about Faile?" The Ogier came striding down the hall in his shirt-sleeves, ink on his fingers and a pen in his hand. "Lan told me I had to go, and then he said something about Faile, in a trap. What did he mean?"

Distractedly, Perrin told him what Moiraine had said. *It might work. It might. It has to!* He was surprised when Loial growled.

"No! Perrin, it is not right! Faile was so free. It is not right to trap her!"

Perrin peered up at Loial's face, and suddenly remembered the old stories that claimed Ogier were implacable enemies. Loial's ears had laid back along the sides of his head, and his broad face was as hard as an anvil.

"Loial, I am going to try to help Faile. But I will be helpless myself while I do. Will you guard my back?"

Loial raised those huge hands that held books so carefully, and his thick fingers curled as if to crush stone. "None will pass me while I live, Perrin. Not Myrddraal or the Dark One himself." He said it like a simple statement of fact.

Perrin nodded, and looked through the door again. *It has to work. I don't care if Min warned me against her or not!* With a snarl he leaped toward Faile, stretching out his hand. He thought he touched her ankle before he was gone.

Whether this dream of the trap was *Tel'aran'rhiod* or not, Perrin did not know, but he knew it for the wolf dream. Rolling, grassy hills surrounded him, and scattered thickets. He saw deer browsing at the edges of the trees, and a herd of some sort of running animal bounding across the grass, like brown-striped deer, but with long, straight horns. The smells on the wind told him they were good to eat, and other scents spoke of more good hunting all around him. This was the wolf dream.

He was wearing the blacksmith's long leather vest, he realized, with his arms bare. And there was a weight at his side. He touched the axe belt, but it was not the axe hanging from its loop. He ran his fingers over the head of the heavy smith's hammer. It felt right.

Hopper alighted in front of him.

Again you come, like a fool. The sending was of a cub sticking its nose into a hollow tree trunk to lap honey despite the bees stinging its muzzle and eyes. *The danger is greater than ever, Young Bull. Evil things walk the dream. The brothers and sisters avoid the mountains of stone the two-legs pile up, and almost fear to dream to one another. You must go!*

"No," Perrin said. "Faile is here, somewhere, trapped. I have to find her, Hopper. I have to!" He felt a shifting inside him, something changing. He looked down at his curly-haired legs, his wide paws. He was an even larger wolf than Hopper.

You are here too strongly! Every sending carried shock. *You will die, Young Bull!*

If I do not free the falcon, I do not care, brother.

Then we hunt, brother.

Noses to the wind, the two wolves ran across the plain, seeking the falcon.

CHAPTER
54

Into the Stone

The rooftops of Tear were no place for a sensible man to be in the night, Mat decided as he peered into the moon shadows. A little more than fifty paces of broad street, or perhaps narrow plaza, separated the Stone from his tiled roof, itself three stories above the paving stones. *But when was I ever sensible? The only people I ever met who were sensible all the time were so boring that watching them could put you to sleep.* Whether the thing was a street or a plaza, he had followed it all the way around the Stone since nightfall; the only place it did not go was on the river side, where the Erinin ran right along the foot of the fortress, and nothing interrupted it except the city wall. That wall was only two houses to his right. So far, the top of the wall seemed the best path to the Stone, but not one he would be overjoyed to take.

Picking up his quarterstaff and a small, wire-handled tin box, he moved carefully to a brick chimney a little nearer the wall. The roll of fireworks—what had been the roll of fireworks before he worked on it back in his room—shifted on his back. It was more of a bundle, now, all jammed together as tight as he could make it, but still too big for carrying around rooftops in the dark. Earlier, a slip of his foot because of the thing had sent a roof tile skittering over the edge, and roused the man sleeping in a room below to bellow "thief!" and send him running. He hitched the bundle back into position without thinking about it, and crouched in the shadows of the chimney. After a moment he set the tin box down; the wire handle was beginning to grow uncomfortably warm.

It felt a little safer, studying the Stone from the shadows, but not much more encouraging. The city wall was not nearly as thick as those he had seen in other places, in Caemlyn or Tar Valon, no more than a pace wide, supported by great stone buttresses cloaked in darkness, now. A pace was more than sufficient width for walking, of course, except that the fall to either side was nearly ten spans. Through the dark, to hard pavement. *But some of these bloody houses back right up against it, I can make it to the top easily enough, and it bloody runs straight to the bloody Stone!*

It did that, but that was no particular comfort. The sides of the Stone looked like cliffs. Eyeing the height again, he told himself he should be able to climb it. *Of course, I can. Just like those cliffs in the Mountains of Mist.* Over a hundred paces straight up before there was a battlement. There must be arrowslits lower down, but he could not make them out in the night. And he could not squeeze through an arrowslit. *A hundred bloody paces. Maybe a hundred and twenty. Burn me, even Rand would not try to climb that.* But it was the one way in he had found. Every gate he had seen had been shut tight and looked strong enough to stop a herd of bulls, not to mention the dozen or so soldiers guarding very nearly every last one, in helmets and breastplates, and swords at their belts.

Suddenly he blinked, and squinted at the side of the Stone. There *was* some fool climbing it, just visible as a moving shadow in the moonlight, and over halfway up already, with a drop of seventy paces to the pavement under his feet. *Fool, is he? Well, I'm as big a one, because I am going up, too. Burn me, he'll probably raise an alarm in there and get me caught.* He could not see the climber anymore. *Who in the Light is he? What does it matter who he is? Burn me, but this is a bloody way to win a wager. I'm going to want a kiss from all of them, even Nynaeve!*

He shifted to peer toward the wall, trying to choose his spot to climb, and suddenly there was steel across his throat. Without thinking, he knocked it away and swept the man's feet out from under him with his staff. Someone else kicked his own feet away and he fell almost on top of the man he had knocked down. He rolled off onto the roof tiles, loosing the bundle of fireworks—*If that falls into the street, I'll break their necks!*—staff whirling; he felt it strike flesh, and a second time, heard grunts. Then there were two blades at his throat.

He froze, arms outflung. The points of short spears, dull so they hardly caught the faint light of the moon at all, pressed into his flesh just short of bringing blood. His eyes followed them up to the faces of whoever was holding them, but their heads were shrouded, their faces veiled in black except for their eyes, staring at him. *Burn me, I have to run into real thieves! What happened to my luck?*

He put on a grin, with plenty of teeth so they could see it in the moonlight. "I do not mean to trouble you in your work, so if you let me go my way, I'll let you go yours and say nothing." The veiled men did not move, and neither did their spears. "I want no more outcry than you. I'll not betray you." They stood like statues, staring down at him. *Burn me, I do not have time for this. Time to toss the dice.* For a chilling moment he thought the words in his head had been strange. He tightened his grip on the quarterstaff, lying out to one side of him—and almost cried out when someone stepped hard on his wrist.

He rolled his eyes to see who. *Burn me for a fool, I forgot the one I fell on.* But he saw another shape moving behind the one standing on his wrist, and decided maybe it was as well he had not managed to bring the staff into use after all.

It was a soft boot, laced to the knee, that rested on his arm. It tugged at his memory. Something about a man met in mountains. He eyed the night-cloaked shape the rest of the way up, trying to make out the cut and colors of his clothes—they seemed all shadow, colors that blended with the darkness too well to see them clearly—past a long-bladed knife at the fellow's waist, right up to the dark veil across his face. A black-veiled face. Black-veiled.

Aiel! Burn me, what are bloody Aiel doing here! He had a sinking feeling in his stomach as he remembered hearing that Aiel veiled themselves when they killed.

"Yes," said a man's voice, "we are Aiel." Mat gave a start; he had not realized he had spoken aloud.

"You dance well for one caught by surprise," a young woman's voice said. He thought she was the one standing on his wrist. "Perhaps another day I will have time to dance with you properly."

He started to smile—*If she wants to dance, they can't*

be going to kill me, at least!—then frowned instead. He seemed to remember Aiel sometimes meant something different when they said that.

The spears were pulled back, and hands hauled him to his feet. He shook them away and brushed himself off as if he were standing in a common room instead of on a night-cloaked rooftop with four Aiel. It always paid to let the other man know you had a steady nerve. The Aiel had quivers at their waists as well as knives, and more of those short spears on their backs with cased bows, the long spear points sticking up above their shoulders. He heard himself humming "I'm Down at the Bottom of the Well," and stopped it.

"What do you do here?" the man's voice asked. With the veils, Mat was not entirely sure which one had spoken; the voice sounded older, confident, used to command. He thought he could pick out the woman, at least; she was the only one shorter than he, and that not by much. The others all stood a head taller than he or more. *Bloody Aiel,* he thought. "We have watched you for some little time," the older man went on, "watched you watch the Stone. You have studied it from every side. Why?"

"I could ask the same of all of you," another voice said. Mat was the only one who gave a start as a man in baggy breeches stepped out of the shadows. The fellow appeared to be shoeless, for better footing on the tiles. "I expected to find thieves, not Aiel," the man went on, "but do not think your numbers frighten me." A slim staff no taller than his head made a blur and a hum as he whirled it. "My name is Juilin Sandar, and I am a thief-catcher, and I would know why you are on the rooftops, staring at the Stone."

Mat shook his head. *How many bloody people are on the roofs tonight?* All that was needed was for Thom to appear and play his harp, or someone to come looking for an inn. *A bloody thief-taker!* He wondered why the Aiel were just standing there.

"You stalk well, for a city man," the older man's voice said. "But why do you follow us? We have stolen nothing. Why have you looked so often at the Stone tonight yourself?"

Even in the moonlight this Sandar's surprise was evident. He gave a start, opened his mouth—and closed it again as

four more Aiel rose out of the dimness behind him. With a
sigh, he leaned on his slender staff. "It seems I am caught
myself," he muttered. "It seems *I* must answer *your* questions." He peered toward the Stone, then shook his head.
"I . . . did a thing today that . . . troubles me." He sounded
almost as though he were talking to himself, trying to puzzle it out. "Part of me says it was right, what I did, that I
must obey. Surely, it seemed right when I did it. But a small
voice tells me I . . . betrayed something. I am certain this
voice is wrong, and it is very small, but it will not stop." He
stopped then himself, shaking his head again.

One of the Aiel nodded, and spoke with the older man's
voice. "I am Rhuarc, of the Nine Valleys sept of the Taardad Aiel, and once I was *Aethan Dor*, a Red Shield. Sometimes the Red Shields do as your thief-catchers do. I say
this so you will understand that I know what it is you do,
and the kind of man you must be. I mean no harm to you,
Juilin Sandar of the thief-catchers, nor to the people of your
city, but you will not be suffered to raise the armcry. If you
will keep silence, you will live; if not, not."

"You mean no harm to the city," Sandar said slowly.
"Why are you here, then?"

"The Stone." Rhuarc's tone made it plain that was all he
meant to say.

After a moment Sandar nodded, and muttered, "I could
almost wish you had the power to harm the Stone, Rhuarc.
I will hold my tongue."

Rhuarc turned his veiled face to Mat. "And you, nameless youngling? Will you tell me now why you watch the
Stone so closely?"

"I just wanted a walk in the moonlight," Mat said lightly.
The young woman put her spearpoint to his throat again;
he tried not to swallow. *Well, maybe I can tell them something of it.* He must not let them know he was shaken; if
you let the other fellow know that, you lost whatever edge
you might have. Very carefully, with two fingers, he moved
her steel away from him. It seemed to him that she laughed
softly. "Some friends of mine are inside the Stone," he said,
trying to sound casual. "Prisoners. I mean to bring them
out."

"Alone, nameless one?" Rhuarc said.

"Well, there doesn't seem to be anyone else," Mat said

dryly. "Unless you care to help? You seem interested in the Stone yourself. If you mean to go into it, perhaps we could go together. It is a tight roll of the dice any way you look at it, but my luck runs good." *So far, anyway. I've run into black-veiled Aiel and they have not cut my throat; luck cannot get much better than that. Burn me, it would not be bad to have a few Aiel along with me in there.* "You could do worse than betting on my luck."

"We are not here for prisoners, gambler," Rhuarc said.

"It is time, Rhuarc." Mat could not tell from which of the Aiel that came, but Rhuarc nodded.

"Yes, Gaul." He looked from Mat to Sandar and back. "Do not give the armcry." He turned away, and in two steps he had blended into the night.

Mat gave a start. The other Aiel were gone, too, leaving him alone with the thief-taker. *Unless they left somebody to watch us. Burn me, how could I tell if they did?* "I hope you don't mean to try stopping me, either," he told Sandar as he slung the bundle of fireworks on his back again and picked up his quarterstaff. "I mean to go inside, by you or through you, one way or the other." He went over to the chimney to pick up the tin box; the wire handle was more than warm, now.

"These friends of yours," Sandar said. "They are three women?"

Mat frowned at him, wishing there was enough light to show the man's face clearly. The fellow's voice sounded odd. "What do you know of them?"

"I know they are inside the Stone. And I know a small gate near the river where a thief-catcher can gain entrance with a prisoner, to take him to the cells. The cells where they must be. If you will trust me, gambler, I can take us that far. What happens after that is up to chance. Perhaps your luck will bring us out again alive."

"I have always been lucky," Mat said slowly. *Do I feel lucky enough to trust him?* He did not much like the idea of pretending to be a prisoner; it seemed too easy for pretense to become reality. But it seemed no bigger risk than trying to climb three hundred feet or more straight up in the dark.

He glanced toward the city wall, and stared. Shadows flowed along it; dim shapes trotting. Aiel, he was sure. There must have been over a hundred. They vanished, but now he could make out shadows moving on the cliff face that was the sheer side of the Stone of Tear. So much for going up that way. That one fellow earlier might have made it inside without raising an alarm—Rhuarc's armcry—but a hundred or more Aiel would have to be like sounding bells. They might make a diversion, though. If they caused a commotion somewhere up there, inside the Stone, then whoever was guarding the cells might not pay as much attention to a thief-taker bringing a thief.

I might as well add a little to the confusion. I worked hard enough on it. "Very well, thief-taker. Just don't decide I am a real prisoner at the last minute. We can start for your gate as soon as I stir the anthill a bit." He thought Sandar frowned, but he did not mean to tell the man more than he had to.

Sandar followed him across the rooftops, climbing to higher levels as easily as he did. The last roof was only a little lower than the top of the wall and ran right up to it, a matter of pulling himself up rather than climbing.

"What are you doing?" Sandar whispered.

"Wait here for me."

With the tin box dangling from one hand by its wire handle and his quarterstaff held horizontally in front of him, Mat took a deep breath and started toward the Stone. He tried not to think of how far it was to the pavement below. *Light, the bloody thing is three feet wide! I could walk it with a bloody blindfold, in my sleep!* Three feet wide, in the dark, and better than fifty feet to the pavement. He tried not to think about Sandar not being there when he came back, either. He was all but committed to this fool notion of pretending to be a thief caught by the man, but it seemed all too probable that he would return to the roof to find Sandar gone, maybe bringing more men to make him a prisoner in truth. *Don't think about it. Just do the job at hand. At least I'll finally see what it is like.*

As he had suspected, there was an arrowslit in the wall of the Stone right at the end of the wall, a deep wedge cut into the rock holding a tall, narrow opening for an archer to shoot through. If the Stone were attacked, the soldiers inside would want some way to stop any trying to follow this path. The slit was dark, now. There did not appear to be anyone watching. That was something he had tried not to think about, too.

Quickly he set down the tin box at his feet, balanced his quarterstaff across the wall right against the side of the Stone, and unslung the bundle from his back. Hurriedly he wedged it into the slit, forcing it in as far as he could; he wanted as much of the noise to be inside as he could manage. Pulling aside a corner of the oiled cloth cover revealed knotted fuses. After a little thinking, back in his room, he had cut the longer fuses to match the shortest, using the pieces to help tie all the fuses together. It seemed they should all go off at once, and a bang-and-flash like that should be enough to pull everyone who was not completely deaf.

The lid of the tin box was hot enough that he had to blow on his fingers twice before he could pry it off—he wished he had whatever Aludra's trick had been, lighting that lantern so easily—to expose the dark bit of charcoal inside, lying on a bed of sand. The wire handle came off to make tongs, and a little blowing had the coal glowing red again. He touched the hot coal to the knotted fuses, let tongs and coal fall over the side of the wall as the fuses hissed into flame, snatched up his quarterstaff and darted back along the wall.

This is crazy, he thought as he ran. *I don't care how big a bang it makes. I could break my fool neck doing thi—!*

The roar behind him was louder than anything he had ever heard in his life; a monstrous fist punched him in the back, knocking all the wind out of him even before he landed, sprawled on his belly on the wall top, barely holding on to his staff as it swung over the edge. For a moment he lay there, trying to make his lungs work again, trying not to think how he *must* have used up all his luck this time by not falling off the wall. His ears rang like all the bells in Tar Valon.

Pushing himself up carefully, he looked back toward the Stone. A cloud of smoke hung around the arrowslit. Behind the smoke, the shadowed shape of the arrowslit itself seemed different. Larger. He did not understand how or why, but it did seem larger.

He only thought for a moment. At one end of the wall

Sandar might be waiting, might be intending to take him into the Stone as a pretend prisoner—or might be hurrying back with soldiers. At the other end of the wall, there might be a way inside without any chance of Sandar betraying him. He darted back the way he had just come, no longer worrying about the darkness or the drop to either side.

The arrowslit *was* larger, most of the thinner stone at the middle simply gone, leaving a rough hole as if someone had hammered at it with a sledge for hours. A hole just big enough for a man. *How in the Light?* There was no time for wondering.

He pushed through the jagged opening, coughing at the acrid smoke, jumped to the floor inside, and had run a dozen steps before Defenders of the Stone appeared, at least ten of them, all shouting in confusion. Most wore only their shirts, and none had helmet or breastplate. Some carried lanterns. Some held bared swords.

Fool! he shouted inside his head. *This is why you set the bloody things off in the first place! Light-blinded fool!*

He had no time to make it back out onto the wall. Quarterstaff spinning, he threw himself at the soldiers before they had a chance to do more than see he was there, hurled himself into them, smashing at heads, swords, knees, whatever he could reach, knowing they were too many for him to handle alone, knowing that his fool toss of the dice had cost Egwene and the others whatever chance he might have had.

Suddenly Sandar was there beside him, in the light of lanterns dropped by men clawing for their swords, his slender staff whirling even faster than Mat's quarterstaff. Caught between two staffmen, taken by surprise, the soldiers went down like pins in a game of bowls.

Sandar stared at the fallen men, shaking his head. "Defenders of the Stone. I have attacked Defenders! They will have my head for—! What was it that you did, gambler? That flash of light, and thunder, breaking stone. Did you call lightning?" His voice fell to a whisper. "Have I joined myself to a man who can channel?"

"Fireworks," Mat said curtly. His ears were still ringing, but he could hear more boots coming, running boots thudding on stone. "The cells, man! Show me the way to the cells before any more get here!"

Sandar shook himself. "This way!" He dashed down a

side hall, away from the oncoming boots. "We must hurry! They will kill us if they find us!" Somewhere above, gongs began to sound an alarm, and more thundered echoes through the Stone.

I'm coming, Mat thought as he ran after the thief-taker. *I'll get you out or die! I promise it!*

The alarm gongs sent echoes crashing through the Stone, but Rand paid no more attention to them than he had to the roar that had come before, like muffled thunder from somewhere below. His side ached; the old wound burned, strained almost to tearing by the climb up the side of the fortress. He gave the pain no heed, either. A crooked smile was fixed on his face, a smile of anticipation and dread he could not have wiped away if he had wanted to. It was close, now. What he had dreamed of. *Callandor.*

I will finish it at last. One way or another, it will be done with. The dreams, finished. The baiting, and the taunting, and the hunting. I'll finish it all!

Laughing to himself, he hurried through the dark corridors of the Stone of Tear.

Egwene put a hand to her face, wincing. Her mouth had a bitter taste, and she was thirsty. *Rand? What? Why was I dreaming about Mat again, all mixed with Rand, and shouting that he was coming? What?*

She opened her eyes, stared at the gray stone walls, one smoky rush torch casting flickering shadows, and screamed as she remembered it all. "No! I will not be chained again! I won't be collared! No!"

Nynaeve and Elayne were beside her in an instant, their bruised faces too worried and fearful for the soothing sounds they made to be believed. But just the fact that they were there was enough to still her screams. She was not alone. A prisoner, but not alone. And not collared.

She tried to sit up, and they helped her. They had to help her; she ached in every muscle. She could remember every unseen blow during the frenzy that had all but driven her mad when she realized. . . . *I will not think about that. I have to think about how we are to escape.* She slid backwards until she could lean against a wall. Her pains fought with weariness; that struggle when she had refused to give in had taken every last scrap of her strength, and the bruises seemed to sap even more.

The cell was absolutely empty except for the three of them and the torch. The floor was bare, and cold, and hard. The door of rough planks, splintered as if countless futile fingers had clawed at it, was the only break in the walls. Messages had been scratched in the stone, most by unsteady hands. *The Light have mercy and let me die,* one read. She blanked that out of her head.

"Are we still shielded?" she mumbled. Even talking hurt. Even as Elayne nodded, she realized she had not had to ask. The swollen cheek on the golden-haired woman, her split lip and black eye, were answer enough, even if her own pains had not been. If Nynaeve had been able to reach the True Source, they surely would have been Healed.

"I have tried," Nynaeve said despairingly. "I have tried, and tried, and tried." She gave her braid a sharp tug, anger seeping through despite the hopeless fear in her voice. "One of them is sitting outside. Amico, that milk-faced chit, if they have not changed since we were thrown in here. I suppose one is enough to maintain the shielding once it has been woven." She barked a bitter laugh. "For all the pains they took—and gave!—to take us, you would think we were of no importance at all. It has been hours since they slammed that door behind us, and no one has come to ask a question, or look, or even bring a drop of water. Perhaps they mean to leave us here until we die of thirst."

"Bait." Elayne's voice quavered, though she was obviously trying to sound unafraid. And failing miserably. "Liandrin said we are bait."

"Bait for what?" Nynaeve asked shakily. "Bait for who? If I am bait, I'd like to shove myself down their throats till they choke on me!"

"Rand." Egwene stopped to swallow; even a drop of water would be welcome. "I dreamed about Rand, and *Callandor.* I think he is coming here." *But why did I dream of Mat? And Perrin? It was a wolf, but I am sure it was him.* "Do not be so afraid," she said, trying to sound confident. "We will escape them somehow. If we could better the Seanchan, we can best Liandrin."

Nynaeve and Elayne exchanged looks over her. Nynaeve said, "Liandrin said thirteen Myrddraal are coming, Egwene."

She found herself staring at that message scratched on the stone wall again: The Light have mercy and let me die. Her hands clenched into fists. Her jaws cramped with the effort of not screaming those words. *Better to die. Better death than being turned to the Shadow, made to serve the Dark One!*

She realized that one of her hands had tightened around the pouch at her belt. She could feel the two rings inside, the small circle of the Great Serpent and the larger, twisted stone ring.

"They did not take the *ter'angreal*," she said wonderingly. She fumbled it out of her pouch. It lay heavily on her palm, all stripes and flecks of color, a ring with only one edge.

"We were not even important enough to search," Elayne sighed. "Egwene, are you certain Rand is coming here? I would much rather free myself than wait for the chance of him, but if there is anyone who can defeat Liandrin and the rest of them, it must be him. The Dragon Reborn is meant to wield *Callandor*. He *must* be able to defeat them."

"Not if we pull him into a cage after us," Nynaeve muttered. "Not if they have a trap set he does not see. Why are you staring at that ring, Egwene? *Tel'aran'rhiod* will not help us now. Not unless you can dream a way out of here."

"Perhaps I can," she said slowly. "I could channel in *Tel'aran'rhiod*. Their shielding won't stop me reaching it. All I need do is sleep, not channel. And I am surely weary enough to sleep."

Elayne frowned, wincing as it pulled her bruises. "I will take any chance, but how can you channel even in a dream, cut off from the True Source? And if you can, how can it help us here?"

"I do not know, Elayne. Just because I am shielded here does not mean I am shielded in the World of Dreams. It is at least worth a try."

"Perhaps," Nynaeve said worriedly. "I will take any chance, too, but you saw Liandrin and the others the last time you used that ring. And you said they saw you, too. What if they are there again?"

"I hope they are," Egwene said grimly. "I hope they are."

Clutching the *ter'angreal* in her hand, she closed her eyes. She could feel Elayne smoothing her hair, hear her murmuring softly. Nynaeve began to hum that wordless lullaby from her childhood; for once, she felt no anger at it at all. The soft sounds and touches soothed her, let her surrender to her weariness, let sleep come.

She wore blue silk this time, but she barely noticed more than that. Soft breezes caressed her unbruised face, and sent the butterflies swirling above the wildflowers. Her thirst was gone, her aches. She reached out to embrace *saidar* and was filled with the One Power. Even the triumph she felt at succeeding was small beside the surging of the Power through her.

Reluctantly she made herself release it, closed her eyes, and filled the emptiness with a perfect image of the Heart of the Stone. That was the one place in the Stone she could picture aside from her cell, and how to distinguish one featureless cubicle from another? When she opened her eyes, she was there. But she was not alone.

The form of Joiya Byir stood before *Callandor*, her shape so insubstantial that the surging light of the sword shone through her. The crystal sword no longer merely glittered with refracted light. In pulses it glowed, as if some light inside it were being uncovered, then covered and uncovered again. The Black sister started with surprise and spun to face Egwene. "How? You are shielded! Your Dreaming is at an end!"

Before the first words were out of the woman's mouth, Egwene reached for *saidar* again, wove the complicated flow of Spirit as she remembered it being used against her, and cut Joiya Byir off from the Source. The Darkfriend's eyes widened, those cruel eyes so incongruous in that beautiful, kindly face, but Egwene was already weaving Air. The other woman's form might seem like mist, but the bonds held it. It seemed to Egwene that there was no effort involved in holding both flows in their weaving. There was sweat on Joiya Byir's forehead as she walked closer.

"You have a *ter'angreal*!" Fear was plain on the woman's face, but her voice fought to hide it. "That must be it. A *ter'angreal* that escaped us, and one that does not require channeling. Do you think it will do you any good, girl? Whatever you do here, it cannot affect what happens in the real world. *Tel'aran'rhiod* is a dream! When I wake, I will take your *ter'angreal* from you myself. Be careful what you do, lest I have reason to be angry when I come to your cell."

Egwene smiled at her. "Are you certain you will wake, Darkfriend? If your *ter'angreal* requires channeling, why did you not wake as soon as I shielded you? Perhaps you cannot wake so long as you are shielded here." Her smile faded away; the effort of smiling at this woman was more than she could bear. "A woman once showed me a scar she received in *Tel'aran'rhiod*, Darkfriend. What happens here *is* still real when you wake."

The sweat rolled down the Black sister's smooth, ageless face, now. Egwene wondered if she thought she was about to die. She almost wished she were cruel enough to do that. Most of the unseen blows she had received had come from this woman, like a pounding of fists, for no reason more than that she had kept trying to crawl away, no reason more than that she had refused to give up.

"A woman who can give such beatings," she said, "should have no objections to a milder one." She wove another flow of Air quickly; Joiya Byir's dark eyes bulged in disbelief as the first blow landed across her hips. Egwene saw how to adjust the weaving so she did not have to maintain it. "You will remember this, and feel it, when you waken. When I allow you to waken. Remember this, too. If you ever even try to beat me again, I will return you here and leave you for the rest of your life!" The Black sister's eyes stared hate at her, but there was a suggestion of tears in them, too.

Egwene felt a moment of shame. Not at what she was doing to Joiya—the woman deserved every blow, if not for her own beating, then for the deaths in the Tower—not that, not really, but because she had spent time on her own revenge while Nynaeve and Elayne were sitting in a cell hoping against hope that she might be able to rescue them.

She tied off and set the flows of her weavings before she knew she had done it, then paused to study what she had done. Three separate weavings, and not only had it been no trouble to hold them all at once, but now she had done something so they would maintain themselves. She thought she could remember how, too. And it might be useful.

After a moment, she unraveled one of the weavings, and the Darkfriend sobbed as much from relief as from pain. "I am not like you," Egwene said. "This is the second time I have done something like this, and I do not like it. I am going to have to learn to cut throats instead." From the Black sister's face, she thought Egwene meant to start learning with her.

Making a disgusted sound, Egwene left her standing there, trapped and shielded, and hurried into the forest of polished redstone columns. There had to be a way down to the cells somewhere.

The stone corridor fell silent as the final dying scream was cut off by Young Bull's jaws closing on the two-legs's throat, crushing it. The blood was bitter on his tongue.

He knew this was the Stone of Tear, though he could not say how he knew. The two-legs lying around him, one kicking his last with Hopper's teeth buried in his throat, had smelled rank with fear as they fought. They had smelled confused. He did not think they had known where they were—they certainly did not belong in the wolf dream—but they had been set to keep him from that tall door ahead, with its iron lock. To guard it, at least. They had seemed startled to see wolves. He thought they had been startled at being there themselves.

He wiped his mouth, then stared at his hand with a momentary lack of comprehension. He was a man again. He was Perrin. Back in his own body, in the blacksmith's vest, with the heavy hammer at his side.

We must hurry, Young Bull. There is something evil near.

Perrin pulled the hammer from his belt as he strode to the door. "Faile must be here." One sharp blow shattered the lock. He kicked open the door.

The room was empty except for a long stone block in the middle of the floor. Faile lay on that block as if sleeping, her black hair spread out like a fan, her body so wrapped in chains that it took him a moment to realize she was unclothed. Every chain was held to the stone by a thick bolt.

He was hardly aware of crossing the space until his hand touched her face, tracing her cheekbone with a finger.

She opened her eyes and smiled up at him. "I kept dreaming you would come, blacksmith."

"I will have you free in a moment, Faile." He raised his hammer, smashed one of the bolts as if it were wood.

"I was sure of it. Perrin."

As his name faded from her tongue, she faded, too. With a clatter, the chains dropped to the stone where she had been.

"No!" he cried. "I found her!"

The dream is not like the world of flesh, Young Bull. Here, the same hunt can have many endings.

He did not turn to look at Hopper. He knew his teeth were bared in a snarl. Again he raised the hammer, brought it down with all his strength against the chains that had held Faile. The stone block cracked in two under his blow; the Stone itself rang like a struck bell.

"Then I will hunt again," he growled.

Hammer in hand, Perrin strode out of the room with Hopper beside him. The Stone was a place of men. And men, he knew, were crueler hunters than ever wolves were.

Alarm gongs somewhere above sent sonorous clangs down the corridor, not quite drowning out the ring of metal on metal and the shouts of fighting men rather closer. The Aiel and the Defenders, Mat suspected. Tall, golden lamp stands, each with four golden lamps, lined the hall where Mat was, and silk tapestries of battle scenes hung on the polished stone walls. There were even silk carpets on the floor, dark red on dark blue, woven in the Tairen maze. For once, Mat was too busy to put a price on anything.

This bloody fellow is good, he thought as he managed to sweep a sword thrust away from him, but the blow he aimed at the man's head with the other end of the staff had to turn into another block of that darting blade. *I wonder if he is one of these bloody High Lords?* He almost managed a solid blow at a knee, but his opponent sprang back, his straight blade raised on guard.

The blue-eyed man certainly wore the puffy-sleeved coat, yellow with thread-of-gold stripes, but it was all undone, his shirt only half tucked into his breeches, and his feet bare. His short-cropped, dark hair was tousled, like that of a man roused hastily from sleep, but he did not fight like it. Five minutes ago he had come darting out from one of the tall, carved doors that lined this hall, a scabbardless sword in his hands, and Mat was only grateful the fellow had appeared in front of them and not behind. He was not the first man dressed so that Mat had faced already, but he was surely the best.

"Can you make it past me, thief-catcher?" Mat called, careful not to take his eyes off the man waiting for him with blade poised to strike. Sandar had insisted irritably on "thief-catcher," not "thief-taker," though Mat could not see any difference.

"I cannot," Sandar called from behind him. "If you move to let me by, you will lose room to swing that oar you call a staff, and he will spit you like a grunt."

Like a what? "Well, think of something, Tairen. This ragamuffin is grating my nerves."

The man in the gold-striped coat sneered. "You will be honored to die on the blade of the High Lord Darlin, peasant, if I allow it so." It was the first time he had deigned to speak. "Instead, I think I will have the pair of you hung by the heels, and watch while the skin is stripped from your bodies—"

"I do not think I'd like that," Mat said.

The High Lord's face reddened with indignation at being interrupted, but Mat gave him no time for any outraged comment. Quarterstaff whirling in a tight double-loop weave, so quick the staff blurred at the ends, he leaped forward. It was all a snarling Darlin could do to keep the staff from him. For the moment. Mat knew he could not keep this up very long, and if he was lucky then, it would all go back to the strike and counterstrike. If he was lucky. But he had no intention of counting on luck this time. As soon as the High Lord had a moment to set himself in a pattern of defense, Mat altered his attack in midwhirl. The end of the staff Darlin had been expecting at his head dipped instead to sweep his legs out from under him. The other end did strike at his head then, as he fell, a sharp crack that rolled his eyes back up in his head.

Panting, Mat leaned on his staff over the unconscious High Lord. *Burn me, if I have to fight one or two more like this, I'll bloody well fall over from exhaustion! The stories do not tell you being a hero is such hard work! Nynaeve always did find a way to make me work.*

Sandar came to stand beside him, frowning down at the

crumpled High Lord. "He does not look so mighty lying there," he said wonderingly. "He does not look so much greater than me."

Mat gave a start and peered down the hall, where a man had just gone trotting across along a joining corridor. *Burn me, if I did not know it was crazy, I would swear that was Rand!*

"Sandar, you find that—" he began, swinging his staff up onto his shoulder, and cut off when it thudded into something.

Spinning, he found himself facing another half-dressed High Lord, this one with his sword on the floor, his knees buckling, and both hands to his head where Mat's staff had split his scalp. Hastily, Mat poked him hard in the stomach with the butt of the staff to bring his hands down, then gave him another thump on the head to put him down in a heap on top of his sword.

"Luck, Sandar," he muttered. "You cannot beat bloody luck. Now, why don't you find this bloody private way the High Lords take down to the cells?" Sandar had insisted there was such a stairway, and using it would avoid having to run through most of the Stone. Mat did not think he liked men so eager to watch people put to the question that they wanted a quick route to the prisoners from their apartments.

"Just be glad you *were* so lucky," Sandar said unsteadily, "or this one would have killed us both before we saw him. I know the door is here somewhere. Are you coming? Or do you mean to wait for another High Lord to appear?"

"Lead on." Mat stepped over the unconscious High Lord. "I am no bloody hero."

Trotting, he followed the thief-catcher, who peered at the tall doors they passed, muttering that he knew it was here somewhere.

CHAPTER
55

What Is Written in Prophecy

Rand entered the chamber slowly, walking among the great polished redstone columns he remembered from his dreams. Silence filled the shadows, yet something called to him. And something flashed ahead, a momentary light throwing back shadow, a beacon. He stepped out beneath a great dome, and saw what he sought. *Callandor*, hanging hilt down in midair, waiting for no hand but that of the Dragon Reborn. As it revolved, it broke what little light there was into splinters, and now and then it flared as if with a light of its own. Calling him. Waiting for him.

If I am the Dragon Reborn. If I am not just some half-mad man cursed with the ability to channel, a puppet dancing for Moiraine and the White Tower.

"Take it, Lews Therin. Take it, Kinslayer."

He spun to face the voice. The tall man with close-cropped white hair who stepped from the shadows among the columns was familiar to him. Rand had no idea who he was, this fellow in a red silk coat with black stripes down its puffy sleeves and black breeches tucked into elaborately silver-worked boots. He did not know the man, but he had seen him in his dreams. "You put them in a cage," he said. "Egwene, and Nynaeve, and Elayne. In my dreams. You kept putting them in a cage, and hurting them."

The man made a dismissive gesture of his hand. "They are less than nothing. Perhaps one day, when they have been trained, but not now. I confess surprise that you cared enough to make them useful. But you were ever a fool, ever ready to follow your heart before power. You came too soon, Lews Therin. Now you must do what you are not yet ready for, or else die. Die, knowing you have left these women you care for in my hands." He seemed to be waiting for something, expectant. "I mean to use them more, Kinslayer. They will serve me, serve my power. And that will hurt them far more than anything they have suffered before."

Behind Rand, *Callandor* flashed, throwing one pulse of warmth against his back. "Who are you?"

"You do not remember me, do you?" The white-haired man laughed suddenly. "I do not remember you, either, looking this way. A country lad with a flute case on his back. Did Ishamael speak the truth? He was ever one to lie when it gained him an inch or a second. Do you remember nothing, Lews Therin?"

"A name!" Rand demanded. "What is your name?"

"Call me Be'lal." The Forsaken scowled when Rand did not react to the name. "Take it!" Be'lal snapped, throwing a hand toward the sword behind Rand. "Once we rode to war side by side, and for that I give you a chance. A bare chance, but a chance to save yourself, a chance to save those three I mean to make my pets. Take the sword, *countryman*. Perhaps it will be enough to help you survive me."

Rand laughed. "Do you believe you can frighten me so easily, Forsaken? Ba'alzamon himself has hunted me. Do you think I will cower now for you? Grovel before a Forsaken when I have denied the Dark One to his face?"

"Is that what you think?" Be'lal said softly. "Truly, you know nothing." Suddenly there was a sword in his hands, a sword with a blade carved from black fire. "Take it! Take *Callandor*! Three thousand years, while I lay imprisoned, it has waited there. For you. One of the most powerful *sa'angreal* we ever made. Take it, and defend yourself, if you can!"

He moved toward Rand as if to drive him back toward *Callandor*, but Rand raised his own hands—*saidin* filled him; sweet rushing flow of the Power; stomach-wrenching vileness of the taint—and he held a sword wrought from red flame, a sword with a heron-mark on its fiery blade. He stepped into the forms Lan had taught him till he flowed from one to the next as if in a dance. Parting the Silk. Water Flows Downhill. Wind and Rain. Blade of black fire met blade of red in showers of sparks, roars like white-hot metal shattering.

Rand came back smoothly into a guard stance, trying not to let his sudden uncertainty show. A heron stood on the black blade, too, a bird so dark as to be nearly invisible. Once he had faced a man with a heron-mark blade of steel, and barely survived. He knew that he himself had no real right to the blademaster's mark; it had been on the sword his father had given him, and when he thought of a sword in his hands, he thought of that sword. Once he had embraced death, as the Warder had taught, but this time, he knew, his death would be final. Be'lal was better than he with the sword. Stronger. Faster. A true blademaster.

The Forsaken laughed, amused, swinging his blade in quick flourishes to either side of him; the black fire roared as if swift passage through the air quickened it. "You were a greater swordsman, once, Lews Therin," he said mockingly. "Do you remember when we took that tame sport called swords and learned to kill with it, as the old volumes said men once had? Do you remember even one of those desperate battles, even one of our dire defeats? Of course not. You remember nothing, do you? This time you have not learned enough. This time, Lews Therin, I will kill you." Be'lal's mockery deepened. "Perhaps if you take *Callandor*, you might extend your life a little longer. A little longer."

He came forward slowly, almost as if to give Rand time to do just that, turn and race to *Callandor*, to the Sword That Cannot Be Touched, to take it. But the doubts were still strong in Rand. *Callandor* could only be touched by the Dragon Reborn. He had allowed them to proclaim him so for a hundred reasons that seemed to leave him no choice at the time. But was he truly the Dragon Reborn? If he raced to touch *Callandor* in truth, not in a dream, would his hand meet an invisible wall while Be'lal cut him down from behind?

He met the Forsaken with the sword he knew, the blade of fire wrought with *saidin*. And was driven back. The Falling Leaf met Watered Silk. The Cat Dances on the Wall met the Boar Rushes Downhill. The River Undercuts the Bank nearly lost him his head, and he had to throw himself inelegantly to one side with black flame brushing his hair, rolling to his feet to confront the Stone Falls From the Mountain. Methodically, deliberately, Be'lal drove him back in a spiral that slowly tightened on *Callandor*.

Shouts echoed among the columns, screams, the clash of steel, but Rand barely heard. He and Be'lal were no longer alone in the Heart of the Stone. Men in breastplates and rimmed helmets fought with swords against shadowy, veiled shapes that darted among the columns with short spears stabbing. Some of the soldiers formed a rank; arrows flashing out of the dimness took them in the throat, the face, and they died in their line. Rand hardly noticed the fighting, even when men fell dead within paces of him. His own fight was too desperate; it took all of his concentration. Wet warmth trickled down his side. The old wound was breaking open.

He stumbled suddenly, not seeing the dead man at his feet until he was lying on his back atop his flute case on the stone floor.

Be'lal raised his blade of black fire, snarling. "Take it! Take *Callandor* and defend yourself! Take it, or I will kill you now! If you will not take it, I will slay you!"

"No!"

Even Be'lal gave a start at the command in that woman's voice. The Forsaken stepped back out of the arc of Rand's sword and turned his head to frown at Moiraine as she came striding through the battle, her eyes fixed on him, ignoring the screaming deaths around her. "I thought you were neatly out of the way, woman. No matter. You are only an annoyance. A stinging fly. A biteme. I will cage you with the others, and teach you to serve the Shadow with your puny powers," he finished with a contemptuous laugh, and raised his free hand.

Moiraine had not stopped or slowed while he spoke. She was no more than thirty paces from him when he moved his hand, and she raised both of hers as well.

There was an instant of surprise on the Forsaken's face, and he had time to scream "No!" Then a bar of white fire hotter than the sun shot from the Aes Sedai's hands, a glaring rod that banished all shadows. Before it, Be'lal became a shape of shimmering motes, specks dancing in the light for less than a heartbeat, flecks consumed before his cry faded.

There was silence in the chamber as that bar of light

vanished, silence except for the moans of the wounded. The fighting had stopped dead, veiled men and men in breast-plates alike standing as if stunned.

"He was right concerning one thing," Moiraine said, as coolly serene as if she were standing in a meadow. "You must take *Callandor*. He meant to slay you for it, but it is your birthright. Better by far that you knew more before your hand held that hilt, yet you have come to the point now, and there is no further time for learning. Take it, Rand."

Whips of black lightning curled around her; she screamed as they lifted her, hurled her to slide along the floor like a sack until she came up against one of the columns.

Rand stared up at where the lightning had come from. There was a deeper shadow up there, near the top of the columns, a blackness that made all other shadows look like noonday, and from it, two eyes of fire stared back at him.

Slowly the shadow descended, resolving into Ba'alzamon, clothed in dead black, like a Myrddraal's black. Yet even that was not so dark as the shadow that clung to him. He hung in the air, two spans above the floor, glaring at Rand with a rage as fierce as his eyes. "Twice in this life I have offered you the chance to serve me living." Flames leaped in his mouth as he spoke, and every word roared like a furnace. "Twice you have refused, and wounded me. Now you will serve the Lord of the Grave in death. Die, Lews Therin Kinslayer. Die, Rand al'Thor. It is time for you to die! I take your soul!"

As Ba'alzamon put forth his hand, Rand pushed himself up, threw himself desperately toward *Callandor*, still glittering and flashing in midair. He did not know whether he could reach it, or touch it if he did, but he was sure it was his only chance.

Ba'alzamon's blow struck him as he leapt, struck inside him, a ripping and crumpling, tearing something loose, try-ing to pull a part of him away. Rand screamed. He felt as if he were collapsing like an empty sack, as if he were being turned inside out. The pain in his side, the wound taken at Falme, was almost welcome, something to hang on to, a reminder of life. His hand closed convulsively. On *Callandor*'s hilt.

The One Power surged through him, a torrent greater than he could believe, from *saidin* into the sword. The crystal blade shone brighter than even Moiraine's fire had. It was impossible to look at, impossible any longer to see that it was a sword, only that light blazed in his fist. He fought the flow, wrestled with the implacable tide that threatened to carry him, all that was really him, into the sword with it. For a heartbeat that took centuries he hung, wavering, balanced on the brink of being scoured away like sand before a flash flood. With infinite slowness the balance firmed. It was still as though he stood barefoot on a razor's edge above a bottomless drop, yet something told him this was the best that could be expected. To channel this much of the Power, he must dance on that sharpness as he had danced the forms of the sword.

He turned to face Ba'alzamon. The tearing within him had ceased as soon as his hand touched *Callandor*. Only an instant had passed, yet it seemed to have lasted forever. "You will not take my soul," he shouted. "This time, I mean to finish it once and for all! I mean to finish it now!"

Ba'alzamon fled, man and shadow vanishing.

For a moment Rand stared, frowning. There had been a sense of—folding—as Ba'alzamon left. A twisting, as if Ba'alzamon had in some way *bent* what was. Ignoring the men staring at him, ignoring Moiraine crumpled at the column base, Rand reached out, through *Callandor*, and twisted reality to make a door to somewhere else. He did not know to where, except that it was where Ba'alzamon had gone.

"I am the hunter now," he said, and stepped through.

The stone shook under Egwene's feet. The Stone shook; it rang. She caught her balance and stopped, listening. There was no more sound, no other tremor. Whatever had happened, it was over. She hurried on. A door of iron bars stood in her way, with a lock as big as her head. She channeled Earth before she reached it, and when she pushed against the bars, the lock tore in half.

She walked quickly across the chamber beyond it, trying not to look at the things hanging on the walls. Whips and iron pincers were the most innocuous. With a small shudder she pushed open a smaller iron gate and entered a corridor lined with rough wooden doors, rush torches burning at intervals in iron brackets; she felt almost as much relief at leaving those things behind as she did at finding what she sought. *But which cell?*

The wooden doors opened easily. Some were unlocked, and the locks on the others lasted no longer than that larger lock had earlier. But every cell was empty. *Of course. No one would dream themselves in this place. Any prisoner who managed to reach Tel'aran'rhiod would dream of a pleasanter place.*

For a moment she felt something close to despair. She had wanted to believe that finding the right cell would make a difference. Even finding it could be impossible, though. This first corridor stretched on and on, and others joined it.

Suddenly she saw something flicker just ahead of her. A shape even less substantial than Joiya Byir had been. It had been a woman, though. She was sure of that. A woman seated on a bench beside one of the cell doors. The image flickered into being again, and was gone. There was no mistaking that slender neck and the pale, innocent-appearing face with its eyelids fluttering on the edge of sleep. Amico Nagoyin was drifting toward sleep, dreaming of her guard duties. And apparently toying drowsily with one of the stolen *ter'angreal*. Egwene could understand that; it had been a great effort to stop using the one Verin had given her, even for a few days.

She knew it was possible to cut a woman off from the True Source even if she had already embraced *saidar*, but severing a weave already established had to be much harder than damming the flow before it began. She set the patterns of the weaving, readied them, making the threads of Spirit much stronger, this time, thicker and heavier, a denser weave with a cutting edge like a knife.

The wavering shape of the Darkfriend appeared again, and Egwene struck out with the flows of Air and Spirit. For an instant something seemed to resist the weaving of Spirit, and she forced it with all of her might. It slid into place.

Amico Nagoyin screamed. It was a thin sound, barely heard, as faint as she herself was, and she seemed almost like a shadow of what Joiya Byir had been. Yet the bonds woven of Air held her; she did not vanish again. Terror twisted the Darkfriend's lovely face; she seemed to be babbling, but her shouts were whispers too soft for Egwene to understand.

Tying and setting the weaves around the Black sister, Egwene turned her attentions to the cell door. Impatiently, she let Earth flood into the iron lock. It fell away in black dust, in a mist that dissolved completely before it struck the floor. She swung open the door, and was not surprised to find the cell empty except for one burning rush torch.

But Amico is bound, and the door is open.

For a moment she thought of what to do next. Then she stepped out of the dream . . .

. . . and woke to all her bruises and aches and thirst, to the wall of the cell against her back, staring at the tightly shut cell door. *Of course. What happens to living things there is real when they wake. What I did to stone or iron or wood has no effect in the waking world.*

Nynaeve and Elayne were still kneeling beside her.

"Whoever is out there," Nynaeve said, "screamed a few moments ago, but nothing else has happened. Did you find a way out?"

"We should be able to walk out," Egwene said. "Help me to my feet, and I will get rid of the lock. Amico will not trouble us. That scream was her."

Elayne shook her head. "I have been trying to embrace *saidar* ever since you left. It is different, now, but I am still cut off."

Egwene formed the emptiness inside her, became the rosebud opening to *saidar*. The invisible wall was still there. It shimmered now. There were moments when she almost thought she could feel the True Source beginning to fill her with the Power. Almost. The shield wavered in and out of existence too fast for her to detect. It might as well have still been solid.

She stared at the other two women. "I bound her. I shielded her. She is a living thing, not lifeless iron. She *must* be shielded still."

"*Some*thing has happened to the shield set on us," Elayne said, "but Amico is still managing to hold it."

Egwene let her head sag back against the wall. "I will have to try again."

"Are you strong enough?" Elayne grimaced. "To be blunt, you sound even weaker than you did before. This try took something out of you, Egwene."

"I am strong enough there." She did feel more weary, less strong, but it was their only chance that she could see. She said as much, and their faces said they agreed with her, however reluctantly.

"Can you go to sleep again so soon?" Nynaeve asked finally.

"Sing to me." Egwene managed a smile. "Like when I was a little girl. Please?" Holding Nynaeve's hand with one of hers, the stone ring clasped in the other, she closed her eyes and tried to find sleep in the wordless humming tune.

The wide door of iron bars stood open, and the room beyond seemed empty of life, but Mat entered cautiously. Sandar was still out in the hall, trying to peer both ways at once, certain that a High Lord, or maybe a hundred Defenders or so, would appear at any moment.

There were no men in the room now—and by the looks of the half-eaten meals on a long table, they had left hurriedly; no doubt because of the fighting above—and from the looks of the things on the walls, he was just as glad he did not have to meet any of them. Whips in different sizes and lengths, different thicknesses, with different numbers of tails. Pincers, and tongs, and clamps, and irons. Things that looked like metal boots, and gauntlets, and helmets, with great screws all over them as if to tighten them down. Things he could not even begin to guess the use of. If he had met the men who used these things, he thought he would surely have checked that *they* were dead before he walked away.

"Sandar!" he hissed. "Are you going to stay out there all bloody night!" He hurried to the inner door—barred like the outer, but smaller—without waiting for an answer, and went through.

The hall beyond was lined by rough wooden doors, and lit by the same rush torches as the room he had just left. No more than twenty paces from him, a woman sat on a bench beside one of the doors, leaning back against the wall in a curiously stiff fashion. She turned her head slowly toward him at the sound of his boots grating on the stone. A pretty young woman. He wondered why she did not move more than her head, and why even that moved as if she were half-asleep.

Was she a prisoner? *Out in the hall? But nobody with a face like that could be one of the people who uses the things on those walls.* She did look almost asleep, with her eyes only partly open. And the suffering on that lovely face surely made her one of the tortured, not a torturer.

"Stop!" Sandar shouted behind him. "She is Aes Sedai! She is one of those who took the women you seek!"

Mat froze in the middle of a step, staring at the woman. He remembered Moiraine hurling balls of fire. He wondered if he could deflect a ball of fire with his quarterstaff. He wondered if his luck extended to outrunning Aes Sedai.

"Help me," she said faintly. Her eyes still looked nearly asleep, but the pleading in her voice was fully awake. "Help me. Please!"

Mat blinked. She still had not moved a muscle below her neck. Cautiously, he stepped closer, waving to Sandar to stop his groaning about her being Aes Sedai. She moved her head to follow him. No more than that.

A large iron key hung at her belt. For a moment he hesitated. Aes Sedai, Sandar said. *Why doesn't she move?* Swallowing, he eased the key free as carefully as if he were trying to take a piece of meat from a wolf's jaws. She rolled her eyes toward the door beside her and made a sound like a cat that had just seen a huge dog come snarling into the room and knew there was no way out.

He did not understand it, but as long as she did not try to stop him opening that door, he did not care why she just sat there like a stuffed scarecrow. On the other hand, he wondered if there was something on the other side worth being afraid of. *If she is one of those who took Egwene and the others, it stands to reason she's guarding them.* Tears leaked from the woman's eyes. *Only she looks like it's a bloody Halfman in there.* But there was only one way to find out. Propping his staff against the wall, he turned the key in the lock and flung open the door, ready to run if need be.

Nynaeve and Elayne were kneeling on the floor with Egwene apparently asleep between them. He gasped at the sight of Egwene's swollen face, and changed his mind about her sleeping. The other two women turned toward him as he opened the door—they were almost as battered as Egwene; *Burn me! Burn me!*—looked at him, and gaped.

"Matrim Cauthon," Nynaeve said, sounding shocked, "what under the Light are *you* doing here?"

"I came to bloody rescue you," he said. "Burn me if I expected to be greeted as if I had come to steal a pie. You can tell me why you look as if you'd been fighting bears later, if you want. If Egwene cannot walk, I'll carry her on my back. There are Aiel all over the Stone, or near enough, and either they are killing the bloody Defenders or the bloody Defenders are killing them, but whichever way it is, we had better get out of here while we bloody well can. *If* we can!"

"Mind your language," Nynaeve told him, and Elayne gave him one of those disapproving stares women were so good at. Neither one seemed to have her full attention in it, though. They began shaking Egwene as if she were not covered with more bruises than he had ever seen in his life.

Egwene's eyelids fluttered open, and she groaned. "Why did you wake me? I must understand it. If I loose the bonds on her, she will wake and I'll never catch her again. But if I do not, she cannot go all the way to sleep, and—" Her eyes fell on him and widened. "Matrim Cauthon, what under the Light are *you* doing here?"

"You tell her," he told Nynaeve. "I am too busy trying to rescue you to watch my langu—" They were all staring beyond him, glaring as if they wished they had knives in their hands.

He spun, but all he saw was Juilin Sandar, looking as if he had swallowed a rotten plum whole.

"They have cause," he told Mat. "I. . . . I betrayed them. But I had to." That was addressed past Mat to the women. "The one with many honey-colored braids spoke to me, and I. . . . I had to do it." For a long moment the three continued to stare.

"Liandrin has vile tricks, Master Sandar," Nynaeve said finally. "Perhaps you are not entirely to blame. We can apportion guilt later."

"If that is all cleared up," Mat said, "could we go now?" It was as clear as mud to him, but he was more interested in leaving right then.

The three women limped after him into the hall, but they stopped around the woman on the bench. She rolled her eyes at them and whimpered. "Please. I will come back to the Light. I will swear to obey you. With the Oath Rod in my hands I will swear. Please do not—"

Mat jumped as Nynaeve suddenly reared back and swung a fist, knocking the woman completely off the bench. She lay there, her eyes closed all the way finally, but even lying on her side she was still in exactly the same position she had been in on the bench.

"It is gone," Elayne said excitedly.

Egwene bent to rummage in the unconscious woman's pouch, transferring something Mat could not make out to her own. "Yes. It feels wonderful. Something changed about her when you hit her, Nynaeve. I do not know what, but I felt it."

Elayne nodded. "I felt it, too."

"I would like to change every last thing about her," Nynaeve said grimly. She took Egwene's head in her hands; Egwene rose onto her toes, gasping. When Nynaeve took her hands away to put them on Elayne, Egwene's bruises were gone. Elayne's vanished as quickly.

"Blood and bloody ashes!" Mat growled. "What do you mean hitting a woman who was just sitting there? I don't think she could even move!" They all three turned to look at him, and he made a strangled sound as the air seemed to turn to thick jelly around him. He lifted into the air, until his boots dangled a good pace above the floor. *Oh, burn me, the Power! Here I was afraid that Aes Sedai would use the bloody Power on me, and now the bloody women I'm rescuing do it! Burn me!*

"You do not understand anything, Matrim Cauthon," Egwene said in a tight voice.

"Until you do understand," Nynaeve said in an even tighter, "I suggest you keep your opinions to yourself."

Elayne contented herself with a glare that made him think of his mother going out to cut a switch.

For some reason he found himself giving them the grin that had so often sent his mother after that switch. *Burn me, if they can do this, I don't see how anybody ever locked them in that cell in the first place!* "What I understand is that I got you out of something you couldn't get yourselves out of, and you all have as much gratitude as a bloody Taren Ferry man with a toothache!"

"You are right," Nynaeve said, and his boots suddenly hit the floor so hard his teeth jarred. But he could move again. "As much as it pains me to say it, Mat, you are right."

He was tempted to answer something sarcastic, but there was barely enough apology in her voice as it was. "Now can we go? With the fighting going on, Sandar thinks he and I can take you out by a small gate near the river."

"I am not leaving just yet, Mat," Nynaeve said.

"I mean to find Liandrin and skin her," Egwene said, sounding almost as if she meant it literally.

"All I want to do," Elayne said, "is pound Joiya Byir till she squeals, but I will settle for any of them."

"Are you all deaf?" he growled. "There is a battle going on out there! I came here to rescue you, and I mean to rescue you." Egwene patted his cheek as she walked by him, and so did Elayne. Nynaeve merely sniffed. He stared after them with his mouth hanging open. "Why didn't you say something?" he growled at the thief-catcher.

"I saw what speaking earned you," Sandar said simply. "I am no fool."

"Well, I am not staying in the middle of a battle!" he shouted at the women. They were just disappearing through the small, barred door. "I am leaving, do you hear?" They did not even look back. *Probably get themselves killed out there! Somebody will stick a sword in them while they're looking the other way!* With a snarl, he put his quarterstaff across his shoulder and started after. "Are you going to stand there?" he called to the thief-catcher. "I did not come this far to let them die now!"

Sandar caught up to him in the room with the whips. The three women were already gone, but Mat had a feeling they would not be too hard to find. *Just find the men bloody hanging in midair! Bloody women!* He quickened his pace to a trot.

Perrin strode down the halls of the Stone grimly, searching for some sign of Faile. He had rescued her twice more, now, breaking her out of an iron cage once, much like the one that had held the Aiel in Remen, and once breaking open a steel chest with a falcon worked on its side. Both times she had melted into air after saying his name. Hopper trotted by his side, sniffing the air. As sharp as Perrin's nose was, the wolf's was sharper; it had been Hopper who led them to the chest.

Perrin wondered whether he was ever going to free her in truth. There had not been any sign in a long time, it seemed. The halls of the Stone were empty, lamps burning, tapestries and weapons hanging on the walls, but nothing moved except himself and Hopper. *Except I think that was Rand.* It had only been a glimpse, a man running as if chasing someone. *It could not be him. It couldn't, but I think it was.*

Hopper quickened his steps suddenly, heading for another set of tall doors, these clad in bronze. Perrin tried to match the pace, stumbled, and fell to his knees, throwing out a hand to catch himself short of dropping on his face. Weakness washed through him as if all his muscles had gone to water. Even after the feeling receded, it took some of his strength with it. It was an effort to struggle to his feet. Hopper had turned to look at him.

You are here too strongly, Young Bull. The flesh weakens. You do not care to hold on to it enough. Soon flesh and dream will die together.

"Find her," Perrin said. "That is all I ask. Find Faile."

Yellow eyes met yellow eyes. The wolf turned and trotted to the doors. *Beyond here, Young Bull.*

Perrin reached the doors and pushed. They did not budge. There seemed to be no way to open them, no handles, nothing to grip. There was a tiny pattern worked into the metal, so fine his eyes almost did not see it. Falcons. Thousands of tiny falcons.

She has to be here. I do not think I can last much longer. With a shout, he swung his hammer against the bronze. It rang like a great gong. Again he struck, and the peal deepened. A third blow, and the bronze doors shattered like glass.

Within, a hundred paces from the broken doors, a circle of light surrounded a falcon chained to a perch. Darkness filled all the rest of that vast chamber, darkness and faint rustlings as of hundreds of wings.

He took a step into the room, and a falcon stooped out of the murk, talons scoring his face as it passed. He threw an arm across his eyes—talons tore at his forearm—and staggered toward the perch. Again and again the birds came, falcons diving, striking him, tearing him, but he lumbered on with blood pouring down his arms and shoulders, that one arm protecting the eyes he had fixed on the falcon on the perch. He had lost the hammer; he did not know where, but he knew that if he went back to search, he would die before he found it.

As he reached the perch, the slicing talons drove him to his knees. He peered up under his arm at the falcon on the perch, and she stared back with dark, unblinking eyes. The chain that held her leg was fastened to the perch with a tiny lock shaped like a hedgehog. He seized the chain with both hands, careless of the other falcons that now became a whirlwind of cutting talons around him, and with his last strength snapped it. Pain and the falcons brought darkness.

He opened his eyes to stinging agony, as if his face and arms and shoulders had been sliced with a thousand knives. It did not matter. Faile was kneeling over him, those dark, tilted eyes filled with worry, wiping his face with a cloth already soaked in his blood.

"My poor Perrin," she said softly. "My poor blacksmith. You are hurt so badly."

With an effort that cost more pain, he turned his head. This was the private dining room in the Star, and near one leg of the table lay a wooden carving of a hedgehog, broken in half. "Faile," he whispered to her. "My falcon."

Rand was still in the Heart of the Stone, but it was different. There were no men fighting here, no dead men, no one at all but himself. Abruptly the sound of a great gong rang through the Stone, then again, and the very stones beneath his feet resonated. A third time the booming came, but cut off abruptly, as if the gong had shattered. All was still.

Where is this place? he wondered. *More important, where is Ba'alzamon?*

As if to answer him, a blazing shaft like the one Moiraine had made shot out of the shadows among the columns, straight toward his chest. His wrist twisted the sword instinctively; it was instinct as much as anything else that made him loose flows from *saidin* into *Callandor*, a flood of the Power that made the sword blaze brighter even than that bar streaking at him. His uncertain balance between existence and destruction wavered. Surely that torrent would consume him.

The shaft of light struck the blade of *Callandor*—and parted on its edge, forking to stream past on either side. He felt his coat singe from its near passage, smelled the wool beginning to burn. Behind him, the two prongs of frozen fire, of liquid light, struck huge redstone columns; where they struck, stone ceased to exist, and the burning bars bored through to other columns, severing those instantaneously as well. The Heart of the Stone rumbled as columns fell and shattered in clouds of dust, sprays of stone fragments. What fell into the light, however, simply—was not, anymore.

A snarl of rage came from the shadows, and the blazing shaft of pure white heat vanished.

Rand swung *Callandor* as if he were striking at something in front of him. The white light obscuring the blade extended, blazed ahead, and sheared through the redstone column that hid the snarl. The polished stone sliced like silk. The severed column trembled; part of it tore loose and dropped from the ceiling, smashing into huge, jagged chunks on the floor. As the rumbling faded, he heard beyond it the sound of boots on stone. Running.

Callandor at the ready, Rand hurried after Ba'alzamon.

The tall archway leading out of the Heart collapsed as he reached it, the entire wall falling in clouds of dust and rock as if to bury him, but he threw the Power at it, and all became dust floating in the air. He ran on. He was not sure what he had done, or how, but he had no time to think on it. He ran after Ba'alzamon's retreating footsteps, echoing down the halls of the Stone.

Myrddraal and Trollocs leaped out of thin air, huge bestial shapes and eyeless faces distorted with a rage to kill, in hundreds, so they jammed the hall before him and behind, scythelike swords and blades of deadly black steel seeking his blood. Without knowing how, he turned them to vapor that parted before him—and vanished. The air around him suddenly became choking soot, clogging his nostrils, shutting off breath, but he made it fresh air again, a cool mist. Flames leaped from the floor beneath his feet, spurted from the walls, the ceiling, furious jets that flashed tapestries and rugs, tables and chests to wisps of ash, flung ornaments and lamps ahead of them as drops of molten, burning gold; he smashed the fires flat, hardened them into a red glaze on the rock.

The stones around him faded almost to mist; the Stone faded. Reality trembled; he could feel it unraveling, feel himself unraveling. He was being pushed out of the here, into some other place where nothing existed at all. *Callandor* blazed in his hands like the sun till he thought it would melt. He thought he himself would melt from the surge of the One Power through him, the flood that he somehow directed into sealing up the hole that had opened around him, into holding himself on the side of existence. The Stone became solid again.

He could not even begin to imagine what it was that he did. The One Power raged inside him till he barely knew himself, till he barely was himself, till what was himself almost did not exist. His precarious stability teetered. To either side lay the endless fall, obliteration by the Power that coursed through him into the sword. Only in the dance along the razor's sharp edge was there even an uncertain safety. *Callandor* shone in his fist until it seemed he carried the sun. Dimly within him, fluttering like a candle flame in a storm, was the surety that holding *Callandor*, he could do anything. Anything.

Through endless corridors he ran, dancing along the razor, chasing the one who would slay him, the one he must slay. There could be no other end, this time. This time one of them *must* die! That Ba'alzamon knew it as well was clear. Always he fled, always staying ahead of sight so that only the sounds of his flight drew Rand on, but even fleeing he turned this Stone of Tear that was not the Stone of Tear against Rand, and Rand fought back with instinct and guesses and chance, fought and ran down that knife edge in perfect balance with the Power, the tool and weapon that would consume him utterly if he faltered.

Water filled the halls from top to bottom, thick and black as the bottom of the sea, choking off breath. He made it air again, unknowingly, and ran on, and suddenly the air gained weight until it seemed every inch of his skin supported a mountain, squeezing in from all directions. In the instant before he was crushed to nothingness he chose tides out of the flood of Power raging through him—he did not know how or which or why; it was too fast for thought or knowing—and the pressure vanished. He pursued Ba'alzamon, and the very air was abruptly solid rock encasing him, then molten stone, then nothing at all to fill his lungs. The ground beneath his boots pulled at him as if every pound suddenly weighed a thousand, then all weight vanished so that a step left him spinning in midair. Unseen maws gaped to rip his mind from his body, to tear away his soul. He sprang each trap and ran on; what Ba'alzamon twisted to destroy him, he made right without being aware of how. Vaguely he knew that in some way he had brought things back into natural balance, forced them into line with his own dance down that impossibly thin divide between existence and nothingness, but that knowledge was distant. All his awareness lay in the pursuit, the hunt, the death that must end it.

And then he was in the Heart of the Stone again, stalking through the rubbled gap that had been a wall. Some of the columns hung like broken teeth, now. And Ba'alzamon backed away from him, eyes burning, shadow cloaking him. Black lines like steel wires seemed to run off from Ba'alzamon into the darkness mounding around him, vanishing into unimaginable heights and distances within that blackness.

"I will not be undone!" Ba'alzamon cried. His mouth was fire; his shriek echoed among the columns. "I cannot be defeated! Aid me!" Some of the darkness shrouding him drifted into his hands, formed into a ball so black it seemed to soak up even the light of *Callandor*. Sudden triumph blazed in the flames of his eyes.

"You are destroyed!" Rand shouted. *Callandor* spun in his hands. Its light roiled the darkness, severed the steel-black lines around Ba'alzamon, and Ba'alzamon convulsed. As if there were two of him he seemed to dwindle and grow larger at the same time. "You are undone!" Rand plunged the shining blade into Ba'alzamon's chest.

Ba'alzamon screamed, and the fires of his face flared wildly. "Fool!" he howled. "The Great Lord of the Dark can never be defeated!"

Rand pulled *Callandor*'s blade free as Ba'alzamon's body sagged and began to fall, the shadow around him vanishing.

And suddenly Rand was in another Heart of the Stone, surrounded by columns still whole, and fighting men screaming and dying, veiled men and men in breastplates and helmets. Moiraine still lay crumpled at the base of a redstone column. And at Rand's feet lay the body of a man, sprawled on its back with a hole burned through the chest. He might have been a handsome man in his middle years, except that where his eyes and mouth should have been were only pits from which rose tendrils of black smoke.

I have done it, he thought. *I have killed Ba'alzamon, killed Shai'tan! I have won the Last Battle! Light, I AM the Dragon Reborn! The breaker of nations, the Breaker of the World. No! I will END the breaking, end the killing! I will MAKE it end!*

He raised *Callandor* above his head. Silver lightning crackled from the blade, jagged streaks arching toward the great dome above. "Stop!" he shouted. The fighting ceased; men stared at him in wonder, over black veils, from beneath the rims of round helmets. "I am Rand al'Thor!" he called, so his voice rang through the chamber. "I am the Dragon Reborn!" *Callandor* shone in his grasp.

One by one, veiled men and helmeted, they knelt to him, crying, "The Dragon is Reborn! The Dragon is Reborn!"

CHAPTER

56

People of the Dragon

Throughout the city of Tear people woke with the dawn, speaking of the dreams they had had, dreams of the Dragon battling Ba'alzamon in the Heart of the Stone, and when their eyes rose to the great fortress of the Stone, they beheld a banner waving from its greatest height. Across a field of white flowed a sinuous form like a great serpent scaled in scarlet and gold, but with a golden lion's mane and four legs, each tipped with five golden claws. Men came, stunned and frightened, from the Stone to speak in hushed tones of what had happened in the night, and men and women thronged the streets, weeping as they shouted the fulfillment of Prophecy.

"The Dragon!" they shouted. "Al'Thor! The Dragon! Al'Thor!"

Peering through an arrowslit high on the side of the Stone, Mat shook his head as he listened to the chorus rising out of the city in waves. *Well, maybe he is.* He was still having a hard enough time coming to grips with Rand really being there.

Everyone in the Stone seemed to agree with the people below, or if they did not, they were not letting on. He had seen Rand just once since the night before, striding along a hall with *Callandor* in his hand, surrounded by a dozen veiled Aiel and trailing a cloud of Tairens, a knot of Defenders of the Stone and most of the few surviving High Lords. The High Lords, at least, seemed to think Rand would need them to help him rule the world; the Aiel kept

everyone back with sharp looks, though, and spears if need
be. They surely believed Rand was the Dragon, though they
called him He Who Comes With the Dawn. There were
nearly two hundred Aiel in the Stone. They had lost a third
of their numbers in the fight, but they had killed or captured
ten times as many Defenders.

As he turned from the arrowslit, his eyes brushed across
Rhuarc. There was a tall stand at one end of the room,
carved and polished upright wheels of some pale, dark-
striped wood with shelves slung between them so all of the
shelves would stay flat as the wheels were revolved. Each
shelf held a large book, bound in gold, covers set with sparkling gems. The Aiel had one of the books open and was
reading. Some sort of essays, Mat thought. *Who would have
thought an Aiel would read books? Who'd have thought an
Aiel could bloody read?*

Rhuarc glanced in his direction, all cold blue eyes and
level stare. Mat looked away hastily, before the Aiel could
read his thoughts on his face. *At least he is not veiled, thank
the Light! Burn me, that Aviendha nearly took my head
off when I asked her if she could do any dances without
spears.* Bain and Chiad presented another problem. They
were certainly pretty and more than friendly, but he could
not manage to talk to one without the other. The male Aiel
seemed to think his efforts to get one of them alone were
funny, and for that matter, so did Bain and Chiad. *Women
are odd, but Aiel women make odd seem normal!*

The great table in the middle of the room, ornately
carved and gilded on edges and thick legs, had been meant
for gatherings of the High Lords. Moiraine sat in one of the
thronelike chairs, with the Crescent Banner of Tear worked
into its towering back in gilt and polished carnelian and
pearlshell. Egwene, Nynaeve, and Elayne sat close by her.

"I still cannot believe Perrin is here in Tear," Nynaeve
was saying. "Are you sure he is all right?"

Mat shook his head. He would have expected Perrin to
have been up in the Stone last night; the blacksmith had
always been braver than anyone with good sense.

"He was well when I left him." Moiraine's voice was serene. "Whether he still is, I do not know. His . . . companion is in some considerable danger, and he may have put
himself into it, also."

"His companion?" Egwene said sharply. "Wha— Who is Perrin's companion?"

"What sort of danger?" Nynaeve demanded.

"Nothing that need concern you," the Aes Sedai said calmly. "I will go and see to her as I may, shortly. I have delayed only to show you this, which I found among the *ter'angreal* and other things of the Power the High Lords collected over the years." She took something from her pouch and laid it on the table before her. It was a disc the size of a man's hand, seemingly made of two teardrops fitted together, one black as pitch, the other white as snow.

Mat seemed to remember seeing others like it. Ancient, like this one, but broken, where this was whole. Three of them, he had seen; not all together, but all in pieces. But that could not be; he remembered that they were made of *cuendillar*, unbreakable by any power, even the One Power.

"One of the seven seals Lews Therin Kinslayer and the Hundred Companions put on the Dark One's prison when they resealed it," Elayne said, nodding as if confirming her own memory.

"More precisely," Moiraine told her, "a focus point for one of the seals. But in essence, you are correct. During the Breaking of the World they were scattered and hidden for safety; since the Trolloc Wars they have been lost in truth." She sniffed. "I begin to sound like Verin."

Egwene shook her head. "I suppose I should have expected to find that here. Twice before Rand faced Ba'alzamon, and both times at least one of the seals was present."

"And this time unbroken," Nynaeve said. "For the first time, the seal is unbroken. As if that mattered, now."

"You think it does not?" Moiraine's voice was dangerous in its quiet, and the other women frowned at her.

Mat rolled his eyes. They kept talking about unimportant things. He did not much like standing not twenty feet from that disc now that he knew what it was, no matter the value of *cuendillar*, but. . . . "Your pardon?" he said.

They all turned to stare at him as if he were interrupting something important. *Burn me! Break them out of a prison cell, save their lives half a dozen times between them before the night is done, and they glower as hard as the bloody Aes Sedai! Well, they did not thank me then, either, did they? You'd have thought I was sticking my nose in where it wasn't wanted then, too, instead of keeping some bloody Defender from putting a sword through one of them.* Aloud, he said mildly, "You do not mind if I ask a question, do you? You have all been talking this Aes Sedai . . . uh . . . business, and no one has bothered to tell me anything."

"Mat?" Nynaeve said warningly, tugging her braid, but Moiraine said, in a calm only just touched with impatience, "What is it that you wish to know?"

"I want to know how all of this can be." He meant to keep his tone soft, but despite himself he picked up intensity as he went along. "The Stone of Tear has fallen! The Prophecies said that would never happen till the People of the Dragon came. Does that mean *we* are the bloody People of the Dragon? You, me, Lan, and a few hundred bloody Aiel?" He had seen the Warder during the night; there had not seemed to be much edge between Lan and the Aiel as to who was the more deadly. As Rhuarc straightened to stare at him, he hastily added, "Uh, sorry, Rhuarc. Slip of the tongue."

"Perhaps," Moiraine said slowly. "I came to stop Be'lal from killing Rand. I did not expect to see the Stone of Tear fall. Perhaps we are. Prophecies are fulfilled as they are meant to be, not as we think they should be."

Be'lal. Mat shivered. He had heard that name last night, and he did not like it any more in daylight. If he had known one of the Forsaken was loose—and inside the Stone—he would never have gone near the place. He glanced at Egwene, and Nynaeve, and Elayne. *Well, I'd have come in like a bloody mouse, anyway, not thumping people left and right!* Sandar had gone scurrying out of the Stone at daybreak; to take the news to Mother Guenna, he claimed, but Mat thought it was just to escape those stares from the three women, who looked as if they had not yet quite decided what to do about him.

Rhuarc cleared his throat. "When a man wishes to become a clan chief, he must go to Rhuidean, in the lands of the Jenn Aiel, the clan that is not." He spoke slowly and frowned often at the red-fringed silk carpet under his soft boots, a man trying to explain what he did not want to explain at all. "Women who wish to become Wise Ones also make this journey, but their marking, if they *are* marked, is kept secret among themselves. The men who are chosen at Rhuidean, those who survive, return marked on the left arm. So."

He pushed back the sleeves of his coat and shirt together to reveal his left forearm, the skin much paler than that of his hands and face. Etched into the skin as if part of it, wrapped twice around, marched the same gold-and-scarlet form as rippled on the banner above the Stone.

The Aiel let his sleeve fall with a sigh. "It is a name not spoken except among the clan chiefs and the Wise Ones. We are. . . ." He cleared his throat again, unable to say it here.

"The Aiel are the People of the Dragon." Moiraine spoke quietly, but she sounded as close to startlement as Mat could remember ever hearing her. "That I did not know."

"Then it really is all done," Mat said, "just as the Prophecies said. We can all go on our way with no more worries." *The Amyrlin won't need me to blow that bloody Horn now!*

"How can you say that?" Egwene demanded. "Don't you understand the Forsaken are loose?"

"Not to mention the Black Ajah," Nynaeve added grimly. "We took only Amico and Joiya here. Eleven escaped—and I would like to know how!—and the Light alone knows how many others there are we do not know."

"Yes," Elayne said in a tone just as hard. "I may not be up to facing one of the Forsaken, but I mean to take pieces out of Liandrin's hide!"

"Of course," Mat said smoothly. "Of course." *Are they crazy? They want to chase after the Black Ajah and the Forsaken?* "I only meant the hardest part is done. The Stone has fallen to the People of the Dragon, Rand has *Callandor*, and Shai'tan is dead." Moiraine's stare was so hard that he thought the Stone shook for a moment.

"Be quiet, you fool!" the Aes Sedai said in a voice like a knife. "Do you want to call his attention to you, naming the Dark One?"

"But he's dead!" Mat protested. "Rand killed him. I saw the body!" *And a fine stink that was, too. I never thought anything could rot that fast.*

"You saw 'the body,'" Moiraine said with a twist to her mouth. "A man's body. Not the Dark One, Mat."

He looked at Egwene and the other two women; they appeared as confused as he. Rhuarc looked to be thinking of a battle he had thought was won and now learned had not even been fought. "Then who was it?" Mat demanded. "Moiraine, my memory has holes big enough for a wagon and team, but I remember Ba'alzamon being in my dreams. I remember! Burn me, I do not see how I can ever forget! And I recognized what was left of that face."

"You recognized Ba'alzamon," Moiraine said. "Or rather, the man who called himself Ba'alzamon. The Dark One yet lives, imprisoned at Shayol Ghul, and the Shadow yet lies across the Pattern."

"The Light illumine and protect us," Elayne murmured in a faint voice. "I thought. . . . I thought the Forsaken were the worst we had to worry about, now."

"Are you sure, Moiraine?" Nynaeve said. "Rand was certain—*is* certain—that he killed the Dark One. You seem to be saying Ba'alzamon was not the Dark One at all. I don't understand! How can you be so sure? And if he was not the Dark One, who was he?"

"I can be sure for the simplest of reasons, Nynaeve. However fast decay took it, that was a man's body. Can you believe that if the Dark One were killed he would leave a human body? The man Rand killed *was* a man. Perhaps he was the first of the Forsaken freed, or perhaps he was never entirely bound. We may never know which."

"I . . . may know who he was." Egwene paused with an uncertain frown. "At least, I may have a clue. Verin showed me a page from an old book that mentioned Ba'alzamon and Ishamael together. It was almost High Chant and very nearly incomprehensible, but I remember something about 'a name hidden behind a name.' Maybe Ba'alzamon was Ishamael."

"Perhaps," Moiraine said. "Perhaps it was Ishamael. But if it was, at least nine of the thirteen still live. Lanfear, and Sammael, and Ravhin, and. . . . Paah! Even knowing that some of those nine at least are free is not the most important thing." She laid a hand atop the black-and-white disc on the table. "Three of the seals are broken. Only four still hold. Only those four seals stand between the Dark One and the world, and it may be that even with those whole he can touch the world after a fashion. Whatever battle we won here—battle or skirmish—it is far from the last."

Mat watched their faces firm—Egwene's and Nynaeve's

and Elayne's; slowly, reluctantly, but determinedly, too—and shook his head. *Bloody women! They're all ready to go on with this, go on chasing the Black Ajah, trying to fight the Forsaken and the bloody Dark One. Well, they needn't think I am going to come pull them out of the soup pot again. They just needn't think it, that's all!*

One of the tall, paired doors pushed open while he was trying to think of something to say, and a tall young woman of regal bearing entered the room, wearing a coronet with a golden hawk in flight above her brows. Her black hair swept to pale shoulders, and her dress of the finest red silk left those shoulders bare, along with a considerable expanse of what Mat noted as an admirable bosom. For a moment she studied Rhuarc interestedly with large, dark eyes; then she turned them on the women at the table, coolly imperious. Mat she appeared to ignore completely.

"I am not used to being given messages to carry," she announced, flourishing a folded parchment in one slim hand.

"And who are you, child?" Moiraine asked.

The young woman drew herself up even more, which Mat would have thought was impossible. "I am Berelain, First of Mayene." She tossed the parchment down on the table in front of Moiraine with a haughty gesture and turned back to the door.

"A moment, child," Moiraine said, unfolding the parchment. "Who gave this to you? And why did you bring it, if you are so unused to carrying messages?"

"I . . . do not know." Berelain stood facing the door; she sounded puzzled. "She was . . . impressive." She gave herself a shake and seemed to recover her opinion of herself. For a moment she studied Rhuarc with a small smile. "You are the leader of these Aielmen? Your fighting disturbed my sleep. Perhaps I will ask you to dine with me. One day quite soon." She looked over her shoulder at Moiraine. "I am told the Dragon Reborn has taken the Stone. Inform the Lord Dragon that the First of Mayene will dine with him tonight." And she marched out of the room; Mat could think of no other way to describe that stately, one-woman procession.

"I would like to have *her* in the Tower as novice." Egwene and Elayne said it almost like echoes, then shared a tight smile.

"Listen to this," Moiraine said. "'Lews Therin was mine, he is mine, and he will be mine, forever. I give him into your charge, to keep for me until I come.' It is signed 'Lanfear.'" The Aes Sedai turned that cool gaze on Mat. "And you thought it was done? You are *ta'veren*, Mat, a thread more crucial to the Pattern than most, and the sounder of the Horn of Valere. Nothing is done for you, yet."

They were all looking at him. Nynaeve sadly, Egwene as though she had never seen him before, Elayne as if she expected him to change into someone else. Rhuarc had a certain respect in his eyes, though Mat would just as soon have done without it, all things considered.

"Well, of course," he told them. *Burn me!* "I understand." *I wonder how soon Thom will be fit to travel? Time to run. Maybe Perrin will come with us.* "You can count on me."

From outside, the cries still rose, unceasing. "The Dragon! Al'Thor! The Dragon! Al'Thor! The Dragon! Al'Thor! The Dragon!"

And it was written that no hand but his should wield the Sword held in the Stone, but he did draw it out, like fire in his hand, and his glory did burn the world. Thus did it begin. Thus do we sing his Rebirth. Thus do we sing the beginning.

—from *Do'in Toldara te, Songs of the Last Age*,
Quarto Nine: The Legend of the Dragon.
Composed by Boanne, Songmistress
at Taralan, the Fourth Age.

The End

of the Third Book of

The Wheel of Time

GLOSSARY

A Note on Dates in This Glossary. Three systems of recording dates have been in general use since the Breaking of the World. The first recorded years After the Breaking (AB). Since the years of the Breaking and immediately after were years of almost total chaos, and since this calendar was adopted a good hundred years after the end of the Breaking, its starting point was arbitrarily assigned. At the end of the Trolloc Wars many records had been lost, so much so that there was argument about the exact year under the old system. A new calendar was therefore established, dating from the end of the Wars and celebrating the supposed freedom of the world from the Trolloc threat. This second calendar recorded each year as Free Year (FY). After the disruption, death, and destruction caused by the War of the Hundred Years, a third calendar came into being. This calendar, of the New Era (NE), is currently in use.

Accepted, the: Young women in training to be Aes Sedai who have reached a certain level of power and passed certain tests. It normally takes five to ten years to be raised from novice to the Accepted. Accepted are somewhat less confined by rules than novices, and are allowed to choose their own areas of study, within limits. An Accepted has the right to wear a Great Serpent ring, but only on the third finger of her left hand. When an Accepted is raised to Aes Sedai, she chooses her Ajah, gains the right to wear the shawl, and may wear the ring on any finger or not at all if circumstances warrant.

Aes Sedai (EYEZ seh-DEYE): Wielders of the One Power.

Since the Time of Madness, all surviving Aes Sedai are women. Widely distrusted and feared, even hated, they are blamed by many for the Breaking of the World, and are thought to meddle in the affairs of nations. At the same time, few rulers will be without an Aes Sedai advisor, even in lands where the existence of such a connection must be kept secret. After some years of channeling the One Power, Aes Sedai take on an ageless quality, so that an Aes Sedai who is old enough to be a grandmother may show no signs of age except perhaps a few gray hairs. *See also* Ajah; Amyrlin Seat; Time of Madness.

Age of Legends: The Age ended by the War of the Shadow and the Breaking of the World. A time when Aes Sedai performed wonders now only dreamed of. *See also* Wheel of Time; Breaking of the World; War of the Shadow.

Aiel (eye-EEL): The people of the Aiel Waste. Fierce and hardy. Also called Aielmen. They veil their faces before they kill, giving rise to the saying "acting like a black-veiled Aiel" to describe someone who is being violent. Deadly warriors with any weapon or with nothing but their bare hands, they will not touch a sword. Their pipers play them into battle with the music of dances, and Aielmen call battle "the dance," and "the dance of spears." *See also* Aiel warrior societies; Aiel Waste.

Aiel War, the: (976–78 NE) When King Laman of Cairhien cut down Avendoraldera, several clans of the Aiel crossed the Spine of the World. They looted and burned the capital city of Cairhien as well as many other cities and towns, and the conflict extended into Andor and Tear. The conventional view is that the Aiel were finally defeated at the Battle of the Shining Walls, before Tar Valon, but in fact, Laman was killed in that battle, and having done what they had come for, the Aiel recrossed the Spine. *See also Avendoraldera*; Cairhien.

Aiel warrior societies: Aiel warriors are all members of one of the warrior societies, such as the Stone Dogs (*Shae'en M'taal*), the Red Shields (*Aethan Dor*), or the Maidens of the Spear (*Far Dareis Mai*). Each society has its own customs, and sometimes specific duties. For example, Red Shields act as police. Stone Dogs often vow not to retreat once battle has been joined, and will die to the last man if necessary to fulfill this vow. The clans of the Aiel—among them the Goshien, Reyn, Shaarad, and Taardad Aiel—frequently fight among themselves, but members of the same society will not fight each other even if their clans are doing so. In this way, there are always lines of contact between the clans even when they are in open warfare. *See also* Aiel; Aiel Waste; *Far Dareis Mai.*

Aiel Waste: The harsh, rugged, and all-but-waterless land east of the Spine of the World. Called the Three-fold Land by the Aiel. Few outsiders go there, not only because water is almost impossible to find for one not born there, but because the Aiel consider themselves at war with all other peoples and do not welcome strangers. Only peddlers, gleemen, and the Tuatha'an are allowed safe entry, and contact even with them is limited. No maps of the Waste itself are known to exist.

Ajah (AH-jah): Societies among the Aes Sedai to which all Aes Sedai except the Amyrlin Seat belong. They are designated by colors: Blue, Red, White, Green, Brown, Yellow, and Gray. Each follows a specific philosophy of the use of the One Power and the purposes of the Aes Sedai. For example, the Red Ajah bends all its energies to finding men who are attempting to wield the Power, and to gentling them. The Brown Ajah, on the other hand, forsakes involvement with the mundane world and dedicates itself to seeking knowledge, while the White Ajah, largely eschewing both the world and the value of worldly knowledge, devotes itself to questions of philosophy and truth. The Green Ajah (called the Battle Ajah during the Trolloc Wars) holds itself ready to counter any new Dreadlords when Tarmon Gai'don comes. There are rumors of a Black Ajah, dedicated to serving the Dark One.

Alanna Mosvani (ah-LAN-nah mos-VANH-nie): An Aes Sedai of the Green Ajah.

al'Meara, Nynaeve (al-MEER-ah, NIGH-neev): A woman once the Wisdom of Emond's Field, in the Two Rivers district of Andor (AN-door). Now one of the Accepted.

al'Thor, Rand (al-THOR, RAND): A young man from Emond's Field who is *ta'veren.* Once a shepherd. Now proclaimed as the Dragon Reborn.

al'Vere, Egwene (ahl-VEER, eh-GWAIN): A young woman from Emond's Field. Now in training to be Aes Sedai.

Amalasan, Guaire (ahm-ah-LAH-sin, Gware): *See* War of the Second Dragon.

Amyrlin Seat (AHM-ehr-lin SEAT): (1) Leader of the Aes Sedai. Elected for life by the Hall of the Tower, the highest council of the Aes Sedai, which consists of three representatives (called Sitters, as in "a Sitter for the Green") from each of the seven Ajahs. The Amyrlin Seat has, theoretically at least, almost supreme authority among the Aes Sedai, and ranks socially as the equal of a king or queen. A slightly less formal usage is simply the Amyrlin. (2) The throne on which the leader of the Aes Sedai sits.

Anaiya (ah-NYE-yah): An Aes Sedai of the Blue Ajah.

angreal (anh-gree-AHL): Remnants of the Age of Legends that allow anyone capable of channeling the One Power to handle a greater amount of the Power than could safely be channeled unaided. Their making is no longer known. Few remain in existence. *See also sa'angreal; ter'angreal.*

Artur Hawkwing: *See* Hawkwing, Artur.

Assemblage, the: A body in Illian, chosen by and from the merchants and shipowners, that is supposed to advise both the King and the Council of Nine, but historically has contended with them for power.

Atha'an Miere (ah-thah-AHN mee-EHR): *See* Sea Folk.

Avendesora (AH-vehn-deh-SO-rah): In the Old Tongue, "the Tree of Life." Mentioned in many stories and legends.

Avendoraldera (AH-ven-doh-ral-DEH-rah): A tree grown in the city of Cairhien from a sapling of *Avendesora*. This sapling was a gift from the Aiel in 566 NE, despite the fact that no record shows any connection whatsoever between the Aiel and *Avendesora*. *See also* Aiel War.

Aviendha (Ah-vee-EHN-dah): A woman of the Nine Valleys sept of the Taardad Aiel; a *Far Dareis Mai*, a Maiden of the Spear.

Aybara, Perrin (ay-BAHR-ah, PEHR-rihn): A young man from Emond's Field, formerly a blacksmith's apprentice.

Ba'alzamon (bah-AHL-zah-mon): In the Trolloc tongue,

"Heart of the Dark." Believed to be the Trolloc name for the Dark One. *See also* Dark One; Trollocs.

Bashere, Zarine (bah-SHEER, zah-REEN): A young woman from Saldaea who is a Hunter of the Horn. She wishes to be called Faile (fah-EEL), which, in the Old Tongue, means "falcon."

Be'lal (beh-LAAL): One of the Forsaken.

Bel Tine (BEHL TINE): Spring festival celebrating the end of winter, the first sprouting of crops, and the birth of the first lambs.

Betrayer of Hope: *See* Ishamael.

biteme (BITE-me): A small, almost invisible biting insect.

bittern (BIHT-tehrn): A musical instrument that may have six, nine, or twelve strings, and is held flat on the knees and played by plucking or strumming.

Blight, the: *See* Great Blight, the.

Borderlands, the: The nations bordering the Great Blight: Saldaea, Arafel, Kandor, and Shienar.

Bornhald, Dain (BOHRN-hahld, DAY-ihn): An officer of the Children of the Light, son of Lord Captain Geofraim Bornhald, who died at Falme, on Toman Head.

Breaking of the World, the: During the Time of Madness, male Aes Sedai who had gone insane, and who could wield the One Power to a degree now unknown, changed the face of the earth. They caused great earthquakes, leveled old mountain ranges and raised new mountains, lifted dry land where seas had been and made the ocean rush in where dry land had been. Many parts of the world were completely depopulated, and the survivors were scattered like dust on the wind. This destruction is remembered in stories, legends, and history as the Breaking of the World. *See also* Time of Madness; Hundred Companions, the.

Byar, Jaret (BY-ahr, JAH-ret): An officer of the Children of the Light.

Caemlyn (KAYM-lihn): The capital city of Andor.

Cairhien (KEYE-ree-EHN): Both a nation along the Spine of the World and the capital city of that nation. The city was burned and looted during the Aiel War, as were many other towns and villages. The consequent abandonment of farmland near the Spine of the World made necessary the importation of great quantities of grain. The assassination of King Galldrian (998 NE) has resulted in a civil war among the noble Houses for succession to the Sun Throne, in the disruption of grain shipments, and in famine. The sign of Cairhien is a many-rayed golden sun rising from the bottom of a field of sky blue.

Callandor (CAH-lahn-DOOR): The Sword That Is Not a Sword, the Sword That Cannot Be Touched. A crystal sword held in the Stone of Tear, in the chamber called the Heart of the Stone. No hand can touch it except that of the Dragon Reborn. According to the Prophecies of the Dragon, one of the major signs of the Dragon's Rebirth and the approach of Tarmon Gai'don will be that the Dragon Reborn has taken *Callandor*.

Cauthon, Mat (CAW-thon, MAT): A young man from Emond's Field in the Two Rivers. Full name: Matrim (MAT-trim) Cauthon.

channel: (verb) To control the flow of the One Power. *See also* One Power.

Children of the Light: A society holding strict ascetic beliefs, dedicated to the defeat of the Dark One and the destruction of all Darkfriends. Founded during the War of the Hundred Years by Lothair Mantelar (LOH-thayr MAHN-tee-LAHR) to proselytize against an increase in the numbers of Darkfriends, they evolved during the war into a completely military organization. They are extremely rigid in their beliefs, and certain that only they know the truth and the right. They hate Aes Sedai, considering them, and any who support or befriend them, Darkfriends. They are known disparagingly as Whitecloaks. Their sign is a golden sunburst on a field of white. *See also* Questioners.

Chronicles, Keeper of the: Second in authority to the Amyrlin Seat among the Aes Sedai, she also acts as secretary to the Amyrlin. Chosen for life by the Hall of the Tower, and usually of the same Ajah as the Amyrlin. *See also* Amyrlin Seat; Ajah.

Council of Nine: In Illian, a council of nine Lords who are supposed to advise the King, but who historically contend with him for power. Both the King and the Nine often must contend with the Assemblage, as well.

cuendillar (CWAIN-deh-yar): *See* heartstone.

Daes Dae'mar (DAH-ess day-MAR): The Great Game, also known as the Game of Houses. Name given the scheming, plots, and manipulations for advantage by the noble Houses. Great value is given to subtlety, to aiming at one thing while seeming to aim at another, and to achieving ends with the least visible effort.

Damodred, Lord Galadedrid (DAHM-oh-drehd, gah-LAHD-eh-drihd): Half brother to Elayne and Gawyn. His sign is a winged silver sword, point down.

Darkfriends: Those who follow the Dark One and believe they will gain great power and rewards, and even immortality, when he is freed from his prison.

Darkhounds: *See* Wild Hunt.

Dark One: Most common name, used in every land, for Shai'tan. The source of evil, antithesis of the Creator. Imprisoned by the Creator in Shayol Ghul at the moment of Creation. The attempt to free him from that prison brought about the War of the Shadow, the tainting of *saidin*, the Breaking of the World, and the end of the Age of Legends.

Dark One, naming the: Saying the true name of the Dark One (Shai'tan) draws his attention, inevitably bringing ill fortune at best, disaster at worst. For that reason, many euphemisms are used, among them the Dark One, Father of Lies, Sightblinder, Lord of the Grave, Shepherd of the Night, Hearstbane, Soulsbane, Heartfang, Old Grim, Grassburner, and Leafblighter. Darkfriends call him the Great Lord of the Dark. Someone who seems to be inviting ill fortune is often said to be "naming the Dark One."

Daughter-Heir: Title of the heir to the throne of Andor. The eldest daughter of the Queen succeeds her mother on the throne. Without a surviving daughter, the throne goes to the nearest female blood relation of the Queen.

Daughter of the Night: *See* Lanfear.

Dragon, false: Occasionally men claim to be the Dragon Reborn, and sometimes one of these men gains following enough to require an army to put it down. Some have begun wars that involved many nations. Over the centuries most of these have been men unable to channel the One Power, but a few could do so. All, however, either disappeared or were captured or killed without fulfilling any of the Prophecies concerning the Rebirth of the Dragon.

These men are called false Dragons. Among those who could channel, the most powerful were Raolin Darksbane (335–36 AB), Yurian Stonebow (circa 1300–1308 AB), Davian (FY 351), Guaire Amalasan (FY 939–43), and Logain (997 NE). *See also* Dragon Reborn.

Dragon, Prophecies of the: Little known and seldom spoken of, the Prophecies, given in *The Karaethon Cycle*, foretell that the Dark One will be freed again to touch the world. And that Lews Therin Telamon, the Dragon, Breaker of the World, will be reborn to fight Tarmon Gai'don, the Last Battle against the Shadow. *See also* Dragon, the.

Dragon, the: The name by which Lews Therin Telamon was known during the War of the Shadow. In the madness that overtook all male Aes Sedai, Lews Therin killed every living person who carried any of his blood, as well as everyone he loved, thus earning the name Kinslayer. *See also* Dragon Reborn; Dragon, Prophecies of the.

Dragon Reborn: According to prophecy and legend the Dragon will be born again at mankind's greatest hour of need to save the world. This is not something people look forward to, both because the Prophecies say the Dragon Reborn will bring a new Breaking to the world and because Lews Therin Kinslayer, the Dragon, is a name to make men shudder, even more than three thousand years after his death. *See also* Dragon, the; Dragon, false; Dragon, Prophecies of the.

Dreadlords: Men and women able to channel the One Power, who went over to the Shadow during the Trolloc Wars, acting as commanders of the Trolloc forces. Occasionally confused with the Forsaken by the less well educated.

Dreamer: *See* Talents.

Elaida (eh-LY-da): An Aes Sedai of the Red Ajah. Former advisor to Queen Morgase of Andor. She sometimes has the Foretelling.

Elayne of House Trakand (trah-KAND): Queen Morgase's daughter, the Daughter-Heir to the throne of Andor. Now in training to be Aes Sedai. Her sign is a golden lily.

Far Dareis Mai (FAHR DAH-rize MY): Literally "Maidens of the Spear." A warrior society of the Aiel, which, unlike any of the others, admits women and only women. A Maiden may not marry and remain in the society, nor may she fight while carrying a child. Any child born to a Maiden is given to another woman to raise, in such a way that no one knows who the child's mother was. ("You may belong to no man, nor may any man belong to you, nor any child. The spear is your lover, your child, and your life.") These children are treasured, for it is prophesied that a child born of a Maiden will unite the clans and return the Aiel to the greatness they knew during the Age of Legends. *See also* Aiel; Aiel warrior societies.

Fetches: *See* Myrddraal.

Five Powers, the: There are threads to the One Power, and anyone who can channel can usually grasp some threads better than others. These threads are named according to the sorts of things that can be done using them—Earth, Air (sometimes called Wind), Fire, Water, and Spirit— and are called the Five Powers. Any wielder of the Power will have a greater degree of strength with one, or possibly two, of these, and lesser strength in the others. Some few may have great strength with three, but since the Age of Legends no one has had great strength with all five. Even then this was extremely rare. The degree of strength can vary greatly between individuals. Performing certain acts with the One Power requires the ability to weave flows in one or more of the Five Powers. For example, starting or controlling a fire requires Fire, and affecting the weather requires Air and Water, while Healing requires Air, Water and Spirit. While Spirit was found equally in men and in women, great ability with Earth and/or Fire was found much more often among men; with Water and/or Air among women. There were exceptions, but it was so often so that Earth and Fire came to be regarded as male Powers, Air and Water as female. Generally, no ability is considered stronger than any other, though there is a saying among Aes Sedai: "There is no rock so strong that water and wind cannot wear it away, no fire so fierce that water cannot quench it or wind snuff it out." It should be noted that any equivalent saying among male Aes Sedai is long lost.

Flame of Tar Valon: Symbol of Tar Valon, the Amyrlin

Seat, and the Aes Sedai. A stylized representation of a flame; a white teardrop with the point upward.

Forsaken, the: Name given to thirteen of the most powerful Aes Sedai of the Age of Legends, which made them among the most powerful ever known, who went over to the Dark One during the War of the Shadow in return for the promise of immortality. According to both legend and fragmentary records, they were imprisoned along with the Dark One when his prison was resealed. Their names—among them Lanfear, Be'lal, Sammael, Asmodean, Rahvin, and Ishamael—are still used to frighten children.

Fortress of the Light: The great fortress of the Children of the Light, located in Amador (AH-mah-door), the capital of Amadicia (AH-mah-DEE-cee-ah). There is a King of Amadicia, but the Children rule in all but name. *See also* Children of the Light.

Gaidin (GYE-deen): Literally "Brother to Battles." A title used by Aes Sedai for the Warders. *See also* Warder.

Galad (gah-LAHD): *See* Damodred, Lord Galadedrid.

Game of Houses, the: *See Daes Dae'mar.*

Gaul (GAHWL): An Aiel of the Imran sept of the Shaarad, a *Shae'en M'taal*, a Stone Dog.

Gawyn (GAH-wihn) **of House Trakand** (trah-KAND): Queen Morgase's son, and Elayne's brother, who will be First Prince of the Sword when Elayne ascends to the throne. His sign is a white boar.

gentling: The act, performed by Aes Sedai, of shutting off a male who can channel from the One Power. This is necessary because any man who learns to channel will go insane from the taint on *saidin* and will almost certainly do horrible things with the Power in his madness. A man who has been gentled can still sense the True Source, but he cannot touch it. Whatever madness has come before gentling is arrested by the act of gentling, but not cured by it, and if it is done soon enough death can be averted. *See also* One Power, the; stilling.

gleeman: A traveling storyteller, musician, juggler, tumbler, and all-around entertainer. Known by their trademark cloaks of many-colored patches, gleemen perform mainly in the villages and smaller towns.

G L O S S A R Y659

Gray Man: Someone who has voluntarily surrendered his or her soul in order to become an assassin serving the Shadow. Gray Men are so ordinary in appearance that the eye can slide right past without noticing them. The vast majority of Gray Men are indeed men, but a small number are women.

Great Blight, the: A region in the far north, entirely corrupted by the Dark One. A haunt of Trollocs, Myrddraal, and other creatures of the Shadow.

Great Game, the: *See Daes Dae'mar.*

Great Hunt of the Horn, The: A cycle of stories concerning the legendary search for the Horn of Valere, in the years between the end of the Trolloc Wars and the beginning of the War of the Hundred Years. If told in its entirety, the cycle would take many days. *See also* Horn of Valere.

Great Lord of the Dark: The name by which Darkfriends refer to the Dark One, claiming that to use his true name would be blasphemous.

Great Serpent: A symbol for time and eternity, ancient before the Age of Legends began, consisting of a serpent eating its own tail. A ring in the shape of the Great Serpent is awarded to women who have been raised to the Accepted among the Aes Sedai.

Grim, Old: *See* Dark One; Wild Hunt.

Halfman: *See* Myrddraal.

Hawkwing, Artur: A legendary king (ruled FY 943–94) who united all the lands west of the Spine of the World. He even sent armies across the Aryth Ocean (FY 992), but all contact with these was lost at his death, which set off the War of the Hundred Years. His sign was a golden hawk in flight. *See also* War of the Hundred Years.

Heart of the Stone: *See* Callandor.

heartstone: An indestructible substance created during the Age of Legends. Any force used in an attempt to break it is absorbed, making heartstone stronger. Another name for *cuendillar*.

hide: A unit of area for measuring land, equal to 100 paces by 100 paces.

High Lords of Tear: Acting as a council, the High Lords are the rulers of the nation of Tear, which has neither king nor queen. Their numbers are not fixed, and have varied over the years from as many as twenty to as few as six. Not to be confused with the Lords of the Land, who are lesser Tairen lords.

Hopper: A wolf.

Horn of Valere (vah-LEER): The legendary object of the Great Hunt of the Horn. The Horn supposedly can call back dead heroes from the grave to fight against the Shadow.

Hundred Companions, the: One hundred male Aes Sedai, among the most powerful of the Age of Legends, who, led by Lews Therin Telamon, launched the final stroke that ended the War of the Shadow by sealing the Dark One back into his prison. The Dark One's counterstroke tainted *saidin*; the Hundred Companions went mad and began the Breaking of the World. *See also* Time of Madness; Breaking of the World; True Source; One Power.

Illian (IHL-lee-an): A great port on the Sea of Storms, capital city of the nation of the same name.

Illuminators, Guild of: A society that holds the secret of making fireworks. It guards this secret very closely, even to murder. The Guild gains its name from the grand displays, called Illuminations, that it provides for rulers and sometimes for great lords. Lesser fireworks are sold for use by others, but with dire warnings of the disaster that can result from attempting to learn what is inside them. The Guild chapter house is in Tanchico, the capital of Tarabon. The Guild established one other chapter house in Cairhien, but it is no longer active.

Ishamael (ih-SHAH-may-EHL): In the Old Tongue, "Betrayer of Hope." One of the Forsaken. Name given to the leader of the Aes Sedai who went over to the Dark One in the War of the Shadow. It is said that even he forgot his true name. *See also* Forsaken.

Karaethon Cycle, The (ka-REE-ah-thon): *See* Dragon, Prophecies of the.

Laman (LAY-mahn): A king of Cairhien, of House Damodred, who lost his throne in the Aiel War. *See also* Aiel War; *Avendoraldera*.

Lan (LAN); al'Lan Mandragoran (AHL-LAN man-DRAG-

or-an): A Warder, bonded to Moiraine. Uncrowned King of Malkier, Dai Shan, and the last surviving Malkieri lord. *See also* Warder; Moiraine; Malkier.

Lanfear (LAN-fear): In the Old Tongue, "Daughter of the Night." One of the Forsaken, perhaps the most powerful next to Ishamael. Unlike the other Forsaken, she chose this name herself. She is said to have been in love with Lews Therin Telamon, and to have hated his wife, Ilyena. *See also* Forsaken; Dragon, the.

league: *See* length, units of.

Leane (lee-AHN-eh): An Aes Sedai of the Blue Ajah, and Keeper of the Chronicles. *See also* Ajah; Chronicles, Keeper of the.

length, units of: 10 inches = 1 foot; 3 feet = 1 pace; 2 paces = 1 span; 1000 spans = 1 mile; 4 miles = 1 league.

Lews Therin Telamon; Lews Therin Kinslayer: *See* Dragon, the.

Liandrin (lee-AHN-drihn): An Aes Sedai formerly of the Red Ajah, from Tarabon. Now known to be of the Black Ajah.

Light, Children of the: *See* Children of the Light.

Loial (LOY-ahl) **son of Arent son of Halan:** An Ogier from Stedding Shangtai.

Malkier (mahl-KEER): A nation, once one of the Borderlands, now consumed by the Blight. The sign of Malkier was a golden crane in flight.

Manetheren (mahn-EHTH-ehr-ehn): One of the Ten Nations that made the Second Covenant. Also the capital city of that nation. Both city and nation were utterly destroyed in the Trolloc Wars.

Masema (mah-SEE-mah): A Shienaran soldier who hates Aiel.

Mayene (may-EHN): City-state on the Sea of Storms that derives its wealth and its independence from knowledge of where to find the oilfish shoals, which rival in economic importance the olive groves of Tear, Illian, and Tarabon. Oilfish and olives provide nearly all lamp oil. The current ruler of Mayene is Berelain, the First of Mayene. The Rulers of Mayene claim to be descendants of Artur Hawkwing. The sign of Mayene is a golden hawk in flight.

Merrilin, Thom (MER-rih-lihn, TOM): A gleeman, and once the lover of Queen Morgase.

mile: *See* length, units of.

Min (MIN): A young woman with the ability to read things about people in the auras and images she sometimes sees surrounding them.

Moiraine (mwah-RAIN): An Aes Sedai of the Blue Ajah. Born in House Damodred, though not in line of succession to the throne, she was raised in the Royal Palace in Cairhien.

Morgase (moor-GAYZ): By the Grace of the Light, Queen of Andor, Defender of the Realm, Protector of the People, High Seat of House Trakand. Her sign is three golden keys. The sign of House Trakand is a silver keystone.

Myrddraal (MUHRD-draal): Creatures of the Dark One, commanders of the Trollocs. Twisted offspring of Trollocs in which the human stock used to create the Trollocs has resurfaced, but tainted by the evil that made the Trollocs. They have no eyes, but can see like eagles in light or dark. They have certain powers stemming from the Dark One, including the ability to cause paralyzing fear with a look and the ability to vanish wherever there are shadows. They have few known weaknesses, but one of these is that they are reluctant to cross running water. In different lands they are known by many names, among them Halfman, the Eyeless, Shadowman, Lurk, Fetch, and Fade.

Nedeal, Corianin: *See* Talents.

Niall, Pedron (NEYE-awl, PAY-drohn): Lord Captain Commander of the Children of the Light. *See also* Children of the Light.

Oaths, Three: The oaths taken by an Accepted who is being raised to Aes Sedai. Spoken while holding the Oath Rod, a *ter'angreal* that makes oaths binding. They are: (1) To speak no word that is not true. (2) To make no weapon with which one man may kill another. (3) Never to use the One Power as a weapon except against Shadowspawn, or in the last extreme of defense of her own life, or that of her Warder or another Aes Sedai. These oaths were not always required, but various events before and since the Breaking caused them to be necessary. The second oath was the first adopted, in reaction to the War of the Power. The first oath, while held to the letter, is often circumvented by careful speaking. It is believed that the last two are inviolable.

Ogier (OH-gehr): (1) A non-human race, characterized by great height (ten feet is average for adult males), broad, almost snoutlike noses, and long, tufted ears. They live in areas called *stedding*. Their separation from these *stedding* after the Breaking of the World (a time called the Exile by Ogier) resulted in what is called the Longing; an Ogier who is too long out of the *stedding*, sickens and dies. Widely known as wondrous stonemasons who built the great human cities after the Breaking, they consider stonework simply something learned during the Exile and not as important as tending the trees of the *stedding*, especially the towering Great Trees. Except for stonework, they rarely leave their *stedding* and typically have little contact with humankind. Knowledge of them among humans is sparse, and many believe Ogier to be only legends. Although believed to be a pacific people and extremely slow to anger, some old stories say they fought alongside humans in the Trolloc Wars, and call them implacable enemies. By and large, they are extremely fond of knowledge, and their books and stories often contain information lost to humans. A typical Ogier life-span is at least three to four times that of a human. (2) Any individual of that non-human race. *See also* Breaking of the World; *stedding;* Treesinger.

Old Grim: *See Dark One.*

Old Tongue: The language spoken during the Age of Legends. It is generally expected that nobles and the educated will have learned to speak this, but most know only a few words.

One Power, the: The power drawn from the True Source. The vast majority of people are completely unable to learn to channel the One Power. A very small number can be taught to channel, and an even tinier number have the ability inborn. For these few there is no need to be taught; they will touch the True Source and channel the Power whether they want to or not, perhaps without even realizing what they are doing. This inborn ability usually manifests itself in late adolescence or early adulthood. If control is not taught, or self-learned (extremely difficult, with a success rate of only one in four), death is certain. Since the Time of Madness, no man has been able to channel the Power without eventually going completely, horribly mad, and then, even if he has learned some control, dying from a wasting sickness that causes the sufferer to rot alive, a sickness caused, as is the madness, by the Dark One's taint on *saidin*. For a woman the death that comes without control of the Power is less horrible, but it is death just the same. Aes Sedai search for girls with the inborn ability as much to save their lives as to increase Aes Sedai numbers, and for men with it in order to stop the terrible things they inevitably do with the Power in their madness. *See also* Aes Sedai; channel; Five Powers; Time of Madness; True Source.

Ordeith (OHR-deeth): In the Old Tongue, "Wormwood." Name taken by a man who advises the Lord Captain Commander of the Children of the Light.

Pattern of an Age: The Wheel of Time weaves the threads of human lives into the Pattern of an Age, often called simply the Pattern, which forms the substance of reality for that Age. *See also ta'veren.*

Powers, the Five: *See* Five Powers, the.

Questioners, the: An order within the Children of the Light. Their avowed purposes are to discover the truth in disputations and uncover Darkfriends. In the search for truth and the Light, their normal method of inquiry is torture; their normal manner that they know the truth already and must only make their victim confess to it. The Questioners refer to themselves as the Hand of the Light, the Hand that digs out truth, and at times act as if they were entirely separate from the Children and the Council of the Anointed, which commands the Children. The head of the Questioners is the High Inquisitor, who sits on the Council of the Anointed. Their sign is a blood-red shepherd's crook.

Red Shields: *See* Aiel warrior societies.

Rhuarc (RHOURK): An Aiel, clan chief of the Taardad Aiel.

Rogosh Eagle-eye: A legendary hero mentioned in a number of old stories.

sa'angreal (SAH-ahn-GREE-ahl): Any one of a number of objects that allow an individual to channel much more of the One Power than would otherwise be possible or safe. A *sa'angreal* is like unto, but much more powerful than, an *angreal*. The amount of the Power that can be wielded with a *sa'angreal* compares to the amount of the Power that can be handled with an *angreal* as the power wielded with the aid of an *angreal* does to the amount of the Power that can be handled unaided. Remnants of the Age of Legends, their making is no longer known. Only a handful remain, far fewer even than *angreal*.

saidar (sah-ih-DAHR); *saidin* (sah-ih-DEEN): *See* True Source.

Sea Folk: More properly, the Atha'an Miere (ah-thah-AHN mee-AIR), the People of the Sea. Inhabitants of islands in the Aryth (AH-rihth) Ocean and the Sea of Storms, they spend little time on those islands, living most of their lives on their ships. Most seaborne trade is carried by the Sea Folk's ships.

Seanchan (SHAWN-CHAN): (1) Descendants of the armies Artur Hawkwing sent across the Aryth Ocean. (2) The land from which the Seanchan come.

Selene (seh-LEEN): A name used by the Forsaken called Lanfear.

Servants, Hall of the: In the Age of Legends, the great meeting hall of the Aes Sedai.

Shadar Logoth (SHAH-dahr LOH-goth): A city abandoned and shunned since the Trolloc Wars. It is tainted ground, and not a pebble of it is safe.

Shai'tan (SHAY-ih-TAN): *See* Dark One.

Shayol Ghul (SHAY-ol GHOOL): A mountain in the Blasted Lands, the site of the Dark One's prison.

Sheriam (SHEER-ee-ahm): An Aes Sedai of the Blue Ajah. The Mistress of Novices in the White Tower.

Siuan Sanche (SWAHN SAHN-chay): The daughter of a Tairen fisherman, she was, according to Tairen law, put on a ship to Tar Valon before the second sunset after it was discovered that she had the potential to channel. Formerly of the Blue Ajah. Raised to the Amyrlin Seat in 988 NE.

Soulless: *See* Gray Man.

span: *See* length, units of.

Spine of the World, the: A towering mountain range, with only a few passes, which separates the Aiel Waste from the lands to the west.

stedding (STEHD-ding): An Ogier (OH-geer) homeland. Many *stedding* have been abandoned since the Breaking of the World. They are shielded in some way, no longer understood, so that within them no Aes Sedai can channel the One Power, nor even sense that the True Source exists. Attempts to wield the One Power from outside a *stedding* have no effect inside a *stedding* boundary. No Trolloc will enter a *stedding* unless driven, and even a Myrddraal will do so only at the greatest need and then with the greatest reluctance and distaste. Even Darkfriends, if truly dedicated, feel uncomfortable within a *stedding*.

stilling: The act, performed by Aes Sedai, of shutting off a woman who can channel from the One Power. A woman who has been stilled can sense the True Source, but she cannot touch it. So seldom has it been done that novices are required to learn the names and crimes of all women who have suffered it.

Stone Dogs: *See* Aiel warrior societies.

Stone of Tear: A great fortress in the city of Tear, said to have been made soon after the Breaking of the World, and to have been made using the One Power. It has been besieged or attacked countless times, but never successfully. The Stone is mentioned twice in the Prophecies of the Dragon. Once they say the Stone will never fall until the People of the Dragon come. In another place, they say the Stone will never fall until the Dragon's hand wields the Sword That Cannot Be Touched, *Callandor*. Some believe that these Prophecies account for the antipathy of the High Lords to the One Power, and for the Tairen law that forbids channeling. Despite this antipathy, the Stone contains a collection of *an'greal* and *ter'angreal* rivaling that of the White Tower, a collection which was gathered, some say, in an attempt to diminish the glare of possessing *Callandor*.

Sunday: A feastday and festival in midsummer, widely celebrated in many parts of the world.

sung wood: *See* Treesinger.

Talents: Abilities in the use of the One Power in specific areas. The best known of these, of course, is Healing. Some, such as Traveling, the ability to shift oneself from one place to another without crossing the intervening space, have been lost. Others such as Foretelling (the ability to foretell future events, but in a general way) are now found only rarely if at all. Another Talent long thought lost is Dreaming, which involves, among other things, interpreting the Dreamer's dreams to foretell future events in more specific fashion than Foretelling does. Some Dreamers had the ability to enter *Tel'aran'rhiod*, the World of Dreams, and (it is said) even other people's dreams. The last known Dreamer was Corianin Nedeal, who died in 526 NE.

ta'maral'ailen (tah-MAHR-ahl-EYE-lehn): In the Old Tongue, "Web of Destiny." A great change in the Pattern of an Age, centered around one or more people who are *ta'veren. See also* Pattern of an Age; *ta'veren.*

Tanreall, Artur Paendrag (tahn-REE-ahl, AHR-tuhr PAY-ehn-DRAG): *See* Hawkwing, Artur.

Tarmon Gai'don (TAHR-mohn GAY-dohn)**:** The Last Battle. *See also* Dragon, Prophecies of the; Horn of Valere.

ta'veren (tah-VEER-ehn): A person around whom the Wheel of Time weaves all surrounding life-threads, perhaps ALL life-threads, to form a Web of Destiny. *See also* Pattern of an Age.

Tear (TEER): A nation on the Sea of Storms. Also the capital city of that nation, a great seaport. The banner of Tear is three white crescent moons slanting across a field half red, half gold. *See also* Stone of Tear.

Telamon, Lews Therin (TEHL-ah-mon, LOOZ THEH-rihn): *See* Dragon, the.

Tel'aran'rhiod (tel-AYE-rahn-rhee-ODD): In the Old Tongue, "the Unseen World," or "the World of Dreams." A world glimpsed in dreams which was believed by the ancients to permeate and surround all other possible worlds. Unlike other dreams, what happens to living things in the World of Dreams is real; a wound taken there will still be there on awakening, and one who dies there does not wake at all.

ter'angreal (TEER-ahn-GREE-ahl): Any one of a number of remnants of the Age of Legends that use the One Power. Unlike *angreal* and *sa'angreal*, each *ter'angreal* was made to do a particular thing. For example, one makes oaths taken with it binding. Some *ter'angreal* are used by Aes Sedai, but the original purposes of many others are largely unknown. Some will kill or destroy the ability to channel of any woman who uses them. *See also angreal; sa'angreal.*

Tigraine (tee-GRAIN): As Daughter-Heir of Andor, she married Taringail Damodred and bore his son Galad-edrid. Her disappearance in 972 NE, shortly after her brother Luc vanished in the Blight, led to the struggle in Andor called the Succession, and caused the events in Cairhien that eventually brought on the Aiel War. Her sign was a woman's hand gripping a thorny rose stem with a white blossom.

Time of Madness: The years after the Dark One's counterstroke tainted the male half of the True Source, when male Aes Sedai went mad and Broke the world. The exact duration of this period is unknown, but it is believed to have lasted nearly one hundred years. It ended completely only with the death of the last male Aes Sedai. *See also* Hundred Companions; True Source; One Power.

Traveling People: *See* Tuatha'an.

Travels of Jain Farstrider, The: A very well-known book of travel stories and observations by a noted Malkieri writer and traveler. The book was first printed in 968 NE and has been reprinted continuously ever since. Jain Farstrider disappeared shortly after the Aiel War and is generally believed to be dead.

Treekillers: An Aiel name for the Cairhienin, always said in tones of horror and disgust.

Treesinger: An Ogier who has the ability to sing to trees (called "treesong"), either healing them, or helping them to grow and flower, or making things from the wood without damaging the tree. Objects made in this manner are called "sung wood" and are highly prized. Few Ogier remain who are Treesingers; the ability seems to be dying out.

Trollocs (TRAHL-lohks): Creatures of the Dark One, created during the War of the Shadow. Huge of stature, they are a twisted blend of animal and human stock. They are divided into tribelike bands, among them the Dha'vol, the Ko'bal, and the Dhai'mon. Vicious by nature, they kill for the pure pleasure of killing. Deceitful in the extreme, they cannot be trusted unless coerced by fear.

Trolloc Wars: A series of wars, beginning about 1000 AB and lasting more than three hundred years, during which Trolloc armies ravaged the world. Eventually the Trollocs were driven back into the Great Blight, but some nations ceased to exist, and others that survived were almost depopulated. All records of the time are fragmentary.

True Source: The driving force of the universe, which turns the Wheel of Time. It is divided into a male half (*saidin*) and a female half (*saidar*), which work at the same time with and against each other. Only a man can draw on *saidin*, only a woman on *saidar*. Since the beginning of the Time of Madness, *saidin* has been tainted by the Dark One's touch. *See also* One Power.

Tuatha'an (too-AH-thah-AHN): A wandering folk, also known as the Tinkers and as the Traveling People, who live in brightly painted wagons and follow a totally pacifist philosophy called the Way of the Leaf. Things mended by Tinkers are often better than new. They are among the few who can cross the Aiel Waste unmolested, for the Aiel strictly avoid all contact with them.

Verin Mathwin (VEHR-ihn MAH-thwihn): An Aes Sedai of the Brown Ajah.

Warder: A warrior bonded to an Aes Sedai. The bonding is a thing of the One Power, and by it he gains such gifts as quick healing, the ability to go long periods without food, water, or rest, and the ability to sense the taint of the Dark One at a distance. So long as a Warder lives, the Aes Sedai to whom he is bonded knows he is alive however far away he is, and when he dies she will know the moment and manner of his death. While most Ajahs believe an Aes Sedai may have one Warder bonded to her at a time, the Red Ajah refuse to bond any Warders at all, while the Green Ajah believe an Aes Sedai may bond as many Warders as she wishes. Ethically the Warder must accede to the bonding voluntarily, but it has been known to be done against the Warder's will. What the Aes Sedai gain from the bonding is a closely held secret. *See also* Aes Sedai.

War of Power: *See* War of the Shadow.

War of the Hundred Years: A series of overlapping wars among constantly shifting alliances, precipitated by the death of Artur Hawkwing and the resulting struggle for his empire. It lasted from FY 994 to FY 1117. The War of the Hundred Years depopulated large parts of the lands between the Aryth Ocean and the Aiel Waste, from the Sea of Storms to the Great Blight. So great was the destruction that only fragmentary records of the time remain. The empire of Artur Hawkwing was pulled apart in the wars, and the nations of the present day were formed. *See also* Hawkwing, Artur.

War of the Second Dragon: The war fought (FY 939–43) against the false Dragon Guaire Amalasan. During this war a young king named Artur Tanreall Paendrag, later known as Artur Hawkwing, rose to overwhelming prominence.

War of the Shadow: Also known as the War of Power, this war ended the Age of Legends. It began shortly after the attempt to free the Dark One, and soon involved the whole world. In a world where war had been forgotten, even the memory of it, every facet of war was rediscovered, often twisted by the Dark One's touch on the world, and the One Power was used as a weapon. The war was ended by the resealing of the Dark One into his prison. *See also* Hundred Companions, the; Dragon, the.

weight, units of: 10 ounces = 41 pound; 10 pounds = 1 stone; 10 stone = 1 hundredweight; 10 hundredweight = 1 ton.

Wheel of Time, the: Time is a wheel with seven spokes, each spoke an Age. As the Wheel turns, the Ages come and go, each leaving memories that fade to legend, then to myth, and are forgotten by the time that Age comes again. The Pattern of an Age is slightly different each time an Age comes, and each time it is subject to greater change.

Whitecloaks: *See* Children of the Light.

wilder: A woman who has learned to channel the One Power on her own, surviving the crisis as only one in four does. Such women usually build barriers against knowing what it is they are doing, but if these can be broken down, wilders are among the most powerful of channelers. The term is often used in derogatory fashion.

Wild Hunt: It is believed by many that the Dark One (often called Grim, or Old Grim, in Tear, Illian, Murandy, Altara, and Ghealdan) rides out in the night with the "black dogs," or the Darkhounds, hunting souls. This is the Wild Hunt. Rain can keep the Darkhounds out of the night, but once they are on the trail, they must be confronted and defeated or the victim's death is inevitable. It is believed that merely seeing the Wild Hunt pass means imminent death, either for the viewer or for someone dear to the viewer.

Wisdom: In villages, a woman chosen by the Women's Circle for her knowledge of such things as healing, and foretelling the weather, as well as for common good sense. A position of great responsibility and authority, both actual and implied. She is generally considered the equal of the Mayor, and in some villages his superior. Unlike the Mayor, she is chosen for life, and it is very rare for a Wisdom to be removed from office before her death. Almost traditionally in conflict with the Mayor. Depending on the land, she may instead have another title, such as Guide, Healer, Wise Woman, Seeker, or Wise One.

CHAPTER

I

A preview of
The Shadow Rising

Book Four of
The Wheel of Time

Seeds of Shadow

The Wheel of Time turns, and Ages come and pass, leaving memories that become legend. Legend fades to myth, and even myth is long forgotten when the Age that gave it birth comes again. In one Age, called the Third Age by some, an Age yet to come, an Age long past, a wind rose on the great plain called the Caralain Grass. The wind was not the beginning. There are neither beginnings nor endings to the turning of the Wheel of Time. But it was *a* beginning.

North and east the wind blew beneath early morning sun, over endless miles of rolling grass and far-scattered thickets, across the swift-flowing River Luan, past the broken-topped fang of Dragonmount, mountain of legend towering above the slow swells of the rolling plain, looming so high that clouds wreathed it less than halfway to the smoking peak. Dragonmount, where the Dragon had died—and with him, some said, the Age of Legends—where prophecy said he would be born again. Or had been. North and east, across the villages of Jualdhe and Darein and Alindaer, where bridges like stone lacework arched out to the Shining

Walls, the great white walls of what many called the greatest city in the world. Tar Valon. A city just touched by the reaching shadow of Dragonmount each evening.

Within those walls Ogier-made buildings well over two thousand years old seemed to grow out of the ground rather than having been built, or to be the work of wind and water rather than that of even the fabled hands of Ogier stonemasons. Some suggested birds taking flight, or huge shells from distant seas. Soaring towers, flared or fluted or spiraled, stood connected by bridges hundreds of feet in the air, often without rails. Only those long in Tar Valon could avoid gaping like country folk who had never been off the farm.

Greatest of those towers, the White Tower dominated the city, gleaming like polished bone in the sun. *The Wheel of Time turns around Tar Valon*, so people said in the city, *and Tar Valon turns around the Tower.* The first sight travelers had of Tar Valon, before their horses came in view of the bridges, before their river boat captains sighted the island, was the Tower reflecting the sun like a beacon. Small wonder then that the great square surrounding the walled Tower grounds seemed smaller than it was under the massive Tower's gaze, the people in it dwindling to insects. Yet the White Tower could have been the smallest in Tar Valon, the fact that it was the heart of Aes Sedai power would still have overawed the island city.

Despite their numbers, the crowd did not come close to filling the square. Along the edges people jostled each other in a milling mass, all going about their day's business, but closer to the Tower grounds there were ever fewer people, until a band of bare paving stones at least fifty paces wide bordered the tall white walls. Aes Sedai were respected and more in Tar Valon, of course, and the Amyrlin Seat ruled the city as she ruled the Aes Sedai, but few wanted to be closer to Aes Sedai power than they had to. There was a difference between being proud of a grand fireplace in your hall and walking into the flames.

A very few did go closer, to the broad stairs that led up to the Tower itself, to the intricately carved doors wide enough for a dozen people abreast. Those doors stood open, welcoming. There were always some people in need of aid or an answer they thought only Aes Sedai could give, and they came from far as often as near, from Arafel and Ghealdan, from

Saldaea and Illian. Many would find help or guidance inside, though often not what they had expected or hoped for.

Min kept the wide hood of her cloak pulled up, shadowing her face in its depths. In spite of the warmth of the day, the garment was light enough not to attract comment, not on a woman so obviously shy. And a good many people were shy when they went to the Tower. There was nothing about her to attract notice. Her dark hair was longer than when she was last in the Tower, though still not quite to her shoulders, and her dress, plain blue except for narrow bands of white Jaerecruz lace at neck and wrists, would have suited the daughter of a well-to-do farmer, wearing her feastday best to the Tower just like the other women approaching the wide stairs. Min hoped she looked the same, at least. She had to stop herself from staring at them to see if they walked or held themselves differently. *I can do it*, she told herself.

She had certainly not come all this way to turn back now. The dress was a good disguise. Those who remembered her in the Tower remembered a young woman with close-cropped hair, always in a boy's coat and breeches, never in a dress. It had to be a good disguise. She had no choice about what she was doing. Not really.

Her stomach fluttered the closer she came to the Tower, and she tightened her grip on the bundle clutched to her breast. Her usual clothes were in there, and her good boots, and all her possessions except the horse she had left at an inn not far from the square. With luck, she would be back on the gelding in a few hours, riding for the Ostrein Bridge and the road south.

She was not really looking forward to climbing onto a horse again so soon, not after weeks in the saddle with never a day's pause, but she longed to leave this place. She had never seen the White Tower as hospitable, and right now it seemed nearly as awful as the Dark One's prison at Shayol Ghul. Shivering, she wished she had not thought of the Dark One. *I wonder if Moiraine thinks I came just because she asked me? The Light help me, acting like a fool girl. Doing fool things because of a fool man!*

She mounted the stairs uneasily—each was deep enough to take two strides for her to reach the next—and unlike most of the others, she did not pause for an awed stare up the pale height of the Tower. She wanted this over.

Inside, archways almost surrounded the large, round entry hall, but the petitioners huddled in the middle of the chamber, shuffling together beneath a flat-domed ceiling. The pale stone floor had been worn and polished by countless nervous feet over the centuries. No one thought of anything except where they were, and why. A farmer and his wife in rough woolens, clutching each other's callused hands, rubbed shoulders with a merchant in velvet-slashed silks, a maid at her heels clutching a small worked-silver casket, no doubt her mistress's gift for the Tower. Elsewhere, the merchant would have stared down her nose at farm folk who brushed so close, and they might well have knuckled their foreheads and backed away apologizing. Not now. Not here.

There were few men among the petitioners, which was no surprise to Min. Most men were nervous around Aes Sedai. Everyone knew it had been male Aes Sedai, when there still had been male Aes Sedai, who were responsible for the Breaking of the World. Three thousand years had not dimmed that memory, even if time had altered many of the details. Children were still frightened by tales of men who could channel the One Power, men doomed to go mad from the Dark One's taint on *saidin*, the male half of the True Source. Worst was the story of Lews Therin Telamon, the Dragon, Lews Therin Kinslayer, who had begun the Breaking. For that matter, the stories frightened adults, too. Prophecy said the Dragon would be born again in mankind's greatest hour of need, to fight the Dark One in Tarmon Gai'don, the Last Battle, but that made little difference in how most people looked at any connection between men and the Power. Any Aes Sedai would hunt down a man who could channel, now; of the seven Ajahs, the Red did little else.

Of course, none of that had anything to do with seeking help from Aes Sedai, yet few men felt easy about being linked in any way to Aes Sedai and the Power. Few, that is, except Warders, but each Warder was bonded to an Aes Sedai; Warders could hardly be taken for the general run of men. There was a saying: "A man will cut off his own hand to get rid of a splinter before asking help from Aes Sedai." Women meant it as a comment on men's stubborn foolishness, but Min had heard some men say the loss of a hand might be the better decision.

She wondered what these people would do if they knew what she knew. Run screaming, perhaps. And if they knew her reason for being here, she might not survive to be taken up by the Tower guards and thrown into a cell. She did have friends in the Tower, but none with power or influence. If her purpose was discovered, it was much less likely that they could help her than that she would pull them to the gallows or the headsman behind her. That was saying she lived to be tried, of course; more likely her mouth would be stopped permanently long before a trial.

She told herself to stop thinking like that. *I'll make it in, and I'll make it out. The Light burn Rand al'Thor for getting me into this!*

Three or four Accepted, women Min's age or perhaps a little older, were circulating through the round room, speaking softly to the petitioners. Their white dresses had no decoration except for seven bands of color at the hem, one band for each Ajah. Now and again a novice, a still younger woman or girl all in white, came to lead someone deeper into the Tower. The petitioners always followed the novices with an odd mix of excited eagerness and foot-dragging reluctance.

Min's grip tightened on her bundle as one of the Accepted stopped in front of her. "The Light illumine you," the curly-haired woman said perfunctorily. "I am called Faolain. How may the Tower help you?"

Faolain's dark, round face held the patience of someone doing a tedious job when she would rather be doing something else. Studying, probably, from what Min knew of the Accepted. Learning to be Aes Sedai. Most important, however, was the lack of recognition in the Accepted's eyes; the two of them had met when Min was in the Tower before, though only briefly.

Just the same, Min lowered her face in assumed diffidence. It was not unnatural; a good many country folk did not really understand the great step up from Accepted to full Aes Sedai. Shielding her features behind the edge of her cloak, she looked away from Faolain.

"I have a question I must ask the Amyrlin Seat," she began, then cut off abruptly as three Aes Sedai stopped to look into the entry hall, two from one archway and one from another.

Accepted and novices curtsied when their rounds took
them close to one of the Aes Sedai, but otherwise went on
about their tasks, perhaps a trifle more briskly. That was all.
Not so for the petitioners. They seemed to catch their breaths
all together. Away from the White Tower, away from Tar
Valon, they might simply have thought the Aes Sedai three
women whose ages they could not guess, three women in
the flush of their prime, yet with more maturity than their
smooth cheeks suggested. In the Tower, though, there was
no question. A woman who had worked very long with the
One Power was not touched by time in the same way as other
women. In the Tower, no one needed to see a golden Great
Serpent ring to know an Aes Sedai.

A ripple of curtsies spread through the huddle, and jerky
bows from the few men. Two or three people even fell to their
knees. The rich merchant looked frightened; the farm cou-
ple at her side stared at legends come to life. How to deal
with Aes Sedai was a matter of hearsay for most; it was un-
likely that any here, except those who actually lived in Tar
Valon, had seen an Aes Sedai before, and probably not even
the Tar Valoners had been this close.

But it was not the Aes Sedai themselves that halted Min's
tongue. Sometimes, not often, she saw things when she
looked at people, images and auras that usually flared and
were gone in moments. Occasionally she knew what they
meant. It happened rarely, the knowing—much more rarely
than the seeing, even—but when she knew, she was always
right.

Unlike most others, Aes Sedai—and their Warders—
always had images and auras, sometimes so many dancing
and shifting that they made Min dizzy. The numbers made
no difference in interpreting them, though; she knew what
they meant for Aes Sedai as seldom as for anyone else. But
this time she knew more than she wanted to, and it made her
shiver.

A slender woman with black hair falling to her waist,
the only one of the three she recognized—her name was
Ananda; she was Yellow Ajah—wore a sickly brown halo,
shriveled and split by rotting fissures that fell in and widened
as they decayed. The small, fair-haired Aes Sedai beside
Ananda was Green Ajah, by her green-fringed shawl. The
White Flame of Tar Valon on it showed for a moment when

she turned her back. And on her shoulder, as if nestled among the grape vines and flowering apple branches worked on her shawl, sat a human skull. A small woman's skull, picked clean and sun-bleached. The third, a plumply pretty woman halfway around the room, wore no shawl; most Aes Sedai did not except for ceremony. The lift of her chin and the set of her shoulders spoke of strength and pride. She seemed to be casting cool blue eyes on the petitioners through a tattered curtain of blood, crimson streamers running down her face.

Blood and skull and halo faded away in the dance of images around the three, came and faded again. The petitioners stared in awe, seeing only three women who could touch the True Source and channel the One Power. No one but Min saw the rest. No one but Min knew those three women were going to die. All on the same day.

"The Amyrlin cannot see everyone," Faolain said with poorly hidden impatience. "Her next public audience is not for ten days. Tell me what you want, and I will arrange for you to see the sister who can best help you."

Min's eye flew to the bundle in her arms and stayed there, partly so she would not have to see again what she had already seen. *All* three *of them! Light!* What chance was there that three Aes Sedai would die on the same day? But she knew. She knew.

"I have the right to speak to the Amyrlin Seat. In person." It was a right seldom demanded—who would dare?—but it existed. "Any woman has that right, and I ask it."

"Do you think the Amyrlin Seat herself can see everyone who comes to the White Tower? Surely another Aes Sedai can help you." Faolain gave heavy weight to the titles as if to overpower Min. "Now tell me what your question is about. And give me your name, so the novice will know who to come for."

"My name is . . . Elmindreda." Min winced in spite of herself. She had always hated the name, but the Amyrlin was one of the few people living who had ever heard it. If only she remembered. "I have the right to speak to the Amyrlin. And my question is for her alone. I have the right."

The Accepted arched an eyebrow. "Elmindreda?" Her mouth twitched toward an amused smile. "And you claim your rights. Very well. I will send word to the Keeper of the

Chronicles that you wish to see the Amyrlin Seat personally, Elmindreda."

Min wanted to slap the woman for the way she emphasized "Elmindreda," but instead she forced out a murmured "Thank you."

"Do not thank me yet. No doubt it will be hours before the Keeper finds time to reply, and it will certainly be that you can ask your question at the Mother's next public audience. Wait with patience. Elmindreda." She gave Min a tight smile, almost a smirk, as she turned away.

Grinding her teeth, Min took her bundle to stand against the wall between two of the archways, where she tried to blend into the pale stonework. *Trust no one, and avoid notice until you reach the Amyrlin*, Moiraine had told her. Moiraine was one Aes Sedai she did trust. Most of the time. It was good advice in any case. All she had to do was reach the Amyrlin, and it would be over. She could don her own clothes again, see her friends, and leave. No more need for hiding.

She was relieved to see that the Aes Sedai had gone. Three Aes Sedai dying on one day. It was impossible; that was the only word. Yet it was going to happen. Nothing she said or did could change it—when she knew what an image meant, it happened—but she had to tell the Amyrlin about this. It might even be as important as the news she brought from Moiraine, though that was hard to believe.

Another Accepted came to replace one already there, and to Min's eyes bars floated in front of her apple-cheeked face, like a cage. Sheriam, the Mistress of Novices, looked into the hall—after one glance, Min kept her gaze on the stone under her feet; Sheriam knew her all too well—and the red-haired Aes Sedai's face seemed battered and bruised. It was only the viewing, of course, but Min still had to bite her lip to stifle a gasp. Sheriam, with her calm authority and sureness, was as indestructible as the Tower. Surely nothing could harm Sheriam. But something was going to.

An Aes Sedai unknown to Min, wearing the shawl of the Brown Ajah, accompanied a stout woman in finely woven red wool to the doors. The stout woman walked as lightly as a girl, face shining, almost laughing with pleasure. The Brown sister was smiling, too, but her aura faded like a guttering candle flame.

Death. Wounds, captivity, and death. To Min it might as well have been printed on a page.

She set her eyes on her feet. She did not want to see any more. *Let her remember*, she thought. She had not felt desperation at any time on her long ride from the Mountains of Mist, not even on the two occasions when someone tried to steal her horse, but she felt it now. *Light, let her remember that bloody name.*

"Mistress Elmindreda?"

Min gave a start. The black-haired novice who stood before her was barely old enough to be away from home, perhaps fifteen or sixteen, though she made a great effort at dignity. "Yes? I am. . . . That is my name."

"I am Sahra. If you will come with me"—Sahra's piping voice took on a note of wonder—"the Amyrlin Seat will see you in her study now."

Min gave a sigh of relief and followed eagerly.

Her cloak's deep hood still hid her face, but it did not stop her seeing, and the more she saw, the more she grew eager to reach the Amyrlin. Few people walked the broad corridors that spiraled upward with their brightly colored floor tiles, and their wall hangings and golden lampstands—the Tower had been built to hold far greater numbers than it did now—but nearly everyone she saw as she climbed higher wore an image or aura that spoke to her of violence and danger.

Warders hurried by with barely a glance for the two women, men who moved like hunting wolves, their swords only an afterthought to their deadliness, but they seemed to have bloody faces, or gaping wounds. Swords and spears danced about their heads, threatening. Their auras flashed wildly, flickered on the knife edge of death. She saw dead men walking, knew they would die on the same day as the Aes Sedai in the entry hall, or at most a day later. Even some of the servants, men and women with the Flame of Tar Valon on their breasts, hurrying about their work, bore signs of violence. An Aes Sedai glimpsed down a side hallway appeared to have chains in the air around her, and another, crossing the corridor ahead of Min and her guide, seemed for most of those few strides to wear a silver collar around her neck. Min's breath caught at that; she wanted to scream.

"It can all be overwhelming to someone who's never seen

it before," Sahra said, trying and failing to sound as if the
Tower were as ordinary to her now as her home village.
"But you are safe here. The Amyrlin Seat will make things
right." Her voice squeaked when she mentioned the Amyrlin.

"Light, let her do just that," Min muttered. The novice gave
her a smile that was meant to be soothing.

By the time they reached the hall outside the Amyrlin's
study, Min's stomach was churning and she was treading
almost on Sahra's heels. Only the need to pretend that she
was a stranger had kept her from running ahead long since.

One of the doors to the Amyrlin's chambers opened, and
a young man with red-gold hair came stalking out, nearly
striding into Min and her escort. Tall and straight and strong
in his blue coat thickly embroidered with gold on sleeves and
collar, Gawyn of House Trakand, son of Queen Morgase of
Andor, looked every inch the proud young lord. A furious
young lord. There was no time to drop her head; he was staring down into her hood, right into her face.

His eyes widened in surprise, then narrowed to slits of
blue ice. "So you are back. Do you know where my sister and
Egwene have gone?"

"They are not here?" Min forgot everything in a rising
flood of panic. Before she knew what she was doing she had
seized his sleeves, peering up at him urgently, and forced
him back a step. "Gawyn, they started for the Tower months
ago! Elayne and Egwene, and Nynaeve, too. With Verin Sedai
and. . . . Gawyn, I . . . I. . . ."

"Calm yourself," he said, gently undoing her grip on his
coat. "Light! I didn't mean to frighten you so. They arrived
safely. And would not say a word of where they had been, or
why. Not to me. I suppose there's scant hope you will?" She
thought she kept her face straight, but he took one look and
said, "I thought not. This place has more secrets than. . . .
They've vanished again. And Nynaeve, too." Nynaeve was
almost an offhand addition; she might be one of Min's
friends, but she meant nothing to him. His voice began to
roughen once more, growing tighter by the second. "Again
without a word. Not a word! Supposedly they're on a farm
somewhere as penance for running away, but I cannot find
out where. The Amyrlin won't give me a straight answer."

Min flinched; for a moment, streaks of dried blood had
made his face a grim mask. It was like a double hammer

blow. Her friends were gone—it had eased her coming to the Tower, knowing they were here—and Gawyn was going to be wounded on the day the Aes Sedai died.

Despite all she had seen since entering the Tower, despite her fear, none of it had really touched her personally until now. Disaster striking the Tower would spread far from Tar Valon, yet she was not of the Tower and never could be. But Gawyn was someone she knew, someone she liked, and he was going to be hurt more than the blood told, hurt somehow deeper than wounds to his flesh. It hit her that if catastrophe seized the Tower, not only distant Aes Sedai would be harmed, women she could never feel close to, but her friends as well. They *were* of the Tower.

In a way she was glad Egwene and the others were not there, glad she could not look at them and perhaps see signs of death. Yet she wanted to look, to be sure, to look at her friends and see nothing, or see that they would live. Where in the Light were they? Why had they gone? Knowing those three, she thought it possible that if Gawyn did not know where they were, it was because they did not want him to know. It could be that.

Suddenly she remembered where she was and why, and that she was not alone with Gawyn. Sahra seemed to have forgotten she was taking Min to the Amyrlin; she seemed to have forgotten everything but the young lord, making calf-eyes that he was not noticing. Even so, there was no use pretending any longer to be a stranger to the Tower. She was at the Amyrlin's door; nothing could stop her now.

"Gawyn, I don't know where they are, but if they are doing penance on a farm, they're probably all sweat, and mud to their hips, and you are the last one they will want to see them." She was not much easier about their absence than Gawyn was, in truth. Too much had happened, too much was happening, too much with ties to them, and to her. But it was not impossible they had been sent off for punishment. "You won't help them by making the Amyrlin angry."

"I don't know that they *are* on a farm. Or even alive. Why all this hiding and sidestepping if they're just pulling weeds? If anything happens to my sister. . . . Or to Egwene. . . ." He frowned at the toes of his boots. "I am supposed to look after Elayne. How can I protect her when I don't know where she is?"

Min sighed. "Do you think she needs looking after? Either of them?" But if the Amyrlin had sent them somewhere, maybe they did. The Amyrlin was capable of sending a woman into a bear's den with nothing but a switch if it suited her purposes. And she would expect the woman to come back with a bearskin, or the bear on a leash, as instructed. But telling Gawyn that would only inflame his temper and his worries. "Gawyn, they have pledged to the Tower. They won't thank you for meddling."

"I know Elayne isn't a child," he said patiently, "even if she does bounce back and forth between running off like one and playing at being Aes Sedai. But she *is* my sister, and beyond that, she is Daughter-Heir of Andor. She'll be queen, after Mother. Andor needs her whole and safe to take the throne, not another Succession."

Playing at being Aes Sedai? Apparently he did not realize the extent of his sister's talent. The Daughter-Heirs of Andor had been sent to the Tower to train for as long as there had been an Andor, but Elayne was the first to have enough talent to be raised to Aes Sedai, and a powerful Aes Sedai at that. Very likely he also did not know Egwene was just as strong.

"So you will protect her whether she wants it or not?" She said it in a flat voice meant to let him know he was making a mistake, but he missed the warning and nodded agreement.

"That has been my duty since the day she was born. My blood shed before hers; my life given before hers. I took that oath when I could barely see over the side of her cradle; Gareth Bryne had to explain to me what it meant. I won't break it now. Andor needs her more than it needs me."

He spoke with a calm certainty, an acceptance of something natural and right, that sent chills through her. She had always thought of him as boyish, laughing and teasing, but now he was something alien. She thought the Creator must have been tired when it came time to make men; sometimes they hardly seemed human. "And Egwene? What oath did you take about her?"

His face did not change, but he shifted his feet warily. "I'm concerned about Egwene, of course. And Nynaeve. What happens to Elayne's companions might happen to Elayne. I assume they're still together; when they *were* here, I seldom saw one without the others."

"My mother always told me to marry a poor liar, and you qualify. Except that I think someone else has first claim."

"Some things are meant to be," he said quietly, "and some never can. Galad is heartsick because Egwene is gone." Galad was his half-brother, the pair of them sent to Tar Valon to train under the Warders. That was another Andoran tradition. Galadedrid Damodred was a man who took doing the right thing to the point of a fault, as Min saw it, but Gawyn could see no wrong in him. And he would not speak his feelings for a woman Galad had set his heart on.

She wanted to shake him, shake some sense into him, but there was no time now. Not with the Amyrlin waiting, not with what she had to tell the Amyrlin waiting. Certainly not with Sahra standing there, calf-eyes or no calf-eyes. "Gawyn, I am summoned to the Amyrlin. Where can I find you, when she is done with me?"

"I will be in the practice yard. The only time I can stop worrying is when I am working the sword with Hammar." Hammar was a blademaster, and the Warder who taught the sword. "Most days I'm there until the sun sets."

"Good, then. I will come as soon as I can. And try to watch what you say. If you make the Amyrlin angry with you, Elayne and Egwene might share in it."

"That I cannot promise," he said firmly. "Something is wrong in the world. Civil war in Cairhien. The same and worse in Tarabon and Arad Doman. False Dragons. Troubles and rumors of troubles everywhere. I don't say the Tower is behind it, but even here things are not what they should be. Or what they seem. Elayne and Egwene vanishing isn't the whole of it. Still, they are the part that concerns me. I *will* find out where they are. And if they have been hurt. . . . If they are dead. . . ."

He scowled, and for an instant his face was that bloody mask again. More: a sword floated above his head, and a banner waved behind it. The long-hilted sword, like those most Warders used, had a heron engraved on its slightly curved blade, symbol of a blademaster, and Min could not say whether it belonged to Gawyn or threatened him. The banner bore Gawyn's sigil of the charging White Boar, but on a field of green rather than the red of Andor. Both sword and banner faded with the blood.

"Be careful, Gawyn." She meant it two ways. Careful of what he said, and careful in a way she could not explain, even to herself. "You must be very careful."

His eyes searched her face as if he had heard some of her deeper meaning. "I . . . will try," he said finally. He put on a grin, almost the grin she remembered, but the effort was plain. "I suppose I had better get myself back to the practice yard if I expect to keep up with Galad. I managed two out of five against Hammar this morning, but Galad actually won three, the last time he bothered to come to the yard." Suddenly he appeared to really see her for the first time, and his grin became genuine. "You ought to wear dresses more often. It's pretty on you. Remember, I will be there till sunset."

As he strode away with something very close to the dangerous grace of a Warder, Min realized she was smoothing the dress over her hip and stopped immediately. *The Light burn all men!*

Sahra exhaled as if she had been holding her breath. "He is very good-looking, isn't he?" she said dreamily. "Not as good-looking as Lord Galad, of course. And you really know him." It was half a question, but only half.

Min echoed the novice's sigh. The girl would talk with her friends in the novices' quarters. The son of a queen was a natural topic, especially when he was handsome and had an air about him like the hero in a gleeman's tale. A strange woman only made for more interesting speculation. Still, there was nothing to be done about it. At any rate, it could hardly cause any harm now.

"The Amyrlin Seat must be wondering why we haven't come," she said.

Sahra came to herself with a wide-eyed start and a loud gulp. Seizing Min's sleeve with one hand, she jumped to open one of the doors, pulling Min behind her. The moment they were inside, the novice curtsied hastily and burst out in panic, "I've brought her, Leane Sedai. Mistress Elmindreda? The Amyrlin Seat wants to see her?"

The tall, coppery-skinned woman in the anteroom wore the hand-wide stole of the Keeper of the Chronicles, blue to show she had been raised from the Blue Ajah. Fists on hips, she waited for the girl to finish, then dismissed her with a clipped "Took you long enough, child. Back to your chores, now." Sahra bobbed another curtsy and scurried out as quickly as she had entered.

Min stood with her eyes on the floor, her hood still pulled up around her face. Blundering in front of Sahra had been bad enough—though at least the novice did not know her name—but Leane knew her better than anyone in the Tower except the Amyrlin. Min was sure it could make no difference now, but after what had happened in the hallway, she meant to hold to Moiraine's instructions until she was alone with the Amyrlin.

This time her precautions did no good. Leane took two steps, pushed back the hood, and grunted as if she had been poked in the stomach. Min raised her head and stared back defiantly, trying to pretend she had not been attempting to sneak past. Straight, dark hair only a little longer than her own framed the Keeper's face; the Aes Sedai's expression was a blend of surprise and displeasure at being surprised.

"So you are Elmindreda, are you?" Leane said briskly. She was always brisk. "I must say you look it more in that dress than in your usual . . . garb."

"Just Min, Leane Sedai, if you please." Min managed to keep her face straight, but it was difficult not to glare. The Keeper's voice had held too much amusement. If her mother had had to name her after someone in a story, why did it have to be a woman who seemed to spend most of her time sighing at men, when she was not inspiring them to compose songs about her eyes, or her smile?

"Very well. Min. I'll not ask where you've been, nor why you've come back in a dress, apparently wanting to ask a question of the Amyrlin. Not now, at least." Her face said she meant to ask later, though, and get answers. "I suppose the Mother knows who Elmindreda is? Of course. I should have known that when she said to send you straight in, and alone. The Light alone knows why she puts up with you." She broke off with a concerned frown. "What is the matter, girl? Are you ill?"

Min carefully blanked her face. "No. No, I am all right." For a moment the Keeper had been looking through a transparent mask of her own face, a screaming mask. "May I go in now, Leane Sedai?"

Leane studied her a moment longer, then jerked her head toward the inner chamber. "In with you." Min's leap to obey would have satisfied the hardest taskmistress.

The Amyrlin Seat's study had been occupied by many grand and powerful women over the centuries, and reminders of the fact filled the room, from the tall fireplace all of golden marble from Kandor, cold now, to the paneled walls of pale, oddly striped wood, iron hard yet carved in wondrous beasts and wildly feathered birds. Those panels had been brought from the mysterious lands beyond the Aiel Waste well over a thousand years ago, and the fireplace was more than twice as old. The polished red-stone of the floor had come from the Mountains of Mist. High arched windows let onto a balcony. The iridescent stone framing the windows shone like pearls, and had been salvaged from the remains of a city sunk into the Sea of Storms by the Breaking of the World; no one had ever seen its like.

The current occupant, Siuan Sanche, had been born a fisherman's daughter in Tear, though, and the furnishings she had chosen were simple, if well made and well polished. She sat in a stout chair behind a large table plain enough to have served a farmhouse. The only other chair in the room, just as plain and usually set off to one side, now stood in front of the table atop a small Tairen rug, simple in blue and brown and gold. Half a dozen books rested open on tall reading stands about the floor. That was all of it. A drawing hung above the fireplace: tiny fishing boats working among reeds in the Fingers of the Dragon, just as her father's boat had.

At first glance, despite her smooth Aes Sedai features, Siuan Sanche herself looked as simple as her furnishings. She herself was sturdy, and handsome rather than beautiful, and the only bit of ostentation in her clothing was the broad stole of the Amyrlin Seat she wore, with one colored stripe for each of the seven Ajahs. Her age was indeterminate, as with any Aes Sedai; not even a hint of gray showed in her dark hair. But her sharp blue eyes brooked no nonsense, and her firm jaw spoke of the determination of the youngest woman ever to be chosen Amyrlin Seat. For over ten years Siuan Sanche had been able to summon rulers, and the powerful, and they had come, even if they hated the White Tower and feared Aes Sedai.

As the Amyrlin strode around in front of the table, Min

set down her bundle and began an awkward curtsy, muttering irritably under her breath at having to do so. Not that she wanted to be disrespectful—that did not even occur to one facing a woman like Siuan Sanche—but the bow she usually would have made seemed foolish in a dress, and she had only a rough idea of how to curtsy.

Halfway down, with her skirts already spread, she froze like a crouching toad. Siuan Sanche was standing there as regal as any queen, and for a moment she was also lying on the floor, naked. Aside from her being in only her skin, there was something odd about the image, but it vanished before Min could say what. It was as strong a viewing as she had ever seen, and she had no idea what it meant.

"Seeing things again, are you?" the Amyrlin said. "Well, I can certainly make use of that ability of yours. I could have used it all the months you were gone. But we'll not talk of that. What's done is done. The Wheel weaves as the Wheel wills." She smiled a tight smile. "But if you do it again, I'll have your hide for gloves. Stand up, girl. Leane forces enough ceremony on me in a month to last any sensible woman a year. I don't have time for it. Not these days. Now, what did you just see?"

Min straightened slowly. It was a relief to be back with someone who knew of her talent, even if it was the Amyrlin Seat herself. She did not have to hide what she saw from the Amyrlin. Far from it. "You were. . . . You weren't wearing any clothes. I . . . I don't know what it means, Mother."

Siuan barked a short, mirthless laugh. "No doubt that I'll take a lover. But I have no time for that, either. There's no time for winking at the men when you're busy bailing the boat."

"Maybe," Min said slowly. It could have meant that, though she doubted it. "I just do not know. But, Mother, I've been seeing things ever since I walked into the Tower. Something bad is going to happen, something terrible."

She started with the Aes Sedai in the entry hall and told everything she had seen, as well as what everything meant, when she was sure. She held back what Gawyn had said, though, or most of it; it was no use telling him not to anger the Amyrlin if she did it for him. The rest she laid out as starkly as she had seen it. Some of her fear came out as she dredged it all up, seeing it all again; her voice shook before she was done.

The Amyrlin's expression never changed. "So you spoke with young Gawyn," she said when Min finished. "Well, I think I can convince him to keep quiet. And if I remember Sahra correctly, the girl could do with some time working in the country. She'll spread no gossip hoeing a vegetable patch."

"I don't understand," Min said. "Why should Gawyn keep quiet? About what? I told him nothing. And Sahra . . . ? Mother, perhaps I didn't make myself clear. Aes Sedai and Warders are going to die. It has to mean a battle. And unless you send a lot of Aes Sedai and Warders off somewhere—and servants, too; I saw servants dead and injured, too—unless you do that, that battle will be here! In Tar Valon!"

About the Author

Robert Jordan was born in 1948 in Charleston, South Carolina. He taught himself to read when he was four with the incidental aid of a twelve-years-older brother, and was tackling Mark Twain and Jules Verne by five. He was a graduate of the Citadel, the Military College of South Carolina, with a degree in physics. He served two tours in Vietnam with the U.S. Army; among his decorations are the Distinguished Flying Cross with bronze oak leaf cluster, the Bronze Star with "V" and bronze oak leaf cluster, and two Vietnamese Gallantry Crosses with Palm. A history buff, he also wrote dance and theater criticism. He enjoyed the outdoor sports of hunting, fishing, and sailing, and the indoor sports of poker, chess, pool, and pipe collecting. He began writing in 1977 and continued until his death on September 16, 2007.